TOTAL
ECLIPSE

TOTAL ECLIPSE

Liz Rigbey

ORION

First published in Great Britain in 1995 by
Orion
An imprint of Orion Books Ltd
Orion House, 5 Upper St Martin's Lane, London WC2H 9EA

A CIP catalogue record for this book is available
from the British Library.

ISBN: 0 75280 122 8 (cased)
ISBN: 1 85797 242 2 (trade paperback)

Typeset by Deltatype Ltd, Ellesmere Port, Cheshire
Printed in Great Britain by Richard Clay Ltd, St Ives plc

My thanks, foremost and wholeheartedly, go to Mark Lucas. In addition, I am very grateful for the advice given, with patience and generosity, by: Professor Alec Boksenberg of the Royal Greenwich Observatory, Cambridge, England; George G. Walker, defense attorney, San Francisco; Diane Hovarongkura. I fear that more generosity still will be required when they read this book and discover the number of occasions I have failed to follow their advice. Thanks also to the following people who helped or supported me in many different ways while I was writing this book: Kevin Jackson; Rosie Cheetham; William R. Grose; Dudley P. Frasier; Kay Rigbey; Adrian and Felicity Cave; Norman Coward; Alan Dressler.

I

It was spring when Julia came to the observatory. Everybody noticed her arrival. Almost no one noticed that it was spring.

The birds on the mountain top were noisy. Some of the low peaks were turning from white to a pale egg-blue. The air warmed and swelled and thickened, impeding progress a little around the steep site. Scientists sweated when they climbed up the ridges where the telescopes were housed. And the tourists arrived.

Far beneath the circling hawks their car hoods flashed at regular intervals as they rounded the bends in a well-spaced line. An hour later the windows of the staff residence trembled as the first of the cars turned, in low gear, into the parking lot.

There were couples clasping each other, families, families with no mother, families with no father, groups of children with one squeaking adult in charge of them and groups of grown-ups with one quiet child between them. They were relieved to reach their destination. Many had driven up here from San Francisco. They were city people and they soothed themselves after their long, unsettling confrontation with the mountains by making small purchases in the souvenir shop. Then there were the restrooms and the cafeteria. Mostly it was the children who dragged their reluctant adults finally to see the telescopes.

The tourists did not realize they were being watched. During the long days' wait for night, the astronomers and their support staff would work or sleep or read or talk. When spring brought the visitors they would stare at them through the lounge windows of the staff residence. The windows were tinted and if the visitors noticed anything it was their own reflection. Lomax had been too embarrassed to stand in the lounge and intercept strangers' glances when he first came to the observatory. It was like participating in someone else's love affair. Messages, ricocheting between the visitor and their mirror image and back again, were personal, swift, subliminal. But after a month or two the sight became so familiar that Lomax allowed himself to watch more intently.

For the scientists, removed from their homes for days or weeks or months, the bickering families were reassuring and the women were interesting. The men commented on their clothes, hair and legs. At the time there was an Italian in residence who loved feet.

'Oh God, oh God, look at her toes,' he moaned as a woman passed by in flipflops.

'Lovely teenager daughter just arrive. She did not want to come to observatory today. She feel sick at travelling road around and around mountains. She prefer to lie by pool in very small bikini. She put clothes on today only with utmost reluctance,' a Russian commented helpfully. A few of the scientists glanced up at the lovely teenage daughter but most of the men were dozing or reading. An Englishman was sulking because the recently arrived copy of the *Astrophysical Review* was on someone else's lap. Someone wrote a letter home. Someone played patience with a worn pack of cards.

'Her first sexual experience still await her. She can dream of this event and imagine what it will be, but nothing can really prepare her for gift of love that awaits her.'

Now almost everyone was looking at the teenage daughter. Only Doberman remained in his corner, shortsightedly bent over his computer printout.

The Englishman seized his moment.

'If you're not reading that, perhaps I could . . .?' He gestured to the *Astrophysical Review* and then eased it out of Lomax's hands. Lomax let it go. He was watching the girl. She sloped along behind her parents and young brother. Her hair had the sheen of frequent brushing. Her lips were dissatisfied. They pouted.

'Good feet, good feet,' said the Italian knowledgeably.

The girl neared the window and, seeing her own image, started as if encountering a lover. She bridled and looked up at herself from lowered lids. Her lips parted to reveal a shining brace of some complexity.

'Aaaaah. So slender, so supple, her walk the self-conscious walk of young woman who is begin to know own body. Face so clean from all stresses and monstrous strains that harass wrinkles. And mouth. Let us take mouth now . . .'

But Yevgeny's audience had been diverted.

Professor Berlins was crossing the parking lot. He was explaining something, waving his arms around and nodding vigorously at his own words. At his side walked a strikingly attractive woman. She was not a tourist. Tourists wore baggy pants and sneakers and sloppy sweatshirts. This woman wore a short, simple dress which touched her body in enough places to reveal its shape. She looked, thought Lomax, as though someone had sculpted her. At this distance he could only see outlines but all the angles and proportions which are most pleasing to the human eye were somehow right about her: of the chin to the neck, the shoulder to the arm, the rise of the breast, the taper of the ankle.

'Oh God, oh God,' breathed the Italian. Lomax concluded her feet were good too.

'Perhaps her mouth is now clang with silver, wires and other hardware but we forgive this because we know that when it is remove we will admire shining row of teeth. Above are yielding lips of young woman anxious to experience romance, below them dampness of tongue. Small: perhaps. Pink: probably. Healthy: we hope so. Yes, all in all, an inviting, a seductive prospect, and we must hope that man who first hand this young woman gift of love is not high school senior but capable to enjoy pleasure of giving.'

Yevgeny paused as the girl moved out of sight and then he, too, noticed Berlins and the woman and joined in the silence. She was reaching the mirror window and they could hear fragments of the professor's monologue: room reserved here for her when weather or work did not permit return home . . . not luxurious . . . privacy . . . friendly working atmosphere . . . scientific community . . .

The men, some of them standing now, rearranged themselves. A few took a step forward. Lomax had long suspected that the signals which strangers displayed to their own image were exciting to some of the scientists. He had occasionally seen Yevgeny or Doberman position themselves in the eyeline of visitors to experience the thrill of someone else's frank admiration. He felt alarmed now at the prospect of this woman gratifying the men. His stomach contracted. He wanted to protect her but could only watch as she advanced innocently towards the window.

Luckily Berlins was walking on the near side, masking her with his waving hands. Lomax already liked Berlins but now his affection swelled with gratitude. The old man had guessed who would be lining up at the window and was trying to shield the woman. But in one large, overdramatic flourish – 'friendly community spirit!' – he had dropped one of the bundles of paper he habitually and unnecessarily carried around the site. Unnoticing, he strode on as the woman fell back to pick it up. She was revealed. There was some spontaneous, unspoken acknowledgement of her beauty among the men in the lounge, a rustle, a murmur, perhaps a sigh. They leaned forward. The woman stooped.

3

As she rose, paper in hand, she caught sight of her reflection in the window. Lomax tensed. The men's faces stretched towards the window.

Her look was surprised. She did not bridle or simper or flirt with her own image but flickered, briefly, with bewilderment. It was only a moment, perhaps not even a full second, before she was handing the papers back to Berlins and he was thanking her and apologizing and holding open the door of the staff residence for her.

Inside the lounge, the men wandered away from the window. They were disappointed. They resumed reading or closed their eyes or shuffled playing cards. Lomax was relieved. He did not know why.

Someone was shouting.

'I think you are all disgusting – yes, each and every one of you, hungry and slobbering over each woman passing by like big, ugly dogs!'

It was Jorgen, a Swedish astronomer who had scarcely spoken since arriving on site. Lomax had thought he must have a speech impediment or poor English but last week Jorgen had overheard two astronomers discussing omega equals one and joined in, not just enthusiastically but heatedly. Onlookers had found themselves participating until at least six different nationalities were yelling at each other in broken English. After that the Swede had resumed his long silences. Lomax now recognized these as the self-restraint of an explosive personality.

Jorgen's words made Doberman look up from his corner. Others began to study their cards or their books intently. A few of the astronomers shuffled their feet. Lomax noticed faces reddening and suspected his own was among them.

'There is data of a most exciting and extraordinary kind now emerging here! Most extraordinary. But what I find in the scientific staff is bizarre because they spend their days not analyzing, not discussing, not attempting to explain, but staring at women! At women! That window is dangerous, it should be removed.'

'Sure we're interested in her, she's Berlins' new assistant,' said McMahon, his tone conciliatory. He always knew everything. He was so well-informed that Lomax occasionally suspected the observatory was bugged.

But the Swede was not to be deflected.

'So the new assistant is of more interest than the startling results produced last night. I see. I see. An assistant is more interesting. I wake up. I have my breakfast. I go to the lounge and I am disappointed to find men playing cards and watching women. I go to the labs. I come back. I am thinking to myself: Aha, there is something highly irregular in our results, the team will be discussing them. There will be animated discussion. Many arguments, many opinions. Debate of the highest quality. But what do I find?'

He gestured around the lounge at the half-played card game, the unfinished letters home, the dented cushions and the blinking Doberman.

'Good God, if I want a stimulating debate I will have to telephone home to my sixteen-year-old son. Because here there is nothing but men with their brains in their pants.'

At that moment, Jorgen glimpsed Kim. Lomax did not know how long she had been in the room. He wondered if Kim had seen the men's reaction, including his own, to the new assistant. He hoped not.

'And the lady, of course,' added the Swede stiffly. Kim grinned at him and sat down by Lomax. Her grin was so broad that a few of the men smiled back at her. They liked her. They liked her grin. They said, in her absence, that Kim could be a pretty woman if she wanted to.

'Come on now, Jorgen,' Doberman said from his corner. 'I've just been analysing the data and I've come to the conclusion that there's an equipment failure. That explains the results.'

Lomax and Yevgeny exchanged glances. They had pointed out at least eight hours earlier that there was an equipment failure. Even now a small team of scientists and maintenance technicians was analysing the computers and the main telescope itself to pinpoint the fault.

'Ah, but they have found no fault! None! Is it possible that these astounding results are not so preposterous!'

Lomax liked the Swede for using words like 'astounding' and 'preposterous.' He recognized excitement as an important ingredient of the man's working life. In fact, there had been widespread excitement and then disbelief last night when results seemed to indicate a remarkable redshift in a nearby galaxy. Only the Swede had been reluctant to believe in an equipment failure. He had crossed the asphalt time after time that morning to ask the investigative team if they had made any progress. On each occasion he had returned to the lounge elated.

'There's no point getting work-up until we know,' Yevgeny said. But Jorgen did not look soothed.

'Are you a betting man?' asked Doberman, getting up and spilling computer printout onto the floor.

'No,' Jorgen told him grandly. Doberman hardly reached to his shoulder.

5

'Well, bet this once. I'll buy the drinks if the results are accurate. You buy if it's an equipment failure. Either way we get blind drunk.'

The Swede stared at him, his eyes bulbous. Lomax thought he was about to start yelling again but Doberman continued smoothly: 'We'll go into town and get screaming, roaring drunk. Maybe we'll find some women. It's just exactly what you need.'

Several people offered to join this expedition. To Lomax's surprise, the Swede seemed mollified.

'On the weekend,' he agreed.

'And maybe,' suggested Yevgeny in a sly voice, 'new assistant would like to accompany us.'

Lomax doubted that.

The men began to disperse. Kim and Lomax looked at each other. Kim had large eyes. Under their scrutiny, Lomax felt himself redden again. She slid her chair closer to his and spoke in an undertone.

'So, Lomax.' Her smile was mischievous. 'So. She makes your beard curl.'

'Er . . . who?' he asked innocently.

But Kim wasn't fooled. She leaned back in her chair so that her neck pressed against the headrest. 'Her name's Julia Fox and she'll mostly be working for Berlins but she's also support on Core Nine,' she said.

'Oh,' said Lomax. He was working on Core 9.

'Plus she has to run the eclipse committee.'

'The what?'

'For the total eclipse of the sun. This fall.'

'Why does the sun need a committee?'

Kim shrugged, rolling her brown eyes expressively. 'Coming with us on Saturday night?' she asked. She had been one of the first to volunteer for the drinking party.

'Probably not.'

'You're scared Jorgen's right and there's really an interesting redshift out there.' Kim knew Lomax well. They had worked on two projects together.

'He's an eminent man. I guess we have to take him seriously,' Lomax said.

'Nah. Haven't you seen the way his eyeballs go round and round when he talks? The guy's at least partially insane. I mean, he's been here, what, two weeks? Everyone starts to crack after about two weeks.'

'Maybe he misses his family.'

'You mean, you miss your family. You don't have any way of knowing that he misses his.'

Kim was right. Lomax's children had been vacationing for a few weeks with their mother and Robert. Lomax had last seen them a month ago. Sometimes, when he thought of Robert and Candice and the children staying at expensive European hotels together, he felt lonely. Waiters and airline staff would think that Helen and Joel were Robert's children.

He looked around at his colleagues. Doberman, nose deep in printouts again. The Englishman, no longer reading the *Astrophysical Review* but keeping one hand on it and regarding beadily anyone who approached it. McMahon and Yevgeny, heads close together, muttering, perhaps plotting, in a corner together.

Lomax felt Kim's warm fingers on his arm.

'Get drunk, Lomax,' she advised. She gave him a tender squeeze and Lomax looked down at her. She was his closest friend here. They had evolved a joint defence, both jaundiced and affectionate, against the routines and irritations of observatory life. They were allies. He ruffled her dark hair.

'Ahem, ahem. I hate to interrupt this tender moment,' said Berlins. He was standing right over them with the new assistant, dazzling, at his side. Lomax's face grew warm. Julia Fox was smiling but he found it difficult to smile back or even to look at her. As Berlins introduced them he nodded, just the way Berlins had when he crossed the parking lot with her. Berlins was saying something about Core 9, and then about the eclipse committee. Standing, Lomax knocked the chair over. Kim shot him a penetrating glare and picked it up.

'Lomax is very excited just now. We had some unusual data last night,' Berlins explained.

Julia said: 'He looks excited.'

She was still smiling and her words were cool but there was a note of apprehension in her voice. She was young, younger than she had seemed from a distance. Lomax guessed that she was shy and that the introductions were an ordeal for her. Briefly, he allowed himself to meet her eye. In a nervous gesture she pushed her hair away from her face; ineffectually, because it at once swung back across her cheeks. He looked at her hair. It seemed to contain many colours – chestnut, blonde, a gleam of red. It fell loosely to her shoulders. She continued to smile at him as she turned to be introduced to Doberman and the Englishman. Her smile may have been, very slightly, lopsided.

Doberman stood too close to her, squinting sideways through thick glasses as if she were something very closely printed which had been spewed out of a computer. The Englishman stepped forward but

Yevgeny was faster. As soon as Doberman had shaken her hand, Yevgeny was pulling it hungrily to his lips. Lomax left.

He crossed the asphalt to the labs, dodging tourists. He was inside the building when he heard Kim puffing behind him.

'Try pretending she's your sister,' she suggested. Lomax ignored her and after a few moments he could no longer detect her breathing. She had turned into one of the offices. His pace slackened. The hallway was deserted. He could hear himself walk in it. The high ceilings and wooden floor and regular rhythm of his footsteps made a pleasing echo. This building had been constructed early in the century when there was just one telescope, a refractor, and it had taken astronomers two weeks by stagecoach from San Francisco to drive north across the valley and the foothills and penetrate this mountain range.

He entered the labs and was back in the twentieth century. They were windowless. The atmosphere was controlled. The light levels were predetermined. There was always a background hum, a low electronic buzz, but often you didn't hear it, even if you listened.

The computers were arranged in rows at individual tables. There was no one else at work. Lomax wove his way in and out of the hardware to his own computer and, after a few moments, pictures of the galaxy he thought of as his appeared on the screen. The familiarity of this room, this computer and this galaxy, was pleasant. But concentration was elusive. He found himself thinking about Julia Fox, the way her fingers had scraped at her hair and it had fallen right back over her face.

He studied his galaxy. In boyhood Lomax had developed a method of observatioon which he still retained. He learned an area of sky and learned it intimately until he knew it as well as the school timetable or the back of the bus driver's head. That patch of sky became a beacon or a landmark and meant he could always find his way. It was the start and end point of all his observations into the unknown. Now this galaxy, an especially attractive barred spiral, was the cornerstone of his private map.

The computer could pull back or move in closer but if you asked it to move in too close it gave you a dense jungle of images that meant nothing. It could produce pictures from information recorded by the telescope here on the mountain top and from the space telescope which had snapped this small piece of sky by chance with its second, roving eye. You could put the shots from the different angles together to form another image. It was not a complete picture but a tantalizing one. It invited guesswork, fancies, theories.

Lomax's finger clicked and clicked and clicked again. He watched the images without thinking about them. He remembered how Yevgeny had kissed Julia Fox's hand when Berlins had introduced them. He felt first unsettled and then disquieted. He did not know why. The sensation was almost physical. Doberman had been clasping Julia's hand and Yevgeny had taken it from him and kissed it and she had looked on him with a combination of warmth and embarrassment. Suddenly, as if jolted, Lomax realized the reason for his discomfort. There was something wrong with his galaxy.

Last night and every other night, he had known this galaxy. And now it was different. It had been altered. The alterations were easily noticeable. Although limited to the galaxy itself, the changes distorted perceptions of the surrounding sky.

He clicked again.

The computer was obedient. At his request it produced and reproduced the same evidence. But when asked to explain itself, the machine was unresponsive. Lomax's attempts to circumvent its systems were blocked. For some time – he did not know how long – he tried to outfox the computer.

Doberman and McMahon came in. McMahon was yawning as though he had just woken up and when Lomax looked at the clock he saw it was late afternoon. No wonder the labs had been so silent. Everyone else had been asleep.

'Any news?' he asked.

They shook their heads. Doberman had visited the biggest telescope, where the faultfinding team was still at work.

'Could lose another night's viewing,' said McMahon. 'And conditions are perfect out there.'

'Lomax, if the telescope's fixed, want to trade places with me tonight?' Doberman asked. He was standing right by Lomax now. Lomax instinctively cleared his screen.

'You want to view?'

'Yeah. I have an interesting little meteor-shower survey for Japan which I can give you next week instead.'

Lomax was booked to supervise viewing that night for a group of Australian astronomers who would be watching gaseous nebulae on screen from Perth. And now Doberman, who had never shown any interest in Australia or gaseous nebulae, was trying to trade this for meteor showers. He squinted at Doberman suspiciously. Doberman blinked back at him.

'You want to view tonight?'

'He wants to view the new assistant,' McMahon explained.

'Oh,' said Lomax.

'I've learned,' said Doberman, 'that women can find a man who knows how to ride the big telescope let's just say . . .' He grinned, his whole mouth ascending his face until it was almost touching his nose. 'Let's just say . . . exciting.'

Lomax groaned. Doberman was a braggart. Kim and Lomax had never believed the tales of his extensive sexual exploits. These generally featured many women, remarkable for their appetite and determination, begging an exhausted but ultimately obliging Doberman for his favours.

Doberman grinned again, his features buoyant with sexual innuendo. Lomax could not imagine a woman as attractive as Julia Fox taking any interest in him. She was an untouchable beauty.

'Want to take her viewing yourself, is that it, Lomax?' asked McMahon shrewdly.

'Of course not.'

Of course he did. At any rate, he wanted to protect her from Doberman's advances.

'It's just . . . well, these Australians have called me a few times to talk about their project and I'm not sure if . . .'

'I can handle gaseous nebulae. Just gimme the gist,' said Doberman, pulling up a nearby chair, reversing it, wrapping his knees around the backrest and flopping his chin over the top.

Lomax wavered. 'I'm not sure.'

'Lomax. C'mon.' Doberman was panting a little. 'She gave me such a helluva smile just now in Berlins' office.'

Lomax's stomach muscles spontaneously atrophied.

'Ple-eeeze,' begged Doberman.

Reluctantly, Lomax told him about the Australian project.

'I sure hope they fix the telescope,' said Doberman, getting up. 'I'll let you know how it goes tonight.' From his tone, Lomax guessed he was not referring to gaseous nebulae. McMahon, chuckling, caught Lomax's eye as they left. Lomax did not respond.

He continued to try and retry the Core 9 galaxy and finally, when there was no room for doubt that the original data had been rearranged, he just stared, defeated, at the screen. He, Lomax, had not altered the data and there was only one other astronomer who was likely to have seen it. This thought was an uncomfortable one.

He jumped when Berlins appeared suddenly, carrying a coffee. Lomax always tried not to look at Berlins' shaking hands, but now they vibrated so badly that the coffee slopped out of the cup. The professor spun around the chair which Doberman had vacated and sat down on it heavily.

'There's definitely a fault there,' he said, sighing. 'But I don't understand why we can't locate it.' He sipped coffee, spilling more. 'At least we've managed to prove last night's results were distorted.' His glasses, slipping down his nose, were endearingly lopsided.

Berlins was one of the most senior scientists at the observatory and Lomax's immediate boss. He would retire in a few years' time. Lomax liked him for many reasons. Berlins had been especially kind to him during his divorce and even now occasionally gave him extra time off to see his children.

Berlins was saying: 'Jorgen really wanted to believe the results were accurate. He was busy concocting an interesting explanation. But we shouldn't dismiss his ideas. There have been occasions when mistakes have enabled us to see the truth more clearly.'

Lomax admired Berlins' professional generosity. However apparently insane your theory, he would listen to it intently, nodding, and ask you questions. He had been a considerable theorist himself. His views on the formation of the universe, published about twenty years ago, had shaped a whole generation of astronomers. His ideas had subsequently been challenged and current thought had drifted away from him. He was still a respected cosmologist but he devoted himself now to nurturing the talents of younger scientists.

'Did you sleep this afternoon?' Lomax asked. He did not want to tell the professor how old and tired he was looking. He just wanted Berlins to go to bed.

'Oh yes. I had plenty of sleep. Very refreshing,' the professor assured him. Lomax studied the older man's face curiously. He did not look refreshed. Lomax coughed.

'Er, Professor . . . could this telescope fault or computer fault or whatever it turns out to be . . . could it possibly affect existing data?'

Berlins stared at him.

'Data already obtained? From viewing on earlier occasions?' he asked. Lomax nodded.

'But you know better than that, Lomax. Why are you asking?'

Now was the time to tell Berlins about the data change in Core 9. Lomax had engineered the moment and now all he had to do was speak. But caution, or perhaps instinct, held him back. He paused.

'Yes, Lomax?'

He floundered. 'I . . . well . . .'

Berlins took another sip of coffee and waited.

'Hi!' said the new assistant. She stood, hesitating, in the doorway. Berlins gestured her into the room. She apologized, Lomax was not sure why, and waved some papers at Berlins.

'I typed most of these but I had problems with your writing.'

'Everybody does,' said Berlins morosely.

Julia had changed into jeans and a sweater, pastel-coloured and soft like baby clothes. Nothing she wore was tight but you were left in no doubt that her figure was perfect. Lomax fixed his eyes on his galaxy.

She took a tissue from her pocket and wiped up the spilt coffee. Then she leaned over Berlins, pointing to places on his scrawled pages which she had marked in green. Lomax noticed that she wore a wedding ring.

'Redshift,' said Berlins, and Julia wrote it out clearly in a large childish hand.

'Doppler effect. Two ps. Bahcall-Peebles. That's B-a-h.'

'Okay, thanks.' Julia turned to leave. Then she stopped and looked at Lomax. 'Still excited?' she asked.

'Well, um . . . not really. I mean, we now know that the telescope's faulty, even though we don't know what the problem is.'

'You look tired. Want some coffee?'

Lomax refused. He didn't know why. He liked the idea of Julia fetching him coffee. Within a few moments he knew he wanted some badly. Berlins returned to his office with Julia, his unfinished conversation with Lomax forgotten, and by the time they had left, coffee was all Lomax could think about. He waited as long as he could and then sneaked to the drinks machine. He pressed the buttons for strong and black and, while he waited, Julia suddenly appeared by his side. He jumped guiltily. The machine finished its hissing and buzzing and he reached into its mouth for his drink.

'I knew you wanted some coffee. I guessed you'd be here.' She paused. 'Would you help me with something? Now that Professor Berlins has gone back to the telescope?'

'Sure,' he said, his hand baking round the plastic cup. They were going to lean over a keyboard together and watch the screen, their faces close, as they checked the spelling of Angstrom.

'Would you read through the paper I've just typed? Because it doesn't make any sense to me. It's not just the words I don't know, it's the sentences. I can't tell where they begin and end . . . I mean . . . I don't want Professor Berlins to think . . .' Her voice trailed away helplessly.

Lomax followed her to Berlins' office.

'What's an eclipse committee?' he asked her.

She turned to reply as they walked and he found himself admiring her forearms. They were long and graceful. He had never admired anyone's forearms before. He tried to remember anything at all about Candice's and couldn't. By the time they arrived at Berlins' office she had told him about the eclipse committee and he had not heard a word.

2

Julia had tidied Berlins' office. A window was open. A small jar of tiny yellow spring flowers stood on the desk. She invited him to take her own seat in front of the screen and then busied herself with one of the stacks of papers. He watched her out of the corner of his eye. She was filing, paper by paper. Even when he looked at the screen he was aware of her presence. She wasn't wearing perfume but he could smell her. It was a soft, clean smell. His small daughter used to smell that way after a bath, when she was sleepy and affectionate before bed.

Julia was sitting on Berlins' desk now, her feet on a filing cabinet, reading something. Her legs were a little apart and bent so that her jeans stretched tight.

'How am I doing?' she asked him over her shoulder.

'It's not your fault. He just forgets about syntax and things,' Lomax said.

'But he's a brilliant scientist, right?'

The brilliant scientist who could construct a theory on the formation of the universe but was unable to construct a sentence. Lomax wasn't going to take her stereotype away from her. He nodded absently and carried on reading.

It was hard to concentrate with Julia so close. Occasionally he glanced up and admired the way her hair fell over her shoulders or the slight curve of her back as she bent forward to read. He supposed he would get plenty of opportunities to study her back. It would be more difficult to gaze long and hard at the other side of her. He wanted to stare not so much at her breasts and hips – although these were of course interesting – but at the almost perfect symmetry of her face. He knew her beauty was classical: you could express it as an equation. This was the sort of thing Doberman would probably do. The cheekbones were high and in perfect proportion to the length of the face which was in perfect proportion to the chin and the forehead. It was possible, he told himself, that he had occasionally met women with faces like hers and remained unattracted to them. But Julia was so heartstopping because of the hint of her imperfections: most of the time she controlled her cool symmetry but occasionally her eyes darted or her smile was crooked or she twisted her lip and, briefly, she ceased to be unassailable.

She turned and found him staring at her. Lomax looked quickly back to the screen, but not before he had noticed the wedding ring again. He erased some of Professor Berlins' 'ands' and replaced them with periods.

'Who exactly is this for?' he asked suddenly, looking up. Julia became flustered at once, fluttering through Berlins' handwritten pages.

'Um . . . I don't know if he told me . . . no. It doesn't say.'

'It's just this is . . .'

'What?'

Lomax paused. He didn't know how to explain. The paper was only two or three pages long. It had no heading and no conclusion. It cited no references.

'It's notes. Ideas. That's why it's so messy. You don't need to worry about this too much,' he said, getting up.

'But is it . . . ?'

'It's fine. You did a good job.'

He wanted to stay and talk to her and watch her face. On impulse he asked: 'How much sleep did the professor get this afternoon?'

'None. He's been here with me pretty well since I arrived.'

Lomax frowned to hide his anger. He tried to regulate it by nodding slowly but it washed through his body all the same. Berlins had lied to him. A small lie, an insignificant one, probably just an elderly man's attempt to hide his fading stamina. But still a lie.

'I shouldn't have shown those notes to you,' said Julia suddenly. 'Something in them bothers you.'

Lomax picked up the stapler and stapled his thumb with it. He almost yelped in pain. He removed the staple and two small dots of blood punctuated the skin. Julia came over and took hold of his hand, turning it to see the damage in the light. Her fingers were long and her touch was cool. She studied his thumb, tutting over it and offering him Band-Aids, disinfectant, a clean tissue. He pulled his hand away and stepped back from her as soon as he could. Too soon, possibly: he thought he detected a slight twist to her mouth and a wounded look momentarily in her eyes but there was no time to rectify this, even if he could, because he had stepped onto a computer cable and pulled it from its socket. The writing on the screen disappeared.

15

Lomax swore, apologized, and bent to replug the cable, knocking the yellow flowers from the desk. Julia seemed to flutter nervously like a bird trapped in the confusion he had created. Red faced, he stood up.

'The file should be stored . . . the system backs up automatically . . .'

'You're too big for this office,' Julia was saying. Reminded of his height, he began to stoop, a legacy from his gauche teenage years, and edged towards the door, apologizing again.

'You're embarrassed because you think you never should have read that paper,' Julia said. The abruptness and accuracy of this remark made him stop. 'He didn't say it was confidential. I wish he'd said. My first day here, and I've already . . .'

Julia's helplessness was more painful to Lomax than his embarrassment, his anger or his throbbing thumb.

'You didn't do anything wrong, really. I'm on the professor's team. We're good friends and we don't have any secrets . . . He was probably planning to show me the paper, that's why he had you type it.'

'When he shows you . . .'

It was a plea.

'I'll be reading it for the first time. Don't worry.' There was a pause. They looked at each other. Lomax realized he was using the soothing voice he sometimes used with his daughter. It seemed to calm Julia. She stood still and parted her lips.

'It's all right,' he said.

Julia's hair fell round her cheekbones, emphasizing them. She looked at him searchingly and then seemed to relax, as though he had passed some test and she had decided to trust him. She bent to mop up the mess around the fallen flowers and Lomax went back to his own computer.

He watched the screen without reading it for a few minutes. He tried to search through long columns of figures but his concentration lapsed constantly. He realized he had left his coffee in Berlins' office.

He printed some pages and carried them back to his room like an animal dragging its meat into a quiet corner. He made some fresh coffee and settled at his desk by the window. He preferred working here to working in the lab. You could open a window and smell the mountains.

He leafed through an old copy of the *Astrophysical Review* in the late afternoon light, remembering the excitement and anticipation he'd felt since boyhood at the close of the day. Occasionally he recaptured it, but only occasionally. Mostly now he did little more than glance out to check on the likely viewing conditions.

Outside his room there had been slamming doors, hurrying feet and voices for some time. Now everyone had gone to the cafeteria for their evening meal and all was quiet again.

He found the article he was looking for and went to join the others. They were finishing their food, but no one was rushing off to work. He noticed Julia at the centre of a group nearby. She looked up briefly as he came in.

Lomax selected his meal and took up a defensive position with the *Astrophysical Review* on the far side of the room. He studied it as he ate. Doberman passed him with a large dish of wobbling, childish dessert.

'Read Proome's theory of CO_2 absorption yet?' he leaned over Lomax's shoulder and peered at the journal.

'No. This isn't the latest issue,' Lomax said.

Doberman returned to Julia's table. Lomax tried to read. It was hard to concentrate when he had to keep hunching his shoulders against the gales of laughter from across the cafeteria.

'So, you've played computers with her already.' Kim's voice tickled his ear. Her breath made his neck itch. He looked up with what he hoped was the unseeing expression of someone who had been completely immersed in his work.

'Who?' he asked vaguely. He noticed that Kim, too, was carrying a dish of jello.

'You know who. She had you read her typing in Berlins' office this afternoon. What was it? Love letters?'

'Kim.'

'You can't deny it. McMahon saw you.'

McMahon was incredible. He must have the entire place rigged with hidden cameras.

'Listen, she just asked me to check through something before Berlins saw it, okay?'

'Oh God, maybe she likes you, Lomax. How did you handle it? I mean, did you faint or something?'

'No, but I stapled my thumb.'

'Dickhead. Show me.'

Kim paused in her eating to examine the ghost of the staple. She lifted his thumb to her mouth and gave it an enormous, smacking, jello-stained kiss.

'For Chrissake!' Lomax looked involuntarily towards Julia.

'It's okay, I'm blocking her view – and, I mean, *I* could blot out the whole of Kansas.'

Lomax wished Kim wouldn't talk that way about her size. He wasn't sure whether her tone was bitter.

'So what was this alleged typing she asked you to check? Allegedly?'

Lomax shrugged unsuccessfully. 'Just some notes, really. Some ideas.' He tried to build the shrug into his voice but that was unsuccessful too. Kim paused in her eating and looked up at him sagely.

'Oh yes, what kind of ideas?'

Lomax considered. 'I'm not sure yet. I'm still thinking about them.'

To his surprise, Kim changed the subject.

'So guess how many guided tours she's had?'

'Who?'

'You know who. Guess how many guided tours.'

But Lomax wasn't playing.

'Three! The official one with Berlins, an extra escorted tour at the end of Doberman's leash, and the de luxe version with Prince Charles.'

Lomax glanced at Julia's table. Next to her sat the Englishman, tall and redheaded, telling some funny story. He spoke on a rising note and the others leaned forward, smiling in anticipation.

'Plus, Doberman's trying to get her to view with him tonight.'

Lomax saw Julia smile politely as the others roared with laughter.

'Want to know something interesting about her? Oh, but maybe I shouldn't tell you this. No, I'm sure I shouldn't.'

Lomax wanted to hear what she had to say very badly. With a superhuman effort, he said: 'Okay, don't.'

'Cool, very cool. But I know you want to know.'

Lomax's face was, he hoped, without expression.

'McMahon told me.' Kim paused and her eyes glistened. 'You *have* to know.'

She was right, and Lomax was about to speak when he heard another bowl of jello arrive at his side. Jorgen sat down.

'Well then, it's a fault with the telescope. Okay. We are all agreed on that.' Jorgen rarely started a conversation, but if he did he seemed to start it half way through. He sounded dejected.

'Too bad,' Lomax said. He wished Jorgen would eat his dinner elsewhere and that Kim would insist, in the face of his continued protests, on revealing the information about Julia. But at Jorgen's arrival, Kim had slipped away.

'It's a shame because, you know, I had some really quite interesting ideas to explain that redshift.' Jorgen looked sadly at his jello. 'I guess you don't want to hear my theory.' He sounded pathetic. He'd been offering his theory round the diners but no one had wanted to listen.

'Okay,' said Lomax. There was, after all, nothing else to do. Now there was believed to be a computer fault, work had been halted on all the telescopes. Dirty coffee cups were accumulating. People were tense. Someone reported that outside it was completely dark and viewing conditions clear. There were groans. A few astronomers were dressed ready for viewing in the bulky heated suits the observatory supplied. Others had already started to nibble at chocolate bars and peanut butter sandwiches from their night snack boxes. An argument had broken out on a table near Lomax and a scientist was banging a fork against a plate to make her point. Jorgen began to yell his theory over the noise. It was a while before anyone noticed Berlins and Dr Yokoto from the fault-finding team standing at the front of the room.

When there was silence, Berlins announced that all the equipment was now working normally. A few people got up to start work, but others demanded an explanation.

Yokoto drew a small box from his pocket and held it up at eye level, removing its lid with a flourish.

'In the box,' he said solemnly, 'is a piece of glass. On that piece of glass is a hair. A small hair, a tiny hair, but a hair which somehow escaped our notice.'

Surprise followed anger.

'Where was this . . . hair?' Jorgen demanded.

Berlins was silent for a moment.

'I regret to report that it was in fact found in the slit end of the spectrograph up at the Fahrhaus.'

Voices began shouting. A few hissed. A slit-end hair should have been simple to diagnose and easy to find. Everyone turned to Yokoto for an explanation. Yokoto stared boldly back until, involuntarily, one eye began to twitch.

'We will, of course, be investigating whose hair this is and how it got into the spectrograph. But . . .' Yokoto's tic increased in intensity like a series of electric shocks. '. . . my first reaction is that it is the hair from a man's beard.'

Lomax was aware that a number of faces had turned towards him, some of them muttering.

'Been near the spectrograph lately?' McMahon called to him.

'How you know it beard hair and not pubic hair?' asked Yevgeny. There was laughter. Yokoto shot Yevgeny a look of disgust.

19

'Lomax, what have you been doing with the spectrograph?' Kim leered.

'I haven't been near the goddam spectrograph,' said Lomax, remembering immediately that he had. But people were scattering. They were gathering their snacks and coffee flasks and sweaters and talking in small groups. Lomax watched them go as Yokoto bore down on him to match the rogue hair to his beard. He dared to glance over to Julia only once. She was looking at him. Their eyes met before she turned away. The expression on her face was kind, compassionate even. Humiliated, he watched her leave the cafeteria with Doberman.

3

'Shave it off,' people advised Lomax for the next few days. He soon grew tired of them calling this across the lab to him or muttering it as they passed him in hallways. They had already renamed a cloud of gas and dust many galaxies away The Beard Nebula.

'I seriously think you should consider shaving your beard off,' Berlins told him when they were alone one evening. Unluckily, this wasn't the first time a hair from Lomax's beard had caused problems in delicate equipment.

Berlins spoke quietly, amusement in his eyes, but Lomax knew he wasn't joking. They had only lost a total of four hours' viewing time, but it added up to many thousands of dollars at a time of financial stringency.

'I couldn't do that, Professor Berlins,' he said.

'Just think about it. Things are changing round here, Lomax.'

Lomax did not like change. The new atmosphere of reorganization at the observatory unsettled him. He ignored the rumours about job cuts. He had no interest in the management training and fund raising courses some senior astronomers were now attending. He had resisted the cultivation of the observatory's new public image. He had argued that money spent on a sound and light exhibition specially for the tourists was money wasted. And he did not intend to shave his beard.

Julia walked in just then. Berlins said: 'How do you think Lomax would look without a beard?'

Julia made a great show of considering this. She put her head on one side and then the other and stared hard at Lomax's chin. It could have been an invitation to stare back at her, but Lomax was still unable to.

'Well . . . Lomax.' She smiled. 'It depends who you want to be.'

'I've had this beard since I was about twenty,' Lomax said. 'Even I'm not sure what's underneath any more.'

'Maybe you could trim it back a bit.' Julia sounded like Candice. Candice was always trying to persuade Lomax to trim his beard or wear different clothes or have his hair cut.

'No, the clippings would find their way into the spectrograph,' Berlins said. 'Lomax is a slob and he's proud of it. He leaves things lying around all over the observatory. Pens, disks, documents, photos. One day he changed desks with someone and they found the drawers were full of half-eaten sandwiches. Most of them were in such an advanced state of decay that they were practically fossilized. He chews the ends of pens ferociously and then walks around with ink in his mouth for the rest of the day. Look at the way buttons are missing from his shirt. Julia, I don't want you to think all scientists are like this.'

'I don't,' said Julia quietly.

Lomax wore a pained expression.

'This untidiness indicates an untidiness of mind which is worrying. Unsettling. Unscientific, even. Because Lomax's mind is otherwise of outstanding quality,' Berlins said, looking directly at him.

'He's telling you to clean up your act,' Kim explained when Lomax repeated the conversation to her the next day.

'Can't I clean up my act without cleaning up my chin?'

A party had gone into town the night before. They had spent the day promising each other how drunk they'd get but Kim reported that they had eaten a respectable meal in a respectable restaurant without a hint of rowdiness. One or two of them had fallen asleep. Doberman had failed to produce the women he'd promised Jorgen.

The party had stopped at a drug store to buy Lomax a cheap razor. 'I'm a smooth operator!' was printed on the handle in gold lettering. It had been presented to him that morning and he had smiled his thanks but still refused to shave.

'I guess he means that if you wore a suit and parted your hair like Jorgen then guys would take you more seriously. It's true you're a mess, Lomax.'

'I thought I was taken seriously,' Lomax muttered. 'I don't like the way this is all turning so personal.'

'Don't ask me what's going on, I'm a mess too. That's why I like you.'

Lomax looked around the room. It was a mealtime, as usual. Family mealtimes had always seemed to Lomax to be about much more than food, but this coming-together of the scientists three times a day was far worse. This is where friendships were made or broken, dominant people exercised their power, and groups formed and re-formed. Whenever you were getting tired of the observatory, the first thing you tired of was mealtimes.

'Five years ago . . .' Lomax began. 'No, even two years ago, there wouldn't have been all these people wearing ties. It's Dixon Driver's fault.'

Dixon Driver was the observatory's new director. Since his arrival he had urged some of his scientific staff to take a more managerial approach to their work.

'I mean, look at Doberman in a crushproof suit. I worked with him at St. Christophe and he never wore anything but jeans.'

Kim shrugged. 'So Doberman's ambitious and the world's changing.'

Lomax thought of Candice and how she had changed. Everyone had changed except for him and now they were telling him to change too. Kim straightened suddenly.

'Okay, Lomax, get a grip on yourself. Breathe deeply and keep your blood pressure under control. She's coming this way.'

As Julia sat down, Kim told her confidingly: 'Lomax is real worried about his image.'

'I'm not worried. Everyone else seems to be,' said Lomax.

'They say he should smarten up. Trim that hair, shave that beard. But I think he's lovable just the way he is, don't you?'

Julia laughed. It was possible to interpret this in a number of ways. 'Everyone needs to change from time to time,' she said.

Kim looked at her in disbelief. 'Did you? Does it hurt? Is it painful?'

'The only thing which makes it difficult is other people. Sometimes they don't want to let you change.'

'Not in Lomax's case. Everyone wants him to change. Everyone except me. I don't want to be the last slob left around here.' She tugged her dark hair first in one direction and then the other. It looked equally dishevelled both ways.

'You could change too,' Julia said.

'You could change too,' Kim mimicked in a little-girl voice as she walked back across the asphalt with Lomax. 'I'm surprised she didn't give me a diet sheet.'

'You don't like her.'

'It's the way she looks so damn helpless all the time, it makes everyone run to help her. What an act. I bet I know why the husband's dead. He hung himself from the nearest tree.'

Lomax stared at her. 'The husband's dead?'

'Oh yeah, I didn't tell you in the end. Husband and daughter. Or was it stepdaughter? I don't remember. Anyway, they're dead. That's why she's here.'

23

'Kim, that's awful.'

'Uh huh.' Kim's tone was not entirely sympathetic.

'God. How did they die?'

'Her lisp drove them to suicide.'

'She doesn't lisp.'

'Lomax, if Barbie could talk, that's how she'd sound.'

'Why don't you like her?'

'There's nothing to like. She's just a great face and a great figure.'

'You're wrong.'

'Your hormones are talking.'

'I'm not the slightest bit attracted to her.'

'If you'd gone to my school you would have got about a million Hail Marys for that one.'

'She's not dumb just because she's pretty.'

'What did she have you read the other day?'

Lomax had to smile. Kim never let any piece of information slip by her. 'I told you. Just some typing.'

'Tell me really, Lomax.'

'There's nothing to tell.'

They were at the door of the lab. Tourist cars cruised gently round the parking lot nearby.

Kim persisted. 'You said it was ideas, or notes or something.'

Lomax frowned. He strolled to the edge of the parking lot where there was a low stone wall looking out across the valley towards the next mountain range and the next until the distance was a milky blur of mountains. The wall was wide enough to sit on but he leaned on it instead, bending his head against the sun. Its heat and light poured down on them, reflected off car hoods nearby with a dazzling intensity.

'I don't know exactly,' he said, 'but it seemed to be some kind of theory out of Core Nine.'

'Big deal. We've all got theories out of Core Nine. Even me. And I'm not working on that project.'

'This theory was constructed on the basis of evidence which to my knowledge doesn't exist.'

Kim was silent for a moment, searching Lomax's face. He stared back. Her hair fell limply around her cheeks. Bloated by the unkind sun, or perhaps by emotion, her face looked balloon-like.

'Do you know it doesn't exist?'

'I'm sure, but Berlins claims it does. Remember the redshift when the hair got in the spectrograph? Well Jorgen went round constructing a theory to explain it. Berlins is working on similar lines.'

'He's lifted Jorgen's theory?'

'No, he's amended it. But Jorgen's theory was based on faulty information. And Berlins is working on a fiction. A fabrication.'

'A fabrication! What's that supposed to mean?'

Lomax told her how he had discovered the altered galaxy in Core 9 and spent the afternoon trying to prove, without success, that no one had been distorting results. Kim's face reddened as he spoke.

'You're not going to try to tell me . . . Jeez, Lomax. No one would do that. Berlins wouldn't do that!'

Her voice was strangled by anger and anguish. When Lomax spoke, he heard the same tone in his own.

'But no one else has access to the data! Only me and Berlins!'

Kim leaned forward in a vomiting position. Lomax saw her knuckles go white as she gripped the warm wall and he knew at once he had made a mistake. He shouldn't have confided in her. He asked himself how, when he knew Kim so well, he could have made such an elementary error of judgement. It proved you never really knew anyone. For all her cynicism about the place, Kim was happy at the observatory. She lived here and worked here and thrived here. She was engrossed in her project and outside the lab the other scientists were fond of her, brotherly even. And Berlins – always kind, always patient, gently guiding the research – played too fundamental a role in Kim's small world to withstand a challenge.

'It's okay,' Lomax said soothingly. He tried to eliminate the angry, urgent tone from his voice. He tried to sound relaxed. 'It's okay. I know Berlins is above reproach. I admire him as much as you do. All it means is he's obviously working along some line of his own and he's basing it on evidence I'm not aware of. I tried reading some articles in *AR* which were relevant but so far I can't see where he's coming from. That's all.'

'So Berlins is smarter than you. That's what you're saying.'

'That's all I'm saying.'

'Good. Because if you thought –'

'I don't.'

'I mean . . . Lomax, just keep your mouth shut.'

This was the same Kim who was usually greedy for a scent of scandal, who was mischievous enough to hint at foul play where there was none just to make life interesting.

'You're a dickhead,' she said and walked away.

He sat on the wall and watched her cross the parking lot. Cars had to pause to let her pass, their occupants staring. Usually dickhead was a term of affection with Kim, but not this time. He stayed sitting on the wall a few minutes more. Near him, a lizard did press-ups. Lomax could not think of Berlins without disgust.

He decided to work the afternoon out and then go home. The telescope was booked by a group of Italians for the next few days; this was an opportunity for a break. He thought of his house, high in the green foothills, overshadowed by the mountains and big trees. Spring would be further advanced at the lower altitude. The branches would already be in leaf and shaking with busy squirrels.

Soon afterwards, he shaved. Taunted just once more by Yevgeny or the Englishman – it didn't matter which – he shaved in front of everyone.

At first, as he trimmed back the beard with scissors, there was cheering and clapping. But when he reached the soap and water stage a silence fell. He took the 'I'm a smooth operator!' razor and everyone listened to the rasping sound it made as he dragged it across his face and neck. He did not hurry and so, incredibly, did not cut himself, but the process nevertheless felt like a mutilation. It hurt, this scraping and peeling, and what lay underneath was tender.

A group of about ten men watched him, fascinated. Lomax had learned in adolescence that he should shave round his birthmark with particular care. He only became aware of his audience because of the effect he knew it was having on them as he gradually revealed it, basking on his lower left cheek. It used to remind him of a lizard sunbathing on a rock.

Nobody broke the silence when the birthmark began to appear, but Lomax did not have to look up to sense the embarrassment in the room. When he finished, he felt elated. The faces on all sides of him were staring and foolish.

He cleaned the razor and ran clear water into the bowl until the pieces of beard were gone. He patted his chin dry. His audience did not move.

'So long, see you in a couple of days,' he said. He picked up his bag and went out to the dark parking lot. As soon as he was inside his car he turned on the light and stared in the mirror. It was only big enough to show him sections of his face, but those sections were new and strange and shocking to him.

He had assumed that trapped under the beard was a young man of about twenty but the young man had been aging in there all this time. He hadn't been cocooned against the disappointments, the bereavements, the late nights and the divorce. He had experienced them all and now here they were, etched onto his face. Lomax wanted to stare and stare.

'Hi!' Julia tapped on his car window. The intrusion made him jump.

'Show me,' she said. He guessed that his shave and his birthmark were already the subject of conversation back in the staff residence. He opened the door and sat under the light while she looked at him.

'Trick or treat,' he grinned ghoulishly.

She put her head on one side and stared at his birthmark.

'You can have it removed with plastic surgery,' she said. 'I just might be able to help you . . . give me your phone number.'

Lomax didn't want a plastic surgeon but he wanted to give her the number.

'Where is that?' she asked.

'It's in the foothills this side of town. You head towards the Interstate and take the Old Mine Road.'

Julia lived less than twenty minutes away from him. They exchanged not just phone numbers but addresses. Julia said she was going home the very next day. When he left the parking lot he had a date for the following night.

Lomax drove especially slowly round the hairpin bends down the mountain because he didn't want to die before his date. Whenever there was a straight stretch of road he reached up to his chin and felt the strange smoothness there. He ran his fingers all over his neck and up under his ears and round the line of his chin and over his cheeks. Nothing had happened at the observatory for weeks and then, in just fifteen minutes, he had shaved his beard and fixed a date with Julia. He could think of nothing else but these two events. His suspicions about Berlins were forgotten. His anger evaporated.

4

Lomax did not know what to wear. His beardlessness and indecision and search through untidy closets for the right clothes all reminded him of adolescence. He found jeans. He wished there was something more likely to impress Julia. He found more jeans. He remembered Candice's exasperation and how he had resisted her attempts to change his appearance.

Now he opened closets and sighed his way through drawers. He tried to tell himself that jeans were what he, Lomax, wore and that a date with Lomax was a date with jeans. But all his defiance must have been spent on Candice. Now he just wanted to wear the right thing. He suspected that shaving might even have been something to do with Julia.

Deputy Dawg watched him knowingly. He had picked up Deputy from the friends who were looking after him while Candice and Robert and the children were vacationing.

'I can't take you, boy. You have to shave before you get a date with her,' he said.

Deputy knew all about dates. He had a reputation for womanizing in the foothills. A number of puppies in this immediate area, and perhaps throughout most of Northern California, were his and now those puppies were growing up. Deputy had even been seen displaying an unhealthy interest in his own daughters.

Lomax washed and shaved. This time the razor slid over his cheeks less painfully. He no longer felt it was slicing off pieces of his face. He appreciated the cleanness of the lines it cut through the soap. There was a possibility Julia might kiss him goodbye, or hello, and he wanted his face to be smooth for her. He momentarily allowed himself to entertain the thought that her kisses might not be restricted to goodbye or hello, or even to his face. He thought of her mouth.

' "I'm a smooth operator," ' he told Deputy through the right side of his mouth as he shaved the left side of his face. But Deputy was trying to copulate with a giant sponge he had retrieved from the shower.

Lomax drove to Julia's house with his chin stinging. He felt apprehensive. Were they going to eat out? Or would they have an evening at home sipping wine and discussing their marriages?

Julia's house was even more isolated than Lomax's. He passed the end of the drive twice because there were dark trees and overhanging foliage all around it. He couldn't reconcile this with his idea of where Julia might live. He had imagined her in a tidy apartment.

The house was large. As he waited on the doorstep, Lomax thought his car didn't look as though it should be parked on the drive, not unless someone had called a plumber.

Julia opened the door and he was suddenly acutely aware of his birthmark. She didn't smile or kiss him hello.

'The garbage disposal's broken,' she said helplessly. She really did think he was the plumber.

'Lead me to it.' He followed her past rooms with high ceilings and pastel walls. He tried to look in through the open doors but she walked quickly, discussing the garbage disposal over her shoulder. She wondered if it was blocked. She had used it just once that evening, she said, when she'd cleared some limp old lettuce out of the fridge. It had gotten blocked once before. It was an ancient garbage disposal unit.

Lomax imagined Candice shoving her hand down into the pipe the way you weren't supposed to, or getting out a plunger or a screwdriver and saying: 'Fuck this.' Now here he was, up to his elbow in decaying lettuce and assorted garbage, and as his fingers reached down among the filth and the chopped up pieces and the blades Julia, wearing a soft blue dress, was leaning on a work surface close by and asking questions about astronomy.

'A redshift is called a redshift because it looks red on the spectrograph,' he said. 'The light it emits tells you two things: it's moving, in fact it's going away from you, and you should get some idea of how fast it's moving.' There was something between his fingers now which felt like small bones, perhaps chicken.

'So, why the fuss over the redshift in Core Nine? I mean, I know it was all a mistake, but . . .'

'Core Nine is a survey of a number of distant galaxies, clusters and superclusters in one area of sky. A core of sky. The galaxy Jorgen got so excited about is much closer, maybe only ten million light years away. That's real close. We can see five, eight, billion light years — that takes us to the edge of the observable universe.' There was a large bone between his two forefingers but he didn't have the dexterity to grasp it, at least not with his left hand. He slowly extracted his left arm and put his right arm down the hole.

'If we see light which is eight billion light years away, that's how long it's taken that light to reach us. So when we're looking back to this light we're looking back to the beginning of the universe. To its formation, the big bang. Almost, but not quite. Anyway, the point is that the universe is expanding. Everything's travelling outwards all the time.'

He searched now for the thick bone. He couldn't find it. He craned his neck to see Julia and make sure she was still listening but she was looking for something in the fridge.

'Are you still listening?' he asked.

'Sure. Everything's travelling outwards all the time.'

'Okay. Well, the further they are away from us, the faster galaxies appear to be travelling. That's what we expect. We can work that out from looking at their redshifts.' He had grasped the bone. He manipulated it gently round the blades and tugged it free. He switched on the unit and it made guttural sounds while he washed his hands. He suspected Julia wasn't interested in what he was saying. He remembered the talk he had given his son's fourth grade science class. He brought the explanation to a speedy conclusion, yelling it over the gurgle of the garbage disposal.

'The hair in the spectrograph made it seem that there was this incredible velocity redshift in a galaxy which is much too close to us to be moving that fast. That's the reason Jorgen got so excited. A high-velocity nearby redshift would challenge many of our assumptions about the structure . . .' His voice was drowned as the machine grappled with an especially stubborn piece of debris. He waited for it to stop. '. . . our assumptions about the formation and structure of the universe.' The garbage disposal had finished but he realized he was still yelling.

'Oh,' said Julia. Suddenly the kitchen seemed very silent.

'The most exciting things,' added Lomax, remembering suddenly what had most pleased the fourth-graders, 'are distant quasars. They're almost as old as the universe. And they emit such bright light that we can see sort of shadows. Ancient shadows from many billions of light years ago. They're the shadows of the young universe developing.'

Julia looked at him.

'So you're watching the universe being formed out there?'

'In silhouette. I guess you could say that, yes.'

30

Julia stared at him incredulously and Lomax felt a flush of triumph.

'Do you need anything else fixed?' he asked her.

'Well . . . oh no, it's okay.'

But Lomax insisted. He wanted to fix things for her. He was good at fixing things. She finally admitted that one of the security lights wasn't working.

'Maybe the bulb needs changing.'

She shrugged.

'Surely you know how to change a bulb?'

She laughed. She was embarrassed. So he tried to show her but it was clear by the end of the lesson that she still didn't know how. Candice hated women like this.

There was a number of other small jobs around the house. He found some tools in the basement and used them to re-align a closet door and change a plug and replace some picture hangings.

This gave him an opportunity to see something of her home and learn about her family, the family which had died, from the bedspreads and the pictures and the keepsakes on the bureau. Except there were no keepsakes.

The only room which had any discernible personality was the basement. The air down here had the thin equilibrium of air which is seldom disturbed so that just moving across it you seemed to release dormant smells of wood and varnish. Someone had hung the tools with affectionate order along the wall. They were all at the same 30-degree angle, in diminishing size from left to right, secured on identical nails. They had been well-cared for but now they were dusty. Lomax admired the wall. It had the immediacy of a cave painting.

Beneath the tools were nails and screws and plugs arranged in a tidy network of wooden nests. The nests were home-made and he found, chiselled on the side of the structure, the word 'Gail'. It was too neat to be graffiti.

The workbench ran all the way along the wall and was endearingly scarred by years of small home woodwork projects. The scars, crisscrossing at many angles, were the only sign of disorder here. Even the dirty rags were folded in a bag marked 'Dirty Rags'. Lomax felt a rush of warmth for Julia's husband.

The rest of the basement was dark, with boxes stacked high into the corners. Maybe after the deaths Julia had packed things up and brought them down here. The crust of family life, its patina, the relics of its different personalities, were missing from the rest of the house. It was probably all in those boxes.

When Lomax had finished his chores he was dusty and dirty. Julia told him to sit down in the living room and she would bring him a drink.

This room was like all the others. Its big old windows filled it with the last long rays of daylight. The walls were painted in the pastel shades he already associated with Julia and large antiques, vases or sculptures stood self-consciously in pools of space. He wandered about, aware that his clothes were now dirty, reluctant to sit in the creamy chairs.

On the bookshelf was a picture of Julia's wedding day. Lomax examined it greedily. He wanted to learn all he could about her. So far she had talked about her childhood and the observatory but she hadn't talked about the ghosts in the photograph, and the longer they went unmentioned the more the tragedy hung between them.

Lomax had time to take in the fact that Julia's husband had been much older than her. The young man and woman in the photo seemed closer in age to Julia. He heard her voice approaching and hastily replaced the picture.

'I have a confession to make,' she said. 'You probably noticed you couldn't smell anything cooking.'

Lomax had noticed, but he tried to look non-committal.

'I bought everything else I needed to make Chinese Chicken Salad. I mean, I remembered the crunchy chow mein noodles and the scallions and the toasted almonds.'

'But you forgot . . . ?'

'The chicken.' She bit her lip anxiously.

He smiled. 'Let's have it without.'

'You can't have Chinese Chicken without the chicken.'

He hoped she wouldn't suggest that they eat out. He wanted to spend the rest of the evening in her house surrounded by her pictures and her bookshelves. He wanted to glean information about her from the way her spare pairs of shoes sprawled on the carpet or from the appointments and anniversaries scribbled on the kitchen calendar. He wanted to be a detective.

'So, let's see, you have . . .'

'Salad. With a lot of different ingredients. And noodles . . . I hope you like noodles.'

'Mmmmm, noodles. Do you have a can of tuna fish?'

'Maybe . . .' He followed her to the kitchen.

'If you do then we can have Spicy Tuna Salad. And noodles. Simple.'

He had guessed some time ago that he would wind up making the dinner. She gave him the ingredients and watched while he opened doors and drawers looking for more.

'I actually like to cook. It's just it's not going to be easy to organize the kitchen now I'll be away so much,' she explained.

'You soon learn how. You need to keep supplies.' He was mixing things together. He hoped he looked skilful.

'My husband couldn't cook at all,' she told him.

'He sure kept a neat workshop, though.' Lomax handed her the can of tuna fish to open.

'In the basement? He never went down there.'

'Oh, it's your workshop, right? That's where you learned advanced woodworking.' He was busy now. He could ask the questions he had wanted to ask about her family in just the right distracted tone.

'It was Mr Weinhart's workshop. He used to look after the house and the yard and other peoples' yards around here and he kept his tools in the cellar.'

So Julia's husband was as much of an enigma as ever. The rush of affection he had felt for the occupant of the workshop had been for Mr Weinhart, some kind of janitor.

'Who's Gail?'

'Gail?'

'Her name's carved on some shelves down there.'

'You took a good look around.'

Lomax reddened.

She said quickly, her voice softening: 'I mean, I've been down in the basement and I've never even noticed that. Gail was my stepdaugther. She used the workbench too. She used to go down in the cellar with Mr Weinhart for hours and he'd show her how to make things. She liked doing that.'

She was still holding the can of tuna. He took it from her and began to open it himself. He didn't want to talk about Mr Weinhart or Gail.

'Your husband's dead,' he announced. He knew that was the wrong way to say it but she rescued him anyway.

'I'll show you a picture.' She went out and came back with the photo from the living room. He stopped cooking to look at it but she did not hand it to him so they each held a corner of the frame.

'That's Lewis. Those are my stepchildren, Gail and Richard. And that's me, of course. Lewis and Gail died in an accident at the end of last year.'

'I'm sorry,' Lomax said and she nodded.

'You look . . . different,' he said. 'I mean, you look great there, and you still look great . . . you just look sort of . . .'

'Older?' she smiled.

'Wiser,' he said and looked at the photo to cover his embarrassment. He noticed again how much older than Julia her husband was: he might have been her father. He was white-haired and distinguished. The stepdaughter, Gail, was plain. Standing next to Julia, a stunning bride, Gail was barely noticeable. Richard was a younger version of his father, his face fuller but with the same bone structure.

'Richard's still alive?'

'Sure. He lives in Seattle.'

Julia seemed to have allotted him time to study the picture and now his time was up. She drew it away from him.

'A happy family,' Lomax said because he felt it was something Julia wanted him to say.

'We were a happy family.' Her voice shook slightly. She returned the photo to the living room. Lomax turned back to his pans.

As they ate she asked him about his divorce and he told her a little about Candice and the children and Deputy Dawg.

'I like dogs,' she said.

It was easy to talk to her. She asked questions and fixed her eyes on him and nodded in the right places. Her comments were intelligent and her evasion was clever. She had a way of turning his questions back around to him with only the briefest of answers so that by the end of the meal he knew there were whole areas of her life she was reluctant to talk about in any detail: all the dead people. The dead father, the dead mother, the dead husband, the dead stepdaughter.

Lomax supposed he should go home. By this time she seemed impossibly beautiful and she had expressed no sexual interest in him. He remembered Doberman, manoeuvering himself into a night's viewing with her. Probably she was bored with the many clumsy sexual advances men made. He calculated that his best move was retreat. He got up to go.

'It's strange. I've hardly noticed your birthmark all evening,' she said.

'Not once?'

'Just when you first arrived. You stood there looking so awkward. Like: I'm the plumber, is this the right house?'

'Plumbers have birthmarks?'

'It's more noticeable when you start acting shy and awkward. Your birthmark sort of walks through the door first and you come sneaking along behind it. Like a riot shield. Did you ever think of having something done about it?'

'Nope,' said Lomax. He remembered that this was the pretext under which he had taken her phone number and address and she had invited him for dinner. Perhaps it wasn't a pretext. Perhaps he was really here because she felt sorry for him.

'Don't be shy about it.'

'I guess it's the reason I grew a beard. That's the furthest I'm prepared to go to disguise it.'

'Why?'

'Well . . . it's me. Lomax. It's a part of me.'

'You could have plastic surgery and still be you.'

'I don't think so.'

'You believe that if your appearance changes, your personality automatically changes with it?'

'I wouldn't be me any more.'

'Lomax, after my Dad died but before I got married . . . I shared an apartment with this girl. Marcia.'

Lomax nodded. He had already heard a little about Julia's apartment-sharing days: it had been established as a safe area in her life to talk about. No one had died.

'Well, Marcia had round handwriting with real big loops in it. She wrote a g and it looked like two big bubbles. Someone told her this was a sign of an aggressive personality. She didn't want an aggressive personality. So she changed her writing.'

'And was Marcia less aggressive after that?'

'Marcia was just exactly the same. If her personality had changed, then her handwriting might have changed too. But not the other way around.'

'So if I get less aggressive my birthmark might disappear?'

Julia sighed for an answer.

He said: 'You think I should have plastic surgery.'

'We-ell . . .'

'You think my birthmark's repulsive.'

'I don't.'

'You do.' His throat, against his will, was constricting and he had to work harder to push his voice through it as if he was working against some force as natural as gravity.

'Don't get upset. You're very attractive. I'm just telling you that if you need any help I know a surgeon who specializes in birthmarks, accidents, burns, that kind of thing. And he's good.'

They were still sitting at the dinner table. She got up, walked around it, leaned torwards him and kissed his birthmark. Her kiss felt cool. Maybe his birthmark was hot.

If he had been waiting for some sexual signal from her all evening, this was it. She slipped her hands into his. But he had to ask her something.

'Julia, did you ever have plastic surgery?'

'Yes.'

He recoiled at the possibility that her perfection was manmade. She watched him, then quietly fetched the wedding photo again. This time she let him hold it.

'A couple of years ago I was in an accident and my nose got smashed up. It looked terrible. That's when I found this plastic surgeon. Now, can you really tell the difference?'

He stared at Julia in the wedding photo. She carried a bouquet. There was a jewel glittering on her dress. Her smile was joyful. He looked from that Julia's nose to this Julia's nose and back again.

'No.'

'Are you sure? You said I'd changed when you saw the picture earlier . . .'

'You haven't changed. You look just the same. Really.'

'You wouldn't be Lomax if you had plastic surgery. I wouldn't be Julia if I hadn't.'

Relieved, he reached out and gently touched her nose. He ran his finger down its fine bridge and then across her cheek and down her chin so lightly that his touch wouldn't have broken the surface of her face if it had been water.

So it was all natural. The surgeon had just restored something which nature had created first.

'What caused the accident?' he asked softly. But she shook her head and got up to return the picture to its shelf.

He surveyed the debris of the meal. He hadn't really noticed whether it was good or not. He couldn't even remember eating it. Now he just wanted her to come back to the table. By the time he realized she was calling him she must have done so several times.

A note in her voice alarmed him. There was no light in the room and at first he could hardly see her. Then he mistook a big, sculptural ceramic for her. Finally he found her. She was standing back from the window, half-hidden by the drapes.

'There's a car out there,' she said.

'Mine?'

'No.'

He could see it, too, now. It was parked against the dark bushes but the light from the house captured points of its metal work and hinted at its shape. Its driver could not have deluded himself that it would be invisible.

Lomax opened the front door and listened. There was no engine running. The car sat quietly outside like a threat. Was it waiting for something?

He had only taken a few steps before he saw that it was a police car. Lomax was relieved. Its occupant did not get out but rolled down the window.

'Is there some kind of problem here?' asked Lomax.

'Just making sure Mrs Fox's okay,' said the policeman.

Lomax stared. He felt some further explanation was required but the man grinned back at him. Lomax did not like his grin. It was big-toothed. The man's other features were coarse, too, and although it was a cold night, perspiration was visible on his face.

'Don't you guys generally work in pairs?' Lomax asked suddenly.

'No sir. I'm a sheriff in these foothills and I'm what some people call a lone wolf.'

There was nothing wolf-like about the man's fat face.

'Well as you can see, there's no cause for worry,' Lomax said. But the fat sheriff grinned.

'Just making sure you're all right, Mrs Fox,' he called as Julia approached. 'Saw a car parked on the drive here and I thought to myself: I'm gonna make sure Mrs Fox's okay.'

'Everything's fine, Sheriff. Thanks for your concern,' Julia said.

The sheriff looked confidentially towards Lomax.

'Mrs Fox's had a lot of disturbance. So I like to make sure she's okay.'

'Well as you can see, she's fine.' Lomax's tone was final, dismissive. It contained a note of irritation. The sheriff was supposed to sense this, nod, start the car and drive off. But he grinned back at them happily, unmoving.

'It's all right, Sheriff. Dr Lomax was just getting ready to leave,' Lomax heard Julia say. He looked at her.

'I'll stay here a while longer, Mrs Fox. I'd like to do that. So I know you're safe,' the policeman said. His smile was fixed. 'You got company, don't let me interfere with your entertaining now.'

But he had interfered. Because of his presence, unasked for and unnecessary, Julia had sent Lomax away.

They went back inside the house but the atmosphere was different now. Lomax was angry. Julia was brittle.

'Does that guy sit outside your house often?' Lomax demanded as soon as they had shut the door.

'I don't know. I don't think so.'

'Who does he think I am? An axe murderer, for Chrissake? And since when have policemen just parked in people's drives without anyone asking them to?'

Julia looked pained.

'You didn't ask him to? Or did you?'

'No,' said Julia. 'I didn't ask him to.'

Lomax felt an explanation was due from someone, if not from the sheriff then from Julia. But none was forthcoming. They stood staring at each other for a moment.

'You really want me to go now?'

'Yes, because I'm tired. I drove down from the observatory this morning, and tomorrow night . . .' She looked at her watch and saw it was past midnight. '. . . tonight I have to drive all the way back.'

'Are you sure you're safe with that big-toothed fat guy outside?'

'He's a policeman.'

Lomax studied her face for signs of tiredness but it looked as perfect as ever. For a few brief moments, during his anger, he hadn't noticed her beauty but now he recognized it afresh. Of course she wanted him to go. She had probably been waiting for him to go for hours.

'Thanks for dinner,' he said.

'Thanks for cooking it,' she said.

They smiled at each other. His hand was on the door handle.

'I guess I'll see you at work . . . I may not mention I visited you here. I mean, there's no reason not to, but people are –'

'It's okay,' she said. 'I won't tell anyone either.'

She kissed him on his other cheek, the one without the birthmark, and then on his lips. It was a soft kiss and it lasted several seconds.

Outside, Lomax looked straight away towards the dark police car. It was still there and he knew without being able to see that the sheriff was grinning at him. He drove down to the road outside and, after a few hundred yards, stopped. He waited a cold, tired twenty minutes before he saw the car finally drive away. Relieved, he went home.

5

Usually Lomax went away from the observatory and came back again and nothing was different. Now everything was different. He was in love. It was as though each molecule in his body had been changed from a solid state to a gaseous one. He was still Lomax, still composed of the same molecules, but suddenly they were highly-charged, their motion frantic and their paths random.

'Lomax, what's up with you?' Kim said.

The symptoms, though, were obvious. Lapses in concentration. Loss of appetite. An apathetic response to any intellectual activity which might divert his thoughts from Julia. An enthusiasm for previously tedious chores, like cleaning his teeth, which he could carry out while musing about her. Sleeplessness. Fantasies. Fatigue, which miraculously vanished when Julia walked into the room.

'I'm worried about you,' Kim said. They were at breakfast. Lomax had asked for a pancake but had forgotten to eat it. He was not listening to Kim and had hardly noticed she was there until she reached out and began stabbing at the pancake with her fork.

'You'll waste away if you don't eat your breakfast,' she said with her mouth full. 'C'mon, tell me. It's to do with this thing about Berlins, right?'

Lomax looked at her uncertainly.

'I'm not too proud to say I'm sorry. You tried to confide in me . . .' Kim finished the pancake in a few gulps. '. . . and all I did was yell at you. Well I apologize.'

'Oh. Okay. Thanks.'

'I upset you and you shaved your beard off. You didn't have to start self-mutilating. We'll sort it out.'

Lomax was careful scarcely to glance at Julia or speak to her if anyone else was around, and he resisted the urge to talk about her all the time, but he had never thought this would fool Kim.

'How will we sort it out?'

'Give me a straight answer. Do you still think Berlins is faking results?'

Lomax shifted his weight around. 'I've no way of checking for sure until we get that piece of sky back.'

'Oh, so it's over the horizon?'

'It won't be back until September.'

'By which time you'll have forgotten about the whole thing.' There was relief in Kim's voice. Her fork scurried around the plate looking for any tiny leftovers. She did not meet Lomax's gaze.

'No,' he said.

'Why not, Lomax? Why can't you just ignore it all?'

'Because . . .' He heard his voice rising and did nothing to control it. 'Because the man's an idiot. An old fool. He's actually planning to present a paper at the Chicago summer symposium.'

'Shhhhh. What kind of paper?'

'An idiot paper.'

'Calm down, or you'll turn into Jorgen.'

'An idiot paper based on his idiot theory based on faulty results which may or may not have been doctored to fit the idiot theory.'

'Shit,' said Kim. They looked at each other.

'That's what kind of a paper.' He was spitting the words.

'Just calm down. Your face is twisting up and you don't look like you.'

But Lomax could not stop.

'I've always trusted Berlins, for years and years I've trusted him and now I see what he's doing. Lying and cheating. I never felt so let down by anybody. Ever. He even told some stupid small lie in the lab the other day.'

Although they were surrounded by the noise of the cafeteria there was a silence between them. The other diners had all left and the room was echoing now as the staff scraped dirty dishes, yelling loudly to each other in Spanish.

'But,' said Kim, lowering her head and raising her eyes to him, 'Berlins wouldn't do these things.'

But Julia had shown Lomax the letter of confirmation. The speech was scheduled for three months' time. There was a whole file of dispiriting correspondence. The organizers had stressed that the symposium was a forum for new theories and ideas and had asked Berlins to confirm that he had something new to say. Berlins had assured them that he had.

'If you're right about all this,' Kim said at last, 'and you're not, but if you are then you have to stop him going to the summer symposium. You can't let him expose himself to . . . well, to ridicule.'

Lomax agreed, but venomously.

'Are you sure it's nothing personal, Lomax?'

'You think I *want* to find he's changing results?'

Kim looked for a moment as if she did. 'You often challenge him,' she pointed out.

'That's what Berlins is here for. That's his unique ability. He invites challenge. The result is progress.'

'Not this kind of challenge. He doesn't invite this kind of challenge.'

'True. This is a different kind of challenge.'

Kim studied his face. 'What are you going to do?' she asked.

'First I can do a bit more research.'

'Like what?'

'Well, I could check the results we currently have in the data bank.'

All results were recorded and printed in the data bank. If any were subsequently altered on disk – and alterations were not easy to make –the bank would still hold a printout of the original results.

'But I don't see how you're going to get into the data bank to check without Berlins knowing.'

Few people had access to the data bank and Berlins was one of them.

'Rodrigues has a key card.'

'You'll have to sign for it.'

'Okay, so I'll sign for it.'

Kim shrugged. 'Let's go fetch it now,' she said. 'I'll come with you.'

'To the Fahrhaus?'

'To the Phallus.'

The Fahrhaus was the largest telescope on the mountain, situated at the highest point. It was named after a dead astronomer but Kim always referred to the crop of domed telescopes as the Penises, and the Fahrhaus specifically as the Phallus.

The Fahrhaus had a separate parking lot and some of the astronomers drove back and forth between the two sites although they were only separated by several hundred yards. There was a trail, too, away from the roar of cars in low gear on the road, which wound steeply between big rocks and pine trees. Lomax would have liked to walk the trail alone.

The sun was already warm. The lot was half full. They crossed it and, as they climbed the steps to the trail, Julia emerged suddenly from the laboratories below, a file under her arm. She saw them and waved but did not break her stride. Lomax allowed himself only a

41

glimpse at her. She walked confidently, the breeze catching her hair and her dress so that there was a slight fluttering around her. He made himself turn and continue the steep climb.

This Julia, walking towards him through a breeze, would probably reappear later as the Julia of his fantasies. He was already alarmed by the range, intensity and frequency of his fantasies.

'Why don't you ask her for the key to the data bank?' said Kim.

'Because she doesn't have one.'

'She could borrow Berlins' without him ever knowing.'

'He carries it around.'

'You mean he takes it to the bathroom?'

'Probably.' He stumbled a little over the rough ground.

'Doesn't it make you sick the way Yevgeny and Doberman slobber over her the whole time?' Kim asked.

She was right. It did make him sick. Only that morning, Yevgeny had greeted Julia by kissing her hand again in his slimy Russian way. Lomax had sat drinking coffee and trying to behave as though he hadn't noticed, when actually the event had caused a strange corporal explosion so that all the molecules in his body had seemed to be hurtling outwards.

'God, the look on your face when Yevgeny was sucking her fingers today.'

'That's what Russians do,' Lomax said, hating Kim's words. He wanted to ask whether Yevgeny had just kissed Julia's hand or really sucked at her fingers.

The ascent was steep and they had to climb between narrow rocks. Kim puffed and sweated and did not speak again until the incline levelled between pine trees and the trail was thick with needles. It was shady here but the heat was intensified by the dizzying smell of the pines. In a moment, the view would open out beneath them.

'So,' Kim began again as soon as she was breathing more evenly, 'did she already let you suck her fingers?' She was sweating and redfaced and she was leering at him.

'No,' said Lomax gloomily.

'Still at the back of the line, eh?'

'Line, what fucking line?'

They were walking on a carpet of pine needles now, Lomax a little ahead. Kim's limp hair clung to her head. Circles of sweat were appearing on the front of her shirt.

'It's only I don't want you to get hurt by a . . . a Barbie doll,' she said.

'What line?'

'Lomax. I'm just saying you're not the only guy who's interested.'
Lomax opened his mouth to protest but remained silent.
'I mean, Doberman's nothing but a brag.'
Lomax tripped over a tree root.
'She wouldn't really look at him,' Kim added. 'He's just a fantasist.'
'What's he been saying?'
'The usual Doberman things.'
Lomax wondered for the first time whether Doberman's tales could possibly be true. He had always found them comic until now.

They rounded a corner and the silver dome came into sight. They had passed Lomax's favourite view and he hadn't even noticed it.

'Better knock before entering or we might catch Rodrigues screwing the telescope,' Kim warned. Rodrigues spent every spare moment lovingly maintaining the equipment in the Fahrhaus. Kim had tried to start a rumour that Rodrigues was actually sleeping with the telescope.

'You see . . .' she began as they passed through a door marked Private and into the steady, clean coolness. Even the metallic corridors were kept dust-free. 'You see, it's all to do with Rodrigues' basic fears of sexual inadequacy. Rodrigues suspects that his own penis . . .'

Her voice was lost for a few moments as they passed through a double membrane of doors, Lomax walking fast and Kim losing ground behind him.

'. . . another penis which projects far above the ground, is erect every night and, in a manner of speaking, ejaculates into deep space. Now. In his childhood. Rodrigues was almost certainly . . .'

Lomax passed through another membrane.

'. . . attempt to resolve this early sexual difficulty in adult life. But his choice of a telescope for a partner indicates that, sadly, he's unlikely ever to succeed. Result . . .'

They were inside the dome now and, as the acoustics changed, Kim dropped her voice to a whisper.

'Result: he's crazy. Terminally out to lunch.'

In the dome, amid the gleaming metal and glass and the ferris wheel of the telescope, Rodrigues' back was visible.

'Hi, Rodrigues!' Kim called cheerfully. Rodrigues didn't turn round but faces appeared over the balcony, high above them. A guide was lecturing a party of tourists. The balcony was transparent and children stared at them through it. Lomax scraped himself against a wall but Kim stood where she would be most visible, smiling.

The guide was saying: 'Maybe you have the idea that every night astronomers sit staring through their telescope. If so, you're many years out of date. Occasionally an astronomer will ask to actually look through the eyepiece . . . he climbs into a special cage to do that. It's over there . . .'

Everyone looked. No one could see anything like an eyepiece. Kim pointed helpfully.

'But it's possible for an astronomer in say, England, or Hawaii, to book skytime here and scrutinize the results from his own laboratory via computer . . .'

Kim stood in full view of the balcony, smiling and indicating parts of the telescope like the cabin crew pointing out emergency exits. Lomax reached Rodrigues. He was taking some small piece of the telescope apart and was surrounded by tiny screws and a complex of wires and terminals and bananas. Rodrigues liked bananas. Some wizened brown skins lay empty on the floor.

'Hi,' Lomax whispered close to Rodrigues' ear, and Rodrigues jumped.

'I thought you were another goddam tourist broken loose from the guide,' he said without bothering to lower his voice. 'We had one down here the other day touching the fucking telescope. Incredible.'

Lomax made sympathetic noises.

'What you want?' demanded Rodrigues.

'The key to the data bank.'

'Oh Christ. Why don't you just ask Berlins?'

'Er . . .' Good question. 'I couldn't find him.'

'That's because he's right here. Ask him. Hey!' Berlins was walking towards them, skirting the wall to avoid the tourists' gaze. He shuffled around the equipment, taking the exaggerated care of the short-sighted not to brush against it. Lomax watched him coldly. Even this simple action of crossing the floor seemed loaded with calculation.

'Lomax been looking for you,' Rodrigues said.

'I've been in my office, did you look there?'

'Er . . .'

'He wants a key to the data bank. I said ask Berlins for Chrissake. He said he couldn't find you. Well now you're here.' Rodrigues did not look up.

Berlins turned a keen gaze on Lomax and Lomax stepped back and tripped over a lump of metal and leads which Rodrigues was preparing to clean.

'Oh Jesus fucking Christ you're so fucking clumsy,' said Rodrigues. Lomax had steadied himself by placing his hand on a workbench, unfortunately on top of one of Rodrigues' bananas. Rodrigues rescued it, swearing.

'Why do you want to get into the data bank, Lomax?' asked Berlins.

Lomax's head felt heavy with its weight of anger and suspicion. He lifted his face with a supreme effort to meet Berlins' stare.

'So I can check something.'

Berlins was standing near Rodrigues' lamp. His pupils had shrunk to tiny points so that his eyes fixed on Lomax with a clear, cold blueness. Lomax looked away. It seemed to him that there was no question in Berlins' eyes, no surprise, only knowledge. Berlins must guess that he had been discovered.

Lomax watched the tourists file out overhead. He heard the clatter and chink of Berlins' keys.

'This one,' said Berlins, holding up a key card so that the other keys jangled loosely on their ring. 'There's some book you're supposed to sign.'

'Oh yeah,' said Rodrigues. 'The signing out book. You gotta sign that fucker out.'

'Well I never bother, personally. It's up to you,' said Berlins. Kim arrived and he added: 'Now if you wait a few minutes I'll give you both a ride back to the labs. That is unless you prefer hiking through the rocks in this humidity.'

'Lomax does. He's the outdoor type,' Kim said.

Lomax muttered something affirmative.

'How about you, Kim?'

'Can I use the carphone?' Carphones held a mysterious fascination for Kim.

'If you like.'

'Okay, I'll wait, Professor,' she said, 'and ride back with you.' It seemed to Lomax that there was a rapid glance of understanding between Berlins and Kim. He searched Kim's face and was reassured when she met his eyes innocently. Lately all his senses had been heightened. He was subject to fleeting thoughts and suspicions which, before he could put them into words, he already knew were absurd. Something was distorting the world, either falling in love or the shock of his discovery about Berlins. He wasn't sure which.

It was hard to choose the right time of day to visit the data bank. It was virtually impossible to do anything unusual without McMahon appearing from nowhere. The labs were less busy at night but the hallways were only quiet in the early morning after dawn but before breakfast.

45

Lomax left his room at seven o'clock the next day. He was awake most of the time now anyway, thinking of Julia. He let himself into the labs and whistled as he made his way to the data bank. He tried to sing quietly to himself but his voice was tuneless. He had only been here once before, when there was a fault suspected. He had felt then that he was being admitted to some inner sanctum. The database, with its silence, locks and seclusion, its concentration of great knowledge in a small space, seemed to have an almost religious significance. It was the heart and mind of the observatory.

He knew that to gain entry you had to use the key in conjunction with a smart card and an accredited password. He had always wondered whether he was accredited. He fed the card and punched in his password and waited. The lock did not accept it. He punched in Berlins' password and the lock slid open.

The data bank was large and windowless. Rows of metal shelving stretched into the darkness. No matter how many lights Lomax switched on, the room was still half lost in pools of shadow. The printers, ranged along one wall, were idle now. Each day Rodrigues or one of his assistants came in to file the data from the night before and now last night's data was stacked near one machine. The air conditioning was almost silent in here, so that Lomax's footsteps sounded especially loud. The air was heavy and unmoving.

He searched the shelves for a reference number, running his finger through the dust and disturbing balls of fluff on the floor. He half-tripped on an empty can of Coke which someone had wedged under a low shelf. He stooped and found more cans and three or four empty whisky bottles. There were cigarette butts too. Further on there was a familiar, human smell. He stooped again and found he had stepped on a wad of tissues which had released the smell of semen. His feet crunched on the shards of glass from more bottles and as he pushed them aside with his heel he found a couple of syringes. Used rubbers were just visible wrapped in more tissues.

He located his reference number. The print-out was there, apparently untouched, about half way up some shelves in the shadows. He left, picking his way through the detritus. He locked the doors behind him feeling that something important had been violated and that it had been violated systematically for some time.

6

When Lomax returned the key of the data bank to Berlins, the professor was not in his office. Julia, smiling, said she would give it to him. Lomax wanted to stay and talk to her but could think of nothing to say. There was a silence between them. He hovered awkwardly before her. He wanted to sit on the edge of her desk like Doberman did. Doberman had shown her how to type equations on the computer.

'There's something arousing about dumb women,' Lomax was anguished to overhear him remark afterwards. 'And they're always attracted to intelligent men.'

Lomax was sure Julia was far from dumb. She simply lacked confidence. But today she was calm and relaxed, her smile symmetrical. He wished he could think of something to say to her. Her whole body, leaning towards him so that her hair and breasts fell forward, was perfect. Her beauty was at its most intimidating. He turned to leave the room.

'Lomax, will you bring Deputy Dawg with you next time you come to my house?' she said unexpectedly. They made a date.

The intervening days passed quietly. The professor did not ask any questions about the data bank. Neither did Kim. Life at the observatory seemed to continue as normal. Only for Lomax had everything changed.

He was agitated and unusually alert. He watched Julia constantly. Whenever she was in the room he was aware of her presence, so that he knew where she was and who she was talking to even without looking at her. When she was somewhere else he bristled with anticipation of their next meeting and if he glimpsed her, in the staff residence or passing through the labs, the chemistry of his body was entirely reorganized. She often smiled at him. He was sure the smile was innocent and friendly but he could not prevent his body responding to it as though it was a sexual invitation. He carried the *Astrophysical Review* around the site with him to hide his frequent erections.

He watched Berlins, too, with distaste. He received an invitation to attend the Chicago summer symposium and refused it. Sometimes he tried to solve the puzzle of the altered data but it was difficult to concentrate for more than a few minutes at a time. His mind always returned unerringly to Julia, the way Deputy Dawg always returned home. Deputy's disappearances resulted in search parties, phone calls to neighbours, sobbing children and disruption. Then, just as his absence was being integrated into the life of the household, he would reappear. He would be found sitting in the yard, thumping his tail on the ground. No one knew where he had been.

On Lomax's next break, he and Deputy drifted around the house together thinking of women until it was time to leave for Julia's. When they arrived, Julia petted Deputy. She sat on the rug and stroked him all over and he fell happily to the ground and she rubbed his belly. Deputy lay with his paws in the air and his eyes half-closed. Lomax watched jealously. He tried to attract her attention but, when she stopped stroking him, Deputy dug his nose into her until she tickled him behind the ears, giggling delightfully.

'Okay, let's go,' said Lomax briskly.

They were to take Deputy to the foothills.

'You should wear hiking boots.' She was wearing soft creamy pants which swished when she walked, and cream shoes.

'I don't have any hiking boots.'

She kissed Deputy on the nose. Deputy scraped his long tongue over her cheek and she squealed, kicking her legs. She exasperated and excited Lomax.

He said: 'Sure you have hiking boots. I saw them in the closet when I fixed the door.'

She looked up and her expression changed and her face reminded him again that people had died. The boots belonged to someone else, someone who was dead now. How could he have forgotten, even momentarily, the ghosts in this house? He was standing near the wedding photograph and the dead family was staring at him unblinkingly.

'Those boots don't fit me,' said Julia. 'I'll see what else I have.'

Deputy followed her out of the room, his tongue hanging louchely from the side of his mouth.

Lomax stared back at the dead family. He eyed Julia's husband, looking for some clue to his character. But he found none. Lewis was attractive. His face was strong. His white hair was cut with care and his skin was lightly tanned. It was hard to judge his age; Lomax could only guess that he was between 45 and 60 years old. Lewis smiled. Probably this was a fixed smile which was reserved for photographs. Lomax could not imagine the face talking or sleeping or doing anything but smiling.

He replaced the picture quietly.

'Ready?' said Julia. She and Deputy were standing together, framed by the doorway, watching him. Deputy rubbed his nose lovingly against Julia's knee.

'How did you meet Lewis?' Lomax asked when they were in the car.

'My father knew him. He was my father's attorney. And they played golf together. Actually, I met him when I was fourteen and my father took me to the golf course because I wanted to drive the golf buggy. Then I met him a few more times. Then I met him again at my father's funeral.'

'How old were you then?'

'When my father died? Eighteen.'

'Would your father have been pleased? If he'd known?'

'Known what?'

'That you married Lewis?'

Julia half repeated the question under her breath as if to grasp it. She was acting dumb again. He recognized this now.

'Would my father have been pleased if he'd known I . . . ? Well I guess so. He would have wanted someone to take care of me, that's for sure.'

When they had parked the car, Lomax insisted that Deputy stay on a leash. Deputy showed his disdain for this and Julia pleaded on his behalf but Lomax was hardhearted.

'Please . . .' said Julia, her arms around the dog, looking up at Lomax with large eyes. Her mouth was slightly open. She pouted. Her lips, scarcely perceptibly, massaged the air. Something about the movement made Lomax's jeans tighten and for a split second he thought Julia's eyes strayed downwards, so briefly that he must have imagined it.

He said: 'Deputy chases after women if you let him loose round here. Just wait a few minutes.'

At first there were people: families hiking and groups of teenagers. Everyone and everything seemed to be coming down the hillside, the people, their dogs, the water in the mountain creeks. Lomax took a fork to the left and their route was shady and still. The trail rose gradually, winding through rocks and trees, and as they climbed higher they passed fewer hikers until there was no one else at all. Lomax unclipped Deputy's leash. Neither Julia nor Deputy noticed.

49

Deputy walked at Julia's side, stopping only to drink when they crossed a creek. He slurped noisily. The path was thinner here and embraced by foliage. Soon they did not speak at all. There was silence on the mountainside. Once Lomax looked up and saw a tiny plane, very high above them, cutting through the sky. He could not hear it. Occasionally their feet snapped a twig.

The trail was mostly shaded. Once or twice they found themselves in hot sunshine for a few minutes but the trees would bend back over them.

When they stopped, sitting on some fallen timber to drink from the water bottle, it was by silent consent. Julia drank first. He watched her lips close around its damp neck. She drank but she looked at him as she drank. It was a look of sexual invitation so unmistakable that, after passing him the bottle, he was not surprised when she stood up before him and stretched. He watched her body openly. It was a relief after all the surreptitious watching. It was a relief to admire the way she was sinewy like a deer and to show his admiration instead of feigning indifference. It was exciting to study this slow, lazy, sexy preparation for what he knew now must follow. Her back lengthened and curved, her bosom pointed. He held the water bottle tightly. He forgot to drink.

Smiling, she stood closer and took the bottle away from him. She laid her arms on his shoulders and kissed him. The kiss was slow and very soft. Then they kissed again. He reached inside her clothes and felt her skin. Her breasts were firm and her nipples hard. She was taking off his shirt now and running her tongue over his body, kissing him and licking him until she had created small vortices of pleasure that seemed to suck him in. When they lay down he tried to swing his body above hers, as Candice would have expected, but Julia was already stretching over him. Her breasts hung before him but as he reached for them she began to kiss him and lick him again, her fingers creeping up his thigh and her mouth circling low so that by the time she opened his jeans he was powerless with pleasure at the soft wetness of her lips.

Her tongue explored the tightening skin and massaged the curves and crevices at the base of his penis, snuffling round the rough skin. She was comic. He smiled with pleasure. She was licking the smooth skin now with slow movements. She kissed him and licked him until the whole of him seemed to exist only where her mouth was. Then he felt her moving her whole body sensuously against him. She was blowing on the skin her mouth had made wet and the mixture of cold and warmth was still more arousing.

'Mmmmmmm,' she whispered.

He was unable to speak. He could only lie still, overwhelmed by the pleasure of further swelling in his groin. She took his penis gently in her mouth and began to massage it with her tongue. Her mouth was damp and smooth and it closed tightly around him. He exhaled deeply. She began to suck a little. He groaned. His penis seemed to stretch away from him, far down into her throat. Her body pressed against him as her mouth began to suck rhythmically. He was close to climaxing when she pulled away.

He could guess what must follow. He already felt guilty at his selfishness. Candice would never have allowed things to go so far. All he wanted was for Julia to continue but he knew that sex was not supposed to be this way. Reluctantly, as if his body was an immense weight, he hauled himself onto his elbows expecting to meet Julia's eye, accusatory, waiting, insistent. But she smiled playfully up at him from behind his penis.

'Julia . . .' he began apologetically.

Her tongue appeared and she licked all the way up his penis from the base to the very tip which was by now so sensitive that the soft pressure made him shudder involuntarily. She saw the movement and smiled.

'Enjoy,' she said, pushing him a little. He remained balanced on his elbows.

'Okay. Okay, but I'll come,' he warned her weakly.

She said softly, 'That's the whole idea.'

He did not lie down but watched her as she kissed his penis and then took it in her mouth again. Her eyes, still looking into his, were enormous. She blinked slowly. The same look – lazy, sexy – as when they had begun. She started to suck again, gently at first, then rhythmically. Lomax sank back, helpless with pleasure.

It was a sexually incomparable afternoon. For Lomax, making love had usually been accompanied by the rustle of domestic preparation, by the comedy of undress, by a child calling from the next room. And there had been the importance, then the priority, and finally the burden, of pleasing Candice. Candice, her mind busy, her life a dissatisfaction, had been hard to please. This sex now, here, with Julia, was a liberation. Pleasure replaced thought for the first time in many years. He climaxed again and then again and possibly again. When he remembered this afterwards, as he often did, it seemed remarkable.

Eventually they lay still. Their debris – shoes and underwear, the water bottle drained empty on its side, Deputy snoring nearby – was unreproachful. They smiled at each other. Lomax remembered that he had been thirsty some time ago and that he had still had nothing to drink.

Before they left the place Lomax looked round at it fondly. The thin grass they had lain on was flattened and bruised. There were growing trees and fallen ones, softly rotting, on all sides. Lomax irrationally wanted to carve something on a tree or on one of the fallen trunks, a mark that would remain for years, but Julia and Deputy had already started off down the hillside. He picked up a piece of wood and walked after them, trying to carry the wood nonchalantly like any old stick.

Their mood was dreamy. They walked close together. Lomax touched Julia a lot, or kissed her. He would have liked her to reach out to him. But she did not. He wanted to tell her how extraordinary sex with her had been but he guessed that she knew. So they talked about other, more mundane things. She told him how happy she was working at the observatory.

'Isn't it sometimes sort of claustrophobic?' Lomax asked.

'Claustrophobic? How? With the view of the mountains?'

'I mean, you could find the atmosphere claustrophobic.'

'Do you?'

'Sometimes. The same faces, day after day, talking about the same things.'

'But I like that.'

'Why?' He was determined she would talk to him now. He would learn more about her.

'It's like a family. I guess it makes me feel sort of safe. And it means I always know what's going to happen tomorrow.'

Lomax put a protective arm around her shoulders. Her life had been too full of shocks.

'And,' she was saying, 'I like to hear you astronomers talk about the stars. Things happen out there but they happen slowly and they take millions of years. It makes earth and all the people and all the things that seem to matter, it makes them insignificant.'

She was slight beneath his arm. Her shoulders were narrow. He squeezed her gently and she glanced up at him.

'How old were you when your mother died?' he asked.

'I was a tiny baby. She committed suicide. She wasn't crazy. She had post-natal depression.'

She looked up at Lomax again. 'It's a clinical condition,' she said defensively. 'It wasn't my fault.'

'Shit, Julia,' said Lomax in alarm. 'Of course it wasn't your fault.'

'I've always felt as if I killed her. Sort of. Deep down. Anyway, my father looked after me real well.'

'He didn't remarry?'

'No. He had a lot of girlfriends but he thought I wouldn't like him to marry. He was probably right. I wanted him all for myself.'

'He raised you alone?'

'He had help. He worked most of the time. I mean, he was chairman of the company. But my favourite day was Sunday because he usually spent Sunday with me.'

She was talking to him. At last, she was speaking.

'What did you do on Sundays?' he asked. He let his arm drop. She seemed happy when she talked about her father and it was difficult to walk with his arm around her, especially as Deputy wanted to be close to her too and kept wedging his body between their legs.

'Oh, we'd go to the golf course. He let me drive the buggy. Or we were just at home together. I went to dance classes and I used to show him my steps and he'd clap and say Bravo. Once I cut his hair but that wasn't a big success. Oh, and I was allowed to cook for him on Sunday. Poor man, he ate some terrible meals but he always pretended to enjoy them. Sometimes, probably when he couldn't face another meal cooked by me, he took me out to restaurants. Nice restaurants. I wore my best dress and tried to order sophisticated food. Oh, and he had these cocktail parties and I used to beg him to let me deliver drinks to the guests. Actually, it was because I wanted to go the party but I was scared no one would speak to me. Anyway, he was sure I'd spill a drink down someone's dress.'

'Did you?'

'Yes.'

'Was he mad at you?'

'Yes.'

'Did he yell at you right there in front of everyone?'

'Oh Lomax, Daddy didn't yell. You knew he was angry without him saying a word. And that's the second time I met Lewis. He was kind to me. He sneaked up to me and he whispered in my ear that it was a horrible dress and it looked much nicer with lemon and cherry all over it.'

She laughed. She was remembering Lewis and her father and the party and the cocktails and the dress. She had an intimacy with her own memories which Lomax could never share. He felt excluded. He felt lonely. There was a creek, a small one, and she jumped across it without his help. He saw the past on her face and guessed that she had crossed the creek without even noticing it. He took her hand to remind her that she was hiking with him right now.

'You don't want to hear all this,' she said suddenly.

'I do!' he protested.

'I think I saw Lewis once more before my father died. At Sachs Smith. That was Lewis' law firm. He had been Daddy's attorney but then they made him managing partner and there were cocktails to celebrate. More cocktails. I was older by then and I didn't spill any but I could see Daddy looking at me the whole time to make sure.'

'Did you guess you'd marry Lewis one day?'

'No! At the party? God, no! He was so big and important and he made a speech and everyone wanted to talk to him. He didn't even speak to me, except when we were leaving and he kissed my cheek and I got confused because I didn't guess he was going to kiss the other cheek too.'

'And then you met him again at the funeral?'

'Yes. And Daddy left his money in a trust for me and Sachs Smith managed the trust. Lewis personally managed it, which he didn't have to but he wanted to. So when I needed some money, I just had to go to Lewis and tell him why I needed it and we'd agree how much I could have. I shared an apartment with Marcia and worked at the TV station and had a good time. Lewis worried about me. I was only eighteen. He said we should have lunch once a month so he could see how I was getting along. I used to tell him everything at those lunches. All about my life. There was a married man. Then I dated this TV sports commentator. He listened to me. He was so sweet. So kind. Then we had lunch once a week. Then we went out for dinner. Then he sent me flowers. Then after a while he wasn't Daddy's friend who was looking after me, he was Lewis and . . . well, I was in love with him.'

There was a quiet warmth in her voice when she talked about Lewis. Lomax became almost handicapped by jealousy. He staggered over rocks and slipped down the trail. He reminded himself that Lewis was dead.

When they returned to Julia's house, Lomax watched her as she faltered around the kitchen preparing a meal. Her movements were uncertain. She was endearing.

'Can we stay the night?' he asked. 'Me and my dawg?'

'I have to go back to the observatory.'

He wanted her to suggest returning in the morning instead. But this idea did not occur to Julia. She opened and closed the fridge a few times but did not take anything out.

He said: 'Kim phoned just as I was leaving today. She's in town and she wanted to go to the movies.'

'What did you say?'

'I said I'd call back.'

'Do you want to go the movies with Kim?' Julia looked up and blinked at him.

'Of course not. I'll stay here with you until it's time for you to go. I'm just trying to decide what excuse to give.'

Julia opened and closed the fridge a few more times.

'What's wrong with the truth?'

'She won't like it.'

'You think she'd be jealous?'

'Maybe. Sort of.'

'She has other friends at the observatory besides you.'

'Sometimes Yevgeny. Sometimes.'

Julia made French dressing. Her fork whirled in a small glass jug. He noticed again the delicacy of her wrist and forearm.

'Oh yes,' she said, 'I'm sure Kim regularly sleeps with Yevgeny.'

Lomax gaped at this suggestion while she looked in the refrigerator again.

'This is a spaghetti and sauce . . . only I don't have . . . oh, no, I forgot to buy any ground beef. Oh Lomax.'

'Kim. Is sleeping with Yevgeny?'

'I have to go to the supermarket right now.'

'Kim. And Yevgeny.' It was true they were often deep in conversation together in the cafeteria. Once or twice Lomax had come across them in the staff residence drinking coffee early in the morning.

'He'd sleep with anyone. He's that sort of man.'

She picked up her purse and stood over him, waiting. Lomax was thinking that Julia, too, was occasionally found deep in conversation with Yevgeny, or drinking early morning coffee with him. Lomax thought of Kim's remark that if he was interested in Julia he would have to get to the end of the line. He remembered the smell of semen in the data bank. The contentment he had felt since making love began to seep away.

'How do you know?'

She was wandering around the kitchen looking for something now.

'Know what? I can't find my carkeys and I don't have enough money for the supermarket. If I only buy ground beef, can I pay by credit card?'

Lomax got up. 'I'll go to the store. Julia, how do you know that Kim's sleeping with Yevgeny?'

'It's hard to imagine, isn't it? They're both so sort of round.'

'How do you know?'

'He told me, Lomax. But I probably would have guessed anyway. It's easy to just sort of tell these things.'

'I can't tell them.'

'Too busy stargazing. Make sure the meat's lean.'

'Are you certain about this?'

'Why are you so shocked? Kim's also very friendly with the professor. That's the way she is. She likes making friends.'

'Don't try to tell me she's sleeping with Berlins. Please.'

'She might be. He's a little bit greedy.'

Lomax sat down again.

'And some dog food or whatever Deputy eats,' she reminded him.

The supermarket was in a small shopping mall in a residential area and he missed the street several times. Once inside he wandered around looking for refrigeration. Kim. Sleeping with Yevgeny and possibly Berlins. Berlins greedy.

The long rows of packaged meat stretched before him. Identical slabs of red muscle bulged through shiny plastic. Julia. Sleeping with Yevgeny and possibly Berlins? After all, Berlins was greedy. The idea was so painful that he could not think about it for long.

He leaned on the display and a blast of cold air hit him under the chin. Over the last few weeks everything had changed. Friends and colleagues he thought he knew well turned out to be strangers. An otherwise tranquil scientific life had been disrupted by suspicion. He, Lomax, had changed his physical appearance. The information centre of the observatory, once a forbidden place, turned out to be open to anyone who wanted a drink or fast sex. And then there was Julia.

Suddenly, unexpectedly, he longed for Candice and the children. He thought of Candice's kitchen and the easy familiarity with which she moved around it. He thought of his children sitting in the kitchen and passing pieces of food to the ever-open mouth of Deputy Dawg under the table. For a moment he ached for the normality of it all. They were coming home sometime in the night. Perhaps their return would change everything back the way it used to be.

When he arrived at Julia's house there were two more cars outside it. Police cars.

He entered through the back door and heard the sheriff's voice, raised.

7

The sheriff and two other men were sitting in Julia's armchairs. For a few moments they did not see Lomax. Almost the first thing he noticed was that one of them was fingering the wedding photo.

Julia was saying: 'I don't recall . . . I guess I was outside in the yard.'

'Can you hear the telephone ring in the yard, Mrs Fox?'

She hesitated. 'No. I don't think so. Although sometimes I can.'

She sat on the edge of the chair, her back straight, her hands in her lap. Her face had lost its symmetry. Her mouth twisted a little and her eyes were mobile. Lomax had time to think that this animation increased her beauty and involuntarily he studied the visitors to gauge their admiration.

The man with the wedding photo watched her from a slumping position, his right ankle hoisted onto his left knee. He was relaxed. He balanced the photo on the arm of the chair like a can of beer. He seemed to be enjoying himself.

'This is Lieutenant van Rose,' said Julia, and a tall, skeletally thin figure stood to shake hands.

'Homicide,' said van Rose. His voice was quiet and the word was spoken softly but still it sounded more like an accusation than a police department. The detective's gaunt face was serious. The skin was stretched so taut across it that the lines of his frown looked like the fissures in his skull.

'And Mr Kee, also from Homicide.'

The man with the photo smiled. He made no attempt to move from his chair but waved the photo happily. Lomax crossed the room and shook Kee's hand. Deputy thumped his tail. Lomax noticed that, with his innate bad taste, Deputy had chosen the sheriff's knee to lean his head against.

'And you know Murph, Murphy McLean.'

It was impossible to ignore Julia's use of the sheriff's first name.

'Hi, Lomax!' said Murphy McLean, as if Lomax was an old friend. 'How are things up on the mountainside?'

The familiarity of the sheriff's tone and the knowing grin which seemed to be engulfing his face made Lomax redden. How could the sheriff know what had happened on the mountainside that afternoon?

'You got a real big telescope up there, I hear.'

The grin widened impossibly. His mouth seemed to be swallowing his head.

'I was telling Murphy about your work at the observatory,' Julia said.

'Clever shit, Lomax, that's clever shit you guys do.' The sheriff nodded to the two detectives. 'Lomax got brains coming out of his ears,' he confided.

'We have a few more questions for Mrs Fox,' the thin man explained. 'We're still pursuing our investigation into the deaths of Gail Fox and Lewis Fox.'

'We'll be through soon.' Kee spoke for the first time. Lomax realized they were inviting him to leave.

'Oh, I'd like Lomax to stay,' said Julia at once.

'Shit, let him stay, guys. We're perplexed. We need all the brains we can get.' The sheriff turned his bloated face to Lomax and winked deliberately at him. Lomax did not respond. He moved to the corner of the room where Julia could see him but her visitors could not, and leaned against the windowsill. He felt unsurprised, as if he had known all along that the deaths had not been accidental.

The thin detective studied his notes for a few moments before speaking. Julia waited, her body tense and her face pale.

'You didn't hear the phone ring because you were outside in the yard. Why might you have been in the yard, Mrs Fox?' Van Rose's voice was soft, his tone sympathetic.

She twisted her fingers and bit her lip. Lomax agonized with her. Finally she looked up.

'Sweeping the leaves, maybe. I like sweeping the leaves.'

'You like sweeping leaves, ma'am, you can come sweep mine,' the fat sheriff said. That familiarity again. It disturbed Lomax. Any moment McLean might wander into the kitchen and make himself a cup of coffee. Van Rose was at pains to ignore him.

'Only maybe. You're not sure?'

'Well, no. I'm not sure.'

'Are you sure you didn't get in your car and drive somewhere?'

'I'm certain.'

'Well, is there any other reason you might be in the yard?'

Julia deliberated again. This time the silence went on for over a minute. The sheriff whistled to himself. Kee yawned loudly.

'Maybe I went to the garage . . .'

Van Rose leaned forward a little. 'The garage?'

'Yes.'

'To . . . ?'

'To check that Lewis shut it behind him. It opens automatically but you have to remember to push the button to close it.'

'So you went out to check the door was shut.'

'Yes. And . . .'

'And . . . ?' Van Rose's expression was dense with anticipation.

Julia frowned. 'And . . .'

Van Rose's body tipped closer towards her as she hesitated.

'And I pushed the button.'

The lieutenant leaned back. Kee smothered a smile.

'Why, that's sensible. The lady goes out to check the garage door's shut. It's not. She shuts it. You big shots from Homicide shouldn't need Mrs Fox to explain that,' said the sheriff, shifting his bulk around in his chair. Deputy looked up at him adoringly.

'Mrs Fox, there were three, four, maybe even five telephone calls to this house between seven and ten a.m. on November twelfth. The caller got the answer machine every time. How come?'

Julia stared at him, wide-eyed. 'I don't know,' she said.

There was a pause. Van Rose studied his notes again.

McLean said: 'Sweetheart, if you don't mind me saying something, the boys here might find that kind of odd. You say you're sitting at home, you expected your husband and his daughter hours ago and they don't come. You're half out of your mind with worry and then the phone rings . . . but you don't pick it up! Now I'm not in Homicide, I'm no ways clever enough, but even I can see these boys are likely to find that, well, let's say . . .' the sheriff shifted his weight again and looked round the room. His expression was one of immense satisfaction. '. . . let's say . . . suspicious.'

'Oh,' said Julia helplessly.

Lomax stood up. 'I'd like Mrs Fox to call her lawyer.'

Van Rose stood up too. 'That's not necessary. We need Mrs Fox to tell us what she can remember. We can't question every witness with a lawyer present.'

'Just sit yourself back down, Galileo,' the sheriff said soothingly.

'But you've described Mrs Fox's behaviour as suspicious.'

Van Rose looked with irritation at the sheriff.

'Me and Mrs Fox know each other from way back! We're old friends. I was just hinting to her, friend to friend, that the boys here may not find her answers entirely satisfactory!' The sheriff raised his hands in a gesture of injured innocence.

'Maybe, sheriff, you should keep your comments to yourself,' said the lieutenant. The fat man did not reply but made the same open-handed gesture, this time to Julia.

'I guess I'm just about through anyhow.' Van Rose scanned his notebook. Kee dragged himself lazily from his chair. But Lomax was angry now.

'Mrs Fox's trying to put this trauma behind her. The police don't seem to be helping much.'

'I know it's been tough for Mrs Fox. But she more than anyone wants us to pursue our investigation,' van Rose said.

'Oh I do. Only . . .' Julia was standing up. '. . . I've answered all these questions before.'

Kee and van Rose exchanged expressionless glances.

'We'll try not to bother you again, ma'am, unless we're sure it's necessary,' said van Rose meekly.

As the men left, Murphy McLean stood too close to Lomax. He tried to take a step back but the sheriff was muttering something in his ear: 'You lucky bastard, you. I seen most of the knockers in these foothills, Lomax, and the best pair around are right here in this room,' He exited, winking and smirking. Lomax said nothing. A series of suitable replies would occur to him over the ensuing twelve hours.

'That guy makes me vomit,' he told Julia before they had even heard the car engines start outside.

'Which one?'

'Fatso, the one you call Murph. He kept leering at you. So did Kee.'

Julia was making nervous circles of the room, fluffing out the chairs and cushions where the men had been sitting. Lomax noticed that Kee had replaced the wedding photo on the wrong shelf and he moved it proprietorially.

'I thought these guys were supposed to be trained in the art of observation,' he muttered. Julia continued to circle the room. He felt his anger increasing.

'Dickheads,' he snarled as the cars turned outside.

'Oh Lomax, they're just policemen. They're not especially clever and when they're off duty they get drunk or play golf. They're no different from anyone else.'

'How do you know so much about policemen?'

61

'I've seen a lot of them since November,' said Julia. Her tone was exasperated. He looked at her as she left the room but she did not catch his eye.

He sighed and sank into the chair in which Murphy McLean had been sitting. He could hear Julia moving around the kitchen as she made the meal. She switched on the TV. He felt excluded.

'For Chrissake, Julia, why won't you talk about it?' he said, bursting into the kitchen. She was crying silently in a room filled with noise: beside her the studio audience of some TV game show roared while at her feet Deputy Dawg guzzled his dinner with atavistic ferocity.

Lomax switched off the television. He put his arms around Julia and she continued to sob noiselessly.

'Talk! Talk, for Chrissake,' he said when the sobbing had eased and she was dabbing at her eyes with a tissue.

All she said was: 'Do I look ugly?'

'No.'

'I do.'

'You don't.' It was true, even with her hair clinging to her wet cheeks and her eyes red. 'I want to help,' he said, kissing her.

'You can't.'

'You need help. If these deaths were . . . if they weren't accidental, and months later your house fills up with suspicious policemen . . .'

'You think they're suspicious?'

'Well, yes.'

'But I liked van Rose.'

'So did I. That's got nothing to do with it.'

She was curling up now, onto his knee. It was a pleasant sensation. She trusted him to hold her and not to let her fall.

'Were they really murdered?' he asked, very softly.

She nodded.

'How?'

'Shot.'

'Both of them?'

She nodded again.

'Where?'

Her words were barely audible. 'In the apartment.'

'They were in an apartment?'

Julia sniffed in reply.

'Whose?'

'Gail's.'

'They were in Gail's apartment and they were murdered there?'

'Yes.'

Lomax thought of Lewis' patrician features, and the nondescript daughter, whose face at present he could not recall. It was hard to believe that the smiling family had been murdered.

'Why?'

She shook her head.

'A random killing . . . a robbery?' he suggested.

But she just shook her head again.

'Can you tell me anything more? Why would the police possibly think you were involved?'

'I don't know. I don't know how anyone could think that.'

She raised her eyes and looked into his.

8

Lomax chose to learn more about the Fox murders from the small branch library in the foothills. He had long ago established a friendship with one of the librarians there. Her name was Mrs Cleaver.

He had met Mrs Cleaver when Joel was small enough to attend her Saturday storytelling sessions. Mrs Cleaver was nicotine-stained ('My favourite smell,' Joel had said when he was five, 'is the smell of Mrs Cleaver.') and she had long grey hair which was yellowed by cigarettes.

'She's like an anti-advertisement for my clinic,' Candice said of her. Candice and Mrs Cleaver had not liked one another. Some small disagreement over a library card or a renewal date had escalated over the years and once, when Lomax and Candice had been fighting about something completely different, Candice had cited his devotion to Mrs Cleaver as an instance of betrayal.

'How's your God-awful ex-wife?' Mrs Cleaver asked him today. He had found her smoking outside the emergency exit. There was no smoking allowed in the library.

'She just got back from Europe.'

'Europe. A plumbing disaster across five latitudes,' said Mrs Cleaver with venom. She was famously angry. Her stories, adored by children, were full of enemies who died horribly. Parents occasionally submitted petitions to the library censuring this violence and Mrs Cleaver would pin an insincere apology on the notice board, dripping with barely concealed bile.

'When are you next seeing your kids?'

'Tonight, I hope.'

'Well, if you see them on the weekend, bring Helen to storytelling. Saturday's session is for her age group and it will feature her favourite character, Mary Mudcap.'

'Mary Mudcap. Where do you get them from, for Chrissake?'

'Mary Mudcap is based on me,' said Mrs Cleaver with satisfaction, allowing herself something like a smile as she lit another cigarette.

Lomax asked: 'Do you know a man called Murph something? A sheriff?'

Mrs Cleaver groaned. 'What's he got you for? Allowing your dog to crap in a thirty-mile-per-hour zone? Driving with a broken brake light in the bicycle lane?'

'Nothing yet.'

'Well stay right away from him. If he takes it into his head that he doesn't like you, he'll hang around until he gets you for something. I found myself in a small dispute with the Stinks –' (The Spinks were Mrs Cleaver's neighbours. She had hated them for many years. They were celebrated among generations of local children for their frequent appearances as the Stinks in Saturday sessions, where they always met with an unhappy end or, if they survived, moved to Seattle. Mrs Cleaver did not like Seattle.) '– and that damn sheriff took their side. She gave him cookies, that's why. Within a week, he caught me smoking in the mall just after a bunch of idiots had declared it a smokefree zone. Plus then there were some minor traffic offences.'

'He's involved in a murder inquiry which I'm interested in. I came over to look it up on microfiche.'

'Why are you interested in a murder inquiry?'

Lomax hesitated. 'Well . . . I met someone who's sort of connected.'

'Which murder?'

'Last November. A man and his daughter, they were shot in her apartment.'

'Oh, yes, some animal name. Wolf?'

'Fox.'

'I remember it. Didn't they arrest the wife?'

'No,' said Lomax, bridling a little. 'They haven't arrested anyone.'

Mrs Cleaver sat him down in a dark corner and fed the machine microfiches. She leaned over him, clicking her brown teeth. Close to, her tobacco smell was mixed with the chemical scent of soap.

'Okay, we have the evening papers on November twelfth and the mornings and evenings from then onwards. Don't forget the Sundays, they probably carried some late comment . . .'

She pulled up a chair. She intended to study the screen with him. She liked Lomax and she liked murders.

'Double Slaughter on West Side,' said the headline. 'Lewis Fox went to the airport for a reunion with globetrotting daughter Gail. But within hours both were dead, mown down by mystery assassins in Gail's apartment.

'When top attorney Fox, 58, father of two, met daughter Gail on her

65

return from a language school in France, he telephoned his wife to say they'd soon be home. But Gail was to travel little further . . .'

There was much newsprint on the subject, but few facts. Detectives said that nothing appeared to have been stolen. They confirmed that the attack seemed motiveless. The same photos, old ones, of Lewis and Gail were reproduced several times. Lewis smiling professionally, Gail looking young and self-conscious. There were quotes from colleagues and teachers. One newspaper revealed, next to a picture of her, that Julia was being interviewed by the police. Others quoted Julia saying that she was shocked and distressed. Mrs Cleaver microfiched rapidly through the days.

Without new evidence to fuel it, the story soon lost its prominence. It had only ever attracted this attention because these were unlikely murders in the professional classes. There were family murders over on the south side of town every day but the south side was tough and the deaths there scarcely merited a paragraph.

One article printed the comments of psychics and mediums on the murders. Another attempted to profile Julia, but the profile was little more than a collection of old photographs. Even in half-shaded magnification, Julia looked beautiful.

'She's a very pretty girl,' said Mrs Cleaver. 'Is she the friend you mentioned?'

Lomax knew that his face would give away the exact nature of the friendship.

'I guess so . . . she came to work at the observatory.'

'And you fell in love, eh?'

Lomax could not meet Mrs Cleaver's eye. She bared her yellow teeth. She was smiling.

'And what,' she asked, 'does the former Mrs Lomax think about it?'

'She doesn't know yet.'

'Going to tell her?'

'I guess I'll mention it.'

'So it's serious? Well just remember what happened to this woman's last husband,' said Mrs Cleaver cheerfully. Lomax left wondering if Candice was right about Mrs Cleaver.

That evening, Helen and Joel and Deputy came to stay. The children were unable to tell him where in Europe they had been or exactly what they had seen there. They roamed around the house just as they always did, making sure everything was where it always was and reprimanding him for any changes.

After a meal they looked at maps together and planned a hiking trip that they would take some weekend soon. There would be backpacks and a tent and warm sleeping bags. They would light a fire and cook a meal over it. It would, Lomax promised them, be fun. The children smiled. Lomax guessed that they were trying to appear enthusiastic for his sake and, not for the first time, he resented Robert and his expensive European trip.

The next day he went to Candice's office.

'I have a girlfriend,' he said.

'That's nice,' replied Candice tautly. She did not look at him. She was flicking through a pile of what looked like resumés.

Candice was always brisk in her office. When he had still been her husband it was a visit to her business premises which had first alerted Lomax to the possibility that his marriage might be ending. People, mostly women, came here for a massage with scented oils or to have grey Austrian mud smeared over their faces, or for various other beauty treatments. They rang the doorbell and were met by a woman wearing a white coat like a doctor who said: 'Please step inside.' The place was referred to as 'The Clinic' to make clients feel their visits were less of an indulgence than a medical necessity. All the surfaces were white.

Candice had long ago told Lomax that he looked like someone who had managed to slip in without ringing the bell. She thought he was bad for business and always ushered him quickly into her office.

'Yes,' agreed Lomax, 'it's nice.'

She turned her back to him, swivelling to a computer screen behind her to punch in some information.

'How old is she?' Candice asked without moving her eyes from the screen.

'Sort of mid, well, early, twenties.'

A long silence indicated disapproval.

He said deliberately: 'I'm kind of worried that she may be arrested on a double-murder charge.'

His words had the desired effect. She swivelled back to him, dropped her arms on the desk and stared, motionless. It was a pleasing moment. Candice was seldom still.

'Well, not really. The police are sort of sniffing around but I don't seriously think they'll indict her.'

Lomax enjoyed carelessly using terms like double-murder charge and indict, but under Candice's unswerving stare he began to feel uncomfortable.

'I mean,' he added, 'I'm sure they won't.'

'What's happening? I go away for a few weeks and I come back and there's stubble all over your face instead of beard . . .' (Lomax had soon tired of shaving daily) '. . . and you've taken up with a murderer. You didn't let her see the kids last night, I hope.'

'Candice, she is not a goddam murderer.'

'You've just said she was. Double.'

'I said the police were sniffing around her. Of course no one's actually going to accuse her of a crime she didn't commit.'

'Who did she kill?'

'No one.'

'Who did someone, possibly this woman, kill?'

'Her husband.'

'Her husband!'

'And her daughter.'

'What!'

'I mean, not her daughter, her stepdaughter.'

'Are you kidding?'

'No.'

'Look, I don't care what you do with this woman but if she's a murderer, suspected murderer, of small children, don't dare let Helen or Joel near her, okay?'

'I would never let Helen and Joel near a murderer of small children or any other kind of murderer, if I knew one, but I don't. And you do care. That's why you're yelling.'

Candice was silent. Her hair was usually sleek but now it fell over her face. She had been leaning forward with such intensity that she had creased the papers on her desk. Her pale suit had twisted around her body. She was no longer immaculate. She looked like the old Candice. Guessing this, she drew a mirror from her desk and began making all the minor adjustments which turned her into this other Candice she had become.

'Want to have lunch?' he asked.

'I'm not going to answer any questions about the Eiffel Tower, St Mark's Square, or the London Planetarium.'

'I'm not going to ask any.'

Candice snapped open a box of powder and began applying it energetically. 'I guess it was inevitable that sooner or later you'd meet someone.'

'I've met a couple of people, actually. I just haven't told you about them.'

'Who?'

68

'It doesn't matter. Want to hear about Julia?'

'Julia.'

'That's her name, yes, Julia.'

'You can't be serious about this woman, Lomax.'

'You don't know anything about her except that her husband and her stepdaughter are dead. That's all you know.'

They went to a French restaurant near Candice's clinic. Candice insisted they sit in a half-lit alcove.

'You don't want to be seen lunching with a slob,' he suggested.

'I don't want to be overheard talking about the slob's girlfriend's double-murder charge.'

'She has not been charged.'

Candice did not retract or apologize.

Lomax said: 'It'll take about five minutes for me to tell you everything Julia's told me, only it took her about five hours.'

'She talks real slow?'

'She doesn't volunteer any information. I looked it up in old newspapers in the library and found out a bit more, but not much.'

Candice's eyes narrowed at the mention of the library.

'Mrs Cleaver sent you her best wishes,' added Lomax playfully. Candice munched on some French bread which had just arrived, warmed, in a small basket.

'I choke,' she said, 'on Mrs Cleaver's best wishes.'

Lomax prepared himself to tell her everything. It was hard to remember a time when he hadn't told her everything. This was a reassuring process. For many years he would confide his problems and Candice would discuss them with him all night, offering a succession of opinions, each passionately held until superseded by the next. By morning, he always knew what to do.

'Well?'

Lomax arranged and rearranged French breadcrumbs with his finger as he spoke. 'Julia was married to a man called Lewis. I don't know how old he was exactly, probably her father's age. I mean fifty-seven, fifty-eight, fifty-nine or sixty, depending on which reporter you believe.'

'So she likes older men,' said Candice. Lomax searched her face for indications of intentional cruelty but she was already asking another question.

'Was he rich?'

'Wealthy. Lewis was her family's attorney.'

Candice's eyes glinted.

69

'And if you're thinking she killed him for his money, you're wrong. I mean, she didn't kill him and she didn't need his money anyway because her father left her money of her own. It's in some kind of trust.'

'What does that mean?'

'I'm not sure. Something to do with attorneys because that's how Lewis and Julia got together in the first place. He was administering her trust fund. Anyway, Lewis had a son and a daughter by a previous marriage, almost the same age as Julia. Their names are Gail and Richard. Richard works up in Seattle and doesn't come home much. Gail was at school here, at Tradescant, and last year she went to Europe to study languages for a few months.'

'Oh really? Where?' Candice had a new interest in Europe.

'I don't know where.' Lomax destroyed the neat line of crumbs irritably. 'She was due to fly back one night last November. Her father went to meet her at the airport, Julia waited at home. Shortly after the plane landed, Lewis phoned the house to say that they were dropping in at Gail's apartment to deposit some of her baggage but then they'd come right on home. And that's the last time Julia spoke to him.'

'She never saw him again?'

'Not until the police asked her to identify the bodies.'

'Which were found at the airport?'

'Which were found at Gail's apartment.'

Candice nodded and stabbed her fork in the air with recognition. 'Ah. They were shot, right? At close range? I remember seeing it on TV.'

'Do you remember what you thought at the time?'

'That it was hoodlums, I guess.'

'The police don't seem to agree.'

Candice waved her fork again. It was one of her few habits left over from the old days. 'Strange.'

'What's strange?'

'Well, all of it, actually, but what I meant was that I can imagine someone having a reason to kill the husband – something to do with his job, maybe – and I suppose it's possible that someone wanted to kill the daughter but why would anyone want to kill them both?'

'Maybe they wanted him but she got in the way.'

'Yep. That explains it. So what makes the police think Julia did it?' Candice pronounced Julia's name awkwardly.

'They haven't said so. It's just the way they act.'

'What evidence do they have?'

'None, so far as I can tell.'

'And what do you think?'

'That they were an ordinary family. Julia had no reason to kill them. And —'

Candice said: 'People in ordinary families often want to kill each other.'

Lomax decided not to waste time interpreting this remark. He said: 'Julia isn't capable of killing anyone.'

Candice was watching him closely.

'It's terrible for her right now. First she has the trauma of their deaths, then the trauma of finding herself under suspicion. There's this fat, dumb sheriff with teeth all over his face who harasses her the whole time. It's obvious he thinks she did it.'

Their food had arrived but Candice didn't start eating. She was still studying Lomax's face. It was such a long, searching stare that he found himself reddening.

'Is that how you look at your clients when they don't pay their bills?' he said.

'You're in love, aren't you, Lomax?'

Lomax nodded mournfully.

This love was not a completely pleasant experience. Later that day he returned to the observatory where he was closer to Julia, but even here the ratio of time spent thinking about her and wanting her was unhappily disproportionate to time spent in her company. The resulting equation reversed fantasy and reality. It seemed their brief meetings functioned only to refuel Lomax's fantasies. In his fantasies the encounters which in real life were punctuated by silences and awkwardnesses became fluid and their undertone of sexual promise was ecstatically fulfilled.

Whenever they met she held his gaze steadily and he would find himself studying her full, damp lips. The sight aroused him and sometimes he thought she knew this and it made her smile.

Somehow, without any discussion, she indicated that the staff residence, with its thin beds and thin walls, was not a possible sexual venue. Lomax wandered in and out of the laundry room to assess its suitability and, in desperation, even found himself considering, briefly, the data bank. There were plenty of secluded trails leading down the valley from the observatory. If the weather would only dry he could invite her hiking and they would get to some quiet place and she would amaze him again. But the weather was unseasonably wet.

Lomax's frustration seemed to infect everybody. He paced the site and, as cloud cover obscured the sky night after night, he met more and more of his colleagues, also pacing. The asphalt was thick with the round silhouettes of astronomers in bulky, heated suits walking stiff-leggedly, their faces pointed at the sky. People were irritable. They gossiped. The atmosphere was dense with rumours of impending job cuts. People speculated on the likely abandonment of whole projects, possibly their own. They discussed the eclipse committee. The rumour spread that, since the observatory had no solar telescope, the director planned to raise funds to move one to the mountain top especially for the occasion. Astronomers estimated how much this would cost, not in dollars but in jobs. There was bickering at mealtimes, followed by arguments. At the drinking parties which now took place nightly in the staff residence, more than one fight broke out. The community began to split into hostile factions. Julia spent a lot of time with Yevgeny and Doberman. Lomax watched her jealously but did not join the group. He felt isolated. He found himself calling Candice more often than usual.

'What's the matter with you? I'm busy,' she said.

Impossible to describe what was the matter with him. The constant heightened state of sexual desire. The professional and sexual frustration. The shiftlessness of life in an observatory where nothing was observed. The tedium of threatened changes which never took place. The weight of his suspicions about Berlins. He chose to tell Candice about the last of these.

'Stop shouting,' she told him. He realized he had been yelling but was unable to stop himself.

'Is that all you can say?' he bellowed.

'Well, frankly, I don't know what to say. I mean, it's unbelievable.'

'Unbelievably stupid,' he agreed. He was sitting on the desk in his room and now he began kicking his chair. It fell over.

'Are you throwing things around?'

'No I am not.'

'Lomax, losing your temper won't help. Why are you behaving this way?'

'Berlins isn't even being careful about it. I keep uncovering more evidence without even trying. Yesterday he left a pile of papers on my desk and on the top I found these calculations . . .'

'What sort of calculations?' Candice's question was crisp. She was at the clinic. This was her white labcoat voice.

'Calculations which changed some figures into something else.'

'Is it possible you were mistaken?'

'I could be mistaken about any one thing but not all of them. God, people, I mean. You trust them. They change. They let you down. They're all the fucking same.'

Candice's voice narrowed.

'Don't get personal,' she said.

'I was talking about the entire human race.'

'Even whatshername, Julia?'

He paused. He did not want to think that Julia would change and let him down. But Candice did not wait for an answer.

'You must be wrong about Berlins,' she insisted. 'Because he would never tell lies to a whole symposium even if he told lies to you. Which anyway I don't believe.'

'You don't want to believe it.'

Candice liked Professor Berlins. She had met him at the observatory on open days and he had called at their home a few times. It was before the divorce, when relations were strained, and Berlins' presence had relieved the tension. He had brought his wife once. She was smiling and white-haired.

'Don't go too near the edge,' Mrs Berlins had called to her husband when, admiring the view, he had strayed close to the railings of the deck.

'It's okay, they're safe,' Lomax had said quickly. He had built the deck and the railings. But Berlins had returned obediently to the group round the table.

'Married to his mother,' Candice had said when they had gone.

'It works for them,' Lomax had replied.

The telephone call ended unsatisfactorily. Candice would not agree that he had grounds to suspect Berlins. He began shouting again and she hung up the phone. He gave the fallen chair another kick and it scuttled across the room. The phone rang once more. A single ring meant the call was internal. He hoped it was Julia or, if it wasn't Julia, he hoped it was Kim. She had been avoiding him lately, ever since he had forgotten to go to the movies with her.

'I'd like to speak to you in person right away,' someone said.

'Um . . . who?'

It was Berlins, his voice scarcely recognizable. Lomax felt his anger thicken.

'What's up?' he demanded. Berlins told him curtly to come to his office.

As Lomax left the staff residence he saw small groups of scientists scattered around the parking lot talking energetically in low voices.

There were Doberman and Yevgeny and McMahon, heads close together, watched by curious passing tourists. Lomax looked at once for Julia but could not see her.

Suddenly Kim was standing in front of him.

'Shit, Lomax, shit,' she said. It was the first time for days she had seemed to notice him and now she was grabbing both his arms and trying to hold him still.

'Lemme go. Berlins is waiting for me,' Lomax told her. He looked at her for a moment and noticed that her brown eyes were big, so big that they seemed to bulge over half her face.

'I know. It's because of me. It's my fault. I did something real bad. I made a mistake.' He could feel her fingers digging into his arms. 'You'll hate me for ever. You'll never ever speak to me again. Only I didn't do it on purpose.'

Lomax wasn't sure if he was supposed to smile. This kind of talk usually meant Kim was joking.

She said: 'I told him you're mad at him.'

What was she talking about?

'The results. The doctored results. We were having like a heart to heart –'

'You and Berlins? Where? When?'

Kim glared at him in exasperation.

'It doesn't matter where for Chrissake but, since you ask, just now in the car when he drove me down from the Fahrhaus. That's where we always have our heart to hearts. And he asked was I going to the Chicago symposium this year and I said maybe and he said I should go because he was presenting a paper and I said what about and he said wait and see and were you going?'

She paused momentarily, gasping for breath.

'So I said no and he said why and I said you were mad at him and he said you'd been real strange these past few weeks and I asked didn't he know why and he said no and I said really? And he said no, was it something to do with Chicago? And . . .' Her voice faltered. 'And I told him.'

'Oh,' said Lomax. 'What exactly did you tell him?'

'That you're walking around seething with fury because you think he . . .' She began to squeak. 'And he went . . . like . . . crazy.'

Lomax left her on the asphalt crying.

Julia was not in the office. Berlins was seated behind his desk. He looked small. He did not smile. His cheeks seemed to have swelled a little, or his eyes had shrunk, but the effect was distorting. Lomax stared at him. The hair on top of his head was thinner and greyer than Lomax had noticed before. Berlins gave a brief, irritable hand gesture. Lomax understood that he was to sit down.

There was a silence. Lomax looked around the neat office. Julia had left her desk tidy. She had not logged out of her computer. Its otherwise blank screen recorded the date and time.

Berlins told him that he would like to know, in detail, exactly what allegations Lomax planned to make against him.

'I wasn't planning to make any allegations at all,' said Lomax. He heard his voice echo around the room. Had he shouted? A small part of him found it almost inconceivable that he would shout at Berlins. The expression of shock and pain on the professor's face nauseated but did not check him.

'I mean, I wasn't planning to tell anyone. Since you decided you wanted to go to Chicago and make a fool of yourself. I was going to let you do it.'

Berlins watched him in silence. There was a hardening around his jaw. But Lomax still could not stop. 'I was planning to let you damage a reputation you spent years building and I was planning to let them laugh at you. Not the action of a friend, you're probably thinking. But then cheating on results isn't the action of a friend either.'

Lomax had finished. He was breathless. He waited for Berlins to reply but the older man continued to regard him in silence. Lomax noticed that Berlins' head and upper body as well as his hands were shaking.

'I see,' he said at last. His voice was high-pitched and quavering. His face was unnaturally pale, even his lips looked white. This, Lomax guessed, was the colour of fury. Berlins said: 'I note, Lomax, that you chose to discuss this not with me but with your colleagues.'

'Only Kim.'

Berlins knitted his fingers together on the desk in front of him. He sat upright, his body taut, though shaking. The muscles in his face seemed to have stiffened.

'And don't bother to deny it,' Lomax added. 'I can prove the galaxy was redrawn because I have copies of the print-outs of the original results.'

'Oh,' said Berlins ominously. 'You can prove it.'

The long silence that followed was oppresive. It was more oppressive even than the weight of suspicion that Lomax had been carrying around these last few weeks. It made him sweat. He wiped his forehead with his arm.

'I'm going to turn down the air conditioning. It's cold in here,' Berlins said, standing suddenly. His face had a frozen translucence. He flicked a switch and the background whirring which you almost never heard was suddenly noticeable because it had stopped. Berlins returned to his seat and the silence continued, deeper this time. Then the professor picked up the phone and dialled an internal number. He spoke to a secretary, urging her to make immediate space in her boss's diary.

'Tell Dixon we'll see him in a few minutes,' he concluded.

'What are you doing for Chrissake?' said Lomax.

'This is something we should discuss with the director.'

'Shouldn't we discuss it with each other first?'

'It seems things have gone too far for that.'

'Why drag Driver into it?' Lomax shouted.

'Because,' he said, pulling his jacket onto his shoulders, 'in the circumstances, it hardly seems worth trying to communicate with you directly.' He opened the door. 'Unfortunately you don't have time to shave. I said we'd go right over.'

Berlins was starting off down the hallway. He walked faster than usual, with his eyes fixed on the ground, his toes pointing out and his elbows flapping. He turned. Lomax was still standing in the doorway of the office.

'Come along, Lomax,' he said briskly.

'You must be going crazy, Professor Berlins.'

Lomax heard anguish replace anger in his voice as it echoed along the hallway. It brought faces to a few of the doors. Lomax loped along behind Berlins, remonstrating, but Berlins did not slacken his pace.

Dixon Driver's office was in the oldest part of the observatory but there had been an attempt to make the interior seem older still. It was wood panelled. There were brass instruments in glass cases around the walls, and photographs of constellations. It was typical of Dixon Driver, Lomax thought, that these photographs had been retouched in unlikely but striking colours. Driver's appointment one year ago had been a controversial one. His academic record and astronomical career were undistinguished but his ability to market the observatory to sponsors, benefactors, the government and the public was outstanding. In spite of the flow of funds, Driver was regarded as a ruthless manager who had been planning since his appointment to trim jobs and projects. Part of the current paranoia on site arose from the belief that Driver threatened the academic standing of the observatory by favouring only the projects with public appeal.

76

Driver had not been expecting Lomax. He dragged another chair up to his desk next to Berlins'.

Since Lomax had last been in this office, more pictures had been added. They had been taken with a faint object camera and their artificial colouring made everything more than a few hundred million light years away look the same electric blue that flashed outside the downtown strip joints.

Berlins was apologizing for their abrupt arrival. 'Lomax will explain why we're here,' he said.

Both men turned to Lomax. He gave an exaggerated shrug. 'It wasn't my idea to come.'

Driver's eyebrows shot up. He looked at Berlins.

'Anthony?'

Berlins cleared his throat.

'Dr Lomax has made some very damaging allegations about results obtained at this observatory. I think you should hear them.'

'Allegations against the observatory?' Driver leaned forward, frowning. His features grew dense.

'Against me in particular. I regret to say that instead of approaching me about all this, he went in secret to the data bank and even discussed his suspicions with his colleagues.'

Lomax opened his mouth to object but Driver spoke first.

'I'm disappointed, Dr Lomax, to find your methods so underhand. If either of you has behaved suspiciously so far, it seems to be you.'

Lomax was aware that Berlins' tone, though taut, was regular, whereas in the course of his confrontation in Berlins' office he, Lomax, had sweated, shouted and sworn. He reddened now and Driver, tugging at his bowtie, watched him intently.

'This is all very disturbing, Anthony. No wonder you insisted on bringing the matter to me,' he said. 'Particularly if Dr Lomax has been telling other people on site about it.'

Lomax said: 'But I discussed my evidence with one close friend who, as far as I know, didn't tell anyone. Professor Berlins, on the other hand, was preparing to discuss the same evidence with an entire goddam symposium.'

'What exactly is this evidence? What are the allegations?' asked Driver. Lomax did not speak. Driver waited and then turned at last to Berlins who explained.

'Dr Lomax believes he has evidence of falsification of results in Core Nine. The falsification is, apparently, consistent, and Dr Lomax concludes from this that someone is trying to substantiate a pet theory. He feels that someone is me, presumably because only he and I have been working specifically with these figures.'

'Hmmmm.' Dixon Driver stroked his chin. He looked at Lomax and then back to Berlins. 'Do you think it's possible that results have been falsified?'

Berlins nodded forcefully. 'Oh, it's possible. And Lomax, Dr Lomax, claims to have proof.'

'Nothing can be proved for sure until that piece of sky comes back over the horizon,' said Lomax.

'Which is when?'

'September.'

'But,' Berlins added, 'Dr Lomax has proof from the data bank which he believes is virtually conclusive.'

Lomax thought of the bottles, the syringes, the semen and other human waste products littering the dirty floor of the data bank. He associated it now with Driver's arrival at the observatory. His predecessor would never have allowed the information centre to become a trashcan. He looked at Driver, a small man in a neat suit, and disliked him. Driver seemed to sense this. He had been leafing through the pages of a hardback notebook on his desk and now he looked up.

'I note,' he began, 'that Dr Lomax paid his visit to the data bank without signing himself in.'

The notebook was the signing in book.

'The professor gave me his key,' said Lomax defensively.

'I see,' said Driver, his voice unpleasant. 'I see. Well, what an interesting situation this is.' He tilted his chair back and looked up at the sky through the glass roof of his office, squeezing the pads of his fingers together.

'Two men in particular have access to one set of results. They both, in varying degrees, acknowledge the possibility that these results have been doctored, but each appears to suspect the other.'

'What?' said Lomax.

'You appear to suspect the professor. And I've known Anthony long enough to be sure, without him uttering a word, that he suspects you.'

Lomax stared at Berlins. 'What?' he said again.

Berlins' face was without expression.

'This is insane,' shouted Lomax.

'Please don't shout, Dr Lomax. Anthony, someone came to you today to tell you that Dr Lomax believes information obtained at this observatory has been falsified. Were you already aware of that fact?' Driver asked Berlins.

'Oh yes,' said Berlins.

'Of course you were aware of it, for Chrissake!' yelled Lomax.

'Your language,' frowned Driver, 'is most unprofessional. Not a good indication.'

Somehow, Lomax silenced himself.

'I've already decided how I intend to handle this,' said Berlins. 'I'm not answering any allegations, and I'm not making any. I've brought the matter to you, Dixon. I'd like to request that you investigate and come to your own conclusions.'

Dixon Driver gave Lomax a reproachful smile.

'Anthony would make a good role model for you. He's not throwing allegations around, let alone at anyone specific. You're a young man, Dr Lomax, and you have a lot to learn from the professor.'

'I've learned a lot from him already and I'm hoping I'll learn more. You don't know how painful it's been for me to suspect a man for whom I've so much personal affection and professional admiration,' said Lomax hotly.

'The affection and admiration are mutual, Lomax. You don't know how painful it's been for me to be on the receiving end of your suspicions,' Berlins said, looking at Lomax for the first time in many minutes.

'Good. Well, I'm glad to hear all this, gentlemen, but it's clearly impossible for you to continue working together in the circumstances.'

Lomax stared at Dixon Driver with incredulity. Driver began pulling at his bowtie again.

'I suggest that you both take a sabbatical until the matter is resolved. Do you think that's a satisfactory suggestion, Anthony?'

For a moment even Berlins seemed nonplussed. Driver looked from one man to the other and back again, registering the shock in their faces.

'There's nothing happening in Core Nine that won't wait for you both – assuming you both return. That, of course, depends on our findings. Now don't look so tragic. Your galaxies will all be there when you come back in September. Or you might return even earlier if we manage to complete our investigations, although it sounds unlikely without this missing piece of sky. Anthony, what do you think?'

Berlins did not move.

'Look on it as a long summer break. You might even enjoy it. And I'll be generous; I'll put you both on half-pay.'

Lomax was aware that his face must be drained of colour. His anger was gone now, replaced with limpness all through his body. He looked at Berlins, who would not meet his eye. The professor seemed to have aged that afternoon. He sat slackly, his shoulders rounded. He did not move.

'When do you want us to leave?' Lomax asked.

'As soon as possible. If you hang around, each garnering supporters to your point of view, this whole thing could blow up into the sort of scandal I'm anxious to avoid.'

'Like . . . *today?*'

'Yes, I think so. I'll have a word with Eileen about it. I suggest you both avoid discussing this with your colleagues.'

'It's going to be kind of difficult to explain . . .' began Lomax, but Driver dismissed his objections with a wave of the hand. Lomax waited for Berlins to say something. Berlins did not speak for some moments. Finally he said: 'It's time I taught my grandson to fish.'

'Sure, Anthony. You'll have a real good summer,' Driver assured him.

'Sarah's been nagging me for some time to . . . well, to rest. It's a notion I've resisted, but maybe . . .'

Lomax did not wait to hear the end of Berlins' sentence. He rose and, unsure what to do next, found himself shaking hands with first Driver and then, mechanically, with Berlins.

Outside, the sun, emerging for the first time in days, was potent. Tourists milled randomly around in the parking lot. There was no sign of the gossiping groups of astronomers he had seen earlier. Lomax felt the sun's rays on his face. Without thought or plan, he began to follow one of the trails that led down the mountainside. The recent rain had left the sandy soil damp. It clung to his shoes. In a couple of places the trail had been washed away. The remaining soil was of a perfect smoothness, broken only by the random deposition of stones. Sometimes he found himself scrambling downwards, clinging to rocks and twigs, but mostly the rhythm of his walk was even. He knew from experience how easy it was to descend too far. Heat and exhaustion on the climb back up could be almost blinding. It was foolish, too, to walk even this early in the year without something to drink. He knew all this but he walked on.

The lower his altitude the denser and greener the vegetation became. There was the sound of running, then crashing, water. Near the bottom of the first valley the water thundered. The rocks were wet and the air was cool and the foliage dripped. Lomax sat on a rock watching the water. His rhythmic descent had dulled the pain of thought and now the noise had the same effect. The water twisted, turned and eddied past him.

He stayed in the valley until the sun had disappeared over the top of the mountain. By lying on the stone he could watch the clouds massing for a thunderstorm. He returned to the observatory sweating, his throat dry. It was early evening and the site was deserted. Everyone must be in the cafeteria.

He went straight to the labs, pausing at each drinking fountain.

Berlins was kneeling on his office floor. His desk drawers hung open and most were empty. The trashcan at his side was overflowing. He had organized his papers into three unruly piles. The fourth pile was more personal: a pen with his name on the side, some photographs, a desk toy, an award. Lomax remembered how Julia had said the watches and wallets and jewellery of her dead family had been handed over to her in plastic bags after their deaths. Here was another sad, random, meaningless collection of personal effects. He watched the professor, noticing again how hairless the top of his head had become.

Lomax glanced at Julia's computer. She had still not logged out of it.

Berlins seemed to see Lomax without looking up. 'Don't loom in the doorway like that, Lomax,' he said mildly.

'You're clearing your desk.'

'Obviously.' Berlins shifted some books from one pile to another. 'This afternoon I cleared my room. In just one hour I've sorted out all this. You should make a start on yours, who knows what you might find.' He held a small, glass box up to Lomax. Lomax knelt down. Inside the box was a tiny model telescope.

'Perfect, isn't it? Swiss. A present from my daughter many years ago. I thought I'd lost it.'

'Professor, we don't have to do this. Driver's just looking to save money. He wants job cuts. Or, even if we come back, Core Nine will be on ice for six months and that's what he wants in his goddam accounts. Let's protest. I'm prepared to apologize if that would help. I mean, I am sorry. I should have talked to you about this right away, as soon as I saw something was wrong. Why don't we tell Driver we're not going, we're just planning to forget the whole thing?'

Berlins blinked. 'I wish we could. Sadly, it's too late for that.'

'But,' said Lomax, handing him the miniature telescope, 'I don't want to go away all summer.'

'I didn't either at first, but I've been thinking of the things I can do. Family things. Grandchildren . . .'

'It's wrong, it shouldn't happen this way.'

'I'll be all right, Lomax,' said Berlins kindly. 'Now go clear your desk.'

'Have you been to the cafeteria?'

'No.'

'You should eat something.'

'Not now, Lomax.'

'Come on. Come with me.'

The professor sighed. Lomax helped him to his feet and they went to the cafeteria together. No one looked up as they came in. The noise level in the room was abnormally high. Everyone seemed to be engaged in intense conversation.

'Let's ask Dixon Driver to reconsider,' Lomax suggested again when they had chosen their meals. He tried not to look at the professor. The sight of his fork shaking as it travelled from his plate to his mouth was disturbing. Lomax looked away, struggling for words. 'I mean . . . we were both angry before. It all happened because we were both angry. Now we're not.'

Berlins chewed thoughtfully before replying.

'No,' he said at last. 'I'm not angry any more.'

'Then let's go see Driver!'

'He's held a meeting for heads of department and told them all. He won't change his mind. Poor Lomax. It's easier for me than for you. At my age the thought of a long holiday is quite acceptable. For you it must seem a big hiccup in your career.'

'I'm not a career astronomer,' said Lomax with a hint of pride.

'It should be you replacing me, not Doberman.'

'Doberman!'

'I thought that news would be salt to your wounds.'

'Doberman.'

'Looks like it. He doesn't know yet. The heads of department aren't telling anyone until tomorrow and I guess we'll be gone by then.'

Lomax had wanted to ask specifically whether Julia knew. He thought she should have found him by now and asked what was going on, where he had been all afternoon, if he was okay. But there had been no sign of her in the labs or the cafeteria.

'It's sort of strange not saying goodbye.'

'A merciful release. It's possible that dread of retirement – I mean the process of retirement: the cards, the presents, the dinners, the speeches, the farewells – has prevented me from going before now.'

'You're not retiring. You're taking a long vacation.'

But Berlins just smiled.

They ate in silence. Lomax wanted to talk but could think of nothing to say. Berlins asked: 'Do you have any hobbies?'

'We-ll . . .'

'I'm planning to build a telescope. I suppose you made your first telescope when you were around ten years old?'

Lomax nodded. He still had it. In the next year or so, he hoped to help Joel make one too.

'Well I never did. A vital stage in the development of an astronomer and I missed out on it. I think I'll do something about that this summer.'

Lomax found it painful to imagine the shaky old hands positioning the mirrors carefully.

After dinner, they paused in the corridor before going their separate ways, Lomax to the labs and Berlins to his office.

'Professor, I'm sorry,' said Lomax. He looked back now on his earlier fury as he might remember a stranger.

Berlins gave him a sad smile. 'At least Driver's inquiry should clear up your suspicions,' he said. He squeezed Lomax's arm affectionately and ambled off. Lomax watched him. The professor's parting words were the nearest to not guilty that he had pleaded.

'I'll call you!' Lomax yelled. He thought the professor might have nodded in response.

There was dense cloud cover again that night. The labs were empty. He telephoned Julia's room but there was no reply. He began clearing his desk but soon found himself just removing the computer disks and papers he wanted to take away with him. He left his collection of beercans, old chocolate wrappers and unwanted printouts untouched. He was digging deep into the bottom drawer for some photos of Joel and Helen when he caught sight of a woman at the doorway. For a moment he thought it was Julia. He smiled but Eileen Friel, head of administration, did not return his smile. She asked him to vacate his room in the staff residence by the next morning.

'I'm coming back at the end of September, for Chrissake,' Lomax remonstrated.

The woman shrugged. 'I could really use that room. I have a group of Russians arriving for the whole of August and the director told me to keep them apart from the Japanese in the other wing.'

'What do the Russians have against the Japanese?'

She shrugged again. For her, international affairs were purely a matter of bedroom allocation.

'Maybe I could just – ' he began but she interrupted him.

'C'mon Lomax, get the hell out of the room. You'll have to apply for re-allocation, that's if you do come back in September.'

The 'if' shocked Lomax. He studied her face. Its blank expression was uncompromising but her voice had betrayed a hint of satisfaction. When she had arrived at the observatory soon after Dixon Driver there had been a room reshuffle. She had allocated Lomax his large room with its fine view, making her sexual interest in him clear. He had pretended not to notice her overtures at first, and after that had avoided her completely. Now, in the silent evening laboratory, she stood over him and he knew that she had not forgiven him. She was enjoying this. She was a small, slim woman, famously active sexually. Doberman had claimed to be her helpless prey on a number of occasions. He said she had a face of 45 and a body of 18.

'I hate to give it up. I like that room,' he said with resignation.

'You'll get another one in September.'

Lomax could guess what it would be like. 'Okay.'

He continued to search for his photos and when he looked up she had gone. He called Julia again. There was still no reply.

He went to his room and began to throw piles of belongings onto the bed. He had no boxes or bags to carry them. He wanted someone to appear – Julia preferably – but no one knocked or even passed in the corridor outside. The phone did not ring. The silence, at a time when the observatory was often at its busiest, was unsettling. He began to feel angry at Julia's absence. When his shirts and underwear and books were piled onto the bed he lifted the corners of the bedspread to make a bundle. But the weight was too great.

There was a knock at the door. It was Kim.

'Where the hell have you been all day?' she asked him. Her eyes were still too big. She was frightened.

'I went hiking.'

'Is everything okay now? I worried about you, but then when you came into the cafeteria with the professor I thought . . .'

She saw the empty shelves and the ransacked closet and the chaos on the bed and stopped.

'Oh God,' she said.

He told her everything that had happened. Her eyes were enormous now.

'Oh Jeez.'

She started to apologize. When she saw that he wasn't angry she began to cry. Her big eyes shed big tears which ran over her cheeks and down her chin. He told her it was okay.

84

'I probably would have confronted Berlins myself if you hadn't done it first,' he said untruthfully. He persuaded her to collect the bedspread from her room to help him move. When she came back with it she was still crying. They pulled it under the piles of clothes and books on the bed and lifted two corners each.

'This is terrible. It's terrible the way it's happened just now with your girlfriend off the site and everything.' Kim sniffed.

'Who?'

'Don't pretend you're not crazy about the Barbie doll. That's probably why I told him. You're crazy about her and I'm mad at you and that's probably why . . .' The rest of her sentence was choked by tears. She sat down on some underpants and a collection of notebooks and sobbed uncontrollably.

Lomax shook her. 'What did you say?' he asked twice or three times. 'Something about someone being off the site?'

'Don't you know about it?' she asked. Her eyes were still big, but now they were red and wet.

'What, what?'

'This morning, when I was talking to Berlins at the Fahrhaus . . . didn't you hear what happened with the Barbie doll?'

Lomax waited. Suddenly he knew that the small gossiping groups, the noise level in the cafeteria, the silence in the corridors, the emptiness of the site all had a significance, and that it was something to do with Julia. He tried to remember when he had last seen her. That morning at breakfast. Since then, she had just been a computer screen that no one had logged out from.

Kim wound the fringe of the bedspread around her finger like a ring. It was her wedding ring finger.

'What's happened?' said Lomax in someone else's voice.

'The police came here and took her away. Then on TV tonight they said she'd been arrested.'

9

The observatory was asleep and the darkness outside dense when Kim and Lomax staggered to his car with the sagging bundle hanging between them like a big baby.

'Why is this so goddam furtive?' asked Lomax, breathless from the load.

'Because you're stealing two bedspreads from Eileen Squeal and she'll stop at nothing – search warrant, citizens' arrest – to get them back,' Kim said, sounding like the old Kim right up until the end of the sentence. Then she broke into sobs again. She did not like Eileen Friel. She requested a room re-allocation on an almost monthly basis and it was always refused.

Lomax ignored her sobs this time. He had already said all the kind and reassuring things he could think of. And despite his protests, he knew he was angry with her. He talked about the bedspreads.

'I could try to ease them out from underneath . . .'

She had stopped crying again. Her face was lit only by the dim glow from the trunk of the car.

'Nah,' she said. 'Fuck it. Compared with the other things people're going to be saying about you, two stolen bedspreads don't figure.'

Lomax squinted at her to see if she was joking.

'I'm not joking,' she said. 'You've been asked to leave because you're under suspicion.'

'I guess it's better than being under arrest,' Lomax muttered as he closed the trunk. Kim stepped closer to him.

'Are you really in love with the Barbie doll?'

'I wish you wouldn't call her the Barbie doll.'

'Are you, are you?'

'Yes.'

'I'll try to stop calling her Barbie. It's just the way she . . . oh, forget it. I only hope you don't spend the rest of your life visiting her in jail. Or worse.'

Lomax squinted at Kim through the darkness. 'What's that supposed to mean?'

'Nothing. Lomax . . .' There were tears in her eyes again. 'I'd come visit you in town if you'd just return my calls.'

'I'll always return your calls from now on.'

To his surprise, Kim suddenly wound her arms around him. She was so small and rounded and she bored her face into his chest with such intensity that he was reminded of Deputy Dawg at his most affectionate.

'I'm only saying this once, Lomax, but I'm jealous of the Barbie doll, okay?'

She looked at him, rolling her chin against his shirt. He rested his arms on her shoulders. He knew this was supposed to be a shared moment of sadness at his departure but all he could think of was Julia.

'I'll be back in September,' he said.

'Sure.'

The hollow tone of these words stayed with Lomax as he drove slowly down the mountain road. There was no other traffic tonight. With the windows open he could hear the crickets and other night creatures. The storm which had been threatening all day still had not come but he could feel the oppressive weight of the air outside. The car, heavy with books and papers and clothes, seemed to cut through it like a big boat. Once, when the car had rolled and rocked its way around a hairpin bend, there was an animal in the road. It froze in the headlights, staring. Lomax braked hard and stared back. It was a mountain lion, smaller than the name suggests but sleek and sinewy and wild. After a few moments it disappeared into the darkness. Its exit was so rapid and so sudden that Lomax suspected he was still seeing the image of the creature seconds after its departure. When he told Joel, later, the child asked many questions which Lomax found himself unable to answer. Joel brought him pens and crayons and asked him to draw the lion and he was unable to do so. Eventually Joel showed him a picture of a mountain lion in a book which Lomax failed to recognize. And so he began to share his son's doubt that he had seen the lion at all.

Finally he rounded the last bend in the mountains and the lights of the city were spread out before him. They shone orange into the distance and their chemical glow stretched up to the clouds.

He skirted the foothills, driving straight to Julia's house.

When she answered the door her face was pale. Her eyes seemed rounder than usual. She looked young – childish, even. She hugged him with the same intensity that Kim had earlier. Unexpectedly she said: 'Where's Deputy?'

'With Joel and Helen . . . I came straight here.'

She led him to the living room. A young man was sitting in the seat where Murphy McLean had sat a few weeks ago. He was clean-shaven, tanned and his short blond hair seemed to strut on his head. Lomax took one look at his suit, his haircut and his jawline and found him repellent.

Julia was introducing her other visitor to him.

'Frances Bauer is my attorney,' she was explaining. Frances stepped towards him, her clothes rustling expensively. Her hair was a pale red. The air around her was perfumed. As she held her hand out to him, jewellery rattled a little on her arm. She smiled at him and it was an attractive smile but he knew she was appraising him. Feeling himself to be under scrutiny, he blushed and stepped back into Kurt, who had stood to shake hands with him. Lomax apologized. Kurt was almost as tall as he was. He tried to match the firmness of Kurt's handshake.

'Kurt's going to help Frances,' Julia said, gesturing to Kurt's notepad. 'He's an investigator.'

'Julia, what's actually happened? I was out this afternoon and . . .'

'Well . . . Murph arrived at the observatory with a couple of guys in uniform and . . .' As usual, when she was explaining anything, her voice trailed helplessly away.

'And what did they do?' coaxed Lomax.

'I was just sitting in the office and I looked up and Murph was standing there . . .'

Julia's voice cracked as she spoke. Lomax put his arm around her. 'What's the charge?'

But Julia did not answer. In a graceful gesture, she bowed her face and hid it with one hand.

'First degree murder. Twice,' supplied Kurt helpfully. 'I mean the murder of Lewis Fox and his daughter Gail.'

Lomax said: 'How can they do this?' He found himself looking at Frances for an answer. She shrugged noiselessly.

'I mean,' said Lomax, 'the police were here just a few weeks ago and it's obvious they didn't have any evidence . . .'

'Well now they think they have evidence.' Her tone was unyielding. Lomax guessed that she did not think he should be present at this discussion.

She said: 'Julia, it's late, you're tired, and your friend's here. We've done what we can for today. We got you bail and we dealt with the press. Now we have to start building your case. Could you come to my office tomorrow morning and tell us everything in more detail?'

Kurt flicked through his notebook with noisy efficiency. 'Eleven fifteen is good,' he said. He had a rasping voice.

Julia looked up. 'I'd like Lomax to come with me.'

Kurt and Frances exchanged glances.

'That's not the way we do business, Julia.'

'Frances might not want even me to be there!' joked Kurt as if there was something astonishing about this.

'But I want him to come,' said Julia, blinking at them with large eyes.

'It's important that everything you say, every line of investigation we pursue, is completely confidential.'

'Lomax is completely confidential.'

'Sure,' said Lomax, trying to sound it.

But Frances was moving towards the door. Her thick hair swayed a little as she walked.

Lomax watched Kurt put a hand on Julia's arm. 'This has been traumatic for you. Facing the press is not a pleasant experience but you did well. Now you need to rest and sleep and lead as normal a life as possible.' Lomax watched the hand steadily to see when he would remove it.

'Normal,' echoed Julia.

'Kurt's right,' came Frances' brisk voice from the door. 'You should go back to work as soon as you can. I'll deal with all reporters. Just make sure none of them sees you with your friend here, it doesn't look good. Probably you should get back up to the observatory as soon as possible. And relax. It'll be months before this case comes to trial.'

Kurt kissed Julia on the cheek. Lomax watched in disgust.

'Eleven fifteen tomorrow,' called Frances. 'Look after her, Dr Lomax. But I'm sure I don't need to tell you that.'

The two attorneys walked towards their cars. Kurt's was long and low. It was easy to imagine it racing other cars away from the intersections. As Kurt passed Lomax's old stationwagon he glanced inside it. Lomax knew he was looking at the pile of books and papers and clothes littered wherever they had been thrown by the hairpin bends and he wished that the storm, which still threatened to begin imminently, would start right now.

When Julia and Lomax were alone they held each other as though they were holding each other up. Lomax was almost overwhelmed by wearinesss. Without speaking they went to bed and, like a child, Julia fell asleep instantly. Lomax lay awake, aroused by the proximity of her body. He slept fitfully until the first dim light of morning and then he slept deeply.

He awoke and knew there had been a storm. The air was clean and the sky clear. He turned to Julia. His erection was painful. There was a frown on her face. She bit her lip. It would be tactless, in the circumstances, to try to make love. He lay beside her remembering everything.

'If you want me to be there, just insist. You're the client,' he reminded her.

'But Frances said . . . Kurt said . . .'

'You're picking up the tab.'

The story of Julia's arrest was on every TV station. Lomax watched the pictures without absorbing them. Lewis. Gail. A small apartment building, the university, a police station, Frances and Julia. Frances making a statement. Julia refusing to answer questions. Kurt and a policeman holding back two jostling men, perhaps reporters.

Julia did not watch. When it was time to leave she stood at the window with her back to the TV.

'They say,' Lomax told her as they left the house, 'that your fingerprints and fibres are all over the apartment where the murders took place.'

'Sure,' agreed Julia.

'You knew that?'

'I knew they must be. I was there less than twelve hours earlier. I went over and tidied it a little and cleaned it so that Gail wouldn't get back from a long trip and find her apartment dusty and empty. I left a welcome home present and I cleaned it all up. So my fingerprints must have been everywhere.'

Lomax smiled at her and touched her cheek. He had known there would be a simple explanation. Probably Frances would sort this out and charges would be dropped in a day or two.

They looked into Lomax's car and then agreed to take Julia's. She drove. Her car was fast but she manoeuvered it with a hesitation that other drivers, especially men, seemed to sense. Julia would catch their eye and something in the way she did this made them wave her across at intersections and allow her into streams of dense traffic with a smile. There was grinning and waving and eye contact right across town. Lomax found it annoying. She was supposed to be talking to him but she kept breaking off to smile at other people. Spasmodically, she told him about Frances. She explained how, when

90

she had married Lewis, Frances had taken over the administration of her trust fund.

'This trust fund,' he asked. 'What . . . I mean why . . . ?'

'Well, Daddy was scared I'd just go spend all his money. He wanted someone to take care of me, so he decided that whenever I needed money I'd have to explain why I wanted it, and Sachs Smith would say yes or no.'

'That's because you were a minor, right?'

She was trying to turn left. She was eying each driver until a man signalled her across.

'Well no, it's for always.'

'For the rest of your life? You have to ask for your own money?'

'You sound like Frances,' said Julia.

Frances was a defence lawyer but when Julia had married the attorney in charge of her trust fund, Frances had been appointed to replace him because she was Sachs Smith's only female partner.

'They thought it would be nice for me to talk to a woman. It doesn't take up much of her time . . . any of her time, really.'

'So you have to ask Frances whenever you want your own money?' It was impossible for Lomax to edit the note of disapproval from his voice.

'That's the rule of the fund. Daddy wanted to make sure I wouldn't do anything stupid with it.'

'You're a grown woman, you're allowed to do stupid things if you want.'

'Daddy couldn't imagine me as a grown woman. I was still a little girl to him.'

'Don't you mind having to ask?'

'Frances always says yes. She's like you. She thinks I'm a grown woman and I shouldn't need to explain why I want it.'

Lomax remembered Frances' attractive, intelligent face. He remembered her eyes. They were green and shrewd. He decided he had probably liked her last night.

'Do you like Frances?' he asked.

He saw Julia hesitate. 'It's sort of different having a woman attorney.'

'How?'

But she was turning left again. Of course it was different having a woman attorney, thought Lomax. She didn't invite Julia to lunch or act paternal or take a personal interest in her affairs. Frances treated Julia like an adult.

They crossed a double line of traffic with the smiling consent of at least three drivers. She was flirting but he no longer found this humiliating. It was one of the techniques a vulnerable young woman had developed to cope when she was left alone in the world. She drove now with a half-frown of concentration. Her face was pale. Her wrists looked thin enough to snap. He wanted to protect her.

Sachs Smith was downtown. Its offices were in the old part of the city, one of a row of historic houses which were a few years older than the century. Not only had the street been named a conservation area but its asphalt had recently been replaced by bumpy stones. One of the houses was open to tourists. Guides stood outside it in bonnets and long dresses and invited you in. Trees had been planted but did nothing to hide the modern blocks beyond.

Julia explained that Sachs Smith's building had originally been the home of a wealthy banker, a Scandinavian immigrant. There was a plaque on the wall to John Christiansen. Inside, the building turned from a house into an office. A receptionist sat surrounded by telephones. A fax machine hummed.

They were led down a hallway. The walls were painted white and ran at uneven angles to the bare floorboards.

Frances did not seem surprised when Lomax was shown into her office with Julia.

'If you insist on Dr Lomax being here, then I suppose I'll have to give in. But I really don't like it,' she said.

Kurt reached for an extra coffee cup. He was wearing a different suit today.

'We're still waiting for the police evidence,' Frances continued. 'However, from the questions they were asking yesterday, I think we can guess what lines they're working along.'

'You mean the money?' said Julia.

Frances paused and Kurt answered. 'This witness coming forward has given them just enough evidence to indict.'

'But,' added Frances, 'they clearly regard the money as significant.'

Kurt agreed with her, hovering over the coffee. Lomax wished he would just pour it, but he said: 'They find big sums of money going from your account to your stepdaughter's account, and they think: blackmail. They're not too smart. So all we have to do is find another explanation. Black or white, Dr Lomax?'

He spoke to Lomax with exaggerated politeness, as if he had not noticed the growth on Lomax's chin or his creased shirt.

Frances said: 'So let's remind ourselves of the last time you came in to Sachs Smith, Julia. Do you remember?'

'Oh yes,' said Julia, 'of course.'

Kurt gave her a winning smile. 'That,' he said, 'was when you met me.'

Julia giggled. 'How could I forget?'

Lomax dropped his coffee spoon. Kurt handed him a clean one.

Frances flicked through a brown folder on her lap. 'It clearly made an indelible impression on you both but actually I have a written record right here. I was on maternity leave. You saw my colleague, Mercedes Gonzales, and asked her for $450,000 from your fund.'

Julia nodded.

Frances stirred her coffee slowly.

'Mercedes phoned me before seeing you and I explained how the fund works. When you want money, we're supposed to establish the reason why. But as you know, I don't actually do that. After talking to me, Mercedes decided not to either.'

There was a note of apology in Frances' voice. Lomax watched her intently. Once she glanced at him and then looked rapidly away. He realized that she was confessing to maladministration of the fund. She explained that she had never approved of the way Julia's father had given someone else the right to veto Julia's access to her money and she believed there was a tacit agreement about this in Sachs Smith.

'You know how I feel, Julia, right? For some time now, although I'm supposed to evaluate your reasons for taking money out and discuss them with you, I haven't actually done so.'

Julia looked pained. She said defensively: 'But Daddy was scared I'd fall in love with someone who'd take all my money away from me. That's why he appointed Lewis to take care of me.'

Lomax shook his head. Lewis had been appointed to take care of the money, not Julia. Although he had ended up taking care of both, possibly.

'Is anything the matter?' Frances asked Lomax.

'No,' said Lomax.

'Well, what I'm trying to say . . .' The apology in her voice was strengthening. '. . . is that maybe I should have inquired in the past why you wanted money. And probably my colleague should have inquired why you wanted that $450,000 on . . . let's see, May 20, that's almost a year ago. Mercedes should have asked you and if she had asked you it would have made the police questions a whole lot easier to answer. But she didn't.'

There was a silence.

'Mercedes will probably have to explain herself in court. But that's not your problem. I have to admit . . . it's a lot of money. I remember Mercedes calling me at home about it. I remember wondering why you wanted it.'

Julia nodded but said nothing.

'Mercedes said . . . you seemed . . . upset.'

'How?'

'She asked you if anything was the matter but you told her everything was fine.'

Julia did not speak.

'So . . . why did you want the money?' asked Frances softly. Kurt's black pen hovered over his notepad like a hawk.

Lomax, Kurt and Frances watched Julia as she stared into her coffee.

'Maybe it was a present for Gail . . . some help you'd offered. To pay off a debt, maybe?'

Silence.

'I mean . . . perhaps she didn't actually demand the money as the police suggest. She might have told you she was in some kind of trouble . . .'

Finally Julia looked up. 'I gave it to Gail but I sort of assumed that it was really for Lewis.'

There was a moment of surprise. Then Kurt's pen was busy. Frances said: 'You took the money from the fund for Lewis? Why?'

'I'm not exactly sure . . .'

'Why did he need it?'

'Well, I don't really know.'

Frances spoke gently now but her voice had tightened a little with anxiety, or agitation. 'For business, for pleasure, a debt . . . maybe the police were right about blackmail but wrong about who was being blackmailed?'

'Frances, he didn't tell me exactly but I got the impression that he needed money for some reason to do with Sachs Smith. So when Gail asked me for $450,000 I guessed it was for Lewis. I knew he wouldn't ask me himself. He used to be in charge of my trust fund, he wouldn't ask me to give him money from it. He wouldn't think that was right. So I assumed Gail was asking for him.'

Frances was incredulous. 'He needed $450,000 for the firm?'

'Gail said she would need $450,000. She hinted it was for her father. I felt sure it was for Lewis. I knew he needed money. So I didn't ask any embarrassing questions. I just paid it into her bank account.'

'I see.'

Kurt said: 'You were a devoted wife.' It was not clear whether his register was ironic.

'Yes,' said Julia, looking directly at him.

Frances asked: 'Did Lewis ever hint to you why he might need money?'

'No. I mean, professional reasons, that's all.'

Frances and Kurt exchanged troubled glances.

'Sachs Smith,' said Frances, 'is playing more of a role in this case than I'd like.'

There was a silence which Lomax could tell Frances was trying to cover by flicking through the brown file. It was a thick file. Some of its early documents looked aged. He could see it consisted of many letters and financial statements. Frances was not really looking at its contents, though. She was thinking. Her cheekbones were prominent, her mouth wide, her chin sharp. She was, he saw, beautiful. Her face was alive even now as she devoted herself entirely to thought. He estimated she was in her late thirties. A few grey hairs were showing among the red and there had been no attempt to hide them. She frowned. She was concerned. Sachs Smith had failed to comply with the terms of Julia's trust and almost half of the fund may have been diverted, by indirect means, to Sachs Smith itself.

'Frances . . .' said Lomax, and she looked up at him shrewdly as if she had been waiting for him to speak.

'Should Sachs Smith be defending Julia? Given the involvement of the firm?'

The nib of Kurt's pen flicked in and out like a tongue.

Frances said slowly: 'It's certainly a question which ought to be asked . . .'

'Oh, Sachs Smith has to defend me,' Julia assured them. 'I mean, it was Lewis' firm. And Daddy always came here.'

Kurt said: 'Our managing partner was murdered. Of course we want to be involved.'

'Lewis Fox isn't on trial,' Lomax reminded them. 'His wife is.'

Kurt insisted: 'It would look bad if we didn't defend her. We're all on the same side here.'

But Frances' green eyes were clouded.

'I'll take advice,' she said. 'I may have to ask you to sign a waiver saying that you want us to take on the case despite our involvement.'

95

Julia nodded. 'I'll sign it,' she said quickly. Lomax tried to catch her eye but she looked away from him.

Kurt's pen nib reappeared. He said he needed to know more about the day of the murders. Julia nodded again. She leaned forward. She was anxious. Lomax found her especially beautiful when her face was alert.

Julia waited for Kurt. Kurt waited for Julia. When, after a long silence, Kurt realized that Julia expected to be questioned, he began too abruptly and she drew back in alarm. He asked the question again, his tone less harsh.

Julia thought hard, twisting hair around her finger. 'We woke up at about four a.m. Possibly four thirty but not later. Lewis said it wasn't worth going to bed at all. But I insisted. He needed the rest.'

'Uh huh,' said Kurt. 'Lewis was tired.'

'He'd fallen asleep in the car a few times recently. I mean, once in the garage when he got home. And once actually at the wheel when he was driving back real late.'

'He didn't tell us,' Frances murmured in surprise.

'Oh, he wasn't hurt. And I guess it's not the kind of thing you want your colleagues to know. I mean, Lewis didn't like people to think he was getting old.'

'So he was falling asleep at the wheel but he wasn't getting hurt,' Kurt said. Lomax noticed that Kurt made statements instead of asking questions. He doubted that much information would be coaxed from Julia in this way.

'I used to worry about him. There's this piece of road about a mile from the house. It's narrow and it sort of waves up and down along the hillside?' There was a question in her voice now. She was asking them to remember the waving road. Lomax recalled it at once. Despite the undulating hillside the road stayed straight, like a drunk who manages to remain upright. He could understand how a car ride here would lull a man to sleep as the wheels hugged the contours.

Julia added: 'Once he drove into the grass bank there.'

'Okay,' Kurt nodded impatiently. He was not interested in the road. 'Okay, so Lewis came to bed and you set the alarm for four a.m.'

'Yes.'

'That's early.'

'Well, Lewis wouldn't go out, ever, without showering and shaving, and it takes at least an hour to get to the airport when the roads are clear and Gail had some cheap ticket because the flight arrived in the middle of the night. Lewis said it usually takes an hour to clear baggage but you couldn't be sure.'

'So. The alarm went off.'

'The alarm went off and Lewis really had difficulty waking. I had to keep sort of nudging him. And that woke me up. I was supposed to sleep for a while longer.'

'You got up,' Kurt told her.

'Um . . .' She seemed embarrassed to contradict him. 'I sort of listened to Lewis having a shower. Then he came and kissed me goodbye. And he looked so tired. His face was puffy and he had shaved badly which is very unusual for Lewis. When he kissed me there was a scratchy place on his cheek. That was the last time he kissed me.'

Lomax thought Julia was going to cry. She looked down, hiding her head with her hand. When she spoke again her voice sounded as though it was being stretched out of her throat.

'I heard the garage door. I heard the car start up. I heard him drive away and I listened for the sound of the car engine on the wavy piece of road. But after a while I couldn't hear anything.'

'You went back to sleep,' Kurt told her.

'I tried to. I reset the alarm, but I couldn't fall asleep for a long time. Then just when I did, the alarm went off.'

'You got up.'

'Yes.'

'Well, what did you do?' demanded Kurt, exasperated into asking a question. Lomax flinched at his tone and Julia looked at him in surprise.

'Just the usual things. Stretched. Showered. Oh, and then the telephone rang. It was Lewis.'

'What time?'

'I don't know. I don't remember.' Julia bit her lip and looked from Frances to Kurt anxiously.

'It's okay, Julia,' said Frances. 'Tell us about the phone call.'

'Lewis sounded real happy. He said that the flight was on time and that Gail looked great. And then Gail took the phone. It was good to hear her. She said she was glad to be back. She said something in French. I couldn't understand it but I sort of laughed. Then she told me they were calling at her apartment to deposit some baggage so they'd be a little late. She said they called because –'

Julia stopped abruptly. They waited for her. When she spoke again her voice was small.

'Because they didn't want me to worry.'

Kurt began to ask Julia questions but now he was too interrogative, Lomax thought, and her answers were short.

'Did they tell you they were calling from the airport?'

'No.'

'Where did they say they were calling from?'

'Nowhere.'

'Where did you think they were at that point?'

'I . . . I didn't think about it.' She began to look distressed.

'So what did you do while you waited?'

'Well, I finished making the welcome home signs. I took one of them, the biggest, outside and put it by the door.' She looked at Kurt nervously. 'I don't know what time that was either. But it was cold and grey out there. Light, but only just.'

'It's all right, Julia, you can't be expected to remember what time you did all these things,' Frances told her. 'Did you make any other preparations for Gail's return?'

'I wrote another sign, a smaller one for the dining room. And I finished putting up the paper decorations. I had intended to do this the night before but I was too tired because I spent so long cleaning Gail's apartment and Lewis got annoyed with me.'

'Okay, we discussed this last night. That's what explains the forensic: you were cleaning the apartment until late the night before the murders.'

'I sort of figured Lewis might take her there first to leave some baggage. I think I left a gift, put up a welcome home sign maybe.'

'But . . . why clean up? I mean, empty apartments don't get dirty.'

'They do if you leave them that way.'

'Oh. Okay. So. You got back from the apartment late in the evening,' Kurt informed her.

'At about ten, ten thirty. I was tired out. I'd stayed longer than I meant to because it was so . . . you know. It needed to be cleaned. I started to make the signs at home but Lewis was annoyed because I'd got myself exhausted over there. He said I should have paid a cleaning firm. Anyway, I said I'd finish the decorations in the morning and so I did. We were planning to have a celebration breakfast with waffles because Gail had written she missed waffles. I prepared everything and I put the decorations in the dining room where we were going to eat. It looked so pretty. It looked like Christmas. I think November can be depressing because the fall colour's finishing. I wanted Gail to find the house looking pretty.'

Kurt said: 'You didn't go to the airport to meet Gail.'

'No.'

'Why not?'

Julia looked startled. 'Well . . . I had to organize our . . . you know . . . welcome wagon.'

'Uh-huh.' Kurt looked at his notes. 'How many guests?'

There was a pause. Julia's lips trembled. 'I'm sorry. . .?'

'How many guests did you invite to the welcome party?'

'Well . . . it was morning. It wasn't a party. It was just a sort of . . . warm welcome.'

Kurt watched her keenly. 'Oh. So no guests.'

'Gail didn't have that many friends. I mean, maybe she had friends but . . . we didn't know who to invite. I mean . . .' Her voice trailed away. She looked as though she was going to cry. 'Do you think we should have invited some guests?' she asked.

Lomax felt triumphant. That was what happened if you were aggressive with Julia. She crumpled into self-doubt. Kurt, unsettled by her response, hurried to reassure Julia that no guests was fine.

He began to ask another question but he stumbled and hesitated, unsure of his ground now with Julia. Frances spoke.

'So the welcome was ready but the guest of honour didn't arrive. When did you start worrying?'

'After maybe nine o'clock. I watched TV. Every time I heard a car or a noise I'd jump up and go to the window.'

This was easy to imagine. Lomax knew the chair she had probably sat in and the place by the window where she had probably stood. 'What did you do while you waited?'

'Watched TV . . . I don't know. I just waited. Swept the yard, maybe. It was full of dirty leaves. And then I got worried. And then I got mad at them for getting me so worried. And then when they still didn't show, I got worried again.'

'Did you go out?'

'No. Yes. Only out into the yard. And to check if Lewis had closed the garage door.'

'Did you call anyone?'

'Vicky. Vicky Fox. I thought maybe there had been a misunderstanding and Gail had asked Lewis to take her over to her mom's first and that when he said the apartment he meant Vicky's apartment.'

'What did she say?'

'Oh, I don't know, nothing I could understand. Nothing sober. Anyway, it was obvious they weren't there.'

'What else did you do?'

'I don't know what I did. I just hung around. But when the police came, I wasn't surprised. I was calm. Ask Murph. I was real calm. It was just like I'd been waiting for them.'

'You guessed something terrible had happened.'

Julia nodded sadly. There was a pause. Lomax was filled with compassion but Frances' voice, when she spoke, was unemotional.

'Are you sure you've told us everything, Julia?'

'Yes.'

'This witness. The super at Gail's apartment . . . how well did you know him?'

'Not well at all. Maybe he did see me, like he said, but not when he said. Probably it was when I had finished cleaning the night before.'

'Did you see him?'

'I don't think so.'

Lomax looked from Kurt to Frances and back to Kurt again. Their expressions were impassive. He suspected that they did not believe Julia.

'You didn't make any more calls, leave the house . . . ?'

'No,' said Julia. Her simple answers seemed to Lomax to shame the two sceptical attorneys. Frances, studying Julia's face, leaned forward. There was the usual rustle of clothes and jewellery that accompanied all her movements.

'Julia. There's something we haven't talked about. Something you haven't even asked about. The penalty. If you're found guilty.'

Lomax felt his internal organs – his stomach, his spleen, his liver, all the soft, spongy, formless places – contract with a power he did not know they possessed. The penalty. He hadn't asked about this either and the reason was that he didn't want to hear what Frances would say next. He glanced at Julia. She waited too, her face turned to Frances, her features sheltered by her prominent cheekbones.

Frances' voice was soft. 'You must already have realized that a conviction would carry the death penalty,' she said.

Julia was motionless.

'The thing is,' added Kurt, 'that there are no deals here. I mean, usually Frances can work something out with the prosecutor but in your case . . . well, for a guilty plea they could only offer you life without parole. That's twice, of course. So a not guilty plea and subsequent acquittal is your only hope.'

Lomax hated him for the bleakness of his words and the unrelenting nature of their delivery. Probably Kurt enjoyed saying that sort of thing. Julia had introduced him as an investigator but he had behaved throughout like an attorney. Not a defence attorney, but a prosecutor.

'I never intended,' said Julia, her voice quiet but strong, 'to plead anything but not guilty.'

Frances lifted her arm to the table. Her jewellery chattered quietly. She cupped her head in her hand and looked directly at Julia.

'Who do you think killed them?' she asked.

Julia looked back at her and said, with uncharacteristic firmness: 'I only know it wasn't me.'

10

When Lomax went home to unload his car, Julia went with him. He wanted her to see his house and had even tidied it a little on his last trip home in anticipation. There were things about the place that he was proud of, like the deck outside and a staircase inside, both of which he had built himself. Candice had attended a class at the community college some years ago called 'Pictures in Ceramics' and her efforts – immense, colourful and consisting of thousands of petals of clay – still lined the walls as you climbed Lomax's staircase. When Candice had moved out, she had left them behind.

'Ugly pieces of shit,' she had said. 'You're welcome to them.'

'Don't you even want one?' Lomax had asked.

'Nope. Now I think people should go express themselves in the bathroom, not all over the walls. Plus they attract dust. Helen sneezes every time she goes up those stairs.'

Helen seldom went near the stairs as they led to Lomax's loft. His den had a glass roof, a small telescope, a computer and a proliferation of books and papers smeared all over the walls and floor. When he showed Julia around he left the den until last.

'Do you like them?' he asked, as she studied the Pictures in Ceramics by the stairs.

'Well, they're kind of . . . well, I don't know. What are they?'

'That one's called Sinister Dexter. I don't remember the name of this one here. But this is my favourite. Motherhood. Candice made it when she was pregnant with Helen.'

'Oh.'

Lomax noticed as he led her to the den that the staircase creaked. He watched her as she stood in the doorway and looked around. One of his numerous fantasies about Julia had involved making love to her in here.

'Oh Lomax, this room is just like your desk, only bigger,' she said.

'You mean . . . a mess?'

'Look!'

Julia had seen a squirrel through the overhead window. The top of the house was in the trees.

'There are a lot of squirrels around here. They aren't scared of humans but they don't like Deputy,' he said.

She stepped over piles of paper to reach the window but the squirrel, perceiving her movement, scrambled along a branch and out of sight. She crossed to a collection of dusty motors and wire in the corner. A child's toy, the colour of dirt, was caught up in the wires.

'What's this?'

He responded to her interest with enthusiasm. 'That was a sort of invention . . .'

He stumbled across the obstructions in the room to join her. He reached for one of the smaller motors and blew the dust off it. The objects remaining in the pile readjusted dangerously for its absence.

'It was for Deputy when he was just a puppy. It was a sort of game to amuse him when we were out and he'd be miserable. It was called Rabbit.'

Lomax pulled the grimy toy from the pile. There was a cascade – slow at first but gaining quickly in momentum – of pipes, wires, motors, blocks of wood, switches, and small circuits. Julia giggled but did not move. When everything was still again, they were knee-deep in debris.

'This is Rabbit. He was suspended on a string, bouncy string like elastic or something, and it was wired to this track overhead so that Rabbit could move both ways. Deputy would be sitting around looking sad and then the programme would start and Rabbit would wake up and play with him.'

Julia was delighted. 'Did it work?'

Lomax hesitated. 'It did for a while. For a long time actually.'

'Oh Lomax, you're so clever,' said Julia. Lomax flushed happily.

'It went wrong in the end,' he admitted, 'when Deputy got real big and fierce. The mechanism couldn't hold up to the treatment. One day he wouldn't go near Rabbit any more. I suspect he may have gotten a small electric shock.'

Before she could react, he grabbed something else.

'Here's the remains of the solar system I made for Joel . . .' He waved a small polystyrene ball. 'I think this was Neptune . . . anyway, it was wired up so he could see the planets rotate but one day the earth stopped moving round the sun and I never did get around to repairing it . . . and this was a small sensor thing I put on the cat, before we had Deputy, which opened and closed the cat door for him but wouldn't let the racoon in – there was this damn racoon which kept coming in – but you can see the sensor's squished because that's what happened to the cat.' He tugged at something under the pile. He noticed that he was out of breath but he could not stop talking.

'God, I'd forgotten this. It goes way back. It's an automatic drapes opener and closer. Very useful for deterring crooks when the family's on vacation.'

'Did it work?'

'We were never burgled. On the other hand, we came home one lunchtime and the drapes were closed. I think it was on some time system of its own.'

Lomax waved a tangle of coloured wires. 'And this was for Joel. He was a really active baby. Candice was worried about him crawling up to this big old stove we used to light sometimes. So I made it a child-sensitive area. If he crawled into the area, a bell rang and we came running in.'

Julia clapped. 'You're so smart,' she said again. 'You can do anything.'

Lomax shrugged. He replaced the wires. The room seemed quiet now it was not filled with his voice. He said: 'Maybe I can help you.'

He looked at Julia but she did not respond. She was peering through the telescope.

'I mean,' he persisted, 'help you to prove you're not guilty.'

'Frances and Kurt are doing that,' she said.

'But I have the whole summer free. You'll be at the observatory and I won't.'

He had tried to explain to her why he was temporarily leaving the observatory. She had been upset, he suspected, on Berlins' behalf. Lomax had hoped that she would decide not to return but she was to see Dixon Driver that day about her future there. He had already hinted that her job was not in jeopardy, at least not until her trial.

'What can you do to help?' she asked.

'A lot. I know that in a case of this kind there are people to see and questions to ask . . . Kurt's an investigator but even for him a lot of it's boring. Routine. But for me. . .'

'You're not a detective, Lomax.'

'Or an attorney. I know. But I am on your side. You need someone on your side, for Chrissake.'

Julia sat down. She touched the telescope. He watched closely as she ran her fingers up its full length and gently felt around the lens cap. She was thinking. He looked at her mouth and saw that her lips were parted, very slightly.

She said: 'You don't think Kurt and Frances believe everything I've told them?'

Her fingers were massaging the metal work now.

'Yes and no. I mean, yes, because you pay them to believe you. But that doesn't mean they really believe you.'

Her fingers dropped. She looked at him.

'Julia, you've been arrested for first degree murder. Two murders. That means a lot of people think you're guilty.'

'Oh,' said Julia, and her head hung. He climbed over the various obstacles with difficulty and held her hand. She moved her fingers between his with gentle pressure. The light from the overhead window shone onto her head. It lit the dust in the air and made the metal points on the telescope gleam. Her knees were squeezed against the desk. He looked at her face. The light seemed to emphasize the fullness of her mouth.

'Let me help you,' he said.

'How?'

'I believe you.'

'That doesn't help me.'

Their faces were close together. They were whispering.

'Someone who believes you works harder and longer than someone who's paid to.'

Looking down he saw that her finger was running round and round the lens cap of the telescope. There was something sensuous in the movement. He felt a strange mixture of arousal and determination.

'Tell Frances and Kurt they have to let me help them. Please.'

She looked up at him. Her lips swelled a little. Then she was smiling. The smile seemed to invite him closer. He could see her tongue. Aroused, he leaned over to her and kissed her. She was receptive. He felt inside her mouth with his tongue. In a moment there would be fewer clothes and more flesh and her damp, warm lips would bring more pleasure.

'Lomax,' she whispered.

'Mmmmm?'

'I have to get back to the observatory by four-thirty for this interview with Dixon Driver . . .'

'Oh God.' Of all the things which had happened lately, this briefly seemed like the worst.

'I'm sorry. I mean . . . there's no time. Look, it's almost three now. I can't be late. He might take my job away from me.'

'You haven't done anything wrong.'

'He may not want an employee with a murder charge.'

Lomax wanted to ask if this job really mattered so much. He wanted to argue and plead.

She whispered: 'I'm sorry . . .'

He looked at her mouth. The lips were swollen to an almost impossible degree now. They were wet from kissing.

'Oh God,' he moaned again.

Lomax could hardly walk down the stupid, creaking staircase he had made. He had wasted his time showing her Candice's pictures in ceramics and some old polystyrene ball which might, once, have been Neptune, when he should have been in bed with her approaching ecstasy.

Julia was promising to telephone Frances and offer Lomax's assistance.

'In fact,' she said, in a tone of someone presenting a consolation prize, 'I'll do it now.'

'Don't offer, tell her. Then she can't refuse.'

'I'll try.'

'It's your case.'

'Well. Okay.'

He opened his mail while she called Sachs Smith. He did not listen to the conversation. There was a letter from Dixon Driver confirming that Lomax would take a sabbatical and saying that he would shortly be contacted about the subject of their last discussion.

Another letter from the observatory, this time from Eileen Friel, asked him whether he knew what had happened to a pair of bedspreads which went missing on the night he left, one of them from his room.

A third, a note from Kim, confirmed what he already knew: Doberman had replaced Berlins as project director. ('PS. Doberman. What a babe hound. He's bragging that he celebrated by screwing three of the kitchen staff. Probably they were making guacamole and didn't even notice.') As he stood in his living room with Kim's letter in his hand and a pile of junk mail, bills and envelopes at his feet, he keenly felt his absence from the observatory for the first time. What the hell would he do all summer? He ran upstairs.

'What did she say?'

'She didn't like it much.'

'And?'

'She said can you go see her today at five o'clock and I said yes.'

'Okay.'

'I think you should shave,' she added surprisingly.

'Okay.'

She was leaving now.

'I'm going to miss you. I even think I'm going to miss the observatory,' he said.

'I'll tell you everything that happens.'

'Don't go near Doberman.'

'Lomax, if Dixon Driver actually lets me stay there in spite of everything then Doberman could be my new boss.'

Lomax had already thought of this. It was one of the least palatable parts of the whole miserable situation.

'That means,' she said, 'that my desk will be three feet away from his. And he's a real nice guy. How can I not go near him?'

'No nearer than three feet.'

'What's the matter with you?'

She was getting into her car now. He bent down. She kissed him slowly.

'Oh God,' he said again.

'Will you call me at the observatory tonight?'

'Sure.'

She drove away.

He was late for his meeting with Frances. The receptionist at Sachs Smith told him to wait for so long that he felt he was being punished for unpunctuality. He found reading difficult today. He read a celebrity interview in a magazine without noticing who the celebrity was.

'Are you sure she knows I'm here?' he asked the receptionist.

'Yes,' she said, without looking up.

Finally he was shown into Frances' office. She greeted him warmly and shook his hand and they sat down not at the desk or at the conference table but in the armchairs.

'Look, you haven't been to law school, you've had no training and frankly you'd get in the way,' she said, pouring him coffee. But she smiled as she said it. Lomax realized that she liked him.

'Aw c'mon, Frances,' he said, winningly.

'Aw c'mon nothing. Do you know how many graduates and students and trainees we have here who'd give anything to gopher on this one?'

'But they're different.'

'Sure, they're qualified.'

'I'm driven by something stronger than career ambition.'

Frances sighed wearily. 'You're in love with her.'

'And I know she's innocent.'

She gave Lomax a knowing look. 'You're in love with her. So your opinion is valueless.'

'I'm in love with her because I know her. And I know she couldn't have committed a crime like this.'

As he spoke the words they sounded hollow. He felt uncomfortable. He remembered that he had met Julia only a short time ago and that Frances might wrongly conclude from this that he did not really know her at all.

'I assume all my clients are innocent. I'm a defence attorney.'

Lomax sighed expressively.

'You think . . .' Frances' face was dense with concentration. She did not look at him. 'You're worried about Sachs Smith's role in all this. You believe that Lewis Fox wanted Julia's money for some reason connected with the firm and that we may try to cover up that reason even if it damages Julia's case.'

Lomax put his cup on the low table. Coffee had spilled into the saucer.

Frances said: 'You're worried that there's a conflict of interest.'

'It crossed my mind.'

'I thought so.'

He said: 'It crossed my mind, but actually I dismissed the whole idea because I don't think you'd do that.'

Frances smiled but her response was swift.

'So without any evidence at all, your verdict on me is: not guilty. And you expect me to take you seriously when you return the same verdict on Julia and announce you're going to prove it.'

'Isn't guilt proven? And innocence presumed?'

Lomax smiled too. He knew that Frances liked him and enjoyed playing games with him and that in the end she would let him in on the investigation.

'Well,' admitted Frances, 'as it happens you're right to trust me. I wouldn't let the firm's interests override a client's. I had to take advice on the ethics of our position. It's borderline. However, there's a strong feeling among the senior staff here that if the managing partner is murdered, we should involve ourselves in his case.'

'It's Julia's case,' Lomax said.

'How come,' asked Frances after a pause, 'how come you have so much time on your hands you think you can help us?'

Lomax told her about his suspicions, his allegations and his suspension from the observatory. She listened intently. At the end of his story she nodded but made no comment.

'Okay,' she said. 'I guess we can find you some work to do on this case. But don't expect to be treated any differently from the way we'd treat a twenty-two-year-old gopher. The work isn't glamorous. Boring phone calls, people who don't know anything and can't help, lots of paperwork, it's mostly routine. Are you on half pay or something from the observatory?'

'Yep.'

'That's good, because we're not giving you a cent.'

Lomax grinned cheerfully.

'And although occasionally it might be a help, for example if you're interviewing someone especially disreputable, most of the time you cannot, cannot, work here looking like that.'

Lomax's grin dropped a little. 'What do I have to look like? Kurt?' Frances eyed him without a flicker or a blink.

'You mean I have to wear a . . . a suit?'

'Yes, go buy yourself one. And it's nice you shaved for our meeting. How about doing it every day?'

'Oh God.'

'Not changing your mind I hope, Dr Lomax?'

'No.'

'Can you be here tomorrow morning at eight-thirty?'

'Yes.'

'Okay, I'll see you then.'

'In this . . . suit I'm going to buy.'

'In your new suit. I have to leave now to get home to my daughter.' Frances turned around the double photo frame on her desk. 'That's Mary,' she said. Mary grinned with tiny teeth. She clutched a fluffy toy cat. Her hair was red.

'She was born around a year ago, right?'

'Nearly. May 30.'

'Cute,' said Lomax. Frances smiled. The other picture showed Frances, dressed casually, with her husband and two small children. It was taken on the beach in winter and the family wore layers of brightly coloured clothes. Frances, in jeans, her hair tugged by the wind and a child in all directions, was nearly unrecognizable. The husband was surprising. He was a couple of inches shorter than her, balding and overweight. The little boy in the photo held his hand and was jumping in the air. The smaller child was half on Frances' shoulders, half on her father's.

Lomax looked at Frances and she was still smiling, her face soft.

He had been driving for fifteen minutes before he knew why he was sad. He wanted to see Candice and the children. Now, at once. Except it was Thursday. On Thursdays, Candice and Robert and the children always went out. They went out to eat or to the movies or occasionally to the theatre. In the summer they might go hiking. Once they had gone all the way down to San Francisco to see a famous European ballet company. Candice thought going out together was a nice family thing to do.

He went to a shopping mall and bought a suit. The sales assistant seemed as unsure as Lomax whether he should make the purchase. It was an uncomfortable experience. Lomax left suspecting the suit was a size too small.

'So I bought a suit,' he told Julia, whom he called as soon as he was home.

She said: 'You bought a suit. Lomax! In a mall!'

Lomax was aware of a male voice in the room with her. 'Who's there?'

'Kurt. He says you can't buy a good suit in a mall.'

'Who said anything about a good suit? And what the hell is he doing there?'

'He drove up to see me. He's asking me questions.'

Lomax seethed. How could he be sure that Kurt would drive all the way down the mountain that night?

'Couldn't he ask you questions over the phone?'

'He brought the waiver for me to sign,' she explained. 'Why did you buy a suit?'

Lomax said that he needed a suit for 8.30 a.m. the next day and then he told her why. There was a long silence.

'Frances is going to let you work at Sachs Smith?'

He wondered if she was repeating everything for Kurt's benefit.

Julia said: 'Are you sure you want to do this? Start shaving in the mornings and going to an office and not even getting paid for it?'

'Yeah, I'm sure,' said Lomax.

'But you could be hiking with Deputy Dawg. Your kids will be out of school soon, you could mess about with them all vacation.'

'I'll still find time for Joel and Helen and the dog.'

'Kurt,' reported Julia, 'doesn't look too pleased.'

'Tough,' said Lomax. He heard muffled voices. Kurt and Julia were talking and Julia had put her hand over the receiver so that he, Lomax, could not hear. His body stiffened with fury.

'Is this for real?' came Kurt's voice, more rasping and abrupt than Lomax remembered it.

'Yes,' said Lomax, holding the receiver away from his ear.

As Kurt spoke, Lomax could imagine his chin jerking angrily up and down. His face would seem to be one enormous jawbone.

'I can't believe Frances is doing this! It's a waste of her time, your time, and – I'll be honest, Lomax – my time. I don't need some fucking amateur hanging around when I'm working, asking dumb questions, holding things up.'

Lomax said nothing.

'I mean, for Chrissake,' Kurt went on. 'Even if you only make the coffee! Do I need a guy with a dozen PhDs and a creased suit from J. C. Penney to make my coffee? For Chrissake. Frances must be out of her box.'

That night it was not Kurt's words Lomax remembered, but Julia's. He had promised himself a sabbatical for years and now he had been given one, although not in the way he had anticipated. Instead of spending the time outside with his children he would be downtown in an airconditioned office all summer where his presence would barely be tolerated and his usefulness doubtful. And every day there would be Kurt.

Lomax thought of Julia and the way she had smiled at him and told him to lie back and enjoy himself. He remembered how he felt last night when her warm body had lain next to his. He remembered her helplessness and soft vulnerability. He had to remind himself of all this before he could understand why he had passed such a harsh sentence on himself.

'Good,' said Frances, looking Lomax up and down. Lomax fingered his collar and the tie he had bought.

'It's choking me. Probably to death,' he said.

'When I first wore earrings I thought they were going to pull my ears right out of my head. And now . . .'

Lomax looked at her ears. Gold pendants dripped from the lobes like tears.

Kurt came in carrying three small, thick cardboard boxes piled one on top of another so they reached up to his chin, wedged in place by his monstrous jawbone.

He deposited the boxes with a thud on Frances' coffee table. 'Hi Lomax,' he said, without enthusiasm. 'Here's the discovery.'

Frances explained: 'The District Attorney's office has to give us copies of just about everything: photos, forensic, statements . . . it all came in yesterday. I guess you haven't had time to go through it yet, Kurt.'

'Sure,' said Kurt. 'Last night.'

Lomax felt relief. Kurt had been reading police evidence last night. He had not been with Julia. He looked at Kurt and saw his face was more shadowy than usual and his speech staccato, as if fuelled by the small uncontainable bursts of energy which now drove him from the room.

'There are some things I can follow up on right now.' He was already near the door.

'Are you going out?' Frances called. 'Because we need to talk soon. Like eleven thirty.'

'Fine, no problem,' said Kurt from a great distance.

Frances caught Lomax's eye. For a moment it seemed she was going to say something, but instead she gestured to Lomax to sit down in one of the armchairs.

'You can look through all this, read things, take notes right here. You may have to move to Kurt's office at ten forty-five if a client arrives but I don't think he'll show. Ask me anything you like. I'll be at my desk most of the morning. Help yourself to coffee.'

Lomax sat down and Frances found the first of the boxes, opened it, and set it in front of him on the low table. She poured them both some coffee from the machine and retreated to her desk.

'I should warn you . . . the police photographs . . . they're not pretty. If you're not used to that kind of thing, even if you are, you might find them . . . well, I've warned you. Make sure you put the pictures away right after you've looked at them in case anyone comes in. Everyone here knew Lewis.'

Lomax could see the pictures about half way through a box. He worked methodically towards them, reading his way through Julia's statement, the statement of the super at Gail's apartment building where the bodies were found, the report from the officer at the scene of the crime and details of fibres, fingerprints and ballistics. There were telephone calls made to and from Julia's phone on the morning of the murder, hazy half memories from people who remembered seeing Gail and her father at the airport, more statements, even a statement from Murphy McLean saying that Julia had hardly responded when he gave her the bad news. He said that in all his years of delivering sad news, he had never seen anyone react this way before.

Lomax was on his third cup of coffee when he drew the photographs from their envelope.

The two corpses had both been shot at close range. Lewis' face remained almost intact, with only a small area behind his left eye missing. In death he wore the livid expression of the horrified or the very drunk. Part of one even row of teeth was visible. The wider pictures showed that his body was turned very slightly towards his daughter, away from the killer.

Here was a man suffering such an extreme of fear and shock that looking at the picture seemed a gross intrusion. And yet Lomax found himself able to study it. The air conditioning whirred. His coffee steamed on the table beside him. After a few moments, he even managed to reach for the cup, but he could not drink from it.

'Are you all right, Lomax?'

He looked up to find Frances watching him from behind her desk. He had known she would be.

'Yes.'

'The pictures of Gail are worse. My theory is that she intercepted her father's attacker so there's not much of her left. Are you sure you want to. . .?'

But he had reached Gail already. He swallowed hard, fighting the urge to retch. Most of her face was missing and what remained might be laughing. The lips were pulled back over the small remaining section of mouth. She was eyeless and there was a bloody cavity where her nose should have been. The back of her skull was visible, cradling blood like a fragment of china cup. He could not see any brains. Probably they were part of the mess covering the couch and the rug.

'Lomax . . . ?'

He looked through the other pictures. The couch was photographed from all angles. Sometimes the half mouth seemed to grimace more than laugh, depending where the photographer stood.

He glanced up. Frances was still watching him. They stared at each other for a few moments until Frances spoke.

'I guess you'll find it hard to forget these pictures.'

Lomax nodded, already knowing that he would never forget them.

'Have you read the reports? She was shot from behind. That's why her face got so splattered.'

He nodded again.

He worked his way through the rest of the boxes, scribbling notes. It was nearly eleven when he finished. Frances' client had not arrived, but she was out of the room. He could not stop himself returning to the first box. He pulled out the package of photographs, unwrapping them like a candy bar.

A green figure rustled at his side. It was Frances. She had swept in without him noticing.

'Lomax, don't, just don't.'

'I'm not looking at the victims. I'm trying to see the apartment,' Lomax told her, although it was impossible to study the couch and the carpet and the shelves and the furniture without his eyes straying to the tangle of blood and corpses in the centre of the pictures.

Frances sat down next to him. 'The apartment? Why?'

Lomax shrugged. 'Astronomer's instinct. I spend my whole time trying to see past the bright light of our galaxy into deep space, which is often much more revealing.'

'And does it reveal anything in this case?'

'I don't know,' admitted Lomax.

'What do you notice?'

'Well . . . in this one here I can just see the corner of something like a sign, a placard . . . it reads "OME". I guess it said "WELCOME HOME". That's no big deal, but it's nice because it proves Julia was in the apartment earlier and it explains why her fingerprints and fibres were there in quantity. And in this one . . .' Lomax pulled out a high shot of the two sprawling bodies. Frances took it from his hand and studied it.

'Think it bears out my theory that she was intercepting his attacker?'

'It's possible. But the police report says there were three bullets and she got two of them . . .'

'They fire at Lewis, she intercepts and falls. They fire at Lewis and he dies at once. Then they suspect she might still be alive so they give her another one just to be sure.'

'Maybe. But it's a sort of devious theory. My project director – Professor Berlins, I told you about him – always says that it's easier to explain facts in a devious way. The simple explanation takes longer to find.'

Frances smiled.

'Unfortunately,' Lomax continued, 'the simple explanation seems to support the prosecution's case. That whoever committed this crime disliked Gail a lot more than they disliked Lewis.'

'Probably likes and dislikes don't come into it. The assassin may well have been hired.' Frances handed back the picture. 'But I hear what you're saying. Anything else?'

'There's something weird I just noticed which doesn't seem to have been mentioned in any of the reports. It's here.'

Frances studied the shot again. It was taken from high above the bodies. Either the photographer was very tall or he had stood on a box.

'Hmmm . . . something weird . . .' She ran her eye over the cluttered bookshelves, the TV set, the couch.

'Look at the bodies, not the background. Actually it's very minor and almost certainly irrelevant.'

'Okay, tell me.'

'Gail . . . she's wearing two wrist watches.'

Frances squinted. 'Oh . . . you think that's a wrist watch? On her other arm there?'

'I think she's got one on each arm.'

Frances nodded. 'You're probably right. I have to admit, Lomax, that I'm impressed by your powers of observation.'

'I work in an observatory.'

'It could just be a bracelet round her other arm . . . let's find the police notation of her personal effects.' Frances was reaching for another box. 'Usually they put it somewhere near the front of the second one . . . oh Lomax, you've left these all in a mess.'

It was true. The boxes had arrived full but orderly. Now envelopes and the corners of pages stuck out at many angles like straw. Lomax drew the list from somewhere near the middle.

'To a slob, a mess is an elaborate but precise filing system,' he explained apologetically.

'But it's inaccessible to anyone except slobs.' Her tone was mild. He glanced at her face but she was not looking at him. She was studying the list.

'It says wrist watch here . . . and again down here. Seems like a mistake.'

'I can't think of any relevance it could have.'

'Me neither. Maybe she always wore two. We could ask Julia.'

'Ask Julia what?'

It was Kurt. They looked up to see him standing over them.

'Lomax just noticed something . . .' Frances waved the picture towards him and Kurt flinched momentarily. 'This arm underneath . . . Gail's wearing a second wrist watch. See here . . .'

Kurt shrugged. He avoided looking at the picture again. 'So what?' he asked.

Neither Lomax nor Frances could answer that question.

'It's eleven thirty, Frances. Where do you want this meeting?' Kurt loomed overhead.

'Well right here, Kurt.'

But he did not move. His face was a question and his eyes were fixed on Frances.

She stared back in silence before she spoke. 'I think Lomax should be here. If he's going to be useful to us, he has to hear this discussion.'

For a moment Kurt's eyes did not leave Frances' face. It seemed he was going to argue. Then he switched on the reading lights, chose a seat across the table from them, and crossed his legs. Lomax shuffled uncomfortably in his armchair.

'Okay,' began Frances, 'you've been through the boxes, tell us what you're thinking, Kurt.'

Kurt took a deep breath. 'It's hard to say this in front of Lomax, but since you insist . . .'

Frances smiled at him sweetly.

'Well, things aren't looking too good for Julia. Her statement doesn't tie up with the evidence. She says she didn't go out the morning of the murders. A witness claims he saw her. She says there were no phone calls. What does the phone company find? Calls. She says she thinks that the $450,000 was really for Lewis. But what does the evidence show? That she gave it to Gail. So.'

'So,' echoed Frances.

'So, we have a lot of work to do on Julia. But let's be positive about this.' Kurt looked positive. 'Prosecution theory: she was being blackmailed and her motive was to kill her blackmailer. That's easily challenged. Evidence at scene of crime: we can explain most of it except this new witness and we can probably demolish him. Our response to all this: destroy theory, prove how weak the evidence is and plant another feasible explanation in the jury's minds.'

He looked at Lomax for the first time. 'You should go read the law reports on Frances' most successful case. People *versus* Theobald. She didn't just flatten the prosecution's arguments; she also gave the jury some new fat to chew on.'

Frances spoke. 'You still think we should pursue the line that Lewis, not Gail, was the intended victim?'

'Yes. But it's a minefield.'

Frances glanced quickly at Lomax. Seeing this, Kurt added: 'I'm not just talking about any financial irregularity here at Sachs Smith.'

'I know,' said Frances. There was a silence. Lomax squirmed. The heat from the reading lights which Kurt had switched on was making him sweat.

'Well, you wanted him here,' Kurt reminded Frances. He stood up and leaned on the back of the chair so that his shadow fell across the table and across Lomax. Lomax was reminded how, hiking once in the open desert, he had stopped to rest on a rock and felt grateful for the sudden shelter of a shadow. Looking up he had found that the protection was not benevolent. It was provided by a vulture, hovering briefly between him and the sun.

Kurt said to Frances: 'You tell him.'

Frances smiled at Lomax apologetically. 'This may make things awkward for you. We're pretty sure that Lewis was having an affair, possibly a serious affair, not long before his death.'

Lomax had been holding his breath. He breathed out now.

'This isn't something Julia needs to know unless we find it's absolutely relevant to the case,' Frances assured him.

'She may know already,' Kurt pointed out. Frances shrugged.

'Basically, Lomax,' said Kurt, leaning towards him, 'this is the way things are. Every way we turn, we find more evidence for the goddam prosecution.'

12

Frances told Kurt that Lomax was to work with him for the next few days. She wanted Kurt to show him how to approach possible witnesses and gather information and for Lomax to understand how that information should be organized. Kurt's jaw was Olympian in its opposition but he was overruled.

'Take Lomax along to your office,' she said, 'and when he needs a desk, put him in with the trainees.'

Kurt's reluctance to admit Lomax to his office was tempered by his pride in it. The office was on the dark side of the building. Just a few yards away from the window big, gleaming buildings started their ascent. The room was sunless. It was painted white and the lights were on. They shone harshly. It was possible to create significant shadows on the bare walls.

Everything was in line with the desk or at 90 degrees to it. There was no other angle. The expanse of white wall was broken only once. Eight small black-and-white photographs were placed at regular intervals. They formed a rectangle. Their subjects, Lomax noted, were places, not people. Mostly they showed strangely empty city street scenes.

Clearly clients did not visit this side of the offices. Kurt sat at his desk and gestured Lomax into the only other chair. It was uncomfortable. Probably it was intended for trainees, secretaries and junior members of Sachs Smith staff.

Kurt sighed. 'Okay, Lomax, let's go,' he said wearily, reaching for a notebook. 'Here's how I generally organize information. Don't waste time arguing with me about it. You guys probably have different ways of doing things at the observatory but this is the method I used in People *versus* Theobald, to name but one success, and it's always worked for me.'

While Kurt talked, Lomax noticed that his profile, perfectly shadowed on the white wall, was magnified to many times its usual size. The shadow jaw hurtled fascinatingly around the wall as Kurt talked. It sank to the floor when Kurt yawned. It disappeared when

Kurt spun to his computer to explain the software. Lomax looked again at the black-and-white photographs nearby and realized they were police photographs from real cases, that the streets were empty because they had been cleared, and that ghosts lay chalked in every picture.

'But don't kid yourself Frances is going to give you any juicy interviews,' Kurt was concluding. He picked up one of the piles of paper and then put it down in exactly the same place. 'Most of the time, you'll be wading through this shit.'

Lomax nodded.

'Right, now let's go.'

Kurt led Lomax through a network of dark passages and down a short, steep staircase. 'These were the servants' quarters in Christiansen's day,' he said. He flung open the door of what seemed to be a closet. 'You can work in here.'

There was a desk jammed against the far wall. The roof sloped so that Lomax had to stoop in order to enter, gradually standing upright when he reached the desk. Above his head was a small, round window.

'Sorry about the size,' said Kurt unapologetically. 'You get these quaint little rooms in historic buildings. This one has the staircase running right over it.'

At that moment someone was climbing the stairs. Each step thudded overhead.

Lomax sat down, wedging himself between the wall and the desk. Kurt put a folder in front of him and explained what he was to do. The telephone company had provided a print-out of the numbers dialled from Lewis' home telephone. Sachs Smith had also obtained a list of numbers dialled from Lewis' office and from his car phone. Lomax's job was to find out whom Lewis had called in the three months prior to his death.

'Here's a reverse phone book. It'll give you the names but that's not good enough. You have to find out who they are and why he dialled them. Now, there are various techniques you can use. You can pretend you're looking for someone else, you can ask to speak to Lewis Fox and see what happens, you can say you're looking for a Lewis Fox, making up any reason which seems plausible, like, he's an old friend and you lost touch . . .'

'What happens if I tell the truth and say I'm helping an investigator look into the death of Lewis Fox?'

Kurt stared at him coldly.

'You can say what you like, Lomax, as long as you come up with the fucking answers. And remember, whenever you do anything, there's some kid at the DA's office, some junior, who's making exactly the same telephone calls and thinking exactly the same thoughts. He's probably around twenty years old.'

He turned to go. 'By the way, the telephone line is shared with Marjorie and Fern, a couple of juniors we have here.'

The room shuddered as Kurt climbed the stairs.

Lomax had lost his pen. He wondered if there was a coffee machine. He was hungry. He wandered around the servants' quarters trying to make friends with secretaries and asking to borrow a pen. He met Marjorie, who groaned when she heard he would be sharing her line.

'Great, just great. Well, I'm going out for lunch right now so you can use it for a while but I'll need the phone when I get back.'

'Where's Fern?'

'On vacation, thank God, or there'd be three of us sharing that line.'

Marjorie's build was heavyweight and she had long, dark, straight hair which she flicked back now over one shoulder. She was unsmiling.

Lomax returned to his desk. No matter how he sat, he was uncomfortable. His first call was to Julia. He wanted to ask whether she had an address book of Lewis' which might reveal whom some of the phone numbers belonged to. There was no answer in her office.

Next, he telephoned Candice.

'You want Joel and Helen this weekend?' she said quickly. He knew it was her wedding anniversary.

'I'd like to take them hiking.'

'Good idea.'

'The weather's warm enough for us to camp now.'

There was a pause. 'Okay,' said Candice cautiously.

'But I really rang to tell you that, if you want me, you'll have to call this number.'

She wrote down the number. 'Are you at the university this summer or something?'

'No.'

'Where then?'

He looked around his office. Someone was walking upstairs. There was almost no light from the window. He felt miserable. 'It's a long story, Candice.'

'Lomax . . . are you all right?'

There was something pleasing about the concern in her voice.

'Well. Yes.'

'Tell me.'

'I can't give you all the details now. I'm supposed to make telephone calls and I share the line with two other people. Only luckily one of them's on vacation.'

'Look. Just tell me where you are and why.'

Lomax tried to give her an edited version of recent events but ended up telling her everything as usual. Speaking did not bring him relief. The story seemed to have happened to someone else, someone who was making a terrible mistake.

'You're making a terrible mistake, Lomax,' said Candice when he had finished.

'Don't you think I wish I was still at the observatory working on Core Nine?'

'So, get back there. Pull out of Sachs Smith, go to Dixon Driver, apologize, get your job back . . .'

'No,' said Lomax miserably.

When he began to make calls to Lewis' numbers, he had little success. If a company answered it was easy to ask them their address and exactly what their business was. But too often machines told him to leave a message, or a hostile voice said that the name Lewis Fox was unknown to them.

He decided to try one of Kurt's suggestions. It worked first time.

'Er . . . I'm trying to contact an old friend of mine . . . His name's Lewis Fox . . .'

'Don't be shy.'

The voice was thick. It fractured at the edges. It belonged to a woman, probably an old woman.

'If you haven't seen him for a few years, you probably don't know about his divorce. He was divorced quite a few years ago. I forget how many.'

Her voice became so thick that it cracked completely.

'I'm sorry,' said Lomax. This must be Lewis' mother.

'I never remarried,' she said.

'No?' Lomax was confused now.

'I could have, but I never did.'

It seemed impossible that the owner of this voice could be Lewis' first wife.

'No. Nope. I never remarried. And there's something else you should know about Lewis. Apart from being divorced, there's something else you should know. And now I have to tell you.'

Lomax suspected that the woman was drunk. 'What's that?'

'He's divorced.'

'Yes . . .'

'And he's dead. Now you're shocked. But if I gave you the details, you'd be more shocked. This morning a young woman telephoned me looking for Lewis. I said, he's dead. She was shocked too. I said: I could shock you some more. I could have shocked her some more . . .' The voice droned on. Was she drunk or insane?

It was the second time that he had been told a young woman had telephoned that very day for Lewis Fox. This must be the someone Kurt had warned him about who was working for the prosecution. A young woman on the other side of town was also dialling her way through Lewis' telephone list. She made the same calls and discussed the same facts on the same case but she was paid to reach different conclusions. He decided to overtake her by starting further down the list.

'. . . my daughter too. His daughter too. It was a wicked crime and a wicked tragedy. Gail. She was just a young girl . . .' the voice was saying.

Lomax concluded the call with difficulty.

He telephoned the observatory and asked for Julia. Doberman answered. Lomax hoped that Doberman wouldn't recognize his voice.

'She's still at lunch, Lomax,' Doberman said.

He called Professor Berlins. Mrs Berlins was cautious.

'Er . . . who exactly wants to speak to him?'

Lomax gave his name and there was a silence. 'Why are you telephoning my husband?' demanded Mrs Berlins. There had been a fragility in her voice before which was gone now.

'To see how he is.'

'Lousy. Thanks to you,' she said. 'A man ends a distinguished career by crawling away under a cloud of suspicion. I think it's predictable that in the circumstances he's going to feel lousy.'

Lomax tried to argue that Berlins' career was not at an end, that there had been a mistake, that the professor would be back at the observatory in September but Mrs Berlins hung up while he was speaking.

Before he had replaced the receiver, he heard Marjorie start to dial at the other end. 'Boy, she was mad!' said Marjorie cheerfully. 'My turn to make a call now.'

Lomax put his head in his hands. He was going to spend the summer assimilating information about the jewellers and restaurants a dead man had telephoned, about the garage which repaired his car, about the insurance salesmen he dealt with, the dental appointments, the infrequent conversations with his daughter in France, the electricity company, the book shops, the AAA, the credit card companies . . . all the flotsam and jetsam which he found so tedious in his own life he was now gathering from someone else's. And it all told him less about Lewis than a look through his trashcan might have done.

'You missed lunch,' a woman behind a nearby door explained to him when hunger drove him out of his office. She was sitting on the floor surrounded by piles of thick brown files. 'We have a delivery from a sandwich house. You give Jay-Jay your order by eleven thirty and then you pick your sandwiches up from her after twelve thirty. They're good. I usually have avocado, nuts and bacon.'

She looked closely at Lomax. 'But of course you can have them without bacon if you're Jewish,' she added.

'Is there anywhere here I can get something to eat?'

'No.'

'Would anyone deliver here now?'

'Not after two p.m.'

'Where's the coffee machine?'

'Standing right in front of me.'

'Oh God.'

'The kitchen's on the second floor.'

'Thanks.'

He turned to go and then turned back again. 'Did you know Lewis Fox?' he asked her.

'Of course I did. He was our managing partner.'

'Was he popular?'

She scrutinized him for a moment. 'He was okay,' she said.

Lomax climbed the stairs. He did not stop at the second floor. The building only had three storeys and when he reached the top he found a way out through a fire exit on to the roof. The traffic sounded far away. Below, a guide in a bonnet was escorting a group of visitors to the open house. Overhead the sky was clear. The sun trickled on to one corner of the roof. His mood began to lift. Tall buildings hung on all sides but there was a crack in the thicket of facades and through this crack Lomax could glimpse, far away, the mountains which ringed the city. He leaned towards them. The blue sky was bleached by the distance and seemed to fade into the snow on the highest, furthest peaks. It was a day to be outside. He went back down the stairs to his office.

123

13

Lomax arrived at Robert and Candice's house with a backpack and the small tent he and Candice had taken hiking with them before the children were born. Candice heard the car and came out to meet him. He wondered if she would recognize the tent lying across the seat.

'I'm worried about this whole idea,' she said.

Lomax groaned.

'Helen's only six and she's scared to go camping.'

'She came camping with us when she was two and she wasn't scared then. Are you going to let me get out of the car?'

Candice was hanging over him, her hands on the roof. She did not move. 'Suppose it rains?'

In response, Lomax pointed to the tent. He watched her closely to see if there was any sign of recognition. She stared at it. Her face began to change. He had only a second to prepare for the spitting ferocity of her reply.

'I remember that fucking thing in the fucking rain. It's a sponge. Touch it and water comes pouring down on you, enough water to fucking drown in. Everything gets wet – your hair, your clothes, your sleeping bag, your spare clothes, your boots. It's misery, sheer misery, and you inflicted it on me and now you want to inflict it on Helen and Joel because you think it's, like, nature. You think it's natural, but it's not natural Lomax, it's wet, it's wet, it's wet.'

Lomax sat in the silent car remembering. He and Candice had hiked all over America and other places besides. They had very often been dirty, sometimes hungry, usually tired and occasionally, yes, wet. Had Candice really been unhappy, or was this the revisionist view of the new Candice?

On one occasion they had been camping in the Rockies when there had been a storm of tropical dimensions. Their tent was a tiny speck on the side of the mountain. Rain seemed to blanket them. Water ran past them and round them until the very ground on which the tent was anchored seemed to shift and slide. But the lightning was worse. Strike by strike it progressed towards them from the distant peaks until their own slope was illuminated. They were at the very eye of the storm. Candice's screams were drowned by the thunder which roared continuously all around them and, more sinister, by the nearby hiss and sizzle of the lightning. Scared to stay in their tent and scared to go out, they had watched in horror while a tree some yards to the left of them was struck, and then a large boulder just a few yards to the right. The frequency of the stabs and unpredictability of the targets overwhelmed Lomax and Candice. They were driven into the tent by fear and helplessness and lay there clutching each other, face down, waiting.

In the morning, Lomax had found that one of the outer tent pegs was burned. He had kept the peg as a souvenir for some years but when the house got turned upside down during the divorce it was one of the things which had disappeared. He presumed it was still there, somewhere.

'There aren't any storms forecast for tonight,' he told Candice. She let him get out of the car. Her voice was calmer.

'Promise me, promise me Lomax, that at the first sign of bad weather you'll turn back. And that you won't camp too far from a car or civilization.'

'Okay, I promise.'

'Are you all right?' she asked him as they walked towards the house.

'I guess so.'

'I'm sort of worried. I mean, your job, this woman, this insane detective idea . . .'

'Well stop worrying. It's your wedding anniversary.'

'Oh,' said Candice, 'you remembered.'

'Of course I fucking remembered.'

The children had small backpacks of their own. Helen was trying to cram a large black-and-white plastic horse into hers.

'Honey, Betty won't fit in that bag,' Candice told her.

'But Betty goes everywhere with me,' said Helen, continuing to struggle.

'We'll be climbing up hills and your backpack will start to feel real heavy,' Lomax warned.

'Then you can carry Betty, Dad.'

'Look what Robert gave me,' Joel said. It was a map of the mountains in a transparent holder which Joel wore on a string around his neck. Lomax had seen hikers wearing maps and secretly despised them.

'I'm not sure we'll need it.'

'Dad. Look. When you want to know where you are, you don't stop and get the map out and unfold it. It's right here, round your neck, all the time.'

'Oh,' said Lomax. 'Good idea.'

Sometimes, when his son spoke, he heard Robert's voice. Robert used imperatives a lot. Whenever he sensed disagreement, he would say: 'Look'. Robert was also inclined to present his ideas as if they were indisputable facts, like the laws of thermodynamics.

Lomax had been trying to put a water bottle into Joel's backpack but Candice had filled it with chocolate and spare socks and T-shirts in watertight bags. There was also a box of Band-Aids.

Lomax sighed. Robert was turning his son into the sort of hiker who wore a map around his neck and Candice was turning the natural world into something you armed yourself against, where disasters might occur and where protection was necessary.

'Dad, what's the matter?' Joel's voice was anguished.

'We don't need a whole box of Band-Aids . . . we're only going for one night. We'll pitch our tent, we'll cook, we'll eat, we'll talk and then we'll probably fall asleep. So when . . .' Lomax pulled a large book from the bottom of the backpack, then a second. '. . . when will you have the time to read these books?'

Candice reappeared.

'Lomax, the children take books everywhere with them. It's a very good habit. When we were in Europe they'd sit at the table when we ordered our meal and . . .'

'Candice, I'm not taking them to a bunch of expensive European hotels.'

Candice's expression flickered. He said: 'Don't you remember what it's like to go hiking, for Chrissake? On a nice day in early summer? Don't you remember anything?'

Candice's face was firm. She and Lomax eyed each other. Joel began to gabble in a small high-pitched voice. At the time of the divorce, when Candice was moving out to Robert's house, Joel had hidden in Lomax's den.

'You gave us this book, Dad. It has pictures of the animals and trees and flowers and things in the mountains. See, here it says about the rock formations, see, right here. When we see something interesting we can look at the book and find out all about it . . .'

His face was unhappy. He flicked some of the pages urgently and held them up. The animals were big and stared right at you. Lomax recognized the picture of the mountain lion. Joel had shown it to him after he thought he had seen one.

'You can bring just whatever you like,' he said soothingly. 'I don't want you to carry too much weight, that's all.'

They drove out into the mountains for about an hour. Helen complained that she felt sick. Lomax parked the car at a lodge by a mountain lake where tourists stayed. The lodge was Lomax's compromise with Candice. If the weather turned stormy, wet, or cold, he was to return with the children and take a room.

When Lomax got out of the car and smelled the mountain air and saw the trail leading away through the foliage, he was eager to start walking.

'Mmmmm. I smell hamburgers!' shrieked Helen, pointing to the lodge coffee shop.

'We should eat, Dad, it may be our last good meal for a while,' Joel advised seriously.

After lunch they took the steep trail up through the trees. The lake, a deep, cold mountain blue, shrank as they climbed. Helen kept looking back for the log-covered roof of the lodge.

'I can still see it,' she said periodically. Finally, when it was out of sight, she asked: 'Daddy, can we stay at the lodge tonight?'

Lomax said: 'Tonight we're going to light a fire on the hillside and tell stories and look at the stars and guess what's up there.'

'Did Mom pack enough sweaters?' asked Helen.

'Yes,' said Lomax.

Gradually they fell into a peaceable silence. Occasionally they stopped and drank from their water bottles and admired the view. Once or twice they commented on a rock formation or an especially steep ascent. Later, they paused to admire a waterfall in complete silence. When they could feel evening in the air they found a place to pitch their tent where the morning sun would shine on them. Lomax discovered he had been carrying the burnt tent peg.

'I'll tell you a story about that later,' he promised. He showed Joel and Helen how to put the tent up and build a fire. Helen was silent with exhaustion. As they cooked their meal, night fell like the closing of drapes. The air was cool and clear.

'Oh wow,' said Joel, 'just look at the stars!'

Refreshed by the food, the children asked for the story of the burnt tent peg.

'I hope that doesn't happen tonight, Daddy,' said Helen afterwards.

'It won't.'

'How do I clean my teeth when there's no faucet?'

They showed her how to clean her teeth, but then she was scared to go into the tent alone.

'What are you scared of, Helen? We're right outside, you can see our fire burning.'

'Snakes.'

'We have a groundsheet. The only way a snake could come into the tent is through the flap and it won't because we're out here.'

'We're guarding it for you,' added Joel.

But Helen wanted Lomax to put her to bed. She said she was too tired to undress herself.

'You're too old for me to do that now.'

'Please Daddy, Daddy, Daddy, please,' she said.

'You can have a sip of my beer,' Lomax told Joel as he went into the tent with Helen. Joel poked the fire with a stone and looked pleased.

It was strange undressing Helen. She was not a helpless baby any more but she pretended to be with evident enjoyment. Lomax took her boots off and then her socks. When he pulled down her pants, she twisted and wriggled with pleasure.

'Now my panties, Daddy!' she said.

'Can't you take them off yourself?'

She danced a little dance. 'You, you!' she giggled.

He unpeeled her underwear. She raised her arms and he lifted the rest of her clothes over her head in one movement. She stood before him, small, naked and smiling.

Lomax's heart beat faster. Here was a human body in a state of perfection, unblemished by pain or time. Helen's limbs were long and slim. There was no excess fat, just a sleekness. Her skin was so smooth that it seemed to glow. The absence of any pubic hair made her sexual parts seem especially vulnerable.

She moved a step closer to him, smiling still. 'I'm growing my hair, Daddy,' she told him. It was almost shoulder length. She had been born blonde and some yellow streaks remained. Lomax reached out. Her hair was still nearly as soft as a baby's.

'It's pretty,' he said.

He gave her a T-shirt to wear in bed and she made him put it on her. To do this, he had to bend her arms gently. They were supple. The T-shirt reached little further than her waist and as she turned to scramble into her sleeping bag, he saw the small curves of her rear. She squirmed and wriggled again.

'Hurry up, Dad,' Joel called from outside. His voice had taken on that strangled, high-pitched tone again.

'Two minutes,' said Lomax.

'I'm going to hunker, hunker, hunker down,' said Helen as she disappeared into the sleeping bag. From inside it, she kicked her legs against Lomax.

'You'll fall asleep quickly now. And you won't even hear me and Joel when we come to bed.'

'Will you sleep next to me?'

'Yes.'

'Kiss me goodnight, Daddy.'

Lomax bent to kiss her and she squealed. 'Your kisses are wet and your face is itchy!'

'I don't even have a beard any more.'

'Your face is itchier without it.'

'I didn't shave today. When I shave my face is smooth.'

In response she reached up and traced his birthmark with her finger.

'Close your eyes now. And if you open them, you'll see the firelight through the tent and hear us talking.'

'Okay. And no snakes will come in.'

'No snakes.'

'Spiders?'

'They're all asleep.'

'Mice?'

'At this moment, mice everywhere are snoring.'

'Okay.'

'Okay.'

'Good night.'

'Good night.'

Joel said irritably when Lomax re-emerged from the tent: 'She doesn't need you to put her to bed, she's old enough to do it for herself.'

'I know, but she asked.'

They talked about home and school and the trip to Europe. Joel managed to do all this without mentioning Robert. Joel never talked to Lomax about Robert.

'Dad,' he said after a silence, 'is it true you have a girlfriend?'

'Yes.'

'Will you marry her?'

'I don't know.'

An unevenness in his tone made Joel look up at him shrewdly.

'Her name's Julia,' said Lomax.

'I know, Mom said.'

'I thought maybe you could meet her tomorrow. If you like.'

'Okay.' Joel was unenthusiastic.

'I have to collect something from her house. We could drop in on the way home. She works at the observatory, but she'll be there tomorrow.'

'Okay, Dad.'

'She's nice, you'll like her.'

'Is she the reason you're leaving the observatory?'

Lomax tried to explain, very simply, that he had only left the observatory temporarily and that he was spending the summer doing something different. He did not want to mention Berlins or the murders and somehow this evasion introduced a complexity to the story. It took a long time to tell and became harder and harder to follow. Joel listened intently and did not ask any further questions. Lomax decided that he would tell the children about Julia's murder charge soon, before they saw her on the television.

They went to bed. They lay on either side of the small sleeping girl and Joel fell asleep immediately. Lomax stayed alert. On several occasions he thought he had heard a strange rustling sound outside the tent and once he got up to take a look, but could see nothing. He thought of Julia. He thought of Lewis. That week he had learned a lot about the man – the stores he went to, the restaurants, the people he called – but the information did not seem to make a real person.

His daughter muttered in her sleep. She moved closer to him and he felt her breath. Somewhere in the distance was the noise of a bird. It must be an owl but he did not recognize its call. He fell asleep wondering what other bird it could be.

14

They arrived back at the lodge in the middle of the afternoon. On the return journey they skirted the lake, stopping every time Joel thought he saw a fish. He made them stand still for whole minutes at a stretch, their eyes scanning the water. Sometimes the surface seemed to pucker but this might have been caused by bugs or rocks. At last they caught sight of something streamlined and speckled in the clear waters and Joel was satisfied.

'Will we eat at the coffee shop again, or will Julia give us cookies?' asked Helen when they rounded the last bend and saw the lodge and parking lot.

Since she had learned about Julia that morning she had asked a lot of questions. Julia's name had been mentioned at regular intervals all day.

'Julia just got back from the observatory. She may not have much food. If you're hungry we should eat right here.'

But they said they weren't hungry.

The drive back to town was slow. Once, on a far peak, they saw the dome of the Fahrhaus shining in the sun. The sight filled Lomax with anguish.

Julia came out of the house to greet them. Lomax had thought about her and even dreamed about her but when he saw her now her beauty still surprised him. His heart lifted and he could not stop grinning, although he knew Joel was watching him.

Julia did not kiss Lomax. Smiling, she put her hands on her knees and bent low to ask Helen about the hike. Helen smiled back at her. Joel stood aside scrutinizing Julia.

'I can't believe you just walked for two days and you're only six years old!' Julia was saying, leading Helen towards the house. Helen giggled happily and took her hand. Joel and Lomax followed.

'Where's Deputy Dawg?' Julia asked.

'He's at home. We couldn't take him on our hike because he runs away in the night. Once Dad tied Deputy to his foot but Deputy still managed to get away when Dad was asleep.'

'How come she knows Deputy?' Joel asked Lomax as Julia took Helen to the kitchen, promising cupcakes and orange juice.

'I brought him here when you were in Europe.'

Joel looked at Lomax reprovingly.

In the kitchen they told her about building the camp fire and sleeping in the tent and seeing the fish in the lake.

'Oh, I wish I could come next time,' said Julia.

'We don't have another tent,' said Joel.

Lomax leaned against the sink, sipping his orange juice. He wished Julia had kissed him. He reminded her that he was here to collect something.

'Lewis' address book. Why do you want it?'

But Lomax said he would explain later. He offered to take the children to Candice's and then return.

'No, Lomax, because I have to get back to the observatory tonight. Doberman asked me specially.'

Lomax tensed. 'Why?'

'It's his birthday. He's organizing some kind of a party.'

'Oh,' said Lomax. He could not meet Julia's eye, or Joel's.

'Plus,' added Julia, 'the press has been hassling Frances and she told me to stay at the observatory and not to answer any questions.'

'Why?' asked Joel.

'I'm going to tell you about it on the way home,' Lomax said.

The cupcakes were sticky and melting. Helen began to lick the chocolate off her fingers. Julia got up to wash her hands, slipping her rings off first. Silently, Helen joined Julia at the sink. She watched Julia rubbing the soap over her palms and sliding her smooth fingers together. She mimed removing rings from her left hand and then tried to copy Julia's exact movements.

'Like this?' she asked.

'You know how to wash up,' Lomax said but, serious-faced, Helen continued her curious, clumsy parody. Then Julia shook her hands loosely and drops of water flew off. Helen did the same. Julia reached for the towel and Helen dried her hands at one end, watching Julia dry hers at the other. Julia put her rings on and Helen mimed the same movement.

'You smell nice,' she told Julia, looking at her in frank admiration. She reached out and touched Julia's necklace, a simple chain with a large pearl. 'This is pretty,' Helen said.

Lomax felt sour as they walked to the car. Julia had not asked him anything about Sachs Smith or how he liked it there or whether he missed the observatory. She had not asked him now, or in any of their telephone conversations. Today she had not kissed him or even squeezed his hand. It seemed that the only way to love Julia was to give and ask for nothing back.

Then, as the children were getting into the car, she appeared at his side, rapidly put her arms around him, and kissed his cheek before either of the children could notice. His mood changed instantly. He felt elated. He felt aroused.

She said softly: 'I'm sorry we didn't have any time alone together.'

'When are you coming back?'

'Soon.' She kissed him again and licked his ear very swiftly.

'Look!' shrieked Helen as they turned out of Julia's drive. There was a police car pressing against the bushes by the side of the narrow road. Lomax, slowing, eased past and found himself a few feet from Murphy McLean.

'Murph! Murph!' Helen called, bouncing in her seat and waving zealously.

McLean was speaking into his radio. He saw Lomax without surprise and, half-turning, gave the occupants of the car a grotesque parody of a wink. It pulled the two sides of his face in different directions, up and down, and made Helen giggle. Lomax accelerated.

'How come you know that man?' he asked Helen.

'That's Murph the sheriff. He comes to our school.'

'Why?'

'To tell us not to talk to strangers or take presents from them. Even if the present is a little puppy.'

Joel said: 'Dad, why's he stopped right outside Julia's house?'

'I can think of no reason,' replied Lomax grimly, 'why that man should be there.'

'Is it anything to do with the press hassling someone?'

'Maybe,' Lomax admitted. And then he told them, with difficulty, about the murders. At first they were silent. They looked at him without speaking.

'Of course,' he added, 'Julia didn't shoot anybody. But the problem is that the police don't have anyone to blame, so they've arrested Julia.'

Joel said annoyingly: 'They need evidence before they can arrest someone.'

'The police often think they have evidence. But they can be wrong. That's why we have courts, so people have the chance to show that they're innocent. I mean, they're presumed innocent. The police have to prove them guilty.'

Sometimes it was hard to remember this. He glanced across at Joel but the boy was not satisfied.

'Look,' said Joel importantly in Robert's voice. 'What evidence do the police have?'

'It's kind of complicated. Someone thinks he saw her. And the police believe that Gail, she's one of the people who died, was taking money from Julia. So they think they've found a reason for Julia to kill Gail.'

'Did they find the gun?' asked Joel.

'Nope.'

'How about fingerprints and things like that?'

'Nothing you wouldn't expect.'

'So all they have for proof is this money?'

'Yup. Oh, and a man who thinks he might have seen her outside the apartment round about the time of the murders. He's only just come forward. I don't know why it took him so long to remember. After all this time, he may be confused about exactly if and when he saw her.'

Helen said: 'Julia didn't kill anyone, did she Daddy?' Lomax agreed with her. But Joel refused to be convinced.

'Did Helen and Joel like me?' Julia asked over the phone that night.

'Yes. Especially Helen adored you.'

'She's cute.'

'So are you. I wish I'd seen you alone.'

She did not answer him. Instead she said firmly: 'It's very important with kids that . . . um . . . well I didn't want them to see us kissing and things.'

'I guess they see Robert and Candice kiss occasionally.'

'I bet they hate it.' There was more insistence in her tone than he had ever heard before.

'What makes you so sure they hate it?'

His interest made her defensive. 'Nothing.'

'Did Lewis' kids see you kissing him?'

'Perhaps sometimes.'

'And?'

'And they hated it.'

Lomax tried to tell her that he would like to know more about Lewis. He explained that he had spent the week dialling Lewis' telephone numbers, speaking to people who knew Lewis, or shops where Lewis had bought goods or restaurants where Lewis had eaten. Lewis was, for him, a series of digits. He said: 'Julia, thanks for the address book, it'll save me hours of dialling. But I'm trying to imagine

Lewis . . . and I can't. Why don't you tell me about him? Is it really too painful?'

'Why?' asked Julia.

'Why what?'

'Why do you need to imagine him?'

'Because you suggested the $450,000 you gave to Gail was really for Lewis. So Sachs Smith are trying to find out why he needed it. They have to peer into all the cracks and crevices of his life to find out where there's a hole big enough to take $450,000.'

There was a silence. The telephone line crackled the way it did when there was a storm somewhere out on the mountains.

'Why do you think he wanted the money?' Lomax asked.

'I told you. For the firm. If they're trying to prove that he was dishonest, they'll never succeed.'

'They seem to think it's your best hope.'

'My best hope,' said Julia, 'is that I'm innocent.'

'I know you are. I just wish you'd help a bit more.'

'What do you want me to do?'

'God, I don't know. Talk about him. Tell me about his mother or his first wife.'

'I never knew his mother, his first wife's a drunk.'

'How about more pictures, then?'

'Pictures? Of Lewis?'

'Do you have any?'

'Sure.'

'Can I see them some time?'

'I keep them with me. They're right here. You want to borrow them?'

'Can I?'

She hesitated, but only momentarily. 'All right. How urgently . . . I mean . . . do you need them soon?'

Lomax offered to collect them from the observatory but he was relieved when she said that McMahon was driving into town that night. He didn't want to see the other astronomers walking around the site looking busy and know he was no longer a part of the place.

Julia said: 'McMahon's going to some restaurant downtown. I'll ask him to leave them at Sachs Smith for you. That way, you'll have them in the morning. But I don't see how they can help you.'

Lomax did not want her to hang up. He tried to think of something else to talk about and remembered Murphy McLean and his monstrous wink.

'Did he drop in? Or was he just sitting outside your home winking at people?'

'He didn't ring the bell.'

'He just sat out there?'

'I don't know. Probably. I've seen him around here a few times.'

Lomax gripped the phone so hard that his fingers hurt. 'What the fuck,' he spluttered, 'what the fuck does he think he's doing? Hanging around and intimidating you like that?'

'He's not trying to intimidate me. He's trying to protect me,' Julia said. Lomax could sense her backing away from his anger. He softened his tone, but shortly afterwards she hung up.

15

On Monday morning Lomax overslept. He did not want to go to Sachs Smith and sit under the stairs listening to the thud of feet all day. He nicked his left ear with the razor as he shaved. The traffic was bad. The sky was overcast. He was late and anxious about being late. Then, as he wedged himself behind his desk, he realized that nobody noticed or cared what time he arrived. He wanted some coffee and remembered morosely that he would have to make it himself.

At least he had Lewis' address book and photographs to study today. The address book was small, old and battered. It was intimate. Once it had been bound in brown leather but over the years the leather had rubbed smooth. Lomax was surprised that Lewis had not replaced it. He examined Lewis' handwriting. It was small and neat and had changed little in the life of the book. Only the colour of the ink varied. When Lewis' friends moved, he crossed them out with thick, straight lines and added their names and new addresses on the next blank page. The lines dissected the names exactly in half. They had been drawn slowly and deliberately. Sometimes, names were crossed through and their owners were not added later on. What had happened to these people? Had they died, or had Lewis lost touch with them, or argued with them and decided to eliminate them from his address book?

Lomax was able to use the book to identify some of the numbers on his list. He decided to reward himself with a cup of coffee. Marjorie was just leaving the kitchen as he arrived. She did not greet him or even look at him but she flicked her hair in his direction.

'Monday,' she stated.

'Yeah,' said Lomax sympathetically.

'Monday. I hate it. I've already burned a hole in the phone this morning and I'm going to burn some more.'

When he returned to his desk, he tipped up the envelope Julia had sent. He had already looked for a note from her but there was none.

McMahon had scribbled on the outside of the envelope: 'Going out to get drunk. Greetings. ATMcM.' He wondered if McMahon had opened it. Probably, knowing McMahon.

The pictures fell out onto his desk. There were many different sizes and colours. His heart throbbed noisily as he shuffled through them. Holiday pictures. Pictures in the yard. Christmas pictures. But most of all, there were wedding pictures. Many of these were practically identical to the picture he had already seen, taken moments before or moments afterwards. While the fixed smiles of Julia, Lewis and Richard were almost unchanging, Gail was often blinking, or pushing her glasses up the ridge of her nose or contorting her mouth in speech. Lomax selected one picture from which to study the family. In it, Julia looked particularly beautiful. Her smile was not quite complete. The perfect shape and fullness of her lips was visible and so were the soft shadows under her cheekbones.

Julia, Lewis, Richard and Gail. Two of the people in this picture were dead and a third faced the possibility of the death penalty. He looked from face to face. Julia's happiness. Richard, a younger version of his father. Gail, wearing a strange, barely-formed smile. He stared hard at Lewis.

Lewis looked the same in this picture as he did in all the others. Same weight, same stance, same smile. His hair was white, but it was as thick as a young man's. The skin was lined but it stretched firmly over strong bones. Why would anyone want to kill him? What were his secrets? Lomax bent closer and Lewis smiled at him. It was a routine smile, without warmth, and at the sight of Lomax's ill-fitting suit and unskilful shaving, the smile would fade. Lomax guessed that Lewis would disapprove of him. Lewis was probably a member of some country club on the edge of town where the tablecloths were white linen and the head waiter deferential. This waiter would look appraisingly at Lomax's suit and know at once that here was a man making a fraudulent attempt at respectability. Lewis would order a good wine and Lomax would knock his glass over and of course it would be red wine. Both the head waiter and Lewis would control their irritation as they mopped up. Probably Lewis was good at self control. He revealed little about himself, and certainly not to cameras.

Lomax put the picture to one side and returned the other photos to the envelope. He placed Lewis' address book in the empty drawer of his desk and picked up the telephone. He heard Marjorie's voice. Without intending to, he found himself listening to her call.

'He's an old friend of mine and I'm trying to contact him . . .' she was saying.

'Oh yeah?' sneered a male voice.

'Does his name ring a bell?'

'Fox?'

'Lewis Fox.'

'Lewis Fox. No. His name does not ring a bell and you don't sound old enough to have old friends, kid,' said the voice.

Marjorie blathered about knowing his daughter, actually, it was his daughter Gail who was really her friend but . . .

'And,' said the man, 'you're the second call I've had lately from someone saying they're looking for their old friend Lewis Fox. And if I get one more dumb-assed, super-nosy call from one more . . .'

Lomax did not hear the rest. When he arrived in Marjorie's office she was replacing the receiver. Her face was pinker than usual. She played with her hair.

'Which case are you working on?' he said.

'Why?'

'Did you know that I'm working on the same case?'

Marjorie flung her hair around. 'Well . . . not exactly.'

'So you didn't exactly know that I've been wasting my time making exactly the same goddam calls to exactly the same goddam numbers and asking exactly the same goddam questions?'

'Er . . .'

'When people kept telling me that a woman had already called asking for Lewis Fox, I thought it must be someone from the DA's office. But no. It was someone down the hall using the same fucking telephone line.'

Marjorie pouted. She said: 'Calm down.' Her voice was not calming.

'No. What were you told about me?'

She sighed. 'They just said – '

'Who did?'

'Kurt. He just said that . . . well, who cares what he said? Basically I got the impression you were here because you're crazy about the client and you've got some kind of idea you can help her and that . . .'

Her voice trailed away. There was a silence. Marjorie broke it. 'You haven't been to law school,' she said lamely.

'No, I haven't been to law school. I've been to other kinds of school.'

'Is it true you work up at the observatory?'

Lomax's voice was loud. 'No. I work here at Sachs Smith on People *versus* Fox.'

139

'Don't shout at me, shout at Kurt.'

'Let's not waste any more time. Just bring your notes and your pen into the closet where I work, Marjorie, the windowless closet under the stairs, and we'll trade information. I'll tell you what I know, you'll tell me what you know. Then we'll agree how to work together so we save time and we don't duplicate. Okay?'

Marjorie gathered the scattered pages on her desk. When she was seated in Lomax's office she looked at him with interest. 'Want me to make some coffee?' she offered. Her voice was friendly for the first time.

As they drank, Lomax showed her the way he had filed the numbers and any information he had gained about them. Marjorie was impressed. Her own system was more haphazard. They worked their way through lists of digits. Generally, Marjorie's calls had been more successful than Lomax's. She referred frequently to a sheaf of photocopied pages.

'What's that?' asked Lomax.

'Lewis' address book. His wife let Kurt photocopy it and it's been real useful.'

Lomax said nothing.

'And this is a copy of his desk diary . . . it also had a few names and numbers in it. I've been able to correlate phone calls he made with subsequent appointments, that kind of thing,' said Marjorie.

'Did you know him?'

'Who, Lewis Fox?'

'Yes.'

'You're an old friend of his and you're trying to make contact, right?'

They smiled.

'Actually, I didn't know him. I only started work here a few weeks ago and this is my first case,' she admitted.

'Do you get the impression he was popular?'

She shrugged. 'I don't get any impression at all.'

When Kurt arrived, looking for Marjorie, they were bent over their work, deep in discussion.

'Oh good, you've met,' said Kurt. Lomax gave him a look which he hoped was contemptuous.

'Shit, Lomax, you seem kind of sick,' Kurt told him insincerely. 'Maybe you're too sick to go out tonight.'

'Go out where?'

'I'm meeting Gerry Hegarty, Lewis' buddy. He's going to introduce me to Lewis' mistress. Frances told me to take you along so you can see how we interview people.'

'Okay,' said Lomax.

'He's taking us to Lewis' club.'

Lomax nodded. This must be the country club.

Hegarty picked them up from the office after dark. Lomax was tired. The monotony of the work at Sachs Smith and the dinginess of his surroundings was fatiguing. He had learnt nothing in the course of his research that might be to Julia's advantage. She had said she would call him from the observatory that day, but had not done so. Probably she had tried and found the line busy.

Hegarty drove. The car was old. It had the size and solidity of a machine from another era but the bodywork gleamed and inside the upholstery smelled fresh. Hegarty had been so pleased with his new car all those years ago that he had kept it new. Lomax placed the evening paper on the backseat, put his feet on it, and sprawled. There was a picture of Julia on the front page of the paper, just visible by his ankles.

Kurt and Hegarty, in the front, talked about the car and then they started to talk about Lewis. Lomax could not hear everything they said. Hegarty's voice was quiet, almost as monotonous as the car engine. He drove them smoothly through the evening traffic, the stops and starts barely perceptible. Once, while they waited at the lights, he combed his hair. Hegarty's words, when they reached Lomax, were hypnotic.

'... tired ... asleep ... more than one occasion ... asleep ...'

Lomax closed his eyes. Kurt's voice crackled.

'How many cars did he write off, Mr Hegarty?'

Hegarty paused.

'Who?' asked Lomax, opening his eyes. 'Who wrote off cars?'

'Wake up, Lomax. Mr Hegarty's been explaining about Lewis' car crashes.'

'No, no, not crashes, that's putting it dramatically. He never caused any damage to anyone else or to their property. He just sort of fell asleep sometimes.'

'Did he drink a lot?' Lomax asked. Passing traffic lit up Hegarty's face in the driver's mirror. Its expression was wary.

'No more,' said Hegarty, 'than anybody else.'

Lomax thought of Lewis leaving his country club. It would be late at night. Deferential as always, the head waiter himself might open the door for him and Lewis would walk to his car, not drunk, not undignified, but with a certain correctness in his stride which suggested some extra effort might be necessary. Then he would drive home to Julia in the foothills, straining to remember to stay awake, until . . .

'Which side of town is this club, Mr Hegarty?' asked Lomax.

'It isn't any side really. It's downtown.'

'Lewis' club? Is downtown?' Lomax was incredulous. He was unwilling to relinquish the country club he had created. He had already added some long lawns and stone walls. Then there were the white tablecloths, the head waiter, the goddam wine list. They were all so Lewis.

Sharp turn succeeded sharp turn.

'It's right here,' said Hegarty as he halted the car.

'Here! Here?' Lomax was astonished.

High brick walls embraced them on all sides. The lights of the city flickered on the tiny weeds which had rooted in the cracks.

'You get that gosh wow out of your voice you fucking, fucking amateur,' Kurt spat at him in a whisper as they climbed out of the car.

Hegarty did not seem to hear. 'It gets kind of crowded,' he said. He led them with a surprising swiftness through the dark, threading his way neatly around cars on some familiar route of his own. Behind him, Kurt and Lomax banged against bumpers and fenders; Kurt swore under his breath. Everything about the place looked low rent: its hidden downtown location, its crumbling walls, its haphazard lighting. Lewis' club was going to be a sleazy dive. It was going to be the kind of place where elderly businessmen eyeball bulging flesh before going home for dinner with their wives. Lomax felt a stab of pain on Julia's behalf.

They were at the entrance now. Lomax looked at the dark windows and the uninviting door, and remembered the country club. But all that belonged to the Lewis he would have chosen for Julia. Behind this bleak facade he would find the real Lewis.

Hegarty rang. He cleared his throat as they waited. There was no sign, no neon light, nothing indicating the existence of the club or its name. What was its name? Had Hegarty called it anything except The Club?

The door was opened by a man in a tuxedo.

The head waiter. Lomax took a step back in surprise and stumbled on the uneven paving. The man greeted Hegarty and then looked Kurt and Lomax coolly up and down. Kurt's face broke into a winning smile and he thrust his jawbone at the man. He stepped forward to speak but Hegarty was quicker, drawing the head waiter to one side and whispering to him with urgency.

As they waited, Lomax found himself rhythmically flexing and unflexing a calf muscle. There was music inside the club and, curiously, it was orchestral music. He did not recognize it but he liked to hear it. He felt hungry and then noticed the smell of food, good food, escaping from the open door.

At last the whispered discussion ended and they were allowed in. Hegarty led. A hall, too narrow to walk side by side, opened out into a surprising staircase. It was wide. It curved gently. It invited you to climb. As they did so, their steps lightened. The music grew louder; impossibly, the sound had all the range and depth of a live orchestra. Lomax felt a sense of heightened anticipation. His heart seemed to thud to the music and, ahead of him, Hegarty seemed to walk to it.

They paused in the doorway at the top of the stairs.

The restaurant was not large but it was loud. At one end, on a raised platform, was a thicket of tuxedos: an orchestra. It consisted of about fifteen players. Their music swelled. It filled the room. It was a delight. The air was dense with their notes and it seemed to Lomax that he was breathing music. Gently swaying chandeliers kept time overhead. The light that fell from them was dim and the walls were swathed in dark drapes so it was some time before Lomax could distinguish the figures of the diners. While the orchestra played, they ate. Some of them had finished their meals and sat back, cigarettes in hand. Their smoke curled overhead and insinuated itself around the chandeliers.

The head waiter appeared mysteriously in front of them. He gestured to a table and they threaded their way towards it. He and Hegarty talked into each others' ears for a few minutes and the man disappeared.

'Nicholas is in charge here,' explained Hegarty unnecessarily. Nicholas could be seen in the distance now, watching the room. He sat at an empty table communicating with his staff in his own languid semaphore. Except for the raising of a finger or an eyebrow he was still.

'This is a great place,' said Kurt, and Hegarty nodded.

'Only,' added Kurt, 'this smoke. It violates city ordinances.'

Hegarty examined his cufflinks. 'Perhaps,' he said at last.

He told them he had ordered food. There was little choice and he always took Nicholas' recommendation.

Lomax glanced around him at the other diners. The tables were small and most held only two people. Conversation was almost impossible while the orchestra played.

'Like it?' Hegarty asked him. It was the first remark he had addressed to Lomax.

'Yes,' said Lomax. Hegarty smiled. He produced a comb from his pocket and began to smooth the hair at the sides of his head. He was careful, raising his elbows high above him. This was the second time he had combed his hair in twenty minutes. The effect was comic because Hegarty was almost completely bald.

A snowy white tablecloth was set before them and covered in a choice of dishes.

'Just help yourselves, gentlemen,' Hegarty instructed.

The food was good. As they ate they watched the elbows of the orchestra flying and their black coats flapping. The music reached a crescendo as they were finishing. Lomax's head absorbed it and he could think of nothing else. Finally it was over. There was enthusiastic clapping from the dark recesses of the room. The orchestra bowed. The conductor bowed twice. They made a disorderly exit from their small platform and a pianist appeared to play for the diners.

'Neat,' commented Kurt. He was leafing through his notebook. 'So, you and Lewis came here often,' he informed Hegarty, who took out a cigarette. Kurt eyed it distastefully.

'I guess so,' Hegarty said. He talked softly. He liked to think before he spoke.

'How did you meet each other?'

'I did some work for Sachs Smith. We got to know one other and Lewis became my closest friend. I expect you want to ask me questions about him. So did the police. Tall, thin man, said he was from Homicide, face like a skull. Extraordinary.'

Kurt looked alarmed. 'What questions did the police ask?'

'It would probably save time,' Hegarty suggested, 'if I told you the answers.' His voice was kind, but he was taking charge of the interview. He was an accountant and he headed an accountancy firm. He habitually took charge of situations. He tugged at the cuffs of his shirt.

'Lewis hadn't been in this city long, I guess it was about fifteen years ago, maybe less, you can check up if you want the exact dates. He was going through a divorce and so was I. We had a lot of other things in common. He had problems with his family, his ex-wife, and so did I. Mine lived right here in this city and his soon followed him here. I got married five years ago and right afterwards Lewis started thinking about marrying Julia. It was just like me and my brother. First time I got married was soon after he did. People don't admit it. People don't say: I got married because my friend did, because my brother did. I mean, Lewis loved Julia. But if I'd stayed single, he might have still been single. By the way, Julia's a good, sweet kid. She could never have carried out a crime like this.'

Kurt wrote hasty notes. When he had finished, he raised his eyes again to Hegarty. 'This girl . . . Lewis was involved with someone . . .'

'Sure. Alice. Nicholas will send her over soon,' said Hegarty.

'You mean Alice is already here?' said Kurt.

'Sure.'

Coffee and cognac arrived. While it was being poured, Lomax looked around at the other tables. He had noticed that the diners were mostly in couples. Now he became aware that many of the couples demonstrated some intimacy. They fed each other or gazed into each other's eyes or stroked one another. Lomax strained to see in the darkness. On the platform the pianist, dressed in black, was playing Chopin softly.

'Is this decaffeinated?' Kurt asked the waiter.

The elderly man's eyes rolled in Kurt's direction. 'No, sir,' he said, and disappeared into the dark.

Lomax was beginning to find the predominance of young women and older men significant. He turned to ask Hegarty about it but the orchestra was taking up their instruments again. After the applause that followed the performance, Hegarty told them: 'There's some talented players there.'

Lomax nodded, although he knew nothing about music or musical talent, and said so.

'Well, the people here aren't necessarily musical. I actually went to music college and Lewis had a good knowledge of the subject but many of the members don't know a sonata from a concerto and that really doesn't matter.'

'So they don't join for the music?' Lomax asked.

'Oh no. They join for the women.'

Kurt and Lomax looked around. In the dim light, most of the women seemed young, and all of them looked beautiful.

'Nicholas supplies them,' suggested Lomax.

Hegarty's expression was pained.

'Well, not like a pimp. These girls are emphatically not prostitutes. Nicholas simply introduces men to lovely women. I don't know how he finds them. Young men too, a few. But what you actually pay for here is the food and the orchestra.'

'So,' stated Kurt, 'this is not the kind of place you'd bring your wife.'

Hegarty looked at him without expression. 'I wouldn't dream of bringing my wife,' he said.

'How do people join? I mean I'd be interested in . . .'

Hegarty's reply was swift. 'You don't. You have to wait to be asked. Now, here's Alice.'

At first Lomax thought she must be a member of the orchestra. She wore a tuxedo and a white bow tie. She moved confidently round the tables, sliding through the spaces by swinging her slim body to the left and to the right. Her hair was blonde and fell over her face. Her movements were graceful.

'Yes, oh yes,' said Kurt. Hegarty kissed Alice's cheek and vacated his chair for her. He left them and a few minutes later Lomax caught sight of him talking to a slim young woman across the room.

Kurt began asking Alice about herself. She had lived with her mother until last year when her mother had married and moved down to Los Angeles. Now she lived alone. She modelled part-time. She was training to be a veterinarian's assistant.

'Oh, you like animals?' said Kurt. 'I have a puppy!'

Alice's face lit up. She said something Lomax could not hear. Although only the lone pianist was now playing, Alice's voice was so small and breathless that Kurt had to lean forward to catch her words. Lomax watched her speak. He was unable to feel anything for this child. Her good looks did not interest him. Her face was unlined, almost uninhabited.

'How old are you, Alice?' he asked.

'I'm nineteen. Well, in eight days I'll be nineteen.'

'Happy birthday, Alice,' said Kurt, his voice warm with admiration. He began to ask her questions about Lewis Fox. She answered haltingly but eventually informaton emerged from her in fragments and monosyllables. She had first been introduced to Nicholas by a friend of her mother's. She had met Lewis at the club last January. They had met again, and many more times. How many was unclear. It was also unclear exactly when Lewis first arranged to see Alice outside the club, but soon afterwards they began sleeping together. Lewis sent her flowers and other gifts to surprise her. One day a man with gold braid on his uniform had delivered a kitten to her home. Lewis had not talked about his wife to Alice at all except to indicate that the marital relationship was a troubled one. Whenever Alice had thought of his wife she had imagined a difficult old lady. She was surprised, after the murders, to see Julia's picture on television.

146

There had been no tearful split from Lewis. Gradually they had drifted apart. Relationships formed at the club were usually like that. Alice met someone else but she still waved affectionately to Lewis across the room or occasionally changed tables to kiss him hello. He had met someone else, too – an attractive brunette whom he was seen with here. Lewis was attentive and charming to this girl. Alice did not know who she was and had not seen her since. She thought the girl was around her own age or probably a little older.

'Thank you, Alice,' concluded Kurt. 'I may have further questions for you . . . can I take your number and address in case I need to visit you at home?'

Alice supplied this informaton and then slipped away to a distant table. Lomax tried to follow her with his eyes but she melted into the darkness. Hegarty returned to his seat.

'Sexy. I mean the tuxedo,' said Kurt.

Hegarty nodded. 'I guess Lewis thought so too.'

'How old's the puppy?' asked Lomax. Kurt grinned slyly at him, then gathered up his notebook. 'So. Well. Ol' Lewis,' he said, admiration in his voice. 'I mean, first Julia. Now Alice. Wow. Young and tender. Do you think it was a serious affair for him?'

Hegarty shook his head. 'I'll be frank with you. Lewis was a few years older than me and I know I don't have the time or the energy to devote wholeheartedly to that kind of thing any more. Alice is just the sort of girl Lewis wanted. But not too often. See what I mean?'

Kurt and Lomax nodded dejectedly.

'Makes you want to kill yourself on your fiftieth birthday,' said Kurt.

'If someone else doesn't kill you first,' Hegarty replied evenly. 'Any more questons, gentlemen?'

'Yes,' said Lomax before Kurt could speak. Kurt glowered at him. 'Did Lewis have another girlfriend after Alice? A brunette?'

Hegarty thought hard. 'No, not that I knew of,' he said at last.

Kurt scribbled a reluctant note of this. He asked: 'Did Lewis ever confide in you that there was some sort of financial problem at Sachs Smith? Or that he had a financial problem of his own?'

'No,' said Hegarty.

'Was anything worrying him, to your knowledge?'

'He would have told me if there was, and he didn't. The police hinted that there was some suggestion of financial impropriety at Sachs Smith. Well, maybe there was, but I know for a fact Lewis wouldn't have had anything to do with it. He was honest. An honest man. How many people can you say that about? Not many. Let's go, gentlemen.'

They stood. On the platform, the pianist's body rolled with emotion as she played up and down the keyboard.

Kurt said: 'Who do you think killed him, Mr Hegarty?'

Hegarty shrugged. 'Either hooligans. That's possible. Or someone who wanted the daughter for something, God knows why, and Lewis got in their way. But a reason to kill Lewis? No one had a reason to kill Lewis.'

They paused to look back and, while Hegarty talked intently into Nicholas's ear, Lomax located Alice. She was sharing a table with a white-haired man.

As they went downstairs, Kurt in front, Hegarty muttered to Lomax: 'Nicholas would be prepared to accept you as a member.'

'Who?' said Lomax. 'Me?'

Hegarty smiled. 'Think about it. Here's my card . . .' Lomax studied it. He recognized the telephone number as one he had dialled that day.

'Call me if you're interested.'

Lomax was hesitant. 'Can I call you if I have some more questions?'

'What kind of questions?'

'I don't know. They're just forming in my mind now. I'm kind of slow.'

Hegarty nodded approvingly. 'I'll be vacationing soon . . .' He reached into his pocket for a small, green diary, and flicked through the pages without breaking his stride.

'We should meet,' he said, then suggested a date and time. It was weeks away. Lomax wrote it down.

Hegarty took them back to Sachs Smith. When the stately old car had pulled quietly away, Kurt said: 'I'll bet that guy's involved.'

'How?'

'He's too cool, too polished. His best friend's been murdered for Chrissake.'

'Six months ago. He's had time to get used to the idea.'

'Nah. If there was some financial mismanagement, that guy would have a finger in it. After all, he's an accountant.'

'Has any mismanagement come to light?'

'We've got some independent financial consultants checking everything at Sachs Smith. So do the police. And no one's found a single discrepancy yet. Probably they won't. Hegarty's clever.'

Lomax asked: 'Was Lewis popular at work?'

Kurt shrugged. The question seemed to annoy him. 'When he gave people raises.'

Lomax persisted. 'And when he didn't?'

'Managing partners are never real popular. You try to do your job and you just want the firm to be managed well. But sometimes it seems that these people get in your way. Once they were attorneys, they should know what it's like, but they forget. They're here to help, and they just get in your way.'

What had Kurt and Lewis argued about? Kurt's expenses? The redecoration of his office? The installation of a new computer system? Towels in the men's room? Lomax nearly groaned out loud. He wanted to investigate a murder, not office politics.

He had a headache when he arrived home. A local TV special on the Fox case was just finishing. The reporter, in a swaggering tie and dark suit, his face serious, predicted that Julia was unlikely to win the case and reminded viewers that the almost certain penalty was death. Lomax reached for the off switch but was arrested by the pictures which appeared now of the observatory. So the press had discovered Julia's hiding place. There was the parking lot with a shot of the ubiquitous McMahon strolling out of the cafeteria towards the labs, deep in conversation with someone hidden from sight. Viewers would assume that the scientists were discussing something extragalactic when they were probably talking about today's lunch menu.

Lomax called Julia but she did not reply. He made coffee and tried to concentrate on Lewis Fox, but Lewis was becoming, if anything, more elusive. The Lewis Fox he had created so carefully earlier that day could never have been a member of the club. The club was nothing but a musical whorehouse. It was sex masquerading as culture. Wealthy men paid to meet pretty young girls there, girls who were young enough to be their daughters, grand-daughters even. Why had Hegarty asked him to join? Did Hegarty think that he, Lomax, liked that kind of thing? Did Hegarty think that there were similarities between Lomax and Lewis?

The phone rang. He hoped it was Julia but when he picked up the receiver he heard Candice and knew at once that she was angry.

'Lomax.'

'Yes.'

'I've been trying to reach you all evening. It's Helen.'

Lomax's stomach lurched. 'What's happened?'

'That's exactly what I want to know.'

'What?'

'You tell me.'

So Helen had arrived home from the hike with a bruised knee or a cut on her finger and Candice had only just noticed. His anxiety eased, he said gently: 'What's the matter, Candice?'

'Lomax. Look . . .'

Perhaps in response to his tone, her voice changed perceptibly. Her anger was cracking. He waited. It was a moment before she spoke.

'Do you have any idea why I'm calling?' she asked. Some sort of uncertainty was diluting her vigour.

'No. Is Helen all right?'

Candice sighed and began to speak. 'Tonight I was putting her to bed. She was talking about the hike and then I kissed her goodnight. I was just leaving the room and she called me back. She had something to tell me.'

She paused. Lomax waited.

'At first she wouldn't. I had to sit on her bed and coax it out of her for half an hour.'

'Coax what out of her?'

'Lomax, did you touch her?'

'What?'

'Did you touch that little girl?'

'Touch her? What the hell is that supposed to mean?'

'She said: "Mommy. I don't want Daddy to kiss me any more." '

Lomax was silent.

'Can you hear me, Lomax?'

'Well, how did she say it?'

'She said she had something to tell and then – '

'She always says she has something to tell just when you try to turn out her light.'

'Lomax . . .' Candice's voice quavered. 'She was upset.'

'Upset! She was crying?'

'No, she wasn't crying, she was upset. Don't yell.'

'She was upset because you'd been sitting on her bed begging her to tell you something for half an hour and she didn't know what the hell to say! That's why she was fucking upset!'

'Let's try to discuss this without shouting.'

'What exactly are you accusing me of?'

'Nothing.' Her voice had taken on a note of false calm. 'I'm not accusing you of anything. I just want to know why Helen said she didn't want her Daddy to kiss her any more. What happened when you kissed her last time?'

'What happened? Well, I kissed her goodnight. Like you did tonight. And she said my face was itchy. That's what goddam happened.'

'Is that all?'

'Christ, Candice.'

But Candice was rallying now. 'Joel says you were in the tent alone with her for a long time. You undressed her and put her to bed and frankly, Lomax, it's unnecessary, and you know it's unnecessary. She's six years old, she doesn't need you to undress her.'

Lomax could not speak. Helen and Joel had both had to endure one of Candice's interrogations, and the subject of the questioning had been their father, whom they loved. Lomax could imagine Helen's unhappy whine and Joel's squeaks and stammers.

'I mean,' added Candice weakly, 'did you have some reason to undress her?'

It was moments before Lomax replied. 'She asked me to.'

'And what did you . . . what did you actually do?'

'I took off her clothes, I gave her a T-shirt to wear, she got into her sleeping bag, I kissed her goodnight, I went outside to Joel . . .'

'Who slept next to Helen?'

'We both did. We slept one on either side.'

'And . . . is that all?'

'I'm not certain,' said Lomax, his heart clapping against his chest, 'that I trust myself to continue this conversation.'

'I'm not accusing you of anything, Lomax. I just want to find out what happened.'

'Well now you've found out.'

There was a long silence.

'I'm sorry,' Candice said at last.

Lomax told her: 'I'm not sure I can forgive you. I'll think about it.'

He hung up the telephone and lay on the bed motionless. He had not moved when it rang again. He allowed it to ring. When it insisted, he picked it up.

Candice said: 'Lomax, please listen . . .'

'No.'

'I may have got the wrong idea. Well, I did get the wrong idea. But I had to understand why Helen didn't want her Daddy to . . .'

'Go away,' he told her, and hung up.

He lay thinking about that night on the mountainside with Helen, everything he had said, everything he had thought and everything he had felt. Strangely, when he was least expecting it, Lewis Fox intruded on his thoughts. All day he had been trying to find Lewis and now, unbidden, here he was.

Lomax fell asleep lying across the bed, fully clothed. The next morning he woke up with a clear head. He washed energetically. He did not shave. He did not wear his Sachs Smith clothes. His jeans felt like comfortable old friends.

He telephoned Julia.

'Are you okay?'

'Yes. I didn't watch TV last night.' Her voice was quiet. 'I stayed in the office doing eclipse committee work.'

'Just what is the eclipse committee?'

'It doesn't exist yet. I was organizing the first meeting and typing for Doberman. Anything, really, to stay busy.'

'I hope no one in the observatory is hassling you?'

'No. Everyone's being real kind. They think it's some horrible mistake. Which it is.'

Just as he was leaving, the phone rang. It was Kurt.

'Still in bed, Lomax?'

'No.'

Kurt was calling from somewhere noisy. He spoke close to the receiver. 'Type up some notes on Hegarty and Alice, and give them to Frances, can you?'

'But I didn't take any notes. You took notes.'

'So type up what you can remember, especially the brunette. Marjorie should start looking for her. And don't ever go to an interview without taking notes again.'

'Where are you?'

'At the airport. I'm flying to Zurich. Zurich, Switzerland.'

'You look like you need a vacation, Kurt.'

'Go fuck yourself, Lomax. I've traced the $450,000 to a bank account there. No time to tell Frances about what happend last night. So you do the report, just the way I showed you. Okay?'

'Okay.'

But when he hung up, Lomax did not write the report. Instead, he drove to the university campus.

16

Lomax's contract at the observatory required him to teach occasional semesters at the university. Sometimes he gave advanced physics lectures which attracted fewer than 15 students. Sometimes he gave broad introductory lectures in cosmology to an audience of hundreds with assorted majors.

The university had high academic standards. Its students studied hard. The campus was famous for its vegetation. There was a thriving biology and botany department here which had grown up around the plant collection given by an early benefactor. Over the years deans had invested in the collection, nurturing and expanding it. Now the campus trees and shrubs and plants had achieved international fame. Some of Lomax's friends were professors at the university, and were embroiled in its politics. They sat on committees. They said that the cost and upkeep of the plant collection was the university's most burning issue. Tradescant was a quiet institution.

Botanists travelled to the campus to admire the trees and committees fought over them, but Lomax, like the students, ignored them. He walked through a grove of tall hardwoods from Northern Europe without looking at them. He passed groups of laughing students without listening to them. There was a solitary girl sobbing quietly on a seat by a rare Alaskan shrub and Lomax ignored both the girl and the shrub.

'Can I see Professor Hopcroft?' he asked Hopcroft's assistant.

'He's lecturing. He finishes at eleven and he goes right away.'

Lomax waited outside the lecture hall. When the students began to exit, he went in. Hopcroft was still at the front of the room, surrounded by students, most of them women. Lomax sat at the end of a row of empty seats where Hopcroft would notice him. Hopcroft saw him without surprise and smiled.

The two men knew each other without ever having met. Once Hopcroft had attended a series of lectures Lomax had given (When Did Time Begin?) and written Lomax a note congratulating him afterwards. It happened that Lomax had been able to return the compliment, as he had attended some of Hopcroft's lectures (The History of Child Rearing).

Hopcroft was as big as a footballer. He was one of the campus' best-known names and one of its few black teachers. He had written a psychology book about ten years ago which was now a standard student textbook. His subsequent work had been more controversial. His views occasionally embarrassed the university. Well-known to laymen, he was now marginalized by most of his peers and idolized by his followers.

'How are things at the observatory?' Hopcroft asked. His tone was familiar.

'I've taken a temporary break from the observatory. To do some other research,' said Lomax awkwardly. Hopcroft gave him a searching look and he reddened.

'What sort of research?'

'It's difficult to explain.'

'I've seen you explain the Big Bang to a room full of gum-chewing, bubble-blowing eighteen-year-olds. You can explain things.'

'I'm helping a firm of attorneys to investigate a murder. Well, two murders.'

Hopcroft raised first one eyebrow and then the other. The effect was comic. Lomax smiled for the first time that day.

'I'd sort of like to ask you some questions. If you have time.'

Hopcroft was gathering together his lecture notes and a pile of student papers.

'My car is parked right over on the west side of campus. It takes fifteen minutes to walk there, twenty if I walk and chew the fat at the same time. Can it be, you ask yourself, that after knocking Hopcroft off two out of his three committees and taking some of his office away to build a men's washroom, can it be that the dean has confiscated Hopcroft's reserved parking space? Your hackles rise in Hopcroft's support. Let those hackles fall, Dr Lomax. My parking space is right over by the chemistry department these days because that's just where I want it to be. Oh my, it was a red-tape nightmare. A psychologist who wants to park outside the chemistry department? Computers didn't like it, bureaucrats didn't like it. But I liked it. People ask me to talk and I say: You've got between here and my car without interruption. Unless we meet the dean. And that's unlikely because mostly he's in committee meetings.'

'Okay,' said Lomax. 'Fifteen minutes starting from here.'

'Twenty if you want me to walk and talk *and* think.'

As they left the building, Hopcroft snatched a few leaves from the ivy which grew round the door.

'But,' he warned, 'if you have some kind of a court case coming up and you're looking for an expert witness, we may need to be a bit more formal about it. Office, notes, coffee with spoons and little square cookies. That kind of thing.'

'Really I just would like to talk to you. I'm trying to get to know a man. Only he's dead. Every time I think I begin to understand him he sort of eludes me. And . . . I've never done anything like this before.'

'No? No? Are you sure?' hooted Hopcroft. Lomax looked at him in surprise.

'Oh, come on, Dr Lomax, you're doing it all the time. You examine stars as they were millions of years ago, knowing they're probably already dead. Of course, studying people teaches you a lot more about yourself and I imagine that's what's taking you by surprise. So tell Hopcroft. Tell him what it is about this corpse that's agitating you.'

'Do I look agitated?' asked Lomax.

'Sure. Sure.' They were passing the girl by the Alaskan shrub now. She had stopped crying. She watched them.

'Sure, Dr Lomax, you're agitated. So, this dead man. Talk about him.'

'He was aged fifty-eight. His sexual preference was for girls about thirty or even forty years younger. He may have been attracted to his second wife when she was as young as fourteen. He marries her when she's around twenty. Before long, he's having an affair with a kid of eighteen. That's the affair I know about, maybe there were more.'

'Hmmmm,' Hopcroft said. His walk slowed noticeably. The branches of a low tree overhung the path and he reached up and plucked a lone, straggling blossom.

'Hmmmm. So you want me to try to take you inside the mind of such a man to explain this attraction?'

'I guess so,' said Lomax.

'Well, put yourself in his position. Think of the pretty girls who sit in the front row of your lectures.'

Lomax thought of them. They were always pretty and they always sat at the front. They had long, clean hair which cascaded down their backs in thick waves. They wrote copious notes. They asked questions at the end of the lectures. They walked around the campus in groups.

'What's attractive about them?' Hopcroft asked.

Lomax thought hard. 'I don't find them attractive,' he said at last.

155

Hopcroft smiled, flinging his blossom delightedly in the air and catching it again.

'Okay, Okay, Dr Lomax, you don't find them attractive. Understood. Fine. But,' he swung round to stare Lomax in the eye, 'what might other people like about them?'

'Oh, I don't know. A sort of doe-eyed admiration. They're kind of eager to please.'

'And sexually. How about sexually?'

'Um . . . sexually . . . well, I guess their bodies are firm and . . . unblemished.' Lomax remembered Helen and blushed.

'Go on.'

'Some of them are sort of . . . perfect. They don't have wrinkles, scars, onesidedness, dimpled old fat. Their personalities aren't written all over their faces, hardship isn't written all over their faces . . .'

'Yes, oh yes, the loveliness of some young girls is quite indisputable.'

Lomax thought of Helen. His palms were sticky.

'The question which has been bugging me, and it's only a hunch . . .'

'Tell me. Tell me your hunch, Dr Lomax.'

'If a man's attracted to young girls the way this man was . . . if he's attracted to girls, and he has a daughter . . . would he be attracted to her?'

'Well probably,' said Hopcroft.

Lomax looked at him. Hopcroft was still throwing the blossom around. It was becoming increasingly ragged.

'You ask me if a man is likely to have been attracted to his daughter. And I say to you: Dr Lomax, most men are.'

'I mean sexually.'

'So do I.' Hopcroft put the crushed blossom in his pocket and snatched a twig from a shrub as he passed. He twirled it like a tiny baton. 'I'd regard sexual attraction between father and daughter as quite natural. Now, society seems to tolerate this idea. After all, it's been around for long enough, we're grown up now, we can handle basic Freud. We only censure fathers who act on their impulses – often, of course, under considerable sexual provocation, or even downright invitation from the daugher. I published a paper recently which suggested that, in some cases – not all cases, Dr Lomax, I stressed this, but in some cases – such sexual activity could be condoned. Of course, a lot of people are very angry with Hopcroft for saying such a bad thing.'

'Condoned?' echoed Lomax.

'I've shocked you. I've shocked you, Dr Lomax. You didn't want to talk about a dirty subject on our nice walk across the campus with all its pretty trees. Did you?'

'I did.'

'Well then, if you'll permit me to continue . . .'

Hopcroft was snatching leaves now, large, thick rubbery ones. As he tore them from the bushes they sounded like sheets of paper ripping.

'In a number of so-called primitive societies it is normal and accepted practice for a girl's first sexual partner to be her father. I'm not suggesting that there is any force or any violence, oh no, just the opposite. Because you see, the first time around, sex can be a very frightening and bewildering experience. My own research indicates that loss of virginity is far from pleasurable for most females, and, if you can remember back that far, Dr Lomax, you might be silently thinking to yourself that it's not so hot the first time for a man either. Now, in other parts of the world this is acknowledged. Here we simply romanticize the event. So who, then, is the ideal first-time partner for a woman? Answer: a man of considerable experience whom she loves and knows she can trust. Someone who will introduce her to sex with kindness and understanding. Like her father, for example.'

Lomax said nothing. Hopcroft paused to snap off a green stem.

'This man you're investigating. He had a daughter?'

'Yes.'

'Aged?'

'Early twenties. She was the other murder victim.'

'I see, I see. And you suspect — no maybe you don't even suspect, it's just a hunch — that there was some kind of sexual relationship between these two corpses? Now I wonder what gave you that idea?'

'His interest in young girls mainly . . .'

'Well, having actual sexual relations with young girls is no indication at all that he acted on his sexual inclination towards his daughter. And what if he did? What then? Do you think this has some relevance to their deaths?'

Lomax had to admit that it was hard to see how this was possible.

'Aha.' Hopcroft's mouth was full. He gnawed on a twig. 'Well, I happen to know that once you're dead our laws of privacy no longer apply. You can't be private and dead in the United States of America. Especially not if you're murdered. So if you're determined to pursue your investigation into these dead people's private and intimate affairs and if you're determined to pursue this line of investigation in particular, no one's going to stop you. In which case, the advice I give you, Dr Lomax, is stop trying to get to know the dead man and try making the acquaintance of the dead girl.'

Gail. Lomax thought hard. He had difficulty recalling her face although he had now seen her in numerous photographs. In the wedding pictures she looked lumpen and awkward. It was impossible to notice her when Julia dazzled in the same picture.

'You see,' Hopcroft explained, 'incest is generally revealed through the behaviour of the daughter, not the father.'

Lomax nodded vigorously. Of course Hopcroft was right.

'Now as a scientist you must know that it's wrong to come over judgmental about the results of your investigations. But as a man, this may cause you difficulties. I ask you to remember the scientist in you. You don't have to subscribe to my views. No. But bear in mind that not every thinking person condemns every incestuous act. Remember that before you make any judgments.'

'I don't make judgments,' said Lomax. 'At least I try not to, because I'm not always sure I'd stand up to judgment myself.'

'Uh huh. Commendable, Dr Lomax. How old is your daughter?'

Lomax was taken aback. 'She's six.'

'Is she very beautiful?' asked Hopcroft sympathetically.

'Yes,' said Lomax. He knew his voice was almost inaudible, but Hopcroft seemed to hear him.

'So are mine, and I've got three of them. God yes. And before you even think the question to yourself, Dr Lomax, no I haven't. Nor will you. So stop worrying about it. Trust yourself.'

They reached Hopcroft's car. On the passenger seat was a pile of dry leaves, twigs, branches and blossoms. Carefully, and without explanation, Hopcroft added the fractured and chewed vegetation he had collected today while Lomax thanked him. Hopcroft waved away his thanks and wished him good luck.

The sky was overcast. The atmosphere was leaden with the anticipation of rain. When Lomax turned into his drive, squirrels scuttled in front of the car without their usual elasticity. He knew he should compile his report for Frances on last night's meetings but last night was a sore, tender area of his mind which he preferred to leave untouched.

Up in his den he leafed through notebooks full of equations looking for a few blank pages. He allowed the equations to distract him. Some of them now seemed incorrect. He sat down to rework them. When he finally looked up again it was mid-afternoon and he felt refreshed as though he had been sleeping.

Reluctantly, he recalled last night. He found some empty pages in a red loose-leafed book and listed there the facts he had learned about Hegarty, about Lewis and about Alice. The equations on the facing page, precise in their small way, were steadying until he came to Alice. She was difficult to describe. She had all the fluffiness of childhood without its innocence. Involuntarily, he thought of Helen undressing in the tent and the memory led jarringly to Candice's suspicions. He remembered his own suspicions about Lewis and decided to take Hopcroft's advice.

Late in the afternoon he called Frances.

'I can't come into the office to say this because I'm not wearing a suit,' he began.

'So, Lomax, you've had enough.' There was no trace of disappointment in her voice. 'Kurt said you wouldn't last a week. If I was a betting woman, I'd have put money on you staying around until the arraignment at least.'

'I'm staying around. Only Marjorie can complete the telephone inquiries on her own. We've pooled information and she'll report to Kurt when he gets back from Zurich.'

'You knew about that?'

'Kurt called from the airport. He asked me to tell you what happened when we met Lewis's friend last night.'

'He did?' He knew she was raising her eyebrows. 'Can you give me some notes?'

'Yes, I will. But the main point Kurt wanted you to know was that, according to Alice, Lewis had another girlfriend. Another recent graduate from kindergarten. A brunette. Alice saw him with her some months before the murders.'

'That's useful. Type up some notes, Lomax.'

'I've been thinking,' he said. 'I've gotten kind of interested in Gail. Would you mind if I talk to people about her?'

'I don't mind. But the case we're trying to build is that Lewis was the intended victim, not Gail.'

'I know.'

'What line of questioning do you propose to pursue?'

'I don't know exactly,' he admitted. 'It's just that this family – Lewis and Gail and Richard – don't seem like they were ever real people at all.'

Frances' tone was unguarded. She said: 'Oh, Lewis was real enough.'

'You didn't like him.'

Frances paused before answering. 'I guess my feelings don't come into it.'

'Frances, why didn't you like him?'

'Well . . . probably I shouldn't say this. But he patronized me. And he put me down. My feeling was that he didn't welcome a woman partner in the firm.'

'Did you ever met Gail?'

'Once. A few years ago. She came to some sort of office function. At Christmas, possibly.'

'Did Lewis patronize her too?'

Frances considered. 'I don't know. I seem to remember he more or less ignored her. To someone like Lewis, looks, the way people looked . . . was important. I guess he would have wanted a beautiful daughter and Gail was sort of strange. Awkward. Difficult. Not pretty.'

'I'd like to talk to people who knew her. Teachers, friends. Maybe I could go to Seattle and see the brother . . .'

Frances sighed. 'All right, Lomax, you can talk to some of those people. But you're not working alone, you're working with us. Come into the office in a couple of days and discuss whom you've seen, what you're doing. Put your suit on and come in.'

'It's so hard to wear that dumb suit, Frances. I don't feel like me in it.'

'Then feel like someone else for a while.'

Lomax groaned.

'And don't talk to the brother. Kurt's dealing with him.'

'But he's the only other surviving family member. He can tell everything about them.'

'That's exactly why I want Kurt to interview him.'

Later that evening, Lomax delivered his notes to Sachs Smith. The receptionist had been replaced by a night security guard who took the letter but was reluctant to let him enter. Finally Lomax persuaded the man to collect the photo of Julia's wedding from his desk. The guard reappeared after a few minutes.

'Pretty girl,' he said, handing over the picture grudgingly.

Lomax agreed. His eyes were greedy for Julia. He promised Gail that, starting from tomorrow, he would apply himself to studying her.

17

The morning was grey. It had rained in the night and the grass was thick with water. Leaves dripped. From his den, Lomax could see that even the trunks of the trees were darkened by the damp. An acrobatic squirrel stared at him from the underside of a branch. The squirrel was damp too.

Gail wore a dress which Lomax guessed had been bought especially for the wedding. Something about her stiffness suggested that she had not worn it before. She had probably not enjoyed choosing the dress or trying it on. She stood awkwardly, her weight shifted to one side.

Lomax's eyes strayed to Julia. The lines of her cheekbones and jaw were so sharp that they cast small, triangular shadows. With an effort, he looked back to Gail. He noticed the thickness of her chin and the fullness of her waist. Julia's waist was hidden by her marriage bouquet. Above it, pinned to her dress, a jewel sparkled. On the hand holding the bouquet a wedding ring was visible. Lomax wanted to examine her fingers, each one of them in turn.

He made himself study Gail's dangling hands. She had not known what to do with them and they were creased into loose fists. She wore a wrist watch. It was one of the two watches Lomax had noticed in the police photographs and it was probably the only feature recognizable in both the police and the wedding pictures. This Gail wore unattractive hornrimmed glasses. Her lips seemed to be parted by dental work. She was smiling but her expression was scarcely formed, so that she might have been about to cry or speak instead of smile. Lomax found the half smile interesting. He liked the way she looked past the camera. Was she looking at someone who had made her smile that way? Or was she smiling at some secret thought?

'She was kind of cute,' he said to Julia over the phone.

'Yes,' agreed Julia, 'I guess so.'

'But not pretty. Did she lose that puppy fat later on?'

'Um . . . I think she dieted.'

Julia's voice was helpful, as if she was anxious to supply information. But, as usual, she revealed nothing.

'How long did she live with you?'

'She moved in around the time Lewis and I married. And she moved out again when she was a sophomore at Tradescant.'

He hovered over his question before asking it. Then he said: 'Did you like her?'

There was a pause.

'Of course, Lomax. I loved her. She was family.'

He had asked a few simple questions and she was already sounding bruised by them. She bruised easily. He made his voice as gentle as he could.

'Was it like having a daughter of your own?'

'Well . . . I guess so . . . But Richard and Gail didn't see me as a mother.'

'Like what then?' he persisted. 'A friend?'

'Or a sister. I mean, Richard was almost the same age and Gail was just a few years younger. I was like a big sister for her.'

'And you. Did you like having a little sister around?'

'Yes! I always wanted one. I used to . . . don't laugh at this, but I used to pretend I had a little sister.'

Lomax looked at the wedding picture. The lumpen Gail smiled to herself. He was sure Julia's imaginary sister had been nothing like this.

'I imagined a sister and then I really did have one. It was nice.'

Lomax found himself thinking about his own sister. As a small boy, he had imagined a sister and then one had appeared, when he was eight years old. It was hard to escape the feeling that he had invented this monster himself. But as time went on, he resented her less. She was a quiet baby and she grew quieter. He remembered a tiny figure in bulging diapers, absorbed in some silent game out in the yard. He was glancing at her through the open window and she did not see him. And later, much later, during a college vacation when he was thinking about girls and math, he could see her from his room, waiting for the school bus alone at the end of the drive. She was tall and slim and stood with her head bowed a little. Her hair was tied in a straight line which ran along the nape of her neck and half way down her back. She carried some musical instrument in a small, square case. What was it? A flute?

He asked: 'Why did Gail move in with you?'

'Her mother was a drunk. She'd been a drunk for years. That's why Lewis left her. And when it just got too much for Gail, Vicky moved into a care facility and Lewis had her live with us here.'

'That was tough on Gail.'

'It was terrible for her. Awful. Looking after her mother, apologizing for her mother, embarrassed by her mother.'

'Good thing for Gail that she found you.'

Julia laughed softly. 'Good thing for me that Lewis found me,' she said, in a tone of such affection that Lomax felt crushed. He did not ask any more questions.

'I've never told you about Doberman's party,' Julia reminded him. 'Don't you want to hear about it?'

Lomax didn't. 'Sure,' he said.

'It was so nice,' she told him, 'because Professor Berlins was there.'

'Oh? How was he?'

'Just as cute as ever. It was fun, you should have come.'

'I wasn't invited.'

Lomax felt sour. He knew this was nothing to do with Doberman or his party. He was still stung by the tone Julia had used when she talked about Lewis. He reminded himself that Lewis was dead. Julia spoke of him in that adoring voice because she did not know Lewis was sleeping with a girl from the club who was barely out of kindergarten. He was tempted, for a moment, to tell Julia about Alice instead of protecting her from the information.

She was listing the people who had been at Doberman's party. 'Everyone expected you. They were asking where were you? And then, at the end, some of us worked out.'

'You worked out after the party?'

Julia's voice was proud. 'After the party. Isn't that something?'

Where was there to work out at the observatory apart from somebody's bedroom? A couple of the astronomers had rowing machines or exercise bicycles in their rooms. Doberman had dumbells.

'Where?' barked Lomax.

Julia was surprised. 'In the new gym.'

He could not control his tone. 'New gym? What new fucking gym?'

'Didn't I tell you about it?'

'No.'

'You know all that noise and dust in C wing?'

Lomax dimly recollected a few whistling, shirtless workmen. He had watched from the staff residence as Julia crossed the asphalt one day and the men stopped work to stare at her.

'Well, they were making a new gym. Dixon Driver had it installed.'

'A gym? How much has this goddam gym cost, for Chrissake?'

'Lomax, don't be a party pooper. Dixon Driver made a pledge to staff in the last newsletter. Better food and more health opportunities. He's improving the cafeteria and he's opened this gym.'

'God,' said Lomax.

'Doberman goes in there and you should see . . .' Julia began to giggle. 'You should see his little legs going round and round on the exercycle.'

She could not stop giggling at the thought of Doberman's legs going round and round.

'It's supposed to be a scientific institution, not a health farm,' said Lomax.

'You're such a grouch. Everyone loves the gym. Everyone uses it. Good health makes work good.'

He was irritated. He was sure Julia was using Dixon Driver's words.

'Everyone?' He was confident that Kim would have had something cutting to say about the gym.

'Everyone.'

'Even Kim?'

'Especially Kim. She's lost three pounds already. She's on a weight-loss programme.'

Lomax was silent for a moment. 'Did anyone say . . . doesn't anyone think that the money could have gone into one of the research projects? One of the projects which is struggling for lack of funds?'

'Professor Berlins said just that at the party but Doberman told him that the gym cost maybe fifteen minutes of telescope time.'

'What did Berlins say?'

'Nothing. He didn't work out with us in the middle of the night but I guess that's because he's too old.'

Working out in the middle of the night. Lomax felt disgust. How did he know whether she had slept with Doberman or Yevgeny or McMahon after working out with them in the middle of the night? The thought of any of these men enjoying Julia's particular talents made his body stiff with rage and jealousy. He was angry with the men but the shots ricocheted around Julia. How did she feel about him, Lomax, for Chrissake? She gave no indication. There were no endearments as the call neared its end. And she gave no sign that she was grateful for his efforts at Sachs Smith. Then, just as they were about to hang up she said: 'Can I see you soon?'

'Well, yes.'

'I mean, alone this time?' Her voice was liquid with sexual promise.

'Yes, of course,' said Lomax. 'When?'

'Just as soon as I can get away from here,' she assured him. And he ended the call aroused instead of angry.

It was a few minutes before he could make any more calls. Without noticing what he was doing he began to rearrange things around the house in an unsystematic way. He moved piles of papers and blew the dust off some of the shelves but not all of them. Then he collected the dirty coffee cups. They were scattered in various rooms and many had interesting mould growing inside them. He studied this for a while in the kitchen and left them stacked by the sink. Then he telephoned Gail's mother. Vicky Fox was unable to remember his previous call.

'Are you a friend of Lewis' or a policeman or are you from Sachs Smith or what?' she asked.

'I'm from Sachs Smith. I'd like to come over and talk to you about Gail.'

'Oh,' she said, her voice neutral. 'Two policemen came by after Gail died, and a few reporters, but none of them ever came back.' It was easy to guess why.

She tried to give him directions to her home. She was unable to remember the number. 'Thirty-nine, thirty. No, thirty, thirty-five. No, maybe there's an eight in it . . .'

It occurred to Lomax that Mrs Fox might have engineered this confusion to prevent him ever arriving. He ended the call with a selection of possible addresses, assuring her that he would find his way. The sun had broken round the side of the house, suddenly, like a crook, and it made him anxious to be outside. He told Mrs Fox he would be over soon.

He made himself a meal, a late breakfast or an early lunch. He carried his food out through the back of the house onto the deck. He wore no shoes. His feet made a pleasant slapping sound on the warm wood and the sun shone onto his toes. They were still winter white. He ate greedily, direct from the pan, looking at his overgrown and sloping acre of land. It was wild, the way it had been when he and Candice moved in, the way it had been before the house was built, perhaps the way it had been when there was a ranch on this hillside. In places, the children had made camps. There were occasional flashes of bright colour where toys lay beneath the trees and bushes. Near the deck a rope swing hung from the largest tree. Below it the ground was scuffed bare. Joel had climbed the tree a few years ago and fallen and he had roared with pain as Lomax had carried him, running, to the car. Candice had driven them to the hospital, her face blanched, hooting and swearing at the other drivers. The doctor had stitched the cut on Joel's head and said he would be fine.

Lomax padded to the edge of the deck and leaned against the wooden railings. The sun was hotter now. He took his shirt off. The deck never failed to please him and annoy him because he had made it himself and it was good in places and imperfect in others. It jutted out over the sloping hillside, embracing a couple of trees which grew there. He had built the deck round them and they had continued to grow through it until now they were almost as high as the house. In another few years they would shade it. The squirrels already climbed them. He remembered the summer weekends when he had cut the wood for the deck and sanded it and treated it and jointed it and nailed it. He remembered a workshop where the tools were neatly hung along a wall at the same angle and even the dirty rags were in a bag labelled 'Dirty rags'. Whose workshop? Not his own, which was chaotic.

A dog barked. For a moment, he thought it was Deputy. Deputy and Joel had not been allowed on the deck while Lomax was working there because the railings were last to go into place and Candice was scared they would fall over the edge. Sometimes Joel and Deputy would watch through the window as Candice brought Lomax an icy cold beer, or they would sit below, in Lomax's shade, Deputy thumping his tail in the dirt.

He remembered Gail. Her name had been chiselled in the neat workshop. She had liked to work in the basement with the janitor. His name was Mr Weinhart and he was another of the people who had died.

Suddenly Deputy Dawg shot into view. He hurtled briefly through the bushes, barking, then disappeared. As Lomax rounded the house he heard voices. Candice and the children, hindered by Deputy, were getting out of the car. It was a complicated procedure which involved yelling and slamming and barking. Lomax's heart leapt at the sight of them. Then he remembered.

'Hi!' said Candice cheerfully, as if nothing had happened.

Helen ran up to him and clasped his legs. He bent to pick her up but remembered again and drew back.

'Pick me up, pick me up,' she said. She was shouting. The air around the three of them was restless and excited. It made the dog bark. He picked her up and she put her arms around his neck.

'Don't scratch me,' she screamed when he kissed her.

'Hi, Dad,' said Joel soberly.

'We decided to pay a surprise visit,' Candice told him. She walked inside the house. Lomax wondered if she still had a key. It was the first time in a long while that she had been back.

'Paint's peeling right here,' she reported.

Helen explained that their mother had taken them out of school that day. She had told their teachers that they had to visit their father.

'Why? I'm not sick,' said Lomax.

'Well I just wanted to bring them over.'

'I was going out.'

'You have time for a coffee,' said Candice. She started to make it, moving with familiarity around the kitchen which had once been her kitchen. She made clicking noises at the pile of coffee cups with their picturesque mould. She rinsed glasses for the children and made them cold drinks. She found two clean coffee cups.

Joel and Helen and Deputy ran from room to room.

'You've cleaned up the house, Daddy!' called Helen.

'Just this morning,' Lomax told her.

'This is clean?' said Candice.

The children went outside. They could be seen crossing the deck now. Candice shouted: 'Don't climb that tree, Joel.'

'Mom,' Joel said frigidly, reappearing briefly in the kitchen. 'I was like four years old then.'

They made a lot of noise in the yard. They knew, without any explanation, that this visit was some sort of reconciliation and they were happy. Their mood was infectious but Lomax was determined to resist it.

'Why are you here?' he asked Candice.

'Now, don't be hostile.'

'If you've come to apologize, why don't you apologize instead of walking into my house like you still lived here?'

'Oh.' She stood still for the first time since her arrival. 'Oh. Oh. You're mad at me.'

'Do you have any idea,' said Lomax, his voice too loud, 'what it's like being under suspicion?'

He knew now, by the misery he had experienced over the last few days, what Berlins had experienced, and what Julia was experiencing. Being under suspicion was destructive. It isolated you until you even began to put yourself under suspicion.

Candice made their coffee in silence. She sat down at the table. The wedding photo of Julia and Lewis and Richard and Gail was right in front of her but she seemed not to notice it.

'I'm sorry,' she said at last. 'You have to forgive me.'

'No I don't have to.'

'Please. For the children. And for my sake too. Sometimes I get hold of the wrong idea and go too far with it. And when I remember the things I said and did I . . . it's just like someone else said and did them. Lomax, you always stopped me from going too near the edge. It's something you've always done for me.'

'Now Robert has to do that.'

'It's hard for him to interfere where our children are concerned.'

'What do you want me to do?'

'Forget the whole stupid conversation.'

He sat down with her. She looked relieved. They were sitting at a table together discussing something intimate over coffee. This was how Candice liked discussions to be. This was how she solved problems. She stirred her coffee unnecessarily. She was at her most potent now.

'Candice. I've never touched Helen in that way and I never will. But it's hard to draw boundaries round your love for a child or any person. Do you understand me?'

Candice nodded vigorously. She did not want any more misunderstandings. But he knew that for her love was simpler. During their divorce she had decided exactly when they should stop sleeping together and the decision had been easy, obvious even.

'I must have been crazy to suspect . . . I mean, when I saw Helen with you right now . . . Tell me you forgive me.'

She had not been crazy to suspect him. He even wondered if Helen's display of affection out on the drive hadn't been some unspoken father–daughter conspiracy.

'I forgive you,' said Lomax.

'Who's that?' asked Helen when she returned to the kitchen with an empty glass. She pointed at the wedding photograph.

'You recognize Julia,' Lomax prompted her.

Candice picked up the photo and studied it with interest. 'She sure is pretty,' she said.

Helen's smile was goofy. She swung on the back of her mother's chair. 'Julia smells nice. And she showed me how to wash my hands.'

Candice pushed her from the chairback. 'You already know how to wash up,' she said.

'Well Julia showed me an extra good way to do it,' called Helen behind her as she left the room.

Candice did not look up from the picture. 'What are the names of the stepchildren?'

'Gail and Richard.'

'So,' she mused, 'Gail's dead now. And the husband.'

'Supposing,' said Lomax, 'that someone looking like Gail walked into the clinic one day.'

'Uh huh.'

'What would you think, what would you say?'

'God. Well. I'm not sure.'

'Try.'

'Um . . . well, she's a mess. I mean, that dress. Did she choose it herself? If she did, then she either didn't look in the mirror at all or she looked and she saw . . . I don't know . . . something completely different.'

'What exactly is wrong with the dress?'

'Lomax, for God's sake, it's horrible. It would be horrible on anyone but in her case it simply emphasizes her weight problem. Then her hair . . . she's just not trying. Split ends. Lifeless. See how it sort of fades away? It's a long time since anyone cut it. It's such a dull colour. I mean, mice are that colour.'

Candice's hair had once been the colour of mice. Lomax shot her a rapid look but she did not return it.

'And the way she's standing, kind of defensive and yet the look on her face . . . it's knowing. Maybe even defiant? She's the kind of kid who would come to the clinic for a makeover and then argue with every recommendation we made. Oh, did I mention the glasses? They're wrong too.'

'Maybe . . .' began Lomax carefully. There had been a time in their marriage, in the early days of the clinic, when it was impossible to discuss Candice's business without arguing about it. 'Maybe . . . she liked herself that way?'

'Then I guess she wouldn't come to the clinic. But I'm not sure she does like herself that way. She's standing next to this . . . well, this beautiful woman; she must be aware of the difference. And, like I said, the posture's defensive.'

'What would you do to her? You and your clinicians?'

Candice scanned him for irony. Her expression was both comical and challenging. 'Well, we'd make her feel better about herself, Lomax.'

They went outside. Lomax pushed the children on the rope swing for a while. It made a comfortable, rhythmic, creaking noise.

Candice talked about the clinic. She told him about a new member of staff. Her real name was Alison but she was called the Nose. She had been the nose of big cosmetics companies in Europe and America and she had come to work here five years ago. She could have chosen anywhere in the world but she came to a small, new perfumery in the mountains because the air was clear. Her nose was so sensitive that everyday smells which most people hardly noticed could drive her crazy. Daily life was almost unbearable. She had left the perfumery after a nervous breakdown. Now she was working for Candice, mixing simple fragrances specifically for wealthy clients.

'She can smell what shampoo you use,' Helen said from the swing.

'She can smell where you dropped sauce on the rug six months ago. She's amazing.'

'I hope I never meet her,' said Lomax.

'Push harder,' shrieked Joel or Helen. They clung together on the rope like insects, a conglomeration of legs and arms. Candice shoved them when they swung close enough and they swung away again.

'She designed a fragrance especially for me,' Candice said.

Lomax sniffed at her.

'Behind my ears.'

He snuffled around her ears. The movement was intimate, the most intimate for a long time, and it reminded him of the distance between them now. The fine lines around her eyes looked sharper than he remembered. She wore earrings. Her hair was lighter. The children watched intently from their swing.

'What do you smell?'

Lomax hesitated. 'Nothing,' he admitted.

Candice's face clouded. 'That's just what Robert said. Her fragrances are wonderful but they aren't strong enough for ordinary noses. I'll speak to her about it.'

Lomax sniffed the air around Candice again. He could smell rope and bruised grass and dust. He could smell that summer was imminent. He could even smell Deputy Dawg.

'Maybe she's putting water into bottles and letting your imagination supply the rest.'

He was playing the cynic. It was his usual stance in these conversations.

'You can smell her fragrances indoors,' Candice assured him. 'Clients love them. We already have more orders than she can handle.'

She liked to talk about the clinic this way, presenting it as anecdotes and gossip and people. It seemed less like the place they used to argue about.

When Lomax said he had to go, explaining that Mrs Fox was

waiting for him, the children chased Deputy Dawg around the garden trying to catch him and load him back into the car. Their exit was accompanied by the same commotion as their arrival. Candice and Helen both kissed him goodbye.

'What's going on, Dad?' Joel asked.

'Search me,' said Lomax.

'Are you sick?'

'No, of course not.'

When they had gone, Lomax locked the house. He had forgotten to ask Candice if she still had a key. If she did, he wanted to take it from her and give it to Julia. Maybe Julia would come here during the arraignment to escape from the press. They could lock all the doors and stay inside together. He whistled tunelessly as he climbed into his car.

He drove west towards Mrs Fox's condominium with the sun in his eyes. He guessed from the three addresses she had given that she lived somewhere on the edge of town and when he arrived he found he was right under the mountains. A sign in the car park asked him to be quiet. It said: 'This is a Care Condominium managed by Medihomes Incorporated' and gave a toll-free telephone number to dial for more information. Lomax wondered whether he should write down the number. Probably Kurt would. He felt under the seats among balls of doghair and sticky candy papers but was unable to find a pen. He parked the car.

It was still only early afternoon. The mountains were already throwing their shadows across the complex. Mrs Fox was already drunk.

She led him through the house. Most of the doors were shut and where they were open he could see nothing because the drapes were closed. Peering into a dark room as he passed, he tripped over a telephone table in the hall.

'Oops!' roared Mrs Fox too loudly on his behalf. She invited him to join her on the patio. As he sat down the chair creaked. He remembered the creaking rope swing in his own back yard. He wished he was pushing Helen and Joel on it still.

The homes were arranged around swimming pools. The windows and terraces looked inward at the pools as if it was dangerous to acknowledge the presence of the overbearing mountains right outside. Lomax and Mrs Fox watched a bony old man swimming lengths. His action was laborious. His thin elbows protruded from the water like blades.

'That man asked me to marry him,' Mrs Fox confided. She shuffled her seat closer to Lomax and leaned towards him. The air around her was thick with alcohol.

'He's too old for you,' Lomax told her gallantly. That was what Kurt would have said. He felt ashamed of himself but Mrs Fox chortled with delight. She began to talk about the condominium, its regulations and its weekly barbecues. Whenever her eyes met his they darted away again. Some private paranoia told her to be scared of him.

'Did you live in town before you moved here?' Lomax asked.

She nodded. 'On Belmont. And before that, in Arizona.' And she recited her Arizona address like a child, giving it a rhythm and stressing the way five rhymed with drive. Lomax memorized it.

'Lewis had a nice house built specially for us. I could stand in the kitchen and call them for dinner and the house was so big they wouldn't even hear me! It was so big . . .' Mrs Fox stretched her arms wide to indicate big, knocking against Lomax's chest as she did so '. . . that the rooms had intercoms. When we ate dinner, we could see all the lights of the city. That was nice.'

Lomax imagined a young woman, aproned, fixing lunch for her family. She was leaning over an intercom saying: 'Lunch's ready,' and there was the sound of approaching footsteps and loud, cheerful, childish voices. It was impossible to pretend Mrs Fox had ever been that mother. Julia said that Gail had looked after her mother, apologized for her, been embarrassed by her.

She sat without dignity, her shoulders rounded, her knees far apart. Her face was cracked by alcohol. Perhaps she had the same nose as the Gail in the pictures. Perhaps. There was a lopsidedness to her grin which was familiar.

'I wasn't beautiful but I was a very pretty girl,' she said suddenly. She had known, without looking at him, that he was scrutinizing her. 'Lewis fell in love with me when he was just divorced.'

'Lewis was married before?'

'Yeah, to this girl who sort of changed. I married him when I was twenty years old. But he sort of changed.'

'How did he change?'

'Ambition. I don't know. Everyone changes. No one stays the same. Lewis changed, Gail changed. I'm the only person who stays the same.'

Unexpectedly she turned to him. 'Do you change?'

'No, Mrs Fox. Sometimes I feel like the only person who stays the same too.'

In the course of the ensuing conversation she lapsed from logic to incoherence and back again. Was she as confused as she appeared? Or, like a child, did she have moments of startling lucidity?

Lomax felt hot and tired. He watched the swimmer and envied him the coolness of the water. The man turned now at the end of a length and began his laborious progress back down the pool. The tiny waves he created caught the sunlight and refracted it with painful intensity. Lomax closed his eyes. Mrs Fox was still talking but her voice was receding.

'See, people change. Lewis changed his name. When he was a little boy. The whole family did. They changed their name to Fox. They wanted to sound American. But his mother couldn't even speak American.'

Lomax learned that Lewis' mother liked to cook. Whenever anyone came to the house they had to eat something.

'It didn't matter if it was ten in the morning or five in the afternoon, she'd come at you with plates of food, talking in her language, shhh this shhh that, she had all these shhh sounds but with enough American words for you to know what she meant. You had to eat. You could not leave the goddam house – ' Mrs Fox was convulsed with laughter – 'without eating.'

Lewis and his new wife had stayed with his mother in the mid-west while they waited for their house to be built in Arizona. Lewis' mother had turned Vicky Fox from a pretty, slender girl into a young version of herself.

'I was a meatball. Fatso. Lewis was disgusted. She showed me how to cook like she did but Lewis didn't want that kind of food. He wanted an American wife who cooked American food and was American slim. He didn't want her kind of food. He was born in America, he was American. But he cried when she died. And you know what she died of? Fat!'

She rose and went into the house. She had offered Lomax a drink on his arrival and he had asked for something cool but Mrs Fox had forgotten to bring it. Throughout their conversation she had regularly disappeared through the sliding doors, sometimes on the pretext that she thought she heard the phone ring, sometimes in mid-sentence with no explanation at all. She always returned wet-lipped. Deputy Dawg's behaviour was similar on a hot day.

When she re-emerged, Lomax tried to ask her questions about Gail.

'We were a very happy family,' Mrs Fox said. She was making a statement. Lomax remembered someone else using those exact words in that exact tone. Julia, when she had first shown him the wedding picture.

She had forgotten who he was again.

'I'm from Sachs Smith.'

This information did not interest Mrs Fox.

'It seems from the telephone records that Gail called you from her apartment early on the morning of the murders,' Lomax said. He had selected this detail from all the other details in the police's three thick boxes as being of special interest. It probably meant that Gail and Lewis had not arrived at the apartment and found the killer waiting for them. It probably meant there was sufficient time before the killer's arrival for Gail to do the most natural thing in the world after returning from a long trip: call her mother.

Mrs Fox shrugged.

'I don't remember.'

'The call lasted about four and a half minutes.'

'Well. Sometimes I think she did call me. And sometimes I think I just dreamed she called me. And sometimes I don't remember her calling me at all.'

Lomax tried to press her further but the answers were rambling and incoherent and the exits more frequent.

'I have to go,' said Lomax, getting up. He tried to feel compassion for this sad, sick woman whose daughter had been murdered, but all he could feel was weariness.

'Okay,' said Mrs Fox.

'Maybe I'll come back and see you one morning? Would that be convenient?'

Her eyes darted. 'I have this leg. I don't get up some mornings,' she said.

Lomax told her he would call. Out in the pool area the old man had completed his swimming regime. He sat on the side, his legs disappearing into the water at knee level. There was a towel around his neck. His ribs and the shadows beneath them were clearly visible.

'Stripy old zebra, see!' exclaimed Mrs Fox. 'He's too old for me and besides, he's a zebra.'

Her hands shook as she unlocked the door at the front of the house for him. She was physically weak. He could not imagine her driving to Gail's apartment, pointing a gun and firing it three times. He could not imagine she would remain lucid for long enough to plan and execute the murders.

'Do you have a car?' he asked her.

She looked up at him. 'No.'

As he was about to leave he asked her whether she knew that Julia had been arrested.

'Yes,' she said. Her face was motionless.

On the way home he detoured to the university. The shops in the small campus mall were closing. He bought some pens and a couple of theme books. The university symbol, a mountain lion, slouched across their covers. The symbol was the subject of occasional debate in college committee meetings. Some people thought the lion should roar or run instead of just grinning and looking louche.

Lomax leafed through the empty pages. He wanted to fill them with notes which he would assimilate after sunset. This was the way he had always worked. His den was full of notebooks. But today there was nothing to write. He decided to go to the French department. He hoped someone there might remember Gail and say something enlightening about her.

The campus was almost empty. Students walked singly, with books under their arms. They moved more slowly than morning students. A class attempted in silence to photograph the weird, knotted shadows of the famous vegetation. They contorted their bodies to keep their own shadows out of their pictures. Lomax found himself walking along Hopcroft's route. Freshly broken leaves and twigs and the occasional evidence of trampled blossom told him that Hopcroft had passed this way recently but, to Lomax's disappointment, he did not appear now.

The French department was closing. An apologetic secretary was switching off her computer and putting pens into her desk drawers. She did not personally remember Gail. When she and her colleagues had read about the murders they had all tried hard to recall her but the two members of the department who had taught her had now left California. One was teaching in Canada. The other was French and had returned to France.

'No one else remembered her?'

'I'm not real sure,' said the secretary. She was standing now, a small purse hanging from her shoulder. She faced the exit instead of facing Lomax and he could smell her hairspray. Lomax guessed that she was anxious not to be late for a date.

'I'm sorry,' she was saying, with a perfect white smile of apology. 'They've all gone home. I'll ask around for you and you can call me, but right now nobody's here.'

Lomax nodded. It was a fine evening. They could read student papers on the verandah or walk the dog up in the foothills or embark on some small home improvements project now that summer was in the air.

He strolled back to his car across the deserted campus. The air was thinning as the evening light dimmed. A couple of security guards cruised by. They parked and sat smoking cigarettes, their arms hanging from the open windows. The smoke rose vertically in the still air. He could hear their speech, occasional and relaxed.

He bought a pizza. The aroma of salami and tomato and cheese and olives filled the car. When he arrived home it was night and the air was cool. He picked up the box and it was pleasantly warm. His stomach gurgled in anticipation. On the kitchen table were the coffee cups he and Candice had used that morning. He moved them aside and opened the box, releasing a wave of warm, edible odours. He ate a couple of slices and the telephone rang. He hovered over the rest of the pizza. But, hoping that the call was from Julia, he picked up the receiver.

'Hello, Lomax,' said Frances. 'I thought I should remind you that Julia's arraignment's scheduled for next Wednesday. It'll be press, TV, newspapers, hassle. So please, stay right away from her.'

'But maybe she could hunker down here,' he suggested. He knew what Frances' answer would be.

'Nope, that's dangerous. If you want to help her then keep away. She has to be the grieving widow.'

Lomax was too miserable at this prospect to reply.

'You can call her,' said Frances kindly.

'Thanks,' said Lomax. He asked Frances what would happen at the arraignment.

'First Julia pleads not guilty. Then there are a few technicalities to sort out. It won't take long.'

'Like what technicalities?'

'Well, I'm hoping Julia will agree to waive time. Basically, that means her case won't come to trial for quite a while. If she doesn't waive, then we're in court within eight weeks. That's this summer. That's soon.'

'But don't you want the whole goddam thing to be over?' asked Lomax.

Frances paused before she spoke. 'I understand that Julia does. But we don't have much of a case yet. So we need all the time we can get. And from a personal point of view . . .' She hesitated. 'Well . . . I admit I was looking forward to a family vacation in August.'

Lomax's silence seemed to prompt Frances into continuing. She spoke faster than usual. 'If Julia wants an August trial, then of course I'll cancel my vacation. Of course. It's just that it's hard for my children to understand why Mommy's too busy to go away with them.'

'It's okay, don't be defensive,' Lomax reassured her. 'This trial is the most important thing for me and for Julia but . . . naturally, it's different for you.'

He could hear insincerity in his voice. He knew he resented Frances' detachment. Julia's life was under threat but at the end of each day Frances could escape to her happy family, her other world, and whatever the outcome of the trial, that other world would still be waiting and her life would continue in just the same way. Frances seemed to sense all this and an awkwardness hung between them. Then she replied just as though he had spoken his thoughts.

'In my job I see the worst. The worst crimes, the worst actions, the worst people. Without my family, I'd go insane. Or even . . .' Her voice twisted. '. . . get down there in the dirt with them all.' When Lomax did not speak she added: 'I'm not exaggerating. I've seen defence attorneys lose their minds.'

'I understand,' he said. It was true for a few moments. Julia's case flickered before him as it was for Frances. Another human mess, with its foolishnesses, its inconsistencies, its protests of outraged innocence, its passionate friends and relatives, its explosion of uncontainable detail. Frances had to impose coherence on all this. And, when she had finished, she would start all over again on another mess.

When they had hung up, he rapidly regained his own perspective. The case became again Julia's misfortune. Her life was in danger and all Frances could think of was her family vacation.

He opened one of his new theme books. Frances had told him it was essential to record everything. On the first page he wrote the date and time of his visit to Mrs Fox. He added her address and Gail's girlhood address in Arizona. But there seemed little else to record. The rest of the conversation had been incoherent, irrelevant or untrue.

He called Julia.

'Wait while I fetch a towel,' she told him. 'I just got out of the shower.'

She came back.

'Now what are you wearing?'

She giggled. 'Almost nothing.'

'Oh God.'

She giggled again. Lomax felt his jeans tighten.

'I wish you were here right now,' she said. Her mouth was close to the receiver. Her voice was breathy.

He said despairingly: 'Frances just telephoned to say we shouldn't meet for a while longer.'

'Oh . . .' She sounded disappointed. 'Why?'

'Because your arraignment's next Wednesday.'

There was silence.

'Didn't you know?'

'Wednesday . . .' she repeated softly and the playfulness was gone from her voice. She was the small and scared and vulnerable Julia again.

'Julia, I thought they fixed the date when they set bail.'

'They did. It's just I put it out of my mind. Because I didn't think it would get this far. I mean . . . I thought everyone would have realized by now that it's a mistake.'

Lomax struggled for words. He was helpless, here at the end of a phone, to comfort her. 'As soon as the press leave you alone,' he suggested, 'we could go away together. On a vacation. Somewhere secret where no one will find us. And we'll forget all about it for a while.'

'I don't like vacations,' she said unexpectedly.

'Everybody likes vacations.'

There was a long, thinking pause. Was she thinking about vacations or arraignments? 'They won't like me taking Wednesday off work,' she said at last. 'There's a meeting.'

'What are all these meetings?'

'Oh, Dixon Driver's eclipse committee.' She sounded tired now. 'We had our first planning meeting today.'

Dixon Driver's eclipse committee. The name implied that Driver was personally organizing the entire celestial event. It was typical of the man's pomposity.

'And what did they plan?' Lomax had no interest in Julia's answer. He only wanted to stop her from retreating into sadness and silence.

'There's going to be about five hundred school children here at the observatory,' she said, 'and a senator and a whole load of important people and possibly the governor.'

Lomax groaned. 'What about movie stars?' he asked sarcastically, but Julia did not recognize his tone.

'There'll be movie stars tracking the eclipse with Dixon Driver in the jet.'

'A jet?'

'Dixon plans to sort of race along with the eclipse for a few hours. Right across California and out over the Pacific.'

Lomax groaned again.

'Why do you keep making those funny elephant noises? I mean . . . it's my job, Lomax. I like it here. I like committee meetings,' she said reproachfully.

He felt ashamed. Of course committee meetings, even for Driver's ludicrous eclipse event, were better than hearing your double-murder charge read out in court.

'I'm sorry,' he said, and when she did not reply he added, 'You know what I did today? I met Gail's mother.'

'Vicky? Was she drunk?'

'Yes.'

There was something strange about Julia's voice. She was saying: 'It's hard to tell whether she's drunk sometimes. The alcohol's damaged her brain.'

Definitely something strange.

'She smelled of liquor,' he said. But Julia did not reply.

'Are you okay?'

He heard her sob softly. He felt a strange movement, a contraction, in his stomach.

'Julia?'

She sobbed again. The sob was muscular. It had fought long and hard for its escape.

'Oh God. God, maybe I should come up to the observatory.' This was torture.

'It's okay,' she said, her voice broken by tears now.

'Julia, why don't I just come right away?'

'I'll be fine in a minute . . .'

But she was not fine. The violence of the sobs shaking her body prevented her from speaking. He listened to her. The sound was causing him actual physical pain now, somewhere high in his belly.

'It's just I sort of thought the arraignment would never really happen and . . .'

There was a knock at her door, so forceful that Lomax could hear it. 'Shit,' he said.

Julia cleared her throat and gathered her voice. 'Who is it?' she called thickly. Lomax could not hear the reply.

'Oh!' said Julia.

'Who is it?' demanded Lomax.

'Just a minute,' Julia told him. She had stopped crying. She put down the receiver and answered the door. Lomax listened. The visitor was male. Lomax's stomach contracted still further. He knew from the tone of the man's voice that Julia's face was tear-stained. He guessed her hair would be wet from tears and clinging to her cheekbones to emphasize their beauty. He clamped the receiver to his ear and held his body motionless. The man was approaching now.

'. . . persuade you that we need more time to construct a really strong defence . . .' he was saying. Lomax recognized Kurt's voice. Kurt was back from Zurich and now he had arrived to persuade Julia to waive time at her arraignment. He was there. He would be able to put his arm around Julia if she cried again.

The receiver was picked up.

'Lomax, it's okay,' came Julia's voice, different now. 'Kurt's here.'

'For Chrissake! I'm coming up the mountain,' Lomax said.

'You don't need to. I'm fine. I'm sorry. I didn't mean to cry. It's just I never really thought it would get as far as this . . .'

'Julia, listen –'

'I have to go change. Kurt's waiting. He wants to explain what happens at an arraignment,' she said.

'Will you call me later, so I know you're all right? When he's gone?'

'I'll try.'

Julia had asked Kurt into her room. She had been wearing only a towel. Lomax's appetite vanished. The pizza congealed on the table. He wanted to get into his car right now and drive through the dark around the hairpin bends and walk straight to her room and knock forcefully on her door the way Kurt had. Who the hell had let Kurt into the staff residence anyway? There was supposed to be keycard entry. There was supposed to be security.

He imagined arriving at Julia's room and finding Kurt comforting her there. What would he do, apart from look foolish? He had no rights or claims over Julia and he was unsure of his status in her life.

He stared at the pizza. The cheese on it had set hard now.

Some time later he was disturbed by a noise, occasional at first and then persistent. He wondered whether the discordant clangs were generated inside his head. Then he knew that there must be someone outside the house.

The noise was coming from the deck. He turned off the lights indoors and suddenly he was alone in the blackness. This was his own home and he could move through the dark here as fluidly as any night animal. He would have the advantage over an intruder.

He made his way to the window. Gradually the darkness thinned. From here, his body half-turned, he could survey the deck unseen. There was a racoon on the bench, its head buried in the pan he had left there that morning. Its feet danced on the table as it rolled the pan from side to side, clawing at the remains of Lomax's meal. Sometimes it lifted its sharp, masked face and looked about. When it had finished eating, it ran away. Lomax went outside and leaned on the railings. He could hear distant rustlings in the undergrowth, perhaps the same racoon.

Julia still had not telephoned to say Kurt had left.

Finally he went to bed, reluctant to shower in case the sound of the water drowned the sound of the bell.

At one o'clock in the morning he called her. The phone rang three times.

'Hallo?'

Had she been asleep? 'It's me. Are you okay?'

'I'm fine, Lomax.'

'When did he go?'

'Who?'

'Kurt.'

She yawned. 'I don't know what time. I went straight to sleep the moment he left. That's why I didn't call you.'

It was morning before Lomax fell asleep and lunchtime when he woke up, his head aching as though he had spent the night drinking.

He showered but felt no better. He made coffee. He sat on the deck eating a slice of cold pizza and compiling a list of people to call. Inside, the house was quiet. It was hard to start work.

He planned to find peers, friends or teachers of Gail Fox. He knew by now that when approaching strangers for information it was important to adopt the right tone but today he was unable to modulate his voice. He sounded gruff and the responses he drew were unhelpful. The people who remembered Gail had little to say about her. Their descriptions of her were conflicting. He was persistent, but by evening he still had not managed to find anyone who claimed to be her friend.

18

Lomax had often passed the court, but he had never climbed the long steps which led to it before. They were grey stone. Feet made interesting noises pattering and clicking against them. The width of the steps was immense and their height sufficient to make some people pause breathlessly at the top.

The court building was not so old as it looked. It seemed solid but perhaps that was an illusion too. The American flag was suspended from a sloping pole high across the steps. Lomax had seen television cameras clustered here under the flag before and he had always forgotten them as soon as he had passed. The cameras and the steps and the imposing building had been a part of other people's lives. It seemed incredible that now they had assumed a significance in his own.

Inside, the dingy halls buzzed with people who knew where they were going. Lomax asked a woman in uniform about People versus Fox. Busy passers-by made it clear that he was in the way.

The woman directed him to another woman in uniform, behind a desk. She looked down a list and then told him to go along the hallway to court three. It was hard to tell when you were outside court three because the number was missing.

'Is this court three?' Lomax asked one of the policemen who stood by the door.

'Uh huh,' said the policeman, yawning.

Lomax opened the door. It was heavier than he expected. He went inside and the door closed on the noise and movement behind him. The courtroom was about three-quarters full. After the bustle of the hallway it seemed still in here, and hot. Someone was actually making a guilty plea as he entered. He edged to a seat near the front and to one side. Several people had to stand to let him pass. Reporters sat in a block with their notebooks and pocket computers on their laps. A few of them were talking in whispers.

He looked around him. Julia and Kurt and Frances were on the other side of the room. He could scarcely see Julia. She was hidden by Kurt, who kept muttering into her ear.

The judge sat high above the court on a raised podium. Attorneys and defendants seemed to mill beneath him. Lomax studied them. A row of prisoners in yellow uniforms sat handcuffed along one wall. A few were conversing, one was asleep, one was crying. Julia could have nothing in common with these street murderers and drug dealers. Their attorneys often asked for their indictments not to be read out, leaving Lomax to guess what crimes they were accused of.

The woman on the desk outside had given Lomax a case number but he had already forgotten it. Every time another number was called he jerked his head towards Julia to see if it was her turn and the scabs which were forming just under his collar where he had cut himself shaving re-opened. After leaving home that morning it had occurred to him that if the press did learn of his involvement with Julia he would not help her case by appearing unshaven in torn jeans. So he had stopped off on the way to the court and shaved hastily at Candice's house and borrowed a suit and shirt from Robert. He was at least a size smaller than Lomax. Lomax felt hot in the small suit.

The court was busy. Defendants and their attorneys shuffled to the front and out again, the door opened and re-opened constantly, loud voices could often be heard in the hall outside and the uniformed policemen slouched against the panelled walls, jangling handcuffs and shifting their weight from foot to foot. Lawyers mumbled to each other in monotones. But when the clerk called another number and Julia finally stood up, everything seemed to stop.

She moved into the aisle escorted by Frances and Kurt. It was some time since Lomax had seen her and, as usual, her beauty took him by surprise. She was wearing a simple cream-coloured dress which might have been designed for some rite of passage, although not this one.

People sat forward, others turned around in their seats, necks craning. There was a whisper of clothes and notebooks. The man sitting next to Lomax stared so hard at her as she walked down the centre of the room that he rocked the whole row of seats. Lomax did not like the expression on the man's face.

The attention seemed to isolate her. She looked young and slim and vulnerable. Lomax wanted to put his arm around her. Involuntarily, his fingers found the scab on his neck and the warm stickiness of the blood there.

Julia's hair fell forward as she opened the small wooden gate which divided the courtroom. Turning momentarily, she pushed her hair back over her shoulders and for a second her face was fully visible. Lomax wanted to catch her eye. She must already have noticed him but she made no attempt to single him out from the rows of staring idiots all around him. Her face was expressionless.

The judge invited the attorneys to identify themselves. Then Kurt and Frances and Julia stood in front of the judge and the court listened as the People accused Julia of murdering her husband and step-daughter. When the words 'malice aforethought' were read, Kurt rapidly put his hand to his mouth as if stifling a cough. Simultaneously, in a nervous gesture, Julia lifted one arm to rearrange her hair. For a moment Lomax thought two birds had flown up in the courtroom.

The People asked Julia how she pleaded and the room was silent. Her back was slender but straight. For no reason at all, Lomax remembered the photographs of the murder victims he had seen in Frances' office. Sometimes they came into his head inexplicably.

Julia said: 'Not guilty.'

The voice was young and soft and clear. It was not possible that its owner was responsible for the brutality Lomax had seen in the police photographs.

The room resumed its bustle and movement. Attorneys with cases now imminent began muttering to their clients while clients who had just arrived wandered the room looking for their attorneys. The prisoners along the wall started talking. There was a handover of policemen. More prisoners were filing in.

Lomax strained to hear what was happening by the judge's podium. There seemed to be a whole army of prosecutors with papers under their arms. One of them, the man who did the talking, was black. His voice was low and it was almost impossible to hear what he was saying to the judge. It seemed that he and Frances were arguing. When there was a lull in the activity of the room, Lomax caught snatches of their discussion. The prosecutor was challenging the waiver that Julia had signed, the waiver that said Frances could defend her. After a few minutes the matter was resolved and they began to argue about something else.

'We don't have so many dates open . . .' the judge said, leaning forward and raising his eyebrows at a court official who flicked through a large book.

Frances was talking. 'Seven months ago . . . memories are already dim, your honour . . . Mrs Fox is having difficulty sleeping . . . suffering . . . as soon as possible . . .'

The prosecutors' protests were inaudible. After further discussion, the official wrote down some dates. There was a random pause in the room when a judge was assigned to the trial. Judge Olmstead.

When Julia turned to leave, the court fell silent again. People seized the opportunity to stare at her face. Some women would have bridled or blushed or looked angry or stared at the ground or, forgetting the ugliness of the circumstances, smiled. Julia didn't move a muscle but looked up over the heads of the people. And without seeming to seek him out, her eyes rested on Lomax. It was a pleasing moment. His mouth twitched involuntarily. He realized that he was smiling. He tried to suppress it but his mouth was now out of control. The smile broadened and he was powerless to stop it until long after the moment had passed and she had looked away again. He was aware that his grin was both wide and foolish.

Lomax skirted around the cameras and microphones and pushing journalists that were orbiting Julia and her attorneys in the hallway. He could not even see Julia at their centre. He drove to Candice's house.

'There's blood on the collar,' Candice said when he had changed out of Robert's suit and handed back the shirt.

'Sorry.'

'Did she try to finish you off too?' Candice peered at the stain. 'Oh God, no I didn't say that.'

'It's not funny,' Lomax told her.

'I unsaid it. I unsaid it.' Candice sprayed something onto the collar and stuffed the shirt into the washing machine. Outside it was a cool day but the kitchen was warm and the windows were half steamed up. Helen's paintings were tacked to the fridge door. There was a bowl of fresh fruit and a bowl of dried fruit on the table. From under the table came the regular thump of Deputy Dawg's tail.

Lomax would not have wanted to admit that he had found the courthouse – with its flight of steps, its busy, echoing halls and its judge sitting at such an immense height – intimidating. He just knew that now he welcomed the cocoon of a family home. His family, even if it wasn't his home.

'Don't put your feet on the table, Lomax,' said Candice.

'Somewhere in your hard little heart you think she's guilty,' he said.

'Of course not.'

'You'd like her if you knew her.' This was probably not true. Although Candice's likes and dislikes were notoriously unpredictable, she would almost certainly dislike Julia.

'I have an aromatherapist working at the clinic right now whom I don't much like. Last week there was a discrepancy in the accounts. It was small but it was noticeable. This week the discrepancy was too large to ignore. I'm forced to confront the fact that a member of my staff is cheating on me. Do I suspect the aromatherapist because I dislike her?'

'I would.'

'Because you disliked her?'

'Yes. And because she has oily hands. I bet there's oil of rosemary all over the books. Get that woman with the nose to sniff them for you.'

'Idiot. The books are on computer. The person I most suspect is the person I most like. Someone I've taken into my confidence, someone who feels so safe in my affections that they think they can steal from me without arousing my suspicion.'

'Robert?'

'Lomax, let's discuss this sensibly. I don't know who's stealing from me but I bet I find out soon, and I'm going to start looking at my favourite employees.'

Lomax felt sorry for Candice's employees. He knew how it was to bask in her affection and then experience its gradual withdrawal.

'Don't open your mouth until you know for sure,' he advised. She ignored this. Now that she had withdrawn her suspicions about Lomax she had probably forgotten ever making them. Candice found her own mistakes easy to forget.

She said: 'So in answer to your original question . . .' She switched on the food processor for a few moments until he'd forgotten the original question but knew he was expected to wait for an answer. This sort of staging was typical of Candice. 'In answer to your original question, disliking her wouldn't be reason enough for me to suspect she was guilty. The reason I know she's not guilty is that you wouldn't have fallen for a murderer.'

'Thanks.'

'No, really . . .' Candice dipped her finger into the goo inside the food processor, and then into her mouth. Lomax tried to do the same but she slapped his hand. '. . . I mean, a double murderer. It's unthinkable. You. No. Not possible.

Lomax went back to the table. Deputy put his head on his knee. Lomax ate some dried fruit from the bowl. It was brown and stuck to his fingers and could have been anything when it was fresh.

'But don't we all have within us the capacity to — '

'You don't.'

'Is it inconceivable for me to fall in love with someone who does?'

'Yup.'

Lomax sighed.

'So how did she look in court? Terrific, I suppose?'

'Terrific.'

'I know, actually. I saw her on the news. Cream. Nice. But she shouldn't look too good, Juries don't like it. I guess her attorney knows all about that.'

'Her attorney looked terrific too.'

'So why aren't you holding Julia's hand now?'

'She left with Frances and some assistants.' Lomax tried to blur the memory of Kurt escorting Julia out of the courtroom by making him plural. He had thought Julia would stop or wait or look for him again when Kurt had held the wooden gate open but she had stepped through it towards the waiting reporters without another glance in his direction. He said: 'She's supposed to be a sad widow. Frances says the jury will be less sympathetic if they think she has a boyfriend.'

'When are you allowed to see her?'

'I'll go home now in case she calls. I just came by to bring Robert's suit back. I hung it up, by the way.'

Candice looked at him sceptically. 'You can borrow it for the trial.'

'I have one of my own.'

Candice faltered in whatever she was doing. Boiling eggs or opening the oven door or washing the salad.

'I didn't wear it this morning because I didn't think of it,' he explained.

'You have a suit!'

'I had to buy it to work at Sachs Smith.' His voice was apologetic. In the past Candice had tried and failed to persuade him to buy a suit.

There was something else he wanted to say.

'I might go to Arizona this summer.'

Candice paused. She put her head on one side. She considered Arizona. 'Arizona . . .' she said. 'Isn't that where we saw that big fat lizard?'

They had seen canyons and spectacular rock formations and the Colorado river. But for Candice, Arizona was a lizard.

He said: 'It was a gila monster.'

'Why do you want to go back there?'

'I'm doing some research into one of the murder victims. She lived in Arizona when she was a kid.'

He had been planning to say more but he stopped. Candice had frowned at him and now she was shaking her head. 'Don't you think you're taking this research thing too far?' she said.

'No.'

She turned away. In a moment she was busy again. She was annoyed. 'That's what Julia's attorneys are for, Lomax. They don't need you stumbling round Arizona asking questions. And what good is it to anyone if you find out about a dead person's childhood?'

She said the word 'childhood' with exasperation and then switched on the food processor, changing settings until its motor roared. Lomax sighed and ate some more sticky brown fruit. He planned to answer the questions as soon as there was a silence again but she spoke before he could.

'It's a murder inquiry. It's serious. It can lead to a death sentence.' She faltered. Even Candice shrank from these words. 'I mean . . .' she continued lamely, 'it's different from a piece of cosmological research.'

He said: 'You have to get to know someone if you want to know who killed them.'

'Back to their childhood?'

'Maybe.'

Candice did not reply. She just shook her head.

'I've tried talking to people who knew Gail more recently. I tried all day yesterday. And I got absolutely nowhere.'

'Why don't you ask Julia?'

He did not want to explain to Candice how Julia always seemed to answer his questions but reveal nothing. Instead he said: 'I was thinking perhaps I could take Helen and Joel.'

'To Arizona? To find out about some corpse?' Her voice had risen a few notes.

'We could go sightseeing.'

'I don't know,' she said.

But it was clear that she did know. She did not want Lomax to take the children to Arizona. Perhaps, in spite of her retraction, he was still under suspicion. Or perhaps she was just thinking of lizards.

'You should have said before if you wanted to vacation with them. I've fixed up a lot of activities this summer.'

'Like what?'

'Like camp. Like a trip to San Diego to see Mom and Dad. Like a gymnastics course for Helen. Like swim club for Joel. Like friends visiting . . .'

'Okay,' he said. He did not want to argue with her again. 'It was just an idea.'

He said goodbye to his children. They were watching TV. They told him they had been channel-hopping to see Julia on as many of the local news programmes as they could.

'Who was that man with her?' asked Helen.

'I guess some security guard,' Lomax said.

'Did you hang Robert's suit up?' his daughter called as he left. 'Robert likes all his clothes hung up.'

'That child is coming out to the foothills just as soon as this trial is over and I'm going to teach her how to leave her room in a mess,' Lomax said to Candice as he kissed her goodbye. She was softer now.

'You look awful. Pale. Are you sleeping?' she asked.

'Enough.'

'Grow your beard back,' she advised. He touched the cut on his neck. To his surprise, Candice hugged him.

'Take Deputy with you.'

'Okay. Why?'

'You can't get lonely when he's around.'

'I don't get lonely.'

'Take him anyway. I'll explain to the kids.'

Deputy had followed them out to the car and when the door was opened, he jumped in. He stood on the back seat waiting for Lomax, his ears hanging and his tail wagging.

'It'll be all right,' Candice said. 'I have this blind faith in the judicial system. Innocent people get acquitted.'

Lomax nodded. Candice was watching him. Suddenly she said: 'Oh Lomax, be careful.'

He smiled and left but her words and her tone surprised him. He had heard her use that tone with Helen and Joel and she often spoke to him as if he were a third child. This was not annoying. He realized that it made his frequent presence around the house more acceptable to Robert. But on this occasion, it unsettled him.

When he and Deputy arrived home the phone was ringing. Lomax ran for it and Deputy, excited, ran too and tripped him. The phone stopped ringing.

'That was probably her,' Lomax said, 'you dumb animal.'

Deputy wandered off, his nose following smells. The phone rang again and Lomax snatched it.

'It's me,' said Kim. 'Shit, Lomax, that white dress, did she think she was at her first communion?'

'Cream. Did you just call?'

'No. Have you been watching the news? Did you see me? They switched on their cameras just when I was crossing the parking lot.'

'I haven't watched the news.'

'Doberman went back and forwards between the staff residence and the labs about fifty times and he didn't get into a single bulletin,' she snickered.

'Oh Kim, it's serious,' he said.

'It's serious for the Barbie doll, it's serious for you, but up here for us it's thrilling to have a murderer, erm, sorry, alleged murderer in our midst.'

Lomax groaned.

'The cameras have gone home now. I think Dixon Driver sort of likes the publicity.'

'The press wasn't supposed to know anything about Julia working at the observatory,' he said.

'Well you know the fourth estate. They're like bloodhounds.'

Julia would have been safer here at home with him. In bed.

'A few reporters are still hanging around but they haven't even realized she's here,' Kim was saying. 'She came in by the back road past the Phallus.'

Lomax's heart beat faster. 'Julia's at the observatory?'

'Sure.'

'She was supposed to be going somewhere secret away from the press.'

'It's okay, she's away from the press.'

'Where is she?'

'In her room with some guy.'

'What!'

'The guy who's always hanging around her these days.'

'What guy?'

'Lomax, you should hear yourself. What are you going to do, club him and drag her back to your cave?'

'What guy, Kim?'

'Tall, blond, with a jawbone that sort of goes ahead and opens the door before the rest of him arrives.'

'Kurt.'

'Who is he?'

'He's from the law firm that's defending her.'

'Her attorney was on the TV news and she's a woman. This Kurt must be some kind of imposter. You should come right over with your axe.'

Lomax wanted to end the call now so that he could telephone Julia, but Kim was in a mood to talk.

'How are you, Lomax?' she said sweetly. 'I've been thinking about you a lot. I still feel bad for dropping you in the shit with Berlins.'

'It's okay.'

But Kim apologized again and then again.

'Please. Stop apologizing.'

'I feel so guilty. I've probably ruined your career.'

'I don't have a career,' he reminded her.

'You don't any more. No, that's pessimistic. Return Eileen Squeal's bedspreads and it's just possible that Science will take you back.'

'Those fucking, fucking bedspreads,' said Lomax.

'She'll put you on the blacklist,' Kim told him. 'You'll be refused accommodation at scientific establishments all over America. Probably all over the whole world.'

Lomax had now received three letters from Eileen Friel. The first had been polite. The second had requested the urgent return of the bedspreads. The third had said: 'You still have not replied to my inquiries about the missing bedspreads. These are observatory property. Please note that this is a time of financial stringency and every dime should be spent on research projects, not replacing stolen goods.' It had been signed E. N. Friel. It was not so much the letter as the observatory letterhead which bothered Lomax. It had been re-designed. It showed the sun appearing or maybe disappearing behind a large dome, perhaps the Fahrhaus.

'I mean,' he asked Kim, 'what's the sun doing there? The sun's what we don't look at.'

'We do now.'

'Look at the sun?'

'Study it.'

'What?'

'Two new guys are here from Cornell. They're both solar specialists.'

'Solar specialists! We don't have a solar telescope!'

'They're taking their results from Colorado.'

'Then why don't they go to Colorado?'

'Well,' replied Kim irrelevantly, 'one of them's Danish.'

'Solar specialists. God.'

'They're on short contracts. They'll be around until after the eclipse.'

'What can they do in a few months, for Chrissake?'

191

'Half the kitchen staff and most of the guides. And that's just the Danish one.'

'What about work?'

'Hey, it's tiring to screw all day.'

Lomax did not laugh.

'Notionally,' said Kim, her voice sobering, 'they're studing solar flares.'

'Then why are they leaving right after the eclipse?'

'They're taking all the results back to Cornell. C'mon, Lomax, it's obvious. The real reason they're here is for the press.'

Lomax heard himself making a strange noise, halfway between a sigh and a groan. It sounded like an animal in pain. 'A total eclipse of the sun,' he said, 'is not a media event.' Kim guffawed so loudly that he lengthened the distance between his ear and the phone.

'Dinosaur! You cute dinosaur you!' she shrieked. 'I thought you guys were extinct!'

Lomax heard himself making his despairing animal noise again. Deputy, slumbering on the rug now, looked up.

'Anyway,' said Kim, 'there's a lot more press than they can handle. We're all doing some publicity work. Even me.'

'You!'

Kim sounded shy. 'Actually, I'm ABC's eclipse correspondent.'

'Oh Kim.' Lomax was reproachful.

'Forgive me, Father, for I have sinned. But they pay well and everybody's doing it. I have ABC, Doberman has CBS, everyone has something and Dixon Driver and the Danish guy are probably doing CNN from on board the jet.'

'You're a bunch of imposters,' said Lomax. 'Not one of you is a solar specialist except this Dane.'

'Explain that to my mom. She thinks that if it's in the sky I must know about it.'

Deputy stood up and stretched lazily. He looked around him. When he saw that Lomax was still on the phone he lay down and went to sleep again.

'Maybe it's a good thing I got you out of here for the summer,' Kim said, 'because this place has, like, eclipse mania.'

'Perhaps.' He was non-committal.

'Are you taking a vacation?'

'I might go to Arizona for a few days.'

'Arizona . . . ?' said Kim in the same tone as Candice. 'What's in Arizona?'

'Lizards. Big lizards.'

'Oh, lizards, nice. I guess you can't take the Barbie doll?'

'I guess not.'

'Then,' said Kim, 'why don't I come with you?'

Lomax thought she was joking. 'I couldn't steal you away from ABC.'

'ABC can wait,' she said grandly, and Lomax realized the suggestion was serious.

By the end of the call it was arranged. They were going to Arizona.

He dialled Julia's room at the observatory without even replacing the receiver.

'Yes,' said Kurt's voice.

'It's Lomax.'

'Lomax. Why the cheesy grin in court? You weren't supposed to know her.'

'I was grinning at you, Kurt,' Lomax replied. 'Just let me speak to her, will you?'

Julia sounded tired. 'I'm okay,' she said, 'it's just been kind of an ordeal.'

'You looked sweet and innocent,' he told her.

'I was scared.'

'I was nervous for you.'

'I couldn't believe it was happening. The pre-trial motions are in a month and then the trial's in the middle of August. Until then I just have to carry on working and pretending everything's normal.'

That was the sort of stupid advice Kurt would give her. How could she possibly pretend that everything was normal when she was staring a death sentence in the face? 'What are pre-trial motions?' he asked. But Julia did not know.

'It's going to be all right,' he told her, because he could think of nothing else to say.

She agreed with him readily. 'They can't convict me for something I didn't do.'

'When's Kurt leaving?'

'Now.'

'Good.'

When they had finished speaking, Lomax could think only of Julia. He sat out on the deck, engulfed by trees, weighed down by her sadness. But later, when he took Deputy to sniff around the yard, his own sadness began to gnaw at him. Talking to Kim had reminded him of observatory life and he admitted to himself that he

193

missed it. He looked up. The night was clear. All the telescopes on the mountain top would be in use tonight. The domes had opened with their distinctive whirring and the mechanical eyes were noiselessly swivelling around the sky at this moment. He let his head fall back and looked up. The earth was wrapped in a thick mesh of stars – its own galaxy, the Milky Way. One hundred thousand light years from rim to rim but still only one tiny galaxy in millions upon millions. Deputy, who had been ambling around the yard poking his nose into the bushes, lay down on his feet.

There was a letter which Lomax had been ignoring. He had left it on the kitchen table for several days, propped up against an old beer can, and he had still succeeded in ignoring it. The letter was from Dixon Driver and it asked him to submit his allegations to the observatory ethics committee. Lomax had never even heard of the ethics committee before. He suspected that Driver had contrived it especially to deal with him.

He had tried on several occasions to call Berlins to ask whether he had received a similar letter but no one had answered the phone. Now he returned to the house and telephoned Berlins again.

'Hallo?' It was Sarah Berlins.

'Could I speak to the professor, please?' he asked. He hoped she would not recognize his voice but the petulance of her response seemed to indicate that she already had.

'What time do you call this?' she demanded.

'Er . . .' Lomax seldom wore a watch. 'Um . . . around ten?'

'It's ten thirty. P.m. My husband is, of course, in bed. I only hope you haven't woken him up.' Lomax began to apologize but she hung up the phone as usual. Why was her husband of course in bed by ten thirty? Up until a few weeks ago, Berlins had often stayed up viewing all night. Lomax's melancholy closed around him like fog.

He found Dixon Driver's letter and began to draft a reply. It covered less than half a page. It explained that a galaxy under observation for project Core 9 had been restructured post-viewing, and it gave Lomax's evidence. It did not name Berlins or make allegations. Finding a clean sheet of paper, a stamp and an envelope took approximately three times as long as writing the letter. When he had finished he took it out to the mailbox. Deputy followed him patiently. He pulled up the rusty flag. Deputy recognized its squeak as a signal to go back to the house.

Inside, Lomax noticed his fatigue for the first time that day. He lay down on the rug next to Deputy. His eyes were weary, his skin was weary, his bones were weary. Probably even his hair was weary. Deputy licked his arm affectionately while Lomax fell asleep thinking about all the bits of him that were weary.

19

They had been driving through hell all morning.

'Is this air conditioning really on max?' Kim asked.

'Yep.'

Lomax had hardly used the air conditioning in his old station wagon before now. In weather like this he preferred to open the car windows and feel the heat whipping round inside the car. 'Just pretend it's cold out there and the hot breeze in here is the heating,' he suggested.

But Kim preferred air conditioning. She regularly switched on the radio to be astonished by the temperature. 'A hundred and six goddam degrees!'

She tuned to country stations and sang along to the music. Sometimes Lomax agreed to air conditioning just to stop her singing.

'Are you sure this is max? she said, reaching for the radio now. 'My Hershey bars are melting.'

'Better eat them,' Lomax advised.

'What a great idea. It never crossed my mind.'

Kim began tearing the candy out of its wrappers. As if by some prior arrangement, Deputy, who had been asleep on the back seat, leapt up and shoved his nose over her shoulder.

'Wow, that dog is fast,' said Kim, her mouth full.

She handed Lomax a rectangle of chocolate. The move was neatly intercepted by Deputy who retired to the back seat to chew it. Kim passed Lomax more chocolate, then turned up the radio and began to sing. Lomax glanced at her. She licked her chocolate-covered fingers. She looked happy.

'Glad you brought me along?' she called over the music.

'No,' said Lomax. He had spent most of the trip wishing Kim were Julia.

The desert stretched on either side of them. Earlier, the landscape had been featureless but now there were desert plants and rocky hills, cracked with age. The vegetation sprang from unyielding dirt. The temperature had risen noticeably. The sun was merciless here.

Kim had planned their vacation. She had enjoyed doing this. She had bought maps from the AAA and guides from the university bookshop. She had decided they would take the back roads instead of the Interstates.

'And we'll trade places behind the wheel after every meal, okay?'

Lomax had been acquiescent. It was going to be a different kind of vacation from the one he had intended. There would be no camping and little hiking and a lot of meals.

'And, um, you won't want to sleep with me by any chance?'

'No, Kim.'

'Then I get Deputy. Curled up on the end of my bed every night like Lassie.'

'Did Lassie try to mate with the pillows?'

'What!'

'Don't expect a peaceful night with Deputy around,' he warned.

She had tried to consult Lomax about their route but he had simply named the city in southern Arizona which he wanted to visit. She had not asked why. By the end of today they would have arrived there.

'This chocolate's making me hungry,' she said. 'How about we stop for some lunch?'

They were following Kim's favourite kind of road. At first it was paved, then for fifty miles it had been a dusty dirt track through the desert and now it was paved again. The yellow lines here had been faded by the sun or not painted in the first place. Sometimes they passed shacks and once they had stopped for gas in a tiny town where the houses and the stores stood baking in silence.

Lomax intended to pull over at the next opportunity but none arose. The road was lined with hostile plants. Finally, since there had been no traffic, he slowed the car and stopped on the sticky asphalt. They opened the doors and the heat fell in on them.

'Wow! It must be a hundred and ten out there,' said Kim.

They scanned the horizon for shade. There was none and had been none for many miles.

'It sure is quiet,' said Lomax.

They listened to the silence. The air was thick. Heat rose visibly. The rocks and cacti seemed to float.

Deputy stared around him but did not jump out of the car.

'Probably his paws would catch fire,' said Kim, opening the trunk and sitting at the back of the stationwagon, her legs pointing back at the road they had just travelled.

Lomax gave Deputy some water. He lapped it and dipped his ears in it and dripped it over the car.

Kim had insisted on bringing a coolbox which she filled every morning. They made lunch from its contents and from the jars and cans and bags which Kim had loaded into the car in California. She constantly supplemented whatever food she was eating.

'Salad dressing? Mustard? I can do ketchup.'

Deputy watched them eat.

'This is bad weather for dogs. We shouldn't stay here in the south too long,' Kim said.

Lomax took some mustard. 'We have to stay a few days.'

And Kim asked the question he had been waiting for since she had begun planning their trip.

'Why?'

'I have some work to do.'

She looked at him. Her face was sly. She stopped munching.

'And I think I know what,' she said

The effects of the air conditioning had worn off. They were both hot now. Lomax felt beads of sweat shooting down his back. 'What?'

She said: 'I think you're applying for something at the observatory down here. Am I right?'

'Smart thinking.'

'I am right!'

'No, but it's a good idea.'

'That's not the reason you wanted to come here?'

'No.'

Kim was disappointed. 'Your reason had better be good,' she said, and resumed eating.

'You won't think it is.'

Kim had never asked Lomax how he was spending his time since his suspension from the observatory. She had just seemed to assume that he slouched around, like the mountain lion on the university stationery. She did not know about his work at Sachs Smith on Julia's behalf. She did not know he had worn a suit for whole days in succession.

They sat in the back of the stationwagon while he told her all this and explained the purpose of his visit. She continued to eat, fixing her eyes on his face.

'Well,' she said when he had finished. She reached for more food. There was a silence. The desert seemed to inch closer to the car. The heat pressed on all sides of them. He looked at Kim but she did not meet his eye. She was folding some large, succulent lettuce leaves into quarters, immersing them in thousand island dressing and cramming them into her mouth. It became clear that she intended to make no other comment. She was punishing him.

They resumed their journey in silence. Kim drove. She switched on the air conditioning and when it was functional they closed the windows. She reached for the radio but did not sing along. Lomax watched the desert outside swelling in the heat. Once they drove up behind a pick-up filled with brown-skinned children. The children's hair blew around their faces and they smiled and waved. Neither Kim nor Lomax responded. The children shrieked and waved more energetically as the stationwagon overtook. There was still no response. Even Deputy ignored them.

When they joined the highway again they began to pass small conurbations. There were places to eat and signs telling them about the motels and tourist attractions which awaited them at their destination. Lomax found himself wishing Kim would sing. He glanced at her but she was staring at the road straight ahead, her face expressionless.

Without warning, she pulled in at a café which stood by a gas station. 'Coffee time,' she said.

Lomax and Deputy followed her into the café. The door was open. Fans buzzed overhead, rearranging the hot air. They were the only customers.

'My husband does the gas and I do all the work in here. We do not trade jobs. No way. He does the gas. I fix the food. That's how it is around here,' the woman in the café said as she poured them coffee. She was answering some friendly inquiry of Kim's but her tone was forceful, as if someone was arguing with her. She gave Deputy a bowl of water. He drank half of it then sat on Lomax's feet. He looked miserable.

'Poor Deputy,' said Kim. 'Did your daddy bring you all the way down here to hell for some dumb detective game?'

So that was what Kim had been thinking during the long silences.

'I may be dumb,' said Lomax, 'but I am not Deputy's daddy.'

'I guess me 'n' Deputy'll just have to go see the sights alone while you get onto the case,' Kim said bitterly. 'Sifting for clues. Asking questions. Delving.'

'Why are you mad?'

His question seemed to trigger her fury. Her face turned red. Her head nudged up and down.

'This is my vacation! It's my vacation! You're spending my vacation indulging all your private fantasies about the Barbie doll. You speak in monosyllables. You sit thinking about her all day long. Then you announce you don't have any time to see the sights with me because you're too busy going places for her!'

The woman who fixed the meals but did not pour gas was staring at them from across the room.

'Shhhh,' said Lomax.

'You're a dickhead, Lomax, you're a complete shit.'

'Julia didn't ask me or want me to – ' he began. But Julia's name seemed to make Kim angrier.

'You said it was a vacation, you said it was a vacation!' she hissed. 'I wish you hadn't changed. I wish you were the way you were before that dumb little girl came simpering into the labs.'

'I'm just exactly the same way I've always been,' he said. But he was feeling uneasy.

'Oh yeah, yeah, you take one look at her and you shave your beard off and start throwing insane accusations around about someone who never did you any harm and then you quit your whole career just so you can become her . . . her slave. Yeah, that's normal. That's just how you were before.'

The woman was leaning on the counter now, openly listening to them. Lomax paid her.

'Phew. Your marriage looks like it's in trouble,' she said quietly. He held out his hand for the change.

'You should decide who does what and stick to it,' she advised him. 'That way there's no arguing. We do it like that round here.'

Outside, clouds were gathering. It was a relief not to walk into sunlight. The pick-up truck with its cargo of children had just arrived. The children ran towards the open door of the café. They wore colourful clothes and their laughter bounced off the bare walls of the café and echoed around the gas station. Some of them held hands and formed a ragged line. They grew more subdued as they recognized the grim faces of Lomax and Kim.

Lomax was tormented by Kim's accusations. He tried to concentrate on the passing road signs. There was a haunted house a few miles ahead. Everyone was welcome and would have a spooky time there. A house was pictured with ghostly figures peeking out of the window.

'How have I changed?' he said at last.

'You used to be fun.'

He admitted to himself that he had probably not been much fun on this trip. And it was true that he had mostly been silent, thinking about Julia.

'Ever since you shaved you've got meaner. I never would have thought you had a jawbone under all that hair, but you do.'

'All God's chillun got jawbones.'

'Well yours is a bit sharper than I would have expected and since you exposed it you've been a bit sharper too.'

Lomax thought distastefully of Kurt. He touched his chin. It was several days since he had shaved. It felt like a cactus.

'You used to be interesting and sort of affectionate.'

'You're jealous.'

'Sure. I admit it. You were my friend and now you're her lapdog.'

Lomax said: 'C'mon, Kim, I'm still your friend.'

But Kim shook her head. Her face had some unfamiliar creases. He hoped she wasn't going to cry.

'You're getting so distant. We've been in the same car all this time and . . . and there's been a whole desert between us,' she said. Perhaps prompted by her own rhetoric, she started to cry.

'Shit,' said Lomax. 'You should pull over.'

'I can still drive,' she sniffed. She continued to watch the road ahead of her, the tears dripping from her sad cheeks. Lomax shuffled uncomfortably in his seat.

They were on the edge of a town now. They were reaching the haunted house.

'Want to go in?' she asked unexpectedly. Lomax thought he should try to prove that he was still fun.

'Sure.'

In the parking lot, Lomax said: 'Kim, don't cry . . .'

'I'm not,' she replied. Her tears were falling freely.

'Well do you want to sit here for a while?'

'No.'

They went into the haunted house. Kim blew her nose. Her face was wet. Her eyes were red. The man who sold them their tickets stared at her uncertainly and then gave Lomax a questioning look.

'Is she okay?' he asked.

'I'm fine,' Kim said.

The man continued to talk to Lomax. 'There's a tour just started. Go right through the door and you'll find them.'

The guide had begun his spiel. He paused as Kim and Lomax entered the dingy room. When he restarted, he was interrupted by a banshee wail. Lomax thought at first that it was a part of the haunted house's special effects, then he realized the noise came from Kim. The guide paused again. The tour turned to look at them. Kim tried to apologize but her words were guillotined by tears.

Lomax led her back through the door.

'I told you she wasn't okay,' said the ticket seller.

'Please don't cry,' Lomax begged.

'I'm not crying.'

They sat in the car again. Deputy watched them.

'Why are you so upset?'

'Because I know you can't help it,' said Kim. 'It's not your fault. You're besotted with her.'

The expression was unflattering.

'I'm in love. Is that besotted?'

She ignored his question. 'You're so besotted that you travel thousands of miles across America because you have a hunch it could help her. Do you think the Barbie doll would do the same for you?'

Lomax paused. 'No,' he admitted. 'But she's in trouble and . . .'

'Is that all she has to do? Look helpless? And guys press the eject button and bail out of their careers for her?'

'I didn't bail out. You bailed me out. Now I have the summer free and I'm spending it trying to make sure Julia goes free. You think I wouldn't prefer to put on a bunch of sweaters and go viewing tonight?'

This reminder of her own role in events seemed to sober Kim. 'I wish you could see through her,' she muttered.

'What's that mean?'

'She does this simpering little girl act and you . . . you fall for it.'

'She does not. She's highly intelligent.'

'There you go again. You're besotted.'

'Julia's had a really difficult time. No mother. Her dad . . . well anyway, he died . . .'

'And she married a rich lawyer. Real tough.'

'And then he died. And now they've arrested her for killing him. That's a terrible thing to happen.'

'What makes you so sure she didn't kill him?'

'Oh Kim.'

'C'mon, c'mon. What makes you so sure?'

'She just couldn't have.'

'And you're going to find the evidence which says she didn't. Right?'

Lomax did not reply at once. 'I doubt it. But . . . I have to try. I'd do it for you too if you were in trouble.'

She turned to him for the first time. Her eyes were moist. 'You would?'

He nodded without hesitation. His enthusiasm seemed to touch her. She leaned across to him and kissed him damply on the cheek. Her wet hair tickled him. His skin felt uncomfortable where her mouth had been.

'Okay, I'll help,' she said.

'Help what?'

'Help you with whatever you came here for. But I'm doing it for you, not the Barbie doll.'

A pick-up drew up beside them. 'Oh Christ,' said Lomax.

The children began climbing out, yelling in shrill voices. Kim left the car, followed by Deputy, and the children yelled their recognition. This time they clustered around Kim and swamped Deputy with their tiny hands. With difficulty, Kim handed the driver their unused tickets for the haunted house. She came back to the car and rooted round for candy bars.

'It's so easy to make friends in the desert. Pass on the road a few times and you're buddies for life,' she said, disappearing again into the midst of the children. They made squeaky noises and reached for the candy. Deputy barked excitedly. The tour party which Kim and Lomax had left emerged from a door at the side of the haunted house wincing in the daylight. They watched Kim and Deputy and the children.

Lomax did not tell her that her help was unwanted and that Frances would not approve of yet another amateur working on Julia's case. 'I'm trying to find out all I can about Gail,' he explained that night. Kim was eating a pancake. She had asked for strawberry but chocolate had arrived. In the end she ate the strawberry and the chocolate.

'Lewis divorced Vicky Fox and left the family in Arizona when Gail was around ten years old. A couple of years later, Gail and her mother and her brother followed him to California.'

'Why?'

'Not sure. I suspect to torment Lewis.'

'What's living in Arizona until you're twelve got to do with getting murdered in California ten years later?'

'I don't know. Probably nothing. Only . . .'

'Only you have a hunch.'

'Well it's weird. A father and daughter both murdered. It's believable if the motive was theft . . . but nothing was stolen. It might be that someone wanted to kill Lewis and Gail happened to be there, but it doesn't look that way to me.'

'Over on the south side people get shot, whole families get shot, for no particular reason.'

'This wasn't a south side murder. The police don't think so either; they've arrested Julia.'

A waiter tried to take away Kim's plate but she would not concede that it was empty. He looked at her strangely and apologized. Lomax was explaining: 'I want to learn about the victims. About the family. That's all.'

'So who will you see here?'

'I'll take a look at the house where they lived, Gail's school, maybe find a teacher who remembers her.'

'What happened to the brother?'

'He works in Seattle. I'd like to talk to him but Frances told me she and Kurt are doing that.'

'Kurt. Is he the guy with the jaw?'

'According to you, I'm the guy with the jaw.'

Kim chuckled. 'It's okay,' she said, 'you don't have Kurt's kind of jaw.'

The next day, Lomax hoped Kim would let him go alone to Gail's house.

'I'll drop you at the Cowboy Museum and pick you up on the way back,' he suggested. They had passed the Cowboy Museum last night when they were looking for a motel which accepted dogs. Kim had said she wanted to visit the museum. But this morning she shook her head.

'I said I'd help you and I'm going to help you,' she insisted loyally. Lomax could not persuade her to change her mind.

She navigated them towards Gail's house. 'What are we going to do when we find it?' she asked. Lomax admitted that he did not know.

'Do you want to go inside?'

'I'm not sure.'

'Lomax, what's the point? They moved away ten, twelve years ago. Other people have been living there. Looking around the place isn't going to tell you anything.'

'But the Foxes built it. It was designed the way they wanted it.'

'It was probably a kit. They just had to say how many bedrooms.'

'Lewis wouldn't buy a kit. He'd have an architect and torment him checking out the small details.'

Kim thought for a moment. 'So how the hell do we get inside?'

'I don't know,' admitted Lomax.

'This town is tough. There's a lot of drug running over the Mexican border and it has one of the highest murder rates in the country. They said so on the local news last night. You think people around here open the door to strangers? Especially a stranger who hasn't shaved in a while? Especially if the crab nebula's clearly visible on his left cheek?'

'You think my birthmark looks like the crab nebula?'

'Yes. I've been meaning to tell you ever since you shaved.'

Lomax was pleased. He had always liked the crab nebula.

It took a long time to reach Gail's suburb. Probably when Lewis and Vicky Fox had moved there, it had been right on the edge of town.

'Wouldn't it be nice to see a tree?' said Kim. But there were no trees. The houses had been built at occasional intervals into the desert twenty years ago and still did not look a part of it. Cacti and mesquite and ocotillo and yucca grew randomly around them. It was hard to tell where one lot ended and the next started. There were no fences.

Some of the houses were faced in adobe, Spanish style. All were single-storey. The Fox house, pink brick, was visible from the road. It was raised high above the pavement and to reach it you had to turn up a steep dirt drive. Its most notable feature was the realty sign right outside it.

Lomax could not believe his luck. 'Think it's empty?' he asked as Kim wrote down the real estate agent's name and number.

They stared at the house.

'Want to go up and see?'

'No. Let's call the realtor and we can be inside it this afternoon.'

The neighbourhood was quiet. There were no animals or birds or people moving in the heat.

'I wish there was someone we could ask about the schools.'

'The realtor will know.'

This was going to be easy. The realtor would tell them everything. They found a shopping mall and then a telephone.

'I want to phone,' said Kim. 'I like make-believe.'

Lomax and Deputy waited for her in the car. She returned smiling and when she sat down the air seemed to move around her excitedly.

'Two o'clock this afternoon! And guess what, the house is empty!'

'What did you tell them?'

'Almost the truth. It's the best way to lie. I said my husband and I –'

'What!'

'My husband and I work at an observatory in northern California and we both had interviews at the observatory down here yesterday and we want to see this house in case we get the job. She said: "I'll see

you there at two, Mrs Fenez," and I said: "Actually it's Doctor Fenez."
Just in case she wasn't completely convinced.'

'We both had interviews? Both of us?'

'We're a renowned husband-and-wife team.'

Lomax guffawed.

'And I remembered to ask the right questions, about the price and
all, and she gave me the names of the local schools . . .' Kim referred to
a scrawled note. 'And you know what else? She said that the neighbour
at the house next door has lived here twenty years and would be able to
tell us everything about the area.'

'That's terrific, Kim.'

'There's more, there's more . . .'

Stimulated by their mood, Deputy began to bark deafeningly.

'Quiet, Dep. She gave me the neighbour's name. It's Knight. So I
looked it up. First I spell it Night, then Nite, then I remember olde
Englande and hey presto, it's Knight and here's her number. I call her,
she's in, she saw us looking at the house earlier and she's waiting for us
now!'

'You're a genius, Dr Fenez.'

'I for sure am smart.'

They drove back to the house.

'By the way. We have two children. A girl aged twelve and a boy
aged . . . um . . . ten.'

'Must we?'

'So we can ask about the schools.'

'Oh. Okay.'

'The girl is clever and cute like her daddy. She has blue eyes and
looks like you.'

'She has a beard?'

'She was born with one. It's our terrible family secret. However,
thanks to the miracle of modern medicine the beard has been erased.
But we, her parents, fear its return at the onset of puberty. We
anxiously scan her chin every morning for telltale signs. Her name is
Tandra.'

'I don't mind if her beard grows back,' Lomax said. 'I love Tandra
just the way she is.'

'The boy has a few difficulties in school right now. He's quiet. Very
shy. Doesn't mix with the other kids. Of course that's because he's
going to be Einstein when he grows up.'

'Name?'

'You name him.'

'Roach.'

Kim giggled. 'Shit,' she said, 'no wonder the kid has difficulties.'

At the top of Mrs Knight's drive there was a view of the city to one side and the distant mountains to the other. The Fox house was a hundred yards away, stark amid the low, sparse desert vegetation.

'We used to have a little path from here over to your house,' said Mrs Knight, as though they had already bought it. The path was no longer visible. It would be possible, but difficult, to pick a winding route between the prickly shrubs.

'Have you lived here long?'

'We had this place built when our kids were tiny. And now they're grown and we're still here.'

'It's a beautiful home,' said Kim. The room they were in was white and simple and the low chairs were comfortable. They had put Deputy in a high-walled part of the yard where Mrs Knight hung the wash. He was panting out there now in the shade of a pair of sheets.

'Did you ever live in Japan?' asked Lomax. He had been looking at the pictures on the white walls.

'Actually, yes, before we started our family. And we visit most vacations. My husband is professor of Japanese Studies at the university,' said Mrs Knight. 'He retires next year.'

Lomax guessed she had become a mother late in life. She was white-haired and full-bodied. Her face was kind. She was intelligent. He liked her. He regretted their deceit.

'It would be wonderful to have nice neighbours living next door, especially if you have little children . . . ' she said as she served them cupcakes and coffee. Kim obliged by making Tandra and Roach five and seven.

'Aaaah,' said Mrs Knight happily. 'Now ask me anything you want to know about the district.'

Kim and Mrs Knight talked about schools, garbage collection and road maintenance.

'The road down there was paved soon after we moved here. Now look at the potholes. It hasn't been repaired once, not once,' she said.

'Were you the first house around here?' said Lomax.

'No, I think your house . . . well, that house . . . I think the Foxes moved in before we did.'

The mention of the Foxes made Lomax's heart beat faster. He tried to make his voice sound casual.

'Did they stay long?'

'They were there for about ten years . . . actually he left and she stayed on with the children for a couple more years, then they all went. It was such a relief. And the other people who've lived there . . .' Her voice fell. 'Well, that's why it would be nice if you moved in.'

'These people, Fox, they built the house?'

'Yes, but you don't need to worry about that. He was a very thorough man. It'll be well-built.'

'So when did you have the connecting path?'

'Oh, years ago. My youngest was the same age as the Foxes' little girl and they were friends for a while.'

Gail. Lomax felt a sense of elation. This is what he had driven so far to hear. Mrs Knight was going to say something which would make the journey worthwhile. He controlled his voice with difficulty.

'Why was it a relief when they left?'

Mrs Knight shrugged and smiled but said nothing.

'I guess they were difficult neighbours,' he prompted.

'You don't want to hear about that,' she said.

Kim and Lomax exchangd the looks of anxious parents. 'Oh, we do,' Kim assured her.

'But why?'

'Well . . .' Kim squirmed.

'They left a long time ago,' she said. Lomax's body stiffened with tension. Mrs Knight knew something and was not going to tell them.

'Mrs Knight,' said Kim seriously, 'if anything terrible happened in that house we should know about it.'

'Oh no, nothing too terrible, nothing which would affect the house in any way.'

'I think you should tell us, though.'

'You're scientists. You're surely not superstitious.'

There was a silence. Even Kim was lost for words. 'We'd really like to know,' she insisted.

'But,' said Mrs Knight, her face folded softly with disapproval, 'I don't understand why.'

'Because . . . ' Kim's voice faded. There was a silence.

Lomax spoke with difficulty. 'Mrs Knight, we haven't been completely truthful with you. We're not really here to buy the house next door. I'm sorry we deceived you.'

He was aware without looking at her, of Kim's face, livid, bobbing somewhere to the left of him like a red balloon. He could hear her breathing loudly. Mrs Knight blinked at him but was otherwise motionless.

'We are astronomers at the observatory in north California like we told you. But, for reasons I won't explain to you now, I'm working temporarily for a firm of defence attorneys investigating a murder, a double murder.'

'Excuse me,' said Mrs Knight, flustered, 'but I don't understand any of this.'

Lomax wondered if he had overestimated her intelligence and resilience. 'We were asking about the Foxes because we're in Arizona to find out about them.'

Mrs Knight put her coffee down on the table. She held her hand to her head in confusion.

'Lewis Fox and his daughter Gail were murdered last year. The case comes to trial soon. We're working for the defending attorneys.'

Mrs Knight stared at him, trying to digest this information. She shook her head slowly but said nothing.

'That's why we'd like to ask you questions about the Foxes, especially Gail.'

'But,' said Mrs Knight, 'you're defending her?'

'No, no, Gail isn't accused of anything. Gail is dead.'

'But I meant,' said Mrs Knight, 'you're defending the mother?'

There was another silence.

'Vicky Fox isn't accused of the murders,' Lomax said quietly.

Mrs Knight's hand fluttered around her hair, arranging and rearranging one small piece of it.

'Is Vicky still alive?' she asked.

'Yes.'

'I see. Please give me a moment to . . . don't tell me anything else yet.'

Her hands were still now and she sat with her head bowed. Lomax dared to look at Kim. Her eyes bulged at him angrily. At last Mrs Knight looked up.

'How did they die?' she asked.

'They were shot at close range.'

'And who is accused of doing this?'

'Lewis' wife. After divorcing Vicky, he married again.'

Mrs Knight bowed her head once more and when she looked up her face seemed older. Her voice was hoarse.

'What do you want to know?' she asked.

'Can you think back to when you first met the family?'

She nodded.

'How would you have described them then?'

209

'Just normal. Well, Richard, the boy, was . . . it was hard to like him. He was younger than Stephen, they were both toddlers, but Richard picked on him right from the very beginning, from the day we moved in. Stephen's my son. He's a choreographer now. Looking back I realize it probably wasn't Richard's fault. Anyway, the rest of the family seemed just normal back then.'

'And Gail?'

'She was a cute little girl.'

'Were you friends with Vicky Fox?'

Mrs Knight hesitated. 'Not especially. But Gail and Anna liked each other and Vicky used to leave Gail over here, or I'd take her to dancing class with Anna. It got so she just arrived any time of the day and joined in whatever my kids were doing like one of the family.'

'How did you feel about Vicky?'

'She was younger than me. I was over forty when we moved here and the kids were still small. It's not so unusual now, but I was a late starter. So Vicky and I didn't have a lot in common.'

'Did you like her?'

'Vicky? Well . . . ' Mrs Knight struggled. 'She wasn't really my sort of person,' she said at last. She looked pained when Lomax urged her to elaborate.

'I guess she was unhappy. She came over here a lot when Gail was still tiny. It depressed me. Her talk depressed me. Whatever I suggested to help her she always had a reason why everything had to stay just exactly the same. She was trapped but no one else was trapping her. I used to take the children out places so that I wouldn't be home when she called. Matt used to tell her I wasn't in. I didn't answer the phone sometimes because it might be her. I feel terrible saying this. She wanted a friend and I didn't want to listen to her problems. Isn't that terrible?'

'No. Not at all,' said Lomax.

'It's normal,' Kim assured her.

'Did you see much of Lewis?'

'Not really. He was always courteous. He organized the neighbourhood campaign to get the road down here paved and he was good at it. He got the road paved. Only after he moved we had a flashflood through here a few times and when the water was gone there were holes in the pavement and they were never repaired.'

She smiled. 'I wouldn't have told you about the flashfloods if you were really buying the house next door. I would have liked you two to move in.'

'We're sorry,' said Kim meekly. Her face was tender now. Her anger was gone.

'So you didn't form an impression of Lewis?'

'Only second-hand. Through Vicky and Gail, the things they said about him.'

'What did they say?'

'Gail adored him. She worshipped him.'

'What did Vicky say?'

'Well the marriage disintegrated . . . I don't know whose fault it was.'

'That can be tough for the children,' Lomax coaxed.

'It was hard for Gail. She took on the responsibility. From a very early age. Lewis just wasn't there. I don't think he was interested in them. But can you completely blame him for that? I mean Vicky was . . .'

Mrs Knight paused and sighed and Lomax realized with relief that she was going to surrender.

'One day when Gail was still small she came here and sat in the kitchen just like she always did. I was busy so it was a while before I noticed she was crying. It wasn't easy to persuade her to say anything. Finally she said she was crying because her Mommy was dead. She said Mommy was lying on the floor in the house and she was dead. Well of course I went right over. Ran over. There's a yucca, several yuccas, one of them caught my leg. Afterwards I had it stitched . . . look . . .'

She exposed a long, thin vertical scar on her shin.

'You see, I can't forget that day even if I wanted to. I must have been bleeding but I didn't notice. I ran right into their house and there was Vicky lying on the floor. She wasn't dead, she was drunk. That was the first time I knew. It explained a lot. I called Lewis at work and kept Gail and Richard at home with me. It was difficult. I had to keep telling them everything was all right and they sat listening to me and they knew it wasn't all right. Lewis came to collect them later. He didn't thank me. Vicky didn't either. Lewis hardly spoke to me again. He was polite but that was all. They could never admit she had a drink problem. Lewis preferred not to think he had a drunk in the family. They liked to do this . . . this happy family act.'

Lomax remembered Vicky Fox's words. 'We were a very happy family.' Julia had said it too, but Julia had meant it.

Kim said: 'It's good for Gail and Richard that someone like you lived next door.'

Mrs Knight looked at Kim keenly but her tone was gentle. 'Someone like me? What am I like?'

'Sort of normal and motherly.'

Mrs Knight's face was sad. 'No,' she said quietly. 'I didn't do enough for those children. Vicky didn't get help, she got worse. Lewis was away more and more. This house could have been a refuge for Gail and Richard but . . . Well, I've thought about it a lot. I guess I wanted to protect my children. Richard was mean. I didn't like him being around Stephen. I didn't encourage him into my home. Gail wasn't always a nice little girl. But she could be sweet as pie. I would have liked her to come here. But she didn't.'

'Did her mother stop her?'

'I don't think so. As the children got wise to the problem over there, they colluded. They helped Vicky and Lewis to cover up. Especially Gail. That meant shutting friends out, shutting me out, shutting out anyone who would guess the truth. It meant taking on the mother's responsibilities for her. Eventually Lewis left and Vicky disintegrated completely. I don't know what happened exactly but I guess Gail was running the house, looking after her mother, doing everything. It was chaotic over there. It smelt. There was food all over the kitchen, old food. It stuck to your shoes if you walked across the floor. There was a dog and no one cleared up its mess.'

Mrs Knight had been shaking her head. When she stopped talking she continued to shake her head.

'Didn't Lewis ever come home to see what was happening?' asked Kim.

'No. No. I don't believe he did. Those children never should have been left with Vicky. Gail never had a chance to be a little girl. Before she was ten she was doing this . . . cover-up for her mother. She started telling lies. Stupid, childish lies, all to protect the mother of course. And she was always saying her father was coming home, or that he had been home. It wasn't true. They did go stay with him for a little. But he always sent them back to her. Maybe he didn't know she was getting violent.'

'She hit them?' asked Kim.

'Probably. I'm not completely sure. I spoke to Gail. I spoke to Vicky. I even spoke to the teacher. But somehow Gail persuaded everyone that everything was fine. Right up until the end. And I think that's why they moved away. Her teacher was beginning to suspect the truth.'

'How about Richard?'

'Gail carried all the responsibilities. I believe Richard simply absented himself from home. I don't know where he went. If he'd gotten himself into trouble, someone would have done something about that family. But he never did. Too smart. Gail was smart too.'

Mrs Knight looked at Lomax. 'I wish I'd done more. I've always felt guilty.'

'What could you do? The children told everyone they were fine,' Lomax said kindly. But Mrs Knight was not reassured.

'They were only children. They didn't know what fine was.'

'Don't blame yourself,' Kim said, adopting Lomax's tone. 'How could you do something when their own father didn't?'

Mrs Knight sighed. 'Lewis was just a mystery to me.'

Lomax studied her sad face. Mrs Knight had been a capable and mature woman when she moved here. She was not the sort of woman who would have interested Lewis.

'Gail pulled off some act,' Kim observed. 'I mean, if she'd looked dirty or uncared for at school, she would have given her mother away.'

'It was one big act every time she left the house. The place was filthy and probably she was most of the time. But when she walked out of that door she was a normal, cheerful little eighth-grader. She could even explain all her bruises away.'

'Gee,' said Kim. She was leaning forward, her mouth a little open.

'She wasn't a pretty child. I think maybe the teacher didn't notice her. When I got so worked up about it that I went down to Oakfield, the teacher said that Gail had never given her any cause to worry about her. I thought: No, Gail's never given you any cause to notice her, and that's different.'

'So,' said Lomax, 'the teacher took no action?'

'She implied that I had some kind of problem.'

'That you had a problem!' Kim's tone was defensive.

'Matt warned me that would happen if I interfered.' She looked down at the floor. 'I believed them both. I believed Matt when he said I was interfering and I believed the teacher when she said I had a problem. I've always regretted it.'

There was a pause. Lomax sensed that she wanted them to leave. But she continued: 'You know, I often wonder what happened to the Foxes. I might even have been thinking about them this morning when you telephoned.'

'Gail was a student at Tradescant when she died,' Lomax told her. 'She majored in French.'

Mrs Knight's sadness was alleviated for a moment. 'Oh!' she said. 'Tradescant's a good college. And Richard?'

'He went to school in Seattle. Now he works in real estate there.'

'Yes,' Mrs Knight said, nodding slowly. 'But Gail's dead and Vicky's still alive. I never would have predicted that.'

'Vicky's badly damaged by alcohol.'

'And Lewis . . . Why were they both killed?'

'We don't know. We don't know who did it or why.'

Kim gave Lomax a rapid glance. He knew this was her comment on his exoneration of Julia.

'Vicky hated that man, even when they were living together. That's why I thought she must have . . . and she had a history of violence. Her mother was violent to her. Violence runs in families.'

'Violence, but probably not murder,' said Lomax.

'I guess they're not the same thing,' agreed Mrs Knight.

Soon afterwards, as they were leaving, Lomax apologized again for their deception.

Her voice was even. 'I'm glad you came. The Foxes have bothered me for years. It's been good to talk about them.'

Lomax called Deputy and Mrs Knight showed them out past a large, simple painting labelled Rocks, Kyoto.

'Are you vacationing again in Japan this year?' asked Kim.

'Yes.'

'That's wonderful,' Kim enthused.

'Not really.' She opened the door. 'I hate Japan.'

At two o'clock, Kim and Lomax waited for the realtor outside the Fox house. It was very hot now. There was no breeze and nothing moved in the yard. Even Deputy, briefly, was motionless. They stood in the carport out of the sun but the walls seemed to radiate heat.

'Do you think she hates him?' Kim asked.

'Who?'

'Her husband.'

'Maybe.'

'I wish she was my mother,' Kim said. 'If I couldn't have her for a mother, grandmother would do.'

'Weren't you mad at me when I told her the truth?' Lomax said, tugging Deputy away from a big moth which he had located clinging to the wall.

'Yeah. But you were right. We'd never have gotten that kind of information otherwise.'

A car could be heard ascending the drive in low gear.

'She's here!' squeaked Kim excitedly. 'Tandra and Roach are about to have a new home.'

'Don't get so carried away that you buy the goddam house,' Lomax warned.

'No chance, we hate decorating.'

Mrs Knight had told them that Vicky Fox had sold the house for a low price in poor condition. Subsequent occupiers had done nothing to improve it.

'And besides,' added Kim, 'Roach is allergic to paint.'

A car pulled up beside the stationwagon. A man was behind its wheel.

'You don't look like the voice on the phone,' Kim observed.

'At P. K. Preen Realty we don't send women out alone on cold calls, Mrs Fenez,' said the man.

'Dr Fenez,' Kim corrected him.

They shook hands. The realtor introduced himself as Arthur Drachman. 'Why the interest in this house?' he asked as he tried various keys in the lock.

'We may be transferring to the observatory down here. We thought we should cruise around and this neighbourhood felt right. So when we saw your sign outside . . .' Kim gave him a warm smile. Lomax thought she was overacting.

'I'll need to take your details,' he told them as the door swung open. 'Okay, I warn you, folks, these empty houses get like hot, hot, hot.'

He was right. As they walked inside they seemed to walk into a wall of heat.

'The brick absorbs heat like a sponge if the air conditioning gets switched off for a while. Of course, if you moved in it would take just one day for the temperature to drop all the way down to a pleasant seventy-five degrees. Your dog would be happy in that.'

Deputy had decided not to come inside. He lowered his head and shot Lomax a look of pure misery before slouching back to the garage.

'Wow,' said Kim moving through the hall in slow motion, 'it's like swimming.'

'Houses sell better when the air conditioning's on, it's a fact,' Arthur Drachman told Lomax confidentially. Lomax sniffed.

'The other thing,' muttered the realtor, 'is that when you shut up a house like this, it holds the smells. You know what I mean?'

Lomax nodded. The house smelt of dirty diapers. He followed Kim down the hall towards the kitchen. The stone floors were covered in places by grey rugs. Matted fluff lined the corners. Colourful fragments of children's toys were startling in the dirt.

'This is the kitchen,' Arthur Drachman said unnecessarily. Lomax looked for the intercom. Kim, flushed in the heat, stood by the glass doors like a pet waiting to be let out. The realtor felt in his pockets for the key and finally the doors slid open. Outside, a low wall stood between the house and the desert. Once it had enclosed a lawn but the grass was now a uniform brown.

'It might grow back if you watered it, sometimes they do, it's amazing,' the realtor said. But Lomax could see the grass was dead.

'We have a clean and green programme at P. K. Preen. People move out, our cleaners move in and we take care of the watering, so that when clients like you come to inspect, the real estate looks clean and the yard looks green. It's nicer that way. Unfortunately the sellers of this choice property didn't subscribe to the programme. They moved east in a hurry. Divorce.'

Kim exited onto the patio and stared at the dead grass.

'Divorce keeps realtors in business,' Arthur Drachman told Lomax. 'Sometimes it makes you feel kind of mean.'

Kim asked questions about the kitchen while Lomax wandered off around the house. Two families had lived here since the Foxes. Two unhappy families, Mrs Knight had implied.

He found the master bedroom, the room Lewis and Vicky had built for themselves.

There was a walk-in closet. He guessed from the telltale holes that mirrors had once been fixed at either end so that you could see yourself from every angle reflected into infinity. He remembered that there was a similar closet in Julia's room with similarly placed mirrors. Julia's mirrors made Lomax feel uncomfortable.

Like the kitchen, this room also had glass doors which led to the yard. In a house where children were welcome in the parental bedroom these doors would be wide open and small children would run in and out with dirty feet and broken toys. Were Gail and Richard ever those children? He peered through the dust on the windows and saw that this area was divided from the rest of the yard by a gate. It had been built for parental privacy.

A fan began breathing asthmatically in the adjoining bathroom when he switched on the light. It was too gloomy to see in here. He turned a dial and the light gradually increased.

The bathroom was windowless and lined in black stone but the first

216

thing he noticed was the bath, sunk dramatically into the centre of the room. It was large enough for several people. The faucets were shaped like mermaids, their round breasts thrust forward provocatively. Lomax saw that the bathroom had been conceived as an adult play room. Lewis and Vicky would not bathe their children here. They had designed their home believing that if they could isolate their marital relationship from the rest of their lives, it would somehow remain intact. He shook his head and switched out the light. The bathroom was tawdry.

He found Gail's room, and Richard's. Gail's was a pale pink. Tape and tacks had taken lumps of paint away over the years. It faced east. Perhaps she was woken by the sun each morning. The mountains, far in the distance, looked pink at this time of day but Lomax knew enough about mountains to guess that sometimes they would look blue, or black or grey. Today the heat made them hazy. On sharp, clear desert mornings they would appear two-dimensional, as if someone had cut them out of waxed paper.

There were more rooms, one of them probably intended for children to play in. It was large enough for table tennis. The living room had an old-fashioned stove, ornamental rather than functional in the Arizona climate. Vicky and Lewis had moved here from the mid-west. Maybe they had intended to pull the drapes in winter and sit by the fire, the snow outside and the smell of burning logs inside.

From the dining room you could see the city. It was uninteresting in the day but probably at night the lights were pretty, as Mrs Fox had told him. It was hard to imagine the family eating meals together in here. Lomax reminded himself that the house could reveal not what had happened to the family but only what Lewis and Vicky had planned would happen.

They had intended their children to sit quietly in front of the fire sometimes. Noisy play would be out of sight and out of earshot in the big games room. Vicky would cook meals and summon them over the intercom when the meals were ready and the family would eat together in the dining room looking across the city lights. At night, when the children were asleep, the adults would play. This is what the Foxes had planned, and when Vicky Fox had described their homelife for Lomax she had described the fantasies on which the house had been built. She preferred this to the reality.

Lomax could hear Kim and the realtor. They were outside in the shade of the terrace. He listened. Kim was arguing about the price.

'. . . terrific views of the town and the mountains . . . ' Arthur Drachman was saying.

'And no goddam pool.'

'. . . Some of the best schools in the area, a very good record for low level noise, the military hardly fly over here, real charming neighbours, who you say you've already met . . .'

'And no goddam pool.'

'. . . plenty of space for your children to play, room for them to grow up, a beautiful big master bedroom with should I say it, yes, let's say it, a really sexy bathroom . . .'

He faltered for a moment and looked doubtfully from Kim to Lomax and back again.

'And no pool,' said Kim.

'Listen,' said Arthur Drachman, 'I don't have a pool either. All the neighbours have pools. Our kids want to swim, they just pick up the phone.'

He was holding a questionnaire which had been completed in Kim's writing. Lomax edged closer and read it over his shoulder. It asked for Tandra's and Roach's dates of birth. They had turned into twins. The questionnaire asked for their interests and Kim had written: 'Equations.'

'I mean,' the realtor was saying, his voice smooth but his face displaying signs of distress, 'redecoration, yes, possibly regrassing, but the price reflects that.'

Kim opened her mouth to make some other comment, probably about the absence of a pool. Lomax said quickly: 'Mr Drachman, thank you for showing us the house. We'd like to talk this over back at our motel now.'

'In the pool,' added Kim snidely.

'Are you going?' asked the realtor, astonished.

'Well, yes . . .'

'But Mrs, Dr Fenez hasn't looked around in there yet!' he exclaimed.

Kim blushed. She had forgotten to look over the house. 'I guess I'll take a quick peek,' she said. 'But my husband and I never disagree on anything. If he likes it, I like it.'

'Oh,' said Mr Drachman, looking at Lomax with admiration. 'I wish my wife said that sort of thing,' he confided as soon as Kim was gone. While they waited for her they looked out at the leathery-skinned yuccas.

'It's kind of difficult to get used to the desert,' Lomax remarked.

'Tell me about it. I came here from Missouri and I thought I'd never get used to it. And now I love it. You're thinking, he's a realtor, they pay him to say this. But it's the truth. I got here, I got out of my car, it was a hundred and twenty-five degrees and my wife said, Arthur, I want to go home. Now she loves it too. We thought the desert was like dead. You know, dead. But it's real fertile! It's teeming with life. There's so much life between here and the next house that you wouldn't believe it. You just have to know how to listen for it and how to look for it. But you work in an observatory. I guess you know how to look for things. I guess it comes natural to you.' He leaned forward. 'Can you tell me anything at all about this new planet, Professor?'

'What garbage did you give him about a new fucking planet?' asked Lomax in the car.

Kim grinned happily. 'I gave him my name and address at the observatory. I said you're too busy with some top secret research to receive mail right now.'

'Top secret research into a new planet?'

'Uh huh.'

'Oh Kim.'

'He deserved it. As soon as he found out that we're astronomers, he started telling me he's a Capricorn.'

'But he's sort of a nice guy.'

'He's a realtor.'

'Didn't you like the way he said he hated making a living from people's divorces?'

'He hates it but he does it. Right here. Then left.'

Arthur Drachman had given Kim directions to Oakfield School.

'Do you want me to go to the secretary's office and try to find the name of a teacher who knew Gail Fox?' she offered.

'No. I guess Mrs Knight said enough. Let's just look at the school while we're out here.'

'I only hope Roach's incredible intelligence won't intimidate the other kids at Oakfield.'

Speed signs told them they were close. A moment later, they drew up outside it.

'Looks like any school in any suburb,' Kim said. Oakfield had no distinguishing features. Its low buildings stretched away to distant playing fields. Lomax tried to imagine Gail arriving on the school bus and walking along the paths past the fire hydrant into her class like the other kids. She would be trying to act like a normal girl. She would be trying to hide the way she held her home and family together. Did she walk alone or with her brother or in a group of friends? It was difficult to see her in a group. Probably she was alone. And she did not carry a lunchbox. She would eat in the school cafeteria each day.

Kim was thinking out loud. 'I wouldn't call the bathroom sexy,' she was saying. 'It was the opposite of sexy. What is the opposite of sexy? Probably sandpaper. I can't think of anything less sexy than sandpaper.'

'Maybe those bathrooms were fashionable twenty years ago,' suggested Lomax. He gave up trying to imagine Gail. 'Where do you want to go now?' he asked.

'Wherever you want to go, Lomax. Remember, me and my husband never disagree on anything.'

'I'd like to take Deputy into the mountains a little way where it's cool and he can walk,' Lomax said. 'But if you want to swim, I could drop you at the motel.'

He liked the idea of walking alone with Deputy in the cool mountains. He would be able to think over all he had learned that day. To his surprise, Kim agreed. 'We'll meet at dinner,' she suggested.

It was a long, hot drive to the mountains. At first, they seemed to get no closer. Deputy sat in the car in abnormal silence. He took little notice of the other dogs they passed. Once the car was within six feet of a horse and he barely looked up.

'Are you okay?' Lomax asked. Deputy ignored him.

They drove to a lake which Kim's guidebooks recommended. It was a relief to leave the desert for the thick shade of the pines. It was late afternoon when they arrived. Most of the other visitors were leaving. As soon as they were out of the car Lomax could feel that the heat had abated. He and Deputy began to walk but it seemed they were walking more slowly than usual.

'Come on,' he called. Deputy ran to catch up. His head was so low that his ears touched the ground.

'I'm worried about you,' Lomax told him.

Deputy had arrived when Joel was small and Helen was a baby. The children were still young but, Lomax realized for the first time, Deputy was growing old. He watched the dog struggling with the climate and the sudden difference in altitude and recoiled the way he always did when confronted by the inevitability of ageing, his own or someone else's. Berlins' shaking hands had the same effect.

Deputy was sniffing round the rocks which lined the trail. He was looking for evidence of other dogs but it seemed to Lomax he was looking without the enthusiasm he might once have shown. Deputy's life was concertina-ed into fewer years but the process was the same for everyone and the next phase and the last were easy to anticipate. The thought that Deputy had already started his decline towards death was so painful that Lomax sat down on a boulder. Deputy looked at him in surprise and then lifted a hind leg at a comical angle against the boulder and urinated on it.

Lomax stroked the dog's head fondly. The gradual nature of ageing anaesthetized you to its effects. Only recent generations, with the invention of the camera, confronted themselves with an unwelcome chronicle of the changes. Lomax regarded himself as a constant in a shifting world but old photos told him that, despite his resistance, even he had changed. Everybody changes, no one stays the same. Who had said that recently?

They resumed their hike, and when they reached the lake Deputy barely paused to look at it. He walked off the trail, onto the lake shore and into the water in a straight line. Lomax watched Deputy's ears floating behind him. He squatted and slipped his fingers through the surface of the water. It was cool. He undressed and followed Deputy into the lake. Its temperature shocked him. He began to swim. The regular motion of his arms and legs was pleasing. The cold numbed his melancholy. When he dropped his head under the water he could hear nothing and see nothing and when he looked up to breathe nothing seemed real.

He remembered watching another swimmer's elbows cutting through calm water. He had been sitting with Vicky Fox back in California. It was then that she had said: 'Everyone changes, no one stays the same.' Today Mrs Knight had assumed that Gail and Lewis were murdered by Vicky.

He swam further. He looked up for Deputy and could not see him. He scanned the wet horizon and then turned back and located Deputy on the lake shore, shaking himself. Lomax resumed the rhythm of his swim.

Gail had grown up before she was ten. Far from showing a sexual interest in her as Lomax had suspected, her father had ignored her. She had shouldered his responsibilities for him. And she had succeeded in fooling her teachers and her schoolfriends and her friends' parents and anyone else who might threaten the elaborate lie she had constructed around her family. He wondered what such a ten-year-old had become by the age of twenty. He resolved to redouble his efforts, when he was home, to find someone who knew her.

20

It was Lomax's turn to drive. Kim was leaning over the map. She told Lomax this made her carsick but she did it anyway.

'Ah, there's Lifebelt Lake,' she said. 'That's where Julia went.'

They had left the desert behind them and were taking a leisurely route home. They had been to the Cowboy Museum and various other sights and now they were heading north on a rising altitude. Even in the afternoon the air was cooler.

'Julia?'

'When I told her I was going to Arizona she said she had this vacation in Arizona at some resort called Lifebelt Lake. And I've just seen it on the map.'

'Julia said that?' Lomax was suspicious. Julia seldom volunteered information about herself.

'She went there last summer. She's real nostalgic about it because she went with her family and it was their last vacation together. In fact, as soon as they got back the daughter, stepdaughter, went to France and Julia never saw her again.'

'She told you that?'

'Why do you have a problem with this, Lomax?'

'Because Julia never tells anybody anything.'

Kim turned to him. She was chewing gum. Her sunglasses looked ridiculously small. 'You mean, she never tells you anything.'

Lomax bridled at the possibility that Julia revealed more to Kim than she did to him.

'People talk to me. You think Mrs Knight would have said half as much if I hadn't been there?'

Lomax did not answer this question. He was thinking about Julia. When he had told her about this trip she had at first encouraged him to go. She had said he needed a vacation. But when he revealed his real purpose in coming to Arizona there had been a silence. 'I don't understand what Gail's childhood has to do with anything,' she had commented at last.

He had telephoned her most nights from the motels and talked about the places he had been and about Deputy and Kim. Gail had been on his mind. Her house in the desert, her mother, her school and her life. But to avoid the awkwardness of more silences he had not told Julia any of this.

'So is Lifebelt Lake on our way?' he asked Kim now.

'Sort of. Want to go there?'

'Yes.'

'I thought so. I thought all I had to say was the magic word.'

'Lifebelt?'

'Julia.'

'But,' said Lomax, 'it's kind of interesting. Three people vacation together. A few months later two of them are dead and the third's accused of their murder.'

Kim nodded. 'Yes,' she said, 'that's interesting. If you start asking questions about Julia, then it gets interesting.'

'Julia? I'm not asking questions about Julia.'

'Why not?'

He tried to sound patient. 'Because I'm on her side, Kim. The prosecution asks questions about Julia.'

Lifebelt Lake was an expensive resort. You left your car in a compound and travelled around by buggy and walkway.

'We can't afford this,' Kim said.

'They don't give any prices so how do you know?'

'Because they don't give any prices.'

But Lomax knew he was going to stay here. Lewis and Gail and Julia had stayed here. It was the last time all three of them were together until Julia went to the morgue to identify the bodies. He hoped someone would remember them.

'Just one night.'

'I don't like log cabins.'

'Sure you do.'

'They have ants.'

'Not these log cabins.'

Lomax went into the lodge. A young woman in white pants and a white shirt smiled at him. 'You can't rent the cabins by the night,' she said. 'And especially not at this time of year.'

Her smile faded and her face fell. Lomax realized she was mirroring his own reaction. 'You could stay here at the lodge if we had a room, but I don't think . . .'

There was the subdued clattering of fingers on a keyboard.

'No. We don't have anything right now.'

'That's a shame,' Lomax said. 'Some friends of mine told me to be sure and stay here. They gave me the number and made me promise to make a reservation but I lost the number.'

The receptionist looked sympathetic. Her hair was neatly brushed into two blonde pigtails.

'Their name's Fox. They came here last year . . .'

'Fox. Fox . . .' The woman wanted to be helpful. 'Oh yes. I think I recall . . .'

She typed something and nodded at whatever the computer told her.

'Lewis!' she said. Lomax was not convinced by her tone of discovery. He believed that she had remembered Lewis at once, before asking the computer's permission to do so. Her hair and smile and figure said that Lewis would certainly have noticed her.

'He came here with his wife and daughter. Did you meet them?'

'I remember his daughter. She was a very pretty girl.'

Lomax did not bother to correct her. Of course she would have assumed Julia was Lewis' daughter.

'And he's charming. He said he'd be back this year but he doesn't seem to have booked.'

Lomax spared her. He said: 'Lewis may not be able to take a vacation this year.'

'I'm real sorry we can't fit you in, as you're here on Lewis' recommendation . . .' she said thoughtfully. Something about her voice indicated that she was going to suggest a way round the problem.

Suddenly Kim appeared. The woman looked at her in surprise.

'No room at the lodge and no cabins by the night,' Lomax told her.

Kim gave the woman a look of desolation. 'Oh, but we're on our honeymoon,' she wailed.

Lomax flinched.

'Wait a minute,' the woman called over her shoulder as she disappeared into an adjoining office. Lomax glared at Kim. She grinned back serenely. They looked around them. The room was painted white. It was bare and of pristine cleanliness. It reminded Lomax of Candice's clinic.

'I nearly crossed myself when I walked in here. It's sort of religious, like a mission,' Kim whispered. They had visited old Spanish missions in Arizona with simple interiors like this. She pointed to a pair of white antlers, bleached by the sun, which hung over the door. 'That's where the Holy Virgin should be,' she said.

Lomax had always assumed Candice's clinic was white because its aspirations were medical. Now he wondered for the first time if it was designed to give a religious significance to the process of transformation which Candice claimed took place there.

Voices could be heard in the office. Finally the woman re-emerged. She said: 'We have an empty cabin due to a cancellation. It's a five-room deluxe, so it's probably bigger than you need, but it's all we have. I can let you take it for a minimum of three nights.'

'How much?' asked Kim.

'Don't say it. Write it down,' Lomax said quickly. He turned to Kim and added in a tone which was supposed to be fond but came out threatening: 'Don't look. Honey.'

He hardly glanced at the sum the woman wrote before agreeing to it. He was going to stay here.

'Our valet will be right over to transfer your baggage to your buggy and put your car in the lot,' the woman said.

'Do you think he's ever parked a car like that before?' asked Kim as the stationwagon, empty but strangely lopsided, disappeared out of sight. She had insisted on transferring all her bottles of salad dressing and tins of food to the buggy. The valet had watched in silence.

Kim drove them along well-swept lanes to their cabin. Deputy ran alongside. 'How much?' she kept asking. Lomax did not tell her.

The cabin was impressive. There was no other cabin close by and it overlooked the lake. There was a verandah with two hammocks. Lomax sat in one of them. He liked its soft, swaying movement. He lay down. He stared out over the lake. Probably all the cabins were the same. Lewis and Gail and Julia had stayed here last year, perhaps almost exactly a year ago. They had swung in hammocks like these and watched the lake. What had they said? What had they thought? What had they done? He closed his eyes.

'Ants!' bellowed Kim close to his ear. She'd found a thin line of red ants progressing purposefully across the verandah.

'They're fake ants,' Lomax mumbled, rearranging himself in his hammock. 'They switch them on when you arrive so you can kid yourself you're having a pioneer experience.'

'Huh,' said Kim, scrambling into the other hammock.

When Lomax woke he lay watching the view and listening to Kim and Deputy snoring. It was almost night. The lake looked a deeper blue now and the wooded slopes looked dark. The shape of the lake was better defined in this half-light: it formed an almost perfect circle. In the middle was a round island.

Moving quietly, he took the winding trail which led past the cabin to the shore. It was not hard to walk noiselessly on the thick pine needles. After a few minutes he felt something brush against his leg. Deputy. When they reached the water Deputy sniffed it and Lomax scooped a little up with his fingers. The light made the water look viscous but it disappeared rapidly between his fingers, leaving them icy with cold.

They followed the trail around the perimeter and eventually it led to a collection of wooden buildings. A bar and a couple of restaurants glittered in the night. The restaurants looked expensive. He went into the bar. The beer was expensive. The other customers watched him. There were small groups, some silent, some talking or laughing. Their laughter was rich. Their faces were bright with the day's sun. They seemed to shine in the subdued light. It was easy to imagine Julia among them. This had been Julia's world, before the murders.

Nobody spoke to him. He took his beer outside and found that during his absence the darkness had thickened. He sat with Deputy on a wooden jetty looking across the blackness of the lake.

He had nearly finished his drink when a man joined him. The man commented on the beauty and calm of the lake but seemed unaffected by either. He talked compulsively. He spewed words at Lomax. He talked initially about a dog he had owned as a child in Washington which had looked like Deputy, but as it grew too dark for them to see each other he began to discuss the fish he had caught that day and then his family. Lomax listened to the voice. The man sounded small and energetic. He said he lived in New Jersey. He owned a timeshare in Lifebelt Lake. His family came here every year for three weeks.

'The same three weeks each year?' asked Lomax, alert suddenly.

'Yup,' said the man. He started to talk about the summer weather, the weather in New Jersey, the weather in Washington when he was a child.

'I guess that if you come back to the same place each year you soon get to know people,' Lomax said when the man paused for breath.

The man confirmed this and began to talk about the people he had got to know. None of them sounded like Lewis.

'A family recommended this resort to me, they came here about a year back. Maybe you met them,' Lomax suggested. 'Their name is Fox.'

'Fox, Fox, I probably knew them by sight.'

'Lewis is around sixty, tall, white-haired. He came here with his wife, very pretty, very young, and – '

'Oh, yeah, yeah, Lewis,' said the man. 'I met him a few times. And her. She was pretty. So, she was his wife. I actually thought she was his daughter. Yeah, Lewis. I met him everywhere. He's like me. I don't just do nothing when I vacation. I fish, I swim, I rowboat, I visit the cave paintings. I met Lewis and the cute girl, the wife, at the cave paintings. Some of them are sort of, you know, explicit. She was laughing. Yeah, I remember them. How is he?'

'He's fine,' lied Lomax.

'Good, that's good,' said the man enthusiastically.

'There was someone else with them . . .'

'Oh?'

'Lewis' daughter . . .'

The man made remembering noises. Finally he said: 'No. Must have been a different Lewis. I don't recall anybody else with them . . .'

Lomax pushed and tugged at the man's memory but the voice refused to supply a daughter. Instead Lomax learned about the cave paintings in the next valley. They looked just a few years old but had actually been scratched into the rock by cave dwellers centuries ago. A few of them showed couples having sex in interesting positions. The man from New Jersey urged Lomax to see them.

Promising to visit the paintings, Lomax returned to the cabin, Deputy leading him along the dark trails. Lomax could not forgive the man for disturbing the quiet night with his noise. He could not forgive him for remembering the wrong Lewis.

'Where have you been?' asked Kim. 'I made us some food. I figured the restaurants here cost a lot.'

Lomax told her about the man.

'Of course it's the same Lewis,' said Kim.

'How can it be?'

'You think many guys called Lewis come here with pretty girls half their age?'

'But he can only remember Julia. Gail was here too.'

'Fine. So Gail stays here swinging on the hammock and Julia's out making whoopee with the cave paintings.'

'Why?'

Kim sighed. They were in the formerly immaculate kitchen. To make the meal, Kim had raided her food supplies and the detritus was strewn over most of the surfaces. Now she rearranged the kitchen chairs to support her knees and ankles. The exertion left her breathless.

'Why does Gail stay home? You really don't know?'

'No, Kim.'

'Lomax, it's time we talked about this.'

'There's salad dressing all around your mouth.'

Kim wiped her mouth. 'I would have told you earlier if you'd asked for my opinion,' she said. She had opened a bottle of wine from the coolbox. It was already half empty.

'I didn't know you had an opinion.'

'Lomax . . .' Kim pulled a face and put her head on one side. 'Lomax, I always have an opinion.'

'Okay, I'm listening.'

'First, you describe Gail.'

'I can't exactly.'

'Try.'

Kim found a glass for Lomax and filled it with wine. She replenished her own.

'Well . . .' he began. 'She was homely. Plain. Sort of awkward. Dressed sloppy. Overweight in the wrong places. She was smart, though.'

'Sounds like me, except I'm overweight in every place,' said Kim cheerfully. Lomax ignored her.

'I don't know much more than that. It's hard to imagine what that childhood would turn her into.'

'Tough? Resourceful?'

Lomax drank some wine. The glass felt cold in his fingers, like the lake water. 'Maybe,' he conceded. 'But that implies a strong personality. I've spoken to people who knew her and they all have trouble describing her. No one can remember much about her.'

Kim dropped her feet to the floor with a thud and leaned towards him across the table. 'It's like that when you're goddam ugly,' she said.

'Aw, Kim . . .' He could not look at her.

'Nobody notices you.'

'C'mon, Kim . . .'

'I mean it, Lomax. I'm trying to tell you how Gail felt. You want to find out about this woman, I'm telling you what it felt like to be her. She was smart but according to you she looked like shit. I can empathize with that. She knew she had a lot going for her but when she reached a certain age . . .' Kim paused and looked thoughtful. 'It doesn't matter what age. With me it was about, say, thirteen, but I was a late developer. Anyway, one day you realize that it doesn't matter what else you've got, if you're not pretty you're not anything.'

'Kim –'

'Nobody notices you. It's a fact, you can't argue with it. But girls with a cute smile who don't have two grey cells to rub together, these girls can have it all. Gail's homely and plain and, what else did you say about her, overweight in the wrong places? Then she's been through that one.'

Lomax tried unsuccessfully to interrupt.

'Shuddup. Ugly girl's talking.'

She drew breath. Lomax was silent with embarrassment. He did not like Kim to make this kind of disparaging reference to her appearance.

'Gail adores her daddy but he doesn't pay her any attention. She shoulders his responsibilities at home and the sonova lets her. Later on, she gets to live with Daddy, but what does she find there? Julia is what she finds. Julia. Julia's stunning by anybody's standards. Of course, she has a shortage in the brains department. And, unlike Gail, who had to fend for herself and others, Julia's spent her whole life sheltered and protected by a rich daddy and then, dammit, by Gail's daddy. This is the daddy who should have been looking after Gail. And all Julia has to do is simper and giggle and look cute and Daddy's all over her. How do you think that makes Gail feel? How?'

Lomax watched Kim closely. Her eyes protruded. The pupils floated in the whites. Her mouth was turning into mean shapes. Her chins were pressed together.

'Awful, I guess.'

'Right. So when you go on vacation with Daddy and Julia and she's the belle of the lake, you stay in your goddam log cabin with the ants.'

'I see.'

'She probably hated Julia,' said Kim, taking gulps at the wine. 'I would have.'

'You're not ugly, Kim.'

'I'm fat.'

'You're pretty,' Lomax told her seriously. It wasn't true just now but it sometimes was. When Kim was in a good mood her face was soft and pink. Her hair could look fluffy. Her teeth were even and she had a neat little nose.

'Julia thinks I'd be prettier if I lost some weight,' Kim said mischievously.

'Don't,' he told her.

'But Julia said!' she taunted him. 'She told me all about weight loss programmes and said she could help with my clothes and told me how I would look slimmer if I changed my hair. She did, Lomax.'

Lomax scrutinized the kitchen floor. There was a slice of tomato under the table. Deputy woud eat anything which touched the ground except tomato.

'Just be yourself, Kim,' he snapped at last.

That night, Lomax slept outside in the hammock. The stars were visible overhead and he lay watching them and thinking about Kim's words. Had Kim revealed more about herself than about Gail? He was falling asleep when he felt a stabbing pain in that place, high in his belly, which told him he was missing Julia. He resolved to call her before she started work in the morning.

She answered the phone on the very first ring.

'We're at a place called . . .' he paused as if he could not recall the name. He was being careful. He did not want her to feel that she was being investigated. 'Um . . . Lifebelt Lake? It's a place Kim says you like.'

'Oh!' exclaimed Julia in surprise. 'Lifebelt Lake!'

'Kim says you had a terrific vacation here once.'

'Did I say it was terrific?' asked Julia.

'Didn't you like it?' He remembered now that she had told him she did not like vacations.

'I was there a year ago. With Lewis and Gail. It makes me feel sad to think about it because it was the last time the three of us . . .' As usual, her voice trailed away.

'It's nice here,' he told her hastily. 'We're staying in a log cabin with ants. There are some cave paintings.'

'About ten miles away.'

'We'll be here for two more nights. Then we're coming home. I want to see you.'

'You think it's okay to meet?'

'The press isn't going to be staking you out every moment between now and your trial. I miss you.'

He waited for her to say that she also missed him, but there was a silence. The dull ache began again in his belly. His voice, when he spoke, was faded. 'You can stay with me and no one will know you're there.'

Julia's silences had the power to rob him of any certainty. When she did not reply immediately he added: 'I mean, maybe. If you want to.'

'Okay,' she agreed. He could hear that she was smiling. 'We'll hide under the sheets where no one will find us.'

The knots inside his belly rearranged themselves. 'Yes,' he said. 'That's a good place to hide.'

Kim had been to the resort supermarket. She returned carrying a brown bag, provisions spilling from it.

'I bought the absolute minimum because of the prices in that place,' she said, heaving the bag onto the table. Inside, cans clinked against bottles. 'We'll have to stop on the road for the rest.'

Lomax was hungry. He began looking through the bag for breakfast.

'What road?'

'The road to the cave paintings. A man told me to be sure go see them. They're dirty.'

'Did the man come from New Jersey?' He found some blueberry muffins. He opened the box and began to tear at the wrapper inside with his teeth.

'No, he and a couple of other guys hire out rowboats. Or speedboats between three and five in the afternoon. They remember Lewis and Julia.'

Lomax stopped just where he was with his mouth full of plastic wrapper.

'Did Lewis have white hair?' asked Kim.

'Yes.'

'So that's him. Lewis didn't like speedboats on the lake. They're so noisy that they're only allowed between three and five. Some people are still out there after five and Lewis complains about it.'

'Did these guys remember Gail?'

'No, Lomax,' said Kim patiently, 'because they never saw Gail because she didn't go out.' She took the muffins from him and put them in the microwave. 'You should see these kids on the boats. They look like Mr Universe. I bet they hire themselves out by the night to rich widows.'

Lomax did not like this idea. Julia was a rich widow.

'They really hated Lewis,' Kim told him.

'Why?'

'Because he complained about the speedboats and because he was always rowing Julia around on the lake trying to look muscular.' Kim's voice was sly. 'I think they found Julia sort of attractive,' she said.

'Uh huh,' said Lomax. Of course they found Julia attractive. It was completely predictable that they found Julia attractive.

'They played mean tricks on Lewis.'

'Like what?'

'Like, Julia gets into the rowboat. Her bikini's too small. Lisp, giggle, simper, wiggle. She sits down. Lewis is just getting in after her and the guys sort of shove the boat so he misses and falls into the water.'

Lomax did not laugh. It was hard to imagine Lewis' dignity being compromised in this way.

'And they let Lewis get right out on the lake, then they ride their speedboat too close to his rowboat so it practically turns over in the swell. Actually, I think they did that because they wanted to rescue Julia.'

The bell rang on the microwave.

'Remind me not to hire a rowboat,' Lomax said.

'Too late. We're booked for this afternoon when we get back from our trip to the caves.'

When they reached the caves a sign warned them that the site was dangerous. The caves were connected by ladders and visitors were warned to ascend only with the utmost care. The sign ended with the words: 'Are you fit to climb?'

Kim did not remark on it but some of the other people in their tour glanced at her when they had read it. Lomax recognized a few of them from the bar last night. He guessed most of the group came from Lifebelt Lake.

They were led by a thin ranger with thick glasses. He was taller even than Lomax. His voice was monotonous and the tourists made no attempt to hide their lack of interest in his talk. He told them about the hunting and cooking arrangements of the pueblo dwellers while his audience mumbled and shuffled their feet and took pictures with noisy cameras. They were waiting to see the sexual wall paintings. They had no interest in ancient cooking implements.

'The pueblo dwellers' lives by the thirteenth century were dominated by their search for water. For a hundred years when the caves were first occupied, water was no problem. But carbon testing in the area reveals that the weather pattern changed and that within the space of one man's lifetime the water supplies in the immediate area had dried. The pueblo dwellers were forced to travel further and further each day for water until they were carrying it twenty-five miles. Probably this led to the evacuation of the caves. We assume they moved closer to a source of water. We don't know. There's no evidence to tell us exactly where they went or what became of them. There are theories that the shortage of water bred disease in the community. There's another theory, thanks to the paintings on the next level, that the pueblo dwellers were the victims of a sexually transmitted virus which eventually wiped out the whole community. There's no evidence for this.'

At the ranger's reference to the paintings a silence fell in the group. The ranger's delivery was unblinking. Lomax suspected that he despised the tourists.

They were invited to climb a ladder to the next level and the ranger waited patiently while they shrieked and giggled their way up it. The slender, more athletic members of the party went first. Lomax could see Kim reddening as her turn drew near. There was a silence in the group as she heaved herself onto the first rung, the weight of her body swinging her to one side, her camera hanging. Everybody watched as her pants stretched tight over her rolling thighs.

At the top they ducked under the curving lip of a cave and clustered intimately. The air inside swelled with anticipation. The ranger discussed the temperature in the pueblo and its seasonal fluctuations and the tourists shifted their weight from foot to foot impatiently. They moved even closer together. Then, when the ranger began to discuss the pictures, suddenly they were still.

'The pueblo dwellers were good record keepers. You've seen some facets of their everyday life recorded on the rocks below. Now you'll see the work of probably just one artist, depicting life as he knew it. We don't know exactly why he chose to make unusually graphic depictions of sexual activity but I warn you that some of the pictures are explicit. Don't complain to me if you're shocked. Just don't look at them if you feel that way.'

The tourists exchanged glances which said they planned to look.

'When you go through the rock arch into the adjacent cave, turn right and follow the pictures around if you want to see them in what is believed to be the correct sequence. You'll learn all about a man who lived in these caves, probably for around eighty years, from approximately 1250 to 1330 AD.'

Lomax was sceptical. He followed the other tourists through a sandstone arch, its threshold worn thin underfoot by pueblo dwellers or tourists or both. He remembered how he had tried to reconstruct Lewis Fox's life from phone numbers and photos. He had simply succeeded in creating a different Lewis. The pictures this man had left would be even less revealing because the artist himself controlled the flow of information.

The group filed silently into the half-lit chamber. They took the route indicated by the ranger, moving quickly past the first pictures in which stickmen made pots and killed animals.

'These walls are generally regarded as the artist's pictorial auto-biography. Contemporary European art was far more developed.

Think of medieval manuscripts with their colourful illuminations. By contrast, these paintings are of course crude cartoons. The predominant colour is red because of the local availability of haematite. The artist shows little understanding of perspective but his work is an earthy and unpretentious representation of daily life.'

The front of the line had discovered the sexual pictures. There was giggling and whispering.

'Maybe,' said the ranger, his voice parched with irony, 'some of you will find it interesting to chart the gradual disappearance of the pueblo dwellers' water supply.'

He fell silent, watching the tourists. His face was hidden by his hat now. Occasionally his Adam's apple moved.

The thick waving line representing the river grew thinner as Lomax progressed past the pictures. It was often shown at night under recognizable constellations: the Big Dipper, Orion, and sometimes the moon. In daytime pictures the sun was red, dangling threateningly behind the heads of the stickmen.

'Look!' said Lomax, grabbing Kim's arm.

'Did you find something dirty?' asked Kim. She was sweating. She pushed her body against him.

'Just look.'

Kim peered at the painting. 'What is it?'

'Call yourself ABC's eclipse correspondent?'

On the flat wall of the cave was painted a linked series of cartoon images. The sun was large and round and red, then something like a big fish seemed to be swallowing it up. It became a crescent, still shining as it disappeared, a few images later, into the monstrous fish mouth. There was darkness, punctuated by stars. In the next image, the sun began to re-emerge from the fish until it was a globe again and beneath it birds sang. But the river, a thin line which had twisted noticeably through the earlier pictures, had disappeared.

'It's a total eclipse of the sun!' shrieked Kim so loudly that people turned to stare. Tourists behind her, misunderstanding her excited tone, pushed forward.

'Just wait 'til I tell ABC about this,' she said.

The ranger came over to them.

'You're right. It's a total eclipse of the sun. It's this which has helped us to date the paintings accurately. It's a rare event. There's one this fall in the western United States, probably the only time most of us will ever see a total eclipse.'

'Don't I know it?' said Kim proudly. 'I'm ABC's eclipse correspondent.'

The ranger did not respond.

'Did the pueblo dwellers think the eclipse was associated with the loss of their water supply?' asked Lomax.

'It seems the two events coincided,' he agreed, 'and the pueblo dwellers concluded that there was a causal relationship. It would have been hard for them, living so close to nature, to imagine that such a dramatic celestial event would have no impact on their lives at all. They saw it as an omen at the very least. I guess that there'll be quite a bit of that kind of speculation about the eclipse this fall, even in so-called enlightened modern America.'

They shuffled closer to the sexual scenes. Stick women were penetrated by stick men with outsize penises. The penetration took place from a variety of angles, some of them unlikely.

'Hey look, some things don't change. She's giving him a blow job,' said Kim, pointing.

A woman curled, fishlike, at a man's feet and swallowed his penis. There was a crescent moon overhead. The man was standing. He threw his arms up and it was this ecstatic movement which made Lomax think of Julia. He stared at the picture. It seemed impossible that this primitive painting had the power to arouse but the tightening inside his jeans was unmistakable. Jostled by people behind, he moved on.

'Pueblo woman. What a life. Fetching, carrying and blowing,' said Kim.

The ranger spoke.

'Perhaps some of you have noticed the way the sun seems to grow in size towards the end of the sequence. And there's no indication of water at all there. One of the more melancholy interpretations of the sequence is that the elderly artist was left here to die when what remained of the community finally moved out in their search for water. The penultimate picture shows some sort of exodus. And in the last the artist anticipates his own death.'

A solitary figure squatted at the mouth of a dark cave, so childishly painted that it might have been the mouth of another dark fish which was about to consume him whole. The sun, now of massive proportions, hovered like an outsize red vulture overhead.

That afternoon, when they rowed on the lake, the water seemed to have increased in value. The sound of the oars was soothing. The size of the lake and quantity of liquid that surrounded them was reassuring.

'Do you think he painted the last picture and then just went and sat in the pueblo until he died?' asked Kim. 'Gee, that's sort of noble.'

'No,' said Lomax. He had been unsettled to meet the young men who rented out the boats. Swaggering and muscle-bound, it was easy to imagine them lusting after Julia and intimidating Lewis.

'How come no?'

'Just because the style of the pictures is naive doesn't mean they're honest. The guy who painted them was a serial killer. The pueblo dwellers didn't evacuate or die of some disease, he murdered them all. The wall paintings are a fabrication for the defence. He made up the story about the water shortage and, a master stroke this, he suggested that the water loss was linked to a celestial event. He guessed that anyone investigating the disappearance of his people would have such a patronizing attitude to them that they'd believe them capable of such ingenuousness. Giggling uncontrollably, he painted a noble death for himself before setting off into the desert to kill other pueblo dwellers in other places.'

Kim had been lying back, one hand drooping into the water. Sometimes her fingers half floated on the surface. She looked graceful. Now she struggled onto her elbows, wobbling the boat.

'This murder investigation is twisting your mind, Lomax,' she said admiringly.

'As for the sexual pictures,' added Lomax, 'they're pure fantasy. No female pueblo dweller would even look at the guy.'

'Did you find them arousing?' asked Kim.

'No,' lied Lomax. Kim lay back once again. She was chuckling. Then the lake was silent except for the slapping noise the water made against the boat.

'Have you enjoyed our vacation, Lomax?' Kim said dreamily.

'Sure.'

'Did you find out anything useful? About the murders?'

Lomax began to row slowly.

'Interesting,' he said finally, 'but I'm not sure if it's useful.'

21

To Lomax's surprise, Frances invited him to her office for a meeting soon after his return to California.

'Is it okay if I see Julia before the trial?' he asked.

Frances looked at him sympathetically. 'Missing her?'

'Yes.'

'Tough,' said Kurt. He had come into the room to hear Lomax's request. He grinned. Gum squirmed between his upper and lower teeth as if it were trying to escape. He said: 'Just take it from me, Lomax. I've seen her twice this week and she's looking good, okay?'

He grinned again and then his jaw began to stab violently and indiscriminately in the air. Lomax realized that he was chewing the gum.

'Meet her somewhere private and just make sure you're discreet,' Frances told him. 'Very discreet.'

Lomax felt elated. He and Julia had already agreed that with Frances' approval they would meet the very next day. There was an acute and involuntary tightening of his facial muscles. He realized he was smiling. To disguise this he looked down at the table and when he looked up a new pile of notebooks and papers had arrived and behind it sat Marjorie.

'Hi Kurt. Hi Lomax,' she said.

'Hair's cool,' Kurt told her. Marjorie blushed and thanked him and began to rearrange the papers unnecessarily. She looked nervous. Lomax guessed this was her first meeting in Frances' office. She glanced up at Lomax. He was studying her hair. It was the same as before only shorter.

'So, where are we on this case?' Frances asked them. 'It's not so long now until the trial, since Julia wouldn't waive time.'

'I tried everything in my power to persuade her,' Kurt said, chuckling and chewing gum at the same time. 'Reason. Emotion. Talking tough. Boyish charm.'

Frances smiled. 'How's our defence progressing?' She looked from face to face. Only Kurt looked back at her. Lomax could not meet her eye because he had already decided that nothing he had seen or learned here or in Arizona would be of interest to this meeting. Frances and Marjorie would listen but Kurt would ask him the relevance of the information, a question Lomax would be unable to answer.

Frances said: 'Lomax has been vacationing. What have you been doing, Marjorie?'

Marjorie jumped like an inattentive student in class. She picked up a notebook and thumbed through it.

'Well . . . you now have an updated list of all the calls made by Lewis Fox at home, at work or from his car in the three months prior to his death. Lomax helped me compile some of it. He did real good work.' She did not look at Lomax but turned a deep red.

'Good,' said Frances kindly. 'Does the list tell us much?'

'Professionally, there are no surprising connections here at all. Absolutely none. If he had a professional reason to ask his wife for $450,000 then it's not obvious from his calls. I've followed up every single one of them.'

'Yes, professionally Lewis seems to be clean,' Frances agreed. She looked directly at Lomax. 'We've chased Julia's suggestion that Lewis needed the money because there was some kind of problem here at Sachs Smith. Two independent auditors have looked at our books and they couldn't find anything.'

Lomax guessed that Frances had invited him to the meeting simply to hear this. There was no other reason for his presence.

'I must admit,' she added, 'that it was a relief for the firm, although it doesn't help our case any.'

'How was Zurich?' Lomax asked Kurt.

Kurt was throwing his pen up in the air. Lomax wished he would drop it. 'Tidy streets. Pretty girls. Fried food.' He caught the pen neatly.

Lomax was patient. 'Did you find the money had been transferred from Gail to Lewis?'

'No,' said Kurt. 'Zurich is the No Tell Motel of international banking. So what if you're dead? So what if you're wanted by the police of fifty different countries? Your secrets are safe in Zurich.'

The room was silent.

'So there's no evidence at all that Gail passed the money along to Lewis?' said Lomax.

Frances sighed. 'We can't prove she did. We can't prove she didn't.'

'It's complicated,' Kurt explained. 'Lewis had money in a whole load of different accounts. When did it get there and how? Unravelling that kind of thing takes a while.'

Frances added: 'If we just had some indication of why Lewis wanted that $450,000 . . . What about his private life? The girl-friends . . . ?

'Girlfriends are cool,' Kurt told them, throwing and catching the pen in one neat movement.

Marjorie said: 'We know there was some brunette who Lewis was seen around with in the early summer before his death. I haven't managed to identify her yet. I've found a few of the other girlfriends, the ones before Alice.'

'Keep looking for the brunette,' Frances told her.

Kurt said: 'I know why Lewis wanted that money. It was nothing to do with girlfriends.'

Lomax and Marjorie and Frances all looked up at him in surprise. Kurt threw his pen around nonchalantly.

'Are you going to stop the demonstration of manual dexterity and explain yourself?' Frances asked. Kurt caught the pen efficiently and smiled from one to the other of them. Lomax guessed that he had been anticipating this moment since the meeting began.

Frances raised her eyebrows at him.

'You know why Lewis wanted the money?'

'Uh huh.' Kurt wagged his jaw happily.

'Really?' The more astonishment Frances showed, the more Kurt smirked. Lomax thought he looked grotesque.

'I followed up on the research Marjorie and Lomax carried out. The answer was there in that list they compiled for anyone to see.'

Marjorie and Lomax exchanged rapid glances.

'In fact, it was Lomax who made most of the relevant calls. He spoke right to them.'

Everyone looked at Lomax.

'Who did he speak to?' Marjorie demanded. Her tone was defensive. She was blushing again.

'Do the names Arnold Carr, Plus Eleven and Lost in Space mean anything to you?' Kurt asked Lomax. There was a loud crash. Marjorie jumped. Lomax realized that he had knocked over his coffee cup. He grabbed it just as it rolled off the edge of the table and saw that luckily it was empty. Frances took it from him to refill it.

'Remember them?' Kurt pressed him mercilessly.

Lomax thought of his days behind the small desk in his office at Sachs Smith. He remembered the white walls and a blur of voices in his ear. It was possible he had spoken to people or companies of that name.

'I dimly recollect . . .' he began. The recollection was getting less dim all the time. He had talked to someone at Lost in Space for a while because he had liked the name of the company. She had explained that they specialized in office space rentals in the city.

'They're all in the real estate business,' Marjorie said.

'Thank you, Marjorie, they're all realtors. Didn't that interest you one little bit, Lomax?'

'No,' admitted Lomax gloomily. 'Realtors don't interest me one little bit.'

Kurt shook his finger at Lomax and put his head on one side. 'Gotta broaden those horizons.'

'That's not fair!' Marjorie said loudly. Kurt turned to her in surprise. She added more quietly: 'Lomax was only helping to compile the list, he wasn't supposed to be analysing it.'

Kurt displayed his teeth. 'He wants to play detective, he has to learn to think a little.'

'Okay, Kurt,' Frances intervened, returning with Lomax's cup and placing it a long way in front of him where it would be harder for him to knock over, 'you've made your point. Now why was Lewis calling realtors?'

Kurt paused again for effect. He addressed Frances: 'I'm sorry I didn't have time to tell you this before the meeting, it may be a shock to you . . .'

Frances sat upright, her coffee in her hand. Her dress fell in soft folds around her body. Her smile was composed. She was challenging Kurt to shock her.

'We've had the overture, Kurt, let's hear the symphony.'

Kurt said: 'Lewis was thinking of leaving Sachs Smith, thinking seriously. He was planning to set up a rival firm of his own here in the city.'

Lomax watched Frances put her coffee cup down in slow motion. The action was elegant. Only her arm moved. The rest of her body was still except that her face had subtly rearranged itself. Her mouth was slackened, her eyes had sunk a little deeper. He glanced at Marjorie. She had been holding some strands of hair, wrapping and unwrapping them around her fingers, but now her hands were still.

When Frances spoke her voice was quiet. 'Lewis was almost sixty, Kurt. A lot of people have retired by his age. They don't start risky new law firms.'

'He wasn't going it alone. There was a whole group of partners from

Sachs Smith with him. And God knows how many clients they would have taken.'

Frances' eyes narrowed. 'How many partners?'

'Haven't worked that out yet.'

'I can make some guesses,' she said. They looked at each other in silent communication. Then the three lawyers began to talk, sometimes at once, sometimes in turn. They talked about Sachs Smith, the people who worked there, the mood of the firm, the shock and subsequent undermining of morale at Lewis' death, the new managing partner and the distant and disliked figure of the senior partner. Lomax listened to them for a while. There seemed to be a split between the older partners and their newer, younger colleagues who wanted to change the style and direction of Sachs Smith. Lomax thought the attorneys sounded like Doberman, McMahon, Yevgeny and all the rest discussing observatory funding. Office politics were the same everywhere. He wished they would talk about Julia's case.

Marjorie was asking: 'These guys who were leaving. Did they need Lewis? I mean, is there still a chance they'll go?'

Kurt shrugged. 'They may have gotten scared after what happened to Lewis.'

Lomax began to take an interest. 'Are you saying that Lewis' murder could have had something to do with his plans to start a new firm?' he said.

Kurt hesitated. He chewed loudly. 'No, no,' he said at last. Lomax did not find his denial swift enough to be convincing. Kurt added: 'I'm just saying I now know why Lewis wanted to borrow a lot of money from Julia.'

Frances turned to Lomax, her expression severe. 'I don't like your implication.' Her tone was chilling. There was a warning in her voice but Lomax chose to ignore it.

'Is it possible?' he persisted.

'No,' said Frances. She was icy now. She spoke from an immense altitude. The air was thinning. Lomax pursued his question breathlessly.

'How competitive are law firms in this city?'

'Oh c'mon, Lomax,' Kurt said, rising to his feet.

Marjorie spoke. 'Lomax has the right to ask this. He's putting the interests of the client before the interests of Sachs Smith.'

'So do we all,' Frances said. The tension in the room was almost palpable now.

Kurt hovered overhead. 'To answer your question, Lomax, we're not so competitive that we murder each other,' he snapped.

Frances nodded. 'You're going too far.'

Lomax persisted: 'Isn't that how everyone would react to the suggestion that a colleague or a friend or a member of their family had committed a murder?'

'Or a girlfriend,' Kurt added, his voice heavy with implication.

'Exactly. It's just how I reacted when Julia was first arrested. I said she couldn't do this, it's impossible. And you said, Frances, you said you couldn't take my opinion seriously because I'm involved with her.'

Frances looked hard at him. 'Did I say that?'

'Yes. So how can I take you seriously when you tell me it's impossible Lewis died for professional reasons?'

Frances and Lomax looked at one another. She had cats' eyes. They were green and steady and the pupils were small.

'Touché,' she said. Unexpectedly, she smiled. The atmosphere thawed. Kurt put his fists on the table and leaned towards her with mock seriousness.

'Frances. Did you murder Lewis Fox?'

Frances guffawed and Marjorie began to giggle. Probably the giggle was nervous but it was infectious. Lomax and Kurt spluttered and then laughed. Once they had started they could not stop. The room rang with laughter. Lomax felt his body shaking and his face hot. Marjorie turned pink. Her mouth was an amorphous black shape which writhed over the lower half of her face. Occasional high-pitched sounds escaped from it, like a horse whinnying. Her shoulders shuddered. Frances, her elbows on the table, dipped her head behind her hands and shook silently. Kurt flung his body back into his chair and threw his legs and arms around, roaring.

'Okay. I confess,' he spat between convulsions, 'it was me. I never liked the guy. I killed him.'

When they had all confessed and their laughter had subsided, Frances said, 'I guess Lomax is right. We have to start asking our colleagues questions.'

'Without telling anyone who doesn't know already that the firm damn nearly split,' added Kurt.

'Yes, that information doesn't leave this room.' Frances looked at Marjorie as she spoke.

'God, how can I go to Egger – ' Kurt guffawed. Egger was senior partner at Sachs Smith – 'and ask him if he has an alibi for the morning of November 12th?'

Frances told Kurt and Marjorie to continue investigating Lewis' proposed new firm. 'Delicately,' she added.

'Delicately,' Kurt agreed.

'Especially the financial side of it.'

'Should be a cinch after Zurich,' Kurt reassured her. He asked Marjorie to have lunch with him to plan their next move.

'Want to come, Lomax?' asked Marjorie.

'Lomax is working by himself,' said Kurt.

They left the office. 'Bye, Lomax, bye,' called Marjorie over her shoulder.

Lomax and Frances were left alone together in her white room. Neither of them stood up. They eyed each other from across the table. Frances wanted Lomax to speak first.

'So . . .' she prompted.

'There was nearly another murder a few minutes ago,' Lomax remarked. She smiled.

'You bring a new perspective to this case.' She arranged some strands of hair which had strayed across her cheek. Lomax noticed again that a few of them were white. 'It's refreshing. Although occasionally painful.'

'Do you really feel this news about Lewis is going to lead anywhere?'

'No. Well, maybe. But everything keeps coming back to Julia.' Seeing his expression she added: 'I'm sorry, Lomax.'

He did not reply.

'What have you found out about Gail?'

'I'm getting some sort of a picture of her.'

'Tell me.'

Lomax told Frances about Gail's house and school in Arizona. She listened intently, frowning sometimes with concentration. If he faltered, she nodded to encourage him. It was easy to talk to Frances. She could be intelligent and silent at the same time. He found himself describing details, like the way you couldn't run between the Foxes' house and the Knights' house under the harsh desert sun without the knife leaves of the yucca slicing your skin. He told her about Lifebelt Lake and how everyone remembered Julia and Lewis but not Gail. He told her Kim's belief that Gail must have hated Julia.

'I guess,' said Frances, her voice husky from the long silence, 'a lot of women envy Julia the easy way she can make men fall in love with her.'

Lomax felt uncomfortable.

'Of course,' continued Frances as if she were making a statement, although they both knew she was asking a question, 'her looks help. But Julia's more complex than that.'

243

'I never know exactly where I stand with her. What she's feeling. Who she's with. It keeps me in a constant state of . . .' Lomax stopped. He was surprised to hear his own words. 'I don't know. It makes her powerful.' Frances was studying him. He could not look at her while he spoke. 'Not that Julia's aware of her power,' he added.

Frances raised her eyebrows a little. 'No?'

'No. She'd be frightened by it,' he insisted. 'She feels real vulnerable.'

Frances said: 'She didn't have the same power over Lewis.'

'You mean the girlfriends. Alice. And the brunette, whoever she was.'

'There were a lot of girlfriends before those two.'

'All young?'

'I think so.'

He hesitated. 'I feel sort of . . . guilty. I haven't told Julia about Alice.'

'Probably Julia knows about Alice.'

'No,' said Lomax, 'I don't think so.'

Frances picked up her empty coffee cup. She turned it around so that it caught the light. She seemed to be examining it but Lomax knew she was thinking. The cup was white with a subtle leaf pattern near the rim. It was made of fine, thin china. Lomax was scared to touch that kind of china because it broke so easily.

Frances was careful. She said slowly: 'Julia can't be under any illusions that she had a happy marriage and a faithful husband.'

'She is, Frances.'

'Maybe it seems that way looking back but it didn't seem that way to anyone at the time.'

Lomax felt himself move into the state of heightened alertness that meant someone was going to tell him something.

'She was a sad figure in this office. People used to talk about her. No one could believe that anyone so young and beautiful would hang around while he treated her badly. But she did. She clung to him. She drove his secretaries half crazy. She called him constantly. There was one occasion when she was actually in this office and ten minutes later she called. She must have gotten as far as the parking lot. One assistant left because of it. Julia was constantly having her break into business meetings and Lewis would have the secretary lie about where he was. To his wife. So one secretary left, one refused to do it. The last lied for him.'

Lomax was silent for a long time.

'Lewis sort of replaced her father,' he said finally. 'I guess that explains the relationship.'

'When Julia came to see Mercedes last May, to ask for the money, Mercedes called me. She said Julia didn't look well. Still beautiful but very thin. Tired. Worried. Nervous. I'd seen Julia myself a few months earlier at the New Year party and she'd made me think of a chicken. Isn't that crazy? My mother kept chickens. Once they're scared about something, there's no way you can calm a chicken or soothe it. It clucks about the place with its bright little eyes looking everywhere. So vigilant. So frightened.'

There was an intimacy in their conversation. Outside, the offices were quiet for lunch. There were no telephones ringing, no voices in the hall. There were no planes passing overhead. Frances' voice had dropped low.

'Mercedes asked whether I wanted to speak to Julia. She said she thought something was bothering her. But I'd just had a baby. I was busy with my family. It was a happy time for us. I didn't want to think about Julia and her problems, her marital difficulties. I told Mercedes that it was Sachs Smith's job to manage Julia's money, nothing more. I didn't call her.'

Lomax listened. He knew that if he moved the rustle of his clothes would seem abnormally loud. He did not move.

'I don't think this is hindsight. I had the feeling that something would happen, something bad. I tried not to think about Julia. Probably I should have called her and talked to her and helped her.'

Lomax was reminded of Mrs Knight. She had said the same about Gail. He adopted Frances' hushed tone. 'I don't know why Julia was distressed at that time.'

'It's hard . . .' said Frances, 'not to connect her problem, whatever it was, with what happened later that year.'

'Why should it have anything to do with the murders? A marriage went through a rough patch. Later the husband died. There's not necessarily a causal relationship.'

Causal relationship. The last time he had heard those words was in the caves near Lifebelt Lake. The ranger had said that the pueblo dwellers assumed a causal relationship between the total eclipse of the sun and their lost water supply. But the pueblo dwellers had been wrong.

Frances did not answer immediately. 'It was a while before I saw Julia again.'

'At the funeral?'

'There was no funeral. Or if there was it must have been private. I wrote to her, of course. But the next time I saw Julia was when I met you.'

Lomax remembered that strange night. His car outside, books and papers and the other accumulations of observatory life scattered all over it. The weather oppressive. Julia's eyes large with shock and fatigue.

'I was surprised. I expected to find the chicken clucking and clawing at the ground. But she wasn't like that any more. She was different. Of course she was upset by everything that had happened. But she had this calm about her. She was in control now. She wasn't before.'

Lomax said nothing. Julia had seemed to him almost completely helpless that night.

'So when you tell me that she controls your relationship, I believe it. A year ago I would have thought it was impossible for her to control anything. But she's changed since these murders.'

'Of course she has,' Lomax said. 'Of course she has, Frances. Wouldn't anyone?'

Frances sighed. 'Yes, Lomax,' she admitted, 'anyone would.'

'You don't have to commit a murder to be altered by it. It's a horrible experience but conceivably a strengthening one.'

Frances looked at him intelligently. He knew for sure that, while Frances the professional was paid to believe in Julia's innocence, Frances the woman did not.

'You think that Lewis' death brought Julia some kind of freedom? Some kind of release?'

She did not reply.

'Even if she benefited by his death, that still doesn't mean she killed him,' Lomax said. 'It would have been easier to leave him than to murder him.'

'Yes,' agreed Frances, but her voice was uncertain.

They parted on warm terms. He felt that Frances had confided in him and he was flattered. He was sure she had not spoken this way to Kurt. It was courageous of her to trust someone so close to Julia with her doubts.

He drove home via Belmont. Vicky Fox had given him the street name but not the number of her previous house. His town map said it was a short residential street and he intended simply to look at it.

Belmont was many intersections away. He had time to wonder before he reached it whether Frances had really been confiding in him,

246

or cautioning him. Perhaps the intimacy of her tone had been intended to warn him about Julia. The possibility was irritating.

The houses in Belmont were large and old. Many families had lived in them and left their fingerprints here. Some were gothic in style with fanciful wooden turrets and arched windows. Most had big verandahs for children's bicycles, stacked by the front doors, over-hanging plants and wicker chairs with faded cushions. There were cars outside, usually large cars.

He could not guess which house might have belonged to Vicky and Richard and Gail. The neighbourhood was a long way from the south side but the large, untidy, comfortable families who lived here probably had problems of their own.

He returned home to Deputy and released the dog into the yard. Deputy rushed in the direction of the carport. He had been sitting at the window watching squirrels when Lomax arrived and now he wanted to catch them. But they were already looking down on him from high up in the trees.

It was four thirty. Lomax estimated there was still some telephone time left in the day. He called Tradescant's French department and asked for the secretary he had met before.

'You probably don't remember this, but you told me a while ago that you'd ask around for anyone who knew Gail Fox . . .'

'Sure I remember. Did you know that she only majored in French in her sophomore year?'

'No. What was her major before that?'

'Biology.'

'Why did she change?'

'No one here knows. I've asked a lot of people but no one said anything useful. Try the biology department.'

He telephoned the biology department but the few staff who were not on vacation seemed to resent this. They made it clear they were about to go home. As usual, calls about Gail led nowhere.

There was a letter from Dixon Driver in the mailbox. The new observatory logo was on the outside of the envelope as well as on the top of the letter. It invited him to a meeting with the observatory ethics committee in a few weeks' time. It did not tell him why. Ordinarily Lomax would have been sunk into depression by this but now nothing could depress him. Julia was arriving some time tomorrow. She would have been working all night, assisting Doberman at a viewing. Afterwards, she would drive to Lomax's house and spend two whole days here before returning up the mountain. No one would know where she was. She would be hiding, as she suggested, in his bed.

22

There was a possibility that Julia would drive straight down to the
foothills after her night's viewing, and this possibility awoke Lomax
early. In the past, tired and euphoric as the dome of the telescope
clicked shut overhead, he had sometimes found himself anxious to see
his family, so anxious that he had returned home at first light, peeling
off layers of clothing as his altitude decreased and the sun rose. He
would arrive still feeling a mixture of happiness and fatigue and
Deputy would wake the house barking. Candice would pour them
coffee in the kitchen and Helen or Joel would sit on his knee and they
would talk, Candice early-morning sleepy, Lomax animated from a
night riding the telescope.

Remembering this made him feel nostalgic, not just for his family
but for viewing. Sometimes Professor Berlins joined him for part or all
of the night. Lomax would sit in the cage where conditions were raw
but you felt closest to space; Berlins watched with the night assistants
on the screen below. Lomax and Berlins talked over the intercom.
Their conversations were intense and excited, not always completely
scientific. Sometimes the only response to the beauty of space was
silence. Sometimes there was nothing to say, sometimes more than
could ever be said. In the morning, the two men would feel a closeness,
although they might not have seen each other at any time during the
night.

Suddenly it seemed imperative to talk to Berlins. What was he
doing? Where was he? He decided to ask Julia to help him penetrate
Sarah Berlins' cordon sanitaire.

Lomax lay in bed watching a squirrel progress confidently along the
high branches outside the window. He listened for the sound of Julia's
car turning into the drive. She would switch off the engine and the door
would open on her tired, smiling face and he would escort her straight
to bed. They would make love and then she would fall asleep holding
on to him while he lay watching the sky behind the trees grow bluer.

There was a strange thumping noise in the room. He sat up. Deputy had dragged a pillow down to the end of the bed and was showing it the kind of attention that usually preceded intense sexual activity. Lomax pulled the pillow away and went downstairs.

He made coffee and heated muffins. He waited a while before eating but Julia did not arrive. He showered and dressed and tried to read but it was impossible to concentrate and listen for her car at the same time. He sat on the deck. The sun was high now. It seemed Julia had decided to sleep before driving down the mountain. This was of course sensible. But disappointing.

Lomax made lunch but by lunchtime there was still no car. He did not feel hungry. He fed Deputy.

Perhaps there had been a misunderstanding. Perhaps Julia thought they were meeting at her house and she was over there right now wondering why he did not come.

He called her. After a couple of rings the phone was answered by a whirring noise and Julia's voice stiffly inviting him to leave a message. It was unusual for Julia to remember to switch on the answering machine. He waited, but this formal Julia was not interrupted by the real Julia picking up the receiver. She was not at home.

At last, in the middle of the afternoon, he heard a car. He leapt to his feet, startling and then exciting Deputy, who ran barking to the door and catapulted through it as soon as it was open. By the time Lomax arrived, Deputy was howling at the driver. But the driver was not Julia. the car was black and white and Murphy McLean was behind the wheel.

The sheriff wound down the window. 'Hi, Lomax! Howya doin'!' he roared.

Deputy stood on his hind legs and thrust his head into the car, licking the sheriff with his long tongue.

'Hey, Deputy!' said the sheriff. 'I didn't know you cared!'

Through the tangle of arms and dog paws. Lomax could see the sheriff's teeth. He was grinning, as usual. McLean wrestled Deputy away and Lomax pulled the dog out by his collar.

'Sure get a warm welcome here!' commented the sheriff. He could only have been referring to Deputy's welcome, as Lomax had so far said nothing. 'This is a fine house.'

'Thanks.'

'Except the paint's peeling along there . . .' McLean pointed. 'I stopped by yesterday and I thought: Lomax got some paint peeling.'

'Why did you stop by?' Lomax asked.

'Looking for you, Galileo.'

250

'How come?'

'I was outside the mall yesterday morning, and you drove right on by. Did you see me?'

'No,' lied Lomax. He had seen McLean but pretended not to. Ever since meeting the sheriff at Julia's he had been passing him on the freeway or in carparks and ignoring him. He tried just not to notice him, the way he had never noticed him before, but somehow that was impossible now.

'Well I saw you, Lomax, and when you pulled up at the intersection, know what I saw? One of those brake lights didn't come on! Can you believe it? One did, one didn't!' McLean delivered his information as if it was astounding. Lomax stubbornly refused to be astounded.

'Oh,' he said.

The sheriff became confidential. This was the tone Lomax most abhorred. 'Just a friendly warning, Lomax. I got some new boys working with me now and they are like shit hot. I mean . . .' McLean licked his finger, touched the steering wheel and then withdrew it rapidly as though the wheel had burnt him. He made a sizzling noise with his tongue. 'That's how hot they are, Lomax. Now, if they see you without no brake light, they would like, straight away, on the spot, no questions asked, ticket you.'

The sheriff mimed one of his new boys writing a ticket with a grim facial expression that was clearly impervious to reason or argument. Lomax wished he would go away. Julia was sure to arrive any minute.

'Beat-up old cars,' added McLean helpfully, 'tend to attract their attention, see.'

'Thank you, Sheriff,' said Lomax without sincerity. 'I appreciate the warning. I'll fix it right away.'

He hoped that the sheriff would go now, but instead McLean sat back in his seat, his round belly pressing against the steering wheel, and winked loudly.

'No problem, Lomax,' he said. 'How's Mrs Julia Fox?'

'Fine, I think.'

'You think! Oh, I guess you haven't seen her. You've been on vacation.'

How did the sheriff know that Lomax had been vacationing? Or was he guessing?

'Well, when you see her, you just say hi from her old friend Murph.'

Julia's old friend Murph had played a considerable role in her investigation and arrest. His statement about how she had received the news of the murders was swollen with a sense of accusation. In the hope that it would make the sheriff leave sooner, Lomax said: 'Sure. I'll say that.'

But McLean showed no inclination to go. He leaned his elbow on the open window and resumed his confidential tone. 'Things are looking bad for her, Lomax. This witness says he woke up on the morning of the murders, went to the window, and saw the lovely Julia getting into a car. Well, when you add that to everything else . . .' He completed the implication wordlessly by folding his face into a grotesque caricature of itself.

'Then why didn't this guy tell the police at once? Why did it take him six months?' said Lomax hotly.

'Well, Homer discovered the bodies later that morning. Not nice, very disturbing. And Homer is a nervous kind of guy.' McLean's eyes bulged with cartoon nervousness. 'See . . . he needed soothing and reassurance before he had the confidence to come forward with what he saw.'

Lomax stared at the sheriff. McLean bared his immense teeth. 'Gotta go, Galileo!' He started the car, still grinning. 'Don't you forget to say hi to her, now,' he yelled over the sound of the engine. 'You lucky sonabitch, Lomax. I mean . . . whooo!'

His face parodied wide-eyed sexual excitement. He mimed wiping sweat from his brow. Lomax thought it was a shame he was only pretending, since McLean's forehead was glistening with sweat. Winking and waving, he drove away. Deputy stared after him, looking crestfallen and wagging his tail very slowly.

Lomax was bending over the brake light with a screwdriver when Julia's car pulled up. Deputy reprised his welcome routine. Lomax straightened and watched Julia silence the dog with a hug. Deputy licked her lavishly.

'Don't be fooled,' Lomax called. 'Twenty minutes ago that dog did exactly the same act for Murphy McLean.'

She walked over to him, Deputy dancing at her feet, and smiled. She did not kiss Lomax. He wanted her to move a little closer and put her arms around him but she stood a few feet away, smiling. He put aside his disappointment and admired her. Her hair was held in a loose braid which flopped over one shoulder. The braid was not neat. Hairs escaped from it and curled around her face. Her smile was wide, pushing her cheeks up high towards her eyes. Her eyes smiled too. She was pleased to see him. He reached out for the braid and gave it a light tug. She laughed. Her hair felt so soft in his hand that he moved closer and began to unbraid it.

'Lomax, it took me half an hour to do that!'

He shook her hair free and arranged it around her shoulders.

'Didn't you like it?' she asked.

He was standing in front of her now, close against her. He was watching her mouth. It was moist and full. 'Damn braid just fell apart in my hand,' he said. He kissed her and then kissed her again and then again. For a few moments he forgot all the time they had spent apart and the ache of missing her and the silences over the telephone and his jealousy. She pulled away from him at last.

'Hi, Lomax,' she said. Her arms had been holding him. Now they fell to her sides. He wanted her to hold him again but as usual he was powerless. Affection demanded did not have the same quality as affection freely given. He rearranged her hair again and traced lines from her neck to her chin.

'What did Murph want?' she asked.

He shrugged and dropped his arms. 'To tell me the car has a broken brake light. And to say that my paint is peeling.'

'I noticed the paint the last time I was here.'

It seemed everybody had noticed but Lomax.

They went indoors, pushing Deputy ahead of them.

'He asked me to say hi to you.'

'Oh.'

They were in the hallway. He had been intending all day to lead her straight to the bedroom but, thanks to the sweating sheriff, he was troubled now and wanted to talk. They went to the kitchen. When she sat down, Deputy put his paws on her lap and pressed his head against her breasts. Lomax poured coffee and began to revive the lunch he had made earlier.

'Julia . . . that sheriff really bothers me. First, he seemed to know without being told that I'd been on vacation. Then, it must be more than a coincidence that he shows up here just at exactly the time when you're expected. Plus . . . he said something odd.'

'What?'

'About this witness. The guy who thinks he saw you outside Gail's apartment at the time of the murders. The super.'

'Homer.'

Lomax repeated his conversation with McLean. Julia listened, unperturbed, and then waited for him to explain its significance.

'Well, I mean,' asked Lomax, 'who exactly soothed and reassured Homer until he had the confidence to come forward?'

Julia sipped her coffee. 'A doctor? A nurse? a psychiatrist?'

'A sheriff?'

Julia was silent.

'How come McLean's on first name terms with this witness? And didn't the guy have some kind of nervous breakdown after he discovered the murders? And aren't people suggestible when they're in that state?'

'You think Murph persuaded Homer to say he saw me?'

'Well, maybe not exactly persuaded. But he might have added to the man's confusion.'

'Lomax, I've already explained why Homer thinks he saw me. I was there, but a few hours earlier than he realized.'

'He's going to stand up in court and swear, under oath, you were there at the time of the murders. Julia, what I want to know is this. Why does that wide-bodied, small-brained sheriff want to get you? Why? Why does he hang around outside your house and encourage Homicide detectives to ask questions, why does he sweet-talk witnesses to testify against you?'

Julia shrugged. She looked down at Deputy. Lomax's voice rose. 'What kind of a history do you have with this guy?'

But Julia remained silent. Defeated, Lomax cooked. The only sounds in the room were the occasional whimper of ecstasy from Deputy and the clang of pans. Lomax clanged them unnecessarily loudly. He was angry. Julia's voice, when at last she spoke, was scarcely audible over the pans. He paused. 'What?'

'I said, don't get mad about it. That's why I didn't tell Lewis. Because I knew he'd get mad.'

'Tell Lewis what?'

She sighed. 'I don't want to go into details. It's just I had a few problems with Murphy a couple of years back when I first met him. One day he came to see Mr Weinhart to tell him his wife had been taken ill. He took Mr Weinhart over to the hospital in his police car. Afterwards he came back.'

'Came back to your house? What happened?'

'He made advances. I said no. That's all. Nothing really happened.'

'Jesus Christ. The man is a reptile, a reptile in uniform. Did he . . . did he try to insist?'

'No.'

'Did he ever try again?'

'Oh yes, over and over.'

'And?'

'And nothing. He sort of stopped when Mr Weinhart's wife got better. I mean, Mr Weinhart was around the house a lot more then. So Murphy gave up.'

'You rejected his advances. And now he's bitter.'

'I don't know. I don't think so. But since you ask me about my history with Murph, that's it.'

'Did you tell your attorney this?'

'Of course not. What difference does it make?'

'The guy's vindictive, that's what.'

Lunch was ready. Lomax glared at it.

'Can we talk about something else?' she asked in a small, sweet voice. He could not help smiling at her.

He carried their food outside to the deck. It was a clear, sunny day and they sat in the dappled shade of the trees which grew through the woodwork.

'I can't eat so much,' Julia protested.

'Sure you can.'

'I ate at the observatory.'

'Eat all you can and Deputy will finish the rest.' Candice used to say this to Helen, who was a picky eater. Deputy recognized the words and gave Lomax a look of low cunning. He had followed them outside and now sat waiting at Julia's feet.

Julia told Lomax how cold and tired she had been during the night's viewing with Doberman. Many of the astronomers listened to music while they viewed. Doberman had chosen a heavy metal tape which he played over and over all night. Lomax at once forgave her late arrival. As an assistant she would experience little of the euphoria of viewing, especially working with Doberman.

'There are two sorts of astronomer,' he told her, 'the sort who got there because they're fascinated by the universe and the sort who got there because they're good at math and physics.'

'And you're the first sort and Doberman's the second,' said Julia. 'I already guessed that.'

He was pleased. He said: 'Did you wear a heated suit?'

'No.'

'For God's sake, why didn't Doberman give you a heated suit?'

'He did.'

'And?'

'And I took it off, it made me look so fat. I could have stood next to Kim and you wouldn't have known which of us was which.'

'Julia, everyone looks fat in cold suits but they keep out the cold.'

'You don't wear one.'

'True.'

'Because you don't like to look like everyone else.'

As usual, Julia had hit on the truth with childlike simplicity. He didn't want to look like a clone of Doberman or McMahon or any of the others. He said defensively: 'I don't wear a heated suit because once a guy who was wearing one got electrocuted while he was peeing.'

Julia began to giggle.

'I mean, I could spill coffee over it and the wires would hiss and sizzle and then . . .'

She giggled still more.

'And then I'd fry.'

Julia laughed outright. She had finished eating now and Deputy was guzzling the remains of her meal. Her laugh was provocative. He watched her and felt aroused.

'You're supposed to be hunkering down,' he pointed out. She nodded.

'Anyone could wander round the house and see you. We should go to the bedroom at once where it's safe.'

She nodded again. He took her hand and led her up the stairs, his heart beating fast. He began to kiss her face and her neck and to run his hands from her waist up her body. He put a hand on her breast. His finger brushed against the nipple very lightly, first one way and then another and he felt the nipple harden. His finger played with it and it swelled and hardened a little more.

'Lomax, I'm going to make you feel real, real good.'

She was whispering into his ear, but the blood was pounding through his body so loudly that he could hardly hear her. Her hands crept down his body and pressed against his penis, bulging inside his jeans.

'Oh!' she said in mock surprise, raising her eyebrows. Her eyes fixed on his and her smile tantalizing, she deftly found her way inside his clothes. She wrapped her fingers around him and gradually tightened them. He felt a surge of heightened pleasure. He closed his eyes. Something grazed softly against his body. It was Julia, dropping onto her knees. She was going to eat him up, here, now, standing in the bedroom and almost fully clothed. He felt for the wall and leaned against it. She was taking more and more of him inside her, sucking him inside her mouth and down the wetness of her throat. Once he opened his eyes and looked at her. She was watching his pleasure. Her pupils were enormous, filling her eyes darkly. Her hair fell down her back. She was looking coyly up at him like a child with some large and delicious candy in its mouth. He closed his eyes and involuntarily saw two small stick people painted on the wall of a cave. His body began to shudder with pleasure and he forgot the pueblo paintings.

After each time they had sex that day he reminded himself to mention the cave drawings later. He did not remember to do so.

In the intervals of inactivity he wished that she would reach out for him occasionally. He liked to put his arm around her or take her hand or stroke her hair. If he did none of these things then she simply lay in silence and isolation.

'What are you thinking about?' he asked and they talked. But unlike him she found it possible to speak in these circumstances without physical proximity. Sometimes their only contact was the sound of their two voices touching softly in the dark. Their talk was intimate. Coaxed by her, Lomax found himself telling stories, some of them painful, from his past. When he told her how his marriage had ended his throat constricted and his chest tightened. Her response was sympathetic but she could have eased his pain more by just touching his hand. She did not. There was a loneliness in knowing that such comfort was only an arm's length away through the dark but was not volunteered. Mostly he overcame this loneliness by reaching out himself. Her skin was smooth as water.

When they at last went down to the kitchen, half-naked, their bare feet silent on the stairs, they discovered that they had left the door to the deck wide open and that Deputy Dawg was missing. They called him and listened for the sound of his claws scratching across the wooden deck but all they could hear were a couple of police sirens wailing a duet far in the distance. Julia had wound an inadequate towel around her body. She crossed the deck and leaned out over the railings and called Deputy's name. Light from the kitchen was scattered across her back. It was long and curved, her spine a network of tiny shadows.

'You look like a fossil,' he said. She turned and smiled. 'That's a compliment,' he added. She walked back to him in her tiny towel. The shadows trickled through all the crevices of her body. In the hollows of her knees, under her chin in a sharp black line, in circles around her collar bones. She was perfectly constructed.

'Now I can see how you were made,' he told her.

'Will Deputy come back?'

'Eventually. I'll call the dog pound tomorrow.'

'We should go look for him.'

257

'Okay. But we won't find him. He'll lie low until he's found a woman.'

They dressed and went out to cruise the neighbourhood. The roads in the foothills wound and rose and fell. There were signs indicating the names and numbers of the houses but the houses themselves were not visible behind the summer foliage. There was no other traffic. Occasionally they stopped and left the car and yelled Deputy's name into the silence. They were answered once or twice by a dog bark but it was not Deputy's bark. They drove further, the view sometimes clearing to reveal the dark shape of the mountains close by.

A car approached slowly. Lomax pulled over so that it could pass on the narrow road. He glanced at Julia as its lights illuminated her and saw to his amazement that her face was wet. He stopped the car and stared at her in the dark.

'How long have you been crying?' he asked, wrapping her in his arms. She did not reply. The tears continued to shoot down her face. Where had she learned to cry so quietly?

'Deputy's going to be all right. He's too sneaky to get run over. Sneaky dog.' Lomax pulled a sneaky face to amuse her. She responded with a sob. He remembered how Kim had wept in this very car. She had cried because of Julia. Even Kim's tears were outsize compared with Julia's.

'Are you thinking about the trial?' he asked quietly.

She shook her head.

'Say something.'

'I've driven down these roads before,' she told him at last, her voice throaty.

'Around here?'

'I recognize some of the landmarks. There was a house back there called Maybush. And underneath it says Kittens Usually for Sale.'

'Who lives there?'

'I don't know. I just remembered the sign and when I remembered the sign I remembered the road and when I remembered the road I remembered . . .'

He had to wait for her to complete the sentence. He could guess how it would end. With some moving memory of Lewis. She would sob over Lewis and he would have to be sympathetic. The way Julia talked about Lewis, in a tone almost dissolving with affection, never failed to make Lomax jealous. He could only control his jealousy by remembering Lewis' distorted face and twisted body in the police photos, and this seemed a cheap trick.

'I remembered the last time I drove down here was night time and I was looking for someone then, too.

'Who?'

'Lewis,' said Julia. 'I was looking for Lewis.' She hid her head in her hands and her body shuddered with sobs. Lomax was reminded of the three attorneys at the meeting. But they had been shaking with laughter.

'Why were you looking for Lewis?'

'I thought he was with some woman who lived around here.'

Lomax held her a little tighter.

'I knew he was having an affair. I found her address. It was around here somewhere. One night when it got late and he didn't come home and I was waiting for him I decided to drive up to her house and see if his car was outside. I wouldn't have done anything. I mean, like ring the doorbell. I just wanted to see if he was here.'

'And was he?'

Her sob was half laughter. 'I couldn't even find the house! I drove around for hours looking until I practically ran out of gas and had to go home and that's just what Lewis would have expected. He thought I couldn't do anything right.'

Her voice disintegrated on the last word. Lomax tried to wipe away her tears but there were too many of them.

'So you weren't happy with Lewis,' he said.

She shook her head.

'He didn't love me at all, Lomax.'

'That's impossible.'

'It's the truth. I don't want people to know this. Only you.'

'At Sachs Smith they already know he had affairs.'

She twisted free of his arms and turned to him for the first time. Her eyes were wet, the lower lid holding water.

'They know?'

'He wasn't real discreet.'

'God.'

'Julia, I've met one of the women,' he said. 'I met her with Lewis' friend, Gerry Hegarty, at a place Lewis used to go to called The Club . . .'

He saw her flinch. 'Do you know about the club?' he asked.

'I never went there. Lewis went a lot but he didn't take me.'

'Well, I met her there.'

It felt good to say this. He had not enjoyed keeping Alice a secret from Julia. She continued to stare at him.

259

'I don't think she had anything to do with the murders. She's just . . .' he swallowed. He did not want to hurt her. 'She's just a kid.'

Her eyes dropped. 'What was her name?' she whispered.

'Alice. Not very interesting. I don't know why he . . . it seems incredible. When he had a wife like you.'

'Alice,' she said slowly. 'I wonder which one she was.'

'Not the last one.'

'No?'

Lomax risked hurting her again. 'If any of these girlfriends are relevant to the murders, it would probably be the last one. A pretty brunette, also quite young. Alice saw them at the club together in the summer before Lewis died. Maybe that's the woman whose address you found?'

She had flinched again when he mentioned the club.

'I didn't know he was involved with anyone that summer.'

Her voice was dull with pain. She had stopped crying but this was worse.

'Oh Julia, I'm sorry.'

He held her again. He said: 'None of those girls matters now.'

'No,' she said huskily.

'Tell me about your marriage.'

'I don't know what to tell.'

'Were you happy in the beginning?'

'Yes. But he got tired of me pretty quickly. I tried to please him but the harder I tried . . . He just didn't want me any more, Lomax.'

'He must have been a goddam fucking goddam dickhead,' said Lomax, so venomously that Julia smiled for a moment. Then she said: 'You know what it's like to watch someone fall out of love with you. When there's nothing you can do about it.'

'Yes.'

'You know how terrible it is.'

'Yes.' Only a few hours ago he had been telling her how terrible it is.

'It destroys you. Your confidence, everything. You live in hope that they'll come back or that they love you really. And part of you thinks that you're not very lovable anyway. But you keep telling yourself it's not over till it's over.'

'Yes,' said Lomax. 'And they give you signs which you just ignore. Even when they finally tell you, well, you don't believe them. If they wrote it in big letters on the back of an envelope: I DON'T LOVE YOU ANY MORE, you'd persuade yourself it's some address in Maryland.'

They looked at each other. The moon had disappeared now and the car was dark but the air between them was dense with understanding. Julia's marriage had been similar to his own, except that her misery had been compounded by Murph's sexual harrassment and later, murders and a murder charge. He cupped his hand under her chin.

'When the trial's over,' he said, 'things will be better and you'll be happy.'

'Yes?' Her voice was gentle and trusting.

'I promise,' he added. He had never loved her so much as he did now in the cold car with the mountains hanging over them, although he could not exactly see where.

23

'Have you notified the exterminators?' Candice demanded as soon as she heard that Deputy was missing. Once, on some lone expedition, Deputy had lost his collar and been assumed a stray. Lomax had rescued him minutes before he was due to be exterminated.

'Yes,' said Lomax patiently. 'The pound and the SPCA.'

'Have you phoned around the neighbourhood?'

'Yes.'

'I hope he doesn't try to come to our house. He'd never get across the freeways.'

'He won't. He's a wise old dog now.'

Julia had returned to the observatory. Lomax missed her. When she had driven away he had watched her car out of sight and listened until it was out of earshot. Then he had begun to feel lonely. She was going back up to the world he knew and flourished in, leaving him to flounder down here at sea level. He was tired of the murder investigation and unsure of his role in it. So far he had discovered little of consequence.

'Just go hiking and leave the questions to the professionals,' Candice advised him briskly. She was speaking from the clinic. It was useless to argue with her.

'When do Helen and Joel get back from San Diego?'

'Tomorrow. Mom and Dad are driving them. I hope Deputy shows up by then.'

'He will.'

Lomax was not so confident as he sounded. Now that Julia had gone the dog's absence had started to bother him.

He changed into his suit. He had forgotten how it seemed to restrict him in all the wrong places. Today was his appointment with Hegarty. Talking to Julia about the club had reminded him.

He aimed to allow about forty-five minutes for the journey but events (Candice, an evasive clean shirt, the mysterious disappearance of his notebook) conspired to delay his departure. As this happened almost every time he had an appointment he knew that he, Lomax, must be responsible and that the delaying events were not outside his control. It was a piece of self-knowledge that he rediscovered every time he was late. It piqued him now as he turned the car key.

The car did not respond. He turned the key twice, three times. The engine did not even groan. The silence was penetrating. Lomax sat in the car thinking. It was a weekday afternoon. Anyone who might have helped him would be far away at work.

A squirrel scrambled along the roof of the carport. He watched its tail make spasmodic progress, hanging comically over the edge. He could hear its feet. He checked under the car hood and found evidence that it had been chewing the wiring there. This had happened before in Deputy's absence. Lomax looked up at the trees which overhung the drive and located the squirrel, frozen in a vertical line against the trunk. It waved its tail a couple of times before vanishing.

He surveyed his workshop. There was no time to negotiate the mess in here and fix the car. He remembered the neat lines of tools and wooden nests in Julia's basement. It would be easy to find insulating tape there. It would be in a nest labelled insulating tape.

He called the library.

'This is the branch library,' said a throaty voice with all the warmth of a bank raider announcing a hold-up. 'Dorothy Cleaver speaking, how can I help you?' Her tone festered with insincerity. Lomax explained his predicament.

'So,' said Mrs Cleaver, 'you thought that I could either a. come pick you up and give you a ride wherever you're going or b. bring you some insulating tape from a hardware store, size and type specified by you.'

'Well, not if you're busy.'

'Where are you going?'

Lomax gave the address of Gerry Hegarty's office.

'And exactly when were you going to be there, and why? Remember, you're begging a favour and that entitles Mary Mudcap to ask questions.'

'No it doesn't.'

'I bet it's something to do with this murder they're trying to pin on your girlfriend.'

'How did you guess, Mrs Cleaver?'

'I'm sharp as a razor. So tell me who's at 2225 Grand.'

'A guy who was a friend of one of the murder victims.'

'And you're interviewing him. You're playing private investigator! Mary Mudcap does that the whole time.'

'I'm helping the defence attorneys,' Lomax said stiffly. He thought of ways to kill squirrels. 'I'm on sabbatical from the observatory.'

'Okay, well that sounds interesting. I'll come with you.'

'You can't come to the interview.'

Mrs Cleaver cackled in reply.

Lomax waited tensely. He felt less friendly towards Hegarty now. The thought of the club depressed him. People joined it for a series of rapid, superficial relationships and arranged sexual encounters. They went there without those who loved them. Anyone who played a stable role in their life, like a wife or a husband, was excluded. Julia had never been to the club but Lewis had indulged his interest in young girls there. And when you got out of the club, you expected the rest of your life – the steady, reliable side of your life – to be waiting for you just the same. Which it wasn't, necessarily. Lomax had come home to an appalling telephone call from Candice accusing him of just the kind of behaviour which would probably be condoned at the club. He hated the place. He hoped Hegarty would not repeat his offer of membership.

He was alerted to Mrs Cleaver's arrival about ten minutes later by the screech of brakes. He looked out of the window and saw a cloud of dust.

'Who are these drives designed for? Rattlesnakes?' she said, without greeting him. 'They expect you to turn the car at forty-five degrees to the road and you're still turning and there's a goddam tree right in front of you and you have to turn back the other way.'

She dragged furiously on a cigarette. Her elbow hung out of the window. The car was full of smoke.

'Hi,' said Lomax.

Mrs Cleaver chuckled. 'I'm a terrible driver. I'll bet you didn't know that when you called me.'

'No,' said Lomax miserably.

'I've never seen you in a suit before. You look God-awful.' She was heaving the car around with strenuous arm movements. 'But you already know that.'

Dust blew in through the open windows and competed with the smoke for space in Lomax's lungs. 'How come you can just leave the library?' he asked.

'Because it's goody two-shoes Gretchen Throw-up's afternoon on the desk,' said Mrs Cleaver, 'and she's happier when I'm not around poisoning the atmosphere. So all I have to say is that I'm going out to help a disadvantaged borrower to access the facilities and it makes her nod and smile.'

'Disadvantaged!' protested Lomax, but Mrs Cleaver ignored him.

'To access,' she was saying. She had an alarming tendency to drive in the middle of the road. 'To access. It's the kind of verb Gretchen Throw-up likes to use.'

A car was approaching. Its driver was gesticulating for them to move aside.

'Educated people know that access is a noun and not a verb. Is Gretchen Throw-up educated? Huh. Is *Little House on the Prairie* set in Manhatten?'

She continued to drive in the middle of the road. The other car was forced towards the edge. There were no sidewalks this high in the foothills, just grassy banks and potholes. Mrs Cleaver was still talking.

'An uninspiring book. But how else are children going to learn the word calico?'

They were about to pass the other car. It veered across the road until two of its wheels were high up the bank and it teetered at a precarious angle to the asphalt.

'Who does she think she's waving at?' muttered Mrs Cleaver. She leaned across and yelled through Lomax's open window. 'Why don't you just go to Seattle, lady?'

Lomax had time to see the bewildered face of the other driver before he shut his eyes. 'What did Seattle ever do to you?' he asked, thinking of Richard Fox. But Mrs Cleaver was busy manoeuvering another car into retreat.

'So, tell me about this man. He's the murder victim's best friend?'

'He's an accountant. I'm visiting him in his office.'

'That would explain the God-awful suit.' Alarmingly, she was looking at the suit instead of the road. 'Even the tie's God-awful,' she said. 'Is it some kind of disguise? I know detectives wear disguises.'

'Yes,' said Lomax, 'it's a disguise.'

'Can I help you do the interview?'

'No.'

'But I know about these things. Probably you guessed that when I was so perceptive about your suit. I know how detectives work. One nasty guy asks all the questions, one nice guy stays quiet and smiles a lot. And you want me to be the nice guy.'

Mrs Cleaver bared her yellow teeth. She was smiling like a nice detective.

'No. I want you just to leave me there on Grand.'

'How will you get home?'

'I don't know.'

'How will you get the wire to repair your car?'

'I don't know.'

'Admit it, you need me,' said Mrs Cleaver cheerfully. Lomax preferred her when she was morose. 'I've read almost every detective story in the library and I usually solve the mystery long before the detective. Most of these guys are pretty stupid.'

'It's not a story you picked out from the goddam Dewey Decimal System. Two people are dead and someone's been wrongly accused of murdering them.'

'You should let me help you.'

'I can't take you in there with me. It would look peculiar.'

'Okay, I'll hang around outside and you can tell me everything that happens.'

Hegarty's office was in a commercial complex. At ground level was a shopping mall. Lomax got lost looking for the elevator to the commercial section and arrived sweating and breathless. The receptionist stared at him in surprise.

'I'm sorry I'm late,' he gasped.

'Save your apologies for Gerry,' she advised him ominously. But Gerry Hegarty was unruffled.

'Relax, it's okay,' he said. 'You're the kind of guy who's always late. You can't help it.'

Lomax was reminded how much he liked Hegarty. When he had begun hating the club, he had forgotten this.

Hegarty led the way to his office down a shabby hallway. The firm was not as big as Lomax had expected and Hegarty's office was cramped. By swinging his chair around a little Lomax could just see the photographs on the cluttered desk. There was a picture snapped at a party of a woman who might have been a daugher or the young wife Hegarty had mentioned. Nearby was a smiling group of children. Tacked unobtrusively onto the edge of a filing drawer was a picture of Lewis Fox. It had been cut from a newspaper. Lomax was touched by this. Hegarty had small hands. Lomax imagined him with a large pair of scissors trying to trim the edges neatly.

Hegarty saw him looking at the picture. He said: 'Lewis and me were close. One day this winter I suddenly thought about him while I was driving along. I often do that; he comes into my head for no particular reason. I'm cleaning the car or dictating a letter and suddenly I'm thinking of Lewis. So I'm driving down Twenty-third thinking about him and I realize that I'm seeing a figure without a face. An impression of Lewis but not actually Lewis. I thought about his face. Feature by

266

feature. I couldn't do it. I couldn't remember Lewis' face. I was horrified. It felt like a betrayal. It seemed to me that Lewis wasn't really dead so long as I could remember him. But if I started to forget him, then I was sort of killing him. Do you see what I mean?'

'Yes. Does the picture help you to remember?'

Hegarty looked pained. He lit a cigarette and turned his head sideways to blow the smoke away from Lomax. He drew on the cigarette for a few moments before he answered. Lomax had time to notice another photo, overexposed, of a young woman holding a baby.

'Not exactly. No, it doesn't exactly,' he said. 'But . . .'

He paused so long that Lomax wondered if he intended to finish his sentence.

'But sometimes I dream about him. Not very often. I go a month or two without any dreams at all and then it happens every night for a week. And in my dreams he's so real . . . God, everything about him's just . . . just so Lewis. The way he speaks and walks into a room. Laughs. Sort of rearranges his lapels.'

'What else does Lewis do in your dreams?'

'Well,' said Hegarty, eyeing Lomax for a moment then blowing smoke up into the air, 'well, actually Lewis could be sort of intimidating. So sometimes he intimidates me.'

'How does he do that?'

'I just reproduce our relationship in my dreams, not the sentimentalized version which my memory likes to supply but, you know, how it was. Lewis had a strong character. He was tough. People were scared of him. He could turn on you and that was scary and, even though I was his friend, he could turn on me too. It was something you always knew could happen when he was around and it made you careful. And sometimes in my dreams, he does that. For no special reason. Lewis is there and I know he's going to turn mean any minute. I'm tense. I'm waiting for it to happen. That's all. My wife says I yell in my sleep these days. Not exactly yell. Sad noises. She doesn't like it.'

'These are nightmares, not dreams.'

'Yes. You're right. You're right. They're nightmares.' Hegarty's voice was even. Only his pauses betrayed his emotion.

'Do you think Lewis ever turned mean with his wife?'

'Which one?'

'Julia.'

'Probably. Yes. He was protective towards her but she used to drive him crazy. Probably that's when he turned mean with her.'

267

'Why did she drive him crazy?'

'I don't remember. He didn't talk about it much. I think she didn't get along with the daughter.'

'Gail?'

'Gail. Gail and Julia didn't get along.'

'They were about the same age. Weren't they like sisters?'

'I don't know. I don't think so. I think Julia's always complaining about Gail to Lewis. She's trying to persuade him that Gail has to move out of the house, that kind of thing. Well he doesn't want to hear.'

'Did he tell you why Julia complained?'

'Not really. We went to the club and we didn't get too domestic there.'

'You didn't discuss your families much?'

'No. No. You forget your family at the club.'

Lomax looked down in case his face betrayed his reaction to this.

'Except of course,' Hegarty added, 'Gail used to go there, but that's different.'

Lomax looked up.

'Gail?' he said. Hegarty was amused at his astonishment.

'Yes, Gail,' he said. 'Why not?'

Lomax groped for words.

'Um . . . well . . . she wasn't any of the things that the club . . . I mean the women there were sort of um . . . um . . .'

At that moment the receptionist arrived with coffee. She placed the tray between them. Hegarty thanked her. She did not respond.

Hegarty poured the coffee while Lomax thought about Gail. She was the forgettable girl in the wedding photos, the college student no one could remember, the daughter at the office Christmas party who was ignored by her father. Gail was emphatically not club material.

'I guess you're trying to say,' said Hegarty, pouring sugar into his coffee, 'that the club isn't the sort of place men should take their daughters?'

'No, no.' Lomax dropped his pencil. 'I mean, it would depend on the daughter.'

'Well Nicholas okayed her immediately. She fitted right in.'

Lomax stared at Hegarty in silence.

'Why the surprise?' Hegarty asked, smiling. He added: 'Forgive my amusement. I'm so old I'm almost never surprised these days. I like it. Don't take offence.'

But Lomax was too surprised to take offence. At last he said: 'I've seen pictures of Gail and she doesn't fit that description.'

'What pictures?'

'Pictures taken at Julia and Lewis' wedding. Pictures taken on holiday. A lot of pictures.'

'Listen, I was at that wedding and I don't even remember seeing Gail there. She was a kid. She grew up. And when she grew up she was . . .' Hegarty paused. An expression fled across his face. It was lascivious. 'She was so goddam sexy.' His voice was a little deeper than usual. Lomax understood that Hegarty had thought about Gail and the thought had aroused him.

'How well did you know her?'

'Not well at all.'

'No?'

'That's what it's like at the club. You have these relationships and you never get to know anyone.'

Lomax was careful. 'But,' he said, 'you slept with her.'

'Just once. Then she went to France. Unfortunately.'

'Did Lewis mind?' The thought of any of his friends or colleagues sleeping with Helen one day was unpalatable. The idea of Doberman seducing her was repellent. More than that, it was enraging.

'Why should Lewis mind?' asked Hegarty curiously.

Lomax did not respond. 'All this happened last summer?'

'She started coming to the club last summer. Then in July she went to Europe.'

'While you were with Gail . . . are you sure Lewis didn't have a special interest in anyone?'

'Last summer? He was through with Alice and . . . no, I don't think so. No one special after that.'

'Alice told us there was a young brunette . . .' But Lomax knew the answer to his question before he had even finished it.

'Oh, now I see,' said Hegarty. 'That must have been Gail.'

There was a loud ticking noise. Lomax looked around the room. On Hegarty's desk was an old-fashioned brass alarm clock. It must have been ticking steadily throughout their talk but until now Lomax would have sworn the room was silent. He listened to its melody, a deep note followed by a light one. Hegarty seemed to be listening too. Then Lomax said: 'Did Lewis also sleep with Gail?'

Hegarty did not speak. He raised his eyebrows.

Lomax reminded him: 'You're too old to be surprised by anything.'

Hegarty looked amused. 'I can't answer your question,' he said. 'I don't know the answer.'

Mrs Cleaver was unimpressed by the shops in the mall downstairs.

'Not nice,' she said. 'I bought this. Isn't it horrible?' She opened a bag and produced a shirt covered with blobs of red and yellow.

'It looks like it's been inside someone's hamburger.'

Mrs Cleaver giggled gleefully.

'Are you going to wear that?' he asked.

'Sure!' said Mrs Cleaver. 'It's so offensive! Now are you planning to buy me coffee?'

'Okay.'

He thought wistfully of how the journey home would have been in his own car. He would have mulled over everything he had learned from Hegarty. There was something about the stop-start rhythm of the intersections as you crossed town which aided relaxation and made thought come easily.

Mrs Cleaver was reversing out of the carpark. Lomax dropped his notebook in his haste to reach for the safety strap. He could think of no reason why she was driving backwards.

'I'm not going right around the one-way system. It's a waste of gas,' she explained. 'What was the dead man's pal like?'

'That's his car right over there,' Lomax said. Hegarty's car was easy to see. It was different from all the others on the lot.

'Oh, bygone days, bygone words,' cooed Mrs Cleaver, halting beside it. 'When we said automobile here in the west, that's how they looked. How could they stay that way when we started calling them cars? Car. Car. We changed their name and turned them into ugly boxes.'

In the dark outside the club, Hegarty's car had looked black. Now Lomax saw it was a deep olive green.

'It's so sleek and shiny,' Mrs Cleaver said.

'And the inside smells of leather.'

'Is he bald?' she asked mysteriously.

'Balding.'

'I thought so.'

Lomax did not ask her to explain. They were merging onto the highway now and it was thick with cars. Mrs Cleaver was lighting a cigarette. She hardly looked at the stream of traffic as she drove unhesitatingly into its midst. It parted for her and a car hooted.

'Get a load of this,' shrieked Mrs Cleaver, waving her new shirt at the driver. He looked alarmed. They stopped at an auto shop and Lomax bought tape and brake-light bulbs. He closed his eyes as they merged back on to the highway.

'Where are we going for coffee?' he asked.

'To a European place downtown. Or maybe it's Russian. I'm not sure but the cakes are good and I can smoke there.'

'You don't like Europe,' Lomax reminded her.

'I don't like anywhere.'

'Russia?'

'Russia. Huh. All their books are in block capitals.'

The coffee house turned out to be Polish. It was on a corner in the old quarter not far from Sachs Smith. Mrs Cleaver led him into a barber's shop where hair lay thickly on the floor. The barbers looked up but did not say anything. A sign in Polish pointed down a staircase and they followed its arrow to the basement. It was dark and smoky here. People were hunched over tables around the edges of the room. They were playing chess.

They found a table in the gloom. 'Coffee and cakes,' Mrs Cleaver told the waitress. She repeated their order slowly when the woman stared at her.

'No one speaks English in here,' she explained, 'so you can tell me about the murders without any danger of being overheard.'

'I don't know anything about the murders.'

She lit a cigarette and eyed him shrewdly. 'You're a small town boy, right?'

Lomax admitted that he was. Worryingly, Mrs Cleaver patted him on the knee.

'How did you know?' he asked.

'I can see the white picket fence along your skull sutures,' she told him.

He scratched his head.

'If you can't tell me about the murders, tell me what sort of problems you're having with your investigation. Maybe I can help.'

He hesitated. She waited, eating one of the cakes and drawing on her cigarette between mouthfuls.

'Well, I haven't been able to find out much about Gail Fox. She's one of the murder victims. I've tried a lot of people at Tradescant where she was a student but no one really remembers her. The teachers who taught her have gone away. The other students don't have anything to say about her.'

'Hmmm.' Mrs Cleaver narrowed her eyes and sucked on the cigarette to indicate deep thought. 'Did she have any hobbies or interests?'

'I don't know.'

'Girls don't these days. How about a room mate?'

'She lived with her family and when she was in her sophomore year at Tradescant she had her own apartment. I guess I'll go there and see if anyone remembers her.'

'How about siblings?'

'One brother, living in . . .' Lomax paused. '. . . Seattle.'

Mrs Cleaver's face curled in disgust. 'If you can face a trip to Seattle,' she said through pursed lips, 'he would probably say something interesting.'

'Julia's attorney told me not to make contact. She wants to deal with him.'

'Ignore that.'

Lomax had already come to the same conclusion himself. He had tried calling Richard's office several times but Richard was always out or in a meeting.

Mrs Cleaver breathed smoke. 'That one's easy. Just say you're from the IRS and you're calling to inquire why he hasn't responded to your letter about his tax refund. It gets anyone on the line.'

Lomax gulped.

'Did the murder victim have a boyfriend?' Mrs Cleaver was asking.

Lomax took a bite of cake to give him thinking time. He decided that Hegarty did not qualify as a boyfriend. 'I haven't found any yet.'

'Know which high school she went to?'

'Lindbergh. I haven't had time to pursue that one.'

Mrs Cleaver stubbed her cigarette out. 'That's where you'll find her,' she said confidently.

'That's where guys find people in detective stories?'

'That's where I find people.'

'You?'

'I like finding out about people.'

Lomax stared at her uncomfortably. 'What people?'

'Anyone who interests me.'

'Who?'

'People who come into the library. Sometimes they interest me, and I find out about them.'

'How?'

'There are all kinds of ways. It's just a skill you develop. People are slimy snails who leave trails of information about themselves everywhere they go and my hobby is to follow those trails. It happens that high school documentation is extremely thorough in this country and, if you know how to find it, that documentation can tell you a lot.'

Lomax had put the cake down, half-eaten. He knew he would not pick it up again. It was cloying. He had swallowed several times but still it stuck to the roof of his mouth. He felt nauseated.

'Are you telling me you find out personal details about people? Confidential details?'

Mrs Cleaver bared her teeth in a saccharine smile. 'Small town boy,' she said. 'Nothing in this country is confidential. There are so many lists. The United Lists of America. It shouldn't be possible for me to do this, but it is. Like I said, it's a hobby. So you don't have to worry about me using information for the wrong reason or selling it or giving it to anybody else.'

He had begun to sweat. His alarm was obvious and a few of the chess players were looking up from their tables at him.

'Why do you do this?'

'I've often asked myself that question. I guess information is power and when people are rude and discourteous to me, which, incidentally, they often are, I like to feel I have this power over them. Even if they don't know about it.'

'But . . . you could misuse it so easily.'

'I'm tempted sometimes.'

'And have you?'

'Blackmail, poison pen letters? No. I've come close to it when I really dislike someone. But I never have.'

He felt unhappy. He could see the faces of the players peering at him from darkened corners through a film of smoke and their stares added to his confusion.

'Don't get miserable. Use me. Give me Gail's exact age and I'll get back to you in a day or two with a list of people who knew her well enough to talk about her.'

'No,' said Lomax. 'I can't do that.'

Mrs Cleaver drew a pen and notebook from her surprising purse. It was large, plump and square and, like the Queen of England, she carried it over one arm clamped close to her body. She opened the notebook and with an air of professionalism wrote Gail's name and the name of her high school.

'She must have graduated three, four years ago . . .'

'Mrs Cleaver. You don't have to – '

'Anything else you want me to find out?'

'No.'

She shut the notebook with a sharp thud. It had a well-worn fabric cover and a snap fastening. It had been opened and closed many times. It looked less amateurish than the university theme books Lomax used.

273

'You didn't need to ask me if I'm a small town boy,' said Lomax, his voice inert. 'You already knew.'

Mrs Cleaver gave him her most saccharine smile.

24

Lomax fixed his car that night. Even in the dim and bug-shrouded light of the carport it was clear that the engine was now in an advanced state of corrosion. The wire was difficult to thread. He scraped his fingers on rusty metal. He swore. He thought about Dorothy Cleaver and her dangerous hobby. The wire punctured one finger and a thumb. He hoped she would forget or fail to find a list of Gail's high school contacts. But if she produced the list he knew he could not ignore it. Gail's metamorphosis in the five years between her father's marriage and his death seemed to have been chronicled neither by camera nor human observation. As he threaded the wire, his hand became trapped between two sharp and unyielding protrusions. Of course, Gail's mother must have witnessed her transformation. But she was incapable of describing it.

The telephone rang inside the house. As he pulled his fingers free he felt warm blood trickling down his knuckles. He cursed whoever was calling him.

'Lomax?' said an elderly voice which he did not recognize at once.

'Yes?' He was impatient. He held his hand in the air and the blood began to run down his wrist.

'Julia telephoned. I must say it was nice to hear from her. She asked me to call you.'

It was Berlins. Lomax had made a slight allusion to his problem contacting the professor and without asking any more questions Julia had sorted it out for him.

'Professor. I'm so pleased you called.'

Blood dripped from his arm. He caught it with the nearest sheet of paper and as he wound the paper around his torn finger he glimpsed the observatory logo. It must be one of Driver's letters, or Eileen Friel's.

'Why, Lomax? Are you in some kind of trouble?'

'I wanted you to know what's happening.' He told Berlins about the ethics committee and said that he had submitted a statement a short time ago.

'Goodness. I submitted mine a while back.'

'I was a bit slow getting around to it.'

'Lomax, Lomax,' said Berlins fondly. Lomax guessed he was shaking his head.

'It didn't fill a page. Do you want to know what I said?'

'No. It's a kind thought but it's unnecessary. I feel sure we've both said the same thing and I doubt the so-called ethics committee will even read it.'

'What?'

'I now suspect the whole extraordinary episode had something to do with the solar eclipse.'

'The eclipse?'

'Have you heard about the events Dixon is organizing to coincide with it?'

'Yes.'

'He needs funds and solar specialists to get something like that off the ground. He's saved himself a job by losing us both for the summer.'

'God,' said Lomax.

'I understand that the scientists observing the eclipse from this tracking aircraft will be joined by movie stars and TV cameras. In my opinion the observatory's turning into some sort of space theme park. Its position as a serious academic institution is being jeopardized.' For a moment, Berlins sounded young and incisive again.

'They've asked me to a meeting,' Lomax said, unwrapping the bloodstained invitation from around his finger.

'Really?'

'Do you think they'll take us back in September when the eclipse is over?'

'I'm afraid,' said Berlins, 'that it may not be the sort of place we want to return to.'

'Who's on this so-called ethics committee?'

'Dixon. Various other people who I can't remember. And Doberman.'

'Doberman!'

'Regrettably, yes.'

'But Professor, if you don't come back, Doberman stands to gain by it! He'll keep your job! How can he be on the goddam ethics committee?'

'Because it's all just a sham,' Berlins told him, laughing a little at Lomax's outrage. He began to talk about the telescope he was making.

'I've joined a club. Yes, really, there's one in the town just for enthusiasts who make their own little telescopes and I've met some very interesting people there,' he said. The idea of a distinguished cosmologist like Berlins joining a club for amateur astronomers was almost too much for Lomax.

'Oh, they aren't astronomers. They just like to make telescopes. I'm not sure they ever actually observe with them. I've learned a thing or two about mirror-grinding from some of the members, including an especially intelligent twelve-year-old.'

Lomax felt a stab of irrational jealousy for the twelve-year-old. Did this smart-ass juvenile know just who he was rubbing carborundum with?

Lomax told Berlins how he was trying to help Julia.

'Oh dear, oh dear,' said Berlins. 'I guess you're hoping to establish her innocence by finding the real murderer?'

This was typical Berlins. He appeared to state the obvious but one comment could focus your thoughts. Lomax realized that he had tried to find Lewis and now he was trying to find Gail but it had never occurred to him to try finding their murderer.

The professor said that he was going to Missouri for a few weeks. He promised to contact Lomax on his return. Lomax went back outside to the carport. Mechanically, he tipped his head back and looked at the sky as soon as he was away from the houselights. It was not a good viewing night. The moon was too bright.

Over the chorus of crickets, he heard bushes shake somewhere further up the yard.

'Deputy!' he called, suddenly hopeful. But he was answered only by crickets. He missed Deputy. He knew that the chances of his ever returning diminished the longer he stayed away.

The next morning, Lomax called Richard in Seattle, as Mrs Cleaver had advised him.

'He's not here right now,' said a helpful assistant whose voice always turned cool when Lomax said he was from Sachs Smith. Lomax gave a false name and tried to sound like someone from the IRS. His voice whined a little. It was the voice of someone he knew, he forgot whose.

'You could say this is a friendly call,' he said, 'no one is compelling me to make it, certainly I am not in any way obliged to under federal law. However, I would like to point out to Mr Fox that if he fails to respond to my letter of . . . er . . . let's see, three months ago, then he is in immediate danger of losing his refund. I can't tell you how much money's involved. It's substantial. I'll just say that. Now, I would like to ascertain from Mr Fox that he did receive my letter.'

'Gee,' said the assistant. She sounded flustered. 'Well, he's actually away at the moment.'

'Oh,' groaned Lomax, 'that's too bad.' His tone said it was a tragedy.

The assistant was upset. 'He's visiting his mother . . . maybe I should take your number and have him call you, Mr . . . ?'

Richard was here in California.

'Erm, Drachman, Arthur Drachman.'

But it was hard to be Arthur now he had the information he wanted. He gave a false number and rang off rapidly. He dressed and, without shaving, drove straight to Vicky Fox's condominium. He could pretend he was calling on Mrs Fox and accidentally meet Richard.

He rang the bell twice before anyone answered it. Then, instead of the crackle of the intercom, the door opened. Richard, carrying a garment bag and briefcase, was easing his way round the door. He looked just the same as the Richard of the wedding pictures, except his face was thinner. There were small, deep lines etched on each side of his mouth.

'Yes?' he said, hardly glancing at Lomax.

'Er . . . is Mrs Fox here?'

'She's swimming. You'll have to wait. Or call someone to let you in. I can't stop right now.' Richard was trying, with difficulty, to lock the door without putting down any of his baggage.

'Can I help?' offered Lomax nicely.

'No,' said Richard.

'Er . . . are you Richard Fox?'

'Who are you?'

'I'm from Sachs Smith.'

Richard turned to face him for a moment. His eyes were a familiar blue but their expression was icy. He was all Lewis. He wore a necktie and blazer and pale slacks. He smelled of something cosmetic, perhaps aftershave or shampoo.

'What now?' he asked, walking towards his car. Lomax followed him.

'I'd like to ask you some questions . . .' he began but Richard was shaking his head.

'I've had enough questions. I've told your colleague all I know. This crap is screwing up my life. Attorneys, journalists, nuts. Just leave me alone now, okay?'

278

Lomax watched him helplessly as he deposited the garment bag in the trunk and climbed into the car. His car moved away at speed. When he had gone, the complex was silent.

Lomax wandered up and down the row of doors, hoping someone would emerge from one of them. No one did. Finally he found a sign saying 'Medihomes Care Personnel'. A voice over the intercom told him to wait and the silence resumed. The mountains muffled noise so that even the traffic was not audible. Dry leaves arranged themselves near his feet. A moment later a lizard crossed the path.

A high wooden gate opened in the wall, scraping across the paving with exaggerated volume.

'Haven't opened this gate in a while,' said a man apologetically. Lomax had been admitted to the pool area. Mrs Fox bobbed above the surface of the water on a floating couch. Her body was bulbous. She wore sunglasses.

'I'm doing water therapy,' she called to him. She kicked her legs a little against the couch.

'Can you swim?' the man asked Lomax.

'Yes.'

'Mind if I leave you to look out for her? Someone should watch her . . .'

'Sure,' said Lomax. The man was grateful. Lomax sat down to watch Mrs Fox. The surface of the water barely responded to her bulk. She kicked her legs lifelessly. The couch propelled itself in slow arcs. It was unlikely that Lomax would be called upon to save her life.

They were at the heart of the complex, surrounded by windows on three levels. Lomax waited. Suddenly, he sensed movement. It was all around him. He looked up but could see no one. The movement, perhaps many small, individual movements, began again. He looked up once more and studied his environment and, after some minutes, he realized that there were people sitting on second floor balconies or lounging on first floor patios or peering from third floor windows. Wherever his gaze fell, there was a face gazing back at him. Outside Gail's house in Arizona the realtor had told him that the desert might seem barren but it was teeming with life.

Vicky Fox was disinclined to finish her water therapy. Her movements had ceased. It was possible that she was asleep.

Lomax coughed. 'Er, Mrs Fox . . .' he said.

She did not move.

'Are you okay?' he asked.

'Yes.' She continued to float.

Eventually she heaved herself from the couch. Only her ankles were wet. She wrapped a large yellow robe from her neck to her knees and sat down near him. Lomax reached for his notebook.

She said: 'Why did you come back?'

'To ask you more questions.'

'Questions, questions, questions.' She fastened her robe protectively. There was a silence. Her face was puffy.

'Did Gail ever visit you here?' he asked.

Mrs Fox shrugged. 'I guess so. She could have come swimming here every day but she didn't want to.'

'She didn't like to swim?'

'Oh yes, she was a real good swimmer.'

Lomax knew why Gail did not like to swim here: because of all the watching eyes. He remembered her defensive position in the wedding photograph. She was ashamed of her body.

He asked: 'Did you ever visit Gail's apartment?'

'Well . . . once or twice when I had a car.'

'Can you remember the address?'

'1245 Yellow Creek.'

Lomax was pleased. The address had been in the discovery but he had not written it down and he had not subsequently wanted to ask Kurt or Julia for it.

'Can you describe her apartment?'

'She had books.'

Lomax waited, but Vicky Fox had nothing to add. 'What happened to it when she died?'

She shrugged again. 'They cleaned it up and cleared it out, I guess.'

Lomax was disappointed. 'Is someone else living there now?'

Mrs Fox shrugged to indicate that she did not know the answer. Her shoulders spoke some language of their own. Then, unexpectedly, she said: 'If you go there, can you pick up her mail?'

Lomax stared at her. She explained: 'Sometimes mail arrives for Gail and I have to write people and tell them what happened.'

It was hard to imagine Mrs Fox with a pen in her hand trying to find the right words.

'The police used to collect it and read it and give it to me but I guess they don't need to see it any more. They haven't given me Gail's mail in a long time.'

'Okay,' said Lomax, 'I'll pick up her mail for you.' He tried not to show his delight.

'Mrs Fox, when we met last time you told me that Gail changed.'

280

She did not respond.

'How did she change?'

'She grew up.'

'How was she different when she grew up?'

'I don't know.'

'Was she pretty?'

'I'm her mother. You don't ask a mother that.'

'Suppose,' began Lomax slowly, 'suppose Lewis was alive and I asked him the same question. What would he say?'

Mrs Fox threw him a look of startling penetration. Involuntarily, Lomax jerked backwards.

'You don't ask a father that either,' she said.

'So what exactly did you mean when you said she changed?'

She did not reply. She seemed to have forgotten the question.

'Mrs Fox?'

She shook her head and stood up. She wrapped the yellow robe around her still tighter. He realized that she was going.

'I mean . . .' he began lamely, 'I'm real interested in how people change.'

She staggered slightly and leaned against him. 'So you've got yourself a nice new notebook,' she said, gesturing to the Tradescant theme book. 'I don't have to fill it for you.'

She walked away, talking quietly to herself, her soft shoes scraping against the paving slabs. She slid a door open. When it clicked shut behind her there was an echo click across the complex. Either she had badly needed a drink or she shared his suspicion of Lewis' sexual interest in Gail.

Lomax looked around him at the watching eyes. Every condominium seemed identical. There was a wall of windows and beyond them the massive mountains. He could not see the gate which had admitted him, nor could he establish from here which was the carer's door. There was no visible exit.

He bent over his notebook to hide his confusion. The pages were still blank except for Gail's address. At least he had that, plus an invitation to collect her mail. When he looked up, a pale, bony figure was shuffling towards him.

'Which way out?' Lomax asked, as the old man slipped into the water as smoothly as a sheet of white paper. The man pointed and began to swim a noiseless length. Lomax left with relief.

He found Gail's apartment not far from the university campus in an old, low building. The neighbourhood was quiet, a mixture of large

281

family homes and small apartment buildings. It was the kind of place visiting lecturers stayed, or the wealthier grad students. He guessed that Lewis had paid Gail's rent here.

He rang the bell labelled Superintendent.

'I'm from Sachs Smith, defence attorneys in the Fox case,' he explained. The super's face fell. 'You must be Homer,' added Lomax. But the super did not confirm this.

'Your colleague was here,' he said, in a tone of despair. No wonder Homer was miserable. He had been interrogated by Kurt. Lomax remembered that a psychiatrist's report in the discovery had described the super's condition as 'fragile'. Now he was asking anxiously whether Lomax intended to question him further. Lomax assured him that he didn't.

He explained: 'I was just with Vicky Fox, Gail's mother. She asked me to pick up Gail's mail.'

The super's expression was disbelieving. He said that the police were supposed to take any mail which arrived addressed to Gail, even junk mail, but for some months now they had not done so. The box had filled several times, mostly with circulars, and he had emptied it.

'I have it, I have the mail, but I don't know if I should give it to you,' he said. He was a small man. He made Lomax feel intimidatingly tall. He shook his head a lot. Lomax's request troubled him. His face pleated with worry.

'Is someone else renting the apartment now?' Lomax asked conversationally.

'Oh,' said the super. 'Oh, you want to rent the apartment.'

Lomax denied this and told him again where he was from. He offered to check with the police before passing the mail to Gail's mother. But the unhappiness in the man's face was now assuming tragic proportions.

'I don't know what to do,' he said.

'Is there someone you can ask?' suggested Lomax. He wondered if he was harassing this sad man.

'Maybe my son . . .' The super retreated towards a nearby door and called out for Jefferson. Jefferson finally appeared. It was hard to believe he was Homer's son. He was tall and slim. He towered over his father. He had an intelligent, bony face.

'Professor Lomax! Oh, wow!' he said.

Lomax recognized the boy as a physics major. A year or so back he had attended one of Lomax's lecture courses and asked a lot of questions.

Lomax explained he was on sabbatical. He told Jefferson why he was here.

'It's okay to give Professor Lomax the mail, Dad,' said Jefferson. 'He's, like, the numero uno cosmologist up at the observatory. I mean, he's like . . .' Jefferson's voice trailed away with admiration.

Lomax shuffled his feet and made modest noises.

'Jefferson wants to be a cosmologist,' Homer said. 'Some people think medicine would have been more secure. Or law.'

'It was when I was listening to you,' said the boy shyly. 'You did one final lecture at the end of the series on the future of the universe. I just didn't want those lectures to end.'

In his final lecture, Lomax had speculated that the sun might burn out of hydrogen in five billion years. He had described the massive, swollen, red, burning ball that the sun would become. He had discussed the end of the earth. He had predicted the scorching and shrivelling and eventual death of the planet. The Milky Way would become black holes, white dwarves and neutron stars and, after billions of years, he had explained, there might just be one single, engulfing black hole left to represent our galaxy.

At the end of the lecture, there was silence. He realized he had been sharing an apocalyptic vision with young people who habitually worried about zits and the sorority rush. He could tell from the tone of the questions which followed that, while some were exhilarated by his words, others were upset. He had tried to reassure them by giving them a sense of how far away five billion years was but he had learned on this occasion and subsequently that any discussion of the end of the world was unsettling for some people.

He talked now about career prospects in cosmology with Homer. This seemed to calm the super. His brow knitted with concern, he fetched Gail's letters. They were in a Safeway bag. He opened the mailbox while Lomax watched and added its contents to the bag.

'See,' he said, 'I only checked it a few weeks ago and now there's a whole lot more.'

'After the murders there were like crowds of weirdos hanging around here, asking questions, trying to see the apartment. It made Dad kind of cautious,' said Jefferson apologetically.

Lomax flushed. 'Who rents the apartment now?'

'No one.'

Lomax's heart beat faster. 'I guess it's been changed a lot?'

'Yes and no. I mean, they cleaned it up.'

'So . . . no one's lived there since Gail?'

Jefferson sighed. 'Dad says it's a lot different but basically, no, no one's lived there since. You want to see it, right?'

He disappeared and then re-emerged with a key. He bounded up the stairs ahead of Lomax, who followed breathlessly, stopping to pick up the letters which fell from the Safeway bag. The third time they fell he discovered the tear in it.

'It was real terrible when it happened,' said Jefferson. 'I was away doing a scholarship semester at MIT. It was like . . . well, just terrible. I mean, my dad found them. He needed help. He was already in counselling. He's still receiving treatment for this. I wish I'd been here. I wish I'd been the one to find them.'

'He also,' puffed Lomax, 'believes he saw the murderer.'

Jefferson turned to look at Lomax. It was a moment before he spoke. 'Yeah,' he agreed.

'Why did it take him so long to come forward as a witness?'

'If you knew my dad you'd know the answer to that. He won't even hurt a spider. He finds a spider and it goes outside. You think he's going to get someone convicted and sent to their death? That's one of the reasons this whole thing has affected him so deeply.'

'So why did he come forward now?'

'There was some policeman who persuaded him it was his duty. Blah blah blah citizen. Blah blah blah justice. Blah blah blah.'

'Who was the policeman?' asked Lomax suspiciously, sure that he knew the answer.

'I forget his name. This is the apartment.'

Lomax had read the super's statement. It described how he had entered the apartment the morning of the murders when he had found the door ajar.

'He gets upset about things anyway. I mean, little things,' Jefferson was saying as he wrestled with the lock. 'So he comes in here and sees . . . you know . . . it wasn't good for him.'

He pushed open the door. Lomax led the way into the apartment. He could not control his thumping heart. He felt as the small, nervous super might have felt that morning: a door ajar in this secure building was unusual, especially the silence behind it. The super had knocked a few times, quietly at first and then loudly. He knew Gail was expected back that day and called her name. But he heard nothing. He would have entered cautiously. Had any instinct told him what he might find here? Did the silence have its own quality?

Jefferson, as though reading his thoughts, said: 'It was the smell. Dad said he could smell it when he came in.'

What could he smell? Blood? Death? Lomax sniffed. Did the house really smell of something, or was it the atmosphere of the place which he sensed?

The hall opened out almost at once into a large room. Ridiculously, Lomax was ready for the scene from the police photographs. The emptiness of the room glared at him. Along one wall were bookshelves. Empty. Along the opposite wall were windows. Sun poured in through them. There were no drapes. There were electric sockets. In places there were shadows on the walls, indicating the ghosts of pictures. There was no furniture, just the indentation of furniture on the rug.

Lomax recalled the police photographs. He tried to place the furniture, the books, the bodies in this room. When he had deduced where the murders had taken place he walked to that spot.

'Did you come here when she was alive?' asked Jefferson.

Lomax explained that he had seen photographs.

Jefferson joined him now. 'I think her couch must have been right here . . . chair here, you can see the marks,' he said.

'How did they clean up the blood?'

'Easy. She had these rugs thrown everywhere. They sort of soaked it all up, I guess. And Dad said a lot of it stayed on the couch.'

Jefferson swallowed hard. Lomax stared at the floor, trying to imagine. But it was just a floor.

'There's a bedroom through here . . .' Jefferson wandered towards the far door. Lomax did not follow him. He was trying to decide where the murderer had stood. He positioned the bodies on the couch. He stepped back twelve to fifteen feet from them as the ballistics report had suggested. At this distance the wall limited the number of places he could stand. He chose the most likely angle. He fired. Once and then again. There was a suggestion that for the third shot, Gail's second, the murderer had moved only six feet away from his victim. Lomax stepped forward. Six feet was very close range. He felt uncomfortably near the body now. What motive could there be to fire so close to a woman who was already dead – ballistics said the first shot had probably killed or at least fatally wounded her. Various explanations occurred to Lomax. Either the killer was panic shooting or he was enjoying himself. Both possibilities seemed to rule out Frances' idea that this was the work of a hired professional. It seemed to him now that the third, unnecessary, close-range shot was all emotion.

And Frances was wrong about something else. He returned to his firing position and remembered the photographs.

It was unlikely that Gail had intercepted a shot intended for her father. The wall made it necessary to shoot from an angle and Gail was facing the wrong way and was on the wrong side for interception. Unless she had received the first shot, staggered, leaving her father a clear target, and then been pushed or pulled back to the far side of the couch. But the killer would have had to step back six feet to shoot her again. Possible, but unlikely. He remembered Berlins' law. The devious explanation is always the easiest. Simpler explanations take longer.

He had another devious idea. Two killers. Two different motives, one cold-blooded, one emotional.

His thoughts were interrupted by Jefferson, who had been watching him curiously. He asked: 'Is it true one of the shots was almost point blank?'

'Six feet.' Lomax's voice was hoarse.

'Maybe she was scared of missing.'

'She?'

Jefferson looked confused. 'I thought . . . er . . . hasn't the step-mother . . . ?'

'Well the murderer might have been a she but Julia Fox is pleading not guilty,' Lomax said.

'Oh, sorry,' said Jefferson. 'You're defending her, right?'

'Helping to.'

'Sorry,' said Jefferson again. 'Only, Dad saw her out in the parking lot that morning.'

'He thought he saw her.'

Jefferson did not argue.

They went through to the bathroom and then the bedroom. It was large, with closets built into the walls. The windows had been shut for a long time, retaining the room's own atmosphere. Lomax noted where the bed had been and where pictures had hung on the walls. But there was little of Gail here. The kitchen was even less instructive. Like the bathroom, it was shiny clean. There was a large spider in the sink. Lomax rescued it.

'Maybe I should leave the windows open and let some air in,' suggested Jefferson.

'No,' said Lomax sharply. His tone made the boy stare at him nervously.

'It's just . . . I'd like to come back here. With a sort of expert.'

Jefferson shook his head, looking momentarily like his father. 'Professor Lomax, this place was crawling with experts last November.'

'Indulge me,' said Lomax. 'I've heard about this woman and I have a hunch she'll be able to help me.'

'Not another psychic?'

Lomax was offended. 'No,' he said.

Jefferson was sheepish. It made him look still more like his father. Lomax said: 'Could you keep the windows shut and not let other people in unless you have to, just for a few days until she's been here? I mean, that's if she agrees to come.'

'We won't let anyone in, we've been told not to. Although the press were pretty insistent. They offered money, but we still didn't let them in.'

'I really appreciate you showing me this place, Jefferson,' said Lomax and the boy ducked his head and moved towards the door.

'That's okay,' he said. He added: 'I'm finishing a paper just now on ... well, do you think ... I mean, if you had time, maybe you could ... ?'

'Sure,' said Lomax. 'What's it about?'

'Redshift velocity. I have a first draft on my computer. If you could wait ten minutes, I'd print it out and maybe you could ... some of the calculations are ...'

'No problem.' Redshift velocity in exchange for one and possibly two visits to Gail's apartment plus all her mail. It seemed a low price to pay.

Jefferson took him down to Homer's apartment. His father was watching TV. He leapt to his feet when Lomax came in.

'Dad, Professor Lomax says he'll read my paper,' Jefferson said. His father looked pleased and frightened at the same time.

'I hope it's no trouble. I mean, if it's a problem for you ...'

Lomax assured him it was no problem. There was the sound of a printer in an adjacent room.

'It was pretty bad around here when they arrested her,' the superintendent said while they waited. He did not seem to want to say Julia's name. 'After the murders it was terrible – TV, newspapers, oddballs. Then it all stopped for a while. Then after the arraignment it happened again.'

He explained that he was trying to forget the murders. Just as soon as he had testified in court and the trial was over and the owners of the apartment gave him permission to relet the place he would put someone else in there and it would all be over.

It was impossible, after this, for Lomax to ask him for information about Gail or about what he thought he had seen that morning. He explained instead that he would like to make a second visit. The super nodded unenthusiastically.

Jefferson emerged with a sheaf of papers and his telephone number.

'I'll call to discuss it,' Lomax said.

Before getting into his car he looked up at the building. Most of the other apartments had plants or drapes or signs of habitation. Gail's windows were blank. He could hear someone on the second floor playing a guitar half-heartedly. There was country music thumping from the open windows of the top storey. All along the street the trees were in leaf. Next door, a woman was strapping a tiny child, clutching its toy, into a car seat. It was an ordinary, quiet suburb. It felt safe.

He drove home via Candice's house. She was there with the children. They had returned from San Diego just an hour ago. It was the first time he had seen Candice's parents since the divorce and he was surprised at the affection of the reunion.

Helen and Joel told him about their trip. They had been to the zoo.

'We saw a mountain lion, Dad, like you did,' Joel said.

'Probably you had a better view. I only glimpsed a mountain lion in the middle of the night.'

'How big was it?'

'I'm not sure. Six feet long?'

'At the zoo the lion was eight feet long,' Joel informed him. 'Did you know that the other word for mountain lion is cougar?'

Lomax told them that Deputy was missing. Helen looked ready to cry. She climbed onto the couch with Lomax. He assured her that Deputy would be back soon, the way he always was, with cuts and bruises and a proud look in his eye.

'Promise?'

'I promise.' He resolved to call at the dog pound on his way home.

'Has anyone solved the murder mystery yet?' Joel wanted to know.

'Not yet.'

'Julia didn't do it,' Helen declared. She stretched across his lap looking at him.

'Of course she didn't.' He held her waist.

'Have they found the gun?' asked Joel.

'No.'

Joel asked Lomax to draw him a plan of the room where the murders took place and indicate the positions of the bodies. Helen found some paper and Lomax marked X for the place the killer stood for the first two shots and Y for the third shot. Joel studied the plan intently.

'Do you think both the people died on the couch or were they dragged there afterwards?' he said.

'The police think they both died on the couch.'

'How were they sitting?'

Lomax mimed the position first of Lewis and then of Gail. He made dead faces. Helen and Joel giggled.

'What the hell are you doing?' asked Candice coming into the room.

'Trying to solve the murder mystery,' Joel explained.

Candice grabbed the plan. 'This is Helen's vaccination card. She needs it for the next five years and you've drawn goddam murders in ink on the back of it,' she told Lomax angrily. She sent the children into the kitchen to eat with their grandparents.

'For God's sake, Lomax, do you want to give them both nightmares?'

Lomax apologized. 'I wanted to ask for your help,' he said.

Her anger cooled a little. She liked to help people.

'This woman you were telling me about. The Nose . . .'

He explained that he had visited Gail's apartment.

'The scene of the murders? Lomax, you're getting so ghoulish.'

'There was nothing there. No furniture, no blood stains, no ghosts. There was just . . . smells.'

'You want the Nose to go sniffing around in there for you?'

'Yes.'

'Are you serious? She's a perfumeuse!'

'But you said she could smell sauce spilled on the rug six months ago.'

'So, she'll tell you Gail spilled sauce on the rug. So what?'

'Candice, when you walk into someone's home it sort of smells. Each house has its own smell. It's the smell of the house and the smell of the people who live there. And if this woman's nose is as sensitive as you say, she could tell a lot from the smells.'

'God,' said Candice thoughtfully, 'you really think every house smells? What does this one smell of?'

'Deputy Dawg. Cooking, sometimes. Kids.'

'Do you think I should use air freshener?'

'No. I think you should call this Nose woman and ask her if she'll help me.'

Candice was doubtful. 'She's kind of strange. She'll probably say no.'

But the Nose said yes. As Lomax arrived home the telephone was ringing. It was Candice saying she had arranged for Lomax to collect the Nose and take her to the apartment the next day.

'Any luck at the dog pound?' she asked.

'No.' The sight of so many sad brown eyes had depressed Lomax. None of the eyes had belonged to Deputy.

'Don't forget that if your dog doesn't come back we have a fine selection here, and they're free,' the assistant had said. But Lomax had replied, with bravado, that Deputy would soon return.

He opened the Safeway bag Jefferson's father had given him. He turned it upside down and Gail's mail thudded onto the rug. He pushed back the furniture and began sifting it into piles. If Deputy was here he would poke his long nose into the piles and try to sit in them. Lomax would have to push him out of the way. He switched on the TV for company. He did not watch it.

The largest pile was for circulars and junk mail. Most of them boasted the sender's name and Lomax wrote these in his notebook. There were catalogues for book and music companies. There were charities. There were insurance and financial circulars.

Another pile consisted of what looked like business mail. Finally, there were about five handwritten envelopes, probably containing cards. Christmas cards, and then more cards from the same places, dated February. Lomax guessed Gail's birthday was in February. There was a postcard from Geneva picturing small figures ski-ing down a big, white mountainside. The message was in French, the writing illegible.

Lomax was disappointed. Ever since the super had handed over the mail Lomax had assumed that just by looking at the envelopes he would discover something about Gail but all he had discovered was that she had a friend in Illinois and another in Kansas City who had not heard, by February, of her death. It occurred to him for the first time to open her letters.

The phone rang and as usual he answered it hoping to hear Julia. But there was a hiss and crackle of people talking and then Kim's voice.

'Is that you, Lomax? Over.'

'Kim?'

'Lomax. I'm talking to you from McMahon's carphone. Over.'

'You don't have to keep saying Over,' came McMahon's voice. He sounded drunk. 'You're not on board a fucking ship.' There were voices yelling in the background and someone was singing. Lomax recognized the unmistakable sound of astronomers having fun. The phone cut out. Lomax guessed that a party was heading down the mountainside.

The phone crackled back into communication.

'We're on our way over. Over,' shrieked Kim.

'Over where?'

'Your house. Do you have any food?'

'For how many?'

'Over! Don't answer until I've said over.'

'Food for how many, Kim?'

'Three carloads, many Italians. Over.'

'No, I don't have that much food. There's a pizza place in the mall just before you turn into Old Mine. I'll phone through an order and you can stop and pick it up on your way.'

People were shouting something. Kim translated. 'Liquor! Beer! Where can we get some? Over.'

'Same mall as the pizza place. How far away are you?'

'Half way. See you later. Over and out.'

Lomax had never been specially popular at the observatory and he was flattered that the astronomers had decided to party at his house. He wondered if Julia was with them. He telephoned her room and there was no reply. Maybe she was on her way here now. His spirits lifted. He cleared away his notebooks and Gail's mail and any other detritus of his investigation. He made some space in the kitchen and pulled more chairs out onto the deck. He looked up. There was a full moon. Observation would be impossible tonight.

It was strange to see them all again. In the first car came Kim, McMahon, Doberman, Yevgeny, the red-haired Englishman and, to Lomax's delight, Julia. They greeted him warmly. Kim carried a pile of pizza boxes into the house and the Englishman followed her laden with beer. Lomax turned to Julia. His Julia. She smiled at him and he held his arms out but she was formal. She kissed his cheek so lightly that he felt only her breath.

'Hi,' she said quietly and followed the Englishman towards the open door.

The second car contained a group of Italians and, looking disgruntled, Jorgen. 'Put the parking brake on!' he yelled at the driver. 'The parking brake!' He climbed out of the car and announced dramatically: 'That was the worst journey of my life.'

When Jorgen caught sight of Lomax his face cracked into about five pieces, the fault lines radiating from his mouth. 'Lomax, Lomax,' he said, shaking Lomax's hand with crushing intensity. 'Your presence is so very much missed at the observatory. Really so much.'

None of the other astronomers had said this. Lomax clasped Jorgen's hand gratefully.

The Italians introduced themselves. They were involved in a meteorite survey and had been at the observatory for three weeks. They liked the mountains but found the food abysmal. They admired Lomax's house.

Everyone went inside except for Lomax and Doberman, who waited to direct the third car. They could hear the noise of the others competing with the noise of the crickets. Kim had found some music. Dogs further round the foothills were barking. Lights from all over the house were shining out into the night.

Lomax and Doberman did not say much. Lomax felt awkward because Doberman was a member of the ethics committee which would decide his future.

'Nice house, Lomax,' said Doberman, 'but you should do something about that paintwork or the wood will warp.'

Lomax noted the new tone of authority in Doberman's voice. With Lomax and Berlins gone, Doberman's position at the observatory was unchallenged.

'How're things?' he asked, embarrassed by the silence into speaking.

'Great,' Doberman told him. 'Dixon's implementing some sound management practices in that place for the first time. Now every dime goes a little bit further.'

The last car arrived. It mostly contained strangers. A couple of the women were tourist guides and the two men were the solar specialists Kim had told him about.

'And this . . .' said Doberman as a female form approached in the moonlight, hips swinging slightly, 'is Madeleine.'

While Madeleine was still out of earshot he added in an undertone to Lomax, 'And boy, is she hot for me.'

Lomax resisted the urge to guffaw. Madeleine was a graduate student who was working with Doberman for the summer. She was French. Her dark hair was cut short so that her neck looked long and curving. Her eyes were large.

'Isn't she something?' said Doberman. 'I'm surrounded by beautiful women up there.'

Lomax was pleased to meet Madeleine. He hoped her good looks would divert the astronomers' attention from Julia. He noticed with satisfaction that Doberman played with Madeleine's hand as the group walked over to the house. When Yevgeny saw Madeleine he removed her hand from Doberman and kissed it, his eyes liquid. The Danish solar specialist fetched Madeleine a drink and the Englishman invited her to sit on the deck.

'Lomax lives in a tree house!' he said approvingly. 'Do come and see, Madeleine.'

It was a busy party. There was dancing and arguing. People shouted even when they weren't arguing. A small group, sustained by cigarettes that the Dane was rolling, told each other long jokes and wept with laughter. McMahon talked intimately on the deck with one of the tourist guides. Doberman and Madeleine and a couple of Italians lay watching a viewing video of Doberman's which had been recorded from the Fahrhaus. Doberman drunkenly replayed the same galaxy over and over, summoning people from other parts of the party to watch it. It was a warm night. It was possible to smell people's bodies. Lomax occasionally perceived a sweet, sharp perfume in the kitchen or on the deck.

Jorgen trapped Lomax outside and told him about his next project. He had been asked to set up a team investigating supernovae and he wanted to discuss the idea. It felt pleasant talking astronomy. It felt good to be asked for his opinion. Lomax was enthusiastic. He forgot to watch Julia and note who she was talking to.

'The project will be based in Colorado. I hope very much that when your present differences have been resolved you will return here to the observatory near your children and your fine house. But if this is not the case, we must of course speak further. I would most definitely choose to work with you,' Jorgen said and Lomax thanked him. He felt a strange physical sensation which spread to his legs and weakened them. He wondered if he could be drunk and instead recognized the feeling as relief. He looked for Julia, wanting to tell her about Jorgen's offer, but she was deep in conversation with Yevgeny.

Watching the party, Lomax could discern that there was a new power structure at the observatory, with Doberman at its centre. Even Kim was more deferential to him than she used to be. Nobody told him that he had replayed his video enough times and that the points he made about it were banal. People laughed more loudly than Lomax thought necessary at his jokes.

Lomax met him outside the bathroom. Doberman swayed against him.

'You know,' he said, 'I probably shouldn't be saying this. But something tells me there'll be a job waiting for you in September. Something tells me I'll be able to sort things out for you.'

Lomax did not like Doberman's reference to his own authority. 'How about Professor Berlins?' he said. 'I sure hope he'll be there too.'

Doberman pulled a curious face and swayed back to the party.

In the kitchen, Kim was emotional. The pictures she had taken on vacation in Arizona had been developed and she had brought them to show Lomax. She waved them in front of anyone who would look. Some of them floated on the beerstained table.

'It was fantastic,' she said. 'It was so fantastic I could cry. We saw these cave paintings where thirteenth-century people were having oral sex. Can you believe they knew about fellatio in the thirteenth century? I thought it was invented in, like, 1969. Get it? 69?' She giggled almost to tears. 'God, it was such a great vacation.'

Either she had forgotten the painting of the total eclipse or she was deliberately keeping the information for ABC. Lomax thought she had probably forgotten.

Suddenly she said: 'Lomax. Where's Deputy Dawg?'

Lomax told her Deputy was missing and she burst into tears. Yevgeny led her away. Julia, who had made a point of ignoring Lomax all night, heard this and spoke to him at last.

'Are you worried about Deputy?'

He nodded. He wanted Julia to feel sorry for him but she bit her lip and looked fragile and he forgot his plan and felt anxious for her instead.

'It's partly my fault,' she said. 'I should have remembered to shut the door.'

'No.'

They were alone in the kitchen. The room smelt strongly of beer. He moved towards her but she said: 'Lomax. We're supposed to be discreet.' She began to clear away the wreck of the pizzas.

He picked up the wallet of vacation pictures. 'Do you remember the cave paintings from when you were at Lifebelt Lake?' he said. He wanted to tell her how one of them had aroused him because it made him think of her.

'I didn't see the cave paintings.'

'Sure you did.'

'No.'

'Everybody does. You went with Lewis.'

She stared at him strangely. 'Lewis and Gail went to see the cave paintings. I stayed in the cabin. I didn't go out much that vacation.'

He scratched his head. He realized he was far from sober.

'Lewis and Gail . . .' he said.

'Lewis and I weren't getting along too well. He took Gail rowing and sightseeing and I stayed behind. There were hammocks . . .'

'You!' Lomax roared. Her eyes widened. 'You swung in a hammock! While they went out together!'

She nodded. Lomax sat down. His head had begun to throb. Kim was leading a sing-song in the next room. Julia was staring at him. People were calling his name.

Doberman came in. 'Lomax, for Chrissake, are you deaf? I said there's a police car outside.'

'Outside here?'

'In your drive. With red and blue flashing lights.'

'A police car?'

'Lomax, sober up!'

The sing-song had come to a ragged end. The Danish solar specialist was running across the deck outside, something in his hand. People were standing at the windows, their faces eerie in the police lights.

'Shit, shit, the neighbours must have complained,' squeaked Doberman. 'If it gets into the papers that a bunch of astronomers . . .'

'Relax,' said Lomax, going out. 'It's Murphy McLean come to look at the paintwork.'

'Hey, you're partying, Lomax, you sonovabitch! And I thought you were such a damn serious ol' Galileo!' called a familiar voice as Lomax approached the lights. They hurt his eyes.

'I have to keep the lights on, nothing else would calm this critter down except a pistol,' the sheriff said. A blue light passed across his face, turning his teeth a ghostly colour. He opened the door with a theatrical gesture and something brown hurtled out and threw itself at Lomax, pushing him to the ground. Lomax felt big paws trampling his face and a long tongue scraping across his chin. He smelt dog. He felt so happy he was close to tears.

'Deputy Dawg!' he yelled, flinging his arms around whichever parts of Deputy's torso he could catch. Deputy danced on top of him and then ran around him and then galloped, barking, into the house. He ran through the legs of the startled company and reappeared, speeding, around Lomax and the sheriff.

'You found my dog!' said Lomax. Murphy McLean grinned. Afterwards, the other astronomers told Lomax tht he had wound his arms around the surprised sheriff and kissed him.

'An immense kiss,' the Dane said.

'Smacking,' Jorgen assured him.

'Right in the middle of his forehead,' Kim added. 'Probably he could have arrested you. But he's obviously a real nice guy so he didn't.'

Lomax did not believe he could have done such a thing. The thought was still filling him with revulsion a few coffees later. He had kissed a man who had first sexually harassed Julia and then made strenuous attempts to see her wrongly convicted for murder. It seemed impossible, but he could not shake off an uncomfortable sensation that the sheriff's big belly had pressed against his.

'Tell me it's Kim's idea of a communal joke. Tell me I didn't kiss that fat moron,' he begged Julia.

'I didn't see. But the word is that you did.'

'Oh God, I want to die.'

'You were overcome with excitement and gratitude. You were happy.'

'I was drunk. Where is the fucking dog now?'

'He's here. I have him on a leash.'

They were in the kitchen. Deputy was under the table. Outside on the deck McMahon and the tourist guide were still talking while Madeleine and the Dane spoke in hushed voices in an intimate corner. Everyone else had fallen asleep on the floor or on the couch or in some other place.

'Come upstairs and sleep in my bed with me, Julia,' said Lomax, reaching for her hand. It rested on the table while he massaged her fingers. He picked it up and examined the joints. He tapped the nails. He tickled the palm.

'No. I don't want anyone to wake up and find me there,' she said. 'Frances says it's dangerous for anyone to know I have a boyfriend. I even stayed out of Murph's sight because I didn't want him to guess I was here.'

They were silent. Lomax could hear the low voices of the other two couples outside. Deputy snored.

'Just listen to him. He's so pleased to be home,' Julia said.

'Then why the hell didn't he come home earlier?'

The owners of an expensive Afghan bitch had telephoned the police because Deputy had sat down outside their house and refused to move away. He had howled incessantly for the bitch to come out. Lomax guessed from Deputy's smug expression that there had been quite a few women between escaping and finding the Afghan.

Fragments of the evening were already beginning to recur to Lomax. Jorgen had practically offered him a job. Doberman had told him he would return to the observatory, although he had hinted that Berlins would not. And Julia had talked about her vacation at Lifebelt Lake. She had said that she did not see the cave or anything else. She had remained in the cabin while Gail and Lewis went rowing and visited the sights. Both the lodge receptionist and the man from New Jersey had told Lomax that Lewis was seen out with his daughter but he,

Lomax, had simply reinterpreted their evidence to fit his own theories.

Involuntarily, he groaned.

'What's the matter?'

'I'm so stupid.'

'Oh no, Lomax, you're real clever. It's one of the things which is attractive about you,' she said. He looked at her gratefully through bloodshot eyes.

'How the hell did Gail change so much?' he asked.

Julia was taken aback. 'What?'

'Gail? How come people keep saying she was attractive? Tell me that.'

'Gail? Gail Fox?'

'How come?'

'You need more coffee.' She stood and, with her back to him, refilled the kettle. At Lomax's feet, Deputy stirred.

'How come? I mean, look at her when she was sixteen.'

'Well,' said Julia, rejoining him, 'I guess I helped her a little.'

'How could you help her?'

'Lots of ways. There are so many things a girl can do to help herself.'

Lomax blinked. Julia sounded like Candice.

'What can a girl do?'

'Oh, you know. Dieting. Make-up. Hair. Clothes.'

'You don't need any of that to make you beautiful,' he said, trying to take her hand again. She pulled away to make the coffee.

'Well it helped Gail.'

'You mean you changed her? She turned from a plain little girl to a lust-inducing young woman and it was because of you?'

Julia was lifting coffee from the jar to the cup carefully. The spoon was heaped full. She did not drop any.

'Maybe I helped.'

Lomax shook his head. 'No,' he said. He put his feet on the chair Julia had vacated and shook his head again. 'No. It's not possible to change another person. Candice tried to change me but she didn't succeed. We got divorced.'

Julia carried his coffee over and placed it on the table in front of him. In a gesture of unusual affection, she ruffled his hair.

'You're still drunk, Lomax,' she told him.

That night she slept in Helen's bed. Lomax found slumbering shapes in his own room and so he went to Joel's. Julia was a wall's width away. Once he heard her cough. He lay looking at a colourful wall chart. It was called Nebulae And Clusters Of Our Universe. It showed a planetary nebula, an emission nebula, a reflection nebula and some spectacular globular clusters. The crab nebula shone blue and fiery. Kim had told him his birthmark looked like the crab nebula. He lay blinking at it. She was probably right.

The cruel first light was already creeping into the room but by looking at the nocturnal pictures he could keep the dawn at bay, at least until he fell asleep.

25

When the three cars had finally driven away, grey faces looking back through the windows, Lomax closed the gate to thwart any further escape attempts by Deputy. The gate had not been used for some time. Its rusty hinges squealed in protest. Lomax winced at the sound. His head felt about twice its normal weight today. Deputy amused himself tyrannizing the squirrels, which had become bolder in his absence.

Lomax fixed the gate and cleared away the debris from last night. Then he took a long shower. He did not want the Nose to smell the excesses of the party on his clothes or in his hair. He drank coffee and felt refreshed. He ate muffins. He drank more coffee. Deputy stared at him through the gate as he drove away.

The Nose lived near Candice's clinic. Her home was one storey high and painted white. It was small and modern and inside it was as clean as a laboratory.

'I have to keep it this way,' she explained, 'or it would be like an assault course, my nose is so sensitive. When they painted the outside I had to move away for a month.'

Lomax eyed her nose. 'It looks just like any other nose.'

'I wish,' she said miserably. She was small with blonde hair. She should have been pretty but her expression, at least anxious but more often pained, prevented it.

Lomax drove them towards Gail's apartment. The Nose was not a good passenger. She clung to the safety strap every time they rounded a corner and sucked in her breath sharply if she thought that Lomax was too close to the car in front.

'You're lucky,' Lomax told her 'to have a supersense.'

'Lucky nothing,' said the Nose. 'It ruined my marriage. It usually ruins my holiday. Just going out for dinner can be like, well, like purgatory for me. You don't understand.'

Lomax wondered how it had ruined her marriage. Did her husband torture her with his body odour? He wound down the window and calculated how long ago he had showered. Two hours.

'You, for example,' said the Nose.

'Me?'

'You use the same brand of soap as your wife. It's really for babies, right?'

Lomax had to admit she was right. When Candice had left he had just carried on buying the same soap.

'You showered maybe two hours ago. You were at some kind of party last night where people were smoking and drinking. Now, you're not wearing deodorant. If you were, I could probably tell you which one, or at least who makes it.'

'Wow,' said Lomax. She was right. He had forgotten deodorant. He fastened his elbows to his sides.

'It's okay,' said the Nose, noticing his embarrassment. 'I can smell you but it's okay. Most people smell like someone smashed open every bottle in K-mart. They use perfume or aftershave, hand cream, soap, deodorant, hairspray, cosmetics, mouthwash . . .'

Lomax flinched.

'Yours is that green spearmint wash which that guy in a lab coat advertises on TV.'

'True,' admitted Lomax. 'It was a special trial offer. Oh God, I think it was in K-mart.'

'Do you begin to understand, Lomax,' went on the Nose, appealing to him and ignoring him at the same time. 'Do you begin to understand what it's like for me?'

She spoke with such intensity that he drew back a little.

'There's nothing wrong with all these smells individually. Some of them are even pleasant. But all at once . . . I mean, it's like every instrument in the orchestra playing its own melody. At the same time.'

Her voice seemed to break with pain as she spoke. He remembered Candice saying that the Nose recently had a nervous breakdown.

'It's real kind of you to use your special skill to help me,' he said soothingly. 'I realize now that it won't be easy for you.'

'I hope they cleaned up the blood. The smell of blood's very upsetting for me. On the other hand, some cleaning fluids can be almost as bad.'

Lomax told her that he had looked for bloodstains in the apartment and found none.

'I wonder which cleaner they used,' said the Nose wearily.

Lomax remembered that he had started to eat a hamburger in the car a few days ago. He had stopped to fill up with gas and when he came back he forgot about the hamburger. It had been lying on the passenger seat this morning when he started the car and, as he was late and had no time to remove it, he had simply put it under the seat. He wondered how long it would be before the hamburger caused the Nose immense suffering.

To distract her, he explained: 'I'm trying to find out all I can about the murder victim whose apartment we're visiting. It's been emptied, cleaned a bit, but nothing else. It has its own atmosphere. I'd like to know what conclusions you draw about her. It won't be easy because the murders happened eight months ago and the woman was absent from the place four months before that.'

'That's hard,' agreed the Nose. 'Once smells are real old it becomes hard to date them. I could tell that you showered two hours ago but if you hadn't washed for a while then I wouldn't know if it was five days or seven days. I mean I hope I can help you with this project.' She began to bite her nails with ferocity.

'I'm grateful to you for trying,' Lomax said reassuringly, but the Nose did not look reassured.

'When did you realize your nose was special?' he asked.

'When my father died of cancer.'

Lomax was curious to know more but nothing was volunteered. And then, just as he was starting to think of other things, she began to speak. He glanced at her and she was smiling.

She said: 'I was just a little girl. Oh my, he smelled so good while he was dying. And when he was dead there was the sweetest smell. Just the sweetest. They took his body away and for days I kept going into that room and sniffing the sheets and when they changed the sheets I'd go sniff the bed. About a year later I came home from school and there was a neighbour talking to my mom and, just faintly, it was there in the room again. That smell. I was so happy. I ran up to this woman – her name was Higham, Mrs Higham – and started to sniff her. Mom was real embarrassed. I said, you smell like my Daddy smelled when he was dying. I couldn't stop sniffing her, my mother had to drag me off her. I remember her face. She was scared. She went to the doctor. He said nothing was wrong but a few months later it was obvious. It was in her throat. They tried to operate but she died. After that people used to ask me to smell them. I found a few more cancers but when I got to about ten years old I knew I couldn't do it any more. I mean, not unless the cancer's real advanced and then everyone knows about it anyway.'

'How come you couldn't do it when you were older?'

'Children have sharp senses. Adults have to train their noses and still they're never so good as kids'. I started to train mine when I was about twelve. Then I worked in cosmetics when I left school and trained it some more. I thought my nose would make my fortune. And it's true you can make a lot of money out of a nose like mine. But it's not worth it. Because it's like torture.'

She was sounding anguished again. Lomax was glad they had arrived.

'I don't think your dog is pure basset, but he has some basset blood,' she remarked with such assurance as they got out that he peered back into the car for Deputy. Then he remembered she could see with her nose.

'It smells like he's left a half-eaten hamburger back there,' she said.

'Probably,' Lomax agreed. 'That's the kind of thing he does.'

He began to feel excited as they crossed the carpark. Would she be able to see Gail with her nose too? He felt close to finding Gail now. He could not resist glancing up at her window, half-expecting to glimpse her face looking down at him.

'More mail here, Professor Lomax,' said the super when they called to collect the key.

'Lifebuoy,' muttered the Nose.

'Um . . . Jefferson said . . . he had to go to work at the pizza place but he said . . . if he could have your telephone number or if you brought any notes for him or you could call him or . . .'

Lomax remembered redshift velocity. He still had not read Jefferson's paper. He was not even sure where he had put it. He tried to conceal all this from the super. He gave his number and said he would be pleased to discuss the paper any time. He promised himself that he would read it as soon as he got home. He put Gail's letters into his pocket without looking at them and led the Nose up to the apartment. His heart was beating fast. He rang the doorbell. The Nose looked at him in surprise.

'Oh God, that was a stupid thing to do,' he said, fumbling with the key. He threw open the door and the Nose walked in. Her body was tense. Her face was alert. Her eyes darted. She was not visibly sniffing. When he watched her closely he could see that she was inhaling with short breaths. He followed her as she walked all through the apartment slowly. Sometimes she turned a little to one side or walked right up to a wall.

'Stay in one place or you'll give me baby soap in every room,' she told him.

He went into the room where the murders had taken place and stood in the corner by the door. As he waited for the Nose in silence he saw small things he had not noticed before. For example, there were triangles of missing paint all over the walls. Long threads of elastic dangled from one of the empty book shelves. He had used elastic threads like these on Helen's birthday to tie balloons. Where the metal fastenings of the bookshelf were broken, an ingenious arrangement of tightly coiled wire secured them. He felt sure this was Gail's work. But he had no way of knowing.

The Nose was in the bathroom now. He could just see her, sniffing at the bath and the walls and into the sink. When she came to the main room she did not notice him. She worked her way systematically in a criss-cross pattern from wall to wall, digging her face into the corners. Sometimes she walked upright, sometimes she stooped so her nose was just a few inches from the floor.

She began to circle when she reached the area where the bodies had been found. 'Hmmm,' she said.

'That's where they were shot, right there,' Lomax told her.

'I know, I know,' the Nose snapped. He thought she was angry and then discerned that she was tearful.

She completed her survey of the room. 'Okay, I'll tell you what I know but it isn't much,' she said. Lomax stepped forward.

'Stay there,' she shrieked so loudly that he jumped back.

'I may need to sniff some more,' she explained. She buried her hands in the front pockets of her jeans, hunching her shoulders.

'This woman. Don't tell me her name. Her perfume was by Dior. I'm sure about that but I can't for certain name the soap she used because the whole bathroom reeks of lemon cleaning powder. If I had to guess about the soap it would be Floralia, something expensive anyway. She used a lot of powder, actually baby powder, which is why your baby soap confused me for a moment there. Oh, and she liked baby oil too. In the bedroom. She had an active sex life. Semen's so incredibly pungent. Why did God make it smell that way? For population control? It's the first smell which hit me when I walked into that room. You can tell where the bed was from the dents in the rug but there's semen other places in there. Some semen in here also. Er, what else?'

The Nose thought hard. Lomax leaned forward. She had taken a few steps from him. He had to strain to hear her.

'Oh yeah, she wasn't a great washer. I mean, some people are always washing their clothes, they spend their money on washing powder, fabric freshener . . . she wasn't like that. She wore her clothes for a little bit longer than she should have.'

'How do you know that?' called Lomax across the empty room.

303

'From the closet. Now the closet's interesting, they always are. I could smell her in there.'

So Gail was in the goddam closet. Lomax hadn't even thought of opening it. He made an involuntary movement now towards the bedroom. But the Nose was talking again.

'She wasn't an especially clean person. Maybe some days she didn't shower and then she'd spray on extra perfume. People like her are an assault on people like me. I'm glad I didn't know her. I'm pretty sure she was unsanitary when she was menstruating. I don't like to be in elevators with menstruating women, especially slobs like her. I think she was a nervous type of woman. I think she got uptight, possibly she had a temper. But that's not, like, scientific. It's just a small theory I'm currently working on about smell and personality. So I don't guarantee I'm right on all that. There's also a possibility . . . well it's just a guess. I'm probably wrong.'

'What, what?' By now Lomax was prepared to believe anything she had to say. It was impossible for the Nose to be wrong. He had stepped closer involuntarily and she had stepped back from him.

'Was she in hospital?'

'Hospital!'

'Why are you so surprised?'

'Well . . . well, because you're a very surprising woman,' said Lomax. The Nose looked at him strangely.

'Hospital!' he repeated. He was unable to hide his fascination.

'Listen, it's just a hunch. In the bedroom. There's a whisper of Drezellin. It's a kind of anti-fungal thing which they use a lot in hospitals. Like I say, it's a whisper and I can't date it and maybe there's something similar now which you can buy in drug stores for dressing wounds or Athlete's Foot or something. So I'm not sure about the hospital.'

She was beginning to relax. Lomax knew she was enjoying his interest. She walked around the room, moving her head freely, her mouth closed, not sniffing but breathing.

'Not too much for me in the kitchen, except the lemon cleaning powder. I'll try again in a minute. And this room . . . like I said, there's definitely some semen. Books are quite strong. I'd guess the bookcase was pretty well-stocked. But the blood's almost overpowering. There must have been some rugs on top which got stained and that's all they removed. The smell permeated the wall-to-wall underneath, even if the stain didn't. It's horrible.'

'Can't you tell which blood group she was?' asked Lomax to

lighten her mood, which was growing dense again. But the Nose did not smile.

'Well no, I can't unfortunately,' she said sadly. 'I can smell the policemen who were here . . . they always smell the same.'

'How?'

'Sort of . . . well, uniformed police are always . . . oh, I don't know, their uniforms have this smell I guess. And they use this chemical for fingerprinting . . .'

Her voice was trailing away.

'Is there any more?' asked Lomax.

She nodded miserably. Her head hung. She looked unhappy, but would not let him step closer.

'What, what?'

She shook her head, unable to speak for a few moments. Lomax wanted to talk to her gently but at this distance all he could do was yell.

'What can you smell?' he bellowed. She was speaking but he could not hear her. Finally she moved closer.

'Fear,' she was saying. 'Fear. It wasn't just that someone came in and shot them. They were tormented. Tortured, maybe. I mean psychologically if not physically . . . they were really terrified and then they were killed.'

They were on the way home before she could speak without crying.

'I can't tell you any more. I smelled the fear in there the minute I walked in. It's stronger than the blood. And the combination of the two is just . . . well . . .'

'Believe it or not,' said Lomax, 'I may have smelled fear on occasions. I mean, I think I know the smell.'

'People secrete unmistakable substances when they're afraid. The smell is real strong. Most animals and humans can pick it up, at least subliminally. Once I rode horseback and he could smell my fear and he tried to gallop away. The strange thing was that, until he ran off, I wasn't actually scared of him. I was scared the way he smelled would be too much.'

'You were brave to try horseback riding. With a nose like that,' said Lomax.

'I always wanted to try it. It looks such fun. Only I knew I never could. Then my husband gave me a course of riding lessons for my birthday so I like had to try it. Just once.'

'It's hard to give you presents,' Lomax observed, and the Nose nodded.

'Yeah,' she said.

'How can I pay you for what you've done today? I can't give you flowers or buy you dinner or . . .'

'No,' said the Nose sadly. 'You don't have to pay me anything.'

'Maybe I can do something? I can fix things.'

'Well . . .' she hesitated. 'Is it true you work at the observatory?'

'Sort of.'

'I've always been fascinated by that kind of place. First because of what you do there. Second because of the environment you do it in. You have to keep it dust-free and clean, right?'

'You'd like to visit the observatory!'

'I'd like to look through the telescope.'

Lomax thought rapidly. 'Mostly people watch on screen . . . but it should be possible. I'll try to organize that.'

The Nose's face lit up into a brilliant and transforming smile. 'Oh gee,' she said.

'It should be possible,' he repeated. She looked so happy that he did not think now was the time to tell her about the oil of the telescope mechanism, about the bananas that Rodrigues habitually ate on duty, or the peanut butter sandwiches the cafeteria prepared for astronomers who were viewing. He said: 'It's real cold at night up on the mountain, even in summer. So bring big sweaters which you can wear one on top of the other.'

'Oh!' she said. 'Oh, that cold, clean air.'

He promised to call her.

As they neared her house, her mood darkened again. 'I'm not sure I was any use to you today,' she repeated several times. He assured her she had been but she shook her head. He dropped her in front of her house and watched her walk to the door, a solitary figure. She was hunching her shoulders again.

'She's weird,' Lomax told Candice when he called her later. 'Sort of sad.'

'God, yes,' agreed Candice. 'I mean brilliant, but weird. And she's always sick. Migraines. We spend so much time cancelling appointments for her.'

It was easy to imagine the Nose lying in a darkened room holding her head and fighting nausea.

'Sometimes I think she's a little bit crazy,' Candice was saying. 'Remember I told you I thought someone was stealing from me? Well, it started just about the time she arrived.'

'You suspect the Nose?' It was hard to imagine that, while the Nose

306

had been helping Lomax to investigate one crime, she had been committing another herself.

'Not exactly suspect.'

'Does she need the money?'

'No. She earned big money from those cosmetic companies. I think stealing may be part of her craziness.'

'Will you do anything about it?'

'Watch her. That's all.'

Lomax remembered how he had suspected Berlins and intended to do nothing more than watch him. The police had suspected Julia and watched her. Experience showed that suspicion was not a steady state. It was a volatile condition which, under pressure, erupted into accusations.

'Did the Nose help you much?' Candice asked him.

'Yes. She said she could smell Gail in the closet and it made me feel like she really was there.'

Candice was still giggling at this when she hung up.

Some of the things the Nose had said about Gail had unsettled Lomax. Not the surprising things, like the hospital and her active sex life, but the things which reminded Lomax of Lomax. Her slobbishness, for instance. It seemed that whoever you tried to investigate, you just found yourself.

He decided to wash his clothes. He was standing in the kitchen and now he took all his clothes off and threw them in the wash. He saw Deputy staring at him and he decided to wash Deputy too. He used the yard hose and Deputy got overexcited and tried to attack it. Over the sound of barking, Lomax heard the phone ring.

'This is — ' said a hoarse voice, breaking into a violent coughing fit before it could name itself. Lomax guessed it was Dorothy Cleaver.

'Are you okay?'

'Gretchen Throw-up's on the desk again. Her sunny smile makes me ill. Plus I'm in trouble.'

'What kind of trouble?'

'The cleaner found a pile of cigarette butts shoved under Archaeology, Ancient History and Primitive Man and Gretchen thinks they're mine.'

'Are they?'

'Probably. I like wandering around here smoking cigarettes when everyone's gone home. That's when I do my research.'

Lomax felt the return of his unease. He had tried to forget how, in the dark coffee bar, Mrs Cleaver had known more about him than he

307

had told her. It was disturbing to think about Mrs Cleaver investigating people, consulting lists, taking notes, for no particular reason.

'I have some information for you. As promised,' she said. 'Do you have a pen there?'

'Yes.'

'Okay, call this number first.' He wrote down the number. 'It's Andrew Drapinski's.' She spelled Drapinski. 'He was Gail's biology teacher in high school. He probably knew her as well as anyone there. She had a few on-off friends but no one special. I can find them if you like but I figured you'd do better with Joe Johnson. He was the high school heart throb. He must have known her. He's studying medicine back east but he's home right now for the summer. He's working as a ranger in the mountain park so you can go there and look for a tall guy in a hat and a badge that says Ranger.'

Lomax thanked her. 'How did you find all this out?' he asked.

'Mary Mudcap has her methods,' she said mysteriously. 'Want me to make any more inquiries for you?'

'No thanks.'

Lomax telephoned Andrew Drapinski.

'Sure, I remember Gail,' he said. His voice was high-pitched. He arranged to meet Lomax at Lindbergh High when it next opened for summer school.

'Come at twelve when my classes end,' Drapinski told him. Lomax realized after hanging up that he had arranged to visit Lindbergh on the same day as his meeting at the observatory. Driver's letter, now bloodstained, lay in a creased ball by the phone. It was difficult to read the time of the meeting. It looked like four o'clock. He calculated that he should have time to drive to the observatory after seeing Drapinski.

The mountain park was one of Deputy's favourite places. It was full of women. If he escaped from his leash he could be relied upon to harass a large number of bitches in a short space of time. Occasionally he persuaded one to submit to his attentions. In the past, owners had threatened Lomax with litigation as he dragged Deputy away.

Lomax disliked the park for this reason and because it was a tame piece of wilderness. It was a section of mountain slope where the trails were edged tidily in timber and every inch of them was well-trampled. There were seats at intervals and a plethora of signs telling you where you were and what you were looking at. Candice often took the children there. She was capable of walking right past a fallen tree, thick with interesting fungi, until a helpful sign saying 'Fallen Tree' halted her. The sign would indicate the interesting fungi, name them, and discuss them. Candice would read the sign out loud in an instructive way.

Lomax had not intended to take Deputy with him but as he drove away he glanced in the mirror and saw Deputy's nose pressed against the gate and his tail wagging in sad slow motion like a flag of surrender.

'Okay, you can come with me. But if you slip your leash I'm leaving you right there in the park,' Lomax told him. Deputy panted loudly, his tongue hanging from the side of his mouth.

It was a sunny day and the park was busy. On the lower slopes there were ad hoc ball games and a few picnics. Deputy strained at his leash. His body was alert. His nose trailed along the ground.

Lomax remembered that blue-uniformed rangers patrolled the park. People were encouraged to stop them and ask questions about the bugs and flowers they had seen on the mountainside. Candice invariably stopped a ranger with a question. Lomax also remembered seeing a rangers' cabin hidden somewhere on the lower slopes. He had to pull Deputy, who had seen an interesting bitch in another direction, to the cabin by his neck. Lomax glanced in the window as he passed. There was a card game, possibly poker, in progress.

He knocked on the door and after a few minutes an unsmiling ranger appeared.

'Yes?' she said with hostility.

'I'm looking for Joe Johnson,' Lomax told her.

'Oh. Okay.' Her tone altered. 'I thought you were going to ask some dumb question about poison ivy.'

She left him waiting at the entrance to the cabin. Deputy did not cease to strain in the direction of the bitch.

'Hi,' said a deep voice. Lomax turned and found, unusually, that he was looking directly into someone's eyes. Joe Johnson was exactly his height. His gaze was steady.

Lomax introduced himself. 'I'm helping to investigate the murder of a girl who was a student at Lindbergh High with you,' he said.

'You must mean Gail Fox.'

'Can I arrange to meet you some time? I'd like to hear what you remember about her.'

The young man shrugged. 'I can tell you now. It won't take long because I didn't know her too well. Just a minute.'

He returned a moment later with a blue hat. 'We're supposed to wear our hats at all times,' he explained. 'Another stupid rule. Okay, follow me.'

309

Joe's hair was cut so that a wave of it kept surging down his forehead and into his eyes. Now he fixed it in place with the hat and strode ahead of Lomax. Lomax was surprised by his confidence. At Joe's age he had still walked with a stoop. Also, he had still been bothered by his birthmark. Joe, who was handsome, had no such problem. Lomax remembered that Mrs Cleaver had described Joe as the high school heart throb.

Lomax asked: 'Is this a vacation job for you?'

'Yeah. I'm studying medicine in Chicago and it gets pretty intense from next semester onwards. This is the last summer I'll work here.'

He led the way behind the rangers' cabin up the slope. To Lomax's surprise, the trail was unmarked and overgrown. Deputy followed, apparently interested by Joe.

'This is one of the trails where we're fairly sure of not meeting the public,' Joe said. 'I'm an expert in avoiding them. We're supposed to circulate the whole time so we circulate on the routes no one knows about.'

'Why?'

'You could go crazy answering dumb questions.'

'Is that what they teach you in med. school?' asked Lomax, but Joe had gained on him over the steep terrain and did not hear. They reached a seat cut from old timber and Joe sat down on it. Lomax joined him breathlessly. Deputy was panting. Lomax pretended to look at the fine view of the city while his breathing evened. He could see Tradescant, surrounded by green vegetation, to the east. Further away, the downtown buildings glittered.

'So,' said Joe, 'tell me about Gail.'

'I thought you'd do that.'

'I mean, tell me who killed her.'

'I don't know.'

'Are you a detective?'

'No. Gail's stepmother has been accused of the murders and I'm trying to help her defence attorneys.'

'Oh? My mom sent me newspaper cuttings about the murders but she didn't send me that one.' He looked thoughtful. 'So. The stepmother.'

'Gail spoke about her?'

'Oh sure.'

'What did she say?'

'That her stepmother was mean to her. I didn't really believe her but it seems now she was telling the truth.'

'The law presumes people innocent until they're proven guilty,' Lomax pointed out.

'Yeah, yeah,' said Joe as if this was as tedious a formality as wearing a hat in the park.

'How well did you know Gail at Lindbergh?' asked Lomax.

'Not real well. I mean . . . I think she would have liked for us to know each other better.'

'She was interested in you?'

'I don't know how to say this . . .' Joe took his hat off and the wave of hair bounced out from beneath it. He looked away from Lomax, across the veiw. 'She was, you know, like hot for me.'

Lomax was reminded of Doberman. Doberman had said the same thing about Madeleine and then she had shown a preference for the Danish solar specialist. But Doberman was a notorious fantasist and Joe was a high school heart throb.

'Right from the time you both started in high school?'

'I don't know. I don't remember even seeing her until we were seniors and she began to throw herself in front of me every time I walked down the hallway. Gail was homely. I mean . . .' He looked at Lomax. '. . . probably you don't remember high school too well. High school students divide into groups. There's a group of pretty girls who wear great clothes and like sex, there's a group of rich kids whose parents give them fast cars, there's a group of smart kids, there's a group of computer buffs, there's . . .'

'Believe it or not,' said Lomax, piqued at the reference to his age, 'the whole of life consists of people dividing into groups. It starts in high school and it doesn't stop.'

'Well Gail wasn't in a group. She didn't fit in anywhere.'

'Can you describe her? Physically?'

'Plain. Overweight. And here's what was so sad. She tried. She really tried. She came to school in these clothes. Well, if Mary Beth Bartel or Gina Martinez had worn them they'd have looked great. But on Gail . . . jeez. She had expensive hair cuts, make-up, you know. But it didn't make any difference. She was still lumpy ol' Gail. Nobody would want to go to bed with her when there were girls like Mary Beth around.'

'Did you date Mary Beth?' asked Lomax jealously. There had been a Mary Beth at his own high school. Kelly Ann Rettinger. Lomax had found Kelly Ann so attractive that he had slunk off in the opposite direction whenever he saw her.

'Well sure,' said Joe, perceiving his tone and turning to look at him. He pushed the wave out of his eyes, but it was designed to spring right

311

back again. 'Wasn't it like that for you? Girls like big guys. Especially if they're intelligent. I mean, you're an attorney, I assume you're intelligent.'

'No, it wasn't like that for me,' Lomax said, twisting Deputy's leash around his fingers. For the first time it occurred to him that it could have been. Self-assurance like Joe's might have made Kelly Ann Rettinger more interested in him.

'Actually Mary Beth was sort of stupid,' Joe admitted, 'and I even got bored having sex with her after a while. God, I was so superficial when I was young.'

Lomax suppressed a smile. 'Did Gail's intelligence interest you?'

'Not at that age. I mean, you can't screw intelligence. She was unattractive. Also, it drove me crazy the way she kept throwing herself in my way. For example, I was president of the astronomy club. So Gail joins. Maybe she has a passing interest in the subject but not so great as her interest in me. We went viewing one night. I don't know what she hoped would happen. What did happen was that she wore some stupid clothes and got real, real cold. She practically died of hypothermia. I thought, tough shit.'

Lomax was silent.

Joe explained: 'You can perish on the mountains, even in summer, if you're sitting still and staring through a telescope.'

'Really?' said Lomax.

'Yeah. I thought about a career in astronomy. But who wants to spend every night with a frozen butt? Plus we went on a club trip to the observatory and there were all these nerds.'

'I've been there,' agreed Lomax morosely. 'The place is full of nerds.'

Joe was thinking about Gail again. 'She used to flirt with me, and that was, you know, embarrassing. It was like she learned the technique out of a book and then tried it on me. Was it supposed to make me feel horny? I mean, jeez.'

'Did you give her any encouragement at all?'

Joe raised his hands in a defensive gesture.

'No! None! I swear it! Not guilty! I didn't want a starring role in some ugly kid's wet dreams! Except . . .'

'Except what?'

'She used to talk about the stepmother. Gail's dad went out of the house and this woman started to hit her. Gail's dad came back and the stepmother was all charm. That kind of thing. I was sympathetic. Big mistake. That encouraged her. Every time she saw me she said something else about the stepmother. Actually, it got so I didn't believe it. I didn't even listen. Maybe some of it was true, maybe none of it.'

'Was there evidence of violence?'

'Bruises. But she could have got those some other way.'

'From the mother, maybe.'

'The mother was dead. That was sad. The mother died when Gail was little and then the stepmother came along. Gail tried to tell her father how mean this woman was to her but her dad just didn't believe it.'

A small group, children heavily outnumbering adults, emerged on the trail. 'Oh-oh,' said Joe.

'Ranger!' called a voice. Joe groaned.

'We've been all over the park looking for a ranger!'

'We're shortstaffed right now. Some of the rangers are sick with a mystery virus,' Joe called back, putting his hat back on.

Lomax rose. 'I'm going to see Andrew Drapinski at Lindbergh,' he said. 'Remember him?'

Joe pulled a face. 'God. Drapinski. What a funny little guy. Good teacher, though.'

Lomax thanked Joe for his help.

'We've seen a shiny blue bird, about this big. Is it rare?' a woman demanded. The children began to argue over how big the bird was.

'Well, if it's around this big, then it's a blue jay. There are various different sorts of jay but the one you're most likely to have seen is the Steller's Jay. It's about thirteen inches long and its call is loud and raucous . . .'

Deputy steered Lomax back down the slope. They rounded the rangers' cabin. The card game was still in progress. Lomax guessed that the name of the mystery virus was poker.

He decided to walk Deputy now that they were in the park but Deputy tugged in all directions. Eventually – irritable, tired and within earshot of the piercing screams of a child who wanted to go home – they rested. Lomax heard the child and looked at the view but his mind was on Gail.

He was unruffled by her lies about her mother's death and about Julia's violence: her untruth was transparent. However, he was baffled by her transformation. She had battled against her own appearance and finally, when she seemed to have won the battle, her efforts had been mocked by death. Like all deaths, it was a sudden, absurd and arbitrary end to her progress. Unless it was deliberate.

Troubled, Lomax leapt to his feet and resumed his hike.

313

26

Joel and Helen had stayed with Lomax for a night and when he took them home Candice had said: 'I hope you're planning to wear this new suit to your meeting at the observatory.'

'No.'

'Lomax.' Her voice was firm. She was using his name. 'Show the ethics committee you're serious about it.'

'But the whole thing's ludicrous.'

'Do you want your job back?'

'Yes.'

'Then shave, wear a suit, and during the meeting don't start yelling.'

'Yell? When do I yell?'

'When you think other people are being stupid.'

Lomax put his suit on with distaste. He had forgotten to hang it up since he had last worn it. There was a network of creases at acute angles across the jacket. The creases, although not the suit, felt appropriate to wear to school.

He intended to arrive on time for his appointment with Drapinski, but Kim phoned just as he was preparing to leave the house.

'Are my Arizona photos there?' she asked.

'Yes. They have beer stains all over them.'

'Will you bring them back today?'

'Okay.'

'Did I tell anyone about the total eclipse painting in the cave?'

'I don't think so.'

'Phew. That's going to be an ABC exclusive. Wasn't it a great party? People haven't stopped talking about it.'

Lomax wondered what they had been saying.

'Doberman's mad because Madeleine and the Dane have turned into a twosome. And did you see McMahon and the tourist guide? Did you just see them?'

'Kim, there's someone I want to visit the observatory.'

'Who?

'A colleague of Candice's. Her name's Alison. She's unusual but nice. She did me a favour and she'd like to look into a telescope. When are you next viewing?'

'On the fifth I'm supervising here for some Germans who're watching on screen in Bonn. Any good?'

'Terrific. What are they studying?'

'Globular clusters.'

'Oh, she'll like that.'

'I mean, grouping and masses of white dwarves within globular clusters.'

'Which telescope?'

'The Phallus. Me, Rodrigues, and his bananas.'

'If she gets there early evening would you show her around the labs?'

'Sure. Tell her to arrive at five, five thirty. What's unusual about her?'

'She has a supersense.'

'She's a human telescope?'

'Not her eyes. Her nose.'

'Shit.'

'She can smell everything. She can smell what you did six months ago. She can smell your thoughts.'

Kim gasped. 'Will she be able to smell when I last went to confession?'

'Probably.'

'Shit.'

Kim told him that details of properties for sale had begun to arrive from Arthur Drachman in Arizona.

'What do Tandra and Roach say?'

'There's been a terrible misunderstanding. They think the realtor comes with the house. Ever since I told them about Arthur they've been insisting on moving in with him.'

'Call Arthur,' said Lomax, 'and tell him Tandra and Roach are on their way.'

'But Lomax – '

'And make sure Tandra packs a razor. Just in case.'

'Good luck at the ethics meeting, Lomax.'

Lomax telephoned the Nose to tell her at once about her trip.

'I have a migraine right now,' she said. 'There's a black disc in front of my eyes. It rained this morning for just a few minutes and the smell of the damp street is still coming into the house. It's worse after light rain. It leaves this sort of dank smell on the earth and the trees which is so . . . so sickly. Do you think I could ask my neighbour to cut down his trees?'

'He wouldn't like that.'

'But they blossom in the spring.'

'That's probably why he planted them.'

'I get depressed,' she said.

'Well next week you can drive up the mountain and the air will get clearer and cooler as you drive up and up and when you get to the observatory at the top someone called Kim Fenez will be waiting to show you around the labs. Then just as soon as it's dark and the crickets are squeaking at each other, she'll take you to the Fahrhaus. It's one of the biggest telescopes in America. A group of German astronomers will be studying something called a globular cluster. Kim Fenez will be directing the telescope for them and they'll be watching on screen in Germany. Kim's going to let you sit up in the cage and look through the eyepiece of the telescope. It's an amazing experience. You'll feel like you're out in space.'

'Oh,' said the Nose without enthusiasm. Lomax felt annoyed. He had arranged one of the greatest pleasures he knew for her, and all she could say was oh.

'A globular cluster,' he continued, remembering how, after the party, he had fallen asleep with his eyes fixed on Joel's picture of a globular cluster, 'may sound like something the dog threw up, but it's actually immensely beautiful. There are about two hundred of them in our own galaxy and it may be that you'll be looking at some of these. They're groups of stars, sometimes as many as a million stars, packed tightly together like a . . .' In the face of her continued silence he tried to find a way to make globular clusters sound enticing . . . 'a firework display,' he suggested lamely.

'They contain some of the oldest stars in the galaxy. Stars called white dwarves, for example, which are so old they're practically dead. When you look at them you'll be able to see what our sun will be like one day when the world's ended and the sun's burning itself out of the sky.'

'Oh,' said the Nose, anguished this time. He remembered too late how talking about the end of the world upset some people. He added: 'But that's billions of years away.'

'Well, thanks,' said the Nose unenthusiastically. 'I just hope I'm well enough to go.'

Lomax arrived at Lindbergh High School at twelve thirty.

'You're sure late for class,' the security guard said. She wagged her finger at him comically. 'Summer school starts at ten and teacher's gonna be real mad at you.'

'I'm here to see Andrew Drapinski in the biology labs.'

She waved him past. 'Okay, go right through. Climb the stairs at the end of the hall, then double back on yourself.'

'Don't you want to check whether I'm carrying a gun?'

She laughed. 'You ain't carrying a gun,' she said. 'I can tell by just looking into your face.'

Lomax smelled the high school and smelled his own teenage years. There was chalk dust and floor polish and something indefinable, possibly testosterone. He began to stoop. He caught sight of his reflection in a window and straightened.

The hallways were deserted. Just once a group of students passed him, staring at him curiously and then ignoring him. A few classes were in progress. Sometimes laughter, and once shouting, was audible from behind the closed doors. He paused to listen. A drama class. At the top of the stairs he smelled paint and clay and heard the buzz of serious activity. He was passing the art rooms. He looked in. The walls were thick with thumbtacks and paint. Most of the students were working with lurid colours, some stood back appraisingly from their work.

'Dr Lomax?' called a voice at the end of the hall. The words echoed so many times before they reached Lomax that he hardly recognized his name. He jumped guiltily and walked towards the small, bald figure which awaited him. There were lockers along one wall and hand-written signs left from last semester advertising meetings after school. He noticed the astronomy club had been out to the mountains to observe some nearby galaxies which were especially visible just now. Recalling Joe Johnson, he wondered if there were any girls in the astronomy club this year and whether they were pretty. He remembered his anguish at the absence of girls in his own high school astronomy club.

'That was the art studio. The biology labs are right here,' Drapinski said as Lomax neared him. Lomax entered and was so transported by the odour of the labs, of chalk and ether, that it was a moment before he noticed the activities of Drapinski. He was circling a large glass jar which contained a cloud of insects.

'Excuse me if I prepare for a class as we talk,' he said. Lomax studied the wall charts. The foetal blood supply. The sex life of plants. The structure of nucleic acids. An analysis of the fitness of one class revealed by their after-exercise pulse rates and their blood pressure.

'Okay . . . I just have to gas these little guys,' Mr Drapinski was saying. 'Drosophila. Fruit flies. Genetics. You probably did this one when you were in high school. Everybody does.' He flicked a switch. Lomax tried to recall studying genetics with fruit flies but was unable to.

'Thanks for agreeing to talk to me about Gail Fox,' he began. But Drapinski interrupted him.

'I'm not sure I'm going to do that,' he said.

'But on the phone . . .'

The biology teacher did not look at Lomax. His eyes were fixed on the fruit flies. Lomax watched them too. Their activity seemed to be slowing.

'Now I've had time to think about it, I'm not sure I want to talk to you.'

The flies were behaving strangely. They were crashing into each other. A few lay dormant at the bottom of the glass.

'Why not?'

'Didn't you say you were defending the stepmother?'

'Yes.'

'That's why not.'

Drapinski wore glasses. Both the lenses and the frames were thick. He dipped his head so that, from where Lomax stood, the rims obscured his eyes. Lomax shifted his weight but the teacher perceived the movement and answered with a corresponding shift of his own. Lomax concluded that Drapinski did not want eye contact with him. He recognized the biology teacher as a fellow slob. The man's clothes were old and ill-fitting.

The drosophila were succumbing to the gas. They lined the base of the jar lifelessly. A few still flew, although erratically.

'There's always one or two which seem to sort of go on and on . . .' said Drapinski. Finally the last fly fell.

'Why are you killing them?' Lomax asked.

'I'm not. This is anaesthetic.'

He opened the big jar and began to tip the lifeless bodies onto a sheet of white paper. They pattered like rain.

'Did you know about the murders of Gail and Lewis Fox?' asked Lomax.

'Sure.'

'Well, I have this problem,' Lomax confided. Drapinski still did not look at him. 'I'm trying to understand the murders and to do this I have to understand the victims. But I ask people to describe Gail Fox and no one seems to remember her. Then I call you and you remember her but when I arrive you say you aren't talking about her.'

'That must be kind of annoying,' agreed Drapinski, putting down the glass jar.

Lomax opened negotiations. 'How about, I ask you questions and you answer them only if you feel like it?'

Drapinski grimaced. His face was rubbery. He twisted his features into a small, white, wrinkly ball. The action nearly dislodged his glasses.

'But . . .' he said, unscrewing his face and then screwing it up again a different way. His glasses stayed in place this time but his tie, loosely and gracelessly knotted, became animated. 'But . . . a long time ago I decided that woman was a monster. Do I want to help a man who's defending a monster?'

'Julia Fox? A monster?'

Drapinski nodded. 'Like a yeti,' he said, looking at Lomax now. 'I always used to imagine her as the abominable snowwoman.'

Lomax did not know what to say.

'I guess,' supplied Drapinski, 'that sounds strange.'

'Yes it does. And unscientific.'

Drapinski flinched. Behind his glasses his eye colouring was weak. As though he were fading away, Lomax thought.

'I mean, have you met Julia Fox?'

'No, but I've heard all about her.'

'Well it's kind of hard to get to know someone from hearing about them. That's why I'm finding it hard to get to know Gail.'

There was no response. Drapinski wandered off to the front of the lab, opened a drawer and returned with a scalpel. He began separating the flies, one by one, into two groups. Lomax was unable to guess what the criteria for his choice could be. All the flies looked the same from this distance. Discouraged, Lomax continued.

'And monster's an unscientific term. I'm not sure of the exact sense of the word for you but the kind of monster you imagine Julia Fox to be may not be the kind of monster who commits a double murder.'

'Oh, you're clever with words,' said Drapinski, scarcely pausing in his work. 'I can tell you're a lawyer.'

'Wrong,' said Lomax triumphantly. 'I'm an astronomer.'

The biology teacher raised his eyes and blinked rapidly at Lomax.

'I'm an astronomer who's on sabbatical and helping to investigate these murder charges. It just proves you can be wrong about someone. Doesn't it, Mr Drapinski?'

Drapinski smiled. His face and part of his bald head puckered.

'You didn't know Gail at all?' he asked. 'That's a shame, she would have liked to talk to you, she was interested in astronomy. Along with a whole lot of other things. She had a lively, inquiring mind. In fact, I think she may have been an occasional member of the astronomy club here.'

Lomax waited for the teacher to continue.

'You don't want to hear what I have to say,' Drapinski told him. 'Plus there isn't much time. You were late. Thirty minutes.'

'Sorry,' said Lomax.

'Hmmm,' said Drapinski. His tone was not forgiving. 'Why exactly were you late?'

'You want a note from my mother?'

'I want to hear the reason.'

'The phone rang as I was leaving.'

'Did you have to take the call?'

Lomax considered. 'Probably not,' he admitted. Certainly not. He would see Kim at the observatory tonight. He could have made arrangements for the Nose's visit then.

'I'm sorry,' he said. 'I try to get places on time but I'm almost always late and I've never understood why that is.'

'Hmmm,' said Drapinski again. There was a silence. He continued to divide the drosophila.

'What are you doing there?' Lomax asked him at last.

'Sorting these flies into mutants and pure types. The anaesthetic only lasts eleven minutes.'

Then, unexpectedly, Drapinski began to talk.

'This is the kind of work Gail was good at. She was a keen student and she helped me in the labs. She'd brown bag in here at lunchtime and help me sort out the experiments. I have a lab technique I've followed for years. Aim, method, result, conclusion. Gail mastered it at once. Good clear methodology. She knew how to record data. Her analysis of the results was, well, outstanding. Graphs, tables, columns, all well-presented. And her conclusions were intelligent.'

'That's quite a report card,' Lomax said.

Drapinski gestured to one of the wall charts. The criss-cross lines on it looked like big insects. On closer inspection Lomax saw that it was a genetic chart. The lines linked the gametes of grandparents, parents and children. Along one side of the chart the experiment was explained.

'Did Gail do this?' Lomax asked. Drapinski nodded. The gift was so unexpected that Lomax's eyes would hardly focus on it.

'Really?'

'Sure.' Drapinski was enjoying Lomax's excitement. 'This is a study of the heredity of red-green colour blindness. Three hundred different families supplied data about the colour blindness of three generations. Unfortunately the survey relied entirely on the subjects' recall, and a control test indicated that this may be only sixty-five per cent reliable. Details of the control test are given in appendix a. The survey indicates that the allele for colour blindness is recessive and sex-linked . . .' The chart became complex. Lomax picked out the words aim, method, result, conclusion. He looked at the writing. It was small. Ts were crossed. Its slant was uniform. It was tidy. Both the style and content suggested the writer had a scientific mind.

'Three hundred different families. That's the kind of effort she made,' said Drapinski. 'She had me circulate questionnaires at PTA meetings. Parents filled them in, students would never bother.'

'She liked genetics?'

'For the intelligent student, genetics is a delight. At high school level there's a logic to it which is pleasing. I think Gail had a special interest because of the mother.'

Lomax hesitated. 'You met her mother?'

'You don't know much about Gail. Her mother died when she was tiny. Tragic. Gail was always worried that the disease which killed her was hereditary.'

'She told you that?'

'On the anniversary of her mother's death she wore this diamond pin to school. I was scared it would get stolen but the other kids knew why she was wearing it and they left her alone. It was the only memento she had of her mother.'

Lomax returned to the bench. 'How come she spent recess in here instead of fooling about with her friends?'

'Maybe she didn't have many friends. Maybe I was her friend.'

'Were you?'

'For a while.'

Drapinski had finished the division. He poured one pile of fly bodies into a jar. He wrote PURE on the paper and inserted it before fixing the lid firmly.

'Are you married?'

'Yes.'

'How long have you been married?'

'Eleven years. No children, to answer your next question.'

'Was your friendship with Gail anything . . . unusual?'

'Yes.'

'You were often alone with her in here?'

'It was against the rules, if that's what you're getting at. But with Gail it seemed okay.'

'Why?'

Drapinski looked Lomax in the eye for the first time. 'Listen,' he said, 'there was no sexual relationship. I was fond of her. We get a lot of rich kids at Lindbergh. These kids think they own the world. Some of them are already adult, sexually mature. The girls . . .'

He paused. Lomax thought of Mary Beth and Gina and Kelly Ann.

'Well, I mean, it's like a fashion show in here sometimes. They don't interest me. I like adolescents who are confused, full of questions, making mistakes, unsure of themselves. And that's how Gail was.'

'Why?'

'Why do I like them?' For a moment Drapinski looked vulnerable. 'That's how I was at their age. Probably my wife would say I still am.'

'Gail's writing seems mature,' Lomax commented. He was still drawn to Gail's wallchart.

'Intellectually she had a maturity.'

'I'm interested in how she became friends with her teacher.'

'It was nothing sexual,' repeated Drapinski.

'Well, what did you talk about, for example?'

'My wife calls me the Useless Information Department. I'm interested in everything. So was Gail.'

'Like what?'

Drapinski sighed impatiently. 'Black holes. The life cycle of the aphid. Whale sonars . . . anything.'

'Especially genetics.'

Drapinski put the rest of the flies into another bottle. He wrote MUTANTS and sealed the lid.

'She was also a keen behaviourist. She wanted to know why animals and people behaved the way they did. So she used to analyse class behaviour, student behaviour, in a detached, biological way. She did experiments on the whole class without them even knowing. She could use aim, method, result, conclusion on real complex subjects, like high school students, and make it stick. See, sometimes seniors argue that it's not a sophisticated lab technique but Gail proved them wrong. She could apply it anywhere.'

'Pupils can fall in love with their teachers,' Lomax observed carefully.

Drapinski threw his head back and emitted a noise which Lomax did not immediately recognize as a laugh.

'Gail wasn't in love with me,' he said. Perhaps Drapinski had been in love with Gail. The teacher was blushing and it was not clear why.

'Do you dream about her?' Lomax asked, remembering Hegarty.

'Yes.'

'Often?'

'Yes. I used to dream about her before she died.'

'What did she do in your dreams?'

'Usually wore this dress. That's all I can remember.'

'A dress she actually wore?'

'Yes. Blue. She had a lot of blue dresses. I saw her wearing this dress once.'

'Here in the labs?'

'No.'

'Where?'

'It was probably the last time I ever saw her. Right down the hallway, by her locker. After school. There was a staff meeting. Science department. The head of science is a chemist and it was the usual story. All the resources go into chemistry. Biology ignored. It drives me crazy. I walked out of the meeting and they watched me go. And there was Gail right outside in this blue dress.'

'What did she say?'

'She looked at me and smiled. Probably she said hi or something.'

'And you?'

'I said hi. I sort of paused. We were strangers by then. I didn't know if she would say anything more. Then the moment to speak was gone. So I just carried on walking, right out of the building. I wanted to get home before my wife. A piece of brinksmanship in some battle, I don't remember. I didn't think any more about it until I started dreaming about Gail and she was always wearing that dress.'

'Do you wish now that you'd stopped and spoken to her?'

Drapinski had been pretending to clear away the experiment, although Lomax had seen that he was simply arranging and rearranging equipment on the bench. He was also aware that eleven minutes had passed and the flies were still lying dormant at the base of their jars. He wondered if he should point this out to Drapinski but the teacher was thinking hard about his last question. His face had creased into a rubber ball again. His glasses were askew.

'What would you have said to her?' Lomax prompted.

'I would have said: Gail. Why? What the hell happened?'

Lomax waited for Drapinski to explain this but he was reliving the moment he had never had with Gail.

'Why are you doing this? Tell me, for Chrissake!'

Lomax said quietly: 'Did she look pretty in the blue dress?'

'Pretty!' shouted Drapinski, throwing his arms into the air and knocking over one of the glass jars. It was the one labelled PURE. The jolt did nothing to revive its occupants.

'She looked awful! That's the point. She looked revolting.'

The jar was rolling towards the edge of the bench. Drapinski had not noticed it. Lomax caught it as it plunged towards the floor.

'The dress didn't fit her. It was like all those stupid dresses she started wearing. It was the size she would have worn if she was slim. But she wasn't slim. So she was bulging against it. Her hair was cut short. It was supposed to look stylish. But it just showed you that she had ten chins and a thick neck. Plus it was supposed to look blonde but you could see that it was dark underneath. She had this make-up on which was supposed to make her look cute and she was goddam flirting with me. She peeks up at me through her lashes and says Hi in this simpering voice. What could I do? Get the hell out, that's all.'

Lomax replaced the glass jar softly on the bench. The flies slid from the side to the base as he righted it. He was sure they were dead.

'She flirted with you?'

'Habit. Not out of interest.'

'You had been friends but – '

'We were friends when she first came here. We talked a lot. She confided in me. She told me some very personal things. I wouldn't tell you what those things are even though she's dead because she was confiding in me. Can you understand that? No, you're thinking there must have been something dirty about it.'

Lomax recognized that Drapinski's aggression masked his pain. 'I can understand and I'm not asking you to betray her confidences. I'm trying to establish how a friend like you turned into a stranger.'

Drapinski's face remoulded itself several times over. 'She changed.'

'She grew up?'

'No. She changed and it was her stepmother's fault.'

Julia had said that she changed Gail. Lomax had told her it was impossible to change someone. And Julia had ruffled his hair and told him he was drunk.

'I don't believe,' Lomax said, clearing his throat, 'that one person can change another.'

'Start believing it,' Drapinski told him. 'Because Gail changed and this woman you're defending's the reason why.'

'How can you change someone else?'

'When Gail came here she wasn't what you'd call conventionally attractive. She sure had something special about her but I guess some people would call her plain. Not me. Some people. She was sweet and simple and just herself but the stepmother wanted her to be like all the other clones.'

'Every young girl wants to be pretty. She didn't need her stepmother to tell her.'

'Julia Fox started Gail on some kind of sadistic improvement programme. That kid wore a brace, a wooden brace, down her back to make her walk properly. She comes to school in dumb dresses which she can hardly breathe in. She cuts her hair off and changes the colour. She goes on a starvation diet although she's probably gorging candy in secret because she doesn't lose much weight. And she limps around with bleeding feet because the stepmother tells her to wear shoes which are way too small. Why? Because small shoes will stop her feet growing even bigger – they're already too big, of course. And they'll make her mince instead of walk. Oh, and they'll cripple her, but who cares about that?'

Lomax took a step back. Drapinski's fury seemed to be directed at him.

'And you're the only person who noticed this?'

'I was the only person who cared about it.'

'What about her father, Mr Drapinski?'

'He didn't give a damn. I examined her feet one day. The shoes had rubbed the skin away in so many places they were like skinless chicken pieces. And the blood. It had actually soaked through the goddam leather. They were expensive shoes, by the way. There was no expense spared. My wife told me not to interfere but I decided to telephone the father anyway. He's some hotshot lawyer downtown and he isn't too interested in anything I have to say about his daughter. He acts like I'm crazy calling him about Gail's footwear.'

'Did she stop wearing the shoes?'

'Yes. She stopped wearing the shoes. But he's her father and he hasn't noticed she can't walk for pain. That's all I needed to know about Gail's family. I took her on one side and I said: Gail, you're great the way you are. Don't listen to this Julia. She's wrong. Your feet aren't too big. Your hair's nice its own natural colour. You don't have to wear these clothes. It doesn't matter what your weight is. Your walk is just fine. Be yourself.'

Drapinski looked out across the biology lab as he spoke. Lomax guessed he was talking to Gail. His face had softened. His tone was plaintive. He was pleading with her.

'Did that help?' asked Lomax, reluctant to intrude.

'No.'

'She didn't listen to you?'

'The stepmother had some kind of a hold over her.'

'How?'

'No mother of her own. Anxious to please. I don't exactly know. But you should hear the way Gail talked about her. I say: Gail, if this Julia wears shoes which are too small she must be disabled. She says: Julia walks with her back straight and her weight evenly distributed. One foot goes down directly in front of the other. If you saw her footprints in the snow they would make one straight line. She has poise. She takes short steps and she walks tall.'

Lomax could hardly prevent himself nodding. This was true. He had often admired Julia's walk. Drapinski was explaining: 'That's when I decided Julia was the abominable snowwoman. I've always imagined her as a line of footprints in the snow. A straight line, of course.'

'I don't know how Julia could make Gail change,' Lomax said.

'Intimidation. Psychological, initially, although experience tells us that often turns physical. Either way, it was cruel. Especially when Gail had no hope of ever being pretty in the conventional way.'

The two men looked at each other.

'Did she stop visiting you in the lab?' Lomax asked.

'Yeah. After that talk. After I badmouthed her stepmother. I was stupid. I made a stupid mistake. I should never have criticized the stepmother. I should have helped her without criticizing. She only came back for classes and it was near the end of the semester anyway and after that she wasn't taught by me.'

'Who told you Gail's mother was dead?' Lomax asked.

'Gail did. The mother died when she was very young. She told me the whole story. Terrible. Just tragic.'

'Thank you,' said Lomax, standing up, 'thank you for your time. I appreciate it.'

'You don't believe a word I've said,' Drapinski stated, his voice flat.

'I believe you. I don't believe Gail.'

'You think she was pretending to make her feet bleed?'

'I think she was pretending it was Julia's fault.'

'No. No, she was an honest kid. Completely honest.'

Lomax shook his head.

'What makes you so sure?'

Lomax paused. He tried to avoid Drapinski's stare but Drapinski seemed to intercept him wherever he looked.

'C'mon. What have I told you that makes you so sure?'

His tone was pugnacious. He was challenging Lomax to hurt him. He did not release Lomax from his gaze in the long pause that followed. Finally Lomax said: 'Her mother isn't dead. She lives on the edge of town in a condominium where they take special care of her. She's an alcoholic.'

Drapinski began to rearrange his face into a small ball of dough. His mouth disappeared completely inside his cheeks. Lomax wished he had been strong enough to resist Drapinski's invitation to cause this damage. He said: 'It's a common adolescent fantasy.' But Drapinski was deep in thought. Lomax did not want to point out that he had overgassed the drosophila and that they were dead. The teacher would find out soon enough.

He had spent longer at the high school than he intended. Even if the traffic across town was light, he would be at least 30 minutes late for his meeting at the observatory. If he stopped to telephone and warn them of this he would arrive even later. The traffic was already thickening for the afternoon rush. As soon as he was out of town he accelerated, but the mountain roads were too steep for the station-wagon to negotiate them at speed. Its gears groaned. He became aware, for the first time, of just how lopsided the car had become. Wherever the road was uneven the car threw him about like a match in a box.

He progressed along the familiar route, recognizing the landmarks and views. The journey should have been a nostalgic one but he did not enjoy it. He was late and apologies would be required and the meeting which now awaited him had the power to decide his future. He reminded himself of Jorgen's offer of work in Colorado. But he did not want to work in Colorado. He wanted to resume his life here in California, dividing his time between the observatory and his home. He wanted to be close to Julia and his children. And he wanted to see Julia tonight. He wanted to touch her. He wanted to tell her about Andrew Drapinski. He wanted to hear her say that, when she told him she had changed Gail, these had not been the sort of changes Drapinski meant.

He passed lines of tourist cars retreating back down the mountain as he neared the observatory. When he arrived, the parking lot was half empty and a sign said it was now closed to the public for the night. Another sign gave details of the eclipse celebrations. Lomax had time to note that the event was called The Big Sun Out. He glanced at the labs, at the silver domes and at the staff residence with something like pleasure and then half ran to the central administration building.

'I'm sorry,' he said to Dixon Driver's secretary.

'They've been waiting for you,' she told him ominously, leading him to one of the meeting rooms.

Sitting at a round table, papers and coffee in front of them, were Dixon Driver, Doberman, the head of the physics department at Tradescant, a woman Lomax did not recognize and, to his delight and astonishment, Hopcroft.

Dixon Driver looked ostentatiously at his watch when Lomax walked in. 'You're forty-five minutes late, Dr Lomax,' he said.

Lomax apologized. He hoped he was still breathless from running across the parking lot. He glanced at Hopcroft who raised one eyebrow at him so comically that Lomax had to stifle the urge to laugh.

'Okay, well, you're here now, so just sit down.' Dixon Driver waved impatiently at an empty chair. On the table in front of him Lomax found a copy of his letter to the observatory, the one he had written when Driver requested his allegations. Lomax nodded to Doberman, whose response was scarcely perceptible, and to Professor Klugman of the physics department who beamed back at him. Klugman frequently invited Lomax to lecture at Tradescant and sometimes attended the lectures himself. Driver introduced Professors Angel and Hopcroft as members of the university ethics committee who had been co-opted on to the observatory ethics committee. Lucy Angel was a member of the philosophy department.

There was a bowl of flowers in the centre of the table. Lomax noticed that Hopcroft was eyeing it dangerously.

'You can hardly blame us for starting to discuss your case in your absence,' said Driver.

'No. But I'm surprised you're discussing it in the absence of Professor Berlins,' said Lomax.

The committee stared at him. Hopcroft took advantage of the diversion to snatch a flower from the bowl. Driver jerked his bowtie to the right and then the left.

'Shouldn't he be here?' asked Lomax.

'You don't seem to understand,' Driver said irritably, 'that your future and not Professor Berlins' is under discussion.'

'Will he be coming back to work in September?'

'That is a separate issue.' Driver's irritation was escalating. 'What the committee hopes to establish is whether or not your behaviour has been unethical. Or the degree to which it has been unethical. And whether it is acceptable or desirable for you to continue to work here.'

'Oh,' said Lomax.

Hopcroft coughed and leaned forward, crushing the flower in his immense palm.

'Now, Dr Lomax, why are you so concerned about your colleague? This seems to me curious. Our evidence suggests that you've tried to poleaxe this guy's work and reputation.'

'No,' said Lomax, 'it wasn't that way at all.'

'No?' Hopcroft's eyes widened. His voice rose. 'No?'

Lucy Angel suggested: 'Maybe we should invite Dr Lomax to tell us exactly what happened.'

Driver sat upright in his seat, spread his hands and pressed the pads of his fingers together. 'I was just about to ask Dr Lomax to do that,' he said, his voice taut with vexation, 'when he produced this red herring about Professor Berlins.'

Hopcroft settled back in his chair and threw the flower in the air, catching it with one hand.

'Okay, Dr Lomax,' he said. 'Shoot.'

27

By the time the committee dismissed Lomax it was dark. He left them debating ethics and, pulling off his tie, walked across the asphalt. He had forgotten the smell and taste of the night air at this altitude. He found Kim in the cafeteria and while she feigned amazement at his suit he gazed around the room, nodding to everyone he knew and searching for Julia.

'She's probably in the gym,' Kim said, without asking him who he was looking for.

He told her about the composition of the ethics committee. Its members had listened to him and asked questions. They had been affectionate rather than hostile. Only Dixon Driver had not thawed and, perhaps out of deference to Driver, Doberman had also remained below zero.

'Did you say it was my fault?' asked Kim.

'No.'

'Did you name me?'

'No. I said "a colleague".'

'Did you remember to bring my Arizona photos back?'

'They're here. But I forgot the bedspreads.'

Kim pulled a ghastly face and drew a line across her throat with her finger. 'You're doomed. If Eileen Squeal walks in right now, she'll get you.'

Lomax retreated to Julia's room before Eileen Friel could get him. Julia opened the door and when she saw Lomax her face broke into a long, lazy smile. She had just showered after her workout and was wearing a sloppy big T-shirt. She closed the door on them and he snuffled around her mouth and neck and ears, breathing her in.

'Mmmmmm,' he said. The Nose had made him more aware of smells. Julia's was delightful. It was clean and fresh. She let him kiss her ears and touch her hair and put his arms around her waist and pull him close to her. She did not ask him about the ethics committee meeting.

He lay on her bed and she made him coffee. It was his first chance to study her room. Little alleviated its institutional sparseness. There was the usual furniture, chipped and stained, but she had replaced Eileen Friel's bedspread with one of her own, the colour of peaches. He sniffed it. It had the same Julia smell.

He was surprised by the bookshelves. There were books on European history and ancient Egypt. He could see several biographies, works by Poe and Fitzgerald, and some children's literature. When he had arrived she had evidently been reading an account of Captain Cook's voyage to Australia. It lay open on the table by the bed.

She saw him looking at all this and blushed. 'Ever since I got to know you I've realized how stupid I am,' she explained.

'You're not stupid,' he protested, trying to haul her down on the bed with him. She resisted, smiling. She sat in the chair nearby. He reached for her hand.

'I don't have any education. I didn't even read children's books when I was little. I'm trying to learn something in my spare time here.'

She was blushing deeply now. The colour of her cheeks made her eyes a fathomless shade of blue.

'You could go to college,' he suggested.

'I . . . well . . . I'm not ready for that yet. I mean, some people are just too dumb to go to college.'

'You aren't. Who told you that you're stupid? Your father?'

'He didn't like smart women.'

'And Lewis?'

'He didn't like smart women either. You're the first man who's made me want to go back to school, Lomax.'

He sat up and kissed her. She hung her head. Her face was hot with embarrassment.

Over her shoulder he caught sight of the usual bulletin board. There was one in every room. Various observatory notices were hung on Julia's but a picture of a dog had been tacked on top of them as if the notices didn't matter and the dog did. It was Deputy Dawg.

'Where did you get this?'

'From Kim at the party. It's a vacation snap.'

Lomax got up to scrutinize it. Probably it had been taken at the Cowboy Museum. Deputy was barking at the photographer. There was a human hand soothing him. 'Hey, I'm in it too!'

'I know.'

'One day maybe my face will be up there as well as my hand.'

She smiled but said nothing. He saw the familiar faces of the Fox family hanging on a wall nearby. Of course he had not yet earned the right to replace them. He was embarrassed now at his suggestion. He got up to look at the picture to cover his awkwardness. It was the usual wedding photograph: Lewis, Julia, Gail and Richard. But something about the picture arrested him. Something which he had seen every time he looked at it but which only now seemed to have a significance.

'Julia . . .'

'Uh-huh?'

'At your wedding . . . you were wearing a pin . . .'

She was by his side now. 'This?' She pointed. At the end of her finger a multitude of facets captured the light and refracted it towards the smile of the bride.

'Was it yours?'

'It was a gift from Lewis. Not exactly a wedding gift. He gave it to me when he proposed to me.'

'Is it a diamond?'

'Yes.'

'Did Gail ever wear it?'

'Gail?' She looked at him sharply. She did not reply immediately. 'She borrowed it occasionally,' she said at last.

'When she was in high school?'

'Perhaps. Probably.'

'She wore it to school?'

'She wanted to wear it for some reason. I don't remember why. I wasn't too happy about it but she brought it home and gave it back to me.'

Lomax said: 'I went to her high school today.'

'Lindbergh? Why?'

'To meet a teacher who remembered her well.'

Julia nodded slowly. Suddenly, and Lomax did not understand why, they were both tense.

'And?' Her voice was soft. She was vulnerable. Lomax had said nothing and yet he felt he had been brutal.

'You told me that you changed Gail. This teacher agreed. That's all.' He tried to make his voice gentle. But he was inflicting pain on her. He was reminded of the birds which sometimes flew into his house. He had to trap them in order to release them and, not realizing his intentions, they flapped in terror. One had actually died of fright.

'But . . .' She was whispering now. 'That's not all. I can see it in your face and I've seen it since you walked into the room.'

He shook his head.

'You go around asking questions about me and Gail and Lewis. You learn new things. And they influence you.'

'No, no, that's not true.'

'Every time you interview someone, you change a little bit.' Her voice was brittle.

'I don't change, Julia,' he said. 'I haven't changed and I won't change.'

'This high school teacher said bad things about me . . .'

'I can never believe anything bad about you.'

'Of course you have to ask yourself whether it's true. Of course you do. And then, in a roundabout way, you have to ask me.'

'No.'

'It's like a cat that goes out hunting and brings home rats and mice and other things which smell bad and lays them right outside the door . . .'

'No!'

He held her wrist. She tried to twist away from him but he would not let her. She gave up the struggle. Her face was so sad that he couldn't look at it. He stared at the floor. Eileen Friel's stainproof rug. She said: 'My whole life is on trial. All the mistakes.'

'There aren't any mistakes.'

She sighed and he let her go. He watched her move away from him. She sank down onto the bed. 'Oh. Lomax, I've made so many.'

'I don't know of any.'

Her face was still sad. 'With Gail. I admit it.'

He sat down on the chair by the bed. 'Everyone makes mistakes.'

'I was a bad stepmother.'

'You were just a few years older than Gail. You couldn't play mother to her.'

'I should never have tried. But she was a little girl, so gawky and plain. Lewis didn't notice her at all. She always wanted his attention but he just didn't notice her. I used to say, Lewis, for heaven's sake, listen to her sometimes.'

'That's not a mistake. That's kind.'

'I put her on a diet. I showed her how to walk straight. I helped her choose some pretty clothes. I told her how to use make-up. I took her to the best hair salon in town. I mean, she wanted to learn. She asked questions. And it all went further than I ever intended. I shouldn't have done all those things.'

'You were trying to help.'

333

'It's wrong. Lomax, it's only since I've known you that I've begun to think about this.'

'Its not wrong to help someone.'

'When I met you . . . do you remember the first time you came to my house? It was because I wanted to give you the name of a plastic surgeon who'd remove your birthmark? Remember that?'

'Yes.'

'I thought it was a blemish, it should be removed.' She reached up and touched his face, very gently. He knew she must be touching the crab nebula. It was prominent just now. He had exposed it that very morning while shaving. He could hardly feel her fingers.

'You said it was just a part of you. And now I agree. It's a part of you and I love it.'

She was telling him, indirectly and with difficulty, that she loved him. He felt a melting sensation throughout his body.

'And,' she continued, 'I've tried to slim Kim. Isn't that terrible? I've tried to show her how to lose weight and I've suggested clothes and . . . and that's wrong, Lomax.'

'It's not wrong . . .'

She was still touching his birthmark. He took her hand and held it in his. He could cover it completely.

'I failed as a stepmother and a wife. And now I'm on trial,' she said.

Lomax drove down the mountain later that night feeling calm. His body was completely relaxed for the first time in months. Julia loved him. He swung the car to the left and the right and the physical action, rhythmic like a dance, pleased him. Julia loved him. Throughout the preceding months of not knowing, of jealousy, there had been an electric current running through his life which had deprived him of true rest. Julia loved him. His torment was over.

The car swung down the mountain curves, past rock formations and solid seams of granite which had been dynamited to make way for the road. His knowledge of the route was reassuring. He knew where the next bend was and which way it would swing. And when the mountain lion appeared once again in the headlights, that seemed inevitable too. The lion paused to stare at him. Then it was gone. This time Lomax slowed the car and switched off the engine. In the moments after the lights were extinguished, the darkness was intense. He left the car and stood looking out across the valley which he knew was there and could not see. He listened for the mountain lion. The only sound was the ticking of the car's hot engine. He strained to hear the rustle of a big cat but the silence filled his ears. Either the mountain lion was far away already or it was, like him, motionless in the cool night. Or it moved soundlessly.

He looked up. Canis Major. Orion. The Seven Sisters. As a teenager, he had chosen to study the Pleiades. At first it really had seemed there were seven stars in the cluster but as he used progressively more powerful telescopes he had discovered that the cluster was both dense and complex. He had chosen to study it again as part of Berlins' nebula survey a few years ago and found it to be of stunning beauty. It was full of young stars, so hot that they burned blue and coloured the gas which surrounded them. He looked at the Pleiades now. He could see no more than when he was a boy but he could never see those stars in the same way again. He gazed at them with affection and then resumed his passage down the mountain.

At home, Deputy was waiting and the crickets were chorusing. There was a telephone message from Frances inviting him to a meeting tomorrow and several messages from Jefferson. His project supervisor expected the paper on redshift velocity within two weeks. Had Lomax read it yet? Lomax groaned. He had looked for the paper but been unable to find it. He began searching again now. He rearranged the piles of papers, bills and observatory material in his den and found Gail's mail, still unopened. He added the letters, more junk mail, that Homer had given him on his last visit. He put them all by the door so that he would not forget to take them to the meeting tomorrow. Deputy, who liked mail, rolled in it. Lomax continued to search without success for Jefferson's paper.

He wanted to telephone Julia to say goodnight but he decided she would be asleep by now. He himself felt capable of deep sleep. His limbs were heavy. Then, just when he was climbing into the hollow in the sheets he had climbed out of that morning, the phone rang.

'I wanted to make sure you got down that twisty road safely,' said Julia's voice. Her tone was affectionate. This was not the kind of call Julia usually made.

'I'm safe and I'm thinking about you,' he told her, wrapping the sheets around him like a warm cocoon.

He could not remember the dream which woke him early the next day but his heart was thumping rapidly and he was sweating. He felt exhausted, as though he had been fighting all night. The sheets were knotted on the floor. His new sense of security had been prised away while he slept by some malevolent force.

He lay in bed trying to relax but his alarm did not recede with his dream. He remembered that Julia loved him but this gave him no comfort. The possibility of a future with her seemed more brittle than ever. Her trial was scheduled to start in under two weeks. Lomax had worked all summer on her behalf but he was no closer to knowing the identity or motive of the real killer. Julia was the only suspect. And even the attorneys who were paid to defend her had judged her privately and found her guilty. A conviction was possible.

There was a crash overhead. He knew this now to be the sound of a squirrel leaping from one of the trees onto the roof of the house.

An Olde Time Event was taking place in the conservation area around Sachs Smith's office when he arrived. The road was closed and men and women in western dress milled about offering the public balloons and traditional candy. A colourful organ played itself, filling the air all around it with its notes. For a dollar you could climb on a stagecoach and ride up and down the street. Cursing, Lomax looked for a parking place and pushed his way through the crowds. He was not just late but very late.

Inside the lawyers were already seated around the table. There was no other similarity to the last night's meeting. The ethics committee had welcomed him with varying degrees of relief and warmth. Here only Marjorie greeted him. Kurt and Frances scarcely looked up. The cheerful organ music outside heightened the leaden atmosphere inside the room.

The lawyers each had different ways of showing their despondence. Kurt's face looked shadowy, the bones in it especially prominent. His speech was clipped. Marjorie was very still, as if there were some delicate balance in the room which motion might upset. And Frances was irritable. Her eyes were a colder shade of green than Lomax remembered.

'I'm sorry I'm late,' he said.

'You haven't missed anything,' Frances told him, 'except misery.'

'Why misery?'

'Because the pre-trial motions are next week and usually by this stage I have a defence case. I mean, I can stand in court in August objecting and challenging the prosecution. But that's the weakest defence there is.'

'Sometimes it works,' pointed out Marjorie. 'It's worked on Morton de Maria. People versus Jabbourer.'

This intervention seemed to annoy Frances. She made a small, impatient movement of her shoulders as if Marjorie had tried to put an arm around her and she was shrugging it away. 'Morton's won almost every one of his cases since,' she said.

Marjorie explained to Lomax: 'Morton de Maria will be the prosecuting attorney.'

'What's he like?'

'Good,' said Frances.

'Damn good,' said Kurt.

Frances added: 'We actually offered him a place in this firm once but he wanted to remain a prosecutor. He's charming, quick, urbane. Also, black. He probably gets a higher than average quota of black defendants. I saw him at a dinner a few nights ago and he told me how delighted he is to have this case. It wasn't brinkmanship. He meant it.'

Morton de Maria sounded like a monstrous black cat who was going to roll Julia around in his paws before dispatching her. Lomax was also disturbed by the thought of the prosecution and defence meeting at dinner. Could camaraderie really turn adversarial when Frances and de Maria walked from dining room to courtroom?

Perhaps sensing his doubts, Frances said: 'My best tactic with Morton is to be one degree more assertive than he likes. He's polite. Correct. He'll find that hard to deal with.'

'Is Julia going to testify?' Kurt asked.

Frances sighed. 'Right now, I don't think she should.'

'You mean,' said Lomax, 'she'll say nothing?'

'It's her constitutional right.'

'But . . .'

They looked at him. 'But what?' asked Frances dangerously.

'If she claims she's innocent, doesn't a jury expect to hear her get up and say so? And . . . well, when she speaks you can tell that she's honest and good.'

'Innocent people have the right to remain silent. You're correct in thinking that it makes juries suspicious but the judge will remind them of our constitution. I also agree that Julia looks good and sounds good. But there are some questions I don't want her to answer.'

Lomax protested silently to himself.

'She wants to testify,' Kurt said.

Frances made a dismissive gesture which Lomax glanced up just in time to see.

'What about this new law firm Lewis planned?' he asked.

'What about it?' said Kurt. 'I was told to ask delicate questions. I got delicate answers. It's led us nowhere.'

'Maybe we should get tough,' suggested Frances.

Kurt's face rearranged itself into a humourless smile. 'It's the *specialité de la maison*.'

'Not too tough,' she warned him. She looked around the table and her eyes alighted on Lomax. He flinched a little.

'What have you been doing?' she asked. There was impatience in her voice.

'I've been talking to people who knew Gail.'

'Who?'

'Her mother, Lewis' friend Hegarty, a kid who was at high school with her, a teacher who remembers her. They said a lot but I don't know how it's relevant to the murders.'

'Like what sort of thing did they say, Lomax?' asked Kurt, his voice crushing. 'Take Hegarty, for instance, whom I've spoken to myself.'

'Hegarty. Um . . .' Lomax tried to recall his talk with Hegarty. It seemed a long time ago. 'Well . . .'

The nib of Kurt's pen sprang in and out.

'Well, he had a brief affair with Gail . . .'

Kurt and Frances looked at one another.

'He did?' said Frances in surprise.

'Yes, Lewis took Gail to his club and she subsequently slept with Hegarty. Just once. Then she went to Europe. It wasn't really an affair.'

'Did you know that, Kurt?' asked Frances.

Kurt narrowed his eyes. His whole face seemed to cave into his jawbone. 'No,' he admitted. Marjorie suppressed a smile. Frances raised her eyebrows in mock amazement.

'I don't know how it's relevant,' Lomax repeated.

'That's not your problem, Lomax. We asked you to give us research notes after every interview. I showed you the system. Frances needs a complete picture, not the pieces you decide to supply,' snapped Kurt. 'I mean, what happened to paperwork?'

'Um . . .'

'An investigator is only as good as his paperwork, right Frances, right Marjorie? But you haven't given us one goddam sheet of paper.' Kurt was snarling now.

'Sorry,' said Lomax.

'You've been doing all this talking, let's see some results. Soon.'

'Okay.'

The room was silent.

'Is there anything else you want to tell us now?' Frances asked. Her voice was kinder than Kurt's but it retained something of his tone.

'Er . . .' Lomax produced the letters addressed to Gail that the super had given him. He dropped some of them and one fell in his coffee. The attorneys stared in stony silence. Outside, the organ played 'Home On The Range'.

'What's that, Lomax?' asked Marjorie sympathetically, retrieving the wet letter. Lomax explained.

'This is her mail?' echoed Kurt, his voice incredulous. 'The murder victim's mail? How long have you been sitting on that?'

'A while,' admitted Lomax. 'I sort of forgot about it.'

Kurt made a sound like an espresso machine. Frances reached across the table for the envelopes. To the sound of 'She'll Be Coming Round The Mountain', Frances, Kurt and Marjorie sifted them into piles and categories, just as Lomax had. Kurt held some of the letters up to the light but was apparently unable to read anything.

'There's a few official-looking things here from Europe,' he reported finally. 'They could be interesting.'

'Details of bank accounts?' suggested Frances.

'Maybe they'll tell us what the hell happened to the money once it got across the Atlantic,' he agreed. 'Maybe they'll even show it heading in Lewis' direction.'

'If only,' said Frances bleakly. Lomax had never seen her mood so grim.

Marjorie explained to Lomax: 'If these letters contain evidence, and we'd opened them without applying for permission, the court might not accept the evidence. So we have to turn them over to the police.'

'You never should have carried them,' Frances told him severely. 'Now you could end up as a witness and that's the last thing we want.'

'Sorry,' said Lomax.

'Okay,' said Frances, sighing and getting up. 'Kurt and Marjorie, we'll meet on Monday to discuss the pre-trial motions. No need for you to be here, Lomax.'

'What exactly are pre-trial motions?' he asked. He knew Frances wanted them to leave now but he felt stubborn.

'It's just where we get a few formalities sorted out before the trial. You don't have to be there.'

'Like what?'

Kurt and Marjorie were standing too. Frances crossed to her desk. Over her shoulder she said: 'Oh, things like Julia doesn't want cameras in the courtroom. I don't want the jury to see the pictures of the crime. And the judge has to agree just how much I can roam about the room when I'm cross-examining because I walk while I talk and some judges think that intimidates witnesses. We have to sort out the discovery, establish the legality of our research, maybe. Nothing which concerns you.'

Marjorie was gathering her papers up.

'Will Julia be there?' persisted Lomax.

'Sure.' Frances sat down at her desk. She opened a folder which her secretary had left full of letters for her to sign. She began signing. Kurt wandered out with Gail's mail in his hand. Marjorie remained, leaning heavily against the table. She seemed reluctant to leave without Lomax.

He felt dissatisfied. If the defence had learned anything during their investigations which was to Julia's advantage, they had not said so. The trial was a few weeks away and their mood was downcast and cynical. They had given him no more work and his own line of investigation seemed to have run out of fuel. He felt dismissed. Reluctantly, he closed his notebook and prepared to leave.

'Is there anything else I can do?' he asked.

Frances did not look up. 'Not really,' she said. 'Just the interview notes.'

'Well . . . phone me if you want me.'

She indicated the unlikelihood of this by ignoring him. Marjorie said reassuringly: 'Sure we will, Lomax.'

To his surprise, Frances called his name as he reached the door. He turned hopefully. But she said: 'Be careful to stay completely away from Julia. And that includes the courtroom.'

He stared at her. 'You mean . . . at this motions thing next week?'

'I mean during the trial.'

He dropped his notebook. 'Are you telling me not to come to the trial?'

'It's a public place so I can't stop you. But I urge you to keep away.'

'No,' said Lomax. 'I won't keep away from the fucking trial.'

'Lomax, the jury are smart. They clock everyone and everything in that room. So do the court reporters.'

'The room's going to be full of people!'

'You show up in that courtroom every day and – don't delude yourself – they'll notice you and they'll guess why you're there. They'll work it out. Believe me. Juries do that.'

Lomax shook his head with an energy that dizzied him. 'No, no, no,' he said. 'I must be there.'

Frances and Marjorie looked at each other.

'Think you can persuade him?' Frances asked Marjorie at last.

'No,' said Marjorie.

'No, she cannot goddam persuade me, goddam it.'

'I have an idea,' said Marjorie. 'You're there because you're my . . . you're my fiancé. You've come to watch the case because of me.'

'Oh, right. I wear a sign saying: I am Marjorie's boyfriend.'

'No. But you wave when you see me, I occasionally communicate with you in our private sign language, we wait for each other during recesses, we're seen together in the park during lunch breaks . . . geddit? And if anyone asks you outright – and one of these court reporters probably will – you explain that you're real proud of me because I've helped the defence team and you've come to watch the case. Okay, Frances?'

Lomax picked up his notebook, smouldering.

'I'd prefer him not to be there,' said Frances, talking to Marjorie just as if Lomax already wasn't there. 'But if he's going to insist on coming, then that's a good idea.'

'I do,' said Lomax, standing upright again. 'I do insist.'

'Then act your heart out,' she said, looking back down at her letters, 'because Julia's life could depend on it.'

When they were outside, and the door had closed, Marjorie whispered apologetically: 'Kurt says that Frances always gets sort of jittery before a big trial.'

He went home and started typing his reports. He typed fast and inaccurately with two fingers. It was hard to know what to include. Would Frances be interested in Hegarty's dreams, for example? Probably not. He reported only facts. He omitted all innuendo about Julia but included a great deal about Murphy McLean. He ignored the suggestions that Julia had been violent.

Outside it was hot. Once he took a break and sat on the deck and felt the sun trickle down into his skin. The summer had reached its height and that meant it would soon be over. This year the season had passed him by. He had worn fewer clothes and felt hot sometimes and taken a brief vacation but he had somehow lost the summer.

The sun was burning the trees. There was a leaf shower as a squirrel clambered overhead. He could see Deputy through the deck, lying stretched out and motionless in the shade like a dead dog. He watched for a few minutes and Deputy still did not move.

'Dep?' he called sharply and Deputy leapt to his feet in alarm, shaking the dirt off his coat.

Lomax went back to work. That night he completed the notes and when the evening was cool he drove downtown and delivered them to Sachs Smith's night security guard. Uniformed street cleaners were clearing away the debris of the Olde Time Event and in the open house

341

there was some kind of party. Lights blazed. Couples, the men in suits, the women in off-the-shoulder dresses, stood talking and drinking in small groups in the ornamental front yard.

Returning to the foothills, he passed Murphy McLean. He looked away, embarrassed, but McLean hooted and waved and smiled, forcing Lomax to acknowledge him.

Jefferson had telephoned while he was out. He began hunting for the redshift velocity paper once more without success. Over the next week he began the search on many occasions but each time he was distracted or defeated. He would find something else which diverted him and forget about Jefferson's paper for days, returning to the search with renewed and guilty desperation. He was unable to concentrate on anything for even short periods. He walked purposefully into rooms to fetch something, then stood clasping his head trying to remember what. He started books but did not finish them. They lay in various positions around the house, their spines flattened on any page up to 50. He half answered letters. He half ate meals. He was unable to sleep most nights but slumped on the sunny deck in the afternoon and woke with his body heavy and his head aching. Julia's trial was approaching. Nothing he did could help her now. Nothing could lift his sense of disquiet. There was nothing more to be done. His efforts this summer had achieved precisely nothing.

The pre-trial came and went. Convinced by Marjorie that it was a formality, he agreed not to go. Julia was unable to tell him afterwards what had happened. He spoke to her every night. He tried to sound calm but it was impossible to hide his trepidation. She seemed to grow more distant. The burning hot days leading to the trial sneaked past him like pickpockets in a crowd.

Deputy slept a lot. He did not bother to chase the squirrels and they became bold again. Once Lomax caught them clambering over the hood of the car. With increasing frequency he heard them galloping and sliding on the roof of the house. He hoped they would not try to come inside.

Joel and Helen returned to school. They spent the last day of the vacation hiking with Lomax. Joel asked whether the murders had been solved yet and then seemed to forget the subject. He was more interested in the forthcoming eclipse.

The eclipse was already news. Most of the publicity centred on the observatory. Various astronomers had appeared on news items, including Kim. Health warnings were issued routinely between commercials advising people not to look directly at the sun.

'Can we go to The Big Sun Out?' Helen asked.

'It's called an eclipse, not a sun out, and you don't have to go anywhere special to see it,' Lomax said. 'You can watch it from school.'

Joel said: 'Can we watch it with you?'

'Maybe.' The eclipse was on the other side of Julia's trial and was therefore too distant to contemplate.

'Are you going back to work at the observatory?'

Lomax paused. 'Probably.' He was still waiting to hear the results of the ethics committee's deliberations. He had hoped to discuss the committee with Berlins but the professor had not telephoned and his own calls had gone unanswered.

The day before the trial began, when his apprehension was at its height, he called Berlins again and, to his amazement, heard the professor's voice.

'Oh yes, I want to see you, Lomax,' he said warmly. 'Sarah goes out at three for a short time this afternoon. She takes an elderly friend to the supermarket.'

For once, Lomax was not late. He was relieved that there was no other car in the drive and that the professor answered the door.

The professor's hair had been bleached whiter by the sun. 'Did you get my letter?' he asked.

'No,' said Lomax, but Berlins wasn't listening. He was ushering Lomax inside, talking rapidly, disgorging information. Lomax understood that Berlins was offering him tea. They were out of coffee and Mrs Berlins was at the supermarket right now buying some more. They were so busy packing that neither of them had noticed supplies were low. They had the flotsam and jetsam of years to sort out. Mrs Berlins had caused eruptions in the family over the summer by evacuating the attic. The Berlins' children, the youngest of whom was 30, were upset that their mother had taken their old soft toys to the dump.

The professor led him to the kitchen, still talking. Boxes were piled at one end of the room.

'But . . .' said Lomax, 'where are you going?'

Berlins was boiling water for their tea. He had to open many small doors to find the tea and as he did so he revealed empty shelves. He paused and tried to look over his shoulder at Lomax and, on failing, turned his whole body instead.

'Why Lomax, you said you got my letter.'

'I said I didn't get your letter.'

Berlins blinked at him uncertainly. After the events of this spring, doubt would always exist between them.

'You mean, you just happened to call?'

'I often call.'

'Really?'

'But Mrs Berlins always hangs up on me.'

Berlins chortled and continued his search for the tea. 'Women,' he said, 'my God, don't they get us into trouble?'

Lomax had an uncomfortable feeling that this was a reference to Julia.

'Is this the letter?' he asked. It was lying addressed to him, stamped, on the table. Berlins' face broke into delighted smiles.

'That's it! That's it! No wonder you didn't get it!'

'Should I open it?'

'Why not? It's yours. It simply explains that Sarah and I are moving.'

Lomax began reading the letter. 'To Missouri,' he observed.

'Our daughter has three children and Sarah thinks we can be useful there.'

The letter invited Lomax to call round within the next few weeks. Lomax struggled. Finally he said: 'But what about the observatory?'

'I'm retiring. I mean formally. Do you drink your tea black?'

'Yes.'

'Sit down. Sit down, put your feet on a stool, drink, read your letter, make yourself at home. At least until Sarah gets back from the supermarket. And that might be soon because she doesn't like to leave me alone for too long.'

'But I don't understand . . .' said Lomax, sitting down. The professor carried his tea over to the table. He carried it carefully, with both hands, like a small child. His back was hunched over it. Watching him made Lomax feel sad.

'I keep dropping things and spilling things and Sarah gets mad at me,' Berlins confided in explanation.

'Professor,' said Lomax, 'you can't retire now.'

'Why not?'

'Because of Dixon Driver's ethics committee.'

'I discussed all that with Dixon. When he could spare me some time from his preparations for the – er, Big Sun Out.' Berlins said the words slowly and looked at Lomax significantly over his glasses as he did so.

'My decision to retire now is unrelated to the ethics committee, but naturally I don't want it to seem that I'm running away from an unfavourable decision.'

'So . . . what . . . ?'

'Dixon will be writing you. I guess he doesn't leave his letters on the kitchen table. Although he's the sort of man who could forget to put a stamp on if he doesn't like you . . . what was I saying?'

'What will Driver be writing me?'

'Ah yes. I understand that you had a meeting with this committee?'

'Yes.' Lomax wanted to tell Berlins about the committee meeting, but Berlins seemed to know more than he did.

'Well. Now. When all this happened back at the beginning of the summer, you were keen to drop your allegations. Dixon's going to give you the opportunity to do exactly that.'

'Drop the whole thing?'

'The committee plans to ask you to withdraw your allegations. That's the word. Withdraw.'

'I didn't make any allegations.'

'He seems keen to give you your job back, Lomax. Although I have a feeling that Doberman will stay in his present position.'

Lomax felt a mixture of fury and relief. 'For God's sake,' he spluttered. 'Why didn't Driver do this before and save us both all this misery?'

'It hasn't been misery for me. I've taught my grandson to fish. And I've built a telescope. Just wait here and I'll show you . . .'

Lomax sat at the table bristling. The hairs on his arms itched with anger. 'I mean,' he yelled to Berlins, whom he could hear shuffling around the next room, 'he could have sorted this out in one week. And it's taken months.'

Berlins was coming back. 'Well, we've both been on half-salaries all summer, and that's paid for a solar specialist.'

Lomax groaned. 'That fucking eclipse.'

'When is the eclipse? I expect you'll find your re-employment dates from the Monday right after it.'

Berlins placed a box on the table.

'Driver blew it all up so big with his letters and his committees. It's probably going to be hanging over both of us for ever,' Lomax said gloomily. He looked at the box. Along its side was written: 'Yes! It's that tasty protein peanut snack!'

'My career's over, but it certainly won't help yours,' agreed Berlins.

'And I used to boast that I wasn't a career astronomer.'

'There's only one of my colleagues whose opinion matters to me,' Berlins told him.

'Driver's?'

'No, Lomax, yours.'

Lomax hung his head in silence. Berlins attempted to open the box. His hands shook.

'You, of all people, accusing me of . . . I just couldn't get over it.' Berlins was wrestling with the lid of the carton now, but his fingers were weak.

'Professor . . . ' said Lomax, 'someone was redrawing a galaxy. I didn't want it to be you. I didn't think it could be. That's why I didn't do anything about it except confide in Kim.'

Berlins raised his eyebrows.

'Which,' added Lomax, 'I agree I shouldn't have.'

Berlins succeeded in levering the lid off the box. With affectionate delicacy, he drew the telescope out. 'I don't want to calculate how many hours I've spent grinding these mirrors,' he said.

Lomax examined the telescope's smooth metal, its detail and simplicity.

'It's perfect.'

'I want you to have it.'

Lomax almost dropped it. 'I can't take this.'

'I want you to.'

'But . . . you spent all summer making it.'

'It was my pleasure. Now it's my pleasure to give it to you. Who knows, you may learn something from it.'

Lomax did not know what to say. He had intended to talk about Julia but this now seemed inappropriate. He left soon afterwards, relieved he had succeeded in avoiding Sarah Berlins. He and Berlins shook hands.

'Will you give me your new address?' he asked.

'I'll send it to you.'

Lomax suspected that he wouldn't and that the telescope was the old man's farewell. The thought that he might never see Berlins again made his throat constrict. He wanted to say goodbye. He wanted to apologize. He was unable to speak. He grasped Berlins' arm for a moment. Berlins nodded at him.

Lomax was a few hundred yards from their house when he passed Mrs Berlins returning home. She did not see him. She was driving slowly, and she looked worried. He remembered Berlins saying that she didn't like to leave him alone for too long. Why not? Was he ill?

Lomax had already decided that he would send Berlins a letter. He would write all the things he had been unable to say.

The telephone rang as he walked into the house. A small voice said: 'Um . . . this is Jefferson.'

'Oh, God, Jefferson!' Lomax was dismayed. He had not thought about Jefferson or his paper for a couple of days.

'I guess you haven't had an opportunity to read my paper yet. It's just that – '

'I know, I know, it's due soon.'

'Actually, I have to submit it tomorrow.'

'Can I call you back later this evening – in an hour or two?'

'It's okay, maybe we should just forget . . .' Jefferson sounded young and unsure of himself on the telephone.

'A couple of hours, okay?'

He started a systematic search. This involved throwing everything to one side that was not Jefferson's. Soon paper was lying all over the house. The more he looked the more letters he unearthed from Eileen Friel requesting the return of the bedspreads. He resolved to telephone Eileen Friel tomorrow. He would pay his unpaid bills and organize the paperwork. He would clean the house. Then he remembered that tomorrow was the first day of Julia's trial.

He found Jefferson's paper in the den where he had looked for it weeks ago. Relieved, he settled down to read it. The telephone rang again.

'Hi, it's Marjorie.'

He adopted a neutral tone. 'Hi Marjorie, how're you?'

'I just wondered what you were doing this evening?' She sounded shy.

'Erm . . . well, I'm discussing redshift velocity with a student.'

'Oh, okay. It's only that I've just interviewed someone in the foothills and I think I might be quite close to you. I mean, maybe I could drop by. But if you're busy . . .' She sounded certain of rejection.

He said quickly, 'No, come – if you don't have to get back to Sachs Smith, that is.'

He directed her to his house. She seemed to know his address. He could not remember giving it to her. He wondered who she had been interviewing so near by.

'And old girlfriend of Lewis',' she explained.

This must be the girlfriend whom Julia had tried and failed to find one night. 'Did she say anything interesting?'

347

'I don't think that kid has said anything interesting in the whole of her short life.'

'Isn't it too late to interview people?'

'It's never to late.'

Marjorie looked hot. Her clothes clung to her body. She clutched her purse.

'What a great house,' she said. 'There are cute little squirrels everywhere.'

'Yes,' agreed Lomax grimly. Deputy looked at Marjorie but did not get up to greet her. He thumped his tail a few times then went back to sleep.

Lomax made her a cold drink and put one of Helen's curling ornamental straws in it. They sat on the deck under one of the trees.

'Oh, neat,' said Marjorie when she saw how the trees grew through the structure. She seemed flustered. She smiled a lot. Lomax wondered why she had called.

'Want to hear something about Sachs Smith?' she asked, rotating the ice in her drink with the ridiculous straw.

Lomax was silent.

'A lot's been happening.' She began to talk about Kurt. 'He has the sensitivity of . . . I don't know . . . one of those big trucks which crosses Nevada and doesn't even slow down when it hits a cow and there's blood all over the windshield.'

'It sounds like you've crossed Nevada a few times,' said Lomax.

Marjorie nodded. 'I lived there when I was small. My dad was in the Air Force. There are dead cows all over Nevada.'

She sucked on the straw and cheek bones appeared in her large face. She looked cooler now. She hooked her hair back behind her ears.

'So,' she continued, 'Kurt starts asking questions around the office. Who knew about this new firm of Lewis'? Who had planned to go? That kind of thing. This is supposed to be low-key questioning but, I mean, have you ever seen a low-key ten-wheeler? His questions must have scared a few people because first thing this morning there's an announcement. Four partners are leaving as of today. They're setting up their own firm, they've found offices, bought equipment, they're inviting a number of the junior staff to go with them and of course their clients are free to join them if they want.'

'Oh,' said Lomax.

'Frances thinks they were going to announce it some time soon anyway but when Kurt started asking difficult questions they moved the whole thing forward.'

'What else does Frances say?'

'Nothing. You know Frances.'

Lomax realized that he didn't know Frances at all. He did not speak.

Marjorie seemed disappointed by his reaction. She said: 'No one can remember when something like this last happened around here. Not to a law firm the size and status of Sachs Smith. We're one of the biggest in northern California. These guys are probably taking literally millions of dollars' worth of clients with them.' On the word 'literally' she opened her eyes wide.

'How about you? Will you go too?'

Marjorie shook her head. 'I like working with Frances.'

Lomax wondered if the news had any relevance to Julia.

'It's good for Julia,' she assured him. 'Frances is planning to argue that Lewis wanted that money to start a new firm and this will support her case. It should help blow a hole in the police's blackmail theory.'

'Good.'

'But,' she added, 'Frances won't want to take any public swipes at Sachs Smith when it's so vulnerable.'

Lomax put his feet on the table and stretched back in his chair. The sky was visible through the trees. The stars and galaxies and clusters and superclusters were all out there and today the sky was such a deep, deep blue that you could almost imagine that you saw them.

'Stop worrying,' said Marjorie suddenly. 'If anyone can get Julia through this, Frances can.'

'You think she will?'

Marjorie was thoughtful. She studied the ice in her drink. She stabbed at it with her straw. 'I think there's a fifty per cent chance,' she said at last. 'And of course, if Julia loses, she can appeal. Er, Lomax?'

Lomax looked at Marjorie. The evening sun was behind her and he shielded his eyes.

'Maybe I shouldn't say this . . .'

He waited, squinting at her.

'. . . but what makes you so sure she's innocent?'

He sighed and looked back up at the sky. 'She just couldn't have done those things,' he said. He knew Marjorie was watching him closely. The sun was illuminating his face. She would be able to see where he had shaved recently and where he hadn't shaved for a while. The lines around his eyes and his mouth would be filled with sunlight. The crab nebula would be clearly defined.

'You're really crazy about her.'

'Yes.'

349

'She's so beautiful.' Her voice was wistful.

'I have to agree with you there.'

'It's hard to imagine her committing these murders.'

'It's impossible.'

'But isn't there some secret part of you which suspects she could be guilty?'

'No.' Lomax did not want to talk to Marjorie about his secret parts. He disliked the intimate tone of the conversation. He was grateful when the telephone rang inside the house and he was able to leave Marjorie under the tree.

'Um . . . Professor, it's Jefferson. I have to go to work now. I work in a pizza place just near here. And . . .um . . . I have to submit my paper tomorrow. If I don't submit it tomorrow, I'll get an incomplete. So I guess it's too late . . .'

Lomax's guilt ran through him like electricity. 'God, I'm sorry, Jefferson. Someone from the office arrived right after I spoke to you.'

'It's okay, really.'

'Which pizza place?'

'It's on the corner of Pine and Fifteenth. But – '

'I'll be there tonight and maybe we could talk during your break.'

'They don't exactly give me a break . . .'

'When do you finish?'

'Tonight . . . er . . . ten.'

'Okay. I'll wait until ten,' Lomax told him. 'I'm sorry about this. I really want to discuss this paper with you.'

He was trying not to reveal that he still had not read it.

Marjorie finished her drink and stood up when he returned.

'I should get back to work,' she said. She looked sad. He knew she had wanted him to ask her to stay a while longer or to eat with him. He explained about Jefferson and the paper.

'Redshift velocity,' she echoed. 'Well. Do you miss the observatory?'

'Yes. Very much.' After he had said this he realized it was true. He led her clumsily towards her car.

'I hope it was okay for me to drop in,' she said. 'I wanted you to hear the news.' Her voice was drained of vitality. Even her walk was disappointed. He remembered how Julia could make him feel that same way just by talking to Doberman.

'I'm sorry about this student paper. I only have a few hours to read it. But next time you're passing, call me and we'll eat. Or we'll go out somewhere and eat,' he heard himself saying. Marjorie nodded and did not look at him as she got into her car. 'I mean it,' he added.

350

She nodded again. 'Yeah. Thanks.'

She drove away. Lomax watched her go. Marjorie did not attract him but he liked her. He wished he had not made her sad.

The pizza place was near the univeristy and it was busy. Lomax had to wait in line for a table. He was the only person eating alone. The lighting made all the diners around him look young and attractive. They filled the restaurant with their voices.

A succession of waiters and waitresses in yellow uniforms supplied him with water and beer and then food. Lomax looked around for Jefferson. He was working the other side of the room. He moved fast up and down the rows. At just after ten o'clock, when Lomax was on his second cup of coffee, Jefferson sat down opposite him. He had changed out of the yellow uniform and looked hot and tired.

'Want something to drink?' Lomax said.

Jefferson ordered a beer. He seemed nervous and he did not look Lomax in the eye. He was almost as tall as Lomax and the table was small. It was hard for them to find anywhere to put their legs. A couple of times their feet touched and Jefferson jerked away, apologizing.

'Maybe it's just too late for you to do this. What time tomorrow do you have to hand in the paper?'

'By three. It's okay, Professor, I'm not tired.'

Lomax showed Jefferson that some of his calculations were faulty. Jefferson had difficulty following. He asked Lomax to repeat his explanation twice.

'It's so noisy in here . . . it's like ten minutes to our apartment. I think I could concentrate if it was quieter,' he said.

Lomax paid and they drove to the apartment house that Jefferson described as his and Lomax thought of as Gail's. He could not prevent himself glancing up at her window again. Of course the window was dark.

Jefferson's father was watching TV. He leapt to his feet when Lomax walked in.

'We met at work and the professor's explaining where my calculations went wrong,' Jefferson said. The super shook his head.

'Now? At this time of night? You can't ask the professor to help you now. He's a busy man.'

Lomax had to offer many assurances that he was not tired or busy before Jefferson was allowed to lead him to his study.

'It's a bedroom too. The bed pulls down like this, see.' Jefferson said, 'Dad made it. He can make anything.'

The room was small and tidy. Lomax recognized some of the

physics books stacked in the corner. The pictures on the walls were mostly galaxies: M13, M104 and M81, the Great Hercules Cluster, the Sombrero, and the Pin-wheel.

They began working at the computer. Lomax was patient. He went through the calculations several more times.

'I guess you think I'm stupid,' said Jefferson wearily.

'No, it's late and I'm stupid for not doing this before.'

'Can I get anyone coffee? Tea?' asked the super, appearing at the door.

'You should go to bed, Dad,' Jefferson said. 'Don't worry about us.'

But Homer re-appeared about ten minutes later carrying steaming mugs. 'I just thought of something nice,' he said. 'Malted milk. Do you like malted milk, Professor?'

Lomax expressed delight at the prospect.

'Thanks, Dad. Go to bed,' Jefferson advised him.

'Okay,' said the super, 'okay, I'll go to bed, but I probably won't sleep so if you need anything . . .'

He put a Safeway bag down next to Lomax on the crowded desk. It was folded slim like an envelope. 'More mail,' he said.

They heard him moving erratically around the apartment. Finally his door clicked shut and there was silence.

Jefferson explained: 'He's getting kind of nervous about his court appearance.'

When they had completed the calculations, Lomax turned to the end of the paper. 'Your conclusion is good but I think it's too categoric. It's okay for you to opt for one theory but only after you've at least examined all the alternatives, and if you decide to ignore some data you should explain why. Even if you're sure you're right you should appear to be interested in the possiblilty that someone else is. You could also include reference to more recent data. The *Astrophysical Review* published something on redshift velocity from Chile in January. I've written a few paragraphs for you. It's just a summary and I'm not suggesting you take it verbatim but maybe you'll want to refer to it.'

Jefferson thanked him.

'Can you read my writing?'

The boy nodded and read the page in silence. He looked younger and possibly thinner than Lomax remembered him from their first meeting. His face was blotchy with fatigue and there were black smudges under his eyes. Lomax felt a moment's alarm.

'Jefferson. Are you okay?' he asked. Jefferson looked up. At first he seemed surprised but when he registered Lomax's concern his face began to change. Gradually, fighting the process and losing, he crumpled. His mouth distorted, he closed his eyes and tears ran rapidly down his cheeks onto his paper. Lomax saw a box of tissues across the room and fetched it for him. Jefferson sniffed on a tissue and blew his nose. He was gathering his strength. Lomax put a hand on his shoulder and this sympathetic action, far from soothing the boy, seemed to make his body shake with sobs again. He dropped his head and covered his eyes, and his neck and shoulders and back heaved. He sobbed in almost complete silence.

When he had finished crying, he began to apologize, as Lomax knew he would. They spoke softly. Lomax wondered how often Jefferson lay crying in silence in this apartment so that he did not wake his father.

'Don't apologize, just tell me what's the matter. Is it tests and papers?'

Jefferson shook his head vigorously. Lomax waited for him to speak.

'I feel terrible,' Jefferson said, blowing his nose again. 'I mean . . . I miss her.' And he dissolved into tears once more. Lomax assumed Jefferson was talking about a broken romance, although it was also possible that he was referring to his mother, as no mother was in evidence at the apartment. He waited for Jefferson to stop crying again.

'Who do you miss, Jefferson?' he asked gently.

'Gail,' the boy sobbed.

Lomax sighed. He did not feel any surprise. There was an inevitability about this and the inevitability was his own blindness and stupidity.

'That's probably the first time I've said her name out loud for months,' Jefferson whispered.

'Gail, Gail, Gail,' Lomax said.

'Gail, Gail, Gail,' echoed Jefferson. He sniffed. 'I was okay until you showed up and we went to the apartment.'

'From the way you spoke I thought you hadn't been there before.'

'I wanted you to think that. I only told the truth. It's just I hadn't been in there since it happened. I was in and out a million times before she went to France. And now they've arrested Julia and the court case is starting and every time we turn on the TV they'll show another picture.'

This time he fought against the tears successfully. Lomax noticed the familiarity with which Jefferson used Julia's name.

'How well did you know Gail?'

Jefferson looked at him, his eyes covered with a film of water. 'Real well,' he said.

'You were a close friend.'

'Friend and boyfriend. I mean, I think that's what I was. I was never completely sure of my status.'

'You slept with her?'

Tears fell from Jefferson's wet eyes.

'I'm not a wimp,' he said. 'It's just that I can't stop crying. You probably think I'm a wimp.'

'No.'

Jefferson told Lomax that he had met Gail when she moved into the apartment. At first they had hardly noticed each other. Jefferson had a pretty girlfriend who majored in history. Gradually he and Gail became friends. The history student met a theologian and decided she preferred him. Gail and Jefferson went to bed together. The experience was a revelation.

'Professor, it was incredible. Amazing. I would have been up in that apartment every day if she'd let me. I probably would have abandoned school and just had sex all day with her if she'd let me.'

'Wow,' said Lomax enviously.

Jefferson whispered, 'After she died I went to a whore. I didn't think I could ever do something like that. I went a bit crazy.'

Lomax listened.

'It was terrible. Just awful. I figured a professional might come close to Gail at least in technique. Huh. Forget it.'

Lomax smiled against his will. He asked: 'Have the police interviewed you?'

'No.'

'Why not?'

'Because I was away doing my scholarship semester at MIT when it happened. Dad said not to tell anyone how well I knew Gail. He thought that if the police and attorneys and reporters started asking me questions I'd never get over it. One reason he's so upset about all this is because he knows how upset I am. And I'm upset because I know he is. I mean, he had to see her like that.'

They looked at each other and Lomax guessed what was coming next.

'You've seen the photos,' said Jefferson.

'Yes.'

'Did she . . . how did she look . . . ? I've never been able to ask Dad that question but I really want to know.'

Lomax stared at the ground but was silent.

'Oh,' said Jefferson, as though Lomax had answered. Lomax knew he had to say something.

'There was a lot of blood. So it's hard to tell. But something I believe is that however you die, whatever the circumstances, the moment of death is peaceful.'

Jefferson was listening with the whole of his body. 'You think so?' he asked.

'Yes. Supremely peaceful. A sensation of complete relaxation.'

Jefferson nodded. He smiled, although his eyes still shone with water. 'Thank you,' he said, 'thank you.'

'I guess,' began Lomax slowly, 'that you could answer a lot of my questions about her.'

Jefferson nodded enthusiastically. 'Yes,' he said. 'I could tell you about Gail. I'd like to. I want to.'

Lomax thought of the Nose trying to sniff out the barest shreds of information upstairs when all the time Jefferson could have told him anything he needed to know.

'Was she ever in hospital?' he asked.

'Yeah.'

'Did she wear perfume sometimes instead of changing into clean clothes?'

Jefferson grinned. 'God yes. Every other girl I've known would like wash all the time. Gail didn't. And you know what? It was sort of sexy to smell her body instead of her soap. It was very sexy. Am I a pervert?'

Lomax reassured him. 'I do,' he added, 'have a lot of questions for you. You're too tired to answer them now.'

But Jefferson wanted to answer them now. He insisted that he wasn't tired. 'It's the first time I've talked about her. I feel terrific.'

Lomax was weary. He glanced at the clock. It was already past midnight. 'I'm going to need some coffee,' he said.

Jefferson made some and brought it back to his room. 'I'll tell you everything I know. I'll tell you everything Gail told me. So far as I can see, there's only one problem,' he said.

'What?'

'You're working for this big law firm that's defending Julia.'

'Sachs Smith.'

'So, like, you're trying to prove Julia didn't kill them?'

'Yes.'

355

'That's the problem.'

'What is?'

'Well . . .' said Jefferson awkwardly. He sat down and wound his legs around the adjacent table '. . . it's obvious to me that she did.'

28

Jefferson went to a network of shelves and drawers which was fixed along one wall.

'My Dad built these too,' he said. He opened one of the drawers. Helen kept her black-and-white horse, Betty, in just such a drawer at Lomax's house. She had made a bed in it and at night she laid Betty in the bed and closed the drawer gently.

Jefferson pulled out a bundle of letters and then something wrapped in tissue paper. All his secrets. Finally there was a small blue box. He carried it with care, just the way Berlins had carried the box with the telescope inside.

He handed it to Lomax. Close to, Lomax could see it was covered in tiny silver stars.

'Open it,' said Jefferson.

Lomax opened it. On top was a card with more tiny stars. He lifted the card and lying beneath it on a gauzy bed was Julia's diamond pin. He raised it from the box. Its facets caught the rays of light and refracted them powerfully. Whichever way he turned the stone it flashed in a hundred different directions. He replaced it in the box and read the card.

'To my darling girl.' It was unsigned. But Lomax recognized the writing as Lewis'. He covered the diamond with the card again and closed the box, looking at Jefferson for an explanation.

'Well? What should I do with it?' the boy asked.

'How did you get this?'

'Gail gave it to me when I went to MIT in May. I was working there in summer for one of the professors before starting my scholarship semester. She knew we wouldn't see each other before she got back from France so she asked me to keep it for her. I kept it. I don't know what to do with it now.'

'How come Gail had it? No, don't tell me. It was a present from her dead mother, her only memento.'

Jefferson looked at Lomax curiously. 'Gail's mother is alive.

Her father gave her this pin. That's her father's writing on the card.'

To my darling girl.

'No,' said Lomax, feeling nauseated, 'there's been a mistake. This pin belongs to Julia. She wore it at her wedding.'

'Probably Gail loaned it to her. She often did that. Kind of. Well, mostly Julia just took it.'

Lomax put the box on the table. 'Keep it for now,' he advised.

'Really?'

'Yes.'

Jefferson returned the box to its drawer. He covered it with the tissue paper and the letters, and the drawer squeaked closed.

'It's a diamond. A big diamond. It's real valuable,' he said doubtfully. 'I don't want anyone to say I stole it.'

Lomax insisted. 'Probably Gail would have wanted you to keep it.'

'Did Julia tell you it was hers?'

'Yes.'

The boy shrugged. 'It was definitely Gail's.'

Lomax recognized his certainty. It was useless to challenge it. It was as absolute as his own belief in Julia's innocence.

'And Julia definitely killed Gail?' he asked, gently.

Jefferson reddened a little. 'Professor, remember the lecture when you told us about the end of the world?'

Lomax nodded.

'You can predict what's going to happen in the future by looking at the past, right?'

'You can make a variety of predictions.'

'Well I could have done the same thing with Gail. I could have looked at the past and predicted the future.'

'Predicted her death?'

'Julia got more and more violent towards Gail. The next thing was to kill her.'

Lomax was silent.

'Maybe you should describe Gail,' he said at last. 'No one really has yet.'

'Oh my.' Jefferson stood up and walked around the room. He had a route, up and down between the bed hinges and the door hinges. He had probably paced this many times. The rug was worn.

'She was just great company. She was interested in a lot of things and that made her interesting. She was fun. She was real smart. And she was nice. A little bit frightened. Lacking in confidence. Nice. Feature by feature, I guess she wasn't so pretty. But she was attractive.

I mean, especially sometimes, towards the end. Maybe that's because of how I felt about her. Or it might have been because of the operation. I guess the operation helped.'

Lomax's body was uncomfortable. He had just finished a coffee but he could still taste the super's malted milk drink and feel its weight lying in his stomach.

'When Gail was in hospital,' he stated slowly, 'she had cosmetic surgery.' This had been obvious for months but he had failed to see it. Gail had turned from the plain high-school student to the attractive young woman with the help of a surgeon's knife.

'It wasn't her fault,' Jefferson assured him. 'She had a fight with Julia. It was the only time she ever hit back. They both needed their faces repaired afterwards. Julia had a broken nose too.'

The malted milk was now a rock in Lomax's belly. He remembered his first date with Julia. She had told him then about the broken nose and subsequent surgery. She had said it was broken in an accident.

Jefferson said: 'Julia hated her. Julia is probably crazy. You don't believe it? Gail's dad didn't believe it either. He just didn't believe a word Gail told him about Julia. It's the one good thing to come out of all this. When Julia came into the apartment that morning and pointed a gun right at them, then he must have seen Gail had been telling him the truth all along. And when I imagine it, I imagine Gail's father turning to her and saying: "Gail. I'm sorry. You were right. I should have listened." And then Julia fires.'

Lomax remembered the photographs. He remembered the apartment.

'Is that possible?' asked Jefferson. He pulled the bed down from the wall as lightly as a balloon. It swung noiselessly to the ground. Jefferson sat on the end of it, close to Lomax.

'Yes. It's possible that Lewis was speaking to Gail when the killer fired at him.'

'The killer was Julia. Why won't you listen to me, Professor?' He thrust his face forward and his features seemed to stretch outwards in a sad mask.

'Is that what you told your father?'

Jefferson did not blink or take his eyes from Lomax's face. Finally he said: 'Yes.'

'Okay, I'm listening, Jefferson,' Lomax told him. 'I'm waiting to hear why Julia hated Gail so much that she killed her.'

'She had this power. Power's something I find very interesting.'

'It is very interesting.'

'Some people can't handle it at all.'

'No. Some people should not be given power.'

'Well . . . Julia's one of those people.'

'What power did she have?'

'In the family. I know about that. I'm in charge of this apartment. My dad will do anything I say. I could treat him mean and it would still be the same. It's sort of a burden when someone gives you so much power.'

Jefferson's face wrinkled. He might have been going to cry again.

'You carry that burden well,' Lomax said softly. 'I've seen you with your father and I know how well you do.'

Jefferson lifted his hands to hide his face. Lomax knew he was fighting tears. 'Okay,' he said, his voice muffled. 'Thank you.'

Lomax stretched across to put a hand on Jefferson's shoulder. He felt the boy shaking with the effort of self-control. When he had conquered his urge to cry he looked up, his face a new shape.

'Sorry. What I'm trying to say is that people give other people power and they expect them to behave well. And it's . . . well . . . hard to do that. I mean some people fail. Julia failed.'

'What exactly was her power?'

'When she married Gail's father, she was worshipped. Gail's father worshipped her. Gail worshipped her. Who else did Gail have? Her brother got the hell out. Her mother was a wreck. Her father had no interest in her. Julia arrives and she's kind and beautiful. Gail was . . . just slavish.'

'And what makes you think Julia abused this power?'

'Probably her first impulse was good. She wants Gail to be happy and she thinks she can't be happy because she's plain and fat. Looks are important in that house. So it starts off with a few beauty tips.'

'Maybe Gail asked for Julia's help.'

'Maybe she did. But it wasn't a routine, it was a regime. Gail had to eat this but not this, she had to exercise, she had to wear this, walk that way, do this . . .'

Lomax remembered the last time he had seen Julia. She had sat on the bed, the book about Captain Cook's adventures lying to one side. He could recall the room with astonishing clarity. There had been the peach bedspread, the photo of Deputy, the wedding picture of the diamond pin. And Julia had told him how she had failed as a stepmother.

Lomax protested: 'She was trying to help.'

'But Professor, it didn't stop there.'

360

Julia had told him: 'It all went further than I ever intended.'

Lomax said: 'A lot of women have beauty regimes.'

'Self-enforced, maybe.'

'Enforced by other people's expectations.'

'They have a choice. This was a regime which was enforced by Julia. She goes too far and no one can stop her. If Gail doesn't follow her regime, Julia can get real mad and there's no one to say: leave that girl alone. Gail's father thinks Julia's a sweet young thing, just the way you do. And she is, when he's around. Of course he refuses to listen if Gail whispers a word of complaint. So Julia can shout and Gail apologizes. Julia can hit her with a big stick and Gail promises to do better. Julia can keep Gail in a state of fear and agitation almost all the time and there's nothing Gail can do about it. Gail has no power.'

'She can leave home.'

'Which she does. And hit back at Julia. Which eventually she does. Actually . . .' Jefferson stood up again. 'Actually, I told her to do that,' he said. 'I think I gave her more confidence. I told her it was the only way to stop Julia. I didn't guess Gail would get so hurt.'

He turned to Lomax. 'Was I wrong?'

'I don't know.'

'It's too late now, anyway.'

'Yes,' agreed Lomax. 'It's too late now.'

'I think Julia killed them when things started to change. I mean, when her power was eroding. Tyrants don't like that. It makes them real mean.'

Julia the tyrant. It was impossible to imagine.

Jefferson was ticking off points on his fingers.

'First, Gail's father is losing interest in Julia. He's having affairs. Her marital relationship is changing. Second, the regime she imposed on Gail is taking effect. Gail's getting prettier, gaining confidence, she starts to feel attractive and that makes her look more attractive. Plus she uses make-up well, the way Julia taught her. Plus she has the nose job after the fight. It all helps. In that house, where appearances matter, looks are power. Julia's weaker now. Third, she can't tyrannize Gail on a day-to-day basis because Gail lives here. When Gail goes home, she makes sure her father's around. Her father means safety because Julia's different when he's there. Plus, now he pays this attractive daughter more attention than he ever has before. That makes Julia weaker still. She hates it. She openly shows how she feels. They all go on this vacation together and Julia sulks the whole time while Gail and her father go out and have fun.'

'Lifebelt Lake,' said Lomax.

'Yeah, some lake in Arizona. Gail actually enjoyed the vacation. Because for the first time, Julia couldn't be cruel to her. For the first time, Gail had some power. I was at MIT. She wrote me. I spoke with her on the phone. She sounded real happy. She said: I'm free from her at last.'

There was a long silence. The apartment block creaked. A car with a noisy exhaust passed on the road outside. Lomax had been sitting still for so long that his legs ached.

'Except,' added Jefferson, 'she wasn't.'

'None of this,' said Lomax, 'explains why Julia would actually kill Gail. And it certainly doesn't explain why she would kill Lewis.'

Jefferson sighed. 'Julia killed Gail, I'm sure of that. She was cruel and violent to Gail and it all escalated towards the obvious conclusion. But Gail's father . . . maybe there were two killers?'

'There may have been. It's crossed my mind.'

Jefferson stood up and stretched. Lomax was silent with thought. Suddenly Jefferson said: 'Professor, want to know one of the things I remember best about Gail?'

Lomax could no longer feel his legs. He rearranged them slightly with his hands. 'Tell me.'

'Putting on her make-up. Have you ever watched a woman do that?'

'Yes.'

'Who?'

'Different women.'

'Tell me one of them.'

'Okay. My ex-wife. Her name's Candice.'

'What does she do?'

'At first she didn't wear any make-up at all. She didn't believe in it. Then one day I caught her smearing stuff over her face that looked like butter only browner. She was defensive. She said she'd been ill, she was too pale. But she started buying all these little pots and jars and bottles. They had thick glass.'

Jefferson was nodding. 'Some of them are kind of unusual shapes.'

'And when she opened and closed them they made a noise all of their own. Like lips, glass lips. Inside the jars there was this colourful goo. So she learned how to apply it. I mean, there was no more smearing.'

'Brushes,' prompted Jefferson.

'Oh God, there were brushes. Different sizes, different colours, different brushes for different places on her face. It was like watching Rembrandt at work. The light had to be right. The brushes had to be right. And the whole idea was that, after all this, she was supposed to look like she wasn't wearing any make-up at all.'

'Did she sort of finish and then look at herself? And you'd think: she's all done. And then she'd reach . . .'

'. . . for the perfume bottle.'

Jefferson was smiling now. 'Gail used to spray some on her wrists and some behind her ears and some down her cleavage.'

'And Candice did this weird thing. She sprayed it in the air and then she walked into it. Like a perfume shower.'

'Yes! It's not weird. Gail did it. When she died I went out and bought a bottle of her perfume. And sometimes, when I think about her, I spray it around the place. Is that crazy?'

'No.' Lomax thought of the Nose, smelling her father's sheets after he had died.

'It helped me imagine her. It doesn't work so well as it used to. It used to be the smell of Gail and now it's sort of become the smell . . .' Jefferson paused. '. . . the smell of grief.'

'It's taken on a new meaning.'

'For me. Not for you. Want to smell her?'

'Okay.'

Jefferson went to another of the drawers on the wall. 'I mean,' he was saying, 'this is her clean, going-out smell. Her dirty staying-in smell was better, but no one's ever going to put that in a bottle.'

He pulled out a colourful box. There was a bottle inside.

'Who makes it?' asked Lomax casually, knowing the answer already.

'Um . . .' Jefferson searched the box. '. . . um, Dior.'

He sprayed the perfume into a void in the centre of the room. It made the sound of a hissing snake and the room was filled with a sweet, sharp scent. Jefferson walked around with his nose in the air breathing deeply. 'Mmmmmmmm,' he said.

Lomax recognized the smell. It reminded him of his party. One of the women, he did not know which one, had been wearing it. He inhaled it now. This was Gail's smell.

Jefferson put the perfume away and sat down again. 'You don't believe me, Professor,' he said. 'You don't believe what I've told you about Julia.'

Lomax was thoughtful. He said nothing.

'You don't believe me,' the boy repeated.

Finally Lomax said: 'I know you think you're telling the truth . . .'

'It is the truth!'

363

'But Gail wasn't always honest.'

'Like when?'

Lomax told Jefferson how Gail had lied at high school about her mother's death. But Jefferson was excited in her defence. 'I can understand. I can understand why she said that. Probably she wished her mother was dead.'

'I understand too. I'm trying to show you – '

Jefferson interrupted him. 'Julia wasn't the first woman to hit Gail around. She was used to it by the time Julia started, she might even have learned to expect it. With a mother like that, I can see why Gail made-believe she was dead.'

'I'm trying to show you that she wasn't always truthful.'

'No one's always truthful. That doesn't invalidate everything they say. Professor, I saw her bruises. I saw her after this fight. I saw how scared she was of Julia.'

Lomax's tone was calming. 'I have to think about everything you've told me.'

Jefferson nodded slowly. Lomax watched the boy's energy drain and realized that he, too, was exhausted. Jefferson dropped backwards and lay back across the bed.

'Aren't you mad at her?' Lomax asked.

'At Gail? Sometimes. It's what happens when someone dies. The first thing is anger.'

'I mean, aren't you mad at Julia? Since you think she murdered Gail.'

Jefferson did not move or open his eyes. 'No. I think she's crazy.'

'But if you wanted to get even . . .'

'I don't.'

'You have power over your father, you said so. And your father is a key witness in this case.'

Jefferson spoke clearly. 'I didn't tell him to say he saw Julia here.'

'I know you wouldn't do that, Jefferson. But your father was in an unhappy, suggestible state after finding the bodies. And it took him months to decide that he'd seen Julia outside here at the time of the murders . . .'

Jefferson sat up. 'Professor, it took him months to decide *to tell*. He knows what he saw. He woke up and looked out of the window and he saw Julia getting into a car early in the morning. Dad wouldn't lie.'

'I hope not. Because Julia's defence attorney is real tough and things could get unpleasant for him in court.'

Jefferson lay back again and closed his eyes. 'I wish to God that he'd kept quiet about it,' he said. 'There must be enough other evidence. Julia's so dumb she couldn't have killed two people without leaving some evidence.'

Lomax did not respond. After a few moments, Jefferson spoke again, his voice weary.

'Gail coerced me into doing this semester at MIT, as she was going away too. But she also told me I should do the summer job with the professor beforehand. I didn't want to go. It meant I wouldn't see her for a whole six months. I didn't know what she'd be doing or who she'd be doing it with. But she said I had to go. She sent me away. I wish I'd insisted on coming back from Massachusetts and meeting her at the airport here. I wish I'd insisted.'

Lomax raised his eyebrows. The action seemed to require a lot of effort. 'Don't blame yourself,' he said. He began to unwrap his body in preparation for leaving. He had been sprawling across a chair and the desk. His limbs were locked into position again and it hurt to move them.

'No. I've been through that one,' Jefferson assured him sleepily. 'One thing I know . . .'

For a moment it seemed he had fallen asleep but after a moment he spoke again. 'One thing I know is that it's not my fault.'

'I'm going now,' Lomax told him. Jefferson still did not move.

'Thanks for listening. You're the only person I've told. I don't know why I told you, except that I think Gail sort of liked you.'

Lomax paused. One foot was still on the desk, the other on the floor. 'What does that mean?'

He had to wait for an answer while Jefferson yawned. 'Well she knew you, a little bit.'

Lomax put a hand on the desk to support himself.

Jefferson said, without opening his eyes: 'She was interested in astronomy. And cosmology. I took her along to your lectures and she really enjoyed them.'

'Gail came to my lectures?'

'Yeah.'

Lomax tried to recall the lecture room. He remembered a sea of faces. He remembered the pretty girls with their long, well-brushed hair and ironed T-shirts in the front row. The serious students, usually comparatively unkempt, were further back, scattered in among the more fashionable clothes. There had been fifteen minutes of questions at the end and a lot of hands were raised. He remembered a small, dark, intense student who always asked questions in an argumentative way. He remembered Jefferson, fresh-faced, enthusiastic, his hand waving.

'There's only time for one more,' Lomax had said, and he had been aware of Jefferson's face bobbing in front of him, his arm outstretched. Jefferson had willed Lomax to choose him. Lomax had nodded and he had started talking.

Lomax strained to remember who had been sitting next to Jefferson. A girl. Probably tall. Probably attractive. His memory – stubborn, uncomprehending, unhelpful – refused to supply a face. No amount of concentration or mental exertion could fill the seat next to Jefferson.

The boy was asleep now. He looked like a child when his face was so relaxed. He lay diagonally across the bed, his shins and feet overhanging the edge.

The computer was still humming. The cursor winked on Jefferson's redshift paper. Reluctantly, Lomax sat back down and altered the faulty calculations. He scrolled to the conclusions. He changed Jefferson's definites to possibles, his certainties to maybes. He added a penultimate paragraph referring to the *Astrophysical Review*. He typed 'The End'. Jefferson snorted and turned over in his sleep. Then Lomax removed the disc and switched off the computer. Jefferson still did not wake. Lomax was about to turn out the light when he saw the flat brown bag the super had given him. He remembered that Frances had told him not to carry any more mail. He ignored her instructions and went back for it. When he left the apartment, he shut the door as quietly as he could but it sounded loud in the still night. He wondered if he had woken the super. He guessed the man was a light sleeper. He reminded himself that no one, not even Homer, was awoken by the three gunshots fired early that November morning. Probably people had heard them and used them unconsciously, like spice, to flavour their dreams.

Before getting into the car he looked up at Gail's dark window, as usual. He drove home slowly. It would soon be light. In a few hours, a prosecuting and a defence attorney would begin arguing over Julia's future.

Deputy wagged his tail sleepily at Lomax. Lomax was so tired he simply went upstairs and took off his clothes and crawled into bed. Deputy curled up at the other end. Lomax remembered Gail's mail. He had left it downstairs. Getting up and going down for it and opening it now seemed a physical impossibility. He ached all over as if punched.

He had not pulled the drapes. Occasionally, if he could keep his eyes focused for long enough, the night breeze rearranged the branches outside his window to reveal an especially bright star burning itself out somewhere in the universe. The universe was of an immensity that could be noted in a tiny equation but not grasped by the greatest of human minds. It was of an age which could be known but not understood.

The thick canopy of leaves closed across the star again. As he lay waiting for it to reappear, he fell asleep.

A few hours later he was in court. His body was stiff with fatigue. The steps to the courthouse had seemed infinite. In the hallway people had bounced around him at high speed, their motion random. And now, inside the room, the jury was being selected. Lomax did not count this a part of the trial and was anxious for it to be over. After a while it became clear that it was a long process and unlikely to finish for some days.

When, in the hot weeks which preceded the trial, Lomax had imagined the court, the judge had been white-haired and paternal. He had looked, in fact, a little like Lewis. At the beginning of the day the court had risen for Judge Olmstead and a robed figure had mounted the podium and he had seen that Judge Olmstead was a woman. But he had been right about the white hair.

The defence and prosecution seemed to be doing some strange ritual dance around the parade of faces, names and ethnic groups who filed into the room. They rejected prospective jurors for no particular reason that Lomax could divine at first. Then it became clear that Frances favoured young males. Lomax could guess the reason and he didn't much like it. She was rejecting young women but accepting older women, preferably much older women. Morton de Maria was trying for the opposite and in addition he seemed to be favouring blue collar workers. Group after group of men and women were led in to be bowled down like skittles by the two lawyers. Sometimes when they were asked to stand down their faces were relieved. Others were disappointed. Others clearly felt they had failed some test. One man tried changing his answer to the last question.

'No,' said the judge. 'Your second answer could be the answer you think we want to hear. I can't allow it.'

'But I didn't mean to say that! It was a mistake!'

'You have been asked to step down,' she said. 'Now please do so.'

Her voice was firm and the man obeyed her with a wistful backward glance at Julia. She was sitting with Frances and Kurt at the defence table, her back to the public. She was motionless. Occasionally

Frances spoke to her. Lomax could not see whether she responded. He suspected she did not.

In the afternoon, as yet another group of prospective jury members was led in, Lomax closed his eyes and felt the strange sense of physical disintegration which immediately precedes sleep. He opened his eyes. In his momentary confusion it seemed to him that the cross-section of humanity before him now was on trial. Then he remembered that this was Julia's trial and among these men and women were the jurors who would decide her fate.

As he was leaving the court at the end of the day, far behind the knot of reporters who surrounded the defence team, a faint scent wafted towards him which he recognized at once as Gail's. He was overwhelmed by the power of smell to re-create not the events but the flavour of the past. He felt again Jefferson's grief, his own discomfort, and their shared anguish. He had been thinking about Jefferson's story all day. Impossible to believe it, impossible to ignore it. He had decided to tell no one, not even Frances, what the boy had said.

When he arrived home Deputy greeted him lethargically, ignoring the squirrel who scrambled up the carport. The air was hot and humid. Lomax hoped that this was the reason Deputy yawned and stretched and then ambled over to him so slowly.

'Want to go for a walk?' Lomax asked. There were still a few hours of daylight. They could climb one of the mountain trails, even though the sun had turned the grass brown and some of the creeks were probably dry. Unusually, the word 'walk' had no effect on Deputy.

In the mailbox was a letter from the observatory, inviting him to return to work the Monday following the eclipse. The offer was conditional on the withdrawal of his allegations against Berlins.

'Not that I ever made any fucking allegations against Berlins,' Lomax said later when he telephoned Julia at Marjorie's apartment to tell her this news.

'I'm glad life will go back to normal for you,' she said. There was a hint of sadness in her voice which made his belly ache a little.

'It will for you too,' he told her.

'I'm not sure I know what normal is any more.'

They talked about the trial.

'Frances thinks the jury selection could continue for most of the week,' she said.

'Okay. Well, I may miss some of it.'

'I like it. I wish this part of the trial could go on forever.'

'The whole thing will be over in a few weeks.'

'Then what, Lomax?'

He had hardly seen her face that day but his rare glimpses had told him that she had looked young and pale and frightened. He said, 'After the trial you'll be free. Everybody will know you didn't do anything wrong. And I hope you'll marry me.'

He had not been expecting to hear himself say this. The words seemed to have spoken themselves. He had thought about when and how to ask her to marry him and decided that it was unfair to add to her pressure now. On the other hand, he wanted her to know that, if something went wrong and she was convicted, his feelings for her and belief in her innocence would not change.

There was a silence. Probably her face was saying something, if only he could see it.

'Oh Lomax.'

What was her tone? Touched? Surprised? Apologetic? He wanted her to speak again so that he could gauge the register of her voice, but she was silent.

'Shit,' he said, 'I didn't mean to ask you now. Will you just promise to think about it?'

'Okay.'

They talked longer but their conversation was stiff. Her failure to answer, immediately and positively, hung between them.

'Incidentally,' he said, 'do you know what happened to that diamond pin Lewis gave you?'

'No.' She sounded sad. 'I loaned it to Gail. I didn't get it back after she died.'

He was pleased with her answer. After the call he intended to go to sleep but when he lay in bed sleep would not come. He opened all the windows. The days were getting shorter and the calendar said it was fall but the weather still burned. The leaves were so big and heavy on the trees that they made loud, shimmering noises when there was only, like tonight, the slightest of breezes. Mostly they hung helpless under the weight of the heat. Hot and restless, Lomax remembered the mail that the super had handed him last night.

This time he went downstairs and opened the bag. He expected the usual collection of circulars. There was just one. The other envelope was blue airmail. He thought that it had come from France but on closer examination he found that it had been mailed from America to an address in France and from there sent back in a half-legible hand to America. The writing of the original sender was familiar. The sender's name was on the back. Mrs Julia Fox. He stood, naked, staring at it. He was holding a letter from Julia to Gail.

He did not open it immediately. He sat down at the kitchen table, sweeping the dirty dishes there to one side. He had a choice. He could hand the letter to Frances. He could hand it to Julia unopened on the grounds that it was hers. He could pass it to the police. Or he could open it and decide what to do with it when he had read it.

He opened the letter as he had known he would from the moment he found it. In it, Julia threatened to kill Gail. She warned Gail that if she was coming home to jeopardize family life in any way she, Julia, was capable of committing murder. The letter was scrawled. The writing was abnormally large and in some places words had been scored out with ferocity. Lomax read it many times, fast and then more slowly.

He reviewed his options once again. He could show the letter to Frances and let her decide the right thing to do with it. He could take it to the police, but that would be like leading Julia directly to the gas chamber. Or he could hide it and do nothing. As an experienced evader of decisions, he chose the last of these options.

He noticed that Deputy had not eaten the meal which had been left for him in the kitchen that morning. This was unprecedented.

Upstairs, Lomax found a drawer like the one where Helen kept her horse and Jefferson kept his secrets. He put the letter at the bottom of it. Deputy was sleeping so soundly that he was unaware of Lomax's presence in the room. He woke when Lomax stroked his ears but he indicated this only by half opening his eyes. His nose felt warm and dry.

It was clear that Deputy was sick. Lomax thought about Deputy's recent behaviour and concluded that the dog had probably been sick for some days. If he was worse or no better in the morning Lomax would miss jury selection and take Deputy to the vet.

Lomax was too anxious now to sleep. He got up twice to re-read the letter. The size and style of the writing indicated that Julia had written it in a state of considerable distress. There was violence not just in the threat it contained but in the thoroughness of the deletions. The writer may have been frightened, possibly terrified. Very late at night it occurred to Lomax that the letter could be evidence for the defence.

The vet could find nothing wrong with Deputy but took some tests.

'He's not like this usually,' Lomax said as Deputy stood obediently on the vet's table while the vet felt him all over. 'Usually he chews your sleeve.'

370

'I remember,' said the vet grimly. He promised to telephone with the results of the tests. Deputy walked meekly to heel out of the consulting room. He did not bark or even growl at the other dogs waiting outside.

By the surgery a street vendor was selling eye protection for the eclipse. As the date of the eclipse drew closer, filter vendors were beginning to appear in shopping malls and on street corners.

'What do you sell when you don't sell these things?' Lomax asked the vendor. The man rolled a pair of bloodshot eyes at Lomax. He did not smile.

'Sometimes balloons,' he said.

The filters came in all shapes and sizes. You held them to your eyes or you wore them like sunglasses. There were designer filters or cheap ones with the date and time of the eclipse stamped on them. Or you could buy a book about the eclipse with a filter tucked into a pouch inside it.

It was eleven o'clock. In court, the tedious process of jury selection would be continuing. The thought of returning there made Lomax's stomach muscles tighten. Yesterday, although anaesthetized by tiredness, he had been unnerved by the grandeur of the court and the weight of history and experience behind its protocol.

He was passing Tradescant. He turned into the campus and drove slowly towards the shadiest parking lot. He planned to leave Deputy lying asleep in the car but the dog jumped out and followed him, his nose low to the ground and his tail limp. Lomax leashed him, although it was hardly necessary for this new, unhappy, obedient Deputy.

The fall semester was about to start. The campus was preparing itself. New titles were on display in the bookstore windows. Teachers walked briskly carrying bundles of paper. Students were arriving.

'Professor Hopcroft is available,' said the receptionist of the psychology department after a brief telephone consultation. 'But the rules say no dogs in this building.'

'But – ' Lomax planned to explain that Deputy was sick.

'That's unless you're visually impaired and the dog is essential to your health and wellbeing. Is that the case?'

'Yes,' said Lomax.

'Okay, take him with you. Third door on the right.' The receptionist smiled at Deputy, who gave her a sad look. 'The professor likes dogs,' she said.

Hopcroft was pleased to see Lomax. He was even more delighted by Deputy. When he learned that Deputy was sick he telephoned his secretary.

'We have one sick dog in here. It's a hot day. What would you prescribe?'

There was a pause. Hopcroft listened.

'Uh huh,' he said. He raised an eyebrow at Lomax. 'My secretary says that some dogs like coffee. Hers, for example.'

Lomax was doubtful. 'He drinks tea sometimes. Water usually. Right now he won't eat or drink anything much.'

'He drinks tea sometimes,' Hopcroft reported to the secretary, gesturing for Lomax to move books off a chair and sit on it. 'Uh huh. Thank you.' He put the phone down. 'We're going to try no milk no sugar,' he said.

Deputy, who had been watching Hopcroft with a flicker of interest, now decided he liked him. He ambled over and put his head on Hopcroft's large knee.

'My!' roared Hopcroft in delight. 'This is promising behaviour. It borders on the promiscuous. I don't think this dog is too sick. Dr Lomax, humour me. I like to tell myself I know about dogs. Would you take it amiss if I examined this dog?'

'Feel free,' said Lomax, 'but the vet examined him this morning and said nothing was wrong.'

'Uh huh. Well, most of my human patients have the same experience.'

Hopcroft knelt down and looked at Deputy's face. He stared into his eyes and pulled them a little to the left and then a little to the right. To Lomax's amazement, Deputy let Hopcroft prise his lips back and examine his teeth.

'Uh huh,' said Hopcroft, touching Deputy's nose and running his hands through his coat. 'Felt any lumps and bumps on him, Dr Lomax?'

'No.'

Hopcroft sat back in his chair. Deputy replaced his head on Hopcroft's knee. 'How exactly would you describe his symptoms?'

'Listlessness. Loss of energy. Loss of appetite.'

'And when did this start?'

'In Arizona earlier this ear. But he seemed okay when I came back and I thought it must have been the heat. Over the past few weeks he's gotten listless and yesterday I came home and he hadn't eaten his food. In the middle of the night he just lay there and wouldn't move, which is the opposite of the way he usually is. Maybe it's the heat.'

'I don't think it's the heat, Dr Lomax,' said Hopcroft seriously. 'I don't think that's the problem. Now tell me how you've been getting along with that matter we talked about last time. I assume that's why you called.'

'Sort of. But also to thank you for getting me my job back.'

Hopcroft held his palms up. Deputy blinked at him. 'No thanks necessary. In my opinion you should not have been suspended. The whole business was an absurdity. I don't trust that little guy in the bowtie, not one bit. Be careful of that man, Dr Lomax.'

'I'll try. It's hard to avoid him when he's my boss.'

'I take it you've been greatly worried by your suspension.'

'That and other things. This investigation . . .'

'Ah, now. This murder investigation. It was causing you some agitation when I saw you before. How is that progressing?'

'It's in court.'

'It's in court? Why aren't you?'

'It's day two and they're still selecting the jury. Plus my dog's sick.'

'So. Hopcroft is going to start putting two and two together, a dangerous game but some say he plays it well. Yesterday morning you fed your dog and went to court for the opening day of the trial. You returned home to find your dog unhappy, his food untouched. In the middle of the night, he took a turn for the worse. Let me ask you a question, Dr Lomax. Why exactly were you awake in the middle of the night?'

'Um . . . well . . . it was hot.'

'I don't think it's the heat, Dr Lomax,' said Hopcroft for the second time. 'I don't think that's the problem.'

Lomax stared at the ground.

'Agitation?' suggested Hopcroft. He gave each of Deputy's ears in turn an affectionate tug.

'Yes.'

'Why are you pursuing this investigation? I understand that you had the summer free. I understand that. But why exactly did you choose to spend it in this way?'

Lomax shuffled his feet around. He said: 'I'm in love with the defendant.'

'The defendant, I take it, is the male or female accused of these murders?'

'Yes. Female.'

'Well, falling in love is an agitating experience at the best of times. When did you fall in love with this woman?'

'Late spring, early summer.'

'Uh huh. Did you vacation with her in Arizona?'

'No. The Arizona trip wasn't just a vacation. You had told me that father-daughter incest is most likely to be evident from the behaviour of the daughter and so I was finding out all I could about her. She lived in Arizona.'

'And did you find out anything distressing?'

Lomax thought hard. 'Yes, it was sort of sad.'

'I see. And this woman you love, she was here in California.'

'Yes.'

'I see.'

Hopcroft's secretary arrived with a tray. On it were two cups of coffee, a bowl of tea and a plate of cookies.

'Sorry it took a while,' she said. 'I had to cool the tea down for him.' She lifted the bowl carefully onto the floor near Deputy. He watched her but did not remove his nose from Hopcroft's knee.

'He knows it's there. I expect he'll take it soon,' said Hopcroft, running a finger down Deputy's muzzle.

There was nowhere to put the cookies. It was not so much that Hopcroft's office was untidy but that it was bursting with books and papers. The shelves were full and books were stacked neatly in all the available floor or desk space. There were little piles of broken leaves, snapped twigs and bruised flowerheads in places around the office. Sometimes Joel and Helen marked trails in this way.

The secretary removed with care a handful of twigs from some files on a chair and balanced the cookies there instead. She passed the twigs to Hopcroft who put them gently on a shelf behind him.

'If you think he should have some milk in that, call me,' she said, looking wisely at Deputy before departing. They thanked her.

'Well, this has all been very interesting,' Hopcroft said. 'Which aspect exactly of this investigation is agitating you today, Dr Lomax?'

'I'm still bothered by this father–daughter relationship.'

'Uh huh. Those are very bothering things.'

Lomax coughed. 'What in your opinion – ?' He interrupted himself. 'Um, this is all hypothetical, by the way.'

'Of course, of course.' Hopcroft was scrunching on a cookie. Deputy had wandered off somewhere now.

'Where consenting father–daughter incest takes place within a family . . . supposing the father was married, I mean, not to the mother. Supposing there was a stepmother, and she knew about it. What in your opinion does she do?'

'She shoots them,' said Hopcroft. Lomax jumped as if Hopcroft's long legs had kicked him.

'Gee, I'm sorry, Dr Lomax, that was a joke and a very poor one.'

Lomax looked at him doubtfully.

'No, really, it's too bad. If Hopcroft hopes to alleviate your agitation, making tasteless jokes is clearly not the right way to go about it. Please forgive him. But he reads the newspapers like everyone else and it's impossible for him not to know which case you're alluding to.'

Lomax was alarmed.

'You can, of course,' Hopcroft assured him, 'rely on my discretion. And Dr Lomax, I do understand that this part of our discussion is likely to make you tense.'

Lomax realized that he was tense. His body was hard all over with tension. Deputy was lying under Lomax's chair now. His legs free, Hopcroft stretched them out and sank lower into his seat.

'As a boy you were subjected to the European cultural influences which told you stepmothers are always wicked. Ever since you knew this woman was accused of killing her stepdaughter, it must have been occurring to some old part of your brain, so old that you think you stopped listening to it a long time ago, that she might have been a wicked stepmother. Remember wicked stepmothers? Sure you do. There was an assumption of jealousy in those children's tales, sexual jealousy of a young, attractive girl who has a special power over the woman's husband. So the stepmother eliminates her. Please drink your coffee and eat at least one cookie, Dr Lomax.'

Lomax took a cookie. He was not hungry but he did not want to offend Hopcroft. He gulped some coffee.

'Step families in our society are full of tensions which often include sexual jealousy. Perhaps as an undercurrent, but it's there. So how does a stepmother deal with a father's sexual attraction for his daughter?'

Hopcroft sank lower into his chair.

'It is hard for me to comment without knowing any of the people involved. But I would say it's possible there's sometimes a little nugget of truth in those old tales. Sexual jealousy could result in the elimination of the daughter. But Dr Lomax, forgive me if my memory deludes me, but the husband was killed too, as I understand it. Please eat the cookie, don't just look at it.'

'Yes, the husband was killed too,' said Lomax. He began to eat the cookie.

'Well now, this is sounding highly unlikely. She wants to get that girl out of her family so that she can hold all the power.'

The word power made Lomax flinch a little. He could not for the moment remember why.

'So she doesn't kill the husband too. No. This is most unlikely. It's unlikely that she'd kill anyone, but certainly not him. Now, evidence indicates that mothers or indeed stepmothers very often collude in incest. I don't mean participate. Although it's not unknown. No, what I mean is that they simply decide to ignore it. Incest is something which takes place inside the family and, unlike most threats from outside the family structure, it can be accommodated.'

Hopcroft had put down his coffee and was using his big hands to illustrate his point. His right hand was the family structure. His left hand was menacing. It represented the outside threat.

'Where there is non-violent consenting father–daughter incest and the continuation of the family unit is important, then the family often accommodates it. As you know, some of us don't think it's necessarily such a terrible bad crime.'

Hopcroft grinned at him for a moment. 'Ouch, Dr Lomax, that one still hurts you just a little. Dr Lomax is saying ouch, only not out loud.'

'Ouch,' said Lomax morosely.

'So, when does a mother, or a stepmother, confronted by incest, take action? When it's violent or abusive or dangerous, although not always then. Usually it's when she's planning to dismantle the family structure anyway. Or – and I wonder if this is relevant to your case – or, where she is, for instance, the divorced mother, and therefore already outside the family structure. And possibly happy to see its destruction. Certainly she is not going to collude, she has nothing to gain by collusion. I would say that the greatest maternal outrage, aggression and potential violence that I have encountered over father–daughter incest is from divorced mothers.'

Lomax was thoughtful. 'I don't think it's relevant in this case,' he said, 'but it's interesting.'

'Am I putting your mind at rest?'

'Yes.'

'Good. Eat another cookie, please.'

Lomax did so. 'On the question of incest itself . . .' he began. 'Suppose the daughter was plain and overweight and of no sexual interest to her father at all . . .'

'I would like to point out,' said Hopcroft, 'that overweight does not necessarily preclude sexual interest. Indeed, there are many cultures in the world where overweight is what women want to be.'

'Agreed. But we know where this man's sexual interests lie and his daughter isn't the kind of girl who attracts him. Except, she changes. She becomes what he wants.'

Lomax paused. 'Is this sounding improbable?'

'Improbable?' whooped Hopcroft. 'I would say that the above or similar occurs in nine out of ten father-daughter relationships. A lot of young women go to great lengths to make themselves sexually attractive to Daddy. But if you told them that's what they're doing, they'd be amazed. And if their father acted on the signals he's receiving, then they'd be even more amazed. How old was this female when she began to interest her father?'

'Say, about twenty-one.'

'Well, I won't say it's impossible, although something doesn't feel right about it. A man ignores his daughter and then suddenly notices her when she's as old at that? If it's going to happen, it usually happens sooner.'

'But she changed. She didn't attract him earlier.'

'Okay, okay, your point is taken, Dr Lomax. Let's say it's possible.'

Lomax did not move.

'You see, Daddy is usually the very first man on the receiving end of his little girl's sexual signals. Is there evidence that this young woman had sexual relations with other men prior to the age of twenty-one?'

'Several. One her own age, one a friend of her father's.'

'Dr Lomax, I see the way your mind is working. I see your logic. She leads an apparently normal sexual existence, all the time changing her appearance in line with Daddy's wishes, and when she finally succeeds in attracting him, their delayed incestuous relationship takes place.'

Lomax nodded and Hopcroft shook his head.

'This father and this daughter were in regular contact from her puberty to her death?'

'Yes.'

'I don't like the delay. It doesn't feel right, Dr Lomax. None of this feels right to Hopcroft. No, no. It doesn't. Although it's not impossible.'

The telephone buzzed.

'Oh,' said Hopcroft, 'that means I have a graduate student waiting to see me now. There's just a few things more I'd like to say, Dr Lomax. May I do that? May Hopcroft speak freely to you?'

Lomax's look invited Hopcroft to speak freely.

'I see now why you've been distressed. This is a distressing period for you. Not only is your loved one in court, but you find yourself turning up evidence which is sort of uncomfortable to contemplate.

377

Well, I hope I've eased that discomfort a little tiny bit. Falling in love is agitating but a trial like this is positively gut-wrenching. Dr Lomax, try to relax. Try to be calm. Just support your woman and let her lawyers do their work now. That's the only way your dog is going to get better.'

Lomax stared at him and then at Deputy, who was now sitting on his haunches, sphinx-like, by Hopcroft's side. The plate of cookies was empty. The bowl of tea was empty.

'What did you eat for breakfast, Dr Lomax?'

'Well . . . I guess . . . nothing.'

'Uh huh. What did you eat when you came home from court yesterday evening?'

'Um . . . nothing.'

'Yesterday lunchtime?'

'A sandwich. About half a sandwich.'

'Now, Dr Lomax. I see you have noticed the absence of cookies on that plate. Clarissa brought approximately fifteen cookies, the small square ones that Hopcroft likes. I had four, you had two, this dog ate all the rest. Plus his tea. If you hadn't eaten any, do you think he would have touched them? No. So please. Hopcroft hardly dares venture a small joke at this point, especially as his last attempt was not well received, but what the hell. Dr Lomax, for dog's sake. Try to take a little more care of yourself.'

29

When Lomax arrived at the court he found he had missed not only the final selection of the jury but the opening of the trial. He persuaded the bailiff to allow him in, but his seat was so near the back that he could hardly see. Only the judge and the jury and the American flag were visible.

Morton de Maria was making his opening statement. Occasionally Lomax glimpsed him, mostly he deduced de Maria's whereabouts from the movement of heads in the room. The prosecutor's tone was declamatory. His voice rose and fell and paused with all the control of an accomplished speaker. Without seeing him and without hearing most of his words, Lomax knew that here was a formidable opponent.

'He can sure deliver,' Marjorie confirmed during the afternoon recess. When Lomax had left the courtroom he had found her waiting in the hallway for him. They had gone to the park behind the building and bought cold drinks and fruit. The courtroom had windows, but they were far above head height and Lomax had lost all sense of the hot day outside. Now he and Marjorie sat on a bench and felt the sun on their faces. Lomax's apple tasted like sand but, mindful of Hopcroft's advice, he kept chewing it.

'What did de Maria say?'

'That Julia's a double murderer and how he's going to prove it. The noise the reporters made tapping on their little computers practically drowned him out. He tells them they're going to get sexual intrigue, blackmail, jealousy and murder and they're shaking with excitement. The jury looked like they just might enjoy the trial too.'

Lomax had difficulty swallowing.

'What did you think of Frances?' Marjorie asked.

A man a few rows ahead of Lomax had vacated his seat just before Frances had started to speak and Lomax had taken it. He was unable to see much of her from here, but at least he could hear her. Frances was caustic.

'I'm going to make an opening statement, not a movie trailer,' she had told the jury, and some of them had smiled sheepishly. 'I can't promise you entertainment. We are not here to entertain. We are not here to sell newspapers. We are here to maintain the innocence of a young woman whose life was unfairly shattered, not once. But twice. First by the destruction of the family she loved. Then six months later, when the laborious rebuilding process had begun, by this astonishing arrest. We are here to show you that the prosecution replaces evidence with sensation. Truth with speculation. And the truth is dull. The prosecution promises sexual intrigue. I will show you a loving wife. The prosecution promises blackmail. I will show you generosity. The prosecution promises jealousy. I will show you fidelity.'

'Good,' said Lomax.

Marjorie nodded proudly. 'Frances is just the best.'

Marjorie looked hot. She shuffled along the bench into the shade and began peeling an orange. She said: 'Frances isn't scared to eyeball with the jury and they like that. I mean, when was the last time that a beautiful, glamorous, intelligent woman like Frances made a passionate appeal to them?'

'This is pure psychology.'

'It's all psychology, Lomax.'

'So what's de Maria's method?'

'He doesn't move in close the way Frances does. He fires from a distance. But he seldom misses.'

'Does Judge Olmstead have any kind of reputation?'

'We-ell . . . not really,' said Marjorie, putting a piece of orange into her mouth. 'It's kind of hard to tell because this is her first murder trial.'

'What! She's a beginner!'

Marjorie threw some peel at him affectionately. He crushed it and its odour filled his nostrils.

'She hasn't been a judge for long, it's true. But everyone has to start somewhere.'

'Couldn't they have given Julia a judge who knows what the hell she's doing?'

'You missed her speech to the jury this afternoon. It's a standard speech, they all make it. They remind the jury of their responsibilities to the defendant and to the truth and so on. It's important, but some judges just sort of mumble it. Well Judge Olmstead didn't.'

'It's the first time she's said it, that's why.'

'The jury heard every word and that's good. And apparently she was a fine attorney.'

'A prosecutor?'

'Well, yes . . .'

'Oh God.'

'Lomax, calm down.'

Lomax remembered that Hopcroft had also told him to calm down. He finished his apple and tried to relax. But as soon as he returned to the courthouse he felt his heart pounding too fast and too hard.

The first witness for the prosecution was Detective Kee. He took his oath and gave his name. His tone was routine and something about the man's unperturbed manner mocked the mood of the packed courtroom. Marjorie had managed to reserve a seat for Lomax close to the front of the room and from here Kee had a clear view of him. When he noticed Lomax he squinted for a few moments, trying to remember who he was. Then his face relaxed into something like a smile. Members of the jury looked around in surprise to see why Kee was grinning.

De Maria was on his feet but he remained behind the prosecution table. He asked Kee who had first called the police to Gail Fox's apartment on the morning of November twelfth. Kee told the court about the super and how he had discovered the bodies.

'And what time did you arrive?'

'At about ten a.m. The technicians were already at work under the supervision of my colleague, Detective Asmussen.'

'Do you believe the scene you witnessed to have been pretty much as the murderer left it?'

'Hearsay, your honour,' said Frances. 'The murderer probably left the apartment hours before Detective Kee arrived; anything could have happened there since.'

'Sustained.'

De Maria continued without drawing breath. 'Detective, assuming nothing much had changed between the time of the murders and your arrival, please would you – '

'Objection. The prosecution cannot make such an assumption. There was a police evidence team at work for one thing. I doubt they were there when the crime was committed.'

The judge sighed. 'Sustained. Please phrase your questions more carefully, Mr de Maria, or Detective Kee won't ever get a chance to answer them.'

Lomax guessed that Frances had begun a systematic attempt to discredit every one of de Maria's assertions.

'Please describe what you observed on your arrival at the

apartment,' said de Maria. Kee paused, looking at Frances. This time she was silent.

'There were two policemen on the door. Crime lab guys were at work in the first room of the apartment. It's a big untidy room and there are two dead bodies on the couch. Gail Fox's face was mostly shot out. She was half lying, half sitting at the far end. Her father, Lewis Fox, was sprawled at the near end. He'd also been shot in the head, but he still had a face. There was blood all over the couch and on the rug.'

Next to the clerk of the court was what looked like a supermarket cart. Several members of the jury, suspecting it contained evidence, were looking at it expectantly.

'I have already ruled,' the judge told them, 'that you should not have pictures of this crime inflicted upon you. The detective's description is quite enough.'

Some of the jurors were visibly disappointed. There was a young man who looked for a moment as though he might argue.

De Maria had a curious habit of pulling at his fingers. He was immaculately dressed. Lomax had to admit, grudgingly, that during jury selection his kindness had been impressive. He had nearly always softened the blow of rejection with a few words of appreciation or thanks. Now he tugged on each finger in turn before saying politely: 'Detective, may I ask you to repeat your description of the exact position of the bodies?'

'Objection! The witness has already answered this question.'

'But,' protested de Maria gently, 'I fear, your honour, that some members of the jury had been expecting a visual aid.'

'All right,' agreed the judge, turning to Kee. 'You may remind the court of what you saw at the scene of the crime.'

Kee did so. Lomax suspected that this description was a shade bloodier than the last.

'It was clear,' de Maria asked, 'that the victims had been shot?'

'Yes.'

'How long have you been a detective?'

'Eight years.'

'You must have seen quite a number of murder scenes in that time, Detective.'

'Yes, many, but this was one of the ugliest.'

'Motion to strike,' said Frances, rising.

'Please give your reasons, Mrs Bauer.'

'The court is not interested in hearing how this crime compares with others the detective may or may not have seen. The detective's career· is not relevant.'

De Maria was indignant. 'Your honour, the jury has not looked at photos of the crime, they have no way of ascertaining the magnitude of its horror.'

The judge wavered for an instant and Frances was quick to plunge into the silence. 'Your honour, the jury can decide its horror for themselves from a straightforward eyewitness account. They don't need Detective Kee to tell them how to react.'

'Overruled, Mrs Bauer. Since I've taken Mr de Maria's photographs away I'm going to allow Detective Kee to give us the benefit of his experience. But no specific reference to any other cases you may have worked on, Detective.'

Frances sat down.

De Maria said: 'How did you react to what you saw, Detective Kee?'

'It made me feel sick. There was a lot of blood because of the way they'd been shot. It was a mean, vindictive crime. See – '

Frances leapt to her feat. 'Motion to strike. Detective Kee is not giving us the benefit of his professional experience but his emotional response.'

'Sustained. Strike that from the record.' The judge turned to the jury. 'That means I have to ask you to forget what you just heard. Try to forget it completely.'

There were two elderly women on the jury who seemed to have forged a friendship in the jury room. They sat next to each other and had occasionally exchanged glances during the opening statements. Now they nodded at the judge. The man who wanted to see the photographs of the crime turned to Julia complicitously. Lomax had noticed with irritation the man's previous attempts to establish eye contact with her. He hoped she was not returning the man's looks. He remembered how she drove across town, catching the eye of the other drivers.

The judge told Kee, 'Detective, please try to keep from getting too emotional about the crime.'

Kee grinned at her. Lomax suspected that the jury – all of whom looked serious, several of whom seemed tense and one of whom kept clearing his throat – did not like Kee's grins.

'You have described the scene as ugly. Indeed, you have told the court that it was one of the ugliest murder scenes you have witnessed,' de Maria said. His tone was portentous.

'That's right,' replied Kee, a fraction of a second before Frances could object.

'The prosecutor is editorializing,' she said accusingly. 'Motion to strike.'

'Sustained.'

De Maria pulled at his forefingers. 'Was your first reaction to this crime that it must have been the work of a professional killer?'

'No, no. I was sure it couldn't be. My first reaction was that it was the work of an inexperienced killer, probably a lady, who was so scared of missing that she – '

Frances was waving papers in both hands like a windmill. 'Your honour, this is an outrage!'

The court began to rustle with interest. The jury watched Frances, evidently enjoying her fury.

She thundered: 'If Detective Kee was a traffic cop, would he dare to stand in that box and tell us about lady drivers!'

'It certainly is an outrage,' agreed de Maria with mock mildness. 'There's nothing ladies can't do so well as men, and that includes killing.'

Some people in the room were amused. But Judge Olmstead was not among them. Kurt muttered something to Julia, shaking his head. Frances' look, as she turned to de Maria, seemed to confirm his last statement.

'Perhaps,' Frances told him icily, 'now that the detective's speculated on the sex of the killer, you'll also invite him to speculate on the colour of the killer?'

De Maria stared back at her, his black face motionless.

'That's enough,' said the judge, 'both of you. Counsel for the defence and the prosecution will not address remarks directly to each other again in the course of this trial or I will hold them both in contempt. I am very displeased. The trial has barely begun and the behaviour of both counsellors has been reprehensible. Detective Kee, your last statement is being struck from the record. You really should know better than to try that one with a lady judge sitting right here.'

'I'm sorry, your honour,' said Kee, without humility. 'I was trying to give an honest account of my thoughts about – '

'That's enough, Detective. Members of the jury, I know it's difficult, but you must try to forget Detective Kee's last remarks.'

But, thought Lomax, they heard those remarks. They can be struck from the record but not from the minds of the jury.

The questioning continued quietly. De Maria asked simple,

technical questions and Kee answered them soberly. Frances seldom interrupted. She had several whispered consultations with Kurt. Marjorie passed her a few notes. Julia seemed not to move or speak.

'Mrs Bauer, your cross-examination, please,' said the judge when de Maria sat down. Frances stood and there was a long pause as she looked down at her papers. Kurt and Julia and Marjorie turned their faces up to her. Lomax could see Julia's profile. Her perfect chin, her fine jawline, the nose which had been reconstructed just the way it was before.

Frances began strolling towards the witness box.

'Detective, as the senior officer at the scene of the crime, is it your job to make full and detailed notes?'

'Yes, ma'am,' said Kee.

'Do you refer to those notes in the course of the investigation?'

'Yes.'

'Does anyone else refer to them?'

'Yes. See, I'm the senior officer at the scene, and it's my case. But I report to my superiors.'

'These superiors didn't actually visit the apartment?'

'No, they saw the photos.'

'And they read your description.'

'And the reports on fibres, fingerprints, ballistics, pathology et cetera.'

'But your notes are obviously a very important part of the investigation. They re-create the crime for those ultimately in charge of solving it. They provide information for others to follow up. They refresh your memory.'

By now Frances was up close to the witness chair and Kee seemed to scent danger. He was anxious to indicate that his notes were not so very vital.

'My notes, the photos, the reports. They're all equally important.'

'I have a copy of your scene-of-crime notes right over here,' said Frances, sweeping across the court to Kurt who reached into a folder and, with efficiency, produced a few sheets of paper. On the prosecution's table, de Maria's aides ransacked files. Frances showed Kee his signature.

'Do you confirm this is your signature and that therefore these are your notes, Detective?'

Kee looked as if he wished that both signature and notes belonged to someone else. 'Yes.'

He watched miserably as Frances withdrew the notes and wandered over to the jury with them.

'How detailed are these notes?'

'Well, they contain information which I think's relevant.'

'That would include peculiarities? Little distinctive features of the room or the victims which you cannot immediately explain?'

Kee was cautious. 'Ye-es.'

'Please remind the jury how many years' experience you have as a detective in our police force.'

'Eight.'

Kee was scared now. He did not know where Frances was leading him but he suspected he wouldn't like it when he arrived.

'Eight years. In that time you have learned to take detailed records of anything which may be useful or interesting or productive in your investigation?'

'Yes ma'am.'

'I'm sure then that you will remember your detailed case notes and will, without difficulty, be able to answer a few of my questions about the scene of the crime.' Frances flicked the notes tantalizingly. 'Were the drapes closed?'

Kee looked nervous. 'Which drapes?'

'You have described a large, untidy room. The murders were discovered at eight a.m. in domestic circumstances. They might have taken place in the middle of the night, in the morning, in the evening. At the time of your arrival you didn't know. So presumably one of the relevant points you noted was whether the drapes were open or closed.'

'Well, ma'am, we don't use the drapes to tell us when a murder was committed. We have a pathology department.'

There was movement in the room, but it was more anticipation than amusement.

'Are you saying that under no circumstances whatsoever can this be relevant? Ever?'

'Well . . . it could be.'

'Then presumably you should have written it down?'

'It didn't seem too important.'

'The drapes are not in any police photographs. They are not in your notes. This information, which may be relevant, is simply excluded.' Frances sounded incredulous. She waved the notes. Kee watched them longingly as they fluttered in front of the jury.

'It didn't seem important.'

'Perhaps you fear that technicians investigating the crime might have found the drapes closed but opened them before you arrived?'

'Objection,' said a cool voice. Frances paused and turned to de Maria, her eyebrows raised.

De Maria said: 'The defence is leading the witness. He hasn't said his staff alters things. She said it. In fact, I think she's said it three times today.'

'Your honour, I'm trying to understand why something which seems important and relevant to the investigation of the crime was omitted from the detective's notes.'

'Then ask him why, don't supply the answer. Objection sustained.'

The judge was trying to establish an authority which was so recently acquired that, Lomax suspected, she even doubted it herself. But she had succeeded only in sounding petulant. This evidence of her fallibility worried him. He felt something like the confusion and anger he had sensed in Joel whan he, Lomax, made mistakes. Helen still believed that Lomax didn't make mistakes.

Frances turned back to Kee. 'Presumably you went to the police academy, Detective, where the rudiments of investigation are taught. Do you therefore agree that this is an oversight?'

'No. Nobody's asked me about the drapes. No one else seems to think they're important.'

Frances glided nearer the witness chair. Kee pulled away from her, turning to the judge.

'Your honour, the counsellor is too close,' he protested.

Frances stepped back. 'I do apologize,' she said charmingly. She put her hands on her hips, the notes lying against her body now. She spoke quietly as if she was telling Kee a secret. Everyone in the room was motionless. Everyone could hear. 'I guess I just wanted to make sure you understood. You see, we know the victims arrived at or around daybreak. They would not have closed the drapes. Nor would the killer if he followed his victims up the stairs. But he might have done so if he arrived before them and lay in wait. That is the relevance of the drapes, Detective.'

She released him from her stare, took a few paces back and gave the jury a conspiratorial glance. Some were staring at her. Others frowned at Kee. The killer was frightening. He was a man. He stalked silently up stairs or sat waiting for his unsuspecting victims behind closed drapes with his revolver on his lap. He did not sound like Julia.

Frances wandered towards the defence table. Kee looked hopeful that she had finished but she swung round to face him, resuming at her usual volume.

'However, as you think it's unimportant, I hope we can agree on another point of interest. I'm sure you must remember something very unusual about the clothing of Gail Fox, the female victim.'

Kee looked alarmed. He was silent.

'To be more specific,' said Frances helpfully, 'perhaps you'll tell the court what you noticed about her wristwatch.'

Kee leaned back in anticipation of another blow.

De Maria was on his feet.

'Your honour, this is a trial, not a spelling bee. The detective can't remember every little detail of every single case over the last year.'

'He has arrested my client for first-degree murder on the basis of such little details!' stormed Frances. 'And now he can't even remember them!'

But de Maria was not silenced by her fury. 'The detective wrote his notes last November. The counsellor should allow him to refresh his memory.'

The judge nodded. 'Stop shoving them in front of the detective's nose, Mrs Bauer, and just give them to him,' she said wearily.

But Frances, from arm's length, was already handing the notes to Kee. He fell on them greedily and began turning the pages.

'You'll find your description of Gail Fox's clothing at the foot of the first page,' Frances told him. There was a silence as Kee read the first page and then the second.

'What do your notes tell you about her wristwatch?' Frances repeated. Lomax knew what was coming next. The whole court knew.

'Well . . . nothing,' Kee admitted at last, still scanning the pages hopefully.

'Nothing? Nothing at all?' Frances was astonished. A few jurors were smothering smiles. 'She was wearing a watch on each wrist. Your report does not mention this although it is evident in the photographs. Later I propose to call someone who was at the scene and is more observant than you to testify to this fact. Do you know anyone who wears two wristwatches?'

'No.'

'Neither do I.' Frances looked at the jury questioningly to include them in this game. A few shook their heads. They didn't know anyone who wore two wristwatches either.

'Maybe,' suggested Kee, 'she just had two watches.'

'Maybe she did. But you said that it was your job, after eight years of experience, to note any peculiarities about the victims and it seems to me that here is one. But you apparently didn't even see it. Let alone write it down.'

Kee was silent.

'Finally, I'm curious to know why no mention has been made of the victim's baggage.'

'Objection,' barked de Maria rising to his feet. 'Your honour, is the counsellor going to list every little thing about the crime which she finds fascinating and which the professionals in their wisdom have dismissed?'

'In their wisdom?' echoed Frances incredulously. 'Your honour, it is my belief that this murder investigation has been dogged by police oversight and supposition. We've certainly seen some startling examples of the latter today. This is the investigation which led to the eventual arrest of my client and I am trying to indicate to the jury how sloppy it has been right from the start.'

'Objection overruled,' said the judge.

'Where exactly was the victim's baggage?' Frances asked Kee.

'I don't know,' he said morosely. He did not bother to open his notes. Lomax thought he had probably decided to take the shortest route possible between the witness box and the exit. He seemed to have lost weight since he took his oath.

'During earlier questioning you told the court that the victims had come from the airport?'

'Yes.'

'And that Gail Fox had been absent for some months?'

'Er . . . yes . . .'

'And that she and her father said they were stopping at the apartment to leave some baggage there. So where exactly did you see this baggage?'

'Erm . . . I'm not sure. Only it wasn't in the room. Or I would have written it down.'

'If it wasn't in the room, then where was it?'

'I don't know.'

'In another room?'

'I don't know.'

'In the hallway?'

'I don't know.'

'In the kitchen?'

'I don't know.'

'In the closet?'

'Objection,' said de Maria. 'Detective Kee did not find the baggage in the bathroom, the freezer, the microwave or the shower. Mrs Bauer has established that the witness does not know where the baggage was.'

'Yes,' agreed the judge peevishly, 'you've made your point, Mrs Bauer.'

'But Mr, I'm sorry, Detective Kee. Even if you did not notice this yourself, as the officer in charge of the case, and a detective of eight years' standing, surely you read all the relevant reports?'

'Well, yes . . .'

'Perhaps you have some reason to distrust the reports of your fellow officers and therefore have disregarded the information they contain?'

'No.'

'You just omitted this very important detail from your analysis of the crime. And this analysis resulted in the arrest of Mrs Fox. I see. Thank you, Detective. I have no further questions.'

Frances returned to her table. Kee's face sagged with relief. He stepped down, stumbling a little as he did so. The judge adjourned for the day. She told de Maria and Frances that she wanted to see them now in her chambers. Lomax watched jealously as Kurt escorted Julia through a web of reporters to a waiting car.

'Probably the judge's ticked off with Morton and Frances for being so mean to each other,' Marjorie explained as they walked down the long stone steps together. 'She's really playing it by the book. I mean, insisting they always give grounds for their objections when the grounds are usually obvious.'

'At least she didn't stop Frances from demolishing Kee,' Lomax commented. He had felt a slight and gradual slackening of the knots in his belly during the cross-examination.

'Constant challenge is our tactic. It slows things up and generally juries hate it but Frances is so sort of scary when she's angry that she can get away with it. Basically, though, it's a sign of a weak case.'

'But she was clever. About the drapes.'

'Actually,' Marjorie said modestly, 'that was my idea.'

Lomax turned to give Marjorie a look of admiration and tripped on the steps, awkwardly righting himself. 'And what about Gail's baggage?' he asked. 'I thought there was another report which said it was in the car.'

'It was in the evidence officer's report. Plus the notation lists everything and where it was found. So we knew where it was all along. But Kee obviously didn't look in the car and he's too lazy to have read the reports. It was pretty easy to make him look incompetent.'

Lomax stopped at the supermarket on the way home. He hovered around the store, defeated by his own lack of interest. There were rows of plump, perfect fruit. All the apples were red and identical in size and shape. They had recently been watered and their skins glistened. He bought from memory, choosing food he had chosen before.

Deputy was waiting for him, wagging his tail and barking, although this seemed more habit than genuine enthusiasm. He had eaten his meal and when Lomax gave him more he ate that too.

Kim had left a message on the answering machine.

'Be sure to switch on the news tonight. Since you've missed all my other appearances. Also, I haven't spoken to you since your peculiar friend with the nose came here. I told everyone to make sure and shower. Then guess what happened? You gotta catch me to find out and mostly I'm viewing.'

She had forgotten that he had reasons of his own for switching on the news. While he was watching it, Julia rang from Marjorie's where she was staying for the duration of the trial. Lomax turned down the TV sound.

'I've decided I don't want to testify,' she said, 'if that's what happens to you.'

'But the way Frances dismantled Kee was just terrific.'

'I wish she'd been nicer. I felt so sorry for him.'

'You are almost unbelievably cute,' he said.

The court case was on the screen now. The usual snapshots of Lewis and Gail, Kurt shepherding Julia out of court. Julia ignoring the questions of the jostling reporters and looking straight ahead of her, scared and proud and beautiful. Distracted by her appearance, he found that she had been asking him a question.

'Maybe you don't want to talk about it,' she was saying. 'I mean, it's okay if you've changed your mind.'

'Changed my mind about what?'

'About what we were talking about last night.'

'What?'

'You remember.'

'I don't. Oh, God, yes I do. I mean, of course I remember. You can just forget that if you don't want to think about it now.' Belly, heart. Scrunch, thump.

'Lomax . . . if I don't get convicted . . . let's do it.'

He hesitated. 'You mean . . . ?'

'Yes.'

'Get married?'

'If I get a not guilty.'

'Even if you get a guilty. I mean, we'll appeal and . . . well, I mean, you won't be convicted anyway. God. Shit. Do you . . . are you serious?'

'Yes, Lomax.'

When she hung up he sat dumbly in front of the TV, Deputy lying across his feet. He was hardly aware of Kim's appearance on the screen. He read the caption across her chest: 'Dr Kim Fenez, Astronomer.' He could not understand what she was talking about then realized he had forgotten to turn up the sound. She was answering questions about the sun's corona. There was some discussion of The Big Sun Out. As usual, a litany of celebrity names was recited in the same breath as the eclipse and routine warnings against looking at the sun were delivered.

Julia was going to marry him.

Deputy rolled over onto his back and wriggled from side to side, his paws hanging jauntily. Lomax scratched the dog's belly. 'Oh, Dep,' he said.

Deputy scrambled up onto Lomax's lap and began to lick his face over and over. This was more than affectionate; it was a thorough and professional cleansing. To push him away would be an act of gross ingratitude. Lomax let him complete his routine then they went out into the yard. Deputy nearly caught a squirrel and raced in small circles with excitement. They both found they were hungry. They had some more to eat. Deputy tried to copulate with a pillow during the night and the next morning attempted to eat Lomax's breakfast off his plate. A combination of all these events made Lomax feel cheerful.

But once again, as he approached the courtroom and took his seat, he was gripped by something like despair. It might have been the smell of the place, wood and polish and people and something else which reminded him of libraries. It might have been the distance of the outside world, invisible and usually inaudible through the high windows. It might have been a sense of his own impotence to influence the events which took place here. He watched as the jury filed in. He envied and feared their power.

Someone across the room was trying to attract his attention. She wore a dazzling shirt and gazed right at him, willing him to face her. It was Mrs Cleaver in the shirt she had bought at Hegarty's shopping mall. She flashed him a wide, jaundiced smile.

Marjorie had warned Lomax that the prosecution was calling a series of expert witnesses today, most of them forensic. She had said Frances could do little to challenge their testimony.

The fingerprint expert was Detective Asmussen. He discussed the prints that were found in Lewis' car and in Gail's apartment. He displayed large pictures of them. He told the court a lot of interesting facts about fingerprinting. He was helpful to the prosecution and, when Frances' turn came, equally helpful to the defence. Lomax suspected he had heard what had happened to Detective Kee yesterday.

'Would the extensive presence of my client's fingerprints be explained by the fact that she was there less than eight hours before the murders cleaning the place up in preparation for her stepdaughter's return?' Frances asked him.

'That's certainly a feasible explanation,' he agreed, 'and it would also explain why there were so many of Mrs Fox's prints and so few of Gail Fox's.'

'But Gail Fox had been absent for some months.'

'I'd still expect to find some prints there, depending how thoroughly Mrs Fox cleaned the place. They last a long time. I found a few, not many. There were some on Gail Fox's baggage in the car, of course, but not so many. Some people leave a lot of prints, some don't and Gail Fox seemed to fall into that last category.'

'Would you repeat the information about the baggage for the benefit of the jury, please, Detective. I'd like them to note it.'

'Gail Fox's fingerprints were on the baggage in the car.'

'Were there other prints in the apartment?'

'Yes, several others.'

'Whose?'

'Well, the super's, who found the bodies.'

'Who else?'

'There were some unidentified prints.'

'Did you make every attempt to identify them?'

'Well yes. We ran them through the computer, we printed everyone we thought they might just possibly belong to . . .'

'And you were unable to establish whose fingerprints these were?'

'Yes. I mean, as prints hang around for so long, most people's houses would have a few mystery prints in them . . .'

'Most people's houses, Detective, are not the scene of a double murder.'

'We did all we could to indentify them.'

'I see.' Frances' facial expression said that she did not feel Detective Asmussen had done enough.

'Is it possible that the prints might have belonged to the killer?'

'Yes.'

'Is it also possible that the killer left no prints at all?'

'Some people leave no prints.'

'Might the killer have worn gloves?'

'Yes, that's possible.'

'If you were carrying out such a murder would you wear gloves?'

'Objection!'

The judge turned to de Maria. 'Your grounds?'

Morton de Maria blinked back at her in surprise, pulled a few fingers and then explained: 'If Detective Asmussen was carrying out a murder, God forbid, he'd know every foxy trick in the book. His murder methods have nothing to do with the case before us. Plus the question is a slur on his character.'

Detective Asmussen smiled cheerfully at Frances. He gave every indication that he spent his sleepless nights planning the perfect murder.

'Please accept my apologies, Detective. I withdraw the question,' said Frances gracefully.

The policeman nodded.

'I'm simply trying to establish whether it is possible that the murderer arrived, carried out these murders, and left no trace of himself.'

'It happens.'

'Or, let us repeat for the benefit of the jury, the unidentified prints could have belonged to the killer.'

'That is also possible.'

There was a brief recess. Many people stayed in their seats but Lomax knew Dorothy Cleaver would be smoking a furtive cigarette somewhere. He found her hiding in a doorway just along the hall.

'Stand in front of me. Stand right there,' she said.

'It will look like my pants are on fire.'

'There isn't a law against burning pants. You can burn all the pants you like. But try lighting a cigarette and they send you to Alcatraz.'

'How are you?' he asked.

'Just fascinated by your murders. I wish I could hear the whole case. I can only get here mornings for a few hours.'

'It's expert witnesses all day today.'

'Fibres, wounds, fingerprints, forensic scientists telling how they do their work. I love it. Were the contacts at the high school any good?'

'They were interesting. I don't know whether Frances is planning to call them for the defence although I kind of doubt it. They were more like prosecution witnesses.'

'Frances. Is that the redhead who seems to find a lot of things objectionable?'

'That's Frances.'

'I wish she'd stop interrupting.'

'It's what she's there for.'

'It's annoying the judge.'

Lomax suspected Mrs Cleaver was right. Frances had attempted to challenge many of de Maria's questions but Judge Olmstead had been sustaining few of her objections.

'Recognize the shirt?'

'It's unforgettable.'

Mrs Cleaver cackled happily. The cackle turned to a cough. She finished her cigarette, stubbed it out surreptitiously, ground the ash out of it, and put the butt in her purse. 'Mary Mudcap doesn't leave evidence for these forensic guys,' she explained. They returned to the courtroom.

The pathologist described in a deadpan voice exactly the effects of the shots which had been administered. She stressed that the murderer's choice of hollow-nosed ammunition had resulted in particularly messy deaths. The jury hung their heads when she answered questions about the detail of the wounds, the speed of death, and the likely effect of the first bullet to hit Gail.

The fibres expert said that there was more evidence of Mrs Julia Fox in the apartment than Gail Fox but he concurred with the explanation Frances had already supplied for this. He showed the jury a large number of plastic bags which contained tiny fibres. He explained how he had gathered and then analysed his evidence. There was little for Frances to object to here. Her cross-examination re-emphasized how the forensic evidence fitted Julia's story.

When the court recessed for lunch, Lomax saw familiar faces sitting in pairs or singly around the room: Jorgen, the Nose, Doberman, Yevgeny and McMahon. As he was near the front he was one of the last to leave. They were waiting for him in a group near the door. So was Marjorie, as usual. When she saw him greeting his colleagues she disappeared into the crowd.

The astronomers all seemed to know that Lomax was due to return to the observatory soon.

'Will the court case be over by then?' asked McMahon.

'Probably.'

'Will it finish before the eclipse?'

'I'm not sure. Personally I think the court should recess so everyone can see it.'

They ate bagels outside in the park. Marjorie was sitting alone, far away on a distant bench. Lomax waved her to come over but she either did not see him or pretended not to.

'How did you like the observatory?' Lomax asked the Nose. He wanted to hear what she had smelt there but it was impossible to ask this in the presence of the others.

'It's just the most wonderful place,' she enthused. He glanced at her suspiciously. But this was not sarcasm. Her face was relaxed and smiling. She looked pretty today.

'One of the reasons I came here was to thank you in person. Everyone said you'd be here. I mean, the telescope was just amazing. And the globular clusters . . .'

'My God, Alison was lucky to see globular clusters on her first viewing,' said Jorgen. 'In my opinion, nothing is so certain to open the heart as a globular cluster.'

The Nose smiled at him. Lomax noted Jorgen's use of her name with surprise. She ate a cheese sandwich. She sat without complaint on the grass a little removed from the bagels with the smelliest fillings. It seemed strange that she had chosen to sit in the courtroom with its distinctive smells and its many warm bodies. Lomax remembered Candice's misgivings about the Nose. She suspected her of stealing from the clinic. Like Candice's other allegations, this was probably groundless. He tried to forget it but once a suspicion had been voiced, it took on a life of its own. Like a virus.

He listened to the others discussing the case. Lomax was irritated by this. First, it was his case. And second, they seemed to regard it as entertainment. He realized that only for a handful of people in the courtroom was Julia's trial more significant than a TV show. He forgave the astronomers when he detected the unstated assumption of Julia's innocence which underpinned their conversation.

'Nothing in fibres, nothing in fingerprints, nothing nowhere says Julia doesn't tell truth,' Yevgeny said, tearing at his bagel.

'If the prosecution want to prove she walked in and shot someone, they need some forensic evidence which the defence can't explain,' McMahon agreed.

Doberman told them: 'I thought about becoming a forensic scientist.'

'Very interesting profession,' agreed Yevgeny.

'But I got this place at Cornell so I took it. I forgot about that until today. And you know what? Watching those guys on the witness stand made me wish I'd done forensic. I mean the detailed study, the theories, the conclusions. It's not so very different from what we do.'

There was ritual agreement from the others. Only Doberman, thought Lomax, could think analysing man's ugliest acts was comparable with analysing the universe.

'Tell me something,' Yevgeny said to Lomax. 'Beautiful woman with red hair and green clothes. She's married?'

'Frances? Yes, she's married.'

Yevgeny shrugged to indicate this was seldom an impediment. He finished his bagel and licked his fingers.

'Hey,' said McMahon to Lomax, nodding to the retreating backs of Jorgen and the Nose, who had gone to fetch everyone an icecream. 'Who would have thought it?'

'Thought what?'

'Is she a friend of yours?'

'I only met her once. She works with Candice. She wanted to look through the telescope.'

'She sure looked through Jorgen's telescope.'

'What?'

The men moved closer together.

'A while ago she rides the Fahrhaus. A little later she's back for some more. Yesterday afternoon she comes back again. And she was still there this morning . . .' McMahon told Lomax, nodding significantly.

'And,' added Doberman, 'they sure weren't viewing all night.'

'They met in cafeteria. Not so romantic but love is found in most surprising places,' Yevgeny said nonchalantly. 'I myself found love one occasion on escalator at metro station.'

Two women in tight jeans and small T-shirts walked by. The men's eyes followed them.

'On the goddam escalator?' Doberman was saying. 'In the subway?'

'Sure.'

Doberman seemed excited by this. 'Going up?'

'I was going up. She was going down. Our eyes met, escalators is highly sex-charged. Practically this is the energy which makes them move at all. Everyone stands looking at people knowing next moment they will pass. But it is not safe to look at me this way. Jenia never lets moment pass.'

The others clamoured to hear more, and when Jorgen and the Nose returned with cold hands and cold icecreams they found Yevgeny halfway through a tale of some complexity. Lomax looked at Jorgen's fair hair and boyish features. He was smiling at nothing in particular. Lomax supposed Jorgen must smell nice.

'Doesn't the smell of the court drive you crazy?' he asked the Nose. They trailed a little behind the others as they returned through the park. Ahead of them, Yevgeny's story was still unfolding.

'Well, the guys said they were coming to support Julia, so I came with them,' she said. She sounded almost normal.

'Did you meet Julia at the observtory?'

'Oh yes. I couldn't smell her at all.'

'But Julia smells real nice!' Lomax protested.

'Soap and perfume, lots of it.'

'Julia? She wears perfume?'

The Nose smiled again. 'She did the night I was there,' she said. Jorgen, who had been disposing of the icecream wrappers, had caught up with them and was now walking by her side.

'I have to thank you, Lomax,' he said, beaming uncharacteristically, 'for sending Alison to the observatory.'

'You're welcome,' said Lomax. He envied Jorgen and Alison. How easy it had been for them to meet and get to know each other! There had been no policemen, arrests, attorneys or trial for them.

After the bright sunlight outside, the courtroom seemed dim. De Maria called his next witness, the ballistics expert. He did not share the calm professionalism of the other expert witnesses. He was an enthusiast. He talked so quickly and with such excitement that the judge had to ask him to stop and repeat himself. He described the gun and where the killer had stood and explained that the killer had moved into almost point-blank range for the final shot, aimed at Gail.

'Why might this be?' asked Morton de Maria.

'Who can tell, who knows, who can get inside the mind of such a killer?' rattled the expert.

'A pathologist has informed the court that the first shot almost certainly killed Gail Fox. Do you think the second could have been fired out of hatred or revenge?'

Frances was on her feet. 'Objection.'

'Sustained.'

'Is there any practical reason for that second shot that you can think of?'

'Perhaps to make sure she was dead. I don't know. It could maybe, perhaps, just possibly, have been fired by mistake if the killer was inexperienced with a gun,' the man gabbled.

'Please slow down,' the judge begged him.

'In your opinion, could this be the work of a professional killer?'

'It's unlikely. Too messy.'

Frances was brief with the ballistics expert. 'Is it possible to be experienced with a gun but inexperienced as a killer?'

'Of course.'

'Please read the prosecution's last question and the witness' reply,' she asked the court reporter. There was a pause. The reporter haltingly read the question and answer.

'Thank you. Now I'd like you to think about your answer again. Are you claiming that the murderer was inexperienced at killing? Or at shooting? Because, as you've just said yourself, they're not the same thing.'

'Hmmm. Ummm. Well, I'm not saying anything for definite, these are probables, but probably the murderer was an inexperienced killer. At shooting . . .' The man paused for the first time. 'At shooting, well I don't know.'

'So the murderer might have been a very experienced shot?'

'Might have been. Although the shots are so close range . . .'

'Experienced gunhandlers only shoot from a distance?'

'Well, no.'

'So your analysis is that, while you think it unlikely the murderer has killed with frequency in the past, he may be experienced at handling a gun.'

'Um . . . yes, I guess that's correct.'

'Thank you,' said Frances, 'for helping me to clarify that point.'

The next witness was the owner of a gun store. Lomax had seen the store. It was situated in a shopping mall next to a shop which sold cosmetics and which had pictures of beautiful women with pink faces in the windows. The windows of the gun store were reinforced with a thick grille and when it was closed metal shutters fortified it.

This man was also of a quixotic disposition. De Maria was friendly. He tried to put the witness at ease but the man remained tense.

'Mr Barzila, how many guns do you sell in a year?'

'It's hard to say. I mean, it's real hard. You see, we run a gun exchange programme in addition to our new gun sales. So it's real hard to say.'

'Well, try to give me an estimate of the number of guns which change hands via your store each year.'

'Including the programme. Oh. Oh.' Mr Barzila scratched his thinning hair. 'I would say in the region of just under . . . well, let's say fifteen guns a day. So that is like, four thousand, five thousand a year. About. Approximately. I can't give an exact figure. This is hard. It's difficult.'

'An approximate figure is adequate. And approximately four or five thousand guns per year pass through your store. How many years have you been in the gun business, Mr Barzila?'

'Fifteen years. Just over fifteen.'

'And when someone comes to your store to buy a gun, how do you choose the right one?'

Lomax thought this part of the questioning may have been rehearsed.

'Well, we suit the gun to the individual.'

'Oh?' asked de Maria, his tone conversational. 'Is that possible?'

'Yes sir, oh yes. That is our policy. See, it's like buying shoes. Or clothes. Or anything real personal. You got to get the gun which is right for you.'

'So if I named a gun, you'd have a pretty good idea of the kind of person who'd be likely to buy it?'

'Well, I could hazard a guess. I could – '

Lomax had been waiting for Frances' intervention.

'Objection, your honour, this game has surely gone far enough. Suiting a gun to an individual is one thing. Deducing facts about the individual from their gun is quite another.'

De Maria was firm. 'This is not unreasonable, your honour. A Smith and Wesson model 36, .38 calibre special may habitually be bought by a certain type of person.'

'Your honour, this is unscientific. None of us wants assumptions made about us from the toothpaste we use or the coffee we drink.'

'Your honour, we may not want this but it happens. Whole research and information industries are built on those assumptions. Plus a gun is more personal than toothpaste. It's more personal like perfume.'

The judge hesitated.

'Your honour – ' Frances began again.

'Please stop, Mrs Bauer. I'll allow the witness to give an indication of the type of buyer this gun is produced for.'

'Well,' said Barzila, 'the point is they're for everyone. Absolutely everyone can use them.'

De Maria paused. This was clearly not what he had been hoping Barzila would say. 'Do professionals use Smith and Wesson .38 specials?' he coaxed.

'Objection.'

'Overruled. Please answer the question, Mr Barzila.'

'They can. Generally not, but there's nothing to stop them.'

'So, this is a very easy gun to use?'

'The easiest. Load, point, shoot. Simple.'

'Do the manufacturers have a special name for this gun?'

'Well, they realized a while ago that it's the kind of gun which appeals to women, see, some women are inexperienced at handling guns. So they started releasing some of their 36s under the name "Ladysmith". See? For ladies. Ladysmith.'

'Move to strike,' said Frances promptly. 'The murder weapon was not a Smith and Wesson Ladysmith. This information is misleading.'

'But,' de Maria protested, 'Mr Barzila says that Ladysmiths are the same as the model used by the murderer.'

Frances glared at him. The judge paused.

'I'll allow it,' she said. Frances sat down.

'Let's just confirm, please,' said de Maria softly, 'that the manufacturers of the murder weapon believe that this gun is particularly suitable for women and they have marketed it as such?'

'Yes.'

'Thank you, Mr Barzila,' said Morton de Maria.

The judge called for the cross-examination and Frances advanced upon Barzila. Lomax could only see her back but it was purposeful. There was a ripple of anticipation in the room.

'You have described a typical user of a Smith and Wesson 36, Mr Barzila. Now please describe someone likely to use a Colt Government .45.'

Over on the prosecution table, de Maria's assistants were shuffling pieces of paper to see where a Colt Goverment came into the case.

'Oh, well, basically a Colt Government .45 is a gun owned by someone with intent to kill, or someone who takes the gun club seriously, maybe someone interested in target discipline, possibly ex-military, almost certainly male, for sure experienced.'

Frances turned to the jury. She held up her arms momentarily, palms outwards, as if someone had just pointed a gun at her.

'The jury can decide for themselves whether or not I fit that description.'

'Objection!'

'They may be interested to know that I have owned a Colt Government .45 for ten years.'

'Objection!'

'Mrs Bauer.'

'It is my first gun. I have never fired it or any other gun.'

'Your honour! Objection!' De Maria was anguished now.

Members of the jury grinned broadly at Frances. She smiled back at them. Barzila began to tell her that she owned the wrong kind of gun. People started to laugh.

'Your honour, please!' bellowed de Maria. 'Mr Barzila accurately described the killer-instinct typical of this gun owner, but that does not excuse her behaviour!'

The laughter had caught and the court was noisy now. Judge Olmstead hammered with her gavel. For a few moments it seemed that control of the room was slipping away from her.

'Mrs Bauer, you heard the prosecution's objection but you persisted with your point. Unlike Mr Barzila you are not under oath and it is not acceptable for you to turn yourself into a witness or, worse, an exhibit. To deter you from further departures from protocol I require first that the preceding exchange be struck from the record and second that you produce your Colt Government in my chambers tomorrow morning with proof of ownership.'

'Certainly, your honour.'

'Loaded,' said de Maria acidly, 'or unloaded?'

In the laughter that followed, it became clear to Lomax that Judge Olmstead now disliked Frances. By charming the jury and intimidating the prosecution she had alienated the judge. This seemed to him dangerous.

Frances turned back to Barzila.

'Forgive me, Mr Barzila,' she said, 'but my client's future – indeed, her life – could depend on the accuracy of your forecasts. Have you carried out any detailed numerical survey to link certain guns with certain owners?'

'Nothing on paper, no.'

'You work by hunch?'

'Well it's based on experience. It's not like intuition. It's based on many years in the gun business dealing with many different people and many different guns. So it's more than a hunch.'

'Are you saying that if murders are carried out with a Smith .38 then for a fact the killer must be someone inexperienced at handling a gun?'

'It's a simple gun to use, attractive to amateurs. And it's not the best gun for the job.'

'But it did the job. Are you saying that for sure anyone using this gun must be inexperienced at firing it?'

'Well, no, not for a fact. They may have all kinds of reasons for using it that I don't know about.'

'Thank you, Mr Barzila.'

This time Lomax saw Marjorie in the hallway ahead of him. He

402

slipped through the crowds and caught up with her as she was leaving the building.

'Why didn't you come over at lunchtime?' he asked.

'I didn't want to interrupt.'

'Those guys were all from the observatory. They would have liked to meet you.'

She shrugged. Lomax looked at her uncertainly. 'What are you doing now?' he asked.

'Going to Sachs Smith. I have a terrible feeling I'm going to spend the night locating a Colt Government .45.'

She pattered down the steps ahead of him. Lomax watched her go. She had not succeeded in bruising his good humour. In the entire day's evidence, nothing the jury had heard indicated that Julia could be guilty.

30

Gerry Hegarty was first in the witness box the next day. He looked nervous. He adjusted his cufflinks. He coughed several times before taking the oath. If he saw Lomax he did not react. He delayed looking at Julia but when his eye alighted on her he gave her a kind smile which must have been noticed by most of the jury. Here was a man who might have been subpoena-ed to appear as a witness for the prosecution but without a word he had indicated that he did not believe Julia had murdered his friend. Lomax, who as usual had begun the day with his belly knotted, began to relax.

Morton de Maria asked Hegarty his name and occupation and how long he had known Lewis Fox. He asked how often he and Lewis had met and requested a description of the nature of their friendship.

'Mr Hegarty, the jury is having difficulty hearing you,' said the judge, 'and frankly so am I.'

Hegarty apologized. For a while he spoke more loudly but soon his voice resumed its habitual gentleness. There was less movement in the room as people listened harder.

'In your opinion was your close friend Lewis Fox happily married?' asked de Maria.

'Objection.'

'Sustained.'

'Did Lewis Fox ever discuss his marriage with you?'

'Not much.'

'A little?'

'A little.'

'What did he say?'

'He made it clear how much he loved his wife,' said Hegarty, looking at Julia. She bowed her head. The two older women in the jury who always sat next to each other smiled at her. Marjorie put an arm around her. Kurt put his hand on her shoulder. Lomax saw her back shudder and realized that Julia must be crying quietly. Several more members of the jury noticed. They looked at her, Lomax thought, with kindness.

'He said he loved her?'

'Oh yes, more than once.'

'But was he a faithful husband?'

'Objection!'

The judge turned to Frances. 'Your grounds, counsellor?'

'My client has endured considerable hardship already and now the prosecution is adding to her distress unnecessarily. The witness has confirmed that Lewis Fox loved his wife and often said so. His fidelity has no relevance.'

'Your honour,' said de Maria, 'I don't want to add to Mrs Fox's unhappiness, but she's on trial for murder here and it's more important for the jury to know the facts than to save her embarrassment.'

The judge paused. She looked at Julia, who was still crying. There was a silence in the room. On the press benches the reporters swayed inward as if blown by a sudden breeze.

'Please step forward, counsellors,' said the judge.

De Maria and Frances stood beneath the judge's podium. Judge Olmstead leaned down to them. They spoke in whispers. Lomax could not hear them. Possibly the jury could. Around the room, people began talking to each other in hushed voices. Lomax wondered what they were saying. No one spoke to him. Finally the two counsellors drew back. Frances returned to the table with an expression of resignation. She said something briefly to Julia. De Maria took up a position near the witness box.

'I have decided,' the judge told the jury, 'to allow prosecuting counsel to pursue this question. But he had better be able to prove to us later that it is a really essential part of his argument.'

It seemed to Lomax that the court was more still and more silent than it had been so far. Morton de Maria turned back to Hegarty.

'Was Lewis Fox a faithful husband?'

'I have reason to believe that he slept with other women,' said Hegarty softly. He added kindly, 'As many loving husbands do.'

People for whom Julia's face was visible turned to her. This included most of the jury. Lomax was pleased to see that she held her head up.

'Was he sexually promiscuous?'

'Objection. Promiscuous means different things to different people.'

De Maria nodded. 'I withdraw my question.' He turned back to Hegarty. 'How many women do you believe he slept with after his marriage to Julia Fox?'

Hegarty pulled at his cufflinks desperately. 'Lewis didn't necessarily confide in me. I can't answer that question.'

405

'How many to your knowledge?'

There was a long pause.

'To my knowledge, two.'

'You know about two but there could have been more?'

'Objection.'

'Sustained.'

'Did these liaisons take place early in his married life?'

'He was only married five years.'

'Did these sexual liaisons occur towards the end of that five years?'

'Yes, I guess so.'

'Do you think that Lewis Fox's interest in other women was an indication of a deteriorating marriage?'

'Objection. The witness is not a psychiatrist.'

'Sustained.'

'Did Lewis Fox ever confide in you fears about his wife's mental health?'

'He never said she was crazy.'

'Not crazy, perhaps. But I understand he expressed some concern.'

'He just thought she got a little touchy at times.'

'Was he sufficiently worried about this to take any action?'

'I can't think of any.'

'Lewis Fox, early in his marriage, had given his wife a revolver for self-protection. I understand he was later so worried about her mental state that he took it away from her.'

'He asked me to look after a gun, that's all.'

'Oh, come along now, Mr Hegarty!' De Maria pulled at a few fingers in turn – one, two, three. 'Surely this was Julia Fox's gun?'

'I'm not sure exactly whose gun it was.'

'He didn't tell you? He just produced a gun with no explanation at all and asked you to keep it?'

'He said that his household was tense and he preferred that no one had access to a gun.'

'By which he meant his wife?'

'Possibly.'

'What kind of a gun was it, Mr Hegarty?'

'A Taurus.'

'To be precise, I believe it was a Taurus 85 model, .38 calibre special. Is that correct?'

'Yes.'

'A revolver that is similar although not identical to the murder weapon. And he removed it from his house. He bought it for defence purposes. For protection. But he feared that it might actually be used to shoot someone. In an act of aggression.'

'He didn't say that. He just said he wanted me to keep it for him, and I did. I still have it.'

'Why do you think he preferred his wife not to have access to a gun?'

'He didn't say his wife.'

'But he indicated that she was in a neurotic state and that he did not want a gun in the house?'

Hegarty was both intelligent and stubborn. 'Mr de Maria, you're making assumptions there. For all I knew, Lewis may have been scared he would use the gun himself.'

Lomax felt sorry for de Maria. His witness was determined to help the prosecution as little as possible. But the attorney showed no sign of concern.

'Did Lewis Fox remove the gun from the house at about the same time that he confided his fears about his wife's mental stability?'

'It's hard for me to remember at this distance.'

'When did he give you the gun?'

'Early last summer.'

'And he was killed in November. When approximately did he confide his worries about his wife?'

'That's what I can't remember.'

'Try hard to remember, Mr Hegarty.'

But Hegarty shrugged. 'Some time last year. Possibly spring. I'm not sure.'

'So last year there were three dramatic events for the Fox family. Lewis Fox was concerned about his wife's mental stability. Lewis Fox removed a gun from the house because he feared its misuse. And Lewis Fox and his daughter were shot dead.'

'Objection,' said Frances. 'There were many events for the Foxes last year. A happy vacation. A study trip to France. Plans to set up a new law firm. The counsellor has selected three random events and given them a spurious significance.'

The judge paused. 'I will allow the question to stand, Mrs Bauer. But members of the jury, I ask you to bear in mind the comments of the defence.'

De Maria said to Hegarty: 'Please confirm that the three events I have listed actually took place in the order I have listed them.'

'I confirm it,' said Hegarty dully.

'Thank you,' said de Maria, sitting down.

There was a whispered conversation between Frances and Kurt

before she stood up. Lomax was sure she would not miss the opportunity to milk a sympathetic witness.

'Mr Hegarty, is it true to say that Lewis Fox worked hard and played hard?' she asked, rapidly advancing as usual towards the jury and the witness box.

'That's accurate,' agreed Hegarty.

'Was he under stress during the last year of his life?'

'He was always under stress but, yes, I guess it was an especially difficult year for him.'

'Was the stress centred mainly at work or at home?'

'At work. At home he had a loving and supportive wife.'

'She helped him through the bad times?'

'I know she did. And he was a great support to her, too.'

'Let us remind the jury, this was a loving marriage.'

'It was a loving marriage,' Hegarty repeated like a catechism. Lomax hoped the jury did not find this over-rehearsed.

'Why was he stressed at work?'

'He was thinking, along with other partners of Sachs Smith, of setting up a big new law firm in town.'

'Quite a major undertaking.'

'Huge. He was very tense about it. Secrecy was necessary, of course, and that added to the pressure.'

'Apart from anything else the project could cause him financial headaches, I presume?'

'Oh yes. Starting up isn't cheap.'

'Therefore he needed to raise funds.'

'Yes.'

'Did he discuss the sum of money he would need?'

'Not in any exact terms. But we threw a few figures around.'

'What kind of figures?'

'Half a million dollars.'

'How did he propose to raise this money?'

'There were various options. All the partners could contribute. Or they could raise a loan.'

'Lewis Fox's wife had a trust fund in her name. It consisted of money left to her by her father. Did Lewis ever suggest that he could borrow this money from his wife's trust fund?'

'He didn't spell it out. However, he did refer to the possibility of an interest-free loan from a sympathetic party. I assumed he meant a grateful client. But I see now he could have meant Julia.'

'Given what you know of their relationship, is it possible that Lewis Fox would have asked his wife for this money?'

'Objection. This is supposition.'

'Your honour, Julia Fox wrote out a very large cheque. I'm trying to establish where it went.'

'Objection overruled.'

'From what I know of Julia and Lewis, Lewis would never have had to ask for the money. If she knew he needed it, she would simply have given it.'

Frances smiled and thanked him.

Hegarty had done all he could to help Julia but his testimony left Lomax feeling uncomfortable. Mrs Cleaver was again in the court-room and when a recess was announced she signalled Lomax to meet her outside.

'Screen me,' she ordered him from a nearby doorway. He stood in front of her while she lit a cigarette. Her grey hair was yellowing with nicotine.

'Was that the guy with the automobile?' she asked.

'Yes.'

'I didn't like it.' She drew fiercely on the cigarette, screwing her face around it. 'By the time the prosecutor had finished it seemed your girl was too dangerous to own a gun. And the redhead didn't manage to eradicate that impression.'

Someone tapped Lomax on the shoulder.

'Your pants are on fire, Lomax.'

He swung round to see a familiar grin dressed in unfamiliar clothes. The sheriff was out of uniform. He wore a shirt of many colours. Hatless, his head was a curious egg shape. His thin hair was slicked to one side. He was dressed for a day out at the theme park or in the shopping malls, but he had chosen the court for his entertainment instead.

'Dorothy!' he whooped, looking past Lomax.

Mrs Cleaver narrowed her eyes and lowered her cigarette.

'You never are smoking in the county courts! You never are!' he roared. 'Didn't you know it's strictly forbidden? Sure you did! But you decided to do it anyway. And after I caught you in the mall!'

People stared as they passed. A uniformed policeman down the hallway was looking at them with interest.

'Shhhh,' hissed Mrs Cleaver. 'Either arrest me or quiet down, Murphy.'

'Well. As it's my day off I won't arrest you. I'm gonna warn you.'

Mrs Cleaver stubbed the cigarette out carefully. 'Okay, you've warned me, now stop attracting attention to yourself.' She walked back to the courtroom, leaving Lomax and McLean in the doorway.

'Women,' muttered the sheriff, smiling ruefully at Lomax for support. 'Women.'

'You didn't have to humiliate her,' Lomax said. 'She's addicted. She can't help it.'

'I did too. She's polluting people's air around here with her addiction. She should go right outside to the park.'

Lomax said nothing.

'How's she doing, Lomax?' asked McLean, standing too close to him as usual. He smelt strongly of something that might have been aftershave, or possibly hair oil.

'Who?'

'You know who. How's she doing?'

'If you mean Julia, okay I guess. I mean, okay yesterday.'

'Decided to come along and see for myself. I like to follow a case through.'

Lomax thought of the sheriff's report, filled with innuendo about Julia's guilt. He remembered the sheriff's numerous unnecessary and intimidating visits to Julia's house and his subsequent role in her arrest. Following a case through, for McLean, meant seeing a conviction. Probably he was disappointed not to have been called as a witness. Lomax looked down furiously at the sheriff's oily hair and, to his surprise, the weird shape of his head and sweaty brow filled him with pity. It was McLean's day off and he had nowhere better to go than the courthouse. And even if he had somewhere to go, perhaps he had no one to go with.

'Are you married, Murph?' he asked in a tone that bordered on the affectionate. The sheriff looked at him strangely.

'Divorced,' he replied, his voice unusually subdued. 'Better get in there or we might miss something interesting.'

They filed back into the courtroom and were separated in the crowd.

De Maria's next witness was an attorney. Lomax guessed that Claire Journeaux had often appeared in court but never in the witness chair. She seemed intrigued by the novelty of viewing events from there. She gazed around her with a confidence which made Lomax uneasy. He did not know why she had been called.

Some witnesses took the oath with embarrassment, other stood straight and announced it like the pledge of allegiance, others were anxious to show their sincerity. Claire Journeaux's oath was dispatched with professional fluency. There was the usual pause as de Maria rose, consulted his colleagues, pulled his fingers. During this silence, Claire Journeaux sat with the compacted stillness of the habitual and compulsive mover.

Under direction from de Maria she revealed that she had been until recently an attorney in the prosecutor's office. She had known Lewis Fox professionally for some years and last spring he had discussed with her the new firm he and other Sachs Smith partners hoped to start.

When she moved her head sharply, as she often did, the globes which hung from her ears orbited dangerously. She was aged about fifty, knife-thin, short-haired and, Lomax sensed, formidable.

She had been invited to join Lewis' new law firm. This had necessitated a number of telephone calls to Lewis, outside the office, last November. At about seven a.m. on November twelfth she had attempted to contact Lewis.

'Forensic evidence shows us that the murders probably occurred between five-thirty and six thirty. At seven a.m. Julia Fox claims to have been at home awaiting the return of her husband and step-daughter. What happened when you telephoned her house?'

'I got Lewis' voice on the answer machine inviting me to leave a message. That was kind of annoying. I felt sure someone must be there at that time of the morning. I didn't know about his daughter coming home.'

The attorney's energy showed in the constant mobility of her face. Expressions flitted across it as she spoke. Surprise at finding the answering machine. Then annoyance. Then some headshaking because she had not known about Gail's return.

'Did you leave a message, Ms Journeaux?'

'I did. I said I thought maybe everyone was in the shower and that I'd call back shortly. I wanted to contact him before leaving for the office.'

'Did you telephone again?'

'About fifteen minutes later.'

'And what happened?'

'I got the machine again.'

'Did you leave a message?'

'Same again. I figured he might be out jogging.'

'That's strange,' de Maria said. He pretended to be bewildered by her answer. 'Because Mrs Fox must already have been worried about the delay in her family's arrival. It's strange she didn't snatch the telephone as soon as it rang. Did – '

'Objection. This is not the place for the prosecution to give us the benefit of his theories in basic psychology.'

'Sustained.'

As usual, de Maria's rephrased question followed within a second. 'Did Julia Fox pick up the telephone, although the machine was on?'

'No, she didn't.'

'Did you call again later?'

'Yes, I called Sachs Smith from my office. I didn't want to do that but I didn't have much choice. They said Lewis would be late to work that day. So I called his home again.'

'What time was it now?'

'Maybe eight thirty.'

'And?'

'Just the machine. So I hung up the phone.'

'How frustrating for you, Ms Journeaux.' De Maria was all sympathy. 'Did you call again?'

'Yes. At maybe nine thirty.'

De Maria looked vexed. 'Still that darned machine, Ms Journeaux?'

'No. This time someone picked it up.'

'Oh!' Delight and astonishment. 'Immediately?'

'Well, no, it rang for quite a while.'

'Who answered?'

'Lewis' wife.'

'Did you tell her of the difficulty you'd had contacting him?'

'Yes. She said she'd been out.'

'She said she'd been out?' Amazement. 'But her statement to the police says she stayed in!'

'She told me she'd been out.'

'How very curious!' Intrigued. 'Did she elucidate, Ms Journeaux?'

'No. She said he wasn't there right now and she was kind of worried about him. She said she'd get him to call when he arrived.'

'How did Mrs Fox sound?'

'Upset. Worried. Sort of faint on the line. I could hardly hear what she said.'

'What was your reaction to all this?'

'It was disturbing. Naturally it didn't occur to me that he was dead.'

'Thank you, Ms Journeaux.'

Throughout Claire Journeaux's testimony there had been whispered discussion at the defence table between Julia, Kurt and Frances.

The discussion continued as the court waited. Kurt and Marjorie leaned in. Julia was talking a lot, shaking her head. The delay made Lomax tense. The wooden seats in the courtroom were uncomfortable and it was so crowded that he was unable to stretch his legs or unfold his arms. The jury began to grow restless. The judge yawned. Claire Journeaux twitched a little with impatience.

Frances rose without apology. 'Ms Journeaux, would you please point out the defendant?'

Journeaux was withering. 'She's sitting right next to you, counsellor.'

Frances and Journeaux must know each other. When Journeaux was in the prosecutor's office, Frances had probably defended cases against her. Lomax wondered what history was behind this exchange.

'Have you seen Julia Fox before?'

'Well yes.'

'When?'

'I've seen her on TV and in the newspapers lately . . .' Claire Journeaux's eyes looked around the room.

'But have you seen her before in person?'

'Perhaps a couple of times at an association dinner or a Christmas party.'

'Did you speak to her on these occassions?'

'I believe so. Perhaps not directly. I don't remember.'

'Try to remember, Ms Journeaux.'

There was a pause while everyone in the room watched the attorney thinking. She placed both her hands on her knees, leaned on them and creased her face with thought. Finally she said slowly: 'I think there was one occasion when we stood together in a large group at a party. I may have spoken to her.'

'Exactly how large was the group?'

'Maybe four, five, six people.'

'Not so very large. What did you talk about?'

'Objection. Is the defence counsellor writing a society column? Why else would she want this irrelevant information?'

The judge nodded. 'Sustained. Spare us the social chit-chat, Mrs Bauer.'

'Your honour, with respect, I'm seeking to establish that my client's failure to pick up the telephone was caused by her relationship with the witness and not by her absence.'

Judge Olmstead looked at Frances with dislike. 'Then get to the point more rapidly, counsellor.'

Lomax felt that the judge was wrong. She had allowed her antipathy for Frances to influence her decision. The judge's mistake increased his uneasiness.

'Ms Journeaux, my client remembers an unpleasant conversation with you at a Christmas party soon after her marriage. Her step-daughter was present and my client recalls you looking from one to the other and expressing amazement that they were not both Lewis Fox's daughters. She says you asked her when she was due to graduate from high school. Do you recall that conversation?'

'Not word for word.'

'Do you recall thinking something along those lines?'

'Who wouldn't? She was less than half his age.'

'Are you a woman who habitually expresses her thoughts?'

'Not always.'

'My client recalls that on this occasion you did. She recalls that your tone of voice was intimidating and that she was upset throughout the party. Is that possible?'

'Most women would be flattered to be told they look young.'

'Evidently my client did not understand your intent as flattering. Is it possible that you upset her on meeting her in the manner I've described?'

Claire Journeaux's face flickered. 'She must be a very sensitive little girl.'

'Ah,' said Frances. 'Ah. I wonder if that is the first time you have used such a patronizing tone about Julia Fox? Perhaps, perceiving your attitude to her, as the court now also must, Julia Fox did her best to avoid you. Perhaps that is why she did not pick up the phone when she heard your voice on the answering machine? Perhaps, when she was tense and worried about her husband, you were not someone she would choose to speak with?'

'I have no idea,' said the attorney, red-cheeked now and throwing her earrings around, 'what went through her mind.'

Lomax felt ready to applaud. Frances walked towards the defence table but she did not sit down. Kurt handed her some sheets of paper. There was another discussion and Frances turned again to face the witness.

'Finally, Ms Journeaux, I'd like to ask you about the financial arrangements which Lewis Fox had made for his new law firm.'

Claire Journeaux frowned. 'Your honour,' she said politely to Judge Olmstead, 'I hope that the counsellor won't use her present position to extract confidential information about the finances of a new rival firm.'

The judge looked back at her unblinkingly. Maybe there was also a history here. If so, only the two women would know it. Unless the judge's decision was influenced by it. Lomax listened to the exact register of the judge's answer.

She said: 'It is my role to see that only information relevant to the case before me is requested. If that information is of a confidential nature, I will take appropriate action.'

Lomax detected the warning note. The attorney nodded, apparently satisfied but perhaps also chastened.

'I don't intend to question you about your firm's current financial position,' Frances told her. 'I want to know about the financial plans made by Lewis Fox.'

'I don't know anything about them.'

'But he proposed to make you a partner in the new firm. Presumably he discussed finances with you?'

'No.'

'Didn't you ask?'

'Lewis said he was able to raise the necessary finance.'

'Didn't you want to satisfy yourself that the firm was built on sound foundations before agreeing to a partnership?'

'Lewis was honest and trustworthy. I'd known him for years. If he said it was sound, it was sound.'

Lomax wondered if Lewis had liked Claire Journeaux. She was not the sort of woman to attract him. But perhaps he respected her.

'It would have been his duty to tell you, as a possible partner, if there was a large loan outstanding?'

Journeaux paused. She shrugged. 'Perhaps.'

'Certainly, if he was as honest and trustworthy as you claim.'

De Maria stood. 'Objection. Who's answering these questions? The witness or the defence?'

'Sustained. Don't lead the witness, Mrs Bauer.'

Frances scarcely paused. 'Would you agree that an honest and trustworthy man would have had a duty to inform you, as a possible partner, if the firm's finances were based on an expensive loan?'

'Yes.'

'But he did not?'

'He did not.'

'Ms Journeaux, it's expensive to start a law firm. New offices, desks, staff . . . you must have wondered where the money was coming from?'

'I guess I assumed it was coming from Lewis.'

415

'You thought he was a very wealthy man? You thought he had very large sums, we have heard that sums of a half a million dollars were under discussion, you thought he had such large sums readily available?'

'I thought it was possible that Lewis, his family and his friends might have that kind of money.'

'Family? What family?'

'I don't know.'

'His son?'

'I don't know.'

'His daughter?'

'I don't know.'

'His wife?'

'I don't know.'

'Don't you, Ms Journeaux? Were you completely ignorant of Julia Fox's financial position? Remember, you are under oath.'

'I don't need to be reminded that I am under oath, counsellor,' said Claire Journeaux, her face turning the colour of old tapestries.

'Please tell the court whether it had so much as crossed your mind that Lewis Fox's wife might be the reason he could assure you that the firm's finances were secure?'

'A lot of things crossed my mind.'

'Including the possibility that Julia Fox was financing the new firm?'

'Including that possibility.'

'Was that because you had knowledge of Julia Fox's financial position?'

'Not knowledge, no.'

'What about rumours? Hearsay?'

'People said she had a large trust fund.'

'People said she had a large trust fund. And it had occurred to you, it had crossed your mind, it was a possibility, that this might therefore give his new project an underlying financial security.'

The witness was reluctant. 'I guess it had occurred to me. That's all.'

'Thank you,' said Frances. 'I have no further questions.'

Claire Journeaux stepped down. Her face was still burgundy.

Marjorie did not wait for Lomax today but he located her on a shady park bench. She was eating an apple, red and perfect, which looked just like the apples in Lomax's supermarket although they were probably from a different store. He sat down next to her, took his bagel out of a white bag and began to munch it.

'Hi,' she said at last.

'Oh, hi Marjorie.'

'I'm being mean to you because of the way you walked off with your friends yesterday.'

'Not true.'

''Tis too.'

'I waved you over to meet them.'

She sighed her discontent.

They ate in silence, except that Marjorie's apple was noisy. She chewed in a bovine way.

'How can I pretend to be your fiancé if you won't talk to me?' he asked. 'I mean, we were dong so well fooling people with all our little waves and smiles.'

Marjorie scowled in reply.

'How do you think this morning's cross went?' he asked.

'Frances did well against Claire Journeaux.'

'And Hegarty?'

'Hegarty I think we lost on.'

'What's coming up this afternoon?'

'You don't want to know.'

'It's going to be tough?'

'It's going to be real tough.'

'So far, Hegarty's the only witness I recognize, except for Detective Kee, of course.'

'They're prosecution witnesses.'

'Will Frances be calling any of mine?'

'What do you mean, yours?' Marjorie turned to him. She was smiling but her smile was not kind. The apple had made her lips especially red, or her teeth especially white.

'People I found.'

'You didn't find anyone. Except maybe that woman in Arizona.'

'Drapinski, the high school teacher. A kid called Joe Johnson. Um . . .'

'Lomax. Just what do you think Kurt and I have been doing all this time?'

His throat tightened. He began to feel uncomfortable. He had been slumped on the bench but now he sat up. 'Splattering cows over Nevada?'

'There isn't anyone you found who we didn't find. Some of them we interviewed before you did.'

Unable to speak, he nodded.

'None of them told me that,' he said at last. 'And neither did you. I thought I was asking questions about Gail and you were finding out about Lewis.'

'Did you really expect us to leave any part of an important murder investigation to a complete amateur?'

Lomax could not look at her. He replaced the remains of his bagel, which seemed dry now, back into the white paper bag and twisted the corners over. Put like that, he could only agree with Marjorie. Of course Julia's future was too important to risk in his hands. Of course it was. Kurt and Frances and Marjorie had been letting him play investigator all summer. They had been humouring him. His face was hot. His whole body was hot. His discomfiture was embarrassing Marjorie, who looked away. They sat staring in different directions. Some small children were playing a ball game on the grass outside the shade of the tree. The sun shone on them. They were fighting over the ball.

'Wanna buy a filter so you can watch the eclipse?' asked a dishevelled man, appearing from nowhere. He was holding a selection of plastic sunglasses. They said they didn't. They watched the man work his way down the other benches. No one was buying.

Simultaneously Lomax and Marjorie rose to return to the courtroom.

Without warning, she linked her arm through his. 'Lomax, you were really cute,' she said, benevolent now, 'with your notebooks and your head-scratching. But there's no way we could have just handed you interviewees.'

He allowed her arm to stay where it was. 'What head-scratching?'

'You sort of scratch your head with your elbow in the air when you're thinking. Didn't you know that?'

'No.'

'Well it's cute.'

He could see now what a shambling and disorganized affair his investigation had been. He remembered how on various occasions Mrs Cleaver and Kim had helped him, and how he had sometimes taken Deputy Dawg along to interviews. And apparently he had walked around with his elbow in the air.

'I may be a complete amateur with some annoying habits . . .'

Marjorie interrupted him. 'Your habits aren't annoying, they're endearing. And if you want to know something funny, Kurt's started head-scratching now. I've seen him do it at least twice.'

Lomax paused but continued: 'I may be a complete amateur, but I turned up some evidence which you guys missed.'

418

'Sure. Evidence for the prosecution. That's the kind of thing amateurs do.'

Lomax thought of Jefferson, whom he was sure the defence – and hoped the prosecution – had not yet discovered. Jefferson made him feel protective. And he remembered the blue airmail letter hidden in the drawer in his room.

Marjorie squeezed his arm. 'A lot of your work was good,' she said. 'Very good. I'm not telling you that again.'

He smiled at her gratefully but he walked into the courtroom feeling diminished. He slid into his seat and after a few moments smelt hair oil. Murphy McLean was beside him. As the room filled, McLean shuffled closer and closer. He had been drinking beer during the recess. Evidently he had some friends. They were here in the courthouse or in the nearby police station.

He leaned across Lomax and whispered loudly: 'They say it ain't looking too good for her.' A few people heard and turned around. The judge entered and the court rose.

De Maria called Lewis' former secretary from Sachs Smith. She gave evidence that, like Claire Journeaux, she had telephoned Lewis early in the morning on November twelfth and subsequently, and that Julia had not answered her either. Asked about her working relationship with Lewis, she said that she had tired of Julia's persistent calls. There had been many requests to fetch Lewis out of important meetings or away from clients and eventually Lewis had asked her to tell his wife he was out of the office. Then Julia had started to call in person, usually on some flimsy pretext. As if she were trying to catch her husband out. The secretary had not liked to lie. She had not liked the atmosphere of suspicion. She had been planning to quit.

Lomax guessed she was a good secretary. She answered with quiet efficiency. Frances chose not to cross-examine her. Murphy McLean indicated the inadvisability of this move by a sharp intake of breath which Lomax felt sure the jury must hear.

People began to mutter as they waited for the next witness. Lomax had time to remember and be stung again by Marjorie's words. So he was cute and endearing but a complete amateur. Then Homer was crossing the room to the witness chair and Lomax's own feelings were forgotten as he stiffened with anxiety on Homer's behalf. It was in Julia's interests for Frances to savage this frightened and harmless man. Lomax had always known this. But now he had witnessed Frances' ferocity. He could guess how many tense and sleepless nights

419

had preceded that walk across the crowded room. He could guess how, for Homer, it seemed a long walk. He admired the steadiness of his step.

Homer wore a suit. He looked surprisingly comfortable, as if he wore it to work every day. He was sworn in. When he took his seat he was still, his head bowed, his feet scarcely touching the ground.

'Mr Craig . . .' began Morton de Maria, and Homer looked up at him. De Maria asked him about his job and how well he had known Gail and how often he had seen members of her family. The answers were short and clear.

'Now Mr Craig, early in the morning of November twelfth an ugly double murder occurred in the very apartment building where you live and work. Do you see anyone in this room who you saw that night?'

Homer looked around him for the first time. The room was silent as his eyes ran over the jury and the rows of people, the bailiff, the prosecution. It seemed that the last place he looked was towards the defence table where Julia sat.

'Yes, sir, I do,' he said. His voice was hoarse.

De Maria was gentle. 'Please point to that person.'

'No,' said Homer, shaking his head repeatedly and nervously, although his voice was firm again. 'I will not point, sir, because I believe, sir, that's a rudeness. I will simply say that she is sitting at the table in front of me and to my right.'

'We must be specific, Mr Craig. We don't want the jury to misunderstand.'

De Maria was walking towards Julia. He moved behind the defence table and the defence team rustled with distaste like a hissing cat.

'Do you mean this woman?'

'I do.'

'Can you name her?'

'She is Mrs Julia Fox. She is the stepmother of Gail Fox who lived in apartment Number Six.'

'Did you see her on November twelfth?'

'Yes.'

'Where was she?'

'Outside. In the parking lot. She was getting into a car. She got in and drove away.'

'What time was this?'

De Maria was approaching the witness stand. There was gravity in his walk. His facial expression invited the jury to believe Homer. Homer's face creased with concentration.

'It was five forty-five a.m.'

'Five forty-five, and the police believe the murders might have occurred shortly before that time.'

'Objection. The police also believe the murders might have occurred after that time. The police are not so precise as the counsellor implies.'

'Upheld.'

'How did you know . . .' continued de Maria. Homer and the prosecutor had continued to look at each other through this exchange, waiting. 'How do you know it was five forty-five a.m.?'

'I had looked at the clock because I had just woken. I thought maybe it was time to get up.'

'What woke you?'

'I don't know.'

'Gunshots?'

'Objection.'

'Sustained.'

'I didn't,' said Homer, 'hear any gunshots. Not that I was aware of.'

'It's all right, Mr Craig,' the judge told him. 'I have sustained the defence's objection and that means you don't answer the question.'

Homer nodded. 'I'm sorry, ma'am,' he said.

De Maria asked: 'You saw the defendant from your window?'

'Yes.'

'Why did you get up?'

'I wondered who was out there. I'm not a nosy man. But I heard the front door close, it has its own special sound. And I heard someone was opening and closing the trunk of a car, they seemed to be out there for some time . . . I wondered if someone was going away . . . I need to know when people are away, it's part of my job. So I got out of bed and looked. She was just getting into the car.'

'Are you sure it was Mrs Fox?'

'Yes.'

'Then later, it was you who discovered the bodies and alerted the police.'

'Yes.'

'Did you tell the police that you had seen Mrs Fox that morning?'

Homer hung his head. 'I did not, sir.'

'When did you tell them?'

'Four, maybe five months later.'

'Why did it take you so long, Mr Craig?'

'I did not want to be responsible . . .' Homer's voice wavered at last. 'I didn't want her to be . . .' He paused, until it became clear that he did not intend to complete his sentence.

'You didn't want . . . ?'

'I didn't want to be the person who sent her to the gas chamber.'

'Motion to strike!' yelled Frances. Unusually, her voice was shrill.

She was overruled by the judge. 'I think this is acceptable testimony. Mr Craig is describing the fears which prevented him speaking earlier. But I would like to point out to Mr Craig that the jury decides whether a defendant is guilty, and their decision is based on all the evidence. It is a witness' responsibility only to tell the court what he saw, not to draw conclusions from it, which may be the wrong conclusions.'

Homer nodded and hung his head.

'So,' continued de Maria, 'you were silenced by your fears of the consequences of your action?'

'Yes, sir. But the police convinced me I should tell what I had seen, just like the lady judge said, and leave others to decide the consequences. The police said I shouldn't take the law into my own hands. It took me a while to see that they were right. I'm very sorry for the delay.'

Lomax thought he felt Murphy McLean swell at his side. He was in little doubt which policeman had convinced Homer he should tell.

De Maria thanked Homer and Frances rose.

'Mr Craig . . . please will you tell the court . . . ' she began. Homer looked scared as she bore down on the witness chair.

'Keep your distance, Mrs Bauer,' warned the judge, checking Frances mid-stride and mid-sentence. It was a second before she recovered.

'Please tell the court whether it is dark at five forty-five a.m. in mid-November.'

'It is dark,' said Homer, gripping his right arm across his body with his left hand.

'Are there lights in the parking lot outside your apartment?'

'There are street lights.'

'In the street. But in the parking lot?'

'There's a street light right outside and we've always thought that's enough. Sometimes I wonder if we need a light and I ask people and they say the street light's enough.'

'But there is no light in the parking lot and it has occurred to you on occasions that the light may be insufficient?'

'Well . . . yes. But everyone else says it's okay.'

'On which floor do you live?'

'The first.'

'And how far away was this car?'

'About fifty yards.'

'And you believe that you could identify Mrs Fox at a distance of fifty yards across an unlit parking lot in the dead of night?'

'Oh yes,' Homer nodded. 'Yes, I do, ma'am. Because of the street light and because her car door was open and the car light was on. I could see her clearly. I wouldn't have come forward if I wasn't sure about what I saw.'

'What colour was the car?' demanded Frances.

'I did not notice.'

'What make was it?'

'I did not notice.'

Frances paused, shaking her head slowly as though vexed. Her hands were on her hips. She looked aggressive.

'You noticed the driver but not the colour or make of the car?' she said, her voice steeped in scepticism.

'Yes,' said Homer. He spoke with quiet simplicity. Frances' tone had failed to discredit him.

'Shortly after you believed you saw Mrs Fox in the parking lot, you had a traumatic experience. Am I correct in describing your discovery of the mutilated bodies as a traumatic experience?'

Homer stared at her. 'Yes, ma'am,' he said.

'What was its effect on you?'

'Well . . . I was upset. I still am upset. I have trouble sleeping and I worry a lot. I don't go out much these days. I don't like going into empty rooms.'

'Do you take medication to calm your nerves?'

'Yes.'

'Have you received psychiatric attention?'

'Counselling. Not psychiatric. It's different.'

'Do you often wake at five forty-five?'

'Sometimes. I wake any time now.'

'Mr Craig, it is almost a year since the murders took place. A year of strong drugs, counselling, fear of empty rooms, worry, sleeplessness, confusion. After such a year, can you really be completely sure of what you saw one night last November, and at what time you saw it?'

'Yes, I can. Because I've been thinking about it ever since.'

'Remember, my client had got into a car and driven away from the apartment seven hours before you say you saw her doing exactly that. Could you have woken twice and confused the time and events? Could you have seen her on some other night? Is there any doubt in your heart, Mr Craig, and could it be this which prevented you from talking to the police for so many months?'

There was a pause while Homer surveyed her face. He was shaking but he spoke out clearly. 'No,' he said.

Frances waited, and when he said nothing more she spoke again. 'You have no doubt in your heart? None?'

'Seeing Mrs Fox wasn't something which happened before the trauma. It was a part of the trauma. When I walked into that room, I saw them with my eyes but with my head I remembered her driving away. I thought she must have killed them. Thinking it and not telling . . . see, that was traumatic.'

Frances turned from him.

'I'm sorry. I'm real sorry,' Homer said to her retreating back.

'No further questions,' Frances said, and there was bitterness in her tone. She had been defeated by Homer's quiet sincerity.

'Not good for your girl,' McLean muttered beerily into Lomax's ear. 'No sir-ee.'

Lomax did not look at the sheriff or speak to him. He was consumed by his own gloom. He hardly noticed Richard Fox's arrival. Only when he sensed an unusual stillness on the defence table did he realize that Richard was being sworn in. He caught sight of Frances' face. She looked pale.

De Maria rose to his feet and it seemed the movement was slower than usual. He murmured with an assistant and pulled at his fingers and then walked around the table and right up to the witness. This was strange too. The room watched him in silence. Lomax could hear de Maria's shoes clicking on the hard floor. Richard Fox stared at the approaching attorney.

There were a few questions about Richard's job and family. At the first mention of Julia, de Maria said pleasantly: 'Please point to your stepmother, Mr Fox.'

Richard looked straight at Julia. She turned her head away. He pointed, holding his arm out straight. It was hard to see this gesture as anything but accusatory.

'What is the difference in your ages?'

'I think she's a few months younger than me. Or I'm a few months younger than her. I'm not exactly sure.'

'But you're about the same age?'

'About.'

Morton de Maria stood near the witness chair and turned to look at Julia. His face was appraising. His tone was chatty.

'Would you describe her as an attractive woman, Mr Fox?'

Richard shrugged.

'Please answer,' said the judge, 'because our records cannot indicate gestures and facial movements.'

'Okay,' said Richard, looking at Julia, who turned away again. 'I guess she's attractive.' His tone was not complimentary.

'When your father married her, five, six years ago, did you find her attractive then?'

'I guess so.'

'Yes or no, Mr Fox?'

'Yes.'

'Did you tell her so?'

'When they married? No. My dad got mad if I just looked at her.'

'He guarded her jealously from you?'

'He didn't like me too near her.'

'Why was that?'

'Because he knew that he was getting old. And she was young and I was young.'

'He feared that you'd find her attractive?'

'Or,' said Richard, smiling, 'he feared she'd find me attractive. See, I look like my father, only younger.'

'And were those fears justified? Did she ever indicate sexual interest in you?'

'Yes.'

'What makes you so sure, Mr Fox?'

'She told me.'

'In what circumstances?'

'In bed.'

Morton de Maria paused for these words to have their effect on the courtroom. Lomax drew back as if punched. The defence table was still. The jury was motionless.

'How many times did you go to bed together?'

'A few.'

'How many?'

'Maybe twice.'

'And who initiated this?'

'Well, both of us.'

Murphy McLean turned to Lomax with a grin which Lomax knew, without looking at it, was wrapped right around his face.

'You were staying in your father's house?' asked de Maria.

'Yes.'

'You made love to your father's wife in his house?'

'In his bed.'

Morton de Maria paused again. Nobody spoke or even murmured but as the pause lasted longer and longer they rearranged their bodies or took deep breaths or in some way used this moment to punctuate the proceedings. McLean reorganized his weight, pressing stickily against Lomax. The sweet smell of his hair oil was suffocating.

Finally de Maria resumed. 'So. Here was a sexual liaison. A sexual liaison between a young man and the young woman married to his father. Was this a secret liaison?'

'My sister knew.'

'Your sister Gail Fox? The murder victim?'

'Gail heard us. Julia was kind of noisy in bed and Gail came into the house and heard us.'

Lomax squirmed, perhaps to free himself from McLean. Richard was answering the questions without emotion. He was unashamed. One hand was in his pocket as if he were reaching for some loose change.

'What did Gail do about it?'

'She waited until she could hear that we'd finished and then she came into the bedroom.'

'You were still in bed?'

'Yes.'

'And what did she say?'

'She laughed.'

'What did she find so funny, Mr Fox?'

'She was laughing at Julia. I mean, it was kind of funny. See, she took a picture of us.'

'Gail took a picture of you in bed together?'

'Yes. Like flash, snap, and she had a picture. When we were still propped up on our elbows staring at her.'

'So . . . what was funny?'

'I don't know. It just was.'

'Did Julia Fox laugh with you?'

'No.'

'What did Gail say?'

'To Julia?'

'To Julia.'

'She said: "I've got you now".'

'What did she mean by that?'

'She said: "This is going to cost you a lot of money, Julia." '

'What do you think she meant?'

'That she planned to charge Julia for not telling my dad.'

'Blackmail?'

'You could call it that. Or you could call it the most expensive sex Julia ever had.' He glanced at Julia. He might have been smiling. 'I sure hope it was worth it.'

'Was any sum of money mentioned?'

'No. She just said: "a lot".'

'There is evidence that $450,000 was paid by Julia Fox into her stepdaughter's account. Would it be feasible that this was money for the photograph?'

Frances stood up in a burst of energy. She was impersonating someone who was undaunted. Her voice simulated confidence. 'Objection. This is conjecture.'

'Sustained.'

De Maria's rephrasing was rapid. 'Are you saying, Mr Fox, that you think Gail charged Julia a large sum of money to keep quiet?'

'Yes.'

'Could it have been as large as, say, $450,000?'

'Objection.'

'Sustained.'

'What was the relationship like between these two women? Julia and Gail Fox. Stepmother and stepdaughter.'

'She was scared of her.'

'Who exactly was scared of whom?'

'Julia was scared of Gail. She was scared of everyone and everything. She was scared of Dad but she was also scared he would leave her. She was scared of being all alone. But mostly she was scared of Gail.'

'Was she scared enough to believe that her only hope of happiness lay in the death or disappearance of Gail Fox?'

'Objection.'

'Sustained.'

'Given their relationship, how do you believe Julia Fox regarded her stepdaughter's departure to France?'

'Oh, I'll bet she was relieved. But, I mean, Julia may have paid extra money for Gail to go away.'

'Motion to strike, your honour.' Frances was a study in relaxation. She stood leaning on the defence table. Her voice was unflustered. 'The prosecution has produced no evidence beyond hearsay and speculation that the money paid to Gail Fox was blackmail money. Now the witness builds further supposition on these shaky foundations.'

Judge Olmstead controlled the room more confidently now. She was sustaining more of Frances' objections. 'I agree that this is supposition and should be struck from the record,' she said.

De Maria wandered over to the jury. Richard's eyes followed him so that it must have seemed to the jury that he was looking directly at them.

'Gail actually came home from France earlier than anticipated. How did Julia feel on her return?'

Lomax thought again of the evidence, hidden in his room, which would answer that question.

'Scared. I didn't see her but I bet she was real happy in those months when Gail was away.'

'Motion to strike, your honour. This is more supposition by a witness who was absent from the family in the period under discussion.'

'Strike that from the record. Mr Fox, confine your answers to your own experience. Don't try to guess what may have happened in your absence.'

Richard Fox nodded, unperturbed by the judge's correction. He faced de Maria. He was working for the prosecution. 'Okay,' he said.

'I have just one more question.'

The court waited.

'Mr Fox, did you ever hear your stepmother threaten the life of Gail Fox?'

'Yes. In the bedroom. When Gail took the picture and said that it was going to cost Julia a lot of money.'

'What were the defendant's exact words?'

'Julia said: "I'd like to kill you. If Lewis hadn't taken my gun away, I'd have killed you by now." '

No further questions, your honour,' said de Maria. As he sat down, he made the strange, pulling gesture with his fingers which Lomax now recognized was the motion of a surgeon removing his gloves after a successful operation. He had just sentenced Julia to death. Frances rose swiftly to her feet, but the judge held up a restraining hand.

'We have to adjourn. We're over time. Mr Fox, you will be recalled tomorrow for cross-examination by the defence.'

'But I was leaving town!'

Lomax remembered something Mrs Knight in Arizona had said about Richard. She had said that he dealt with the family's problems simply by absenting himself. He had been leaving town when Lomax met him at the Medihome condominium. Richard was always leaving town.

'I'm sorry, but the court requires you to prolong your visit here in California. And let me warn you that overnight you should discuss absolutely nothing relevant to this case with anyone. You can take this to mean that you must not, under any circumstances, talk to members of the press. If you do, I will hold you in contempt and that is not a pleasant experience. This court is adjourned.'

The noise which followed the adjournment did not rise gradually. As if someone had flicked a switch, the silent room was filled with voices. On all sides of Lomax people were talking. McLean was shaking his head and saying something which Lomax did not listen to. Journalists were shoving to get out of the room first. Strangers were discussing the case. Over the heads of the crowd Lomax glimpsed Julia leaving with Kurt. A uniformed policeman preceded her. He knew the man was helping her to exit but the sight of Julia being led away by a policeman was disturbing. Kurt's face was grim. Julia's was white.

The people began to clear. Murphy McLean was lost in the crowd somewhere. Lomax noticed that Frances and Marjorie remained behind at the defence table. They were looking through their files, murmuring to each other. A couple of members of the press called to them across the wooden barrier, more psychological than physical.

'Will Julia Fox testify?' they asked. De Maria must have been wondering the same thing. Frances turned only to give them a quick smile.

Lomax paused when he reached the barrier. Then he opened the low gate and entered the arena of the court.

At first, Frances and Marjorie did not see him. He looked around. Everything was different from here. He was a member of the audience who had strayed onto an empty stage, so recently evacuated by the actors that the air was still thick with their presence. Their tension still hung here. He was surprised by how small the distances seemed: between the prosecution and the defence, between the jury and the witnesses. The judge's podium, backed by the flag, towered overhead. It was made of solid wood which Lomax guessed was oak. Stately old trees had been cut down to construct the courtroom. They brought it something of their antiquity and nobility. The wood was varnished. The brass rails around the podium were polished.

'Lomax.'

Frances' voice echoed a little. The room was practically empty now. He turned and saw her face clearly for the first time in days.

'You're tired,' he said.

Marjorie watched them.

'Do I look terrible?' asked Frances.

As he moved towards her his shoes made the same sound on the tiled floor that he had noticed earlier as Morton de Maria advanced towards the witness chair. The defence, by comparison, moved silently.

'No. You just look damn tired.'

'Trial fatigue. It's normal.'

'Your family . . .'

'They know there's a trial on. The children stay out of my way. My husband keeps quiet. Sometimes he holds my hand.'

Lomax felt something like jealousy for this silent support. He had wanted to do the same for Julia.

'Can I see her, Frances?'

She sighed. 'Maybe,' she said.

Lomax sat down in Julia's chair. From this position the judge would seem elevated to an almost impossible altitude. The witnesses were powerful because they sat by the podium, under its shelter. The jurors watched you with their fidgets, their smiles, their shakes of the head, their glances, their facial expressions and, ultimately, their verdict. Behind your back was a murmuring crowd, waiting for the moment when you turned around. There was nowhere to hide. All you had to protect you was the flimsiest table in the room.

Frances had resumed her search among the files. Marjorie was still watching him. Lomax said: 'Frances, I want to tell you how much I admire what you've done during this trial.'

This quiet, sad Frances whom he had not seen before paused for a moment and looked up. Briefly, a smile illuminated her drawn face. 'Thank you, Lomax. Thank you. But it may not be enough.'

He asked: 'Were you expecting Richard's testimony?'

'Yes.'

Marjorie said: 'I warned you. I didn't tell you exactly what was coming because I guessed you'd get upset.'

He nodded.

'Actually,' admitted Frances, 'it was worse than I thought.

Far worse. The problem is this, Lomax. She hasn't told us everything.'

'Excuse me,' said a soft voice. It was the court bailiff, a black man in uniform who had controlled the room and the crowds with quiet courtesy. 'Will you be here much longer, Mrs Bauer?'

'You want to lock up. We'll leave now.'

Lomax helped them gather their papers. He would not let Frances carry any of the large pile of files. He and Marjorie divided it between them, Lomax taking the bulk. Marjorie drove them without speaking to Sachs Smith.

'Nothing that Richard Fox said explains Lewis' murder,' said Lomax suddenly into the silence. 'I guess you've thought of that already.'

'I'm interested in anything you have to say,' Frances told him. There was resignation in her voice.

'If she paid Gail money to keep quiet it was to preserve her marriage. So why would she shoot Lewis?'

'I'll certainly stress that to the jury. But some of them may be feeling they have enough to convict. I mean, Hegarty's testimony about Lewis taking the gun away from her. Homer Craig's insisting he saw her on the morning of the murders. Richard's allegations of blackmail. And the threats. It's all adding up.'

Marjorie said: 'I bet Morton's planning to suggest Lewis' death was a mistake. That Julia didn't intend to kill him.'

Frances turned to Lomax. He was sitting in the back of the car submerged under files. 'You want to help Julia. Please talk to her, Lomax. We need to know the truth now. This trial is careering out of control. I can't keep riding this bronco.'

'Okay,' said Lomax, pleased with the suggestion that he alone might be persuasive to Julia. 'I'll talk to her.'

She was in Frances' office with Kurt. She was standing at the window. Kurt was leaning on Frances' desk like counsel for the prosecution, speaking to her with low intensity. She did not turn around when Lomax walked in with the two women.

Kurt ignored Lomax. He looked at Frances with a gesture of defeat. 'I don't know what to do with her,' he said.

'Just fuck off, Kurt,' Lomax muttered as he passed the desk, deposited the files and took Julia in his arms. She submitted willingly to this. She buried her face in his chest.

'Cute,' said Kurt.

Marjorie watched them curiously. Lomax stroked Julia's hair.

'Call us,' said Frances, ushering the others out of the room.

Lomax began to kiss Julia. First her eyes, which were damp, and then her mouth. He had forgotten how soft her lips were. At first their kisses were small but when he found that her mouth was wet and yielding he began to reach into it and their kissing became passionate. Lomax thought he had never loved her so much. When they stopped kissing they stood locked together by the fading light of the window looking at each other. He stroked her hair again.

'Is any of it true? What Richard said?'

'Enough. What am I going to do?' she whispered.

'Tell it like it is.'

'I can't.'

'Why not?'

'I can't.'

'Can you tell any of it?'

'Maybe some. It's painful.'

'I'll be here.'

'I know.'

'I'll help you.'

'I know.'

'Don't leave Frances floundering out there.'

'Today was terrible.'

'Tell. Tell.'

'Okay. I'll try.'

'I'm going to call them in. Right now.'

'Okay.'

'Except I can't.'

'What?'

'I have a hard-on.'

She giggled. It was a sweet, sad sound. He kissed her nose. Then he went out into the hall. There was no receptionist or security guard. The other offices were empty. Frances and Kurt and Marjorie were sitting in the foyer together like patient clients, their bodies listing in different directions. Kurt was reading a magazine. Marjorie was shuffling papers on her lap. Frances rested on a low table, her head propped in one hand. She looked up. He nodded to her.

'If this is going to take a while,' she said, 'I'll call my husband.'

'I think it may take a while,' agreed Lomax.

Julia appeared at his side. 'There's something I should show you. A few things. They're at home.'

'Do you want to fetch them?'

'Yes. Or we could go there.'

432

They went to Julia's house. The sun had gone down and the temperature had fallen. There was a cool wind. Lomax looked up but he could not see the moon. The house was in darkness. It had been empty for a while.

'Will you go in first?' Julia asked Lomax, handing him the key. The others were right behind him under the security lamp but he felt apprehensive. There were ghosts in this house. He pushed open the door.

'Move it, Lomax, it's cold here,' said Kurt. The rasp in his voice was no longer grating. It was reassuring. Lomax walked inside. The house had the chill of vacancy. He switched on the light and it threw shadows. Some of them were inexplicably large.

'Go right in,' Julia said to the others, gesturing to the living room. They sat down without taking their jackets off.

'I have to go into the basement . . . will you come with me, Lomax?' she asked in a small voice.

'Of course I will.'

He led the way through the kitchen, switching on every light as he passed. He wanted the house to burn with light like a ship in the dark ocean. He wanted the moths and bugs to buzz around it. He wanted to bathe his fears, which were too deep to express, in electric light.

She followed him down the steps to the basement. The air was not just cool here but damp. He admired again the neat workbench, the rows of tools, the bag marked Dirty Rags. It was a comforting sight, like some memento of childhood. Julia began to reorganize the boxes around the walls noisily. He remembered seeing these dark shapes at the edges of the basement on his first visit here, and guessing they must be associated with the ghosts.

'Do you need any help?' he called to her.

'No.'

After a few minutes she returned to his side carrying some books. At the top of the basement steps she looked at him. 'Thank you,' she said.

Lomax was glad to rejoin the others. They were sitting close together in silence. Frances' eyes were shut.

Wordlessly, Julia handed them the books, one each. Lomax recognized them at once as Tradescant theme books. The mountain lion on the front gave him its usual complicitous grin.

'Whose are these?' he asked.

'Gail's.'

Frances did not open her book. 'Julia. What have you been keeping from us?'

433

'I haven't told lies,' Julia said. 'It's just no one asked about all this except for Lomax.'

Lomax dropped his book. Marjorie and Kurt, who had opened theirs, looked up. 'Me?' said Lomax.

'I tried not to answer your questions.'

'I noticed.'

'You've been interested in my relationship with Gail all along.'

There was silence as the attorneys scanned the theme books. Lomax opened his at random. He recognized Gail's writing from the wallchart in Drapinski's biology lab.

'Subject anxious to please in evening because husband displayed signs of irritation with her a.m. (shortage of favourite breakfast cereal). Note: source of irritation food, so subject attempts to recover position with food. Subject laid table, candles etc., prepared meal in advance. (Note: rings off to wash salad, dries fingers, then rings back on immediately afterwards. DOES NOT LEAVE RINGS LYING AROUND EVER.) Listens for husband's return. Greets him at door. Kisses him. At this stage subject is endeavouring to ascertain his mood. TELLS HIM THERE IS A SPECIAL MEAL TONIGHT. Husband washes. Drink ready for him when he reappears. Note: husband enters living room and subject WALKS towards him with his drink. Note: husband has not walked towards wife once. Before husband enters dining room, subject checks table. Surveys table first on entering room. Then walks to husband's seat. Does not sit down. Leans over table with weight balanced on thumbs and fingers raised from table. Estimates his eye height. Subject fetches husband. Note: subject does not raise voice to attract attention but actually drops voice and stands closer. NBNB Yelling does not attract attention . . .'

Lomax recognized not just the writing from Drapinski's lab, but the bleakly scientific tone.

'THANKS. Subject wishing to indicate sincerity of gratitude puts head on one side (Note: angle is sharp, maybe 20 degrees to shoulder) and smiles without showing teeth. Mouth a long line. Eye contact maintained. Words minimized (eg, Thank you) with head still on one side, fixed smile position immediately regained.'

When Lomax and Julia had emerged from the basement just now she had thanked him in exactly this way.

He looked around him at the lawyers. Their faces were startled and confused.

'What does this mean?' asked Frances at last. Julia was silent.

Kurt said impatiently: 'Well I take it you're the "subject" referred to here?'

Julia still did not reply. She looked at them with a white face and large eyes, the pupils dark. Lomax remembered again the airmail letter. He remembered Richard's testimony. He said: 'You were scared of Gail. Terrified.'

She turned to him and, almost imperceptibly, nodded.

He continued: 'Gail was a keen behaviourist. She could apply simple scientific methods to analyse the behaviour of complex subjects. Like humans.'

'Like you,' Marjorie suggested softly.

'Yes.' Julia spoke so quietly that Lomax wondered if he had imagined her reply. She was sinewy and frightened like a young deer. She hardly moved except, he noticed, that she was trembling a little.

She said in the same half whisper: 'Gail also had videos. They're probably down there somewhere, I'm not sure.'

'Videos . . . which she used to study you?' asked Marjorie, her voice matching Julia's volume. Julia nodded slowly.

Kurt projected his jaw to create a hollow on one side of his face. He scratched at the hollow. When he spoke his voice sounded unnaturally loud. 'Okay, so she studies . . .' his fingers scuttled through his notebook, 'your clothes, your walk, your hand gestures . . .'

'Your sex life,' added Marjorie.

Julia blushed. She reached out and tilted the cover of Marjorie's notebook and, when she recognized it, grimaced a little. 'Oh. You got that one.'

Marjorie held it out. Julia dipped her head and Lomax took it for her. He opened it.

At the front there was a rough graph with dates and times. Parts of the graph were shaded in red. 'Maybe subject menstruating?' was written across these areas. There was a key at the bottom of the page. Green indicated intense activity initiated by husband. Blue was intense activity initiated by subject. Yellow was less intense activity.

Over the page Gail had written a date and then: 'Subject initiated sexual activites on husband's return from work. Subject appeared to reach orgasm 18 minutes and 35 seconds after bedroom door closed. May be faking. Husband reached orgasm exactly 35 minutes after door closing, subject appeared to climax concurrently. Stage three, simultaneous and rhythmic grunting (subject: oh, oh, oh) lasted 4 minutes prior to climax. Recovery time (ie time between climax and speech) 30 seconds. Subject first to speak.'

The last entry in the book said: 'Subject initiated sexual activity. Husband less willing, subject insistent. Husband climaxed 25 minutes after bedroom door closed. Subject silent throughout except for significant non-linguistic means of communication (Mmmmmmm on rising note. Ooooooooh, increasing in intensity) early during foreplay. Possibility of oral sex? Subject uses oral sex as means of capturing interest of reluctant husband? Recovery time: rapid. Husband first to speak. Apparently no reciprocal arrangements for subject. No apparent attempt by subject to demand further sexual congress. Subject now more likely to give than receive sexual satisfaction. See last three records of activity. Decline in frequency of intercourse: 85 per cent since marriage, 35 per cent over one year period.'

The attorneys had watched his face as he read. Now he closed the book.

'Gail was insane,' he said.

'Why did she do this? I don't understand. It's late and I'm tired. I'm sorry, I don't understand,' said Frances.

Julia looked at them. She opened her mouth to speak but said nothing. She swallowed.

'Gail wanted to be you,' said Lomax gently.

Julia faced him again. 'So. You did know. I wondered.'

'No, no,' he protested. 'I had the information. But I've only just worked it out. She wore your clothes, right?'

'Yes.'

'And your cosmetics. Your jewellery. Your perfume. Your shoes. Except they didn't fit.'

'She was bigger,' Julia whispered, leaning towards him. 'None of it fitted. You can't be someone else. It's impossible.' There was a note of desperation in her voice which was on the edge of hysteria. The attorneys scrutinzed her.

Kurt coughed. 'Julia. Why did Lewis let this go on?'

'He didn't know.'

'You tried to tell him,' Lomax supplied, 'but he didn't believe you. He thought you were crazy.'

'Like . . .' said Julia, 'like you're all thinking now.'

The attorneys did not move or speak. The edge was still in Julia's voice.

'I knew there was no point in telling you. I knew you wouldn't believe me.'

Lomax reached out for her hand. It burned in his.

'What's kind of hard to believe is that Lewis didn't know any of this was happening,' Kurt said.

'But,' Lomax protested, 'Gail was different when he was around.'

Julia nodded again.

Lomax turned to her: 'She was your affectionate little sister when he was there. Right?'

Suddenly Marjorie stood up as if sprung by tension from her seat. 'For God's sake, Julia,' she said angrily. 'Why were you such a little goddam mouse? Why didn't you show him these notebooks? Then he would have believed you. He would have done something about it.'

Julia's face looked for a moment as though it was going to melt. 'Oh Marjorie. You don't understand at all. She kept them locked up. If she caught me hunting for them . . .' She looked down. Her teeth were clenched. Her jaw was tight, her mouth was pulled into a line.

'She was violent,' Lomax explained to the others.

'She hit you?' asked Marjorie in the same tone of exasperation. She was standing over Julia now. Julia's head was bowed. She nodded without looking up.

'Holy shit,' said Kurt. 'Okay, so she was crazy. But why did she think she was doing this?'

Marjorie sat down again. There was a long silence. Julia's trembling had become shaking which was so violent that the three lawyers must notice it.

At last Lomax supplied the answer for them. 'She wanted to take Julia's identity for herself. And . . .' He looked at Julia for confirmation. 'And she wanted to destroy what was left of you.'

'Well,' said Julia in a small, hoarse voice, 'there couldn't be two of us.'

'But once you hit back,' Lomax reminded her.

'Finally I hit back.'

'And she broke your nose.'

'She broke hers too. I don't think I did it. I think she did it. Afterwards she had her nose reconstructed. Like mine.'

'Oh,' said Kurt. 'Your nose on her face? No.'

'It didn't make her look like me.'

'But she did look different,' Lomax added.

'Yes. She looked different.'

Marjorie said, her voice still antagonistic, 'Are you saying that Lewis still didn't guess something was wrong?'

'He thought we were silly little girls. He was mad at us for fighting. But . . .' she appealed to them, 'he thought I was crazy. Ever since she learned to do my voice.'

There was a silence into which Lomax groaned. 'Oh God. Of course.'

The others waited for him.

'All those phone calls to the office. That wasn't you. That was Gail being you. And once . . .' he glanced at Frances, 'once she nearly tripped up. You had called by at the office and just after you left, she telephoned him. Everyone thought it must be you calling from the parking lot . . .'

Julia blinked. 'I didn't know it so nearly happened. I kept slipping into the office with lots of stupid excuses because I knew that if she called when I was there he'd have to believe me. But she never did.'

'What did she say to him?' asked Marjorie.

'I don't know. I know some of the calls were very sexy. At first he liked it. Then he asked me to stop. I said: I don't know what you're talking about. It took me a while to understand that over the phone she could fool him, and other people, into thinking she was me. I mean, also my friends. I don't know what she said to them. I just knew they weren't my friends any more.'

The lawyers looked at each other in the night silence. Julia began to speak. Her voice was low. The words came rapidly.

'You don't know what it was like. You can't imagine how it felt to be studied and to see someone gradually acquiring everything you thought was yours and couldn't be taken away. I used to find her talking on the telephone in my voice, wearing my clothes, my make-up, my jewellery, laughing my laugh. I used to look up and see myself walking down the stairs. And all the time I knew this clone, no, this parody, all the time I knew she wanted to damage me. And what kind of a wife did Lewis think I was? A scared, neurotic wreck at home, jibbering about his daughter. An obsessive voice on the phone as soon as he left the house. I couldn't even have sex with him once I'd found that notebook.' She gestured to the book which Lomax still nursed on one knee. 'I couldn't blame him for having affairs.'

Lomax put his arm around her. She was still shivering.

Frances had been silent but alert. Now she spoke. 'Julia, how much did Richard know about this?'

'I think he knew a lot. They were close.'

'Anyone else?'

'No.'

'His blackmail story. It's true, I guess?' said Kurt.

'Probably. I mean, the way he described it, that's how it was. A part of me liked to think that afterwards, when she asked for the money, it was for Lewis. A part of me didn't care. I just wanted her to go away so I could have my life and my husband back.'

'Great motive,' said Kurt, 'for killing her.'

Julia's mouth almost smiled. 'I wished her dead so many times. But I didn't kill her.'

'Shit,' said Kurt. He looked at Marjorie.

'Shit,' said Marjorie.

'I know for sure now that you won't be testifying. I want to continue suggesting to the jury that the money was a gift to Lewis via Gail. If you testify De Maria will have you practically confirming the blackmail story and we'll be sunk.'

'We're sunk anyway,' said Kurt, sprawling back in his armchair. It was the one he had sat in when Lomax had first met him.

'No,' said Frances, her voice strengthening. 'I'll try to get this information about Gail from Richard in the witness chair tomorrow. It certainly doesn't make you look innocent, Julia, but it will have the jury asking who was really the victim. I'll need these notebooks.'

Julia stared at her. 'Why?'

'They're the nearest we have to evidence for the defence,' Marjorie explained.

'You mean people will read them?'

'Perhaps.'

'Including the sex notebook?'

Frances hesitated.

'Frances . . .' Julia's face was frightened. 'Please.'

Kurt told her: 'You have to let Frances help you, even if it's painful.'

'Not the sex notebook, then,' said Frances. 'But all the others.'

Julia looked at Lomax helplessly. He nodded.

'Okay,' she agreed.

'I'll call the DA's office,' Kurt announced, standing up. 'Let's submit this evidence tonight so Frances can screw Richard tomorrow. I mean, it's about time someone screwed him.'

31

Early the next day, rain threatened. Lomax could smell it. So could Deputy. It excited him. He chewed playfully at Lomax's clothes and tried to pull him outside. Lomax decided to take the dog to court. He could wait in the car and take walks in the park during the recesses. Then this evening, when the rain had refreshed the hillside, they could go hiking and try to forget the trial for a few hours.

Lomax drank his first cup of coffee standing on the deck and waiting for the rain. There was a wind blowing onto his feet and between his brown toes. It blew softly but it felt like a fall wind. The clouds were thick overhead and the mountains were less visible than they had been for months. Finally the drops came. At first it smelt unclean as it mixed with the summer dirt. Then, as Lomax drove to the courtroom, it intensified.

It was a long time since he had last switched on the windshield wipers. Their sloshing seemed frantic. For a while they just smeared dead insects, dust and accumulated grease across his vision. But soon the violence of the rain began to cleanse the car and the roads and the whole of the city. There was alarmed speculation on the radio that rain might obscure the eclipse next week.

Dixon Driver's voice addressed the listeners. He explained in his irritating even-toned way that the eclipse would last a total of three minutes and twelve seconds. He had started to speculate on the chances of cloud cover at the observatory in any three-minute-and-twelve-second period in mid-September when Lomax switched stations. He parked the car and left Deputy with his nose protruding into the rain through the part-open window.

Water ran down the courthouse steps. People ran up them. Inside, the hallways smelled of damp clothes. Lomax had thought he was early but he found the room already crowded, cameras clustered by the door. Richard's testimony had probably led last night's news bulletins.

The bailiff gestured to a front seat he had reserved, evidently at

Marjorie's request. Lomax thanked him. He took the seat and looked around him. Many of the faces had become familiar. The same reporters were here every day. The policemen looked the same even if they weren't. The bulk of the onlookers in the public gallery changed constantly, except for the hard core of recognizable regulars who came most days. The regulars nodded to each other or discussed the case in semi-professional tones in the court cafeteria.

It seemed to Lomax that there were more young women in the court today. Two sat on his left, looking around with interest, and another on his right. Their clothes said the summer was over. Overhead, rain streamed down the high windows.

Kurt and Marjorie escorted Julia into the room. The noise in the court always dipped when Julia arrived. Her entrances and exits were the only opportunity for people to see her face. Today she wore a simple dress that was the colour of chestnuts. She had the tired, bright-eyed look which Lomax guessed was fuelled by anxiety and nerves.

'She's cute,' agreed the two girls on Lomax's left. 'She's dressed like fall.'

'I want a jacket in russet.'

'I have one but it's too last year.'

Every night on the evening news, Julia's and sometimes Frances' clothes were described and discussed.

Marjorie's eyes found Lomax and gave him a sweet and secret smile which half the room must have noticed. Frances and de Maria were absent. There was no sign of Judge Olmstead. As the delay lengthened, word spread around that the counsellors were in the judge's chambers. Lomax could guess why.

When Frances emerged, she was perceptibly made-up. She began unloading papers from her briefcase, muttering rapidly to Kurt, Marjorie and Julia. A moment later, de Maria arrived. His face seemed set hard and he also talked in urgent undertones to his colleagues. Of the two of them, Frances seemed the more buoyant.

The jury filed in and took their seats. There was the usual rustle of limbs and scraping of feet as the court rose for the arrival of the judge.

As Richard Fox reappeared on the witness stand a collective nerve twitched in the room. Lomax recognized it as a frisson of sexual excitement. Was Richard the reason there were so many women in court today?

'Cute,' agreed the two young women next to Lomax.

Richard sat straight. He placed his hands lightly on the arms of the

441

chair, unintimidated by the gravity of the court or size of the crowd. He watched the artist drawing him without embarrassment. When the judge reminded him that he was still under oath he nodded briskly. He was impatient with her tone but principally, Lomax guessed, he was irritated by her power. She was a plain, white-haired woman and under all other circumstances would be inconsequential for Richard.

The tone of Frances' opening questions was friendly. Richard's answers were short but they told his story. He had left home at the age of eighteen for college in Seattle. At this time his mother had moved into a special condominium where carers were on hand, and his father had remarried. Richard had felt that he no longer had a home in California and had subsequently returned here only for a week or two annually.

Richard's answers were more brief when Frances asked about his father.

'Sure. We got along okay. So long as I agreed with him.'

'He had a strong personality?'

'You could put it like that.'

'Were you fond of him?'

'He was my father.'

'Were you fond of him, Mr Fox?'

'I'm not sure.'

'Yesterday you described how you slept with my client. She was married to your father. Did you feel any guilt about sleeping with her?'

'No, why should I feel guilty? She's an adult, I figured it was her decision.'

'You say there was a photo taken of you in bed together. Were you anxious for your father not to see it?'

'No.'

'Perhaps you would even have liked him to see it?'

Richard smiled. 'Maybe,' he admitted.

Frances paused. Every face was turned to Richard. Frances had distanced herself from him. She was standing near the jury as if she was seeing him from their point of view. Perhaps Richard was suddenly aware of the loneliness of his position. He said: 'I was just a kid when he left us. My mother was ill. He could have helped, but he didn't. I don't owe that guy anything.'

Frances was sympathetic. 'I'm sure we can understand your bitterness, Mr Fox. Do you think that these feelings about your father were one of the reasons you wanted to go to bed with his wife?'

'I guess it made her a challenge,' he agreed.

'Was it easy to persuade her to have sex with you?'

Richard's eyes wandered lazily around the room and settled on Julia. She looked back at him. They stared at one another for a moment and the court watched that stare. At last he answered.

'She made me work hard,' he admitted, 'but it's more exciting that way. I guess she would agree.'

'How did you set about persuading her?'

'The same way I always do.'

'The court would be fascinated to hear your methods.'

Richard smiled. 'You're asking me to give all my secrets away here,' he said. There was the murmur of a smile in the courtroom and a few giggles. Several members of the jury looked amused.

'Yes, please share with us the secrets of your success,' continued Frances, her voice warm with admiration. 'What did you say to persuade her to go to bed with you?'

Richard allowed himself to enjoy this admiration. 'I paid her a lot of attention. I told her she was beautiful. I told her she was gorgeous. I told her I was hot for her.'

'Did you tell her that you were in love with her?'

'Maybe. I don't remember.'

'But in your experience, a declaration of love tends to persuade reluctant partners into bed?'

'In my experience, women like to be loved and appreciated. And I mean it when I say it.'

'Is it possible that Julia Fox thought you loved her?'

Richard shrugged. 'I don't know what she thought.'

'She may have gained the impression that you felt that way?'

'Maybe.'

'Mr Fox, you are a very attractive young man. Do you have an active sex life?'

Richard's mouth was fighting against a smile.

'Objection,' yelled Morton de Maria.

'Party pooper,' muttered one of the women next to Lomax.

De Maria sounded distressed. 'Mr Fox lives in another state. His sex life there has no relevance to this case.'

Frances said: 'Your honour, I'm simply trying to indicate my client's psychological condition last year and this is vital information.'

'Objection overruled. Make absolutely sure these questions are relevant, Mrs Bauer.'

Frances said distinctly: 'Do you have an active sex life?'

This time, Richard could not hide a smile. 'I guess so.'

'Do you have a regular girlfriend?'

'No.'

'You have many casual relationships?'

'Sure.'

'Is this a policy? Or are you looking for that special girl?'

'It's my policy. I don't get too involved. For me the really interesting part of a relationship is the beginning.'

The press gallery was alive with tiny movements, pens on paper and fingers on keyboards.

'Are you referring to the thrill of the chase?'

'Well, my theory is that women only have power over me while I still want them. So it's kind of fun at that stage. Afterwards I have all the power and it can get a little dull.'

'And this was a policy you applied to Julia Fox?'

'Sure.'

'Perhaps she wished to prolong the relationship?'

'Yes. She was a clinger.'

'What does a clinger do?'

'Calls a lot. Cries a lot.'

'How do you deal with clingers like Julia Fox?'

'The answer machine was invented especially for me.' His smile was charming.

'You mean you avoid talking to clingers?'

'Yeah. I screen the calls. It's the kindest way to do it. It's better than pretending. See, I'm honest. I don't pretend to feelings I don't have. Most girls pretty soon get the message.'

'Did Julia Fox try to contact you on your return to Seattle?'

'Yes, she did.'

'Was she in love with you?'

'I don't know.'

'You've said that women like to be loved and appreciated. Did Julia Fox's husband love and appreciate her?'

'Well no. I mean, he was married to her.'

Laughter moved swiftly around the room like some noisy, invisible person. Lomax looked at the judge. It was possible she was suppressing a smile.

'Would it be fair to say Julia was lonely?'

'Maybe.'

'And unhappy?'

'I think she was unhappy.'

'Because her husband had ceased to notice her?'

'He didn't notice her, she thought he was having affairs and, I mean, he didn't even have sex with her any more.'

'Did her stepdaughter, Gail, add to her unhappiness?'

'Well, she didn't get along with Gail.'

'You said yesterday that she was scared of her stepdaughter. Why was that?'

'Gail was stronger and she was smart.'

'Julia Fox, though, was more attractive.'

'But Julia was sort of weak. She would cry and get upset about things.'

'Did Gail make her upset?'

He paused. Then shrugged. 'I don't know.'

'Would Gail have liked to be more attractive?'

'Well, sure.'

'Did she try?'

Richard was hesitant. 'Probably.'

'How?'

'I don't know what women do. They try new hair, new hair colour, make-up . . . all those things.'

'Did she want to look like anyone in particular?'

For the first time, Richard averted his eyes from the court. He began to study something on the floor by the witness chair. He did not reply.

'Did you hear the question, Mr Fox?'

'Yeah, I don't know the answer.'

'Was there anyone whose looks Gail admired?'

'Are you trying to make me say that she wanted to look like Julia?'

'I'm not trying to make you say anything, Mr Fox. It is my intention simply to establish the truth.'

'Look, I only saw her once a year.'

'You were her closest confidant. She spoke to you on the telephone.'

'Not that often.'

'What did she tell you about her relationship with the defendant?'

'She didn't tell me very much.'

'Nothing?'

'She used to laugh at her sometimes. Because she thought Julia was sort of stupid. And because it was so easy to frighten her. Once she hit Julia. Not hard. After that, all she had to do was like, raise her hand and Julia scuttled away. I mean, Gail thought that kind of thing was funny.'

'I see. She enjoyed terrorizing her stepmother?'

'Julia was so scared that she would have gotten terrorized by a chipmunk.'

'Yesterday you told the court how my client had threatened to kill Gail Fox. Please remind us of the exact words that were used.'

Richard stared at her. 'Um . . . "I'd like to kill you." '

'And then?'

' "If Lewis hadn't taken my gun away, I'd have killed you by now." '

'So even before the scene you described yesterday, it seems my client hated Gail Fox. Was this because she was a lonely young woman who lived in terror of her stepdaughter's violence?'

'Maybe.'

'I suggest to you that Gail Fox's attempts to terrorize her lonely stepmother were cruel and systematic and centred on her determination to steal for herself from Julia Fox everything which made her attractive.'

'Objection.'

'You have allowed that I may submit evidence, your honour, and the evidence has been authenticated.'

'All right, Mrs Bauer.'

A court official reached into the cart and produced a handful of Tradescant theme books. The public and jury all craned to see them. Frances picked one, apparently at random, and passed it to Richard.

'Open the book, Mr Fox, and tell me if you recognize the writing.'

There was a pause. The jury's attention was unwavering.

'It's Gail's writing.'

'Sure?'

'It's definitely Gail's.'

'It is one of a number of similar books found among her effects when she died. Please read me a paragraph.'

'Any paragraph?'

'Any paragraph.'

Richard turned a few pages. Finally he read: 'Laughing. Subject indicates big amusement by throwing back head AND NB NB NB RAISING SHOULDERS. Stresses end of last peal of laughter. So: ha ha ha ha ha ha HA. Dips head and drops shoulders on last HA and raises head again smiling. Regains eye contact.'

Frances said: 'Who do you think the subject referred to here could be?'

'Julia,' said Richard.

'What makes you say that?'

'Well, it's how she laughs.'

'This and the other notebooks found indicate that Gail Fox made a scientific study of her stepmother in order to extract her very identity for herself. There is evidence that she wore her stepmother's clothes, inflicted violence on her if she objected and, on one occasion, broke her nose. Does any of this surprise you?'

Richard shook his head. 'I thought it was like . . . a game. I knew she did it. I didn't know it was so . . .' He waved the theme book. '. . . so serious.'

Lomax looked around him at the sad, sympathetic faces of the jury and the public. It was impossible to view Julia without compassion. She was the accused, but she was clearly the victim.

'You were surely aware,' Frances persisted, 'of Gail Fox's strange and unhealthy obsession with her stepmother?'

When Frances asked the question, Lomax assumed that she would be answered by a reluctant and monosyllabic affirmative. Probably Frances did too. But there was a pause, and in what followed it seemed that she had pulled a trigger and was powerless to prevent the resulting shots from ricocheting around the courtroom.

'It wasn't an obsession. Gail hated Julia. But she wanted to be like her. Gail was smart and it was obvious to her that men wanted Julia. See, my father did. When they first got married they were always in the goddam bedroom. Gail wanted my father to be that way with her too. It was because of my father. She wanted him. You say she was strange and unhealthy about Julia but what was really strange and unhealthy was that she wanted her own father and in the end I guess she got him. I guess that's really what all this is about. Not me and Julia having sex, not that. It's about Gail and Dad having sex.'

Not for the first time, Lomax greeted the reappearance of the truth with a sense of tired recognition. He had a habit of ignoring it or misinterpreting it or just allowing it to slip through his fingers but when it bobbed back to the surface it had a certain familiarity. He guessed that he and Julia alone now heard Richard without astonishment.

There was silence in the court except for the sound of the rain on the high windows. The room was immobile except for the water that ran down the steamy glass. The jury stopped fidgeting. The press stopped writing. The prosecution counsellors stopped taking notes or shuffling the papers or sorting through files. Every face was turned towards Richard. Only the fingers of the court reporter continued to move soundlessly over her keyboard. Hers were the only eyes not focused on the witness chair.

Frances, temporarily speechless, returned to the defence table. Kurt began to whisper to her. Richard watched them, his composure gone.

He looked hot. His hair fell over one eye. He clutched the polished arms of the witness chair. Then gradually, his self-awareness returned. Watching it was like watching a man wake up. He pulled his face into a different shape and put his hands in his pockets and the marks left by his fingers, his prints, were visible on the chair.

'Mr Fox,' said Frances, 'these are surprising assertions. Do you have any evidence at all that your sister and your father had a sexual relationship?'

'Not evidence, but – '

'By evidence I mean photographs, letters or diaries?'

'No.'

'Did either of them actually tell you that sexual intercourse had taken place between them?'

'Not that it had, but I know Gail wanted – '

'Mr Fox, I have the most intimate notebooks of Gail Fox, a paragraph of which you have read to the court. The jury will be invited to look through these notebooks if the judge wishes them to do so. They will find that no reference is made anywhere to a sexual relationship between Gail Fox and her father. I move that Mr Fox's assertion be struck from the record.'

'No,' said the judge, 'we'll keep it on the record, along with your subsequent questions and the witness's responses, Mrs Bauer.'

But Lomax realized that, in discrediting Richard and his ugly evidence against Julia, Frances had disposed of the truth. The cross-examination continued but Lomax hardly heard it. He felt his belly twist. Frances, confronted unfairly and unexpectedly by the truth, had simply discounted it. But it was still the truth.

The last questions were efficient. Did Richard know for a fact that Gail carried out her theat to blackmail Julia? Did he see any evidence of it? Did Julia ever confide in him that she was being blackmailed? And finally, if Julia's marriage was as unhappy as Richard suggested, why would Julia have paid such a high price to preserve it? All Richard's answers were to Frances' satisfaction. She sat down and the judge released Richard from the witness stand.

Judge Olmstead told the jury they were to be given an opportunity to examine Gail's notebooks. They would help the jurors to understand more the state of mind of the deceased. She called for a recess, followed by lunch.

People stretched their legs and stood up and adjusted their clothing or pushed their hair around or began to talk.

'Whooooooo,' said the girls next to Lomax.

448

The rain continued to run down the windows. Lomax watched the defence team leave. He tried to follow them but there were too many people and he was forced to file out behind the public and a group of journalists who, he knew, would be hunting Richard out in the hallways. He had never discovered where the defence recessed to but, even if he had to open every door in the building he knew he must find Julia. Mrs Cleaver was waiting for him. She was sucking a cigarette, unlit.

'Where the hell did they go?' he asked her.

'In one of those doors. Try the second past the elevator.'

The door led to a busy hallway. There were many more doors leading from it. He began to open each in turn, glimpsing snapshots of the small human dramas that were behind them. Other people's dramas. Sometimes their faces turned to him, startled. Sometimes the occupants did not notice his intrusion at all. He guessed that this was where attorneys talked with clients. He passed de Maria in the hall, an assistant muttering softly, de Maria nodding. Finally he found them in a windowless room. Julia was sitting to one side with coffee in a plastic cup on a table in front of her. The three attorneys were conducting a discussion which excluded her. They broke off when he walked in.

'What the hell are you doing here?' Kurt asked.

Lomax ignored him. He sat down by Julia who looked at him without surprise, without smiling and without speaking.

'It was true,' he said.

She remained silent.

'It was true,' he repeated.

He took Julia's shoulders and pushed them gently until she looked up. The coffee spilled. It ran over the edge of the table and dripped onto the floor. No one moved to clear it up. Julia's eyes were clear and blue.

'What happened that morning?' he demanded. 'For Chrissake, Julia.'

'I didn't want everybody to know about Gail and Lewis,' she said, in answer to some other question.

'Julia. What happened?'

'I knew he was sleeping with her. I suspected it but Vicky knew because Gail told her. I thought it would be over when Gail went to France. But when she got back . . . can you believe . . . can you believe he took her straight to the apartment?'

Her face was distorted with pain.

'Vicky knew that?'

449

'I called her. I told her.'

'You told her that Gail and Lewis were in the apartment together?'

'Yes.' Her head dropped gracefully.

'What did she say, Julia?'

'She said. "I'll kill him." '

'Vicky said that? Vicky?'

'She was drunk. I didn't think she could do it. She still had her car then but she hardly ever drove it. I didn't think it was possible. But they didn't arrive. They didn't arrive. Then I knew . . .' Her voice broke.

'Then you knew Vicky had killed them.' Lomax turned to the three attorneys. 'You should go see Vicky right away. Now,' he said.

'Yes,' agreed Frances. 'Oh Julia, why all the secrecy?'

'We can't go anywhere, we're in fucking court. Fuck it,' spluttered Kurt.

'I can go,' said Marjorie. 'Lomax should come with me.'

'Wait,' said Julia. 'Wait. You don't understand. She's a drunk. She's sick. She didn't know what she was doing. It's my fault. It's right that I'm on trial. Because I was stupid enough to call her that morning. I practically pulled the trigger.'

Everyone looked at Frances. She said to Marjorie: 'Go.'

Marjorie and Lomax took his car because Deputy was waiting in it, his nose still sniffing at the rain. He barked when he saw Lomax coming. Lomax let him run around the parking lot for a few moments and then they started driving west. The windows became opaque with steam when they closed them. They opened them again and the rain blew in.

'Don't you have a steam control?' asked Marjorie irritably.

'No. I mean, it doesn't work.'

'How is it you can keep your brain in working order but not your car?'

'My brain?' hooted Lomax. Deputy barked. 'My brain is getting very slow and stupid. I've been talking to a psychologist about Gail and Lewis and he practically told me that Vicky had murdered them and I ignored him. And when I met Mrs Knight in Arizona – she was Vicky's neighbour by the way – she just assumed Vicky was the killer. And instead of listening to her, I corrected her. Jeez. Brain, what brain?'

They drove towards the mountains. The rain turned the roads black. In places it had flooded and the cars slowed down and wings of water shot up all around them. When the stationwagon plunged into the water, it flew in through the window.

'Jesus Christ,' said Marjorie, wringing her skirt.

'Just pretend you're at a theme park on a white-knuckle ride,' Lomax advised. She did not reply.

'What are we going to say?' he asked as they drew closer to Vicky Fox's condominium.

'I'm going to say it. You're going to look for the gun.'

'What?'

'I'll talk to her. You go through the house looking for the gun.'

'If I killed someone, I'd throw out the gun.'

'We don't know this woman's killed anyone.'

Lomax looked at her.

'Keep your eyes on the road, Lomax.'

'We're waiting for the lights, Marjorie. Now tell me what you mean.'

'Well, all we know is that Julia says she killed someone. I know you think Julia's just perfect but even you have to admit she's withheld the truth for a helluva long time. If it is the truth.'

'She explained. She feels responsible. She didn't physically pull the trigger but she thinks it was her fault.'

'Go!' said Marjorie. The lights had changed.

'Plus,' he continued, 'I guess she didn't want anyone to know Lewis and Gail had an incestuous relationship.'

'I've met Vicky Fox. How could she drive across town and murder someone? Seriously? She doesn't even have a car.'

'Not right now. Maybe she did then.'

'She still had to drive it. She's half crazy. She wouldn't notice whether the lights were red or green.'

'Maybe she found some other way of getting there.'

'Mmmmmm,' said Marjorie sceptically. Lomax thought that she was becoming more like the Marjorie he had first met at Sachs Smith, the Marjorie who had told him to get off her telephone line.

The rain stopped. The roads were warm enough for steam to rise off them. The parking lot outside the condominium was pitted with puddles. Lomax, who did not like leaving Deputy in the car, tied him to the door handle with a long leash. The dog smelt around the car then watched them go forlornly.

'Guard. Guard dog,' Lomax said.

Vicky Fox's voice crackled over the intercom.

'Hi, Mrs Fox!' Marjorie sounded friendly. 'We're from Sachs Smith. Could we speak with you?'

'Uh huh,' said the voice. It was supposed to be followed by the buzz of the door opening but nothing happened. They looked at each other. Marjorie rang the bell again.

'Yes?'

'We're from Sachs Smith. We'd like to talk to you. Would you open the door?'

There was a long pause. It seemed the answer was no. Then footsteps could be heard. A tall, white-coated woman stood in the doorway. She wore a badge. It said 'Cindy', and underneath her name was printed 'Care Assistant.'

'Mrs Fox isn't feeling too well,' she said.

'It's really imperative that we talk to her.'

The woman shook her head. 'She don't want to see you today.'

'We're not asking, we're telling,' began Marjorie impatiently. 'The alternative is policemen and search warrants.'

The woman leaned towards Marjorie and held a warning finger up. 'You,' she said, 'ain't telling me nothing.' To Lomax's alarm she began to push the door shut.

'No! Please let us – ' Marjorie shouted, trying to prevent her closing it. Lomax felt something warm brush past his legs. It was brown. It shot into the house at high speed. Deputy Dawg had slipped his leash again.

'What the hell was that?' asked Cindy.

'I'm real sorry,' Lomax said, following Deputy through the door. 'That's my dog. I left him tied up but . . .'

He was inside now. Marjorie was right behind him.

'My,' sighed Cindy in a tone of resigination. Lomax followed the sound of Mrs Fox's squeals.

'Oh! You big bad dog, where did you come from? Oh! Oh!' People sometimes said oh that way when Deputy licked them. His tongue was so long and wet and smooth that it could take you by surprise.

Vicky Fox was lying on the couch with a drink by her side and some bottles of pills scattered over the floor. Deputy's front paws were up on the couch and he was leaning over her like Prince Charming. He licked her face repeatedly.

'Down!' said Lomax in a masterful voice. Deputy gave him a sly look and continued licking. His prey was convulsed with laughter. She had turned a dangerously unnatural colour. Lomax grabbed Deputy by the collar and pulled him away. Vicky continued to laugh uncontrollably. Deputy watched her, his tongue hanging so far out of his mouth that it almost touched the floor. He had shown a propensity to adore drunks before. When her laughter began to subside, Lomax apologized.

'Hi,' Vicky Fox said cheerfully. She ignored Marjorie but gestured to Cindy.

'Cynthia,' she said. 'This is a young policeman who comes to visit me here sometimes. Can I offer you a drink when you're on duty, officer?'

Cindy was picking up the bottles of pills

'Not really,' said Lomax.

'He don't look like no policeman to me,' muttered Cindy meanly, narrowing her eyes. When she had retrieved all the bottles she said: 'Okay, Mrs Fox, I'm gonna leave you with your friends now. I'll be back tonight with some more pills.'

'Okay, Cynthia,' said Mrs Fox. 'John's taking me to the shopping mall today. Or maybe it's tomorrow.'

'Gotta be back by six for these pills,' Cindy called over her shoulder.

'Okay.'

Marjorie knelt down beside Vicky Fox. 'Do you remember me?' she asked. 'I'm from Sachs Smith, and this is Lomax.'

'Sure. Sure I remember.' She smelt strongly of liquor. 'It's nice that you brought a police dog with you.' She was sitting up now and Deputy's muzzle was pressed against her knee. She patted his head. It was hard to imagine any dog less like a police dog.

Marjorie began talking to Vicky Fox about how she was feeling today. She gave Lomax a fierce glance. It was a moment before he realized why. He tried to slip out of the room but skidded gracelessly on a bottle of pills which Cindy had missed. Mrs Fox did not notice. Marjorie rolled her eyes.

In the hallway, he opened and closed doors. One was a bathroom. One was a closet. One had the unused smell of an extra bedroom. Probably this was where Richard stayed on his occasional visits. Lomax was looking for wherever Vicky slept. He assumed that women kept guns by the bed.

The last door he tried opened into a large room. The drapes were closed. He switched on the light but it was still dingy in here. The room had the furniture but not the personality of a bedroom. Only some photos on one shelf and some dusty cosmetics by the vanity mirror made this more than a motel.

Lomax pulled at the drawers by the bed. They contained bourbon bottles, all empty. There were scissors and Sellotape and Band-Aids and a few magazines and pill capsules and a pair of gloves. What were gloves doing here? Lomax closed the drawers. Probably Medihomes had the room cleaned and the help threw into the drawer anything that was lying around. That explained the clean surfaces. Then he remembered that the killer might have worn gloves. He retrieved them and put them on the bed.

He looked through more drawers. Underwear, jewellery, socks, a pile of postcards and letters tied together with ribbon. He felt guilty as he stretched to the back of drawers and ran his fingers over Vicky Fox's most personal possessions. He tried not to look too closely at anything which wasn't a gun. But nothing was a gun. He lingered for a few moments over the photos on the shelf. Richard. A pretty girl he did not recognize. One small picture of Vicky's wedding, the bride slim and smiling shyly. Lewis, dark-haired, handsome, leaning towards her. All that had followed mocked the wedding and mocked the picture. He replaced it silently. He noted Gail's absence. Until he picked up the photo of the pretty girl. There was something familiar about her. She had been caught trying to turn away from the camera. It had captured a smile and an impression of a girl but the detail was lost.

He continued his search. He looked through the clothes and shoes in the closet. He pried around the very back of the closet and the sides. He pressed everything soft in case it was hard. He found a collection of hair-styling equipment. More bourbon bottles. One, two, three hairdryers and a pile of pillows which he squeezed mercilessly. There were several hats. Ridiculously, he felt inside the lining of one. He simply crushed the other. It did not spring back into shape. He replaced it guiltily inside its bag, dented. He reached for a suitcase and opened it and felt all over that too. There was no gun. He was close to defeat. He remembered Marjorie's sceptical tone in the car. Even if Vicky Fox had a gun, how could she drive across town and back to shoot anyone with it? Maybe, after all, there was no gun. He remembered Julia, sitting in the windowless room in the courthouse. She had looked straight into his eyes while the coffee dripped onto the floor nearby. She had been telling the truth.

He shut the closet. Where else could he look? He paused and stood thinking in the large, bare room.

Why would anyone have three hairdryers? He reopened the closet and dragged out each of them, one, two, three.

The first was compact and metallic. It looked like a gun, but it was a hairdryer. The second looked like a hairdryer and was a hairdryer. The third thudded when he moved it. There was something inside the outer casing. He felt for the clips. Security stores and mail order catalogues sold this kind of decoy. They also advertised safes that looked like books or milk cartons. He knew before the case had sprung open that there was a gun in here and that it was a Smith and Wesson .38.

He looked at it without touching it. It was small and grey and perfect, just like Berlins' telescope. It was smooth except for its wooden handle which was criss-crossed with regular and precise indentations to give its user better grip. It had killed two people.

Lomax put the gloves into the hairdryer shell with the gun and clicked it shut. He readjusted the room. He turned out the light.

Vicky Fox was half wailing, half sobbing on the couch.

'I don't know, I don't remember, I can't tell you anything, I don't remember.'

Lomax gestured from the doorway for Marjorie to pass her purse. She stared in disbelief at the hairdryer. Lomax grinned and mimed hairdrying. Then he pretended to shoot himself with it. Marjorie fought laughter. Lomax placed the hairdryer in the purse. It made the sides bulge.

'I can't help it, I can't help it,' Mrs Fox was telling Deputy, who looked at her with sad, brown eyes.

'Mrs Fox,' said Lomax, 'how's your friend? The thin guy we watched in the swimming pool? The man who proposed to you?'

'John is just fine. John is always just fine. And if he wasn't fine, he wouldn't say. That's the way John Fusco is, see.'

'He drives a car.'

'Sure. John drives a car.'

'Where does he live?'

'In Fifteen. John lives in Fifteen and Mona lives in Thirty. They're my friends.'

'Okay, Mrs Fox,' said Marjorie, getting up. 'You'll probably be the first witness for the defence on Monday morning. It shouldn't be too much of a problem for you. Just tell the court what you've told me.'

'There's nothing to tell,' Vicky Fox said. 'Because I don't remember anything.'

'I have a subpoena right here and we're going to fill it in. That means you have to appear. You don't have any choice. There'll be a car for you. We'll talk to the carer here to make sure sure you're ready in time. Probably people will want to ask you more questions over the weekend.'

Vicky Fox nodded dumbly. She stared at Marjorie as she scribbled the subpoena and then handed it over.

'It's okay. Don't get up, we can find our way out,' Marjorie said. Deputy had to be dragged away. He and Vicky parted like old friends.

'For Chrissake, Dep,' Lomax said when they were out of the house, 'that woman murdered two people and all you can do is lick her all over.'

Deputy jumped into the car.

'Okay,' said Marjorie, 'so why the hairdryer?'

'I figured it's wet, we may need one.'

Marjorie sat in the passenger seat and opened her purse and then the hairdryer and took the gloves out and stared at the gun.

'Yes,' she said. 'Yes, this is it. A ballistics expert will be able to confirm not just that it's the right model, but that it's the right gun. They're sort of individual. Like fingerprints. Like perfume. Did you know that the same perfume smells different on different people?'

'No. I didn't know that.' Lomax was smiling.

'Don't open any champagne yet. Don't see Julia on the weekend. Don't do anything,' Marjorie warned him. 'We still have a way to go. For a start, Vicky's still insisting she was home on the night of the murders.'

'I have an idea,' said Lomax.

'Oh-oh.'

'It's just a hunch.'

'What?'

'There's someone else we should talk to while we're here.'

32

Lomax spent the weekend with his children. They bought some filters for the eclipse in a department store which had a whole corner devoted to scientific gadgets. Helen chose a pair of pink frames which made her look like a tiny movie star. Joel selected a heavyweight instrument which you held to one eye only.

'It's expensive, but I'll be able to use it again and again,' he explained as Lomax paid for it.

'How many eclipses are you planning on seeing?'

'Probably a lot. I've made a career decision.'

The store assistant, who was wrapping Joel's filter in blue tissue paper, smiled.

'I'm going to be an astronomer,' Joel announced.

'I'm going to work in an observatory like Julia,' Helen said.

'You could be an astronomer also,' suggested Lomax.

'Is Kim an astronomer?'

'Yes.'

'I want to be like Julia.'

Helen was wearing the pink filter glasses. She walked blindly into Lomax and then Joel.

'What cute kids,' said the store assistant.

'Sometimes,' admitted Lomax. But he felt proud. And although he knew Joel was unlikely to become an astronomer he was pleased that the boy had not said he wanted to be a corporate lawyer like Robert.

Lomax took them down to the department which was painted the same pastel colours as Julia's house and where beautiful women asked other women if they could spray them with perfume.

'Yes please,' said Helen to one of them. The woman sprayed perfume into the air. A nebula of tiny droplets was visible and she told Helen to walk into it. That was just how Candice applied perfume, how Jefferson had said Gail applied perfume.

'Mmmm.' Helen sniffed like Deputy Dawg sniffing rain. 'Daddy, can we buy some?'

'No. We're going to choose a gift for Julia.'

Joel wanted to know why. 'If it's not her birthday, how come she gets a gift?'

'Because her trial will end this week and she'll be free and I'll give her a present from you so she knows that you're pleased.'

They looked at the feminine things in white and pink and cream and pale, pale blue. There were lipsticks and hair combs and gloves and scarves and earrings and small purses for evening and big purses for the day. Helen chose a silk scarf.

'Julia will like this,' she said with certainty.

'All that money on a dumb scarf,' said Joel. Lomax laughed and bought it anyway. He had laughed a lot today. He was happy. They found the children's toys and books and he had difficulty preventing himself from buying everything they asked for. Eventually they chose some books which he thought Candice would not disapprove of.

'Not more Hardy Boys!' she groaned. Joel stood between his parents, looking from one to the other. His body was tense and his face anxious.

'It's okay, there's also some Wittgenstein,' Lomax said cheerfully. Candice smiled. Joel melted away with the Hardy Boys.

Candice was up a ladder painting the master bedroom. The furniture was in the middle of the room, including the bed. It was covered with dustsheets. There were no rugs. The room echoed a little.

'Why white?' asked Lomax.

'I like white.'

'It will feel like you're at the clinic. You'll dream about work.'

'I dream about work anyway.'

'Want some coffee?'

'Okay. Don't let the dog in here.'

Lomax made them some coffee and found a brush and helped her to paint. Perhaps a year ago it would have been painful to paint his ex-wife's marital bedroom. Now it seemed like just another room. He asked her where Robert was.

'Working,' she said. He recognized that tight-lipped tone. She was mad at Robert. There had been an argument.

His brush made a pleasant slapping noise. There were little bubbles in the paint.

'I think Helen and Joel should see the eclipse with you,' Candice told him. 'Will the trial be over by Thursday?'

'Yup.'

'You sound pretty confident.'

'I am confident.'

As usual, he told her everything. He told her about Vicky. He told her about Gail and Lewis and when he described their incestuous relationship, the room felt bigger and more hollow. Candice said nothing. He told her how Frances hoped she would be able to make Vicky confess on the witness stand on Monday. He described his search for the gun in Vicky's closet. Proudly, he told her how, just as they were leaving, he had recognized the importance of another witness and, as a result, uncovered evidence vital to Julia's case. But although Candice habitually commiserated with Lomax's failures she seldom shared his triumphs. She was more interested in the gun.

'In a hairdryer! I never would have thought of that.'

'Not a real hairdryer. A special hollow hairdryer.'

'Maybe I'll get one.'

'What would you keep in it?'

'My gun.'

Lomax stopped painting and looked at her. She was working on the wall close by now. He noticed that the flesh around her chin was thickening. Candice was ageing. He thought of Julia's jaw, which was smooth like the edge of a knife.

'When did you get a gun?'

'Robert wanted me to have it for when he's away on business trips. Do you disapprove?'

'This gun of Vicky's. I realized it's the first time I've looked at a real gun, really scrutinized one. They're such neat little machines. But . . .'

'But I know. They're for killing people.' She put her head on one side and looked quizzical. 'Are you going to marry her?'

'Yes.'

She moved the ladder and climbed back up it and balanced the paint can on the top.

'Actually,' she said, 'I guessed the mother was the murderer months ago. I worked it out. She was the only person it could have been.'

That night, Lomax scarcely slept and by morning his confidence had ebbed away. He was tense and tired. He was convinced that the day would end with Julia's guilt still an invisible but widely acknowledged presence in the room. He tried and failed to eat breakfast, Deputy watching him.

When he reached the court, he found less of a crowd than usual. The press benches were half empty. There were few people standing by the door. The atmosphere was thin. It was Monday morning. Next weekend was Labor Day and some people were already holidaying. The defence was opening its case. Interest was flagging.

Frances called John Fusco and the undercurrent of murmuring and movement in the room did not cease as the old man sank into the witness chair. He wore a dark suit. Probably he had owned it for a long time, keeping it at the back of the closet for funerals and other sombre, significant events. He could never have anticipated that one day he would wear it in court. There was a tie around his thin neck. Even from Lomax's seat, two rows back, the gap between the man's neck and his shirt collar was visible. The jacket flapped a little on his thin body. Did his clothes date from the era of loose suits or had he shrunk since he bought it? Lomax remembered his body climbing out of the pool, shadows under every rib, shoulders bent. This was age. Lomax looked away from Fusco. He saw Julia, Frances, Marjorie and Kurt sitting in a row, strong and upright. Their shoulders were reassuring.

There was activity, some of it frantic, at the prosecution table. Lomax knew Fusco's subpoena had been delivered on Friday but he sensed disarray around de Maria now.

'Your honour,' he said, standing. Lomax tried to see the attorney's fingers. They were still. 'Your honour, may counsellors approach the bench?'

'You may approach.'

Frances joined de Maria and the judge. She was taller than the prosecution attorney but she was hardly tall enough to see over the podium. The judge leaned forward. De Maria whispered. Lomax guessed that he was challenging the witness, or perhaps pleading for more time. The judge was talking. She was nodding. Frances had said something but the judge was looking at de Maria when she spoke. Lomax gauged that de Maria was winning his challenge. His heart began to pound. His mouth was dry. He knew that, without Fusco, the evidence on Vicky Fox was strong but not conclusive.

Finally the counsellors returned to their seats. The judge said nothing. De Maria began talking to his colleagues. Frances stood.

The challenge had been overruled and Frances was going to question the witness. Lomax was so relieved that he hardly heard the first two questions. Something about Fusco's career. Perhaps the word engineer was mentioned. Something about living at the condominiums. By the time Lomax began listening again, Fusco was describing the pool and the mountains and the weekly barbecues. Then he explained how Medihomes provided help and managed the facility.

'The people who live there are real old or real sick,' he said, his face deadpan. 'In case you hadn't noticed, I'm real old.'

Frances smiled. Some members of the jury smiled.

'Are you happy there?' Frances asked.

'As happy as you can be,' said Fusco, 'when you know that you'll be leaving in a box.'

He spoke quietly with the trace of an accent. Had he come to America from some other place many years ago? Time had bleached the colour from his thin hair and the distinctive features from his face.

'Do you drive a car, Mr Fusco?'

'I have a car.'

'How often do you drive it?'

'As little as possible.'

'How often?'

'Maybe a few times a month, maybe less. I like to think it's not me who's gotten slower but the traffic in this town which has gotten faster. Not that it scares me. I'm eighty-four and nothing can scare me any more. Even right now. I'm not scared. Probably when most people say their oath and sit here, they're scared. I'm not. This is because I'm eighty-four.'

Frances was genial. 'You're not scared of driving but you prefer to drive at times when there's least traffic?'

'Yes.'

Lomax looked across to Morton de Maria. His eyes were following Frances around the room. His colleagues were busy.

'Do you drive your car at night?' Frances asked. Fusco tilted his head further in her direction.

'I don't hear so well,' he told her.

She repeated the question twice.

'Not much at night. I like night-time but not for driving. Everything's reversed at night. You can see shapes in the dark which aren't there in the daytime. It's dangerous to drive when you see shapes. So I like to walk around the complex at night, sometimes I swim. But I don't like to drive so much.'

'Mr Fusco, have you driven out any night in the past year?'

'Lady, let's not play games. You're interested in just one date. You want to know about early in the morning of November twelfth.'

'You drove your car then?'

'I drove my car then.'

Lomax's legs and arms were crossed. Now his body uncurled a little.

'Was it dark?'

461

'Sure it was dark.'

'You have told the court you don't like to drive at night. Why did you do so on November twelfth?'

'To help out a friend of mine.'

'Who was that?'

'Vicky Fox.'

'Vicky Fox,' repeated Frances, turning helpfully to the jury. 'Vicky Fox, mother of Gail, and former wife of Lewis. A woman with close ties to both murder victims.' She turned back to the jury. 'Can you describe your friendship with her?'

'I like her.'

'What do you like about her?'

'She's smart. You have to get to know her before you see how smart she is. And she's nice. I never heard her saying anything real mean about anyone. And she's a drunk. I'm teetotal myself but I can empathize with that lifestyle.'

'Are you a close friend?'

'Sometimes.'

'On November twelfth, how did she ask for your help?'

'In the night, early in the morning, she telephoned me. She said she had to cross town right away.'

'Was she drunk?'

'Sure.'

'Very drunk?'

'Probably. It's hard to tell.'

'How would you describe her mood?'

'Upset. Or maybe . . .' The old man was thinking. 'Maybe angry. Anyway, drunk, yes.'

'Why did she have to cross town?'

'Her daughter Gail had called. Gail had been in Europe. She came home that night.'

'And why did she telephone her mother?'

'As I understood it, she was in some kind of danger.'

'What kind of danger?'

'I'm not exactly sure. Something to do with the father.'

'She was in danger from the father?'

'Something like that. I didn't ask too many questions.'

'Had Vicky Fox ever talked to you about relations between Lewis and Gail?'

'We didn't talk about that kind of thing.'

'What did you do on receiving the call?'

462

'I got my car out of the garage and drove Vicky right over to Yellow Creek. That's near the university. It's where the daughter's apartment was.'

'What did she take with her?'

He paused to think again. 'A purse.'

'What else?'

'Nothing else.'

'How big was her purse?'

'Well, I'm not sure.'

'Big enough to hold a small revolver of the kind that will now be shown to you?' Frances turned to the official. 'Exhibit, please,' she said.

The official drew from the cart the gun which Lomax had found in Vicky's room. After asking the judge's permission, Frances took it and crossed to Kurt who handed her a leather purse. Frances put the gun in the purse showily.

'Witnesses I later propose to call will confirm that this is the murder weapon. And the court will note how small a purse such a gun can be hidden inside.' She lifted the gun out. 'So I ask you again, Mr Fusco, was Vicky Fox carrying a purse large enough to hold such a gun?'

'I don't know. It was too dark to see her purse.'

'But only the smallest of purses would not – '

'Objection, your honour. Mr Fusco has said it was dark and he could not see the purse. He doesn't know if it was big enough to hold a revolver or a washing machine. He couldn't see it.'

'Sustained. And please stop waving that gun around now, Mrs Bauer.'

'Certainly, your honour.' Frances returned the exhibit as she asked her next question. 'Was Vicky Fox wearing or carrying gloves?'

'I don't remember. I didn't see.'

'What time did you leave the condominium?'

'I didn't exactly notice. I guess five, five thirty. But that's only a guess.'

'And where exactly did you take Mrs Fox?'

'To her daughter's apartment.'

'What happened when you arrived?'

'Vicky went in alone. She had a key. I offered to go with her but she said it was a family problem.'

'Was she still upset, angry, drunk?'

'Yes.'

'How long was she in there?'

463

'A short time. Less than fifteen minutes. Maybe less than ten. I was thinking. I didn't notice the time.'

'And when she reappeared?'

'She didn't say anything at all.'

'Nothing?'

'Nothing.'

'Not a word?'

'Not all the way home, not when we arrived back at the condo.'

'Not even to thank you for the ride? Goodnight?'

'No.'

'Was this normal behaviour for her?'

'It's normal behaviour for someone in shock. And Vicky gets silent when she's depressed. I myself am also a depressive. I understand when someone wants to be silent.'

'So.' Frances was standing by the jury now. 'Without asking any questions you drove Vicky Fox to her daughter's apartment early in the morning of November twelfth. You waited while she was inside for a period of up to fifteen minutes, and then drove her home again?'

Fusco looked at Frances. He paused and blinked. 'Yes,' he said.

There was a short recess before de Maria's cross examination. Lomax guessed that Dorothy Cleaver would be smoking a hurried cigarette somewhere nearby but he did not move. He watched the people standing, talking, a few reporters hurrying from the room, the prosecution table in frantic consultation, a rustle of self-congratulation at the defence table, although Julia's body was still. He saw a flock of birds, large ones, perhaps geese, fly past the high windows.

When the room was quiet again for the prosecution's questions, Lomax was stiff with immobility but he still did not move.

Morton de Maria walked towards the witness stand. Lomax wondered why. When de Maria spoke his voice was louder than usual, perhaps slower. He wanted Fusco to hear him.

'Sir, where did you wait in your car for Mrs Fox that night?'

It was the first time in the course of the trial that de Maria had called any witness sir, although he and Frances had occasionally used the word during jury selection. Perhaps Fusco's age qualified him for this small mark of respect. Perhaps in the course of his testimony he had earned it.

'I was right outside in the parking lot.'

'How close to the apartment building?'

'Right outside.'

'Did you hear anything?'

'No.'

'Did you hear any shots?'

'Objection!' Now that Frances' witness was on the stand she was different. Brisker. She was no longer demolishing de Maria's arguments but constructing and protecting her own.

She said: 'The prosecution has already insisted that the witness could not see what Mrs Fox carried in the dark. The counsellor should realize that neither could the witness hear shots fired at some distance. After all, no one in the apartment building was even awoken by the shots. Plus, the witness has already demonstrated his hearing problem.'

De Maria said: 'Your honour, the shots were not fired from a distance and would have been sufficiently loud for someone who was already awake to hear them.'

The judge paused then said: 'I'm going to let Mr Fusco answer but I want the jury to note Mrs Bauer's objection and for it to stay on the record.'

'So,' repeated de Maria clearly, 'can you hear me right now, Mr Fusco?'

'Perfectly.'

'Objection! The prosecution is trying to prove the witness can hear when someone stands right by him and yells in his ear but – '

'I just wanted to make sure the witness could hear the questions!' protested de Maria with an open-handed gesture of innocence.

'Stop this, both counsellors,' the judge said, frowning at them. 'The witness can hear you now, Mr de Maria, please continue with your questions.'

De Maria said, every word distinct: 'Please tell the court whether you heard shots, sir.'

'No.'

'Are you sure?'

'I'm sure. That's because they were already dead.'

'You believe that the murderer had been and gone before Vicky Fox arrived?'

'Oh yes. As soon as I heard about the murders the next day. I guessed that. I went right over to Vicky and that's what she told me. It didn't occur to me she could have done such a thing. She couldn't, I mean, physically. She can't even throw a milk carton in the garbage without missing. And anyway, she couldn't have done it. Emotionally. It's impossible.'

465

Lomax had said exactly this, exactly these words, so many times. About Julia. One of them was wrong and it was Fusco.

'Did you discuss this with Vicky Fox?'

'Yes. She told me she had walked in, seen the mess, looked at it and then walked right out again. We agreed not to tell anyone about this in case they thought she was involved. I said that if anyone asked me any direct questions I would answer them. We don't have anything to hide. But I didn't think anyone would ask. Vicky said she just looked at the bodies, she didn't touch anything. She hadn't left finger prints. Maybe she wiped the door, I'm not sure. But we thought there was no evidence and that no one would know she was there. No one did, until a man who needed a shave arrived on Friday.'

Lomax's hand moved involuntarily to his chin.

De Maria thanked Fusco and sat down but Frances was already on her feet. She was asking for a redirect. Despite de Maria's objections she was allowed it.

'Mr Fusco, you now claim that Mrs Fox walked in, looked at the murder victims and walked out again. But earlier you said she was in the building for perhaps fifteen minutes.'

'I'm old, but I'm not so old I can't remember what I said. And I said it might have been less than ten.'

'I see.'

Frances walked towards the witness stand with that sense of purpose that Lomax now knew was dangerous for whoever sat there. She said: 'Mr Fusco. Without looking at your watch or a clock or anywhere but at me, please estimate how many minutes have passed since you took your oath.'

There was a long silence. Fusco screwed up his eyes at Frances, perhaps in dislike, perhaps because he was thinking. He looked at Frances and everyone looked at him. It seemed to Lomax that Frances was taking an immense and public risk. He stopped breathing until Fusco spoke.

'I would estimate . . . twelve. No . . . maybe . . .' The old man looked shrewd. He was going to increase his guess. He straightened his body. 'Fourteen,' he said clearly.

'Fourteen minutes?'

Frances bent her arm and stared ostentatiously at her watch. 'No, Mr Fusco. Twenty-four and a half minutes have passed.'

Lomax breathed out. The invisible man, rustling and murmuring, ran around the courtroom.

Frances added: 'It's a long time just to stand and look at two bodies.

466

Most of us cannot even look at pictures of them for more than a few moments.'

Although de Maria's motion to strike Frances' last remark from the record was successful, Lomax knew it would have had its effect.

'You may step down,' the judge told Fusco. He did so with care. Like other witnesses, he had been humiliated. Lomax's pain at this outstripped his relief. He thought of the skeletal body hidden by the loose suit and his pain increased.

Vicky Fox was taking her oath. At first her lips moved soundlessly as she tried to repeat it. She spoke on her second try, her words barely audible.

She wore a suit. Her hair had been cut. She looked smaller than he remembered her. The make-up on her vanity had been dusted and opened and its contents applied, but this only emphasized the deep crevices in her face. She was looking around at all the people now. She saw Julia and waved to her jauntily. The movement was inappropriate. The two elderly women on the jury exchanged shocked glances.

Frances asked questions about Vicky's medical condition. She tried to ascertain her physical strength by asking how many bags of sugar she could lift but de Maria challenged this successfully. Then Frances said: 'Mrs Fox, I'd like to ask you about your marriage.'

'Uh huh.'

'Were you and Lewis happy in the early days?'

'When?'

'In those early days of your marriage?'

'Well, everyone's happy at first. They all are, that's how it is.'

'When did things start to go wrong for you?'

Vicky Fox shrugged and rolled her eyes as she thought. 'Maybe . . . when we moved to Arizona.'

'That was about four years after you married. What went wrong there?'

'We had a big house.'

'Did that cause you difficulties?'

'It was big. There was an intercom from the kitchen to the other rooms. I could call the kids into the kitchen on the intercom. And there was a yard. They could play in the yard. See, a man sprayed all around against the black widow spiders so they could play in the yard.'

There it was again. The myth of the happy family.

Frances ignored Vicky's failure to answer her question. She said: 'Well that sounds nice. How come your marriage began to change?'

Another voice broke in. It was deep and calm. 'Objection.'

467

Frances turned to face de Maria.

'This isn't direct questioning, it's psychotherapy,' he told her. The judge looked at Frances.

'Is this necessary, Mrs Bauer?'

'Yes, your honour. I want the jury to see how the family structure here has a direct bearing on the murders of two members of this family.'

Lomax saw Vicky flinch.

'You may continue.'

Frances said: 'In Arizona you had a beautiful house with a yard and the children played there happily. But your marriage changed. How did it change?'

'Lewis changed.'

'How?'

'I don't know.'

'Think hard, Mrs Fox.'

But Lomax could guess how he had changed. Probably just the way Candice had changed. First the impatience, then the distraction, then the distaste for physical contact, then a certain tautness. Finally shouting, tears, declarations. A house silent with misery. This last memory made his body jerk backwards suddenly, rocking the row of seats. A few annoyed faces turned to him.

When Vicky did not answer, Frances persisted. 'How did Lewis change?'

'He wasn't there.'

'He seldom came home?'

'He forgot he had a family.'

'Did he have love affairs?'

'Yes, yes, yes. Yes, he had affairs, he was never in the house, he never had anything to say when he came home, he just forgot about us. That's how he changed.'

'That must have been depressing for you.'

'It was depressing. It depressed me.'

'What did you do when you were depressed?'

'Nothing's what you do when you're depressed. Depression's about nothing. You look at the people walking around the stores and driving their cars and you pity them. If they look happy you pity them because they're kidding themselves. If they look sad you pity them because they know. They know what you know. They know there's nothing. See? See? That's depression. It's knowing.'

'I do see.' Frances' voice was gentle. 'You are describing a clinical condition which must have been very hard for you to bear. Some people find a refuge from such a condition in an understanding family.'

'Refuge?' shrieked Vicky Fox, her voice dangerous. Some of the jury drew back a little. The press watched her without writing. The judge cupped her chin in her hand and ran her finger up one cheek. Her expression was grave.

'You mean they hide there? They hide in their families thinking it won't find them? Huh. Huh.'

She flung her arms about extravagantly. 'It gets you. Wherever you go, it gets you. You can't hide anywhere. Not behind children and sisters and husbands and uncles and in-laws. Because you know the truth and you can't cover it up with lovey-lovey families because you know it's still there.'

'So your family was not a source of comfort for you?'

'No.'

'And depression is not a condition you were able to control. For example, for the sake of your family, to make their lives more pleasant?'

'Life isn't pleasant. Don't kid yourself. You know that. You knew it when you stood in front of the mirror this morning, before you put on your make-up. You were so goddam tired you wanted to go back to sleep. You didn't want to come here to ask me questions. You put your make-up on to help you pretend. And then you came here. You had to forget what you knew. See?'

Lomax wondered if, by some uncanny perception, Vicky was right. But Frances did not falter.

'As a matter of fact I looked forward to coming in here because I knew I would be talking to you and that you would be able to clear up this whole case for us.'

'Move to strike, your honour, we're not interested in what the counsellor was thinking while she cleaned her teeth this morning.' De Maria's voice had lost some of its firmness.

'Please strike the record,' agreed the judge.

'You have described the sadness of your depressions, Mrs Fox. Understandably, many people try to escape from such a condition. Drugs and alcohol can provide an escape. Alcohol was your chosen route. Is that correct?'

Vicky Fox shrugged. 'Maybe,' she said. 'It used to make a difference.' She was staring at the jury. There was an unwritten rule in the courtroom that witnesses scarcely acknowledged the presence of the jurors. Lomax became aware of this convention only now, when Vicky Fox broke it. She gazed unblinkingly at the jury as if any one of them might have been the defendant instead of Julia. She picked them out, one by one, and stared at them. One by one they looked away from her, embarrassed. She had been doing this since she entered the room. She seemed drawn to them. Lomax was reminded of a cat he and Candice had once owned. It had always been able to sense who in the room disliked cats and had walked right up to them and rubbed itself against their legs.

'Things must have been real tough for you, Mrs Fox. An alcohol addiction and bruising depression which you could not control, a husband who did not help or support you but gave every indication of his loss of interest in you. Two children.'

'It was tough.'

'You don't seem to believe in happiness.'

'I don't seem to believe in happiness,' repeated Vicky Fox mechanically.

'Do you think you passed this sense of futility on to your children?'

'No.'

'They had the capacity, which you lack, to be happy?'

'They were ambitious and they wanted things. They thought: if I had that, I'd be happy. That's how most people are, see. They think happiness exists but it's just outside of their grasp. They think it exists for everyone else and if they just had something – a husband or a lot of money or a pretty face – then it would exist for them too. But it isn't really there. No one has it.'

'So when your children expressed aims, ambitions, you did not encourage them?'

'No.'

'Perhaps you even laughed.'

'Perhaps I even did.' Vicky Fox's face curled itself meanly.

'The same with your husband?'

'He was ambitious too.'

'And early in your married life you were able to share his ambitions. Later you could not.'

'We didn't share anything. He didn't share.'

'Finally, he moved out of the state.'

'Well he didn't get away from me. I followed him. I figured he owed us something more than that. The kids. Gail.'

'What about Gail, Mrs Fox?'

She shifted her eyes from side to side. 'She was his daughter.'

'Did she want to see her father after your divorce?'

'I guess so.'

'They were close?'

'I don't know.'

'But you implied that you followed Lewis to California for Gail's sake.'

'She was entitled to see her father. So was Richard.'

'You believed that at the time. Do you have any regrets about that now?'

'I don't know. I'm tired. Can I go now?'

The judge said: 'Not yet, Mrs Fox.' Vicky sighed expressively.

'Did Gail want to move in with her father?'

'I don't remember. I wasn't too well at the time.'

'Did she ever tell you that she wanted to live with him?'

'Maybe.'

'She was very fond of him?'

'Oh, she thought he was just great. When you don't see someone so often and they take you out to movies, then you think they're just great. It was easy for him to impress her. She used to come visit me with plans and ideas and all the things she was going to do.'

'And you laughed?'

Vicky Fox shrugged. 'Sometimes I just didn't say anything at all.'

'How did Gail get along with her father when she lived with him?'

'Objection,' said de Maria. 'The witness can't answer this. She wasn't living there too.'

'Your honour, Gail talked to her mother about her father and her words are significant,' said Frances.

The judge nodded. 'Then I'll allow the question.'

'How did Lewis get along with Gail?' Frances repeated.

'I don't know.'

'I think, Mrs Fox, that you do.'

'Then why are you asking me?'

There was amusement. The public had grown restless with the sadness and incoherence of this witness. They were ready to laugh.

De Maria said: 'Objection. The witness has a point, your honour. Just why exactly is the counsellor answering her own questions?'

There was a rustle of noise which might have been laughter or it might have been part of the movement in the room which had increased during Vicky's testimony. People left or entered or changed seats or jingled coins in their pockets or shuffled their feet.

'Your honour,' said Frances, her tone so severe that the front few

471

rows of the public froze, but only the front few rows. Lomax was motionless. He willed the room to stop. Frances would not succeed in controlling Vicky Fox's testimony in the face of the public's disinterest and the jury's distraction. She needed an audience, a receptive one, to make her drama succeed.

'Do you have any quarters for the chocolate machine?' whispered the woman next to him. Lomax ignored her.

Frances said, her voice electric: 'Your honour. I am asking these questions because I now believe that Gail Fox told the witness she had a sexual relationship with her father. I intend to show that their relationship was relevant to their deaths.'

And magically, the room was still.

'Who told you that? Who told you?' asked Mrs Fox.

'Objection overruled,' said the judge.

'Who told you?' repeated Mrs Fox.

'Your son.'

'He didn't know anything.'

De Maria walked round the prosecution table to appeal to the judge. His tone of ridicule which, Lomax now realized, had skilfully undermined Frances, was strained.

'Your honour, move to strike. Surely Richard Fox's allegations were struck from the record. Why, I believe the counsellor even made the move herself! And now ...' The pitch of his voice rose with indignation. 'And now she's basing her questions on his testimony.'

'I don't believe I did strike,' Judge Olmstead said. 'I can allow these questions.'

Frances turned back to Vicky Fox, who was gazing at the jury again. She called Vicky's name, several times, to attract her attention.

'Did your daughter tell you that she had a sexual relationship with her father?'

'I don't know.'

'Mrs Fox, you are under oath. That means you must tell the court what you know.'

'Well I don't know anything. I don't know.'

'Mrs Fox. I believe that Gail confided in you that her father had a sexual interest in her. She told you she was scared and frightened. You were angry. You talked to the defendant about this, Julia Fox, whose presence you have already acknowledged in this room.'

Vicky looked around wildly. She had forgotten where Julia was.

'Objection.' De Maria said: 'Your honour, the defence counsellor is supplying testimony for the witness.'

472

'Sustained.'

'I don't know,' said Vicky Fox mechanically, although no one had asked her a question. Lomax's body was solid with tension. Vicky Fox was not going to give way to Frances. Something in the chemistry of the room – the mood, the silences, the timbre of Frances' voice, the tone of de Maria's objections – something was wrong and the defence would fail.

'Mrs Fox. Why did your daughter go to France?'

'She was studying.'

'Was that the only reason?'

'I don't know.'

'Whose idea was it?'

'I don't know.'

'Was it your idea?'

'Maybe.'

'Did you think it was a good idea?'

'What?'

'Did you encourage your daughter to go to France?'

'Well it's the same everywhere you go. You might as well be in France.'

The defence was imperious. 'Did your daughter have a good reason to leave this country, this state, this city, and this family? A good family reason?'

The witness wavered.

'You are under oath, Mrs Fox. Please tell us if you had some other reason for encouraging your daughter to leave for France.'

Vicky did not reply.

'You must answer the question,' said the judge. Was it the question or the note of kindness in the judge's voice which made Vicky's face crease again?

'But I don't even remember the fucking question.'

The room rustled but it was not the rustle of distraction.

'Mrs Fox,' said the judge routinely, 'please remember you are in court.'

Then Frances spoke: 'Your choice of words is interesting. I wonder why, when questioned about the relationship of Gail Fox and her father, that word comes to your mind, Mrs Fox?'

When her witness only blinked in reply, Frances continued.

'Perhaps you encouraged Gail to go to France, far away from her father, to release her from the burden of a sexual relationship with him?'

473

'I don't know.'

Frances was loud. She was distinct. She was demanding. 'Was Gail sleeping with her own father?'

'Oh God. Oh God,' said Vicky Fox, anguished. 'Oh God, I thought there might have been some sort of thing like that because Lewis liked young girls. That was the problem. He liked young girls.'

'But Gail was not small or helpless. She should have been able to refuse her father's sexual advances.'

'Well it's not so easy to push your father away when you've spent your whole life trying to persuade him to notice you.'

'So when you spoke of your children's aims and ambitions, which you found so futile, perhaps this was one of them?'

'No. What?'

'Perhaps you knew your daughter looked to her father for a love which was more than paternal?'

'No.'

'Perhaps when you learned this you asked yourself whether some of the responsibility for this unnatural relationship lay with you?'

The note of Vicky Fox's voice was rising. Her face seemed to be swelling. 'I didn't ask myself anything. I got drunk, okay?'

'You encouraged your daughter to extract herself by going to Europe. And when you knew your daughter was coming home you feared the unnatural father-daughter relationship would be resumed. And on the night when Gail was due to return you received a phone call.'

'Gail called me. She called me.'

'She asked for your help?'

Vicky bellowed. Sometimes her voice cracked with its own volume and her words were lost. 'She was in the apartment. Her father was there. He was doing something in another room or getting something. I don't know. She said that he wanted her to have sex and she didn't want to but she was going to.'

'She wanted you to stop her.'

'She wanted me to stop her. She wanted me to stop her doing that.'

'And you wanted to help her because you knew that this family was your family and its problems were your problems.'

Frances was accusatory. Vicky drew back.

'Your personality, your depression, your alcoholism, Mrs Fox, were responsible for this situation.'

'I had to help her.'

474

'The court has heard that you drove to the apartment with your friend, John Fusco. Did you take a gun, Mrs Fox?'

'They were dead! They were dead! There was blood everywhere. She'd been shot through the head.' She was sobbing. 'I always knew it was awful to live. I saw them. I saw them, and I knew it's awful to die too. I didn't know that before. It was awful.'

'They were dead after you shot them, Mrs Fox.'

'No!'

'You found them in the preliminary stages of sexual intercourse. Your former husband was behaving like a young lover, the way he was with you once, many years ago when you were happy together. And now he was behaving this way with his own daughter, who gave every indication – '

'No!'

'Every indication of finding her own happiness here. That's where she found it. Right back where you had all those years ago. With this man in this way.'

There was no reply, just an animal noise of pain and anguish. But Frances was merciless.

'You told them to put their clothes on. And then you shot them.'

'No!'

'Objection.'

'You took this gun and fired it, one, two, three times.'

'Objection, your honour!'

'Mrs Bauer . . .'

But Frances would not stop.

'You fired once at your husband. Twice at your daughter. Then they were dead. Then there was blood. Then, as you say, death appeared just as awful as life.'

Vicky made a choking noise, half a sob. 'Oh God!'

'You killed them, Mrs Fox. Why else would you put on your gloves and go to the apartment with a gun?'

'I just wanted to tell him to leave her alone!'

'But the problem was deeper than that. Not a father molesting a small child but a grown woman who went to unusual lengths to seduce her father. It was unnatural. Twisted.'

Vicky Fox was rocking now, her hands on the rail, her face a distortion, her voice a wail. 'It was my family. It was my fault.'

'It was your fault?'

Vicky's face was bloated with tears. Her mouth was large. 'I did it. I made it happen.'

475

'You had to stop them. It had all gone too far and it was your fault.'

There was half a wail, half a scream. 'It was my fault.'

'You shot them.'

'Objection.'

'Mrs Bauer.'

'I shot them.'

The judge leaned forward and stretched a hand towards Vicky. 'Mrs Fox.'

'The whole fucking thing was my . . .'

'Mrs Fox. Please be calm now.'

Vicky spat the words. 'My fucking fault.'

Her body doubled over the witness chair. Her hair, disarrayed, fell forward. Her sobs were piercing. The judge, the prosecution, the public, watched her in silence. A few members of the jury shielded their faces with their hands. Others gaped openly at her. Frances turned back to the defence table and looked down. Lomax caught sight of the expression on her face. Pain mixed with something else. Shame.

Then Julia stood. There had been some barrier, invisible, unspoken, around the defence table but now Julia walked through it. She crossed the arena, her shoes whispering. Watched wordlessly by the judge, she took the dangling hand of the sick woman. She held it tight. He saw Vicky grasp it back. It was all she had to hold on to. Her wails pierced deep into some fund of human sadness and all anybody did, except for Julia, was listen helplessly. Lomax felt sick. Finally the judge said: 'This court is in recess.'

33

TV stations were ecstatic. Today was the day when the sun would be totally eclipsed by the moon, and the weather was perfect.

Berlins' telescope did not work. Lomax had lifted it out of its box that morning and tried to use it. Of course, everything was upside down. He had expected that. But he had not been prepared for the distortion. He had opened the window and looked out at Helen and Joel. They had the day off school and were messing about in the drooping grass and first crisp leaves of fall, right over by the boundary. He had seen two children playing, and a dog, but the children had not been Helen and Joel and the dog had not been Deputy.

Lomax did not know exactly what error Berlins had made in his mirror-grinding. Perhaps he had been ill advised by the smart-alec twelve-year-old star of the telescope club. But some distortion of the light made everything, even subjects as familiar as his own children, look unrecognizable. Lomax had wanted to be impressed. He had wanted to write to Berlins, telling him of the collapse of Julia's trial and inviting him to their wedding, and he had wanted to say that he had used the telescope and admired it. Now he did not know what to say.

The failure of the little telescope, which worked so nearly perfectly, made Lomax unreasonably irritable. He did not know why. He called the children and they fetched their hiking boots.

'Scram,' he told the squirrels which ran up the walls of the carport. As he waited for the children he thought of Vicky Fox. It was hard to forget the way her body had seemed to crumple behind her hands in the witness chair. When she was led away her movements were slow and laborious as if her body was an immense weight. There was a helplessness about her which touched him.

They reached Julia's house. She was ready. As they pulled into the drive she came out, locking the door behind her. The sight of her, walking briskly towards the car, her hair swinging a little from side to side, lifted Lomax's heart. Joel grudgingly gave up his front seat.

Deputy could not decide whether he wanted to travel in the front with Julia or the back with the children and became wedged between the two. Julia laughed. She thanked the children for her pretty scarf. She was wearing it now.

Lomax leaned across and kissed her, cupping her head towards him.

'How far do we have to walk when we get there?' asked Helen suspiciously.

'A mile?' suggested Lomax.

Helen was dangling over Julia's seat. 'Julia can't walk a mile in those shoes!' she pointed out sensibly. Lomax couldn't decide if she was getting more like Candice or more like Robert.

'I think I can,' Julia told her.

'When Dad says a mile he means vertically,' Joel said.

'When Dad says a mile he means five,' Helen said.

'Oh . . .' Julia looked at Lomax for advice.

'Give me the key and wait there,' Lomax told her. 'I know where you have some better shoes.'

He entered the cool house. Julia was going to leave this place with its bad memories and its ghosts and its perennially blocked garbage disposal unit. She was going to move into Lomax's house. She would remove Candice's dusty ceramic pictures and replace them with something interesting that she had chosen. She would sleep with Lomax every night. Sometimes Helen and Joel would be sleeping in the house too, and Deputy Dawg. Julia would be happy. Good memories would accumulate and gradually, over many years, they would replace the bad memories and the ghosts would fade.

He ran back to the car, throwing the hiking boots into the trunk.

'Daddy never ran before he met you,' Helen told Julia as they started off along the straight stretch of road that rose and fell with the terrain, the stretch of road where Lewis had fallen asleep and crashed his car.

'If we see a good picture you have to stop,' Joel instructed. For his birthday a few weeks ago Robert had given him a camera. He sat with it on his lap.

The day was hot but it did not have the scorching edge of a summer's day. Once they had left the houses behind them there was little traffic. The mountain road twisted then twisted back on itself like a rope. The car climbed higher. Occasionally they passed a house, roof steeply sloping, surrounded by trees and gates and dogs. Deputy stared at the dogs and then barked at them deafeningly. The dogs volleyed back.

'Are we going to the lake again?' the children asked.

'No,' said Lomax, 'same road, different place.'

Helen wanted to talk about Julia's trial. 'Did the judge sit very high up?'

'Yes.'

'Were there a lot of people there?'

'Yes.'

'Did he bang a hammer to stop people talking?'

'It's not a hammer, stupid,' Joel said. 'It's called a gavel.'

'Plus it was a lady judge,' Julia told them.

'Are they going to put that bad woman in jail?'

Lomax did not know how to answer this. Just the name of Vicky Fox touched something painful in him. He remembered again the childlike way she had allowed herself to be led from the courtroom. 'Probably she's too sick,' he said at last, his voice gruff.

Frances had said that it was unlikely that Vicky would be charged, and when he had pressed the question she had said: 'I hope not,' and looked away. When they were alone together, briefly, she had said simply: 'People *versus* Fox. My greatest triumph, and a completely sickening one.'

'She isn't really a bad woman,' Lomax said now, and Julia and the children turned to him.

'But killing people is bad,' Helen said.

'Yes, what she did was bad but it's possible to do something bad without . . .' His voice trailed away.

'She was so sad in that courtroom,' Julia told the children, 'that it would have made you cry.'

Lomax, discomforted again, allowed himself to be distracted by a streak of maples high up the mountain. Their leaves had changed colour already and they looked for a moment like a bloodstain on the hillside. Once you had been startled by them you could acknowledge their beauty.

Julia was explaining: 'She's sort of crazy, so she probably didn't know exactly what she was doing.'

After a silence Joel said: 'There's something I don't understand about this murder mystery.'

Lomax and Julia looked at each other out of the corner of their eyes, dangerously, as the car passed along an unfenced road with a steep drop just a few feet away. They smiled. 'What don't you understand?'

'Look,' said Joel. 'Why did they practically have to send Julia to jail before they realized the crazy woman was the murderer?'

'That's a difficult question. I have to think about it.' He could not explain to the children how Julia had almost been convicted rather than admit her failure. Her failure as a wife and as a stepmother. It would be hard for the children to understand. Even Frances had not understood. After the trial's abrupt conclusion, Frances had been cold to Julia. She had announced that she was handing over the administration of her trust fund to another partner.

When the time came to say goodbye, Lomax told Frances that he was to return to the observatory. Instead of congratulating him or even wishing him luck she said: 'Be careful, Lomax.' Then she stood on her toes and kissed his cheek affectionately. Lomax had struggled to remember who else had told him to be careful in that tone of voice and later he had remembered. Candice. After Julia's arraignment, when all the evidence seemed to be against her. He wasn't sure that it was an appropriate farewell remark for Frances to make but he liked her too much to query it. He had kissed Marjorie and shaken hands with Kurt who had displayed all his teeth in a neat line a few inches above his jaw. Lomax had hoped he would never see them again but Julia wanted to invite them all to the wedding.

Since nobody had answered his question, Joel asked it in a different way. 'Look,' he began again in his Robert voice, 'didn't the police take this woman's fingerprints? Didn't they interview her? Didn't they check on her alibis?'

'Maybe they never read the Hardy Boys,' suggested Lomax.

Julia giggled.

'It's a serious question,' Joel told him, 'and you should give me a serious answer.'

Robert again. Lomax asked himself if he had spent enough time with his children this summer.

'Actually,' Lomax said, 'I met Vicky Fox a few times and I forgot to ask her whether she had an alibi. She told me she didn't have a car. She really has a drink problem. I didn't think she could have committed the crime and I guess the police didn't either.'

'Oh Dad,' said Joel in a tone of such disgust that Julia giggled again. 'You actually interviewed the murderer and you didn't even ask her for an alibi?'

They were high in the mountains now. On one side the drop was sheer. On the other, above their heads, menacing boulders lined the steep slopes. There didn't seem to be much holding them in place.

'I guess I wasn't a very good detective,' Lomax admitted to Joel.

'I guess not,' agreed Joel. But he added kindly: 'You're probably a good astronomer, though.'

Julia and Lomax exchanged glances. 'Thanks,' said Lomax.

480

They found a place to park near a creek. Deputy Dawg drank greedily from it, showing his long pink tongue. 'Believe it or not,' Lomax told the children as they put their boots on, 'Deputy adored the crazy woman who carried out those murders.'

Joel blinked at his father.

'He just kept licking her over and over,' Lomax said.

'Probably he was trying to clean her because he knew she was dirty,' Helen suggested.

Lomax was watching Julia. She was struggling with her foot half in and half out of one of the boots he had brought from the house for her. Finally she took it off.

'What's the problem?' he asked.

'They don't fit,' she replied, changing back into her shoes. 'It's okay. I can walk in these.'

Lomax realized that he had run into the house without thinking. He had remembered the hiking boots he had seen all those months ago in the closet when he had first visited Julia's house. He had fetched them instead of Julia's walking shoes. They were Gail's boots.

'God, how could I have been so stupid?' he said.

'It's okay. Really,' she insisted, but her voice was taut.

'I'm sorry.'

'They're good boots and I meant to give them away but I never got around to it.'

'Whose boots are they?' demanded Helen, but they had started walking rapidly behind Deputy Dawg up the trail and both Lomax and Julia pretended not to hear.

The trail was rocky. Lomax helped Julia over the stream in her unsuitable shoes. Joel snapped a picture of them with his new camera. 'Who has the filters?' asked Lomax suddenly.

Everyone looked at everyone else. They had left them in the car.

'How could I have been so stupid?' Lomax said. This was the second time within twenty minutes that he had used this phrase. The repetition annoyed him. 'I'll go back for them. I'll catch up with you,' he told the others.

'There isn't time!' wailed Helen.

'We have one hour until the eclipse,' Joel announced.

Lomax said it would take just half an hour to reach the summit. They all looked up at the sky. It was milky blue. The sun burned down.

'It thinks it's so hot,' said Helen, 'it doesn't know what's going to happen to it in an hour.'

The others walked on while Lomax scrambled back downhill for

481

the filters. He moved fast to counter his irritation, often sliding, sometimes loosening rocks. He soon reached the car. He grabbed the filters and turned and started back up the slope immediately. He was hurrying but his progress seemed slow. The slides he had made on the way down hindered his ascent. His curses broke the silence. Soon he was sweating and breathless. When he recrossed the creek for the third time he stopped. Cupping his hands he lifted the water to his face, relishing its temperature. He looked at his watch. He had forgotten to wear one. He looked up at the sky.

There was the white trail of a jet far overhead, so loose that it was close to disintegration. It was some minutes since the jet had passed. Lomax thought of Dixon Driver on board the research flight that was tracking the eclipse across Oregon and the north of California. He hoped the jet wouldn't fly over this mountain at the moment of total eclipse. He did not want the experience ruined by Dixon Driver's jet engines. The possibility irritated him. He was angry. He asked himself how it was that on a perfect day, with a spectacular celestial event imminent and a lifetime with Julia ahead, his good humour could have frayed so easily.

He found himself thinking of Vicky Fox once again. The children's questions about her had been painful. On Labor Day he had tried to call Homer and Jefferson, but Jefferson had said his father was too upset to talk to anyone. He had been very anguished since his cross-examination.

Inexplicably, he felt angry with Berlins. It was Berlins' telescope which had started this vexation. It had dogged him all day and now it was dogging him as he climbed the mountainside.

After a few moments he saw the others far above him. They were walking in single file, Joel in front, and had nearly reached the summit. Lomax began to concentrate on climbing rapidly towards them, pursued by his darkening mood. Was it possible that Berlins had made a major error in refraction? It occurred to him that the error might have been deliberate. The possibility was startling at first, but after a few minutes it had begun to seem likely and when he had climbed a little higher, probable. Soon it was obvious. The errors in refraction were so subtle and consistent that they could only have been deliberate. Using Berlins' telescope and your imagination you could fool yourself that you knew what a child or a dog looked like in the distance. When in reality they looked completely different.

Lomax sweated profusely. Why would Berlins spend so many hours grinding a distorted mirror?

'Who knows, you might learn something from it,' Berlins had said. About what? All you could learn from a distorting mirror was something about the nature of distortion.

Lomax remembered the falsified results in Core 9. Was it possible that they had been doctored with the same intelligence and consistency as the telescope, not to subvert but in an attempt to discover something about the nature of distortion?

The thought halted him. He was hot now, not because the sun was fierce or because he had been climbing, but from some other heat. It came from inside him and seemed to warm his whole body. It was shame. If he examined the figures more closely he would almost certainly discover that Berlins had been accounting for some distorting factor, perhaps something Berlins had noticed that Lomax had been blind to. Perhaps something obvious.

'Hurry, Dad!' he heard Joel yelling from the distance. He completed his ascent. At the summit he found the others lying on flat rocks like seals. They had decided to watch the eclipse on their backs. They were arranging T-shirts and sweatshirts underneath their heads.

'It's like going to the movies with the screen on the roof,' Julia explained.

'Don't anyone look at the sun except through their filter,' warned Lomax, handing out filters.

'Dad,' said Joel patiently, 'we know that. They've only been giving warnings about it every day for about three months.'

Shortly before Joel's watch told them that the eclipse was due to start they lay down, sprawling at acute angles to each other across the broad, flat rocks. Lomax sat up and looked at Julia and the children as they lay waiting. He was reminded of the pictures on the walls of Kurt's office, where the outlines of people lying in the street were drawn in white chalk. The pictures were unpleasant. The people drawn in them were all dead. Why had he remembered them now?

He lay down. A lizard scurried across his hand. He sat up again. He thought about Julia, trying the hiking boots. He remembered her face as she had put her own shoes on instead.

'Lomax, why do you keep sitting up?' asked Julia.

He lay down again and put his filter to his eyes. Deputy brushed past him. 'Aren't you going to tell us about it, Daddy?' asked Helen.

'Tell you what?'

'About the eclipse,' said Julia.

'C'mon, Dad,' urged Joel. 'You're an astronomer. You're supposed to sort of explain it to us.'

483

They were coaxing him. They could sense there was some change in him. His reply was rapid.

'You already know this. The moon's going to pass between the earth and the sun. It's much smaller than the sun but it's much nearer. So it can actually seem to cover the sun for a few moments. That's all you need to know.'

Deputy, who had been shuffling from person to person, settled by Lomax and scratched himself vigorously with a hind leg. They all watched the sun through their filters.

'It's starting!' shrieked Helen.

The eclipse had begun. Slowly, they became surrounded by silence and darkness. Lomax had not been aware that birds were singing and creatures were rustling in the grass nearby until they stopped. Even Deputy was soundless by his side. As the sky darkened, the earth became still. A big black disc was gliding slowly across the sun. Lomax knew it was the moon, he had just explained it was the moon, but it was not the familiar pale moon. This was a dark, menacing sphere and, like a big fish, it was gradually swallowing the sun.

Night came swiftly. Lomax removed his filter. The blackness all around them was absolute. After a few moments, stars became apparent. It was not really night. It was day. It was day without light and without hope.

'Daddy?' Helen whispered.

'I'm here,' Lomax whispered back.

The sun glowed helplessly from behind the smothering shadow. It had been extinguished. The whole world was still and silent and dark and cold. Despair settled on Lomax like a thick dew.

The moon continued its journey. The sun began to sparkle and then its shape to re-emerge. The earth started to breathe again. Birdsong could be heard far down the mountain. Lomax could feel warmth returning to his face and arms and he could hear Deputy scratching again. The others started to talk in high-pitched, excited tones. Soon the sun was restored. It was a globe again – massive, invincible and whole. But Lomax's misery was unchanged. All the things which had mattered a few minutes ago were replaced by emptiness. His limbs were heavy. He could hear the voices of his children without listening to their words. He did not care what they were saying. He did not care whether he ever got up off his rock.

A shadow fell across him. 'I'm eclipsing the sun,' Helen explained.

'Let's go down now,' said Joel.

'Here, Deputy,' called Julia. Deputy's claws scratched against the rock.

'Come on, Dad,' said Joel.

Lomax got up and they started down the mountain.

'You'll be able to tell your grandchildren about that,' Julia was saying to Helen. 'There may not be another total eclipse of the sun in this part of America for many years.'

'It was amazing,' said Joel.

'I thought it was beautiful,' said Julia. Helen agreed. She held Julia's hand for some parts of the trail. They walked on ahead of Lomax. Their voices echoed a little. The children were loud and unselfconscious. Julia's tones were more measured.

'Are you okay?' She stopped and turned to him.

'Fine, fine,' he said, waving them on. They continued, still talking.

Lomax knew he was not okay. When he arrived back at the car he opened the trunk to throw in the children's boots and saw Gail's hiking boots. He looked away from them.

'I'll drop you at your house, then I'll take Helen and Joel home,' he told Julia as they neared the city.

She stared at him in surprise. 'Why?'

'I have some things to do . . .'

'Okay,' she said, looking at him closely. He did not look back at her. 'Are you sure you're all right?'

'Yes.'

When they reached Julia's house she invited them in for a cool drink.

'No time. I promised Candice I'd take the children right home,' he lied.

Helen kissed Julia an affectionate goodbye.

'Come on,' yelled Lomax from the car and Helen ran back. Julia watched them go. She looked hurt and confused. She held her hands up to her face to shield the sun but for a moment she looked like Vicky Fox, holding her hands to her face to defend herself against Frances. Helen waved to her energetically.

'I have some questions for you,' Lomax told Candice as soon as she came home from work. She was wearing a white labcoat.

'Oh, and I have a few questions for you. About the eclipse. Wasn't it really something? Everyone was standing outside their offices like fire practice.'

'Candice, I need this information now.'

Candice took her labcoat off and hung it up by the door. 'What the hell is the matter with you?' she asked in a hushed voice.

'It's okay, Helen and Joel are watching TV,' he said. They had switched on to see the eclipse again and again. The TV images were taken through a telescope. The sun looked a violent shade of red. The children watched in reverent silence. Lomax could occasionally hear the voice of Dixon Driver or the movie stars who were on board the tracking jet.

Candice led him to the kitchen. 'Lomax. You look so weird.'

'I feel weird.'

'What's happened? Apart from a total eclipse of the sun?'

Lomax sighed. He looked at the table with its bowl of fresh fruit and bowl of dried fruit. He looked around the kitchen and its pictures tacked to the fridge and its gleaming jars of nuts and pulses. He looked at Candice, leaning over him, small criss-crossed lines around her eyes, her face concerned.

'Everything's happened,' he said.

34

It was dark and Lomax was in his den. He had left the glass roof open that day by mistake and when he had come up to the den this evening there was a squirrel inside. It had bounded about in panic, toppling piles of papers, scratching the desk, knocking over Berlins' telescope, upsetting old coffee cups with its tail. In a moment it had run along the bridge of Lomax's telescope and leapt out through the open window.

Lomax had watched darkness fall and the stars appear just as he had once before that day, only the process was slower and less frightening this time. He had looked at the sky with Berlins' telescope for a while and then he had looked through his own. He had telephoned Berlins but his wife had answered.

'He's in Missouri. He's gone ahead. I'm following tomorrow,' she explained. Her voice was unfriendly. When Lomax asked for their new address she refused to give it.

'Well . . . will you give him a message?'

Mrs Berlins was silent, but she had not hung up so he continued.

'Please tell him that I understand. I'm phoning to say I understand . . .' Lomax's voice was strained.

'That's not a message. What I am supposed to say you understand?'

'I believe now that he deliberately distorted results in Core Nine to increase his perception . . . I mean, to understand distortion. There was a correct and proper scientific motive for what he did. I just failed to see it.'

'Ah,' said Sarah Berlins.

'I don't know exactly because I don't have all the figures here. But what I suspect is that there was some kind of gravitational lens in Core Nine.'

'A what in what?' She was beginning to sound impatient.

'We might have been looking at a galaxy, actually probably a cluster of galaxies, through a sort of lens out in space. A gravitational lens can come between the earth and a distant galaxy. It bends the light rays . . . it distorts the image we receive. It consists of dark matter which we can't see and we don't know is there, although sometimes we can make deductions about its presence. If we're intelligent enough. If we aren't, we think we're looking at a galaxy just the way it is. I think the professor deduced the presence of some sort of lens and adjusted the image accordingly but I was so stupid that I thought he was distorting it to prove some point and – '

'So,' said Mrs Berlins, 'you admit you were wrong?'

'Well,' said Lomax with difficulty, 'yes, I was wrong.'

'I'll tell him that. I can't understand all the rest. I just hope you know all the trouble you've caused by being so sure you were right.' Her voice was still hostile.

'Yes,' said Lomax meekly. 'I'm sorry. Can I have his address so I can write him?'

'Write to this address and the mail will be forwarded. Anthony knows how to contact you. If he wants to,' said Sarah Berlins. She hung up the phone.

Lomax continued to stare at the night sky. He chose the Seven Sisters. The Pleiades. His old friend.

The phone had rung three times and he had ignored it each time. He knew he should go downstairs and lock the doors but he did not move. He heard a car pull up outside. The doorbell was broken. She had to bang hard on the door. Then she tried the handle and found it was unlocked and walked right in, calling his name. He heard her voice getting closer and closer until, sneezing, she was climbing the stairs to the den. She pushed the door open.

'Lomax?'

'Yes.' He spoke without energy.

'Why are you sitting up here in the dark? Are you looking at the stars?'

'Pleiades.'

'Oh . . . That's the one you like, right?'

'I used to think I knew it.'

She crossed the den gingerly, trying to avoid the books and wires which lay on the floor. She sat on the desk next to him, her breasts at eye level. The soft starlight that fell through the roof cast shadows under her chin and cheekbones. He did not try to touch her or kiss her.

'What's wrong?' she asked him.

For a few moments he did not reply. He looked at her beautiful face. She studied him gravely. 'Lomax, what is it?'

He said very quietly, so quietly that she leaned a little towards him to hear: 'I know.'

'Know what?'

'The truth.'

'What do you mean, Lomax?'

'I know the truth about you. I know who you are.'

She watched him. Only her eyes moved.

'You're Gail,' he said.

She still did not move. 'Lomax . . . ?'

'You're Gail,' he repeated, his voice firmer now.

'I'm me,' she whispered at last.

'No. You took over her identity. And then you killed her. Julia's dead.'

Her lips parted but she said nothing.

'You learned how to think like her and laugh like her and walk like her and then you used her money to look like her. I know it's possible. I know what surgery can do. I asked Candice today. You can become someone else. All except your feet. They can't make your feet smaller.'

She was breathing deeply now. Her face was colourless.

'I know a lot,' he said, 'but I don't know everything. You had surgery somewhere in Europe. I don't know where. Maybe you did go to language school for a while, just long enough to get used to your new face. To being Julia. I haven't called France but if I did your professor would say that you came late but you were so beautiful that it was easy to forgive you.

'The witnesses who thought they remembered seeing Lewis at the airport with a young woman saw Lewis and Julia. You had arrived earlier, perhaps a day earlier, maybe just hours. You had to steal your mother's gun, change it for some other gun. You left some kind of message at the airport saying you'd gone to the apartment. They found you there. I don't know what you said to them. I don't know how Julia felt when she looked right at herself. I don't know how Lewis reacted when there were two Julias and one of them had a gun. You had Julia change at gunpoint into some of your old clothes, the clothes that were yours when you used to be Gail. She put on your wristwatch but she didn't take hers off. You had her fingerprint the baggage before you put it back in the car. I don't know how much you humiliated her during all this. Maybe a lot, because the room still smelled of fear months later. But I like to think Lewis apologized to her. That he said he was sorry for not believing the things Julia had been telling him about you. While he was saying it, you shot him. I don't know how it felt to shoot your father. I think you loved him. I don't know how it felt to shoot Julia's face off. Sort of like shooting off your own maybe. It was easy for you to return Vicky's gun, maybe you did it some other night. Maybe you planted more evidence on her which we just didn't find. I don't know. When you were still Gail you'd given her a load of garbage about you and Lewis and incest and all you had to do, probably, before the murders, was agitate her a bit more over the telephone. As Gail. The last time anyone heard Gail's voice: please come, Mommy, and help me.'

He faltered. 'I don't know. But . . .' There was hesitation in his voice. '. . . it was garbage? The incest?'

She still did not speak or move.

'Of course when Vicky woke up, she thought she'd done it. She's a drunk. She wakes up every morning and finds things she did yesterday. Probably her first call of the day was from you, sounding like Julia, sounding accusatory. There are two people dead. Your mother's taking the blame. You've been tried and acquitted for your own murder. I don't know how that feels either.'

'That woman is not my mother,' she said.

She felt for her purse. It was on the desk next to her. Lomax guessed it contained a gun. He said: 'Vicky's pathetic. And she's going to take the blame for a crime you committed. You let Frances destroy that woman. You let her humiliate John Fusco. And you let Homer suffer. He wasn't wrong. He did see you that morning.'

She did not reply.

'And then,' he said, 'there was me. Jefferson brought you to my lectures.'

She nodded. 'Gail chose you right back then,' she said.

'So it wasn't just by chance you came to work at the observatory?'

'No,' she said. 'It wasn't completely by chance.' She paused. 'Gail sat with rapt attention at every one of those lectures. Every single one. And you didn't even notice her. You can't remember anything about her. Right?'

'I've tried and I can't.'

'She wasn't the sort of woman you'd notice,' she said with disdain. 'But when I arrived at the observatory, you noticed me.'

'You're the same woman. You look different, but you're still her.'

When he spoke he knew he sounded like Joel sometimes sounded. Wounded and confused and protesting.

She pulled her purse on to her lap. 'No,' she said. 'Gail's dead.'

She reached out and placed her hands on his shoulders. She looked into his eyes. He admired her soft skin, the fall of her cheeks, her full lips, her sad eyes.

'I love you so much, Lomax,' she told him.

He watched her perfect mouth speak the words. But the weight of her hands on his shoulders was immense.

He whispered: 'How can I love you? I don't know who you are any more.'

'I'm still the same woman you loved last week, last month. You'll love me next week, next year. I won't change.'

She was pleading with him. The perfect mouth moved closer. It kissed his eyes, very gently, and then his cheek. Every place it kissed it seemed to own. It left its mark of dampness and sensation. The unkissed parts of his face and of his body waited, vulnerable, powerless, wanting to submit to her. He smelled her hair and felt it flutter a little against his neck. He smelled her. The Nose had said she was perfume and soap. He reminded himself that this smell was synthetic. He reminded himself that her face and parts of her body were synthetic. The whole entity she had created was synthetic. She found his mouth now and was massaging his lips with her own. He loved this entity. He felt her tongue. She had changed, but everyone changes. No one stays the same.

He found himself kissing her. He felt her lips and her teeth with his tongue. She was warm and receptive. She stroked his hair with soft, smooth, sensuous movements. When the kiss ended, one hand slipped down his body, arousing him and filling him with anticipation wherever it touched him.

His thoughts were involuntary.

'Subject strokes man's hair. Subject looks directly into man's eyes. NB subject's eyes not big but creased a little eg looking hard for something on horizon. Subject moves head to right towards shoulder through 20 degrees.'

He lifted her hand, resting lightly on his jeans now, and placed it on the table. He said: 'You killed twice.' His voice was a whisper. It was not an accusation. It was simply a fact.

She stared. She removed her other hand from his hair. The movement created a small disturbance and a sense of loss. She looked down. He watched her open the purse.

'Are you going to kill me too?' he asked.

She stared at him for a moment. 'Kill you?'

'Now that I know.'

'Oh, Lomax.' She reached into the purse. He wondered what kind of gun she would produce. 'Don't be ridiculous.'

Her shoulders were shaking. She was crying. 'I'm looking for some tissues.' Tears were running down her cheeks. 'How could you possibly think that I'd kill you?'

Her face was wet. Some of her tears shone a little in the starlight. 'I want to marry you, not kill you.'

She moved closer to him. He studied her ears and her eyelashes and her lips and her throat. Sadness pervaded every one of her features. Her shoulders bent a little. She looked as small and frail as a tiny bird.

'You're the only person who ever loved me. Really loved me,' she told him, her sobs competing with her words.

He remembered her house in Arizona. Mrs Knight's compassion. Gail had carried her mother's mistakes and her father's and all she had ever received in return was violence or indifference. She was, Mrs Knight had said, just a little girl.

He did not move his body but he allowed himself to lift his arm towards her. Gently, he tried to erase her tears with one finger. But it slid over her face. Her cheeks were tear wet. She moved her head and in a sad, swift movement, kissed the finger he held out to her.

'I know it wasn't easy to be Gail,' he said hoarsely. After a moment, she replied: 'It isn't easy to be Julia.' She scraped the tissue across her eyes in an unselfconscious, unself-regarding movement that he suspected that other Julia might not have made.

'No?'

'No. Because I'm not her. I'm not Gail either.'

'Do you have to remember all the time?

'At first. Not after a while. I mean, people change. They develop. But Lomax, I know. I know I'm not Julia. And it's . . .' Tears intervened. The sobs seemed to have been generated by some violent force outside of her slim body. He could not watch her suffering. He stretched towards her. No matter what she had done she did not deserve this. He gripped her arm in a gesture of support. She was trying to say something. 'Lonely.' He watched her mouth trying to form the words. 'It's so lonely,' she said at last. He nodded. Of course it was lonely not being Gail and not being Julia.

She looked up at him. 'It's not so lonely when you're there. You make it all right. You're kind and good and when you believe in me I can believe in myself. You make me kind and good. You help me.'

Lomax thought about her loneliness. It was something he had recognized in her from the beginning, something which had attracted him to her because he felt it too. With his dog and his children and his devotion, he had alleviated her loneliness. And Julia, with her past and her problems for him to solve and her beauty, Julia had alleviated his.

492

If he sent her away now, his loneliness would return. He thought of the future. Long and empty. He would watch the children growing up and himself growing older. Deputy would die, and there would be another dog and then another. There would be events. Perhaps a few more affairs. Eventually, retirement. Not retirement into a family, like Berlins, but retirement into aloneness. It was a bleak, dull vista.

'Lomax?'

'Yes?'

'Can't we be together?' Her eyes were dark. Her voice was a whisper. 'The world won't be such a bad place if we're together. But if we're apart . . . how can we be apart? I still love you. You still love me. I haven't changed since you loved me yesterday.'

With an effort that felt more immense than he was himself, immense like a locomotive, he shook his head and said: 'No. Because I've changed.'

35

As Lomax drove higher up the mountains he seemed to drive into fall. In some places the trees were sad and beautiful in reds and yellows and golds.

The road to the observatory was longer than he remembered. Every time he rounded another curve in the mountains he expected to see the domes winking in the distance and then was disappointed. Finally he did see them but the sight did not fill him with anticipation or even pleasure. He felt nothing at all.

When he reached the lot it was so thick with tourists that he was unable to find a parking space. Finally he drove up to the Fahrhaus and walked down the trail to the staff residence. He passed one of the guides. She explained that the eclipse had stimulated interest in astronomy and The Big Sun Out had stimulated interest in the observatory and the result was a 100 per cent increase in tourist admissions.

Soon there would be no more tourists. The fall would be spectacular. Big red leaves would line the mountain roads and then the leaves would be matted and brown and cars would slide dangerously on them. Later the snow would come and the astronomers would be trapped here for days or weeks on end.

He went to Eileen Friel's office. She did not greet him.

'Lomax. Did you bring the bedspreads back?'

'Yes.'

'At last. You're in B wing, first storey, room twenty.'

She handed him a key and a book to sign. He did not argue with her. First storey rooms were the worst because you had to lock the window every time you went out. Otherwise tourists climbed in and stole your wallet or your TV or even your clothes. Some scientists locked their windows when they were only in the shower.

He passed the one-way glass in the staff residence self-consciously. You never knew who was looking at you. On an impulse, he stepped into the lounge on his way to B wing.

Doberman was reading a print-out. It cascaded down his legs into a pile on the floor. There were two cups by his side. One was empty, the other steamed with fresh coffee. A group of men, some of whom he did not recognize, were sitting with magazines on their knees or card games on the table in front of them. Whatever else they pretended to do, they were all looking out of the window at the tourists. Yevgeny was asleep in the corner, snoring occasionally.

McMahon was the first to notice him. 'Hi, Lomax,' he said, as if Lomax had just woken up from a nap after an arduous night's viewing.

'Hi,' said Lomax.

Doberman looked up momentarily. 'How're you?' he asked.

'Fine.'

Lomax had turned to leave the room when Doberman's voice called him back. 'What's with Julia? Why did she quit?'

'Um . . . I think she's decided to move away after the trial, probably out of state,' said Lomax. 'I'm not real sure.' He hoped that his vague tone would indicate that he did not want to talk about Julia.

'She isn't even coming back for a goodbye party?'

Lomax shrugged for an answer and turned again.

'I'd like to discuss Core Nine with you. I mean, like soonest. It wasn't working. I've restructured the whole project,' Doberman called. This was his new project director voice, commanding and decisive.

'Okay,' called Lomax over his shoulder.

'Are you all right?'

'Yes.' His voice was without expression and without feeling.

'Did you know you have viewing time tonight?'

Lomax stopped. 'Who, me?'

'Yup, your name's up on that board.'

Lomax went straight to the noticeboard. It was true. He was viewing tonight and Rodrigues was night assistant. Suddenly he was elated. He was viewing again, and at the Fahrhaus where the telescope was so big you could get lost in space. It was months since Core 9 had been allocated viewing time and more months since he personally had been given a chance to ride the Fahrhaus.

'Welcome back,' said a voice behind him. It was Jorgen. They shook hands enthusiastically.

'How's Alison?' asked Lomax. Jorgen's face became illuminated at the sound of her name. He had already been smiling but now his smile took on a foolishness and vulnerability that Lomax recognized as the smile of a man in love. He looked away.

495

'She's fine, fine, most well,' Jorgen assured him, still shaking his hand.

Lomax immersed himself in data to prepare for the night's viewing. Then he found Rodrigues in his workshop surrounded by bolts and screws and motors and pieces of metal he had salvaged from old machines. The shelves were oily.

'I never want to hear the word eclipse ever again not as long as I live,' Rodrigues told him.

They discussed Lomax's viewing requirements for the night.

'I know you, you fucker, you won't get out of the goddam cage,' said Rodrigues.

Over the years, Lomax had accumulated viewing clothes. When it was nearly dark and the temperature in the mountains had begun its rapid descent you put the first layer on. You went to the cafeteria and picked up your night viewing pack – coffee and a flimsy hamburger in a hot box or peanut-butter sandwiches and cookies and chocolate – and at regular intervals through the night you added another layer so that when the dome was finally closed you could hardly walk for clothes.

The parking lot was empty by the time Lomax made his way up to the Fahrhaus. When he had entered the labs there had been a long line of tourist cars starting back along the mountain road. Mostly the cars were full of adults. Grey heads bobbed in the back seats. A few contained couples only. Across the valley whole mountainsides were already shocking fall colours, yellow or red. Lomax had watched the sun begin to slide away. The yellows turned to brown, reds turned to black, the shadows gathered in crags and gullies. He had seen that the sky was clear and the moon was absent and he had felt the excitement that still preceded a promising night's viewing. He had tried not to think of Julia. He did not want to look into that void.

He heard his own footsteps echo in the metallic hallways of the Fahrhaus. There was a smell of bananas. That meant Rodrigues was already here. He was surrounded by gadgetry as usual, talking to someone who was wearing a heated suit. Probably Doberman had decided to supervise. Lomax groaned silently. He had hoped to observe alone tonight.

'Hi Lomax,' said Kim.

'Kim!' Lomax felt relief and pleasure.

'Lemme give you a big kiss,' she said, wrapping the heated suit around him.

'Don't electrocute me,' he begged.

'This is a touching reunion. Very touching. Anyone wants a banana, just let me know,' Rodrigues said.

'I tried to call your room but – '

'I've been in the gym.'

'Oh God, Kim, the gym. What's going on?'

'I do maybe half an hour's torture on the exercise bike every day. Maybe less.'

'Why?'

'Good question,' said Rodrigues. 'Why?'

'I saw myself on TV. God, I look fat.'

Lomax said dully: 'You should stay the way you are.'

'Did you see me?'

'Once.'

'Was I good? Will my mom be proud? Will Tandra and Roach be able to hold their heads up high in school?'

'Yes, yes and yes.'

'Once they gave me this long, thin stick and there was a big sun behind me and I had to point to the core, the photosphere, the chromosphere and the corona. I felt like the weather forecaster. And another time they filmed the caves near Lifebelt Lake and I had to answer questions about the eclipse paintings. I said that was the last time there was a total eclipse over the western USA and it gave us a unique link to the past of a forgotten people. Good, eh?'

'Terrific.'

'Except . . .'

'Except what?'

'I really wish I'd followed the diet Julia gave me. Plus I should have let her help with my clothes.'

'No,' said Lomax. The mention of Julia's name seemed to add weight to his body. His heart felt heavy. Kim watched him. She could have asked him about Julia but perhaps his face warned her not to.

Rodrigues wandered off to talk to his equipment. 'It's a fine night, dark sky. You're in luck, Lomax,' he said. 'You got about ten minutes till lift-off.'

'What room did Eileen Friel put you in?' asked Kim. 'No, don't tell me. First floor, B wing.'

'Right.'

Kim's face was pained. 'A room with a view?'

'Of geological strata.'

The hillside had been exploded to make space for the building.

The lower windows at the back of the wing were a few feet from solid rock.

'You either learn to see in the dark or bulk-buy light bulbs,' Kim said.

'I'd forgotten how thin the walls are. There was a guy in number twenty-one singing "Guantanamera" over and over again.'

'Welcome back, Lomax.' She reached into the pocket of the heated suit and pulled out about a dozen candy bar wrappers. Empty. They fluttered to the ground.

'Pick that up,' yelled Rodrigues from across the dome.

'Shit, don't tell me I've eaten them all.'

Kim rummaged around in another pocket. Another dozen wrappers fell out. Two of them contained chocolate. 'Phew. That was nearly a crisis,' she said.

'How can you eat all that and still go to the gym?' asked Lomax affectionately.

'The goddam exercise bike makes me hungry.'

It was impossible to tell from the cold suit whether she had lost any weight.

'No Lomax. Not one pound. Some things don't change,' she said, filling her mouth with candy bar.

Rodrigues was yelling: 'This babe's ready for you, Lomax.'

They looked up in silence. There was a soft rumbling overhead. Above them, a crack appeared in the dome. It widened. There were stars, millions of them, wrapped around the earth like a blanket. The dark shape of the telescope was silhouetted close by. Lomax began to climb the metal stairs. He enjoyed the smell of oil. He sniffed the thin night air of the mountain. He heard the sound of his feet, echoing a little on the steps. He held onto the handrail and swung his body happily into the cage. The seat was small. Someone had lined it with foam rubber recently. He had to bend his head. He could hear the whirr of the oil pumps and the distant hum of a transformer. He switched on the intercom and he and Rodrigues checked focus and co-ordinates.

Kim's voice crackled overhead. 'Hey, Lomax, I'm here all night. I'm watching on screen. If you need anything, any notes, any help, any coffee . . .'

'Any bananas . . .' added Rodrigues.

'Thanks,' said Lomax.

'We have music. We can do soul, rock and roll . . .'

'Give him a symphony,' Lomax heard Kim say, 'it doesn't matter which one, he doesn't know the difference.'

Lomax's heart began to beat faster. He put his hands on the guide motion buttons and his palms felt sticky. He heard Rodrigues switch control of the telescope over to the prime focus cage. Now the big eye was his.

Lomax pressed his head against the eyepiece and manoeuvred the telescope, gently at first and then, as he began to remember old skills, more adroitly. Soon he was hurtling through space and time. He passed the curious shapes of galaxies lit up in the dark. They spun and burned and spiralled and collapsed but were perfectly still. He saw the bright searchlights of distant quasars. Pinpoints of light passed him like shoals of shimmering fish. Impossible to tell without a spectrograph what was near and what was far. Impossible to guess the depth of this vision. Impossible to know whether the unlit passages of his journey were empty or just dark. His spirits soaring, oblivious to the cold, and unaware of the symphony, Lomax travelled through the night.